The fifth book in the mighty fantasy

For the first time in a thousand years, the lands that make up the Isles have been united under one leader, young Prince Garric from Haft. This is also the moment when the cosmic forces that provide the elemental power upon which magicians draw are at a thousand year peak. Wizards of even small learning are immensely powerful. Human greed and evil are reinforced by supernatural energies.

Starting in *Lord of the Isles,* and continuing in *Queen of Demons, Servant of the Dragon, Mistress of the Catacombs,* and now *Goddess of the Ice Realms,* David Drake tells the continuing, interlocking story of Garric and Sharina, Cashel and Ilna, young brother and sister pairs who journey together from a small town to the capital, and whose destiny is to re-unite the kingdoms of the Isles into one empire for the first time in a millennium.

• • •

"With *Goddess of the Ice Realm,* Drake once again shows that originality is possible in the fantasy realm. It's not just another 'beat a wizard, slay a monster' epic, although there are wizards and monsters of the best style; things happen for a *reason.* This series shows a real understanding of how politics in a monarchic system works. Prince Garric can't just slash his way through things—he has to work at governance, and he has to win the cooperation of others to do so. The ensemble cast of characters continues to charm, and at the same time to change. Serious issues of choice and moral responsibility face them along with the ghouls and spells. All in all, a solid addition to an outstanding fantasy series."   —Steve Stirling

Tor Books by David Drake

The Dragon Lord

Time Safari

From the Heart of Darkness

Skyripper

The Forlorn Hope

Birds of Prey

Cross the Stars

Killer (with Karl Edward Wagner)

Fortress

Bridgehead

The Jungle

The Square Deal

The Voyage

Tyrannosaur

Patriots

LORD OF THE ISLES

Lord of the Isles

Queen of Demons

Servant of the Dragon

Mistress of the Catacombs

Goddess of the Ice Realm

Master of the Cauldron

The Fortress of Glass

The Mirror of Worlds

GODDESS
of the
ICE REALM

DAVID DRAKE

TOR®
fantasy

A TOM DOHERTY ASSOCIATES BOOK
NEW YORK

GODDESS OF THE ICE REALM

Copyright © 2003 by David Drake

Edited by David G. Hartwell
Maps by Ed Gazsi

A Tor Book
Published by Tom Doherty Associates, LLC
175 Fifth Avenue
New York, NY 10010

www.tor.com

Tor® is a registered trademark of Tom Doherty Associates, LLC.

ISBN-13: 978-0-8125-7541-5
ISBN-10: 0-8125-7541-5
Library of Congress Catalog Card Number: 2003055984

First Edition: September 2003
First Mass Market Edition: July 2004

Printed in the United States of America

0 9 8 7 6 5 4 3 2

Acknowledgments

As usual, my first reader, Dan Breen, has worked to make this a better book. Dan isn't always right, but he's always worth listening to.

I didn't have an exceptional number of computer adventures with this one, but there were still occasions when the familiar conclave of Mark Van Name, Allyn Vogel, and my son Jonathan muttered things like "I've never seen that happen before. . . ."

A number of people provided me with background material for *Goddess*. Two who were particularly helpful were Marcia Decker and my British editor, Simon Spanton.

My webmaster, Karen Zimmerman, has been of inestimable value.

And finally, a general thanks to the friends and family, in particular my wife, Jo, who bore with me as I focused, getting increasingly weird—as usual—until I finished the job.

Dave Drake
david-drake.com

Author's Note

As is the case with most of my books, a good deal of the background to *Goddess of the Ice Realm* is real. The general religion of the Isles is Sumerian, though in some cases I've interpolated cult practice from the late Roman Republic where we simply don't know the Sumerian details.

The magic, which is separate from religion in virtually every culture and in at least my fiction, is that of the Mediterranean basin during the Classical period. The words of power, technically *voces mysticae,* are the language of demiurges who act as intercessors between humans and the gods.

I prefer not to voice the *voces mysticae,* but I have done so in conjunction with the audiobook versions of the Isles series. So far as I can tell, there was no ill result. On the other hand, I've also dropped loaded firearms without anything bad happening—that time. I don't recommend doing either thing.

The works of literature imbedded in *Goddess* are Latin classics. Rigal equates with Vergil, Celondre with Horace, and Pendill is Ovid, whom I find to bountifully repay the close readings I've been giving him this past year.

SANDRAKKAN

Gonalia

BLAISE

Erdin

reefs

TEGMA   PANDAH

HAFT

Barca's Hamlet

the

Carcosa

Inner

North

CORDIN

SHENG

TISAMUR

the Outer Sea

the ISLES

ORNIFAL
LAUT
ATARA
KEPULAKECIL
BIGHT
CHARAX
Sea
TELUT
PARE
KANBESA
SIRIMAT
SERES
reefs
BOWWKAN
DALOPO

EHM '98

Prologue

The blue and crimson flickers were as pale as the Northern Lights. They quivered through the ice of the high-domed ceiling, along the struts and down the heart of the thick crystalline pillars on which it rested. The creak and groan of the vast structure filled the half-dark like the sound of moonlit surf. The ice was alive, but it was coldly hostile to all other living things.

In the hall below were things that looked like men but were not, and things that could never have existed save here or in nightmare. Lower still, beneath the transparent ice of the floor, monstrous shadows glided through the phosphorescent water.

She sat on a throne of ice in the center of the hall, white and corpulent. In the air before Her, wizardlight twisted and coiled; and as it moved, the whole cosmos began to shift.

The ice groaned. . . .

Chapter One

I think the rain's going to hold off after all," said Garric, eyeing the sky to seaward where clouds had been lowering all day as the royal fleet made its way up the western coast of Haft.

If it didn't, well, he wouldn't shrink. For most of his nineteen years he'd been a peasant who herded sheep and worked in the yard of his father's inn, often enough in the rain. But now he was Prince Garric of Haft, making a Royal Progress from Tisamur, through Cordin, and to Carcosa on Haft. He was here to convince the folk living in the West that there was a real Kingdom of the Isles again and that they were part of it. It's hard to impress people in a downpour; all they really care about is getting under cover as soon as the foreign fools let them.

"Ah, you can believe that if you wish, your highness," said Lobon, the sailing master of the *Shepherd of the Isles*. His voice mushed through a mouthful of maca root, which oarsmen claimed gave them strength and deadened the pain of their muscles. "What *I* say is that we'll have a squall before we've settled half so many ships into their berths."

He nodded glumly toward the harbor mouth ahead. "That's if Carcosa even *has* berths for a hundred warships. We're at the back of beyond!"

"Carcosa can berth a hundred warships," Garric said, a trifle more sharply than the sailing master's comment deserved. "A thousand years ago when Carus was King of the Isles and Carcosa was his capital, the harbor held as many as *five* hundred."

Lobon was a skillful judge of winds, currents, and the way to get the best out of even a clumsy quinquereme like the *Shepherd,* but he'd been born on the island of Ornifal. He was just as much of an Ornifal chauvinist as a landowning noble like Lord Waldron, commander of the royal army.

Garric came from Barca's Hamlet on the east side of Haft. All the time he'd been growing up, Carcosa was the unimaginably great city that held all the wonder in the world. And besides Garric's own background—

"Aye, lad," said the ghost of King Carus, alive and vibrant in Garric's mind. *"Five hundred ships in harbor—but only when I wasn't off on campaign with them, smashing one usurper or another. And that was most times, till the Duke of Yole's wizard smashed me instead and the kingdom with me. But you'll do better, because you know not to solve all your problems with a sword!"*

Garric smiled at the image of his ancient ancestor. He and Carus could have passed for son and father: tall and muscular with a dark complexion, brown hair, and a quick smile unless there was trouble to deal with. Carus had never fully mastered his volcanic temper, a flaw that'd proved fatal as he'd said. But—

If I'm doing better, Garric said in his mind's silence, *then in part it's because I have your skill to guide my swordarm when a stroke is required.*

"I wouldn't know about what went on before my time," muttered Lobon. He spat over the stern railing, threading the gobbet between the helmsman at the starboard steering oar and one of Garric's young aides. The helmsman remained unconcerned, but the aide jumped and smothered a curse.

Generally an aide was somebody's nephew, a second son who could run errands for the prince and either rise to a position of some rank at court or be killed. Either would be a satisfactory outcome, since a family of the minor nobility couldn't afford to support another son in the state his birth demanded.

This youth, Lord Lerdain, was an exception. He was the heir presumptive of Count Lerdoc of Blaise, one of a handful of the most powerful nobles in the kingdom. Lerdain's presence at Garric's side made it more likely that Lerdoc would remain loyal.

Lobon understood Garric's glance toward Lerdain. He scrunched his face into a smile and said to the aide, "Don't worry, boy. I've been chewing maca root since before your father was born. I won't hit you less I mean to."

His face shifting into a mask of frustration, he added, "Not room to swing a cat aboard this pig, there's so many civilians aboard. Ah—begging your pardon, your highness."

"I understand, Master Lobon," Garric said with a faint smile. "We'll be on land shortly . . . and I fully appreciate your feelings."

The *Shepherd of the Isles* was as large as any vessel in the royal fleet. She had five rows of oars on either side and a crew of nearly three hundred men. Despite the quinquereme's relative size, she was strictly a warship rather than a yacht intended to carry a prince. Garric's personal bodyguard, twenty-five Blood Eagles, took the place of the *Shepherd*'s normal complement of marines, but he and the dozen members of his personal entourage were simply excess baggage so far as the ship's personnel were concerned.

"Though as for being civilians . . ." Garric added mildly. "I think you'd find I could give as good an account of myself in battle as most of the marines the *Shepherd*'s shipped over the years."

For his formal arrival in Carcosa, Garric wore a breastplate of silvered bronze and a silvered helmet whose spreading wings had been gilded. If the sun cooperated, Prince Garric would be a dazzling gem in a setting formed by the polished black armor of his bodyguards.

Garric's armor this day was for show, but the sword hanging from his belt had a plain bone hilt and a long blade of watered steel. There was nothing flashy about the weapon; but swung by an arm as strong as Garric's, the edge would take an enemy's head off with a single stroke.

"Yes *sir,* your highness!" Lobon said, looking horrorstruck to realize what he'd said to his prince. To avoid a further blunder, he stepped forward on the walkway and bellowed through the ventilator, "Timekeeper! Raise the stroke a half beat, won't you? This is supposed to be a royal entry, not a funeral procession!"

Obediently the flutist in the far bow of the oar deck quickened the tempo of the simple four-note progression on his right-hand pipe; the other pipe of the pair continued to play a drone. The rate at which the oars dipped, rose, and feathered forward increased by the same amount. In time the *Shepherd* would slide marginally faster through the water, but a quinquereme was too massive to do anything suddenly. Even the much lighter triremes, which made up the bulk of the fleet, accelerated with a certain majesty.

"The trouble is, lad," said the image of Carus, *"you don't act like a noble and they treat you like the folks they grew up with. Then they remember who you really are and they're afraid you'll have them flayed alive for disrespect to Prince Garric of Haft."*

I'd never do that! Garric thought in shock.

"No more would I," Carus agreed, *"though I showed a hard enough hand to enemies of the kingdom. But there's some in your court who'd show less hesitation over executing a commoner for disrespect than they would over the choice of a wine with their dinner."*

"I don't belong here," Garric whispered, but he didn't need the snort from the ghost in his mind to know that he did indeed belong. The Kingdom of the Isles, wracked by rebellion and wizardry, needed Prince Garric and his friends more than it needed any number of the courtiers and Ornifal landowners who'd claimed to be the government of the Isles for most of the thousand years since the Old Kingdom collapsed in blood and chaos.

Thought of his friends made Garric look toward the bow where his sister Sharina, his boyhood friend Cashel, and the wizard Tenoctris leaned against the railing. Like Garric they were mostly concerned with keeping out of the way. This was a particular problem for the women since they'd dressed for arrival in Carcosa in spreading court robes of silk brocade: cream with a gold stripe for "Princess Sharina," sea green for the aged wizard. In a manner of speaking, Tenoctris was much older than the seventy years or so she looked: she'd been flung a thousand years into the future—and onto the beach at Barca's Hamlet—by the same wizard-born cataclysm that had brought down the Old Kingdom.

Sharina wore a fillet, but the golden flood of her hair streamed out beneath it. She was tall—taller than most men in Barca's Hamlet—and blond unlike anyone else in the community. Her mother Lora had been a maid in the palace in Carcosa when tall, blond Niard, an Ornifal noble, had been Count of Haft through his marriage to Countess Tera. . . .

Even a brother could see that Sharina's willowy beauty would be exceptional in any company. "But I know a prettier woman yet," whispered Garric, and smiled wider to think of Liane bos-Benliman. She'd be meeting him here in Carcosa for their wedding.

Sharina felt the weight of her brother's glance. She turned and waved, her smile like sunlight.

Tenoctris and Cashel turned with her. The old wizard was cheerful, birdlike, and as doggedly determined as any soldier in the army. Cashel was almost as tall as Garric, but he was so broad that he didn't look his height unless you saw him with ordinary men. Mountains would crumble before either Cashel or his sister Ilna, aboard the two-decked patrol vessel following the *Shepherd*, ever failed their duty. Sharina was fortunate to love a man so solid and so much in love with her.

There's never been a man luckier in his friends, Garric thought as he smiled back. Then he turned and waved to the small woman in the stern of the patrol vessel astern.

"And never a better time than now," Carus said, *"for the Kingdom of the Isles to have friends—and luck!"*

When Ilna saw Garric wave, her first thought was, *What does he mean by that?*

Then, feeling foolish—feeling more of a fool than she usually did—she waved with her right as her left held the cords she was plaiting. The movement was polite and a little prim, the way Ilna os-Kenset did most things.

Garric didn't mean anything by it. He was just making a friendly gesture to a childhood friend who didn't, after all, mean very much to him.

Near Ilna—and on a deck-and-a-half patrol vessel like the *Flying Fish,* anyone could be described as near everyone else aboard—Chalcus talked with Captain Rhamis bor-Harriol, a nobleman younger than Ilna's nineteen years.

From what Ilna had seen of the captain during the voyage up the western shore of the Isles, he was a complete ninny.

That didn't matter, of course; or at any rate, it didn't matter any more than if Rhamis was being a ninny in some job on shore. The *Flying Fish*'s sailing master took care of navigation and the ordinary business of the ship, limiting the captain's responsibilities to leading his men in a battle. In Ilna's opinion, ninnies were quite sufficient for *that* task.

"Is something wrong, Ilna?" Merota asked from Ilna's elbow, unseen till the moment she spoke. The nine-year-old was, as Lady Merota bos-Roriman, the orphaned heir to one of the wealthiest houses on Ornifal. Ilna was her guardian, because . . . well, because Ilna had been there and nobody else Ilna trusted was available.

The girl was related to Lord Tadai, who acted as chancellor and chief of staff while Garric was with the fleet and those who held the posts officially were back in the palace at Valles. Tadai would've taken care of Merota, but to Tadai that meant marrying the child to some noble as quickly as possible. Merota was young? All the more reason to pass the trouble of raising her on to somebody else.

Ilna and her brother Cashel had been left to raise themselves after their grandmother died when they were seven. Their father Kenset had never said who their mother was; he'd kept a close tongue on the question of where he'd been when he went off adventuring. The only task Kenset applied himself to after coming home with the infants was drinking himself to death, and at that he quickly succeeded.

Ilna and Cashel had survived—survived and prospered, most would say. They were honored members of the royal court, after all. But Ilna wouldn't willingly see another child deal with what she'd gone through herself. If that meant she had to take responsibility for the child, well, she'd never been one to shirk responsibility.

"Nothing's wrong with the world, Merota," Ilna said. She smiled faintly and corrected herself, "Nothing more than usual, that is."

Which is enough and more than enough! she thought, but it wasn't the time to say that, if there was ever a time.

"And as for myself, I'm in my usual state," she continued, still smiling. "Which is bad enough also, I suppose."

When Ilna had last glanced at Merota, the girl was amidships with Mistress Kaline, the impoverished noblewoman who acted as her governess. Mistress Kaline was still there, lying flat over the ventilators—the *Flying Fish* had no amidships railing—and looking distinctly green.

Ilna's stomach flopped in sympathy, but she'd learned early in the voyage not to eat until they'd made landfall for the night so that she could digest on solid ground. The patrol vessel was agile and quick in a short dash, but it pitched, rolled, and yawed in a fashion that Ilna didn't have words to describe. It wouldn't have been her choice for the ship she wanted to travel on, but she'd never wanted to travel in the first place.

The rest of Garric's staff was aboard quinqueremes or the three-banked triremes that made up most of the fleet. The bigger ships were equally crowded, but they were a great deal more stable. Chalcus had picked the *Flying Fish* because it was similar to the pirate craft he'd commanded in the days before he met Ilna; and since Ilna had picked Chalcus, that was the end of the matter so far as she was concerned.

Chalcus caught Ilna's eye; he bowed to her and Merota with a flourish before resuming his conversation. Chalcus was no more than middling height. He looked slender from the side, but his shoulders were broad and he moved with the grace of a leopard. If you looked closely at his sharply pleasant features, you saw the scars; and when Chalcus was stripped down to a linen kilt like the sailors, you could see he had scars of one sort or another over most of his body.

From taste and habit Ilna dressed plainly, in unbleached woolen tunics and a blue wool cloak when the weather required it; Chalcus by contrast was a dazzle of color whenever circumstances permitted. Today he wore breeches of red leather, a silk shirt dyed in bright indigo, and between them a sash colored a brilliant yellow with bee's pollen that matched the fillet binding his hair. Ilna knew that the nobles gathered on the quay to meet them would think Chalcus looked like a clown; but they wouldn't say anything, at least not the ones who took time to note the sailor's eyes and the way use had worn the hilt of his incurved sword.

"I do hope Mistress Kaline won't still be sick when we're introduced to Count Lascarg," Merota said in a carefully polite voice. "She'll never be able to live down the embarrassment if that happens."

Ilna looked sharply at her ward, thinking for a moment that she was serious. Then Merota's angelic expression dissolved in a fit of giggles.

"Yes," Ilna said, allowing herself to smile minusculely before her face stiffened again into its accustomed sternness. "But if necessary we'll both help her stand. I've found it settles me to hold on to others."

She didn't care for Mistress Kaline as a person; but then, she didn't care for very many people. Ilna had continued to employ Mistress Kaline after Merota became her ward, in part because the stern old snob did in her way truly love the child, but also because Ilna was more afraid of her own power than she was of anything else in this world or beyond it. It would be easy to dismiss the governess who'd sneered at Ilna as an orphan with no culture and no forebears . . . but for Ilna, it would have been equally easy to weave a pattern that would rip Mistress Kaline's soul straight to Hell.

That way lay damnation. It was a path Ilna had once traveled, and from which she would never fully be able to return.

"You're really all right, Ilna?" Merota asked softly.

Ilna reached down with her right hand and squeezed the girl's. Sometimes Merota acted younger than her nine years, but at others it seemed that she was taking care of Ilna instead of the other way around.

"Yes, child," Ilna said, deliberately resuming the pattern she'd been knotting from the hank of short cords she kept in her sleeve. "I've made some bad decisions in the course of my life, and I'll probably make more mistakes as I get older. But in the main, the pattern's not one anyone has a right to object to."

Ilna glanced at the fabric her fingers were knotting while her mind considered other, less pleasant, things. Her pattern in coarse twine would calm those who looked at it, raise their spirits or cool their anger. Ilna didn't weave *charms* any more than the sun was a charm because it warmed those on whom its rays fell. What Ilna wove had the same natural certainty as the wind and the rain, as daylight and death.

She put the finished fabric in her right sleeve, then took a fresh hank of cords out of her left and began again. The patterns were just a way of occupying her fingers; the work didn't calm her, exactly, but her irritation was more likely to come to the surface if she *wasn't* doing something.

A trumpeter signaled from the flagship, the five-banked monster to the right of Garric's. Captain Rhamis looked as startled as a mouse surprised in the pantry. "What's that?" he cried on a rising note. "What're we to do, Plotnin?"

Before the sailing master could answer, Chalcus laid a hand on the nobleman's shoulder and spoke reassuringly. A trireme pulled ahead, but nothing else about the fleet's stately progression changed. Rhamis bobbed his head, rubbing his hands nervously together.

Ilna smiled at an idle thought. She gave her completed patterns to oarsmen and soldiers, common people. She'd been around the rich and powerful enough in recent days to know that they had problems also, but somebody else could worry about them. Ilna would take care of her own first.

She'd always had a talent for fabrics. As a young girl she'd woven so skillfully that the other women in the borough surrounding Barca's Hamlet brought Ilna the thread they'd spun and instead of weaving themselves took a share of the profits from the cloth she finished. That as much as her brother's early strength explained how two orphans had survived in a community which, while not unkind and fairly prosperous as peasant villages went, had no surplus for useless mouths in a hard winter.

Ilna's talent was natural or at least passed for it, but when Ilna left Barca's Hamlet she'd taken a wrong turning that had led her to Hell. She'd met what looked like a tree there. The skills the tree had taught her gave Ilna the power to let or hinder souls, to change a heart or steal a life. She'd used her new abilities for what she thought at the time were her own ends but which she knew now were the purposes of Evil alone.

While Evil ruled her, Ilna had done things that she couldn't forgive and which couldn't be put right. She knew that she'd never be able to make amends for the evil she'd done casually, callously, if she spent the remainder of her life trying.

So be it. Ilna would try anyway, in small ways, in all the ways that she could. Eventually she'd die with her job undone. She assumed death would end her responsibilities. If it didn't, well, she'd deal with what came then.

Chalcus sauntered back from where he'd been talking to the captain. His stride anticipated the deck's motion with the same unconscious ease that Ilna's fingers demonstrated when weaving. The *Flying Fish* was short, narrow, and relatively high. She carried fifteen oarsmen in the upper tier on either side with ten more below them in the center where the hull was wide enough—barely—for them to work. Chalcus said the design made the patrol vessel nimble and fairly fast, but she wobbled like a slowing top.

"There's a shipload of Blood Eagles gone ahead to make sure things are safe for Master Garric," Chalcus said, hooking a thumb over his shoulder in the direction of the trireme that was already driving through the harbor entrance. "Not that the lad showed much need to be protected the times *I've* seen him with a sword in his hand."

Ilna wasn't a seaman, but she could judge patterns like few other people: the men on the trireme's flashing oars were strong and willing, but their timing wasn't as smooth as that of other vessels in the fleet. The bodyguards were picked men, but they weren't picked *oars*men.

She smiled again, recognizing a familiar truth. Every task has its special skills, rowing and weaving no less than the sweep of words that poets use, or that wizards speak for other purposes.

Merota took Chalcus's left hand in hers and began to sing in her clear soprano, *"Lord Lovel he stood by his ship so fine, a-rigging her snow-white sails . . ."*

The sailor himself had taught Merota the ballad along

with many others. For a wonder this one wasn't as bawdy as those the child usually chose to sing in public. Perhaps she didn't think any of the folk aboard the *Flying Fish* would care; except for Mistress Kaline, perhaps, but as sick as the governess looked, probably not even her.

At another time Chalcus would have joined in with the child, singing about the nobleman who came back from a long voyage just in time for his true love's funeral, but the admiral's trumpeter sounded another signal. "Chalcus!" Lord Rhamis called, trotting up the deck toward them. "What do they want us to do?"

Chalcus slipped his hand from Merota's, tousled her hair, and gave Ilna a quick nod of regret before turning back to the dithering captain. Chalcus was determined that the ship he'd brought Ilna and Merota aboard should proceed smoothly, or at any rate without needless embarrassment. It was a responsibility he'd accepted without having sought it, much as Garric was ruling a kingdom though Ilna was sure that he'd have been happier helping his father run a village inn and reading the verses of Old Kingdom poets in his free time.

Garric's big ship began to draw ahead of the other vessels. Prince Garric of Haft would enter the harbor in solitary state, with the rest of his mighty fleet following at a respectful distance.

Ilna's fingers wove twine. She knew that Merota was speaking, but for the moment she didn't have attention to spare for the child.

Being a prince was a great burden, she was sure. Ilna didn't care about "the Isles" as a thing in itself; but she cared about people because it was her duty to care about people, and she knew that the people of the Isles were far better off with Garric ruling the kingdom than if he hadn't been.

A prince deserved a wife worthy of him; a well-born, well-educated, beautiful woman like Liane bos-Benliman. It was far better for everyone that Garric should marry Liane than that he throw himself away on a peasant girl who couldn't write her own name; even if the peasant happened to have a talent for weaving.

"Ilna?" called a child's voice from far away. "Please Ilna, what's wrong?"

And Ilna's fingers knotted a pattern that would bring warmth and calm to the man she offered it to.

"It's more like standing on the seawall at Barca's Hamlet than it's like being in a boat," Sharina said, looking down at the sea almost a dozen feet below the level of the deck on which she stood to the left of Cashel and Tenoctris. Foam boiled back as the *Shepherd*'s bronze ram dipped and rose minusculely at the thrust of the oars. The water was gray today; all Sharina could see in it was an occasional bit of weed churned up as the quinquereme's huge weight slid past.

"We're moving," said Cashel simply. "I don't think I'll ever get used to that. I don't mind, but it's not like being on solid ground."

Sharina laughed. "Cashel," she said, "so long as you're around, *everything* seems solid."

She hugged herself to him, a great, warm boulder. He didn't respond—they were in public, after all—but he smiled as he continued to watch the approaching shore. The long stone moles that extended Carcosa's fine natural harbor had survived the thousand years of neglect following the collapse of the Old Kingdom. One of the lighthouses that originally framed the entrance remained also, streaming a long red-on-white pennon to welcome the fleet, but the other had fallen into a pile of rubble.

The lighthouses had been built in the form of hollow statues: one of the Lady wearing the crescent tiara of the moon, the other of the Shepherd holding the sun disk. Celondre had written a poem when the lighthouses were dedicated, likening them to the children of King Carlon, the hope of the Kingdom's future.

Sharina's arm was still around Cashel's waist. She felt it tighten involuntarily, drawing her to Cashel's solidity in an inconstant world. She'd first read Celondre's verse as a child in Barca's Hamlet where she and Garric were tutored by their father Reise. The twin statues, decorated with gold-washed bronze, had seemed the most wondrous objects in the world, and the kingdom when Celondre lived and wrote was the next thing to paradise. She'd never dreamed that some day she'd see the statues herself.

But these weren't the shining triumphs of a child's imagination. One had fallen and time had so worn the other that Sharina couldn't be sure which deity it was meant to represent. The twin children Celondre praised in the same lyric had both died within a year: the boy had drowned on a sea voyage, while the girl was carried off by a fever. Carlon had died old and bitter, withdrawn from the world and his duties to the kingdom; and a generation later, when the forces that turned the cosmos rose to their thousand-year peak, the Golden Age had fallen in mud and slaughter.

And those forces were rising again. . . .

"Is anything wrong, Sharina?" Cashel asked. He'd felt her tremble, so he shifted his quarterstaff to his right hand in order to put his left around her. His strength was more reassuring than stone walls or a sheet of iron.

"No, nothing that we can't take care of," she said, sorry to have caused the big man to worry. "I was just thinking about a poem Celondre wrote a thousand years ago."

Cashel nodded. Sharina knew that he wouldn't understand what she meant, but now he knew that it wasn't anything he needed to be concerned about. If it was about books, then there were plenty of other people around to take care of it. "Well," he said, "that's all right, then."

In Barca's Hamlet, few people could read or write well. Reise came from Valles on Ornifal, the royal capital, and had been unusually well-educated even there. He and the children he'd taught were unique exceptions. Cashel and Ilna were almost completely illiterate—able to spell out their own names, and that with difficulty. As best Sharina could judge, Cashel regarded books much as he did the depths of the sea: they were vast, hidden reservoirs of the strange and wonderful.

Tenoctris glanced at Sharina, leaning over the bow railing to see past Cashel's bulk. The old woman raised an eyebrow in friendly question at the concern she'd heard in Sharina's voice.

"Celondre wrote a poem about the lighthouses," Sharina explained, embarrassed to have brought the matter up. "And now they're, well . . ." She waved her hand at the timeworn figures.

Tenoctris nodded, seeming to understand more than the younger woman had actually said. "I never visited Carcosa in my own day," she said. "It must have been marvelous. But what I think is important, dear, is the direction of things. A thousand years ago Carcosa and the kingdom were greater than either is now, but they were on the verge of ruin. Today we're rebuilding. It'll be a long time before we—"

She gave a quick, flashing grin.

"—before your children's children will have built a city as great as Carcosa was when Carus reigned, but we're going in the right direction."

So far we've been going in the right direction, Sharina thought, because that was the whole of her fear. But she didn't say that aloud, because as soon as the words flashed into her mind she saw how silly she was being. *So far* was all you could say about anything, ever. Life was temporary; sun and rain and the seasons came and went and returned. Sharina's task was to help Garric and all the other people on the side of peace and order to succeed for as long as she lived.

Wizards like Tenoctris directed onto human affairs the forces that turned the very cosmos and which waxed and waned on a thousand-year cycle. Their peaks were neither good nor evil in themselves, but they gave greater scope to wizards who attempted evil—and greater effect to the mistakes of wizards whose pride was greater than their knowledge.

As if responding to Sharina's thought, Tenoctris smiled wryly and said, "If all we had to worry about were a handful of conscious evildoers, life would be much simpler than it is in the present world of fools, wouldn't it? Though—" she frowned at her own comment "—I'm being needlessly unkind."

Tenoctris was the first to admit that she wasn't a powerful wizard, even now when powers were far greater than they'd been for a millennium. But she didn't make mistakes; and so far as Sharina was concerned, Tenoctris had every right to condemn the powerful fools whose blundering imperiled the kingdom.

A sailor—a petty officer wearing a broad leather belt over his kilt instead of a rope tie like the common seamen—ran out on the jib, shading his eyes with a hand as he peered into the sea ahead of them. He rode the ship's dips and risings with the practiced grace of a courtier making gestures in accordance with palace etiquette. He must have seen—or not seen—what he expected, because he turned and bellowed sternward, "Aye, we're clear, Master Lobon!"

"Such a lot of people," Cashel said, shaking his head in pleased amazement as his eyes swept the moles. "I never knew there were so many people in all the world."

The wealthy nobles of Carcosa would be on the quay to greet Prince Garric formally, but the common people had come out also. The nobles' retainers would keep them away from the quay, but by standing on the long, curving arms that enclosed the harbor they got an earlier view of the visitors. There were thousands of them—many thousands. Even as a shade of its former self, Carcosa remained a great city.

"Waiting to see us," Cashel marveled aloud. He grinned broadly. "Well, waiting to see Prince Garric. And that's just as amazing a thing as, well, all the rest."

He gestured clumsily with the arm that encircled Sharina, indicating the pomp and glitter of the royal fleet: flags and bunting, soldiers in gleaming armor; a hundred bronze rams glinting across the western horizon as the ships approached the harbor, and the sea running in jeweled droplets from the blades of thousands of feathering oars. The commander of the *Shepherd*'s Blood Eagles was trying to array them, though the deck even of a quinquereme was so narrow that only two could stand abreast. Sailors hopped over the ventilator gratings above the oarsmen, cursing the soldiers but going on about their tasks regardless.

The spectators started to cheer while the fleet was still a quarter mile from the mole. The sound was faint at first, from only a few throats and attenuated by distance; but it built, and soon the whole crowd was cheering. Scarves and sashes waved, improvised flags to greet the prince.

"I wasn't sure they'd be glad to see us," Cashel said. "An army coming, after all; an army from Ornifal."

"They're cheering for Prince Garric of *Haft*," Sharina reminded him. "The people who've held power in Carcosa, Count Lascarg and his cronies, may not be happy to see us, but the common people are proud that a man from Haft rules the kingdom for the first time in a thousand years."

"I guess the count'll keep his mouth shut if he has a problem," Cashel said. He spoke with a hint of quiet anticipation. Cashel was for the most part a gentle man; Sharina didn't remember him ever having started a fight. But he'd never quit one either while there was an opponent left who wanted to keep going.

"Yes," said Sharina, thrilled to be reminded of the other side of her fiancé, the part that was never directed at her. "I think he'll be *very* quiet."

She cleared her throat, then added, "And I think that the people cheering know that even if Garric were a tyrant, they're better off ruled by a bully who's in Valles most of the time than they are with the gang right in their midst."

"Prince Garric . . ." called the crowd on the mole. They were shouting in unison now so that Sharina could make out their words. "Prince Garric . . ."

"Garric's not a bully," Cashel said, his voice a soft rumble. His muscles had stiffened, and his thick hickory quarterstaff quivered slightly in his right hand. "And if the people running Carcosa *are* bullies, well, so much the worse for them now."

Sharina felt a surge of pride: in her brother, in her friends, and in the Kingdom of the Isles that they and she were bringing back to life, so that there would be peace and justice for people like the ones cheering them on; peace and justice for the first time in a thousand years.

No matter what wizards or usurpers tried to do to stop them!

"Prince Garric of Haft!" the crowd called.

Cashel stood by the forecastle rail, careful not to rest his weight on it. The hoardings were canvas over a wicker backing, and salt had dried the wood of the frame timbers, leaving long splits. The structure was meant to keep head seas from combing over the prow, not to support the weight of a man Cashel's size.

Cashel could no more swim than he could fly. If he fell overboard he'd try to grab an oar as the ship drove past him, but he'd just as soon not put the question to the test.

For display when they entered Carcosa, the fighting tower was set up in the bow. Its walls were canvas-covered wicker—they were painted to look like stone—but the cross-braced frame was of timbers as sturdy as any to be found on the ship. It had to be to take the recoil of the balista mounted on top.

Today the weapon wasn't cocked, of course. Instead of serviceable iron the head of the bolt in the weapon's trough was of brass polished to look like gold. The four crewmen wore plumes on their helmets and dangled silver gorgets across their linen corselets. The padded linen gave them some protection but was flexible enough they could crank the windlass to draw back the balista's arms.

Sharina seemed cheerful again. Her hand was on Cashel's left shoulder as she stood in companionable silence, which suited him fine. Until he'd left Barca's Hamlet less than a year ago, he'd spent more time with sheep than with humans. Since then he'd learned that many folks thought that unless people were talking there was something the matter. For the life of him, Cashel couldn't understand that.

Cashel was pretty much pleased with the world and with his part in it. That was mostly the case with him. He supposed that was because he didn't have big problems like Garric, who had to keep the kingdom from crashing into ruin and taking everybody's lives and hopes with it.

All Cashel needed to do were simple things like keeping safe whatever he'd been told to take care of. Once that'd meant sheep; now as apt as not it was a person, and that was all right too. He squeezed Sharina gently with his left hand, just reassuring himself that she really was there.

The only trouble that Cashel'd ever found too big for him

was when he'd fallen in love with Sharina os-Reise. She was beautiful, a scholar like her brother, and she'd inherit half the inn—making her by the standards of the borough a wealthy woman. Cashel had known that she was far too good for him.

And so she was: he remained sure of that, as sure as he was that she loved him anyway. Cashel couldn't imagine why, but when he woke every morning he thanked the Shepherd for granting him a gift greater than any he would have dared to ask.

Sharina leaned forward slightly, lost in her own reverie; the railing creaked. Wicker alone would be strong enough to support her weight—though tall, she wasn't a blocky mass like Cashel—but his grip tightened reflexively. She patted his hand reassuringly and eased back to humor him.

Thought of the way salt dried wood made Cashel glance at his quarterstaff, a wrist-thick shaft of hickory, seven feet long and as straight as a sunbeam. He'd made the staff himself as a boy, taking one perfect limb as his payment for felling the tree for a neighbor. He'd shaved and polished the wood, and in the years since he'd continued to wipe it down with wads of raw, lanolin-rich wool whenever he had the opportunity. The staff had taken hard knocks and given harder ones; but today its surface remained as ripplingly smooth as a wheel-turned jug.

Sea air had painted a tinge of rust over the quarterstaff's black iron buttcaps, but that could wait till they were on land again. If Cashel wiped them now, they'd rust over again in less time than it'd taken him to clean them. He'd have liked to rub the hickory, though, but doing that would've meant taking his arm from around Sharina's waist. The quarterstaff, trusty companion though it was, didn't need his attention *that* bad.

Cashel looked past the girl nestled against his shoulder. Their ship—Garric's ship—was two full lengths ahead of the rest of the warships. Following them was a second line, of light craft like the one Ilna traveled on with her beau Chalcus and also of triremes used for transport. Those had only one bank of oarsmen with the rest of the space in the narrow hulls given over to cargo and soldiers who hadn't been trained to pull an oar—another kind of cargo so far as the sailors were concerned.

To count the ships Cashel would've needed a bag of dried peas, like he'd have used to tally a flock of sheep. There were many times more ships than he had fingers, though. Sharina was right: if Garric said *jump,* Count Lascarg would ask "How high?"

He felt his skin prickle; an itchy feeling like the first hint of sunburn after a day's plowing. Cashel's brows knitted in a frown. It wasn't sunburn today; and the other thing that gave him that sort of feeling was wizardry close by.

"Tenoctris?" he said, disengaging himself from Sharina without bothering to explain. "Are you working a . . . ?"

But he could see that she wasn't, so he didn't bother to finish the question. If not Tenoctris, then . . . ?

The wizard sat down cross-legged more forcefully than could've been good for her old bones. She had a satchel of books and the paraphernalia of her art—Cashel carried it for her when the two of them were together—but she didn't bother with it now. Instead, she took a split of bamboo from the sleeve of her court robe and drew a pentacle with it on the soft pine deck between her knees.

Using the bamboo where a less-cautious wizard would use a specially forged athame, she tapped the flats of the pentacle murmuring, *"Cbesi niapha amara . . ."* in time with her beat. A spark of crimson wizardlight winked into existence in the center of the symbol, waxing and waning as she spoke.

Cashel shifted his body slightly to hide Tenoctris as much as possible from the sight of nearby sailors. He trusted the old woman's skill and instincts both; but for most people, wizardry was as surely to be avoided as the plague. Nobody'd object aloud to what a friend of Prince Garric was doing, but the business would make people who saw it uncomfortable or worse. Cashel didn't want that if he could help it.

Sharina spread her court robe with both hands, providing an even better screen than Cashel's bulk. Her eyes looked questions, but she didn't speak. She knew that Cashel or Tenoctris would tell her if there was something she needed to know, and she didn't want to distract them from what might mean everybody's life or death.

"I don't see anything," Cashel said quietly. "It just doesn't feel right."

"Ialada . . ." Tenoctris said. *"Iale."*

The spark suddenly cascaded into a shape or series of shapes, like a wall of damp sand shivering to repose; an instant later it blinked out. Tenoctris dropped her wand and swayed, her frail body drained by practicing her art. Cashel steadied her with his left hand.

Some people believed that wizards merely waved their wands and their wishes took form effortlessly; those folk had never seen real wizardry. Cashel's muscles allowed him to lift weights that few other men could manage, but his feats didn't become easy simply because they were possible. Similarly, a truly powerful wizard could move mountains or tear chasms in time—but that work had a cost.

Tenoctris looked up. "Garric's in danger," she said, forcing the words out in a whisper. "I can't see what—there's a wall my art can't penetrate. But it's something terrible, rushing toward Garric."

"Sound the alarm!" Sharina called. Her clear voice rang over the grunt of hundreds of oarsmen and the *thump* of their bodies slamming down on their benches at the end of each stroke. *"We're being attacked!"*

"Watch her!" Cashel said, releasing Tenoctris so that he could grip his quarterstaff in both hands. Sharina would hold the old wizard if she still needed help to keep upright. As for Cashel himself—

He stepped past the women and leaped outward to the long wale supporting the rowlocks for the uppermost banks of oars. The narrow deck was clogged with Blood Eagles slipping the gilt balls from their spearpoints, turning them back from ceremonial staffs into weapons. Rather than force his way through the soldiers, Cashel was going around.

"Keep clear!" he bellowed, running like a healthy young ox heading for water after a day of plowing. The wale creaked, and the quinquereme itself wobbled as Cashel's weight pounded along so far outboard.

The young aide at Garric's side began to hammer on the rectangular alarm gong set in a framework on the stern railing. The boy's eyes were open and staring.

"Keep clear!"

Chapter Two

*S*ound the alarm!" Garric said. He didn't know what was going on, but he drew his sword with no more than a whisper against the iron lip of the scabbard.

Cashel was running sternward, so the danger wasn't in the bow. Garric turned, looking past the high, curving sternpost. The 127 ships of the royal fleet were arrayed behind the *Shepherd* in order as good as that of so many soldiers at drill. He didn't see any danger, neither in the water foaming past in the oar-thresh nor in the sea to the horizon or the clouds above it. Rain perhaps, but from this sky it would be warm and slow, not gusts with lightning slashes.

There was danger somewhere. The warning must have come from Tenoctris, and she didn't make mistakes.

The trumpet and coiled horn on Admiral Zettin's *Queen of Ornifal* blew together, the raucous call that signaled fleet action. Zettin was commander of the fleet just as Lord Waldron commanded the royal army: Garric could give orders to either man and expect them to be obeyed before they were fully out of his mouth, but the prince didn't get involved in the mechanics of maneuvering ships or battalions.

The prince had other matters to take care of. At the moment, the most important was learning what was the matter.

"Clear the yards, you stupid scuts!" Master Lobon shouted to the sailors who'd gone aloft for show. "Action stations, don't you hear!"

Wiping his face with the end of his red sash-of-office, he snarled—to the gods, not to any of the humans nearby, "Sister take me, the mast's raised! Won't that be a fine thing if we have to ram?"

King Carus took in the world through Garric's eyes, but he analyzed what he saw with the mind of the foremost man of war who'd ever ruled the Isles. A glint on a hilltop that Garric assumed was merely a quartz outcrop was to Carus a possible ambush; the tension in a courtier's posture might precede an assassination attempt. Carus had personal experience of those threats and a thousand more—

But he saw nothing of concern in the surrounding seascape.

"Your majesty—" Zettin called through a speaking horn from the stern of his flagship. Water spewed up as his oarsmen laid into their looms with renewed vigor, trying to close the gap they'd allowed to open between them and Garric's ship.

"Your majesty?" called the captain of the Blood Eagles aboard the *Shepherd*. He held his men in a double rank facing both sides of the ship. Their spears slanted forward, the points winking, and their left arms advanced their shields slightly.

Lerdain was saying something also, though Garric couldn't hear him through the racket of the gong he hammered. Garric pointed at the youth and bellowed, "Enough! Let me think!"

Lerdain froze. Garric knew he wasn't being fair—the lad was only doing what he was supposed to—but there wasn't time to worry about that. The gong continued to vibrate on a note that drilled all the way to Garric's marrow. He tore it from its mountings with his left hand and hurled it into the sea. Water danced briefly as the bronze block sank through the waves.

Cashel hopped onto the quarterdeck, brushing the end of the rail as he went past; it broke. "Tenoctris says you're in danger but she doesn't know what from!" he said, turning to face outward. His hands were on either side of his quarterstaff's balance, ready to swing or stab, whichever the situation called for.

"Well, at least I know where I stand!" Garric said, turning so his back was to Cashel's.

With my friends, and with a sword in my hand. What better place was there?

He and the warrior king in his mind laughed amid the shouts and the horn signals.

The gong's rich note echoed between sea and sky. *They could hear it in Barca's Hamlet,* Ilna thought, and didn't chide herself for exaggerating as she usually would've done.

As the first note sounded, Chalcus began to survey the horizon. He didn't unsheathe his sword or razor-sharp dagger, but he was as tautly poised as a drawn bowstring.

"Ilna, what's the bell?" Merota said, only a child again as she tugged on Ilna's outer tunic. Merota had seen a great deal of horror in her short life. She'd come through it, and given a moment to compose herself she'd come through this as well; but the sudden clanging shocked her into panic. "What's going to happen?"

Chalcus spun and pointed his left index finger at the child's face. "You!" he said. "Crouch under the sternpost behind Glomer, that's as safe a place as there is. *Now!*"

"Yes, Chalcus," Merota said, scuttling past the frozen helmsman to obey. When she'd huddled behind the flutist who blew time for the oarsmen, she began bawling her eyes out.

"Mistress?" Chalcus said softly; his eyes on Ilna's, his muscles rigid as iron but not moving, not yet. Trumpets and horns called; the oarsmen looked up through the ventilators in frightened surmise, and half the sailors on deck were shouting something to someone or everyone. Captain Rhamis tugged Chalcus's tunic much as Merota had done Ilna's, and for much the same reason.

Ilna looked down at the cords she'd been knotting and in their pattern saw the answer to the question Chalcus hadn't put in words. Even strangers could have read the coarse fabric, though they'd have called it a feeling, an impression. To Ilna there was no more doubt than there was in the direction of dawn.

"From there," Ilna said, pointing northwest with her outstretched left arm. She hadn't woven the pattern consciously, but a part of her mind had provided the information she was going to need. "An enemy, coming for Garric. Fast!"

Chalcus's gaze followed her arm. Ilna herself could see only swells and troughs; the sea was a little rougher than earlier this morning before the clouds darkened. The sailor shaded his eyes with his hands stacked, looking through the narrow slit between left palm and the back of his right hand.

Chalcus turned to the helmsman. "Bring us along the *Shepherd*'s side," he ordered crisply. Then, loud even against the clamor all around them, he shouted, "Glomer, play a sprint!"

Glomer was the flutist. Ilna had marveled to see that within a day of boarding the *Flying Fish* in Donelle, Chalcus had known the name of every sailor aboard the vessel. Indeed, she was sure he could give an appraisal of each man's strengths and weaknesses as clear as she herself could've done about the folk of Barca's Hamlet where she'd lived all her life.

"Hawsom—"

The stroke oar, a swarthy man with huge shoulders and an opal the size of Ilna's thumbnail in the septum of his nose.

"—every man of you on the benches, put your backs into it like never before! We're going to save our prince, that's what we're going to do!"

He pointed to Glomer, seated where the upper bank of oarsmen could see him. The men down in the belly of the ship had little enough air, let alone a glimpse of the outside world; they took their cue from the men above them. "*Play*, I said!"

The flutist had been sounding a dirge as the fleet proper marked time while Garric's ship drew ahead. Now he swung into a jig; the high notes from the double-flute's short right-hand pipe syncopated the lower tones of the left. Together the rowers breathed deeply, then drew back on their oars with the deliberate motion of men well used to hard work and willing to continue till they dropped.

The ship moved ahead. It didn't leap like a kid in springtime, for though small compared to the quinqueremes it was still a massive object, but it accelerated noticeably.

"No!" cried Rhamis, reaching out to grab the flute. "Our orders are to keep back from—"

Chalcus caught the captain by throat and swordbelt. Rhamis barely had time to squawk before Chalcus flung him over the side.

"Row!" Chalcus cried to the oarsmen. "It's not your lousy lives you're saving, it's Prince Garric's!"

A coil of rope hung from a post on the afterdeck; it had something to do with the sails, now furled, Ilna supposed. She lifted it, judged her distance, and made sure one end of the rope was still attached to a cleat. Finally she spun the coil toward the floundering captain. It opened as it flew through the air, then splashed in the water in front of Rhamis; he had just enough presence of mind to seize it before it and he both sank.

Ilna turned again. The captain would've been no great loss; but small goodnesses were worth doing, if they didn't get in the way of larger ones . . . like saving Garric.

"Pull, you sailormen!" Chalcus called over the flute's skirl. "There's a devil from Hell after your prince, but we'll have something to say about that!"

Ilna stepped into the far stern, behind Glomer's stool, and offered her left hand to Merota huddling there. By squinting to the northwest she could see but a seeming oiliness on the surface, the track of something moving swiftly underwater toward Garric's huge vessel. The *Flying Fish* continued to accelerate, but the other thing would be there ahead of them.

"Pull!" and the men pulled with the strength of the damned grasping for salvation; but it would not be enough. . . .

Cashel waited, ready but not really tense. If there'd been more room on the *Shepherd*'s stern, he'd have given his quarterstaff a few trial spins to loosen his joints; there wasn't, so he'd make do when the time came.

The helmsman at the port steering oar looked seaward instead of keeping his eyes on the sailing master for orders the way he should've done. He suddenly screamed and lunged away from the railing, slamming into Cashel and bouncing back as though he'd run into the mainmast.

"Here we go!" warned Cashel, bringing his staff around

in front of him despite tight space. He clipped the shoulder of the helmsman, now scrambling away on all fours. The fellow yelped, but the contact didn't slow the staff's motion—which was all that mattered to Cashel at the moment.

The creature came straight up from the water with its huge jaws open. The pointed head was two double-paces long, ten feet as city folks would put it. The teeth were longer than Cashel's middle fingers. Those at the front of the jaw were pointed, while teeth farther back became broadly saw-edged.

"A seawolf!" Master Lobon cried, but Cashel had seen seawolves, great marine lizards, when they came ashore on Barca's Hamlet to snatch his grazing sheep. This creature had a smooth hide instead of a reptile's pebbled skin; and besides, this thing's head was as long as a big seawolf's whole body.

This was a whale, but not one of the sluggish, comb-toothed monsters that browsed on shrimp at the edge of the Ice Capes. This was a meat eater like the seawolves, only much, much bigger.

Still rising, the whale twisted to angle its gaping jaws toward Garric. The railing splintered. Instead of striking as he'd have done with a smaller opponent, Cashel stuck his staff vertically into the beast's maw.

He acted by instinct, but his instinct was correct—as it generally was in a fight. The whale's jaws slammed down but not shut, because the thick hickory didn't flex at the creature's bite. Its bunched jaw muscles only drove the staff's iron ferrules deeper into its own tongue and palate. From its throat came a hiss like a geyser preparing to vent.

The whale started to slip back into the sea, dragging Cashel with it. He wrapped his legs around the stanchion to which the steering oar was attached, continuing to grip the staff with both hands.

The quinquereme listed, dragged over by the weight of the whale. Blue fire rippled through Cashel's muscles; he wasn't sure whether human strength or the wizardry that sometimes filled him allowed him to keep his grip, but he knew that if he let go the monster would find another, better way to attack.

Cashel would anchor the whale so long as his staff held and his strength held, and neither one had ever failed him yet.

Garric hacked twice, leaving bone-deep cuts in the whale's jaw, but the creature's head was so large that a sword couldn't do it real damage. Instead of a third cut he stabbed, slanting his long blade through the underjaw and out through the black-veined tongue. Cashel saw the tip of pattern-welded steel glittering in a spray of blood, but even the blade's full length was unable to reach the monster's vitals.

A Blood Eagle hurled his spear into the whale's skull, just behind the eye. It was a good cast, but the point stuck less than a finger's length into dense bone; the spear fell into the sea. Three more spears drove uselessly into the whale's shoulder.

The whale's nostrils were on the top of its head, in front of the rear-set eyes. They voided a miasma of stale air and rotten flesh, then drew in a fresh breath with the roar of a windstorm.

Cashel was hanging over the sea as the oak stanchion creaked between his legs. Huge as the whale's head seemed, it was small in comparison to the snake-slim body. Far in the depths, Cashel saw the creature's flukes lashing in an attempt to pull itself away from the staff it couldn't spit out.

Very soon the quarterstaff would break, or Cashel would lose his grip on it, or the post would tear loose from the ship's hull. Whatever happened after that would no longer be the concern of Cashel or-Kenset.

Sharina let go of Tenoctris and rose to her feet. The old wizard still sat cross-legged, but she'd reached up to grip the bow railing to steady herself. Now that Sharina's hands were free, she reached under her loose-fitting court robes and drew the Pewle knife she wore concealed under the silk.

The knife's blade was heavy and the length of her forearm. The back was straight but the cutting edge had a deep belly. It was the knife carried by Pewle Island seal hunters, a weapon and every sort of tool all in one package. The knife and her memories were all Sharina had left of Nonnus, the man who'd guarded her through the fringes of Hell and who had died still guarding her.

When Sharina knew him, Nonnus had been a hermit dedicated to the Lady; earlier as a mercenary soldier he'd done things he never spoke of, but which Sharina had heard others whisper of him. She kept the Pewle knife for his memory; but in times like this, it was also a weapon that the bravest enemy would think twice before facing.

Garric's platoon of black-armored bodyguards had rushed to put themselves between their prince and the monster that had leaped toward him from the sea. Small chance of that: Garric stood firm-footed on the sloping deck, using both hands on his sword hilt to hack at the huge head.

The soldiers' weight made the ship list even more; water was gurgling through the lowest oarports, and the commotion belowdecks meant some of the rowers were about to abandon their benches. The sailing master was screaming at the sailors on deck to run out on the starboard wale to balance the load before the ship foundered.

Sharina had been hearing the click of ratchets against pawls from the fighting tower behind her, but it wasn't until the captain of the balista crew shouted, "She's ready! Swing her round!" that she realized the sound was capstans drawing back the balista's arms. She looked up.

The crewmen were rotating their weapon to point back over the *Shepherd*'s deck. Even with the sail furled the mast and cordage would interfere with their aim, but some part of the monster rising like a gleaming black crag beside the vessel should be clear.

The captain stooped to aim, disappearing from Sharina's viewpoint on the main deck. The bolt's bronze head, cross-shaped to smash instead of stabbing cleanly, winked as the captain adjusted the weapon's bearing. Instead of shooting, he rose with a troubled look while his crewmen waited expectantly.

"Shoot!" Sharina screamed. "Shoot or it'll pull us under!"

Over the shouts and clash of metal, Sharina heard the deep groan of the ship's timbers working. The monster's weight was twisting the hull like a bad storm.

"Mistress, I can't!" the soldier cried in agony. "Mistress, I might hit the prince!"

The fighting tower's notched crenellations were eight feet above the deck, higher than Sharina could reach but well within reach if she jumped. She sprang up without thinking further, catching the lip in her left hand and swinging her legs over the upper railing. Her robes got in the way, but that didn't stop her.

There wouldn't have been room for her on the narrow platform if her muscular body hadn't slammed one of the crewmen aside. The Pewle knife was still in her right hand.

"Is it aimed?" she shouted to the captain, his face only inches from hers. He stood with the release cord in his right hand. "Will it hit the thing?"

"Yes, but mistress—" the man said.

Sharina jerked the cord out of his hand. She started to whisper a prayer to the Lady, but the Lady brought peace and good harvests; she had no place here. Instead Sharina murmured, "Nonnus, help me and help my brother. . . ."

She didn't bother bending so that her eyes could follow the line of the bolt; she didn't have the skill to second-guess the captain, nor the time either. She pulled the release cord.

When the trigger claws released the thumb-thick bow-cord, the balista's arms slammed forward against the leather-padded stops on the frame. The double *Bang!* shocked a cry from Sharina; she'd seen balistas and catapults in use before, but she'd never been so close to one when it loosed.

A crash like that of a wedge splitting oak rang on top of the balista's release. Sharina looked toward the stern. The bolt was buried to its wooden vanes in the monster's head where the left eye had been. The impact had distorted the whole long skull like the hull of a rammed warship.

Garric staggered backward, unharmed. None of the thronging soldiers had been touched. *Nonnus, may the Lady show you the peace you did not find in life.*

As her eyes took in the scene, the patrol vessel with Ilna aboard drove into the monster's body alongside the *Shepherd*. The bronze ram bit deep with a sound like an axe chopping into a hog's carcass, but so much louder that it over-whelmed all other noise.

The creature's nostrils spurted a mist of blood high in the air. The patrol vessel's mast cracked and tilted forward, breaking some of the decking ahead of the mast step. The *Shepherd* shook violently; Sharina might've stumbled over the wooden battlements if a balista crewman hadn't stead-ied her.

The patrol vessel continued to slide forward, pulling the monster along with it. Timbers crashed and the *Shepherd* rolled upright with a shudder. The great jaws spasmed open as the carcass rolled onto its back.

Cashel was flying through the air, still holding his quarter-staff and gripping a broken post with his legs. Sharina didn't have time to cry out before he landed in the sea thirty feet from the quinquereme's stern.

Chapter Three

Cashel couldn't feel anything, not even the water when he belly flopped with a splash that would've been immense under most circumstances. Since the sea still roiled with the creature's death throes, he guessed nobody'd notice even that.

He plunged beneath the surface. The cold shock of the sea hadn't revived him, but not being able to breathe did. He tried to flail his arms and realized he was still holding his quarterstaff. He let go with one hand and paddled. Though he still couldn't feel anything and he knew he was very weak, his face lifted into the air again and he was able to gasp in a breath.

Like the whale, Cashel thought and might've laughed, but his nose dropped underwater. Breathing salt water seared his lungs worse than near suffocation had moments before. He kicked to the surface again, knowing that he'd shortly drown.

The water was red with the whale's blood and blotched with crimson froth. The monster lay on its back between Cashel and the *Shepherd,* floating low. Rhythmic spasms rippled down the creature's belly muscles; its underside was a pale contrast to the blotched gray-black of the upper surfaces.

A huge flipper lifted, then slammed back into the sea only inches from Cashel's face. He grabbed it instantly. He could feel bones beneath the slick, gristly surface.

The whale would probably sink also; Duzi, he could see that it was already sinking! But it didn't sink quite as fast as Cashel alone—all bone and muscle, with no fat to buoy him up in the water—so he clung to it and waited.

He might be rescued after all, though he didn't care much. Struggling with a monster the size of a ship had burned all emotion out of him. How long had the fight gone on, anyway?

Because Cashel lay so close to the whale's carcass, all he could see of the *Shepherd* was its mast top. The ship had continued on ahead after Cashel and the whale tore loose, swinging in a wide circle to port. It was so big that it kept going for a long time, even after the oars'd stopped.

Cashel could see and hear fine, and his muscles did what he told them—though not nearly as well as he expected. The numbness in his body was passing too, though of course all he could really feel now was pain.

Something was going on to Cashel's other side also. He'd have to turn his head to see what it was. With a real effort of will—it meant ducking his face underwater again—he did.

The *Flying Fish* was nosing back toward the whale, its prow smeared with blood and its ram skewed upward. Cashel had a vague recollection of the little ship hitting the whale at the moment everything let go in his mind and the world around him. Now its oars were backing to bring it to a halt in the crimson water.

Ilna stood in the bow with a coil of rope in her hand. "Can you catch if I throw this to you, brother?" she called. Her voice would've sounded unemotional to somebody who didn't know her as well as Cashel did.

"I can catch," he croaked, the first words he'd spoken

since he shouted a warning as the whale arrowed up from the depths. Ilna tossed the coil underhanded, landing it in the water so close that Cashel could've grabbed it with his teeth if he'd needed to.

He used his right hand instead, letting go of the whale's flipper. Just then Ilna's man Chalcus dived off the bow, stripped naked and holding the end of another coil of rope.

"I'm all right!" Cashel said, but Chalcus cut the water cleanly and didn't reappear for long moments. Ilna didn't look worried so Cashel figured things must be all right, but where *was* the fellow? A sailor on deck continued to pay out rope; a second coil was spliced onto the first.

The *Flying Fish* halted, drifting slowly toward Cashel. Ilna'd tied her rope to a stanchion, but Cashel wasn't quite ready to clamber up the ship's sheer side. The fight with the whale had taken a lot out of him; almost more than there'd been. He tried to remember exactly what'd happened after he thrust the staff into the monster's jaws, but it wasn't so much a blur as tiny broken pieces of a scene painted on glass.

Sailors at the stern of the *Flying Fish* were dragging a fellow dressed like an officer from the sea at the patrol vessel's stern. Had he fallen from the *Shepherd* the way Cashel had? There might've been more things going on than just the whale too.

"Hoy!" somebody shouted. Cashel turned his head. Chalcus stood on the whale's twitching body, spinning the end of his rope overhead; it must have been a lead line, loaded to sink quickly to check the depth. He'd gathered a triple loop in his left hand. "Ready?"

"Read—" called the sailor on deck. Chalcus loosed the line in an arrow-straight cast that took it into the hands of the waiting sailor. As soon as the fellow caught it, Chalcus jumped feet-first into the sea and bobbed up beside Cashel.

Cashel had begun to shiver. Not from the water, he thought; the sea wasn't nearly as cold as nights he'd watched his sheep through storms of early winter with no shelter but his sodden cloak. He'd strained even his own great strength; it'd be good to get some food in him, if he could keep it down. Or at least a mug of ale to sluice the foul dryness out his mouth. Right now it tasted like an ancient chicken coop.

Conversationally Chalcus said, "We'll be towing our prize in with us; the harbor's not so far, after all, and I've never seen or heard of a creature like this one. Have you, friend Cashel?"

"I never saw anything like it," Cashel muttered. "It's a whale, but it's nothing like the ones that pass in spring by Barca's Hamlet."

Talking helped; he suddenly understood why Chalcus paddled beside him in the bloody water, chatting like they were relaxing on a sunlit hillside. The sailor's tone was cheerfully mild, but his eyes missed nothing. If Cashel suddenly lost consciousness, Chalcus would grab him before he sank and keep him up till he could be hauled on deck like a netful of cargo.

"Neither have I seen its like," agreed Chalcus. "Nor heard of such, more to the point, for my dealings have been more in southern waters and the east than in these western wastes."

He grinned wickedly. His arms floated motionless on the surface, but his legs must be windmilling to keep him so high in the water. Chalcus's nude body looked like a deer skinned at the end of a hard winter. There was no fat on his scarred frame, none at all. His muscles stood out like the individual yarns of a hawser.

"Though perhaps I shouldn't say that, you being a western lad yourself," he added.

Cashel shook his head. "I'm from Barca's Hamlet," he muttered. "I don't know anything about oceans. As for Carcosa, if we get there—"

"Indeed, we'll get there, lad," the sailor said, bobbing like a child's toy in a puddle.

"—all I could say about it is, I've passed through the city and I was glad to get to the other side."

The mild banter was bringing Cashel back from the abyss his struggles had taken him to the edge of. He was aware of himself as a person again. Raising his head, he tried to find Sharina; the huge carcass was still a quivering wall between him and the *Shepherd*.

"Come on, you lazy buggers!" Chalcus bellowed at the crew of the *Flying Fish* as they tugged on the rope he'd tossed them. They were using the light line as a messenger to draw an anchor cable around the whale just behind the flippers. "The sun'll have set before we've got this brute to land, and where's the honor if folk can't see our trophy?"

"Can you really carry this on the *Flying Fish*?" Cashel asked, pitching his voice low so that no one on the deck above would hear the question. "It looks to me like it's as heavy as the whole ship."

"Aye, as heavy and more," Chalcus agreed. "But we'll be all right towing the toothy devil, so long as he doesn't sink; which may happen yet, if they don't make that hawser fast some time soon. I think perhaps I . . ."

He looked sidelong at Cashel, judging how far he'd recovered.

Cashel laughed, snorted salt water from his nostrils, and laughed again. "I think I'm ready to go aboard, Master Chalcus," he said. "I may not have all my strength back, but I think what remains will prove an aid to hauling that rope."

He looked at his sister on the deck above. "Ilna?" he said. "See to it that this line is snubbed off, will you? I'm coming aboard, and I don't look forward to spilling myself in the water again because something slipped!"

Cashel tugged to test the line himself, then walked up the side of the vessel using his left hand on the rope to steady him. Oh, yes; he was ready for work again!

Sharina swung down from the fighting tower's battlements with a great deal more care than she'd displayed climbing it. She'd sheathed the Pewle knife; it hadn't been required as a weapon but its smooth steel weight had settled her mind at a time she needed that. Now that she had leisure and both hands, she worried that her billowing robes would catch a projection and she'd break her neck as she fell.

"Mistress?" said the balista captain as he bent to grab her hand. "Princess, I mean! Let me—"

"No!" Sharina said. As if she didn't have enough problems already!

She dropped to the deck with no problem except that her robes flew up. She smoothed them and looked around to see if anybody was laughing at her. They weren't, of course:

quite apart from her being Princess Sharina of Haft, everybody aboard the *Shepherd* was too shaken to laugh at anything for the moment.

Tenoctris had a hand on the railing, but she'd recovered to her normal state of indomitable fragility. She said, "Your Cashel is really quite remarkable. What he did just now was . . ."

She shook her head, then grinned wryly and added, "*Our* friend Cashel, and very definitely the world's friend Cashel. The wizard who made that attack won't have expected anyone to be able to block it. *Quite* remarkable."

"Yes, he is," Sharina said, a smile of contentment spreading over her face. She hadn't had time to be frightened till it was all over. Before she hopped down from the tower, she'd seen Cashel catch his sister's line. Now with the *Flying Fish* at a wobbly halt beside the monster, there was nothing to worry about.

"Was it a demon, Tenoctris?" she added, then frowned. "*Is* it, I mean. It's still there, after all."

"Not a demon," Tenoctris said, shaking her head. "It's an animal, but one that doesn't belong in this world or time. The wizard who could bring such a thing so far could have opened the way for a demon, of course; but demons are hard to control. Generally impossible to control. Though there's no end of fools with more power than sense who might have tried it anyway."

The old wizard smiled with a mixture of humor and disdain for those who had the great powers that she lacked, but who themselves lacked her judgment and knowledge. Sharina stepped close and hugged Tenoctris. She was inexpressibly glad to have a friend who *understood* the powers that were threatening to overwhelm the Isles.

The forces that turned the cosmos were neither good nor bad; but when they were at their peak, human evil and human error had an immense capacity for causing destruction. Mistakes as much as malice had shattered the Old Kingdom; similar mistakes and malice could grind the slowly-rebuilt civilization of the present too deep into the mud to ever revive.

"Sharina?" Tenoctris said, touching the back of the girl's wrist.

Sharina came to herself again; her fingers had knotted so tightly that her nails were cutting the backs of her hands. "Sorry!" she said with a bright smile. "I was thinking about things that we're not going to let happen."

"No, we're not," agreed Tenoctris approvingly. She patted Sharina's wrist again before looking over the scene around them.

The fleet that'd been arrayed like pieces on a chessboard was now clumped like a crowd watching a street fight. At least a dozen warships were close enough that Sharina could've flung a stone aboard them. Officers shrieked to their own crews and to the *Sister-cursed idiots!* on other vessels. She heard oars break as ships fouled one another, and the chance of accidental ramming must be making the sailing masters scream.

Sharina gave faint smile. She was an excellent swimmer; needs must, she could strip off her robes and make it to shore. She smiled even more broadly. If she had to pull Tenoctris along with her, she could manage that too.

Horns and trumpets began to call, issuing orders instead of just adding to the noisy chaos. Flutists blew time to the rowers, and on a trireme from Third Atara—not all the royal fleet was from Ornifal—a drummer beat a similar rhythm. The clot of ships edged apart, their prows pointing again toward the harbor mouth.

Big as quinqueremes were, they carried more of their weight above the waterline than a merchant captain would think was safe or even sane. The *Shepherd*'s deck wobbled when Garric and his entourage of Blood Eagles started forward. He grinned as Sharina raised her hand in greeting.

"We're heading for the harbor along with the whole First Squadron," Garric said conversationally, nodding toward the Admiral Zettin's flagship. "I don't know that we'll be any safer with ten other ships around us than when we were going to enter in lonely majesty—"

He grinned again. For the moment he was the brother Sharina'd grown up with, not the prince ruling the Isles with a quick mind and hard hand. Garric was both those things, of course; but when he was being a boy, Sharina could let herself be somebody younger and perhaps happier than the princess in court robes.

"—but Admiral Zettin made it clear that the only way I'm going to get rid of my escort is to sink every one of them. He's a former Blood Eagle, you know."

"And he's got the right bloody idea," the captain of the bodyguards aboard the *Shepherd* muttered out of the side of his mouth.

Garric glanced at the man, paused, then smiled. "Yes, I think maybe he does," he said.

The *Shepherd* got under way again. The five banks of oars stroked together to get the rhythm, their blades barely rippling the sea's surface. On the next stroke they bit deeper and the vessel shuddered, though Sharina wouldn't have been able to say that it'd resumed forward motion.

"There won't be another attack today," Tenoctris said with a nod of certainty. "No matter how powerful the wizard who attacked you may be, he won't be able to follow that very easily. Though he *is* powerful. He is, or she is, or it is. And clever as well."

"That's good to hear," Garric said, in the absent fashion that people mouth pleasantries that aren't going to change their behavior in the least. "That there won't be another attack for a while, I mean."

He touched the pommel of his sword, and Sharina smiled brightly because at the same moment her fingers were outlining the hilt of the Pewle knife beneath her robe. They were brother and sister, and their instincts were the same. "Of course it leaves the ordinary business of dealing with Count Lascarg and the factions in Carcosa. That'll be unpleasant enough."

The *Shepherd* was moving at a walking pace; other warships stayed close by either flank. The harbor mouth drew rapidly closer. The sailing master shouted to the starboard vessel, "Watch yourselves, Capsana! We don't have a portside rudder anymore!"

"Should we be leaving Ilna and Cashel?" Sharina said,

bending over the rail to look toward the patrol vessel still wallowing beside the monster's carcass. Its oars had just begun to move again. "Are they damaged?"

"The *Flying Fish*'s in fine shape, better than we are," Garric said. "Master Chalcus, who appears to have taken command—"

There was cynical humor in his smile. Sharina judged that Chalcus would take almost anything he chose to, and apparently her brother shared that opinion.

"—has decided that he wants to bring the whale to the quay in order to amaze folk. He's something of a showman, that fellow, but I think he's earned the right."

Garric's expression sobered. "As have you, sister," he added. "You saved my life when you shot. And Cashel's too."

"The crew—" she said, nodding her head to indicate the men in the fighting tower above "—cocked and aimed. But they were afraid they'd hit you. I was afraid too, but I knew that if I didn't take the chance. . . ."

Garric nodded, grim and far older than his nineteen years. "Yes," he said. "The risk you don't take is the most dangerous one of all."

He cleared his throat, looking toward the harbor. The *Shepherd* and its consorts were passing through the entrance, the lighthouse and its time-wrecked twin were to the left and right of them. The crowds on the mole had fallen silent when the monster attacked; now they resumed cheering. The docks of the inner harbor were covered with spectators wearing their brightest and most expensive garments.

"Well," Garric said, hitching up his sword belt. "Count Lascarg won't try to swallow me whole. But I don't mind telling you, sister, that I'd be happier if Liane were here to keep me from making some terrible blunder in etiquette. Father gave us a wonderful education in the classics, but he didn't teach us how to behave when meeting counts."

"No," said Sharina. "But I doubt that matters. Lascarg will know how to behave when his king comes with twenty thousand soldiers at his back."

And as she spoke, she realized that Garric wasn't the only

one who'd changed. That wasn't the observation of Sharina os-Reise, the girl who'd grown up in a village inn.

She gave her brother a smile—of a sort.

Carcosa's harbor was huge, more a lake than an anchorage to Garric's eyes. Barca's Hamlet had only a rocky, steeply sloping beach. Above that stood a seawall, built during the prosperity of the Old Kingdom and the only reason winter storms hadn't washed the village away during the past thousand years.

This harbor was magnificent: stone quays framed slips where merchant vessels of a thousand tons could lie. To the south were stone ramps where the crews of warships could drag their fragile vessels out of the water and pillared sheds to house those same warships safe from the weather.

"It's a ruin!" King Carus said, the thought despairing and out of keeping for a spirit to whom wrath and laughter were common but sadness almost never came. *"Oh, lad, I did this with my haste and my anger. Would I'd never been king so I wouldn't have to see this!"*

As Carus spoke, Garric saw the harbor through his ancient ancestor's eyes. The harbor should've been thronging with merchant ships from every port in the Isles; instead there were less than fifty—

"Thirty-nine," snapped Carus. He had a warrior's eye for numbers and location.

—vessels above the size of a rowboat. Half of what had been harbor was now a marsh, silted in where the Olang River entered the bay from the north; it hadn't been dredged in a thousand years.

And why should it have been? Even constricted, the harbor had room to anchor many times the present traffic. The sheds that had sheltered half a thousand triremes, the fleet that had scoured pirates and usurpers from the Inner Sea, were half-fallen; not one retained its roof of red tiles.

The city beyond, rising in terraced steps up the hills surrounding the harbor, was a half-populated wasteland to eyes that remembered Carcosa when it ruled the Isles. This Carcosa looked as though it had been sacked by an enemy . . . and so it had, Garric knew from Gostain and Wylert and the other historians of the Dark Age that had succeeded the Old Kingdom. The city had been sacked a score of times, but the worst of the damage that'd thrown Carus into despair was caused by time, not human enemies: a thousand years, over-powering the hand and will of men.

"We'll build it again," Garric whispered under his breath. "Or our grandchildren will."

"Garric?" Sharina asked, not so much concerned as . . . interested. She knew Garric shared his mind with his ances-tor, though he doubted she understood how complete the in-tertwining of soul with soul was.

"I was just thinking about how much work we have before Carcosa's back to what it once was," he said, telling the truth if not quite the whole truth.

Count Lascarg and the chief folk—the most richly dressed, at any rate—of Carcosa stood six feet above the level of the docks that lowlier residents thronged. "Did they build a reviewing stand?" Sharina asked, her eyes narrowing.

Garric viewed the scene superimposed with Carus's memories. "No," he said. "That was the base for the statues of the Twelve Nymphs who guided King Car to the place the Lady had blessed for his new colony."

He smiled without humor. "The statues were bronze," he added. "I suppose after the Collapse, some warlord or an-other decided he needed coinage more than he needed art—or the Lady's blessing either one."

The *Shepherd* slowed as the sailing master and his petty officers snarled orders to the crew. Only one bank of oars was still moving and even those stroked slowly, just to keep steerage way. The rest of the squadron held station; the near-est ships were so close that Garric found it hard to tell who was shouting what.

"Are they all so angry?" Sharina said. She'd wrapped her arms around her torso, hugging herself unconsciously. "They sound as if they were."

Garric put an arm around his sister's shoulders. The ges-ture'd probably raise eyebrows among the spectators used to the formality of court etiquette. Nobody'd say anything to Garric—and if they did, they'd find themselves swimming in the harbor faster than they might think possible.

"They care about their duties," he said. "The officers, I mean, though the men do too. They're nervous that things'll go wrong, and the Shepherd knows how much there is to go wrong maneuvering like this."

Sharina reached up to squeeze his hand, then relaxed. They eased apart. "They're pretending to be angry because they're frightened?" she said with a grin. "Well, I guess that's a good choice for soldiers. Fighting men."

Blood Eagles from the trireme, which'd entered the harbor ahead of the rest of the fleet, had cleared the quay below where Lascarg's party waited. The black-armored guards stood facing the crowd with their shields locked. Gilded wooden balls turned their spearheads into batons for the occasion, but when the monster attacked, Garric had seen how quickly the blunts could come off.

"Hold up there!" a man bellowed from the water. "Don't let this ship dock till you've taken me aboard! Do you hear me?"

The petty officer conning the quinquereme from the bowsprit looked down, spat, and said, "Keep clear of Prince Garric's ship, pretty boy, or you'll swim back to land where you belong."

Sharina understood at the same time Garric did. "That's—" she said.

"Right!" said Garric, squeezing between two sailors and the stanchions bracing the butt of the bowsprit. He grabbed a rope coiled from the railing and bent over the side. Lord Attaper, the Blood Eagles' commander, stood in a skiff that two paddlers—armored infantrymen like himself—were trying desperately to balance.

Garric snubbed his end of the rope and tossed the coil. Attaper caught it, then dragged himself and the skiff six feet across open water to the quinquereme's bow. As he started to climb the ship's side, the lead oar swung forward and swatted his legs away; he dangled like a toy on a string, pulling himself up hand over hand.

Two of the guards on the Shepherd hauled their commander aboard; Attaper was cursing with a fury Garric wouldn't have expected in the man. Planting himself on the deck before Garric, Attaper said, "What happened here? I heard there was an attack! I knew I shouldn't have gone ashore! Didn't I tell you that?"

Lord Attaper was a stocky man in his forties, taller than most, and extremely fit for someone whose duties were largely administrative. All the Blood Eagle officers were nobles, generally younger sons from minor houses, but they and the men they commanded were also veterans who'd been promoted to the royal bodyguard as a reward for exceptional service in the regular regiments.

Garric sometimes wondered how much of a reward it really was. The Blood Eagles got higher pay, fancy armor, and the right to swagger in any military company . . . but their casualty rate was several times that of the other regiments, especially now that they had to guard a prince who was determined to lead from the front. There was no lack of recruits to fill vacancies, though.

"And after all, boy," whispered the image of Carus in his mind, *"you're no more the man to tell them they're fools to go where it's hottest than I was. Good soldiers like to serve with a leader they can respect, and these are some of the best."*

"Good morning, Lord Attaper," Garric said. He kept his tone mild—he wanted to shout back, a natural reaction like the snarling anger of the ship's nervous officers—but he knew this was a time to quietly remind Attaper who was the prince and who was the servant. "We went fishing on our way into harbor; Master Chalcus is following with the catch. Now I have business with local dignitaries, so—"

"It's too dangerous for you to go ashore here if there's already been one attack!" Attaper said. "We'll—"

"Lord Attaper!" Garric said. "My duties as prince require me to greet local dignitaries. Hold your tongue now, or you'll find your duties will involve running the Valles city administration five hundred miles from here."

Attaper paused, his face blank. Then he gave Garric a grim smile and an officer's salute, crossing his right forearm over his chest with the fist clenched. A regular soldier would clash his spear against his shield face instead. "I understand, your majesty," he said.

The *Shepherd of the Isles* bumped against the dock. The starboard rowers had shipped their oars to keep from breaking the shafts, and the deck crew had hung straw-stuffed leather fenders between the outrigger and the stonework. Despite the crew's skill, Garric heard the ship's timbers complain. Lightly-built warships weren't intended to be tied up against stone quays; every extra ounce had been pared from the *Shepherd*'s hull to increase her speed and the endurance of her oarsmen during battle.

"If you're agreeable, your majesty," Attaper said in a formal voice, "my men will conduct the locals past you as you stand on the dock, rather than you climbing the plinth to join them."

Garric smiled with a mixture of humor, amusement, and pride. "Thank you for the suggestion, Commander," he said with equal formality. "I believe your plan will be more consonant with the dignity of the Prince of Haft."

A pair of Blood Eagles on the dockside were struggling to fit a makeshift boarding bridge between the quay and the quinquereme's deck. It'd started life as a door and wasn't long enough to reach the deck safely because of the outrigger for the upper banks of rowers.

Instead of waiting for the soldiers to figure out an answer, Garric stepped on the outrigger and hopped up to the dock. The ship shuddered, rolling to boost his departure. Sharina had Tenoctris to look after, so she stayed where she was.

Attaper swore—under his breath this time—and followed Garric. Drawing his sword, he bellowed to an officer wearing a captain's red plume, "The prince will receive them down here. Start our distinguished hosts moving!"

Two aides—they'd been clerks of Lord Tadai—came quickly toward Garric. Attaper raised his bare weapon by reflex.

"Please!" one of the aides said. Both carried notebooks of thin boards hinged with leather straps. "We're his highness's nomenclators! We have to be at his side to tell him who he's meeting!"

"Let them pass, milord," Garric said, again irritated by the bodyguard's caution; the nomenclators could scarcely have looked more harmless if they'd been mice scurrying on a pantry floor.

He remembered what he'd just said to Sharina, though, and kept his tone level. Whatever his rank now, Garric knew very well that he was nervous about meeting those who'd been his distant rulers while he'd grown up in Barca's Hamlet.

"The first will be Count Lascarg," the aide on Garric's right murmured. His index finger marked a place in the notebook, though he didn't bother referring to it. "His twin children, the honorable Tanus and Monine, were to accompany him, but they don't appear to be present."

The Blood Eagles had started the line of dignitaries moving before Attaper bothered to ask Garric about the plan. That was all right; good subordinates had to be able to take initiative—within limits.

Count Lascarg's scabbard was empty and a guard walked to either side of him. They were more likely to have to support the count than to restrain him: he was a tired old man, overweight and—Garric had served in his father's taproom since childhood—more than half drunk.

Lascarg knelt before Garric, bracing himself with his hands to keep from falling over. He looked up, avoiding Garric's eyes, and said in a rusty voice, "Your highness, I offer the loyal submission of Haft to the Kingdom of the Isles."

"Rise, Lord Lascarg," Garric said. "The officials who've preceded me have made arrangements to allow you and your personal servants quarters in the west wing of the palace. So long as you remain there until I've made permanent dispositions, I can guarantee your safety. Of course you're to take no further part in the government of the island."

"Of course," Lascarg muttered. He didn't sound regretful; perhaps he was even relieved. He rose to his feet more easily than he'd knelt and walked away straight-backed.

Garric watched him go without expression. Lascarg had been commander of the Household Troops the night riots in Carcosa had led to the death of the Count and Countess of Haft; afterward Lascarg had seized the throne himself. That didn't prove he'd been behind the riots in the first place, but the best that could be said was that the Household Troops hadn't protected their employers as they were sworn to do.

Garric wouldn't have had much liking or respect for Lascarg under any circumstances, so nothing important changed when Garric had learned that Countess Tera was his real mother. He'd been born the night she died, and Reise had carried the infant to Barca's Hamlet on the opposite coast with his wife and her own newborn daughter.

The next dignitary through the wall of Blood Eagles was an older man in priestly robes of the traditional gleaming white. Instead of the bleached wool that priests in Valles wore in at least the affectation of modesty, this man's garment was of silk trimmed with ermine.

"Lord Anda, Chief Priest of the Temple of the Lady of the Sunset," said the left-hand nomenclator, "and head of the congregation of the Lady on Haft."

Anda knelt before Garric with the deepest respect, but as he did so he looked over his shoulder with a sneer of triumph toward the next person in line. He said, "The prayers of the servants of the Lady are always with you, your highness."

"He and Lady Estanel, Priestess of the Temple of the Shepherd of the Rock, nearly came to blows over precedence!" the other aide added in shocked amazement. "Can you imagine that? Of course the priests of the Lady have precedence!"

"Rise, Lord Anda," Garric said. "My friend Lord Tadai will shortly discuss with you the means by which the office of the Chancellor in Valles will improve its oversight of the temples here on Haft."

"In fact if you have a moment, your highness . . ." Anda said, rising smoothly. He had the sharp features and bright eyes of a falcon. "My associates and I have a proposal which you as a Haft native yourself will find very—"

"I do not have a moment," Garric said, suddenly so angry that his vision blurred. "Lord Tadai will instruct you."

The priest opened his mouth to speak further. Garric felt his right hand fall to his sword hilt. If the whale's attack hadn't drained him so completely . . .

Lord Anda was too good a politician to push on where he could see there was no hope. He bowed and smiled, passing back through the guards with his dignity undiminished.

Carus was a calming presence in Garric's mind. The ancient king knew more about gusts of rage than most men did. Garric's anger didn't frighten him. *"Just priests being priests, lad,"* the ghost murmured. *"Part of life, like rain running down the inside of your cuirass."*

"Lady Estanel is next," a nomenclator said. "She entered the priesthood after the death of her husband, a major landowner to the south of Carcosa."

The priestess of the Shepherd was short and round. The collar of her white silk robe was trimmed with sable, and her magnificent ivory combs were arranged to give the impression of a tiara.

She curtseyed with supple ease; though fat, Lady Estanel was obviously in good health. "We servants of the Shepherd are delighted to greet you, Prince Garric," she said. "We look forward to discussing methods to reform the current religious situation with you."

"Your discussions will be with my agent, Lord Tadai," Garric said; he heard his voice coming from a thousand miles away. "And milady? You'd best arrange matters so that I *don't* have to get involved, because you'd like that result less than anything Lord Tadai tells you."

Garric couldn't see the priestess's expression through the red haze that clouded his vision, but she passed on quickly. He felt a touch on his right elbow. He turned. Sharina was there. Though relief made him stagger, he could see clearly again.

Attaper must have signaled to the guards, because the line of dignitaries in embroidered brocade stayed on the other side of the black shields. A good bodyguard observes *everything,* and Garric didn't guess he'd ever meet anyone better than Attaper.

"I'm a little dizzy from the voyage," Garric called with a cheerful smile toward the waiting nobles. "A moment, please, and I'll be with you."

He turned again and muttered into Sharina's ear, "We weren't god-ridden in Barca's Hamlet, you know that. A pinch of meal and a sip of ale to the household altar at meals—for the people who could afford that. And we gave when the priests from Carcosa came around with the statues for the Tithe Procession every summer. But we worshipped the *gods,* and these people are just politicians. Politicians who think they'll make me one of them!"

"Yes," said Sharina, holding his wrist as she scanned the nearby spectators with a harsh expression. "Well, they're not going to do that."

Garric looked at the crowd also, really for the first time. He'd been too concerned with the dignitaries on the raised plinth to think about the rest of the folk waiting. Those close by were retainers of the nobles. They stood in discrete blocs of six to twenty-odd men—all men, of course—wearing their employers' colors as cockades. They weren't openly armed, but Garric knew their caps had metal linings and there were truncheons—if not swords—concealed under their tunics.

He'd expected that; there'd have been similar men at a levee in Valles or Erdin or any other community in the Isles big enough to have a range of wealth and therefore rivalry. What he hadn't expected was that the two largest groups would be those of the priesthoods, big scarred men in white tunics. The Lady's gang carried censers on the end of three-foot metal rods, while their rivals held similar rods bent into the shape of a shepherd's crook.

"If any of them saw a sheep in their life, it was as roast mutton," Garric grated under his breath.

Then he straightened, smiled, and said, "Lord Attaper, I've recovered from my indisposition. I'll be pleased to meet the rest of those waiting to offer their respect to the kingdom."

Still grinning, he added to Sharina in a voice only slightly less audible, "You know, sister, for the first time since I became . . ."

He gestured with his palms upturned. Prince, regent; leader. It didn't matter what word he used or if he didn't bother to speak; Sharina understood.

"Anyway, for the first time I'm really looking forward to making changes in the way a government works!"

Garric laughed aloud. His sister laughed with him, squeezed his hand again, and then stepped aside so that the horrified nomenclators could resume their duties.

"Look, you fine folk of Carcosa!" Chalcus called from the bow to the crowd filling the waterfront. "Come look at the dreadful monster that your prince vanquished without so much as mussing his hair! Ah, the kingdom is blessed indeed to have such a ruler as Prince Garric of Haft!"

"Ilna?" said Merota with a troubled frown. She was shouting so that Ilna, holding her hand in the prow of the *Flying Fish,* could hear her. It was a measure of Chalcus's lungs that much of the crowd was able to understand him over the noise not only of civilians but from the crews and equipment of the royal fleet as it docked.

"Yes, child?" said Ilna, turning to face Merota so that the girl could see her answer. Ilna didn't like either to shout or to be shouted at; a poor orphan gets enough of the latter early on.

Chalcus now openly commanded the *Flying Fish.* Captain Rhamis huddled amidships with a cloak over his soaked garments; water dripped from the tip of his scabbard to pool on the deck beneath him.

The harbor had scores of unoccupied docks, though many were only rubble cores which'd lost their facing stones. Instead of bringing the patrol vessel to one of them, however, Chalcus had anchored half a stone's throw out from the shore where more people could see it.

The crew, released from the oarbenches, was hauling the great carcass alongside and lashing it to the *Flying Fish* with a second loop. The whale had begun to sink even before they'd entered the harbor; water was filling the body cavity through the hole the ram had smashed.

Ilna smiled grimly. Chalcus was too fine a showman to lose his wondrous attraction because of inattention.

"Is Prince Garric really as great a man as Chalcus, Ilna?" Merota asked in her high, piercing voice.

The question so shocked Ilna that she burst out with a gust of loud laughter. Merota gaped: Ilna's reaction was almost as unusual for her as a fit of crying would have been.

Ilna's expression settled. A fit of crying was the other alternative. She'd always considered showing emotion to be a sign of weakness; but she'd never denied that she was subject to weakness, either.

Rather than raise her voice, Ilna lifted Merota to speak into the child's ear. Ilna was slightly built—all the bulk in the family had gone to her brother Cashel—but she did much of her work with double-span looms, which often as not she set up by herself. She took her physical abilities for granted.

"Garric is a great man, child," Ilna said. "The kingdom is lucky to have so wise and strong a leader, and Garric's friends are lucky too. As for Chalcus . . ."

She looked toward the bow. Chalcus stood on the railing, gesturing extravagantly as he described the way Prince Garric had winkled out the monster's brains with one thrust of his mighty sword and then had used his pommel to crush its ribs.

Ilna smiled. It was a lie and she *hated* lies, but from Chalcus's lips it sounded like one of the ballads he and Merota sang. It was a pattern of the sort that Ilna wove into her fabrics, one that made the listeners a little happier and the world around them better by some small amount as well.

"Chalcus is a great man also," she said. "But in a different way from Garric. As I am different from Princess Sharina, say."

"But you don't *love* Garric, do you?" Merota demanded.

Ilna laughed again. *The choice is to cry, and that's not a choice.* "I don't know what you mean by love, child," she said, squeezing Merota before she set her back on the deck.

Because she was looking toward the city to avoid meeting Merota's eyes or those of anyone else nearby, Ilna saw the procession enter the harbor area and make its way toward the waterfront where Garric stood. The escort was a platoon of Blood Eagles. They moved forward despite the crowd, using their shields to push people aside and their knob-headed spears to convince those who didn't want to be pushed.

Despite feeling miserable and empty, Ilna smiled wryly. The Blood Eagles had been set a task; they were doing whatever was necessary to get it done. Ilna could appreciate their attitude.

The guards had been sent to Barca's Hamlet. There they'd waited for the arrival of a party from Ornifal to make landfall and come overland to Carcosa. Ilna couldn't see the people in the party who were on foot because the escort's plumed helmets blocked her view, but the two chief members rode horses.

Could you carry a horse on shipboard all the way from Valles to Barca's Hamlet? But of course you could, if you were important enough; and this pair was important.

The middle-aged man rode stiffly. Ilna recalled that he'd been clumsy with any physical task when he was Reise the Innkeeper in Barca's Hamlet. He was Garric's, *Prince* Garric's, father. He was coming to Carcosa at his son's call to direct the nobleman who'd have the title of Vicar of Haft and Agent for the Prince.

The dark-haired woman beside Reise was supple and perfectly at ease. She looked about the crowd with the pleased smile of a goddess blessing her worshippers. Though she'd had a long voyage and a difficult trek across the island to reach Carcosa, she was more beautiful than any other woman Ilna had seen.

She was Lady Liane bos-Benliman, the woman whom Prince Garric was to marry.

I don't know what you mean by love, Ilna repeated in her mind; and hated herself for the lie.

Chapter Four

oes it suit you then, mistress?" said Chalcus as Ilna's left hand gently explored the frame of the loom he'd had erected on the second floor of the building to which he'd brought her when they disembarked. "I chose a house close to the harbor where I could see the water, but if you'd prefer something inland . . . ?"

Ilna sniffed. It wasn't like Chalcus to sound so uncertain. Was she so terrible, then, with her whims and her anger?

Grinning coldly—her anger was indeed a terrible thing, but so was that of the sailor—she said, "Every morning I looked out of my window in Barca's Hamlet and watched the sun rising over the sea, Master Chalcus. The view suits me well, and the building you've taken for us suits me better than I ever imagined."

Her eyes narrowed and she added, "How did you come by it, then? Because a place like this—"

It stood in a row of brick buildings with shops on the ground floor and the merchants' quarters above. There were two full stories, a garret, and a railed walk around the roof of sheet lead. In back was a walled courtyard behind with grape arbors.

"—shouldn't have been empty for us to walk into."

"Nor was it," Chalcus agreed with a touch of irritation, "till my agents rented it last month from the owner and ousted the business being conducted here at the time; which was a brothel, mistress, since you're so suspicious that you might think I'd put a whole flock of innocent orphans on the street in my arrogance. And as for the money I used for the purpose, the Children of the Mistress had amassed a fine collection of plate and jewels in the course of their child-murdering monster worship. When I left Donelle, some part of that left with me. Perhaps this offends you?"

Ilna stood without expression. *I've been a fool many times; but perhaps never so great a fool as I'm being now* . . .

Rather than speak—for she'd say the wrong thing, she always managed to say the wrong thing—she took two steps to Chalcus, put her arms around him, and squeezed as hard as she could. It was like hugging a tree till Chalcus put his arms around her also and held her as gently as if she were spun glass.

"I'm sorry," she said. She wasn't crying because she never cried; or almost never. "If you'd cut the throats of everybody in the building I'd support you, I know you'd have had a good reason. I'm sorry."

"Now mistress," Chalcus said lightly. She loosened her grip on his torso but didn't push away; his touch remained the same. "The pirate who might have done such a terrible thing as that is long dead, buried in southern waters and the past. I'm a simple sailor and a loyal supporter of Prince Garric."

In the garret above, Merota caroled, *"I never will marry, nor be no man's wife. . . ."* The child couldn't have been happier to have a house on the waterfront instead of being shut up in the palace as she'd expected.

Merota was happy more times than not, but Mistress Kaline—who'd sleep in one garret room while her charge had the other—was bustling about in a good humor also. Ilna smiled faintly into the sailor's shoulder. Chances were that Mistress Kaline would've been cheerful in a dungeon, so long as it wasn't on shipboard.

Ilna'd expected to be lodged in the palace—a suite or perhaps a separate bungalow if it was a sprawling complex like the royal palace in Valles. Where she lived—or what she ate and other questions most folk worried about—didn't matter a great deal to her, but here Chalcus had arranged a place where she wouldn't stumble unexpectedly into Garric, or Liane; or Garric *and* Liane. This was much better.

Ilna squeezed Chalcus again before stepping back, embarrassed for half-a-dozen good reasons but refusing to show it in her expression. "We'll need to get cleaned up," she said. "There's to be a dinner with Garric tonight. And I'll need to tell my brother that Merota and I are—aren't in the palace as he'll expect."

"Aye, the prince and all his chiefs and nobles," Chalcus said with an unreadable smile.

He turned to play with the door latch, a heavy arrangement that could be locked from outside but not from within; probably something to do with the building's former use as brothel. Ilna'd known many sorts of hardship and discomfort; but not *all* sorts, and if she'd believed in the Great Gods she'd have thanked them for that mercy.

"Not an assembly I'd ever expected to be part of," Chalcus continued, now looking out the bank of casements facing east over the courtyard. He glanced sidelong at Ilna. "Of course if you're determined to greet all your friends and the new lot from Valles . . . ?"

Ilna's smile was grim. Did he think she was a child who knew nothing of his tastes? Chalcus *loved* gatherings of the great and powerful, as surely as he loved clothes that focused all eyes on his swaggering form. But he was trying to be kind, and that was no cause for anger.

"I'll go to the dinner, Master Chalcus," she said, "and I'll go to Prince Garric's wedding when that's held in a few weeks time. There's nothing forcing me to be elsewhere, and I'm not afraid to recognize the truth. Any truth."

"No, nobody'd be fool enough to think you were afraid, dear one," Chalcus said very softly to the open windows.

He turned to meet her eyes and said, "Do you have regrets, Mistress Ilna?" His voice was flat, stripped suddenly of the lilt that was as much a part of him as the smile generally crinkling his eyes.

"Chalcus," she said, "things are as they should be—for the kingdom, for Garric. For me as well! I wouldn't change a bit of it if I could."

She smiled like a demon carved from ice. The skills she'd learned in Hell gave her powers beyond the imagining of anyone but Tenoctris of those who knew her. She *could* force Garric, and in time she could force the whole world, to her desire; but she *would* not.

"I'm glad for the way things are, Master Chalcus," she said. "Though because I'm often a fool, it tears my heart out to see them."

Ilna opened her arms. Chalcus came to her and swept her up, kissing her; gentle as a cat with her kitten, for all the strength in his scarred body.

Merota continued to sing as she came down the stairs. She'd reached refrain again, and her voice trilled like springwater, *"I'll always be single, the rest of my life. . . ."*

"Well, said Cashel, looking around the overgrown garden, "the palace seems a nice place, doesn't it, Tenoctris?"

"It's quiet," the old wizard agreed. She was being agreeable, at any rate. "I'd hoped the building might have a library that would give me some guidance about the creature that was loosed on us, though."

The palace of the Counts of Haft was brick and three stories high on the front where pillars rose from the ground to the roof. Back here in the private areas there were only two stories and all the rooms looked out on little gardens like this one. Sparrows and finches hopped about on the ground, picking at seeds; a pair of gray squirrels were chasing each other up and down the ancient dogwood tree by the back wall, changing places for no reason Cashel could make out; and in a basin filled by the shower earlier in the day, frogs chirped furiously.

The garden wasn't home, exactly, but for Cashel it seemed more homelike than any place he'd been in Valles, let alone shipboard. He didn't mind ships, but he was glad to be on solid ground again.

"Maybe the library's in the part where the count's still living?" he said, nodding toward the back wall. Garric had taken over the front and east wing of the palace, but the count and his personal servants still occupied his private apartments in the west wing. The other side of the back wall here was also a garden—Cashel could see the tops of what he thought were redbuds and a huge weeping willow—but it was part of the west wing, with no entry from where Cashel stood.

"No, I asked some of the older servants," Tenoctris said. "The library burned in the riots when Count Lascarg came to power. There were volumes in it dating back to the Old Kingdom, the chamberlain thought."

She smiled wryly. "Volumes as old as I am," she added.

The Old Kingdom fell when a wizard drowned King Carus—and drowned himself as well in the backlash of the forces that he couldn't control. An event so enormous had distant effects, the way a stone flung into a pond makes waves slap the far edges. One result had been to throw Tenoctris a thousand years into her future, to fetch up on the shore of Barca's Hamlet where Garric had found her.

Cashel cleared his throat, letting the thought form fully

before he spoke. Then he said, "I guess you were sent here for a purpose, Tenoctris. And I guess that means you're going to stay while you're needed. Which I guess is going to be a good long while yet."

Tenoctris had lived a long life before the cataclysm scooped her up, but she'd already brought more to the present than she'd been allowed to give her own day. Without her wisdom and skill, Cashel knew that the present kingdom, reborn with Garric leading, would have vanished like chaff in a bonfire.

The old woman sniffed as she knelt to look more closely at a stone bench. "I don't accept your notion of purpose, Cashel," she said. "I believe in chance, and I believe in the forces that I can see and sense; but I've never seen the gods you pray to."

Cashel grinned. "Chance?" he said. "You mean luck? Then I guess Garric and me and everybody else in the Isles who wants to live a normal life without wizards smashing things is awfully lucky, seeings as you just happened to appear right where we needed you to keep everything from flying apart again."

Tenoctris laughed as she ran her fingers over the moss-covered carvings on the top of the bench. "Cashel, just as you have faith in the Great Gods," she said, "I have faith in the blind machinery of the cosmos. Sometimes, I'll admit—"

She turned to meet his eyes, laughing with a serious undertone.

"—I have to stretch farther to justify my beliefs than I would yours."

Cashel smiled, holding his quarterstaff out at arm's length just for exercise. He wasn't bragging, though he knew there weren't many men who could grip the end of the thick staff in one hand and keep it straight. Cashel didn't have to brag about his strength; it was there for all to see, as surely as Sharina's beauty.

Tenoctris was giving her full attention to the bench, now. "Cashel," she said, "this is very old. It was part of an altarstone, originally."

"Brought here from an old temple, you mean?" he said.

He looked more closely at the bench, but that was just politeness. The marks on the stone wouldn't have meant anything to him if they'd been clear. Now, worn by time and under a fur of moss, he'd have had as much luck trying to read words in the wave-tops.

"I'm not sure," said Tenoctris, eyeing the rest of the garden from where she knelt. "Those seats there—"

She nodded toward chairs made by cutting down sections of a fluted pillar; her fingertips continued to touch indentations in the top of the bench.

"—are made out of column barrels, and there on the wall—"

Nodding again, this time toward the partition between this garden and its twin in the east wing. Blocks of sandstone formed the foundation, though the rest was old brick.

"—are parts of a frieze. See the triglyphs?"

Cashel wouldn't have known a triglyph if it bit him, but he supposed some part of what he was looking at was a triglyph. Maybe even a family of them.

"I think there was a temple here before the palace was built," Tenoctris continued. She rose, frowning. "I think the inscription's to the Lady, though I'm more guessing than reading."

Cashel cleared his throat. He had the staff in both hands, now. He could hear the concern in Tenoctris's voice. He didn't understand what was causing it, but he was ready for anything that appeared.

"Sharina'll be back soon, I think," he said as his companion continued to ponder the bench. "Can she help you read, do you think, Tenoctris?"

Sharina'd gone off to the temple of the Lady to pray as soon as the formalities of greeting the locals were over. She hadn't asked Cashel to let her go without his company, but they knew each other pretty well by now. Her friend Nonnus had worshipped the Lady, and Cashel figured this visit had something to do with him. That was Sharina's private business.

Tenoctris laughed and put her hand over Cashel's where it gripped his quarterstaff. "I didn't mean to disturb you," she said with a hint of embarrassment. "There's nothing wrong, nothing *evil*, about there being a temple here. It's just that places where people worship tend to focus the forces that turn the cosmos. Reusing the sites for other purposes is, well, dangerous."

She pursed her lips in sour expression though her eyes continued to smile. "As are quite a lot of other things, I know," she went on, "including worrying myself into a tizzy because everybody else doesn't feel the same way I do about what I think is important. And—"

She turned again to survey their surroundings, her hands on her hips.

"—when I let myself think about it instead of just reacting on instinct, there're few more innocent uses for the site than as a quiet garden. Forgive me for being silly, Cashel."

"I don't think you're silly, Tenoctris," Cashel said. His voice was a trifle huskier than it'd have been if he was completely settled, and though he held the staff at his side again, he hadn't forgotten about it.

A shepherd learns that instinct can warn him about a lot of things that his conscious mind could never explain to other people. And Cashel knew Tenoctris well enough by now to trust her instincts just as far as he did his own.

There were probably other temples to the Lady in Carcosa, but the nomenclator Sharina had asked sent her to that of the Lady of the Sunset. It stood on a knoll near the northern wall of the city. She hadn't been able to see the temple itself from the harbor, but the gilded bronze statuary on its roof blazed above all the surrounding buildings.

"Huh!" snorted one of the Blood Eagles escorting her. "This is what the hicks call a temple, is it?"

"Shut up, Lires, or you'll be sweeping out stables with your moustache!" snarled the lieutenant commanding the squad. "She's here to worship and you're here to guard her while she's doing it!"

Sharina pretended not to have been listening, but the soldier's comment angered her on many levels. The temple wasn't large, certainly not by the standards of Valles or ancient Carcosa, but it was perfectly proportioned and had been built by expert craftsmen. The life-sized statues on the roof were winged dancers, probably meant for the four phases of the West Wind; they were modeled as ably as anything Sharina had seen in the capital.

The temple had six slim columns across the front, two more than normal on a width of thirty-five feet or so. The design gave the building a look of airiness, and the ceiling-high glass panels—diamond panes set in silvered bronze instead of lead—lighted the interior as well as displaying the cult statue to those sacrificing outside.

Nothing but Ornifal chauvinism could object to the temple, and Sharina was from Haft. More important, though— she *had* come here to worship, just as the officer said.

Sharina'd been raised to be conventionally religious, since a peasant community doesn't have much scope for complete surrender to the Gods. A farmer who spent all his days praying would starve when winter came, and his neighbors would have as little sympathy for him as they did for his drunken neighbor.

Her mother Lora mouthed platitudes with the same empty formality as she taught Sharina court etiquette: it was the done thing. Reise said nothing about how he felt regarding the Gods; people in general found it politic to conceal their opinions around Lora unless they wanted to listen to her diatribes on where their beliefs were mistaken. Sharina suspected that her father was as much an unbeliever as Ilna declared herself to be, but he'd paid his share when the priests from Carcosa made their annual Tithe Procession and he'd raised his children to offer a pinch of bread dipped in ale at meals to the shrine on the wall of the inn's common room.

Nonnus the hermit was the only person Sharina knew to whom the Lady was a real part of life. Perhaps even to Nonnus She was only a hope, the possibility that Someone could forgive the things he had done as a soldier. For Nonnus's sake, Sharina had come here to pray and to sacrifice. No one had a right to sneer at that impulse.

But she held her tongue—as Nonnus would have done.

In the plaza fronting the temple were seven altars. The one in the center was ornately carved and surrounded by a waist-high marble screen to separate those sacrificing from the common people. An attendant, one of the priestly thugs, lounged in the enclosure to keep out anybody who might try to use a site meant for his betters.

An old woman waited by the simple altar on the right end, where a priest was lighting a small fireset. Two other priests sat in a kiosk to the side, talking and keeping a desultory eye on the plaza. The courtyard behind the temple got a good deal of traffic both of priests and laymen, but only the woman was sacrificing at the moment.

Sharina turned to the officer of her guard. "You'll wait here," she said. "When I've finished, we'll return to the palace."

"Milady," the man said, "we'll come—"

"You will *not*," Sharina said. The anger—at what had happened to Nonnus, at the chaos that was so much a part of life, at herself for the risk she'd taken with the lives of those she loved best when the whale attacked—boiled out in her tone. It shocked her and slapped the soldiers like a gush of fire. "I'm here to worship."

She turned and strode stiff-backed toward the kiosk. One of the priests waited, standing with his hands tented before him. The other walked briskly into the porticoed compound.

The Blood Eagles remained where they were. She heard a man—not the officer—snarl, "Lires, you've disgraced the Regiment!"

"I wish to make an offering," Sharina said to the priest in a clear voice. "I'll need to purchase the incense from you as well. What's the fee for this? Just a basic sacrifice."

An elaborate sacrifice with animal victims and all the pomp of majesty would've offended Nonnus. To the hermit, the offering and even the prayer were merely symbols of the heart; but symbols *are* important.

"Of course, Princess Sharina," the priest said, bowing low. "If you'll wait here just a moment, Lord Anda will be right out. Please accept my apologies on his behalf for our not being properly prepared to greet you."

"I don't want Lord Anda," Sharina said, her eyes narrowing and her anger rising again. "I'm here to make a sacrifice for the soul of a friend. You can—"

The high priest came out of the courtyard, his expression supernally placid but his legs moving very quickly indeed under his long robe. With him—actually straggling a pace or two behind—were half-a-dozen junior priests, men and women both. One had lost her sandal in her hurry, and another appeared to have tugged his robe on back to front.

An alarm clanged within the compound. The burly thugs at the entryway straightened up in the passage, holding their censers like the clubs they really were. Twenty more of the same sort came boiling out of the courtyard and ran toward Anda and his aides.

Anda glanced over his shoulder at them with a look of cold fury and gestured them to a halt. Returning his attention to Sharina, he said blandly, "It's better that we not discuss our business here in public, I think you'll agree, Princess. If you'll come—"

"We have no business!" Sharina said. "I came to burn a pinch of frankincense in memory of a dead friend!"

Lord Anda put his hand on her arm. In a blast of fiery rage, Sharina's mind turned to the Pewle knife. She'd left it at the palace because she was going to worship.

Steel rasped. "Hey!" grunted one of the thugs. The aides clustering with their chief started like deer surprised at a spring; Anda looked up with a blank expression.

Lires stepped between Anda and Sharina. He'd dropped his shield on the way, so he had a hand free to grip the priest's arm and twist it up at an angle.

A pair of thugs started toward them. "I wouldn't!" said the Blood Eagles' officer, his sword bare in his hand.

Lord Anda was struggling; the soldier lifted him a little higher so that his toes just touched the ground. Because of the way the priest's arm bent, if it took all his weight either his shoulder or his elbow would be dislocated.

"Now, let me tell you how it is, master," Lires said. "This is a temple, a place of worship, so I won't shed blood here. But if you'd actually *touched* the princess instead of just looking like you meant to—"

"But—" another soldier protested.

"Shut up!" the lieutenant snarled.

"—then I'd break your arm, and break the other arm; and then I'd break your legs," Lires continued in the tone of a mother chiding her newborn. "After that, well, I'd decide depending on how I was feeling at the time. Do you see?"

"Princess Sharina . . ." the priest whispered. Sweat covered his brow. "I sincerely apologize if anything I said was—"

The soldier jerked him a little higher. "The right answer is *yes,* priestling. Can you say yes?"

"Yes, may the Sister take you!" Anda shouted.

Lires flung him back. Anda stumbled and instinctively tried to put his hand down to catch himself. He screamed and collapsed on the ground.

"Aye, She may," Lires said, clashing his spearbutt against the cobblestones. "And if She does, then I guess you and I get to meet again."

"I have no more business here," Sharina said, wondering at how little she felt. She spun on her heel and added, "Lieutenant, we'll return to the palace now."

"Sorry, your highness," Lires muttered from behind her as the other Blood Eagles fell in on both sides.

"You have nothing to be sorry for, Trooper Lires," Sharina said. "I was the one who mistook this for a place of worship."

She caught the officer's eye as she went on, "I hope you'll be a regular member of my escort in the future, Lires."

If she let herself feel anything, then she'd fly into a screaming fury that wouldn't, that couldn't, change anything for the better. She'd go back to the palace and in a quiet corner scratch an image of the Lady on a stone wall to receive her prayers. It's what Nonnus would've done in the first place.

Lires bent to pick up his shield. He looked back over his shoulder and said musingly, "The building kinda grows on you, though, don't it? Especially the girls on the roof."

Sharina coughed, then began to laugh aloud. "Yes," she said. "Yes they do. Now, if we could only find some way to install the statues as priests!"

Garric knew he was dreaming, but the scene was as real to him as memories of his life in Barca's Hamlet. *The sun beat down on a grassy hillside; there was a grove of oaks on the crest, and the higher slopes in the middle distance were covered in forest.*

"Greetings, Chief Garric," called the eldest of the trio waiting for him. His name was Anda and he owned one of the larger flocks in the community. He was priest of the Lady as his father had been before him. Also as his father had done, Anda lent money on the only security poor men could provide: their bodies. All his herdsmen were bond servants, working off the debts they'd incurred. "We bid you welcome in the name of the Gods whom we serve."

"Greetings," echoed Mistress Estanel, the butcher's wife and the priestess of the Shepherd. She looked a jolly woman, but everybody in the borough felt the rough side of her tongue on a regular basis. Her husband's business required him to make a progress of the surrounding communities. Folk believed he spent as little time at home as he could manage, a plan that all applauded. "The Gods have blessed us already with the weather they've sent for the midsummer sacrifice."

The kid sprawling across Garric's shoulders twisted. Its fore and hind legs were tied; Garric held the hooves to keep it from kicking. Though the kid's jaws hadn't been strapped, the only sound it made was to pant through distended nostrils.

"Greetings, Chief Garric," said Short Horan, the priest of the Sister. He had a field of barley and a nut grove, as well as being the community's thatcher. Horan roofed new-built huts and sheds and also beat old roofs firm in Spring so that they continued to shed the rains. "We're prepared for the sacrifice. Do you come with clean hands?"

"I come with clean hands," Garric said, echoing the ritual phrase. "I bring this kid to the Gods in the name of the communities of Wastervale."

Garric lifted the sacrifice over his head and laid it on the turf altar, then stepped back. It began to bleat. Estanel felt for a point at the back of its jaw, and pinched. The animal fell immediately silent, though its eyes spun in abject terror.

Several hundred people stood near Garric on the hillside; some had come from more than a day's hike away. Not only was the sacrifice important for the health of crops and cattle, there would be a fair in the afternoon with mummers and peddlers from other islands. Some of those visitors watched at a little distance from the locals, remarkable for bright, outlandish clothing.

Because this was a peaceful sacrifice, Garric carried neither his shield of seawolf hide nor his heavy, bronze-bladed spear; the knife thrust through his sash was simply a piece of male attire. His tunic had an embroidered border and his short wool cape had originally been red; it had faded to a rusty color. Because of the ceremony he wore a headdress made from tail feathers of the black sea eagle instead of his usual broad-brimmed leather hat.

"May the Lady accept the sacrifice of our community!" Anda said. All the priests wore a fillet and sash; his were yellow, the color of the Lady, made of wool dyed with the pollen washed from beehives in the Fall. Turning, he took an obsidian-bladed knife from the servant who was assisting him. The stone had a greenish cast and was almost transparent.

"May the Shepherd bless the flocks of our community!" said Estanel, taking the kid by the muzzle. Her fillet and sash were black linen. She wore gold combs and rings set with garnets and sardonyx. The jewelry had nothing to do with the sacrifice save that it gave her an excuse to display her wealth.

"May the Sister make the way of our community easy in the coming year!" said Short Horan, stumbling a little over the formula. He'd been chosen for the priesthood this Spring when Voder died. Usually priests were the wealthiest members of the community, but after a day of arguing by supporters of two rival landowners the assembly had finally picked Horan. Everybody liked him personally, and he was known to be devout. That was more the exception than the rule among priests, but Garric was among those who thought it was a good thing.

Horan gripped the kid's hind legs and stretched them back. His white fillet was coming loose and he'd smudged his sash by unconsciously wiping his sweaty hands on it.

"In the name of the community!" Anda said and expertly cut the kid's throat. Its blood fountained for a moment, soaking into the sods of the altar as part of the ritual. When the animal had bled out, two of Anda's servants carried the carcass aside to be cleaned. A pot was already heating to seethe it for the feast.

"We give this gift to the Gods that they may look kindly on us!" Garric said. "Bless us, Lady! Bless us, Shepherd! Bless us, Sister!"

"May the Gods bless us all for our gift!" the assembly cried, the voices echoing from the other side of the valley.

As Anda lit the fire with a coal from the hollow gourd a servant carried, Garric felt the scene tremble away like reflections in the water when the wind rises. Sunlight slanted through shutters onto the bed. He'd been napping . . .

Garric sat up abruptly. "I didn't mean to fall asleep," he muttered, angry with himself. There was so much to do, especially on the first day on another island.

"You needed your sleep," said Liane, raising her arms to let the silk undertunic shimmer down over her like pale blue water.

"There's never time to do everything a king needs to do and sleep," said the image of Carus. He appeared to be looking out over a landscape that wasn't part of the vision in Garric's mind. *"But you have to sleep."*

Garric pulled on his own inner tunic. He wore silk robes in court, but his undergarments were always wool because he felt uncomfortable with smoother, harder, fabrics next to his skin. He grinned: Duzi knew that he was uncomfortable enough at public functions as it was.

"I'd have awakened you shortly," said Liane as she looked critically at the robe she'd laid on a chest, then put it on again. "You asked your friends to meet with you for dinner."

"Right," said Garric. "I trust my council, but I'm not an Ornifal noble and most of them are. They don't have the same instincts that I do—and frankly, I *prefer* my instincts."

"And mine?" Liane said, smiling sidelong.

Garric took her in his arms and kissed her; with love if not with the passion of a few hours earlier.

"Liane?" he said, turning to choose an outer tunic from the rack; he wouldn't wear his cuirass to dinner. He cocked the shutters farther open as he mused. Then he went on, "Is there a shrine to the Sister here in Carcosa?"

"I think there probably is," Liane said. If she was surprised, her calm face didn't betray it. "If I can't find it in the gazetteer I brought, I'll check with my local agents. How public is your interest?"

She made sure her dress was presentable, then walked toward the adjoining room of the suite where servants had laid out the luggage she'd brought from Valles. Most of her gear consisted of document cases, generally in code. Liane's father had been a far-traveled merchant, and she'd turned his shipping contacts into an intelligence service that reached into every major city in the Isles.

"It's not a secret," Garric said, strapping on his right sandal. His footwear was functional, not a pair of court slippers. He'd sooner have been barefoot in this weather, but that would've shocked the palace servants—though not his friends. "I just had a thought."

He was glad Liane didn't question him about his interest; he wasn't sure what he would answer.

But just maybe, *maybe,* his dream had solved a problem that he'd known he'd face as soon as he decided to come to Carcosa.

Chapter Five

The chamberlain suggested we eat in the roof garden," Liane explained as Garric opened the door to the corridor. "He says we can move under the marquee if it starts raining again."

The squad of Blood Eagles jumped to attention. It was Garric's whim not to have guards or even attendants in his rooms while he was present. He wasn't as fiercely hostile to the idea as Ilna was, but he'd been too long waiting on others in his father's inn to be able to ignore the fact that servants were people who saw and who heard and who spoke to their friends.

"So long as you know how to get there," Garric said, wryly amused. He'd always thought of himself as having a good sense of direction, but that was before he had to get around palaces like this one, which covered as much ground as all of Barca's Hamlet. While he was outdoors he'd been picking up cues from the sun and stars without ever being conscious of them; in a maze of corridors he was as lost as if he were trapped in a cave.

Not that there was ever a likelihood that he'd be *alone* in that cave. As soon as the door opened, half-a-dozen voices chorused, "Your highness, if I could have a moment—" or some close approximation of that. Garric recognized three of the speakers—one was Lord Tadai's chief clerk—but the others were strangers, and they all had either a document in their hands or some other person in tow.

"*Not* now," Garric said. Carus had been right: there weren't enough hours to do all the things he was expected to do. Having people pick at him like yarn thrown to a litter of kittens didn't make the job easier. "See my clerks!"

The Blood Eagles forced the petitioners back with an enthusiasm that showed they'd been waiting for a chance. They were present to protect Prince Garric, and the crowding civilians—any of whom could be an assassin—made the guards' job difficult. Add to that the fact that the soldiers thought of all civilians as soft, cowardly parasites, the thumps and shoving of the ball-blunted spearshafts were more than was strictly required to get Garric room to move.

Garric touched the guard officer's arm and said, "More gently, Captain Physos. The Shepherd knows it's as hard to find good clerks as it is good soldiers. Despite that I don't have time to deal with them right at the moment."

He grinned in response to the image of the king in his mind. Carus was nodding in morose agreement.

The petitioners stepped back; they'd made their attempt, one which at least the courtiers themselves had known was unlikely to succeed. The outsiders fell into agitated conversation with the palace personnel who'd gotten them within sight of the prince but hadn't been able to breach the final line of black armor. Powerful armies hadn't been able to get through the Blood Eagles. . . .

Transoms over the doors to the rooms on either side, and clerestory windows around the half-story above the second floor, were the corridor's only illumination, so Garric's eyes were still adapting. The man waiting in an open doorway was only a blurred figure to him until he raised his blackwood staff-of-office; its three gold bands glinted in a shaft of light.

"A moment, Captain Physos!" Garric said, touching Liane's shoulder to warn her he was halting. "Councilor Reise, did you need to speak with me?"

Garric hadn't had time—hadn't taken time—to give Reise more than a cursory greeting when the new advisor to the Vicar of Haft arrived with Liane during the assembly on the waterfront. He felt a pang of remorse at not having done more, but he thought Reise could understand why the younger man had set his priorities as he had.

"I'd appreciate a moment of your time, your highness," Reise said, bowing and making an elaborate gesture with his left hand. That was Valles etiquette, more complicated than anything required by the court in Carcosa; but it was in Valles that Reise had learned his trade. Several men stood in the room behind him.

Reise or-Laver was a middle-aged man of average height and appearance. He'd succeeded as a servant in the royal palace and later in the household of Countess Tera of Haft. When the countess died during the riots that put Count Lascarg in power, Reise had bought a rundown inn in Barca's Hamlet and managed it so ably that he'd become one of the wealthiest men in the borough. There he'd raised a son and daughter who read classical literature and who were fit to rule the kingdom when fate made them rulers.

The only thing at which Reise had failed was life itself. He was a sad, frustrated man, burdened with a shrewish wife and an indelible awareness of what might have been.

He was Garric's father.

"Yes, of course, Councilor Reise," Garric said. "Liane, if you'll go on and tell people I'm on my way . . . ?"

She squeezed his hand, curtseyed to Reise, and gestured the four Blood Eagles who were her personal escort to proceed. The other nine soldiers and their commander remained with Garric. Captain Physos planted himself squarely between son and father.

"Captain," Garric said, feeling his anger mount. "I vouch for this man."

"Maybe," the soldier said. "But there's the other three."

Garric opened his mouth, not quite sure what his next words would be nor where the business was going to end. *Reise is my father!* But all the guards cared was that Garric not be murdered—or at least not be murdered while they personally were on duty.

"There's no reason soldiers shouldn't be present," Reise said calmly. He motioned the men accompanying him back into the chamber so that four of the guards could push through and check it for threats. The room was servants' quarters for a suite; the connecting door was barred from this side, and the men with Reise were no assassins.

One of them was elderly and the other two were well into middle age. They were expensively dressed, though with a degree of flashiness that suggested they'd made their money rather than inheriting it. The scar across the cheek of the balding man wasn't the result of a shaving accident, though it might well have been done with a razor.

"These gentlemen are Masters Tartlin, Bennerr, and Wates, representing the Northern Shippers' Association here in Carcosa, your highness," Reise resumed. His tone was pleasantly modulated, though seemingly without emotion. "I had dealings with Master Wates—"

A man of Reise's age nodded. He was a close physical double for Garric's father, except that his features were as hard as an axe blade.

"—some years ago when I needed to leave Carcosa quickly with my family. Without Master Wates's help I might not have succeeded, so when he asked me to arrange a meeting if that were possible . . . ?"

"Understood," Garric said, suddenly hard-faced. Since the newborn Garric had been part of that family, Reise wasn't the only man present who owed Wates a favor. He looked at the eldest delegate, assuming he was the leader, and said, "If you can do it quickly, tell me what you need from me, Master Tartlin."

"These past three years, there's been winged demons preying on the shipping coming down the passage between Haft and Sandrakkan," the old man said. When he turned his head slightly, Garric saw that his left ear had once been pierced; the hole had scarred over in the time since Tartlin stopped wearing a ring there. "Lascarg appointed a Commander of the Strait, that's Lusius. If we pay through the nose for Lusius to put his own guards on our ships, they get through; but if we don't, well, there's just as many attacks as before."

"Commercial houses here have been switching to ships doing the southern route," Wates put in. "I don't blame them—but we can't eat Lusius's charges, we'd be bankrupt in a month if we did. The old count wouldn't listen to us but we're hoping you will, your princeship."

Garric nodded. "I *have* listened," he said. "Give me three days—"

He'd learned when he first became ruler that nothing was as simple as it looked when one of two interested parties described it. Reise had brought these men to him, but even so Garric would take the time to understand the problem before he promised to act.

"—to study the matter and I'll take the action that seems good to me."

"You mean—" said the scarred delegate, Bennerr.

Reise touched the end of his staff to Bennerr's lips, a perfectly calculated gesture that startled Garric as much as if he'd heard his father start to sing.

"His highness means," said Reise, "that he will take the action best suited to the needs of the kingdom. You all, as good citizens and supporters of the crown, will be grateful for that action whatever it may be."

"Right," said Master Wates. "That's exactly right, your highness."

Garric turned. "Captain Physos," he said as he started for the door, "do you know the way to the roof garden or do we need to find a guide?"

"If you don't mind I'll take you there myself, your highness," said Reise unexpectedly. Garric turned and faced his dry smile.

"I should remember the way quite clearly," Reise continued. "Countess Tera was fond of dining there whenever the weather permitted."

Garric made a brusque gesture of agreement. He didn't trust himself to speak, because he was afraid if he did he'd say something to embarrass both himself and his father.

Sharina chewed her second bite of meatloaf with a carefully neutral expression. It wasn't bad; it was good, in fact, once she got her mind around the fact it wasn't mutton as she'd assumed but rather beef. They raised cattle in the north of Haft; Count Lascarg came from there, so the palace cooks and their larders emphasized beef dishes.

"I've been thinking about my coronation," Garric said, staring into his tankard as he swirled the last of his beer. He seemed oddly unsure. "As Prince of Haft, on the site of the old royal palace down by the harbor."

Sharina's eyes narrowed. Garric wasn't the sort who pretended to know all the answers, but—always, and especially since he'd become regent of the kingdom—he'd picked a path and proceeded along it. He knew that he might be wrong but he knew also that he was better off acting than dithering.

Cashel stood, taking his empty mug and Sharina's by the rims in one hand. He walked to the serving table at the side, out of earshot of the diners. Across it was a line of Blood Eagles, and beyond them stood servants in nervous frustration at not being able to dispense the dishes and cups themselves. The guards let them reach through to the table to exchange full platters for empty ones, but Garric and his friends were serving themselves.

Sharina winced to see her lover carry the mugs that way, then smiled faintly. Cashel had taken most of his meals alone on a hillside while he watched his sheep; the rest were with his sister Ilna who cooked and washed for the pair of them. Nobody'd ever told him not to stick his fingers into the cups and bowls he was carrying.

Sharina wouldn't have to either, because Ilna had seen the incident. She'd explain the etiquette to her brother, in private because she loved him. Nobody needed a second explanation when Ilna had provided the first one, though. Sharina's smile widened.

To Garric she said, "Judging from the crowd in the harbor, the people here are at least as enthusiastic as those in Valles that there's really a kingdom again. Are you worried about how the other islands will react if you're crowned on Haft?"

"My sources say that folk on Sandrakkan and Blaise understand that because Garric's of the old royal line of Haft, it's appropriate for him to be crowned here," said Liane, speaking as Garric's spymaster rather than merely as a friend; though a friend too, of course.

She smiled broadly. When she didn't have to be formal, Liane had a boisterous sense of humor well matched to Garric's own. "While the Earl of Sandrakkan has his own view of his island's proper place in the restored Kingdom of the Isles," she continued, "I would *not* recommend Prince Garric be crowned in the Earl's palace in Erdin."

Twenty years before, the uncle of the present Earl of Sandrakkan had claimed to be King of the Isles. The royal army—the army of Ornifal—had defeated and killed him, but his heir and the Sandrakkan nobles more generally hadn't lost the notion that they were better men than those sniveling merchants from Ornifal.

"They're more pleased than not, the ones I've talked to," said Chalcus said as he refilled his cup from the beaker he'd brought to the dining table. He, Liane, and Tenoctris were drinking wine; the others stuck to beer as they'd been raised on in Barca's Hamlet—though here it was brewed with hops instead of the dark germander bitters of home. "They're not the nobles, as you'd guess, but sailors and shopkeepers. . . ."

He grinned, swigged, and went on, "Nobody minds that it's Carcosa, so long as it isn't Valles. You're one of theirs, Prince Garric, not somebody who's on the throne because an ancestor owned twenty acres of pasture on Ornifal."

Cashel settled himself again between Sharina and Tenoctris, setting down the mugs without spilling them. He licked ale from his thumb. Sharina hugged him.

There was no formal requirement that Garric be crowned prince, here or anywhere else. King Valence the Third had publicly acknowledged "Prince Garric of Haft" as his son and heir apparent; that was sufficient for legality. The government and royal army had accepted Garric as regent as well, which gave him the real authority—so far as Ornifal went.

For the past several hundred years the King of the Isles had been little more than a Duke of Ornifal to whom the rulers of other islands paid lip service. Garric was determined to reform the Isles into a real kingdom with unity and a degree of universal peace unknown since the fall of the Old Kingdom, so he'd decided to be crowned Prince of Haft in Carcosa where King Carus and his predecessors as Kings of the Isles had their coronations.

His friends, his formal advisors, and even the officers of the army led by Lord Waldron, a stiff-necked noble from northern Ornifal, had agreed with the plan. Sharina didn't understand Garric's apparent hesitation now.

"The problem is deciding who'll offer me the diadem," Garric said, still frowning into his beer. "It was always the Chief Priest of the Lady. It never crossed my mind to wonder about it."

He looked around the circle of his friends with a fierce expression. "But here in Carcosa, that'd mean I was joining a gang. And I'm *not* going to do that."

The anger faded back into the previous look of troubled doubt. "If I can't be crowned by the priest of the Lady or the priest of the Shepherd . . ." he continued.

Liane turned and stared at Garric with dawning horror. Sharina had seen Liane face a demon with equanimity; her present expression was completely inexplicable.

"Then I thought, maybe the third aspect of God," Garric

said. He was barely muttering, obviously ill at ease. "I thought I could be crowned at the shrine of the Prophesying Sister. Liane says the priest is just a functionary; the temple doesn't have any part in the politics of Carcosa."

Now Sharina understood Liane's look of horror. Her own face probably mirrored it.

"Garric, you can't be crowned by the Sister," Sharina said, controlling her voice with an effort. "If you're worried about what people will think, they'll think it's disgusting!"

"The Sister rules death and the underworld," Garric said, straightening and speaking with obvious anger. "Death isn't evil. Death is a part of life!"

"That's words!" Sharina said. "People don't swear by the Sister, they *curse* by Her."

Liane nodded firmly. "Sharina's right," she said. "It isn't politically *conceivable* that you'd be crowned in a Shrine of the Sister. Besides, it's a little place on the side of the High City, the old citadel. The only reason the shrine still exists is that it's an oracle. I doubt there'd be room for twenty people to stand in it."

She looked around the table. "Am I wrong?" she demanded. "What do the rest of you think? Mistress Ilna?"

Ilna looked at Liane without expression. "I don't know," she said, as calm as ice over a stream. No one could guess how swiftly the current might be tumbling beneath that frozen sheet. "Mistress, I don't believe in gods and I don't know anything about how cities are run. I just don't know."

Sharina glanced back at her brother, set-faced and grim. Garric was much more fiercely determined about this than she could understand.

Thinking that, Sharina looked into her own heart. She didn't understand why she was so strongly opposed to the idea, either, but she began to shiver.

Cashel put his left arm around her. Sharina smiled. There was danger and there would always be danger; but evil would never be as strong as the good that supported *her*.

Cashel tore another chunk from the round loaf of bread with his teeth so he could sop the last of his sauce. Since he started to travel he'd learned to eat a lot of new things. He wasn't fussy, but generally he'd rather have had the simple fare he'd been raised on. The wheat bread he got whenever he ate with rich people was a treat, though. He'd gotten used to rye and barley loaves the same way he got used to sunburn, but they weren't things he looked forward to.

Liane wrung her hands, then laid them flat on the table and managed a laugh. "I'm sorry I'm so vehement," she said, letting her soft smile slide across the faces of her friends. "The truth is I had a dream while I was napping this afternoon. It isn't . . ."

She reached over to squeeze Garric's hand without looking up from the empty platter in front of her. In the silence Tenoctris leaned forward slightly and said, "Did you dream of the Sister, Liane?"

"I don't know," Liane fiercely. The words came tumbling out as though the old wizard's question had loosened the keystone of an arch. "I think I dreamed about the Underworld. About Hell, ice and demons and someone in the middle of it all."

She looked at Garric with a desperate expression. "It was evil," she said. "She was evil, Garric. Not just death. I didn't tell you about it because . . ."

Liane brightened, suddenly the educated, sophisticated noblewoman again. She grinned at all of them. "Because I was afraid," she said, enunciating carefully, "that saying it would make it come true. I haven't felt that way since I was three years old."

Cashel chewed his bread as he listened to the others. He didn't understand why Liane and Garric and Sharina—who still occasionally trembled—were upset. There were lots of things Cashel didn't understand; that was all right. Eventually there'd be something for him to do, either that somebody else told him about or what he figured out for himself.

Until then he'd wait, and watch, and listen. Life in general was a lot like herding sheep.

Garric continued to hold Liane's hand. "I had a dream too," Garric said, "though it wasn't a bad one."

In a businesslike tone he added, "Tenoctris, what do *you* think about holding the coronation in a temple of the Sister?"

He'd stopped being worried and angry; Cashel was glad of that. Garric was back to being the man Cashel had grown up with, the fellow who figured he could do most jobs and willing to give even the impossible ones a good try.

"Like Ilna . . ." Tenoctris said carefully. She held her left hand palm in front of her and touched it with her right index finger as if she was counting. "I don't believe in the Great Gods."

She smiled at the company. She seemed decades younger when she smiled, and she smiled often.

"I've never seen Gods, you see, so as a matter of faith I believe that other people haven't seen them either." She cleared her throat and went on, "But I do believe that places of worship can be repositories of power. And—"

Tenoctris smiled again. This time her expression held a touch of the cynicism Cashel had heard when the wizard talked about what a long life had taught her about people.

"—some of those who've worshipped the Sister over the years may not have thought of Her merely as the symbol of life's natural end. Whether or not Liane's dream was prophetic or connected in any way with the Sister—"

She nodded toward Liane; Liane nodded back.

"—I believe there *could* be danger."

No one spoke for a moment. Cashel found the squabbling of finches in the cedar tree behind him familiar and soothing; it helped him think. It was funny to be up on the roof of a building and have full-sized trees growing out of planters beside you, though.

"There's danger in everything," Garric said mildly. He wasn't angry and defensive anymore, just saying what they all knew already. "We can't make our plans based on what's safest, Tenoctris."

He grinned. "That's not safe. Not with what's loose in the world now."

"Tenoctris?" Cashel said as his thought finally formed itself into the right words. "Could you tell about the temple, the Shrine of the Sister, if you were there? Tell whether it was, you know, a bad place to be?"

Tenoctris frowned thoughtfully. "I could tell . . . many things," she said. "I could determine what powers are focused on it, and I *think* I'd be able to tell what uses they'd been put to in the past. Cashel, would you like to escort me to the Shrine of the Prophesying Sister in the morning?"

"Sure," said Cashel. "Or right now, if you like."

"I think I'll be more useful after a night's sleep," the old woman said with a wry smile. "I'm not at my most comfortable on shipboard, and I haven't wholly recovered yet."

"All right," said Garric, nodding three times for emphasis. "Cashel and Tenoctris will view the shrine tomorrow. Does anyone else want to join them? Sharina?"

Sharina shook her head without speaking. Her right arm was around Cashel's waist; she squeezed harder.

"Liane?" Garric went on. "I could go myself if—"

"No!" Liane said. "Garric, please don't go. Humor me in this!"

"Very good," said Garric, his voice calm. "Tenoctris, I'll await your report before making any decisions on the matter. And now—"

Chalcus came sauntering back from the serving table with a pitcher in either hand. He'd been standing there to remove himself from the discussion without making a fuss about it. Cashel smiled. *The same as I did by filling my mouth with bread,* he thought.

"And now, my friends," Chalcus said, lifting the pitchers to call attention to them. "I think a toast to the Isles is called for, if folk will let me fill their glasses."

Cashel joined in the laughter—but Sharina didn't. She and Liane stared at each other across the table with identical worried expressions.

Ilna set her cup back at the corner of her empty platter, precisely where it had been before she raised it to drink the toast. *"To the Isles!"* were fine-sounding words, no doubt, but what did *the Isles* mean? Not a string of islands, surely; and not the people on those islands either, with their own wishes and plans and anger. People weren't a thing or even a thousand things: they were every one of them as different as the spools of yarn from which Ilna wove her fabrics.

She smiled coldly. Most people thought wool was all the

same except for the color it might have been dyed. They were wrong. And maybe Ilna os-Kenset was wrong in not seeing the great fabric of the Isles that someone, perhaps Garric and the rest of them here at this table, were weaving out of individual people.

It wasn't dark yet, but servants were bringing out lanterns to hang from hooked poles. Chalcus would probably suggest they hire a chair to take them to the house they were renting . . . and Ilna would probably agree, because she disliked the feel of cobblestones underfoot and in the dark of unfamiliar streets she might well slip in filth and turn an ankle.

Across the table Cashel, Sharina, and Tenoctris—with Cashel's help—were rising. Ilna rose also, but as Chalcus stood he touched a hand to her elbow for attention and said, "Prince Garric, might I have a talk of a private nature with you and Mistress Ilna before we're off about our business for the evening?"

"Yes, of course," said Garric, his tone friendly but guarded. He didn't have any idea what Chalcus wanted to discuss, but he knew it wasn't a slight thing if the sailor requested privacy.

Ilna didn't have any idea either. What she *did* know was that surprises were usually unpleasant.

"Though you won't mind," Garric continued, making a statement rather than asking a question, "if Lady Liane stays with us to take notes."

Garric seemed much older than he'd been when he and Ilna both left Barca's Hamlet. He'd been a happy boy and a friendly youth; now—he was often happy and usually friendly, but he was beyond question a man.

Ilna smiled, though the expression didn't reach her lips. She didn't think she'd ever been young herself, but she regretted her old friend Garric's loss of childish playfulness. No doubt "the Isles," whatever they were, were better for the change.

"I have work to do with the reports, your highness," Liane said calmly. Her eyes met Ilna's and she made a respectful half-curtsey of acknowledgment. "Good evening, Mistress Ilna, Master Chalcus."

She slipped into the line of guards before Garric could

protest, if he'd intended to. Chalcus didn't want her present—he would've worded his request another way if he had—and Liane didn't choose to be where she was an embarrassment. Ilna could have liked the girl if circumstances had been different. Maybe she liked her anyway.

Chalcus watched Liane go with a speculative grin, then returned his attention to Garric. "So, your highness," he said. "There's trouble in the Strait, monsters from the air preying on shipping. Lascarg's Commander of the Strait, who is now your Commander of the Strait, one Lusius, does nothing but count the bribe money he squeezes from the shippers. Is this old news to you?"

"I'm listening," Garric said; and so he was, with a hard expression which Ilna could read no more than she could look through a block of granite. "Though if you're bringing information, you'd do better to have offered it to Liane directly. She handles that aspect of the government."

"Aye, the pretty Liane learns things for you," Chalcus said. He was poised, standing on the balls of his feet. He was generally tense when he talked with Attaper or Lord Waldron; men of war who never lost the awareness that Chalcus was one of them, but was not necessarily on their side. And the new Garric was one of them as well . . . "But you, I think, are the one who acts or does not act. Is that correct, your highness?"

"I make the final decisions, Master Chalcus," Garric said evenly. "I have wise friends and good advisors; but *I* am the prince."

"Then shortly, when the Northern Shippers' Association asks you to send someone to deal with the monsters, your highness," said Chalcus, "I suggest you send Mistress Ilna and my own self in place of some commodore or other with a squadron of wallowing great warships. That is what I would ask—if Ilna is willing, and if you can spare us from the wedding preparations, which I'm sure must be absorbing much of your time just now."

"Ah!" said Garric, understanding at last; and Ilna understood as well.

Garric's attention had been wholly focused on Chalcus thus far during the discussion. Now he looked at Ilna and said, "Ilna? Is this what you want? Because if it is, or whatever you want . . . ?"

He smiled at her, a boy again; the boy she'd loved for as long as she could remember.

"This is the first I've heard of it," Ilna said. "Any of it. And as for your wedding, Garric, I expect to attend with my good wishes. Certainly I'm not looking for an excuse to be absent."

Her face went cold. She added, "I don't look for excuses."

If it hadn't been for Garric's smile, she'd have spoken the same words in a snarl—angry at Garric, angry at Chalcus; angry at the world. She chuckled at the notion. *Pretty much as always, of course,* she thought.

"But as for what I want," she continued, letting the words roll out as her mind formed them, "I want to make the world a better place."

Her grin was hard, self-mocking. Neither of the men smiled at all.

"If you—" her glance included both men "—or Tenoctris or anyone has a better use for, for *me* than to sit in a room weaving, then tell me. Just tell me what you want me to do!"

"As it chances," Garric said, "the Shippers' Association has already spoken to me. I said I'd give them a decision in three days after I'd studied the matter. What do *you* know about it, Master Chalcus?"

"Have they indeed?" said Chalcus in a tone of pleased surprise. "What a quick set of lads they are! I thought they'd be a week at least getting through the folk who keep the prince from being bothered."

He raised the carafe of wine and poised with it as though he considered pouring himself another mug. Continuing, the banter gone, Chalcus said, "I know that it's real, that ships are stripped and the crews gone without a trace."

Chalcus's smile was as hard as the curved blade of his dagger. "Easy enough to guess where the men are, the sea having so many hungry mouths in it, but the cargoes are another thing."

"The winged monsters?" Garric said. "They're real?"

"Aye," said Chalcus, "they're real. And—"

He leaned back against the table, though he didn't let it really bear his weight. When Chalcus and Garric faced one another, there was always the danger that their poses would become threatening. Because they were the men they were, they both worked to avoid the problem.

Men, thought Ilna. But she had even less use for the other sort, for all her irritation at the dangerous posturing that was marrow deep in the Garrics and Chalcuses of the world.

"—I can only imagine what your shippers told you about Lusius," Chalcus continued, "but if they said he's a crook who's dealt with pirates himself in past years . . . well then, they said the truth. To my certain knowledge."

"I see," said Garric. He grinned. "Pour me some ale, would you, Chalcus? My throat's dry from all this talking. Ilna?"

"No," she said without dressing up the word. She wasn't thirsty, so she wouldn't drink; and the offer had been merely for courtesy, as Garric's request was really a place-holder to let him think. Humans wove their lives through the lives of others in patterns; because the patterns worked, more often than not, and you had to suit your fabric to your materials . . .

Garric took the filled mug and met Chalcus's eyes over it. "I can give you a battalion," he said. "Of any troops you choose, save the Blood Eagles. And some of them if you like."

Chalcus laughed. "And what do I know about leading soldiers?" he said. "Or fleets either one, eh? There's a ship I've marked out to hire, a trim little vessel, and six men from your army I'll take to crew her if they choose to come."

"Yes," said Garric. "And?"

Chalcus still smiled, even his eyes, but the lilt in his voice had an edge. "That much I could do by myself," he said, "as you well know. What I want from you, your highness, is your blessing; and this is not a small thing that I ask, as you know also."

"To go off and settle the problem?" Garric said. "I've *given* you that, Master Chalcus."

"I ask that afterward you accept what I've done, my friend," Chalcus said. His tone was hard, his words very clear. "That whatever promises I make, you will keep as though you'd made them. That whatever deeds others do in my name, you say were done in yours; and that you will honor the doers, no matter what those deeds may have been."

"Ah," said Garric, nodding again. "No, not a small thing at all."

Garric wore his sword always in public during this tour of the kingdom's western islands; Ilna supposed he was reminding people that they were part of the kingdom, and that the royal army was available to enforce anything that its prince couldn't manage with his own right arm. Ilna understood the value of symbols, after all.

Though Garric had worn the weapon to dinner, he'd unbuckled it and hung it, belt and all, over the back of his chair while he ate. Now, moving with a deliberation that showed he wasn't making a threat of any kind, Garric drew the blade and let lantern light quiver along its patterned steel.

"The sword hasn't any guilt for the things it's done while I wielded it," he said quietly to Chalcus. "Nor will I punish the men who act for me. But you're right, Chalcus; it's not a promise I would make were I not sure of the folk I send to act in my place."

He turned to meet Ilna's eyes; and, smiling, still holding her gaze, he shot the blade back home in the scabbard.

Chalcus laughed. "Oh, I wish I'd had a few of your sort in my crew in the bad old days, my princeling!" he said. "Well, never mind. I'll be for you what you'd have been for me—and in a better cause, I'm sure!"

Garric stepped forward and clasped his right arm with Chalcus, each man's hand gripping the other's elbow. They backed apart and Chalcus moved to the side, only a hairbreadth but enough to take him out of the way. Ilna met Garric's eyes again.

"Ilna," Garric said, "I would rather lose my right arm than to lose you from my life. Go and teach whoever's behind the trouble what it means to do evil when there's a force for good like you in the world. And then come back to me and your other friends, because we need you."

A force for good? But yes, she supposed so. It was an odd way to think about herself, though.

Ilna extended her arm to Garric. As he'd done before, as she'd hoped he'd do again but never would have asked him to do, Garric stepped closer and hugged her with the delicate care of a very strong man for a woman half his size.

They stepped apart; Chalcus moved to her side. "Travel safely," Garric said to both of them. "Though—I know there're risks, but there'll never be a day I wouldn't feel safer at your side than I would facing you, either one."

"Never fear, good prince," said Chalcus with a laugh as he turned away, his hand on Ilna's waist. "We'll bring the ears back for you!"

"We will *not*," said Ilna crisply; knowing that it was probably the sort of joke men share, knowing also that with these men there was no certainty that it was a joke at all.

"Ah, then we will not, dearest," agreed Chalcus cheerfully as he handed Ilna through the line of Blood Eagles. In a more businesslike tone he went on, "In the morning, I'll ask you to come with me to see the factor who handles the Serian trade in Carcosa. His name's Sidras or-Morr, and you'll be no end of help to me dealing with him."

"I'll come, of course," Ilna said without emphasis. "But I don't see what I can do that you can't. I don't know the man—I don't know anybody in Carcosa."

"Ah, you'll see, dear one," the sailor said. This back staircase was too narrow for them to walk abreast. Without asking or probably considering the question, Chalcus stepped ahead of her and sauntered down. Behind them on the roof were friends and bodyguards, but who knew what might be waiting below? In all likelihood nothing whatever of a hostile nature; but if something was there, it would have to get through Chalcus before it reached Ilna.

"And another thing, sweetest," he added over his shoulder. "Do you think that your friend Sharina would be willing to join us for the outing?"

Ilna thought for a moment. They reached the landing and Chalcus touched her waist again as they continued.

"You'd have to ask her, of course," she said at last, "but yes, I think she would. She won't be going with Cashel and Tenoctris, and I think she'd like something to take her mind off whatever it is that's worrying her."

"Then we'll indeed ask her, before we leave the palace tonight," Chalcus said with satisfaction. "And if it's why? you're wondering, dearest—let's just say that from all reports this Sidras is a canny fellow who'll recognize a hawk however many swan feathers it drapes itself in. Were I to go alone to see him, the interview would be very short and not at all to my liking. But with a pillar of unquestioned rectitude like yourself, and with the sister of the prince on my other side—then I think he'll listen even to an old pirate long enough to hear that he's reformed!"

Chalcus laughed merrily. As they started down the hallway to the suite Sharina shared with Cashel, he began to sing, *"Dig a hole, dig a hole, in the meadow, dig a hole in the cold, cold ground. . . ."*

Chapter Six

As they paused at Harbor Street, Sharina massaged her left calf where a thorn had caught her as she left her suite by means of the window. Her foot had slipped on the terra-cotta pipe and she'd flailed her leg into one of the roses trained up the palace wall.

"Aye, there they are," said Chalcus, gesturing with his open left hand toward the three large vessels in the reed-choked water just beyond the stone embankment. "Before I'm hanged, I'll be able to navigate the nasty, narrow lanes of a city as well as I do the sea."

"I thought we were going to a warehouse," Sharina said, eyeing the ships. "Though I don't mind, of course."

This morning she wore an eared bonnet and matching beige muslin shawl, both garments borrowed from her maid. Even so she'd decided to climb down the pipe which funneled rain water to the cistern in order to avoid the guards who'd otherwise insist on coming with her. The Princess of

Haft had the power to do many things, but she had a lot less control over her*self* than plain Sharina os-Reise had taken for granted.

Sharina didn't think it was a good exchange, but when it was important she could work around the problem. She'd decided that joining Ilna and Chalcus to see a merchant, three friends together on an outing, was important; especially in her present mood.

"Master Sidras is a clever fellow," Chalcus said, sauntering along with Ilna on his right and Sharina on the other side. "Instead of a building on shore, he bought a hulked transport and dredged a trench for it into the mudflats. The bridge to the embankment is easy to guard. Save for that, you can't reach his store by land or by boat either one, at least not a boat big enough to carry off any amount of loot. And as he prospered, he bought two more hulks to increase his space."

The broad waterfront pavement would allow the largest goods wagons to pass in opposite directions. Ages without maintenance had tilted the paving blocks one from the next, but since there was little other traffic this morning the trio walked toward the hulks with reasonable ease.

Less than half of the ancient harbor was in active use. The northern portion where the river entered had become a mud bank. The huts of eel fishermen and bird catchers stood on stilts over the vegetation, and freshwater streams meandered across the mud to reach the brackish water of the harbor proper. Small animals—probably rats—scurried and splashed among the coarse reeds, and once Sharina saw what she thought was a snake slither across the mud like a riffling breeze.

She didn't mind snakes, particularly. She'd faced more danger from human beings than from any other animal she'd met.

At the landward end of the bridge to the hulks was a wicket gate and behind it a guardhouse. The watchman hadn't rung his large brass gong in the shape of a lion's face, but he must've communicated in some fashion as he watched the trio approach: two more men came out of the hulk and walked down the bridge. The well-dressed one was on the other side of middle age, while his younger companion was a squat troll carrying an iron-bound club.

"There's a cord running under the wharf," Ilna said without pointing. "It must ring a bell in the ship."

Trust Ilna to notice a line . . . but Sharina should've seen it herself, since she'd known it must exist.

"Hello, good sirs!" Chalcus called, still ten feet short of the gate. "We've been told that Master Sidras or-Morr handles the Serian trade here, so we've come to see him."

"Have you?" said the well-dressed man, Sidras himself by his demeanor. His hair had been blond and his beard a deeper red when he was younger; now there was more gray than not in both. He set his left hand on the wicket and glared out at his visitors. "Maybe you're here to tell me to stop dealing with foreign devil-worshippers?"

"We are not," said Chalcus, his tone no longer cheerfully bantering; at best that would inflame Sidras's obvious hostility. "And while I've had my problems with the Serians in years past, they do not worship demons, sir."

"Huh!" said Sidras. "From the look of you, lad, it wasn't the Serians who caused the problems."

The watchman had gotten his crutch under his left arm and lifted himself off his stool. He held a mallet in his free hand and tried to look threatening, though without much success. The bruiser with the club was another matter, though, and Sidras himself looked like he could give a good account of himself in a fight despite his age and fat. . . .

Sharina smiled at the way her mind was running. She'd learned to size up strange men quickly when she tended bar in her father's inn during the Sheep Fairs. Today she and her friends were here to do business, not to brawl.

Chalcus had halted a double-pace back from the gate to make clear that he didn't intend to push beyond his welcome. Sidras looked from him, to Ilna, and finally to Sharina. The situation obviously puzzled him.

"Who are you, then, mistress?" he said, nodding to Sharina.

"I'm Sharina os-Reise," she said, making the choice of words in the split second between the question and her answer. "My friend is Ilna os-Kenset, and we're accompanying Master Chalcus, who wishes to bargain with you."

She didn't know Chalcus's father's name. For that matter, she wasn't sure that Chalcus himself knew.

"Huh!" Sidras repeated. "I suppose I'm to think you're Princess Sharina of Haft, am I, because you're tall and a blonde?"

"You're to think I'm a respectable woman from Barca's Hamlet on the east coast," Sharina said. "Because I'm telling you that, and you needn't flatter yourself that I think you're worth lying to!"

Sidras smiled faintly, though the unsettled look didn't leave his eyes as he switched his gaze to Ilna. "If your father's name's Kenset . . ." he said. "And you come from Barca's Hamlet too . . . ?"

"I do," Ilna said. From Ilna's expression, Sharina judged she wasn't best pleased to be interrogated this way, but she was holding her temper. Ilna had a lot of experience not being pleased, after all.

"Would you chance to know a fellow named Cashel, then?" Sidras said, surprising Sharina as much as if he'd suddenly jumped off the dock.

"He's my brother," said Ilna simply. "Though we're not a great deal alike."

"Huh!" said Sidras. "That's not what *I* see, mistress, despite him getting all the bulk of the family. Unlock the gate, Mattion."

As the watchman fitted the four pins of his key into the slots in the padlock, Sidras looked his visitors over again and shook his head. "I'm letting you in," he said, "because if you two trust Master Chalcus I'll trust him too. But we may all three of us be the greatest fools ever born!"

Chalcus laughed. He bowed and gestured the women ahead of him with his left arm.

The bridge to the nearest of the three ships was wide enough for carts and as solid underfoot as the stone pavers of Harbor Street. Sidras walked alongside his three visitors while the guard stumped behind the group.

Sharina glanced at him over her shoulder; the fellow's expression was sullenly angry though she couldn't tell whether he was still worried about Chalcus or if he were simply a sullenly angry person. The Lady knew there were enough of them in the world, and the attitude was probably less of a handicap in a bodyguard than in most professions.

"We're here to see the goods you trade to the Serians," Chalcus said. "Not the silks and ceramics they bring to Carcosa, Master Sidras. I'm on a voyage to Valles by the northern route, and there's a few trifles I want to take along to make up my lading."

The freighter's original deck had been raised two levels with wood framing, increasing the enclosed volume considerably. It had already been a large vessel, much bigger than anything anchored normally in Carcosa Harbor now.

Echoing Sharina's thought aloud as they entered through the open doorway, Chalcus said, "She was in the grain trade from Tisamur to Blaise, was she not?"

He bent to scratch the deck with the nail of his index finger, illustrating his question and probably checking the soundness of the wood at the same time. "Great wallowing pigs, but as sturdy as the rocks of the shore itself, to be sure."

"Aye," said Sidras, not displeased. "She was to be broken up for her wood. I bought her in Blaise and had her towed here in the summer when the winds were as much to trusted as ever you can."

"As ever you can," Chalcus agreed. He put his hands on his hips as he surveyed the room the factor had brought them into. It was a vast echoing hall, open save for wooden piers and the frames holding goods in bales and baskets.

Sharina's eyes took a moment to adjust to the light filtering through side windows. Half-a-dozen clerks, men and women both, were at work among the shelves; one of them was using a lantern.

"I'm readying a back cargo for the Serian ship docked at Clasbon's Factory," Sidras said, leading the way through the racked merchandise. The cross-aisles were offset from one another, so crossing the width of the ship was like walking a curving forest path. "Otherwise you'd have to come down into the hold if you wanted to see my Serian stores."

Sharina could only guess at most of the goods stacked about her. She walked around a pile of sacks whose contents had been emptied into wide storage jars. Ilna paused to run her fingertips across the coarse fabric; then she jerked her hand away and shook it with a look of distaste, as though something foul was sticking to her skin.

"Here, then," Sidras said with a gesture toward a row of pallets. Though it was morning, Sharina's eyes had adapted well enough to see by the light diffused through the broad windows in the west sidewall. "Anything in particular you're looking for, or do you plan a general cargo?"

The odors of the goods in the vast hall mixed with the miasma of the mudflats on which the vessel stood. The combined smell was a thing Sharina felt she could touch.

The pallet nearest to her held a pile of small sharks; they'd been sliced down the middle, sun-dried, and pressed flat. Blotches of orange mold grew on their dull gray skins. Next to them was a pallet stacked with dried sea cucumbers whose salt pungency reminded Sharina of the marsh grasses along Pattern Creek in the borough. The goods farther down the line continued the varied assortment of the sea's produce. Few of the items were food in Barca's Hamlet—or, Sharina suspected, in Carcosa either.

Chalcus and Sidras were examining a large unglazed pot that sat on a tray sealed with pitch to hold an inch of seawater. The bottom of the pot was dark because water was wicking through the raw earthenware.

Sidras lifted the lid; the smell of camphor breathed over the air around. The men bent forward cautiously, keeping well back from the opening as they looked within. Sharina hadn't heard their discussion; she stepped closer.

"Careful!" Sidras warned. "The camphor keeps them quiet, but you don't want to take chances with these."

Sharina glanced over to see that Ilna was examining bolts of dyed linen, which had probably come from Blaise. Nodding—*Why do I feel responsible for Ilna, who's managed her life with as little help as anyone I know?*—Sharina peered into the pot. For a moment she saw only slick iridescence; then a small oval head rose.

"Enough," said Sidras, straightening up. He replaced the lid.

"Reef snakes," Chalcus explained. He grinned, but there

was sweat on his brow. "They're little things that live on the reefs west of Haft and hunt fish. I've never heard of one longer than a man's arm."

"If they bite your hand," said Sidras, "it feels like you've stuck your arm in molten bronze. You start to swell right away, and after an hour or so you die."

"If you're bitten, you die," Chalcus said. His fingers were twitching where his swordhilt would've been if he'd not left the blade behind to seem less threatening. Some men fear spiders, some fear cats; and some men, even unquestionably brave men, are terrified by snakes. "And you're screaming to the end."

"The Serians eat these too?" Sharina asked. Compared to the sea cucumbers, a meal of snake meat didn't strike her as particularly disgusting.

"I think their healers use the poison," Sidras said, shaking his head. "They buy the snakes live and pay well for them, let me tell you. They have to, for there's few enough fishermen willing to risk the bite. I've heard men say that there's no real danger if you're careful, that they're sluggish devils and nearsighted besides. But I've never known anyone to gather them unless he was in more need of money than usual."

Ilna hadn't seemed to be paying attention, but as Chalcus looked up from the container of snakes she opened her hands to display the pattern she'd woven while she was turned away. Sharina caught a flash of it and felt momentarily warm, as though a cat had brushed her leg. Chalcus looked fixedly into the knotted cords for a moment, then hugged Ilna tight.

"You must think I'm a weak, frightened man, Master Sidras," he said with a laugh. He stepped away from Ilna and bowed to the factor.

"I do not," said Sidras. "An assistant of mine reached into the container on a dare once. He was a clumsy boy, and a fool, and a pilferer besides I shouldn't wonder. But he didn't deserve that death. Nobody does."

"Now these . . ." said Chalcus, moving to wicker baskets of conical seashells packed in straw mats to keep them from chipping one another. "Are new to me. You fish them from these waters?"

"We do now," said Sidras, pulling out one of the shells. It was slender and only a little longer than the merchant's middle finger. When he held it to catch the light, it shimmered with the colors of a brilliant sunset: purples and magentas and reds that shaded suddenly into indigo. "Lusius does, at any rate. Three years back the sea bottom rose west of the Calves—"

He glanced at Sharina and raised an eyebrow.

"Those are the three islands north of Haft," Chalcus explained. "Commander Lusius has his base on the easternmost, Corse."

"Aye," agreed Sidras. "And if I *did* refuse to deal with folk because of the way they live, it wouldn't be the Serians and their idols I'd start with. But Lusius controls the belemnite shell, and there's no lack of buyers for it."

He handed the shell to Chalcus, then drew out another one and offered it to Sharina. It was as delicate as eggshell, with a faint spiral pattern. She could see the shadow of her finger through the side.

Chalcus held the shell up and turned it. He said, "So the bottom rose and these—the belemnites?"

"Aye," said Sidras, nodding. "They're little squids with shells, and that's what Lusius says they're called. He's got a wizard with him who learns things, I don't know how."

Sharina heard the strong implication that Sidras didn't want to know what wizards did. Sharina knew more about wizards than most people did—and based on her experience, Tenoctris was the only one who didn't deserve Sidras's prejudice.

"And the winged demons came at the same time?" Chalcus said.

"The Rua, right," said Sidras, scowling thoughtfully. "I don't know about them being demons, but they fly. They're sure not men like live around here."

He barked a laugh. "They fish for the shell too," he added, rummaging between baskets and coming up with a swatch of coarse fabric.

A net, Sharina thought, but Sidras shook it out and she saw it was a bag. The meshes were open enough to hold objects the size of belemnite shells but nothing smaller.

"Lusius fights the Rua for the shell," Sidras explained. "From what I hear he doesn't do a lot better than he does keeping them from raiding ships, but one of them dropped this bag when an archer pinked him."

"May I look at that?" Ilna said. Everybody turned, startled to be reminded that she was still present. Grinning wryly she went on, "I'm not interested in snakes or seashells, but cloth is another matter."

"Of course," said Sidras. Chalcus had already swept the bag from him and offered it to Ilna. She held it in one hand and ran the tips of the other fingers along the loose meshes.

Chalcus and the factor began talking about the Commander of the Strait and his troops. Sidras seemed to have lost his wariness of Chalcus, and their mutual dislike of Lusius added to their warmth.

Sharina examined the shell again. Then, turning her head, she glanced toward Ilna. Her friend was motionless; her eyes were open, but they weren't looking into anything in this world.

Sharina looked away, licking her lips. Ilna had a talent for fabric; it told her things that no one else could hear.

But Sharina herself had learned that not all secrets are good to know.

"Your highness . . ." said the servant, his face lowered so that he wasn't actually looking at Garric. He was one of the staff Lord Tadai had summoned from Valles, not a member of Count Lascarg's establishment. "The delegation from the Temple of the Lady of the Sunset has arrived under Senior Priest Moisin bor-Sacchiman."

The room Liane and Reise had chosen for Prince Garric's public business was on the ground floor of Lascarg's palace; Garric supposed it was meant for small entertainments or the overflow from large ones. The high ceiling had scenes painted in each coffered cell, though even now in daytime there wasn't enough light to be sure of the subjects. They weren't terribly well-drawn, either: the Counts of Haft didn't attract artists as able as those who decorated the palaces of nobles on the more powerful islands.

From above shoulder height the sidewalls were frescoed with a design of birds on a seashore, but the lower walls were wainscoted in age-darkened oak. During a party there'd be crowding and drunken spills; rough usage wouldn't harm the wood, but plaster would flake off with the expense of repairs.

"His highness will see them now, Master Bessin," Liane said coolly, then returned her attention to the three stacks of documents laid out on the long table before her.

During the intervals between petitioners, she and Garric were going over proposed lists of officials for the new royal government on Haft. All of Garric's senior staff had clients and relatives to place, so the decisions had to be made as much on politics as merit.

Garric would've been happier to answer the servant himself—by Duzi, he'd rather have opened the *door* himself!— but everybody else seemed to want things complicated. Part of the point of his travels through the capitals of the western islands was to convince people that Garric was a prince, not some mumbling shepherd from the boondocks as they might have heard. That meant he had to act like a prince, however silly and uncomfortable he felt doing it.

"A lot of life is playacting, lad," remarked the grinning image of Carus. *"The silver plate on your armor won't turn a blade one whit better than plain bronze, but you have to wear it so that all your men can see you there leading them."*

Behind Garric trilled birds in a silver cage, a gift from the Shepherd's priesthood earlier this morning. The birds were literally gold: four creations of metal that fluttered on their perches and sang with undiminished musicality so long as anyone was present in the room. A system of weights powered the device; the priestess who delivered the automaton said that it should be wound every morning, but that the task could be performed by any scullion capable of turning a spit. The birds' song was oddly soothing, more so than the music alone should have been.

The servant made a signal to the ushers on the other side of the door; they drew back the double panels and bowed. Moisin, a tall man in silken robes, entered. He was flanked by a pair of Blood Eagles. The priest was bald to mid-skull and had an ascetic expression, belied perhaps by the fact his garb must have cost as much as a good horse. Behind him, four underlings carried a large object draped in brocade on a hand barrow.

Moisin bowed deeply. "Your highness," he said, "the congregation of the Lady asked me to bring this token of our joy at your visit to us here in Carcosa."

He turned and nodded an order to his juniors; they set the barrow on the parquet floor and stepped aside. With a conjuror's flourish, Moisin whipped off the cover. Beneath was a wide-mouthed urn more than four feet high. It was made of translucent, gray-green stone polished to a mirror sheen.

"It's lovely," murmured Liane under her breath. She got up from the table where she'd been working on accounts and walked toward the urn as if entranced. Moisin smirked minusculely. "The pattern is . . . lovely!"

Garric rose also, even more impressed than he'd been by the mechanical birds. Neither gift would change his behavior toward the priesthoods of Carcosa, but they were marvelous things beyond question.

Light from the room's north windows behind him struck a pattern through the walls of the urn. The gray to gray-green to green shadings were as faint as the mergings of color within a rainbow, but they made Garric feel happier and *safe;* as safe as when he was an infant wrapped in his featherbed, knowing his parents would protect him.

"The stone is cryolite, ice spar," Moisin said, anticipating the question that Garric hadn't gotten around to asking. "It's only found on the Ice Capes and rarely in blocks so big as this one. Some say that it's ice from the bottom of glaciers, compressed into stone."

"It's lovely," Liane repeated. She reached out but didn't quite permit her fingers to touch the smooth walls. They had the sheen of liquid light; it was hard to tell where the stone ended and the air began.

"I want to be very clear," Garric said, raising his voice beyond what his arm's-length separation from Moisin required. "My government will almost certainly make major changes in the structure and power of the priesthoods in Carcosa. You already know that. Absolutely nothing you give me, not this—"

He gestured without looking. It was hard to keep his train of thought and his necessary harshness if the urn were in his line of vision.

"—not a pile of gold as big as this palace, *nothing,* will affect the decisions of my government."

"That much gold would pay the army's wages for three years . . ." mused Carus. His image was smiling, but his reminder that everything—even rectitude—required moderation was serious.

"Of course the congregation of the Shepherd understands your honesty and the needs of the kingdom, your highness," Moisin said, bowing again. "Our concern is only that you realize that those who worship the Shepherd rejoice as warmly in your visit to Haft as every other citizen does."

The priest smiled knowingly. His half-nod *might* have been meant to indicate the birds twittering in their joy.

Garric cleared his throat. "Very well," he said. "You may assure your fellows that their gift has been accepted on the terms that they offered it."

Moisin bowed again and turned. His underlings continued to stare at the urn, as entranced as Liane herself. With an angry snap of his fingers Moisin recalled them to their duty; they trailed from the room with him. The Blood Eagles marched out also, though one darted a final glance over his shoulder at the stone's lustrous beauty.

Liane's hand sought Garric's. Only when she touched him did she meet his eyes and smile, then walked back to her duty.

"I'm leery about accepting gifts from the priesthoods," Garric said, "even if we're not going to change our minds because of them. But I guess these things may as well be here with us as in vaults in the basement of some temple."

"Yes," said Liane. "I think so too."

And the birds trilled music sweeter than anything that came from a living throat.

Ilna stood silent, her mind looking out over the warm, lush world where the net bag had been woven. A shallow sea stretched from horizon to horizon, marked by coral heads and masses of vegetation that hid whatever land there was for them to root upon.

A soft wind barely riffled the water. Through it, some as high as the sun itself while others skimmed the glassy surface, flew the winged men, the Rua. They were as inhuman as so many cats, but like cats their slimly-muscular bodies were beautiful and their movements were perfectly graceful.

Ilna's fingers stroked the bag, barely touching it. The long, strong fibers spun to form the meshes came from the inner bark of shrubs growing on the distant islets; she *knew* that as she would know the sun was shining by the feel of its rays on her skin. Her body wasn't in this waking dream, but the senses that made Ilna a weaver like no other person alive saw and heard with a clarity that her eyes and ears could never equal.

The Rua called to one another in high, fluting voices. Had Ilna heard the sound in Barca's Hamlet, she'd have taken it for gulls' cries, but these were rich and didn't have the birds' metallic timbre.

When a flyer passed close to her vantage point, Ilna saw that its skull was more oval than a human's and that its teeth were small and blunt. Its wings stretched from little fingers longer than a human forearm and back to its thighs. The material was stiff though thin as air, like a fish's fin rather than the taut skin membranes of a bat.

Ilna was standing on—she was watching from; she had no body, only senses—the top of a volcanic cone, which rose steeply from the water. Only a few shrubs with small waxy leaves managed to grow on the gray slopes beneath her.

One of the Rua coursed the sea just below Ilna's vantage, dipping its legs with the quick, precise motion of a bird drinking. After each dab the legs kicked forward, tossing a gleaming object into the bag the creature held in both hands.

After the fourth grab, the creature flew up the side of the cone with the short, powerful wingbeats of a hawk. It—she: the Rua had two flat dugs to either side of her deep breast-bone—swooped past Ilna to drop into the volcano's sheer-walled interior. Her bag was full of belemnites, their tiny tentacles writhing over their iridescent shells.

Ilna opened her hands, feeling the rough fibers fall from her fingers. With the bag, the world of her vision slipped away. She blinked in the dim light of Sidras's warehouse.

Sharina was watching her sidelong with a worried expression. Ilna smiled tightly, picked up the bag—it was only a network of tough cord now—and handed it her friend.

"They'll be delivered to your vessel tonight, then, and I wish you joy of them!" Sidras said.

"Aye," said Chalcus with a laugh that wasn't as wholly carefree as it usually sounded. Ilna's eyes narrowed. He spat on his right palm and held his hand out to Sidras to grip, sealing the bargain they'd made while Ilna was in her reverie. "It may be that I'll find myself in a place where they'll be the only hope of joy there is. Though that's not a thought that pleases me, Master Sidras."

Chalcus threw up his outer tunic to reach the money belt he wore beneath it. Before he could open the supple leather flap, Sidras laid two fingers on his wrist.

"Hold a moment, lad," the factor said. "You mean this cargo for Lusius, is that not so?"

"It may be that I do," said Chalcus. Then with an edge of challenge in his voice as he went on, "Aye, if I deliver it at all, I'd judge it would be to your Commander of the Strait. What is that to you?"

"Just this," said Sidras, withdrawing his hand. "Take the goods on consignment for me, then, rather than paying for them. I'm an old man or perhaps I'd go with you myself to help with the delivery."

Chalcus laughed merrily and clasped arms with Sidras. "You're not such an old man now, Master Sidras, that I wouldn't press you to join us were not my crew full for the voyage," he said. "But aye, I'll deliver them in your name."

He turned with laughter bubbling behind his eyes and said, "Now, my fine ladies, let's take ourselves to the palace. You have your duties to attend, my blond friend; Mistress Ilna and I have good-byes to say and many a thread of business to tie up!"

"Halt!" ordered the officer of the guard. The Blood Eagles in front of and behind Cashel and Tenoctris clashed their boots down on the flagstones. Cashel didn't see why soldiers had to do everything with flash and noise, but it wasn't his place to tell them their business.

The guards were with Tenoctris. Cashel figured that if he needed help, it wasn't something a bunch of soldiers could give him. Garric had agreed.

Temples weren't a part of Cashel's life before he left Barca's Hamlet less than a year before, so he hadn't had any clear notion of what the Shrine of the Prophesying Sister would look like. It turned out to be a trim little semicircle of pillars with a tile roof, built into the rocky slope. It looked down on Carcosa Harbor and what Garric had said was the oldest part of the city.

It all seemed pretty old to Cashel. The millhouse where he'd grown up dated from the Old Kingdom, but that was home; he'd never thought of it as being ancient, the way he did Carcosa's crumbling city walls and the weed-grown hills that once were buildings.

The two hired bearers set down the sedan chair in which Tenoctris sat reading a scroll. One man wiped his forehead with the dangling ends of the kerchief he wore as a sweat band. "It's heavy work," Cashel said in sympathy.

"Yeah, but she don't weigh nothing," said the bearer. He patted the seat back. "All the weight's in the chair, and that's a right plenty when the road's so steep they cut steps."

"We're there, then?" Tenoctris said, looking around brightly while her fingers rewound the book. It was a simple leather scroll wound on sticks of plain wood without the gilding and decoration some books had. It looked old, though, and if Tenoctris was choosing to read it now, it was probably important.

"Yes, milady," said the palace servant who'd been the party's guide up the path's steps and switchbacks. "The Shrine of the Prophesying Sister."

The roofed portion of the building was small, but Cashel

could see that the rock had been dug out deeply beyond. A stern-looking man with a full black beard came from the doorway and bowed to the newcomers. Instead of priestly robes, he wore a pair of gray tunics—plain but of cloth tightly woven by a skillful craftsman.

Cashel grinned as he helped Tenoctris out of the chair. Ilna'd approve of the tunics, both of their workmanship and their simplicity.

"Lady Tenoctris," the bearded man said, ignoring Cashel as well as the guards and attendants, "it's an honor to greet a scholar of your stature! I'm Horife or-Handit and I've written a little work debunking the superstitious belief in prophecy. I'm sure you won't have read it . . . ?"

He bustled toward them, apparently expecting to push past the soldiers. The officer of the guard grabbed a handful of Horife's beard and jerked him back. The priest—he *was* a priest, wasn't he?—gave a startled squawk.

"I'm afraid I haven't read your book, Master Horife," Tenoctris said. A faint smile was her only acknowledgment of the way the guards had handled the fellow. "My reading is sadly out of date, which I regret. I used to wonder what it would be like to live an active life. Now that I'm living one, I find I have very little time to read, my greatest pleasure when I was a poor scholar."

"Ah," said Horife, smoothing the beard, which the soldier had released when he stepped backward. "Well, of course, I didn't think you had . . ."

Though he'd certainly hoped it.

Horife cleared his throat and continued, "In any case, Lady Tenoctris, I'm happy to welcome you to the Shrine of the Prophesying Sister. Ours is, I'm proud to say, the oldest continuously used religious structure in Carcosa."

He raised his right hand with the index finger extended. "Now, I know what you're thinking—that the Temple of the Lady of the Sunset is older, but in fact that temple has been rebuilt seven times since its original construction. The excavated portion of *our* shrine dates back to the predynastic settlement of the area. The—"

"Excuse me, Master Horife," said Tenoctris, politely but

firmly. "While this history would be interesting in its place, we came here hoping to enter the structure and examine it. Would that be possible?"

"It sure would," growled the officer of the guard, who'd been promoted from the ranks. He was a scarred veteran, bald when he took off his helmet. "And if you'd like Master Fuzzy here to stop chattering in your ear, you just say the word and you won't see him again. All right?"

"What?" said Horife angrily. Then he must have realized what the soldier meant—and that he *did* mean it. "Oh my goodness!"

"I'd like Master Horife to come with us quietly," Tenoctris said with her faint smile. "I'd like him to be able to answer any questions we have."

"I've got a question," said Cashel. He guessed he sounded like he was offering a fight; which maybe he was, if he'd heard what he thought he had. "You're a priest, right? And your shrine tells the future, that's what prophesy means, Sharina told me. So how did you write a book that says it's superstition?"

Horife blinked and turned to Tenoctris. "Pardon me, milady, but who is this person?"

"My companion, Cashel or-Kenset," Tenoctris said dryly. "I've never in our association found his judgments to be flawed. I'm sure that's more important to a scholar like you, Master Horife, than the fact he's Prince Garric's closest friend from childhood."

Horife gaped at Cashel, his eyes lingering longest on the thick, polished length of the quarterstaff. Cashel wasn't even angry. Horife was a puppy; he didn't know how to behave, but you don't kick puppies.

"Ah," said Horife. "Master Cashel, I assure you that no one could be more faithful in the preservation and restoration of this wonderful cultural icon than I am. I've spent years . . ."

His voice trailed off as he realized that he wasn't answering the question. Starting over, Horife said, "The basin in which Carcosa lies is an ancient volcanic crater, you see. Gas seeps through cracks in the rock and into the cave that was the original sanctum of the Sister. I, ah, describe this fully in my book. The gas induces, ah, dreams which, ah, *conventionally* religious people have believed were prophetic."

Horife cleared his throat. "Ah, in recent generations there haven't been gas flows of the strength of those in the past, but if you'd care to enter the sanctum I'd be delighted to show you the cracks?"

"Yes, we would," Tenoctris said. To the officer of the guard she added, "I don't believe that Master Horife will be a danger to us, sir, and space inside is obviously limited."

"You've got that right," the soldier said, probably referring to both Tenoctris's statements. "Siuvaz, you're the smallest. You go in with them and the rest of us'll stay out here. Just take your sword."

A soldier who wasn't any taller than Ilna handed his spear and shield to his fellows, then took off his helmet as well and drew his sword. Cashel didn't see much need for a guard, but there probably wasn't need either for his quarterstaff, which he was going to take anyway. "Go ahead," he said to Horife.

The priest led them into the pillared porch. He paused and gestured to the floor, a mosaic of simple white rosettes on a black background. "When I became director, that is *priest . . .* " Horife said, "of the shrine, I had the garish modern pavement taken up and restored the pattern that we found on the lowest level."

Tenoctris nodded and gestured him on. Horife bowed, then bowed again to Cashel when he recalled that Cashel was a person. He entered the square anteroom.

As Cashel followed Horife, he glanced at the black-and-white marble and wondered what the garish decorations had been. He liked pictures; they were the best part of living in cities, it seemed to him. Of course, to Cashel there weren't many other good parts about cities.

Horife pulled back the curtain of white linen, which separated the anteroom from the tunnel in the back. It'd started as a natural cave, but it'd been squared up and the walls polished a long time ago. Somebody'd even cut fluted half-columns to either side of the opening to look like pillars.

"The curtain was black when I was appointed," Horife said in a disgusted tone. "I'm sure it'd been black for generations, but that's quite wrong. Rank superstition!"

Tenoctris looked about her with a bright, quizzical expression. When wizards spoke their incantations, the spells gave off a kind of light that anybody could see; but Tenoctris was able to view the raw forces with which she and other wizards worked. It was like being able to see the wind, not just watching trees move. Judging from her smile, she wasn't finding anything that bothered her.

"Now here," said Horife, "is the sanctum and the incubation couch."

He drew in his lips at a thought, then added for Cashel's benefit, "That is, the couch where the petitioner sleeps in order to receive dreams from the goddess, according to tradition. In some periods the priest recounted his dream to the principal, but as far back as records go there are examples of the principal himself sleeping in the sanctum. Either practice is quite authentic."

"I'd like to go in, please," said Tenoctris. She started forward, but Cashel held her arm till gently the priest had hopped in ahead of them. Cashel followed him, letting the little soldier bring up the rear.

It wasn't likely anything was going to happen. But things did happen sometimes, to sheep and to people besides. Cashel liked to be in the way of trouble if there was going to be any.

When you got in a double pace, the cave swelled to the size of a peasant's hut or a bit more. The inner walls had decorative carving, but the workmen hadn't had to open them out the way they'd done the entrance. This was hard rock, not limestone that dripping water could eat away. Cashel wondered if a bubble had cooled in lava back when Carcosa had been a volcano.

Wax candles burned in wall sconces, lighting things better than Cashel would've guessed. The black rock shone like polished metal and reflected each flame into many.

Across the back wall was a couch carved into the rock. Cashel judged he could lie there without knocking his head, but Garric—who was a handsbreadth taller—would have to bend his knees to fit. Not that either of them was likely to try.

"Now," said Horife, kneeling beside the end of the couch raised for a headrest, "if you'll look here, milady—run your fingers across the stone here if you will, that'll show you better. And Master Cashel too, if you'd like."

Tenoctris obediently sat on the couch, then bent to touch the floor with her fingertips. Cashel could see that there were little cracks all across the bottom of the chamber, like the glazing on an old pot. Frowning, he ran his hand over the wall. So far as he could tell, that was solid. He didn't want to be in here if there was a cave-in. They were well up the hill, but there was still enough rock overhead to squash them flat if it landed on them.

The soldier, Siuvaz, was looking around the same as Cashel was; there was no way for an enemy to come at them except by the way they'd entered. Cashel tried to figure out the reliefs carved into the walls, but no matter how he held his head the glint of light on the glassy stone kept him from being sure what he was seeing. It wasn't anything ugly or sick, anyhow. Some of the things he'd seen since he started to travel made him wonder about people, Duzi knew they did!

Horife was talking to Tenoctris about gas entering the chamber through the cracks in the floor. Cashel didn't see what that had to do with having dreams, let alone seeing the future, but so long as Tenoctris was happy it didn't matter. There was a funny smell in the room with maybe a hint of sulphur, but nothing so bad it even made his nose wrinkle.

Tenoctris got up from the stone couch. Cashel offered her a hand to grip if she wanted, but she ignored it. Nobody likes to be treated like they're helpless, and Tenoctris was pretty spry except when she was completely exhausted.

"I think we've seen what we needed to, Master Horife," she said. "Your shrine has interesting resonances, but there's nothing here that need concern Garric."

Except how you're going to make it hold more than a double handful of people, even if you do it out front, Cashel thought, *just like Liane said.* But that was no concern of his.

An earthshock threw Horife off his feet; Tenoctris bounced back onto the couch. When Cashel instinctively braced his staff against the sidewall to stay upright, the iron buttcap sparkled with red wizardlight. Rock squealed like ice cracking under enormous weight.

Cashel lifted Tenoctris and cradled her in his left arm. She was moaning faintly. He hoped she hadn't been badly hurt, but you couldn't tell with old people.

The cracks in the stone floor had widened. Smoke poured out of them, but it wasn't just smoke: it glowed with the same unearthly color as the sparks Cashel's staff had struck from the wall.

Siuvaz stood groggily, rubbing his eyes with his left hand. He'd hit the wall hard and dropped his sword, which he didn't seem to have noticed yet.

The strands were merging into something with the head of an enormous snake. It was between Cashel and the only exit from the stone chamber.

Horife was on all fours, shaking his head to clear it. He looked up and saw the serpent of wizardlight, growing increasingly solid as the vapors from deep in the earth congealed into its body. Horife screamed and sprang like a sprinter toward the exit.

The creature of smoke struck, sinking its glowing fangs into the priest's torso. His arms and legs shot straight out. Cashel expected Horife to scream, but only a froth of spittle came out of his mouth.

Cashel tossed Tenoctris to the soldier. "Get her out!" he shouted, his voice echoing louder than the rumbling aftershocks.

Cashel didn't wonder whether the passage was blocked, whether Suivaz would obey, whether the half-stunned soldier would even be able to catch the wizard so casually thrown to him. He didn't wonder about anything, just *did* the only thing that might help—slamming his quarterstaff endwise into the serpent's flat head.

The staff's ferrule struck the glowing smoke. A roar of blue wizardlight flung Cashel into the wall behind him. He didn't notice hitting the rock, but both his hands tingled where they gripped the staff.

The serpent of smoke jerked upright, releasing its victim. Horife bounced off the ceiling and dropped to the floor. His limbs were still rigid and his face was turning black. The serpent didn't show any injury, but it'd felt the stroke; now it wove slowly side to side as it watched Cashel. Its head was as long as a horse's but wedge-shaped and much broader at the back.

"Ready!" Suivaz shouted, hunched over Tenoctris whom he held in both arms.

The iron buttcap Cashel struck the first time still glowed red hot from the impact. He rotated his staff a half-turn and shouted, "Go!" He struck again, his quarterstaff a battering ram crashing into the serpent's skull.

Azure thunder surrounded him. He didn't feel the staff strike, but the stone floor was no longer beneath his feet. He was falling and his lungs burned. He fell for a lifetime until—

A figure stepped through the fiery darkness to face him. A woman, Cashel thought, though it might have been a boy; she wore a shift of some shimmering material.

"Who are you?" he said. His throat felt like it'd been rasped.

"I'm Kotia," she said, her voice more clearly female than her form. "I've come to find a champion. Will you follow me and do my will?"

The serpent had disappeared. So had the cave and anything but the sparkling whirlwind encircling them. "I want to go back to my friends!" Cashel croaked.

Kotia shrugged. "You can come with me or you can stay and die," she said. "You can't go back. If you choose to stay, I'll find someone else. There are many souls in this place."

Her eyes narrowed as she examined Cashel again. With for the first time a touch of emotion she added, "Though you would be very suitable."

Cashel paused, his big hands squeezing hard on the quarterstaff. He didn't know what being Kotia's champion would mean; but he did know about death, at least from this side of existence, and the rest could wait at least a little longer.

"All right," he said. "I'll come with you."

Kotia reached out a hand. Cashel took it in one of his. Together they stepped through the wall of wizardlight.

Chapter Seven

Cashel stepped out of a cave in a hillside, coughing and wheezing. His eyes watered from the bitter smoke. He blinked and rubbed his eyes with the back of his left wrist. When he opened them again, he got his first look at an unfamiliar valley. The sides were steep, particularly the opposite wall. Everything had a jagged rawness, though the slopes were green with shrubs and spiky grasses.

Kotia lay crumpled at the entrance to the cave, in the middle of a many-sided figure. Words were written around the outside in the curvy letters of the Old Script. Cashel couldn't read them, but he'd helped Tenoctris often enough to be able to recognize the shapes.

So Kotia was a wizard. Well, it wasn't a surprise, given what she'd plucked him out of.

Thinking about that, Cashel looked back into the cave. The smoke was disappearing swiftly, vanishing like frost in the sunshine rather than drifting out in a haze that spread through the still air.

Cashel clenched and unclenched first his left hand, then his right, working out the numbness. His fingers tingled a little, but his grip was back to full strength. He checked the buttcaps of his quarterstaff. The iron of both showed a dull rainbow discoloration and was warm to the touch, but it hadn't been blasted away by the wizardry it'd channeled back in the shrine.

Cashel didn't know where he got the power that filled him when he faced wizards. He didn't think about it, didn't *want* to think about it.

But he was glad it was there. Especially when he stood between his friends and evil.

Kotia was beginning to stir. Cashel squatted close by but he didn't touch her. Wizardry was just as hard work as breaking rocks, and the incantation that'd brought the girl to Cashel's side must have wrung her out. She'd recover by herself; and anyway, there was nothing Cashel could do to help.

As he waited, he looked into the cave. He couldn't tell for sure because of the changes stonemasons had made on the shrine in Carcosa, but he'd be willing to bet that the original cave there was as like to this one as twin lambs.

The rock wasn't, though. This valley's walls were granite, not basalt like the ridge above Carcosa. Chunks of mica glittered coldly in the stone.

Though the sky was bright, the sun was about to dip below the sawtoothed crags across the valley. The night would be pretty cold, and the only shelter Cashel could see was the cave they'd just come out of. He figured he'd rather stay out here on the slope if that was the choice.

Kotia rolled over and raised herself on an elbow. She stared at Cashel with the expression of a drover buying mutton on the hoof.

"Mistress," he said simply, since she didn't seem ready to start a conversation.

"You really are a big one, aren't you?" Kotia said musingly. She twisted her legs under so that she was sitting upright, facing him. "I thought it was just the image your soul projected. You don't see real bodies in that realm, you know."

"I don't know anything about that, mistress," Cashel said. So long as he remained squatting, their heads were pretty much on a level. "Where am I, please?"

Kotia got up with a fluid motion that meant she'd recovered completely. She was young and seemed in good health, but Cashel suspected she was also a very powerful wizard. He rose also, holding his staff out crosswise in front of him to balance his weight.

"You're in my world, where I brought you," Kotia said. "My father cast my brother and me out of our manor. I intend to go to our neighbor, Lord Bossian, but there's a . . . a spirit hunting me. He's already killed my brother. I need you to protect me from the spirit."

Cashel frowned. "Spirit?" he said.

"All right, then, a demon!" Kotia said with a flash of

anger. "His name is Kakoral. But you're sworn to protect me. I warn you, your oath has power here!"

"I don't need threats to make me keep my word, mistress," Cashel said. "I just needed to know what I'd be dealing with."

He took the wad of raw wool out of his belt wallet and began rubbing his staff down with it. The hickory felt as smooth as glass to his familiar touch.

"If you help me . . ." Kotia said, sounding a little unsure of herself. Cashel had noticed lots of times it bothered people because he didn't get upset and carry on when they thought he should. "That is, Lord Bossian is a great wizard. He may very well be able to send you back to your own world. But you'll have to save me from Kakoral first."

"I've already said I'm going to help you, mistress," Cashel said quietly. He looked at the sky, indigo in the west and in the east a silky violet in which stars already glittered. "Is Lord Bossian's place close enough that we can get there before dark? Because we don't have much time if we're going to do that."

"No, no," said Kotia. "I'm too exhausted to travel farther anyway. We'll stay here for the night, then in the morning . . ."

She knelt beside the pack leaning against the rock at the cave mouth. It was a small thing, no bigger than the satchel in which Tenoctris carried the books and tools of her wizardry. Kotia took out a bundle no bigger than her clenched fist, then bit her lip and looked up at Cashel again.

"I'm sorry," she said. "My shelter is only big enough for me alone. Will you be all right . . . ?"

"I'll be all right," Cashel said. And he would. It was going to get nippy, of that be was sure, but at least he didn't have to contend with rain or sleet. "I probably wouldn't be sleeping anyway, seeing's as this Kakoral's hunting you."

"Oh, he won't attack tonight," Kotia said briskly. She'd undone her little bundle and was spreading it into a tube as long as she was. It was as fine as gossamer and of the same shimmering material as her shift. "He'll come in the light. My brother and I built a fire. When the flames burned a particular shade of red-orange, Kakoral appeared and . . . took my brother. While I ran."

"Oh," said Cashel. He gave his staff a practice spin. When he and the hickory reached the right rhythm, there was no finer feeling in the world. It was like the way sunlight sparkles on a waterfall, all shimmering beauty and *he* was a part of it . . . "Well, we don't have a fire, so we'll be all right."

"He *will* come," Kotia insisted angrily. "I went into the Place of Souls when I knew I couldn't reach Lord Bossian before morning, but I doubt you'll be able to really help. I was desperate, that's all!"

"Well, I'll do what I can," said Cashel.

He turned his back and walked a few steps away to where the slope wasn't so steep. He resumed whirling his staff, a full series of exercises this time: in front of him, then overhead and jumping to use the shaft's spinning weight to turn him so that he was suddenly gazing back into Kotia's furious eyes.

"Are you a wizard?" she demanded. "You had to be a wizard to have survived as long as you did in the Place of Souls!"

"I'm not a wizard, mistress," Cashel said, working the staff in a figure eight—back under one armpit, then up over the opposite shoulder, then reversing. "My friend who was with me's a wizard, but I think she got clear before—"

Before what?

"—before things happened."

"I don't . . ." Kotia said. She probably meant "I don't understand," but she didn't bother to finish when she heard what she was saying.

Cashel nodded approval. He'd long ago decided most people didn't listen to themselves or they couldn't possibly talk all the nonsense they did. Kotia had her ways, but she was better than that.

She cleared her throat. "You're sure you'll be all right, then?" she said.

"Yes, mistress," Cashel said. "Though if you had something to eat in your wallet, I wouldn't turn down a bite of it."

"No," said Kotia. "I'm sorry, there isn't . . . I didn't have much time to prepare, you see."

"Sure," said Cashel. "Good night, mistress."

It was solid dark by now. The moon wasn't up, if there even was a moon over this place. Cashel heard a rustle as Kotia got down into her cocoon.

The stars were diamond points in the clear sky. The constellations weren't the ones Cashel was familiar with, though one in the north was close enough to the Seven Plow-Oxen that he could imagine it was familiar if he squinted.

A horn called, then another one from a much greater distance. The sounds were silvery and seemed to echo for many miles.

For a time, Cashel squatted with his back to a rock, looking out in the darkness. Then he got up and resumed his slow pirouettes with the quarterstaff. The exercise kept him warm.

And for all he hadn't let himself react to Kotia's warning, he didn't in the least doubt that come morning he'd have more than just the empty air to swing the staff at.

The bay horse skidded on the cobblestones as Garric negotiated the final left-hand switchback below the shrine. It might've gone down in a clash of bones and equipment if King Carus's reflexes hadn't taken over at the critical moment. Garric leaned right, jerking the reins and the bay's head with him. It got its hooves under it again and hunched up the short remaining distance to the plaza.

On this stretch of roadway there wasn't room for two to ride abreast, so Lord Attaper, a noble from northern Ornifal and a horseman from early childhood, was following immediately behind. He grunted with approval at what he took for Garric's horsemanship.

In all truth Garric didn't like to ride, but it was faster than running a mile uphill in armor to the Shrine of the Prophesying Sister. If it'd been his decision alone he wouldn't have paused to put on his helmet and cuirass, but the Blood Eagles wouldn't have allowed their prince to get within bowshot of trouble without the armor.

The dozen bodyguards ahead of Garric were dismounting

in front of the shrine. He leaped from his saddle before the bay had drawn up. His boots skidded on the cobblestones but he kept his balance with the same borrowed skill that made him a rider.

"Your highness, the lady's safe but your friend Cashel has vanished!" said the officer standing with his sword drawn.

Tenoctris was all right; she sat cross-legged on the floor of the porch where she'd drawn a hexagram across the mosaic in vermilion. The officer of her escort had sent one of his men as a messenger back to his palace; the rest of the squad surrounded the wizard.

Tenoctris chanted an incantation while tapping the symbols with one of her disposable bamboo splinters. These Blood Eagles probably didn't like to be around wizardry any more than most other non-wizards did. They stood with Tenoctris because it was their duty to stand; and they would stand until they died or were relieved.

"Vanished where?" Garric snarled, drawing his long sword. He didn't bother Tenoctris—what she was doing was probably more important than anything she had to tell him—but instead headed toward the carved entrance to the sanctum. He could see a body sprawled on the floor inside.

"Your highness!" said Attaper, but he followed rather than trying to get in the way. In Garric's present mood, that was a good thing. Cashel had been here because Garric sent him on a mission which both Liane and Sharina had warned was a bad idea.

"Siuvaz, go with them!" ordered the commander of Tenoctris's escort. A short soldier, bareheaded and without his spear or shield, trailed Attaper into the sanctum.

The air inside had a vaguely sulphurous taste, enough to make Garric blink but not a problem for breathing. Attaper rolled the corpse faceup with his boot. The man was nobody Garric remembered seeing before, though his features were so black and swollen that he couldn't be sure.

The candles had burned almost to their sconces. There was nothing else in the chamber except a Blood Eagle helmet.

Siuvaz snatched up the helmet. In a clear, carrying voice, he said, "I was here with the lady, the priest, and Lord Cashel. There was an earthquake and I hit my head. A giant snake came up from the floor and bit the priest. Lord Cashel told me to get the lady out. I took her out while he fought the snake. When we came back, Lord Cashel was gone. Your highness."

Though the soldier seemed to speak normally, his gaze was directed somewhere past Garric's right shoulder and his eyes weren't focused. He was terrified . . . and not, Garric suspected, because of what had happened in this chamber previously. His concern was that he'd abandoned Prince Garric's friend.

The officer of the escort had come in behind Siuvaz. To Attaper he said, "Sir, we were outside and nobody felt an earthquake. But I trust Siuvaz, sir. I wouldn't have sent him in if I didn't. And he was right to get Lady Tenoctris clear."

The officer was sweating also. Both men were frightened because they'd done exactly what they were supposed to do in a crisis . . .

Garric said, "Good work, Siuvaz. The kingdom's lucky to have men who'll do their duty. Captain—"

"Sub-Captain Orduc, sir," murmured Attaper.

"I assume you entered this chamber immediately after Siuvaz gave the alarm. Did you see any sign of Cashel or the snake?"

"Nothing, your highness," said Orduc, shaking his head. "The lady was bruised and somebody'd rung Siuvaz's bell good—you can see the dent in his helmet."

"From the wall," the soldier said in embarrassment, fingering the blackened bronze. "The earthquake bounced me into it hard."

Garric squatted and ran the fingertips of his left hand over the floor. There were cracks in the stone but nothing that would've let an earthworm slip through, let alone a man-eating snake.

He rose. "All right," he said. "Knowing Cashel, I'd guess he was in a better place than the serpent is now."

He strode out of the chamber ahead of the others. Tenoctris had finished her incantation. She gave Garric a wan smile as she tried to get up. He lifted her, marveling again at how little she weighed.

"I'm sorry, Garric," she said. "All I can tell you now is that the person behind the attack also directed the whale that we met outside the harbor. Perhaps I can learn more from books I have back at the palace."

"Yes," said Garric. "We're going back there now."

He frowned and added, "Tenoctris? Who was the target of the attack? It couldn't have been me, could it?"

"I *think* . . . " Tenoctris said, emphasizing the doubt because she never stated a certainty that was merely a probability. "I think that Cashel himself was meant to be the victim. Because he'd protected you against the earlier attack, you see."

"Yes," said Garric. "I do indeed see."

As he handed Tenoctris into her sedan chair, he viewed the world through a red haze. Through his mind echoed the words, *"He was there because I sent him."*

And he was going to have to tell Sharina that.

"Why didn't I go?" said Sharina. Her eyes were filling with tears. She could no more stop crying than she could stop her heart beating, and it made her furious. "I could've gone with him, and instead I let him go alone. I knew there was something wrong!"

"Yes, you did," said Garric. His face was like stone. "So did Liane, and I was a pigheaded fool who wouldn't listen to either one of you. Cashel's gone because I sent him into a dangerous place."

Sharina was glad he didn't say, "You couldn't have done anything." That was probably true, but it wasn't the point. She hadn't been *with* Cashel when he went into danger.

A cageful of birds twittered on the marble-topped serving table beside the door. Sharina didn't remember them from the previous time she'd been here in her brother's reception room. When her eyes cleared momentarily, she realized that they were mechanical, not real as she'd thought previously. Awareness of her mistake made her sob. She turned away, biting her wrist to stifle what would otherwise have been a scream of frustration at her own weakness.

"There was nothing wrong with the shrine, Garric," Tenoctris said. "Our enemy had laid a trap there, but it wasn't because the site was dedicated to the Sister."

"It doesn't matter why I was wrong!" Garric shouted. "I was wrong, and Cashel's paid for my mistake!"

Ilna put her hand on Sharina's and turned her slightly so that she was facing what at first was a pale blur. Her vision cleared again: she was staring into the side of a tall urn made of gray-white stone. The instant Sharina saw it, her stomach settled. She touched the stone with her fingertips. It was smooth and soothing, like a bath in warm oil.

Chalcus stood with his back to the hallway door, his eyes pointedly focused on the windows looking onto one of the palace's many small internal gardens. He, Ilna, and Sharina had returned from Master Sidras in a cheerful mood. Chalcus was drawing fantasy pictures of the wonderful sights they'd see on their voyage; Ilna brought up practical considerations—clothing, the house they were staying in, arrangements for her ward, Lady Merota; and Sharina herself was feeling foolish and contrite for the scene she'd made the evening before.

But she hadn't been foolish. Hadn't been wrong about the Shrine of the Prophesying Sister, at any rate.

"Tenoctris, what should we do next?" Garric said. "In your opinion?"

A year before, when Garric was a boy in Barca's Hamlet, he wouldn't have bothered to add, "In your opinion?" to make it clear that he'd make the decision no matter what anybody else thought. As prince he'd had to learn that, and the kingdom was fortunate that he *had* learned; but when Sharina thought of the responsibility that came with the words, her heart went out to her brother.

And here I'm crying because Cashel's gone but not necessarily in trouble. The priest was dead in the shrine, but Cashel had been fine the last time anybody saw him.

Sharina stroked the urn with her palm. She was feeling more like herself again. There'd been so many changes, so many things that she'd taken for granted had been snatched away . . .

"I'll go through the library I've gathered since I came to

this age," Tenoctris said. She smiled faintly. "It's far more extensive than anything I had in my own time. I couldn't afford . . . well, much of anything."

"Yes," said Garric grimly. He was being polite, but he was obviously impatient. Liane moved a little closer to his side, but she didn't touch his hand as she'd started to do. "And then what?"

"I'll use my art to search for references that have bearing," Tenoctris continued. "I'll tell you whatever I find. If that doesn't help, I'll seek information by other means; but until I know more, I can't suggest a course of action."

"What help can we offer?" Garric said. "What help could *anyone* offer?"

Only the six of them were in the room: the six who'd discussed plans at dinner the night before. The six of them, and last night Cashel . . .

Sharina felt a rush of nausea and rested her forehead against the urn. She felt her fears soften, remembering many times Cashel had faced danger and returned to her side.

"At the moment, nothing," Tenoctris said crisply. "There may be volumes elsewhere in the city that I find I want to look at. If so, then the help of Prince Garric might be useful in getting to see then."

"Yes," said Garric, grinning. "And the help of the whole royal army including battering rams, if *they* would be useful."

Despite the words, his tone was boyishly cheerful again. Tenoctris had offered him something to do instead of waiting for the next threat, the next disaster.

That decided Sharina. She faced her friends and said, "All right, what can I do? Because I don't want to do nothing while Cashel's in danger."

"Perhaps you can help me," Tenoctris said. "Handing me books, finding things that I've dropped or misplaced. As Cashel would, but—"

She smiled softly.

"—while I don't expect any heavy lifting, it might be useful having someone with me today who can read."

Sharina hugged the old wizard and said, "That's perfect. Shall we get started at once?"

It struck Sharina that Tenoctris must've been lonely most

of her life. Normal people don't like being around wizardry, and wizards didn't seem to socialize with one another any more than hawks did.

"Garric?" said Ilna. Eyes turned to her. She'd remained at Sharina's side, unobtrusively supportive much the way Cashel would have been if he were here.

"Yes?" Garric said, still smiling.

"This urn," Ilna said, running her finger along its curved neck while looking at Garric, "was made by someone very skilled."

Her lips twitched in distaste, even though she hadn't added the words, "As good as I am." Ilna didn't like to boast; nor did she have to, among friends who knew her abilities.

"I suggest that you loan it to Sharina for a few days," Ilna continued, pointedly not letting her eyes meet Sharina's. "I don't care for stone, but the pattern that light gives *this* stone is something that I'll try to duplicate. Now that I've seen someone else do it."

"Done!" said Garric cheerfully. "I'd thought nothing good would come out of the priesthoods here in Carcosa, and I'm glad to have been wrong."

To Sharina he added, "Shall I have servants take it with you now? Duzi, I'll carry it myself! It's not that heavy!"

Liane looked concerned. Sharina laughed and said, "In this warren of steps and corridors, it's heavier than any one man should be carrying. Even you or Cashel. But thank you and . . ."

She paused, thinking. "Could you have it taken to my suite, Garric?" she said. "While I'm helping Tenoctris, I won't . . . I mean, I'll be fine. But sometimes when I wake up before dawn, I could use . . ."

Sharina didn't know how to finish the sentence, but she didn't have to. Not for her friends. Perhaps everyone wakes sometimes with the thoughts and the despair that come before dawn.

"Done!" Garric repeated. Sharina turned to go out of the room; but before she did, she stopped and hugged Ilna, the friend she was sure knew better than most about the hours before dawn.

Chalcus closed the door behind Sharina and Tenoctris, then grinned as he met Ilna's eyes. He stood with one foot lifted back against the wall and his arms folded across his chest, well able to convince most people that he was cheerful and relaxed.

Cheerful the sailor might be; he usually was, in Ilna's experience—even in circumstances that would leave those same "most people" screaming in terror or vomiting in disgust. He was *not* relaxed.

Ilna turned to Garric and Liane, who waited as Chalcus did for what Ilna had hung behind to say. Light flooding through the windows behind them shadowed their expressions.

"Master Chalcus and I will be leaving shortly to deal with the Rua in the north," Ilna said. She spoke without the time-wasting pleasantries that others might have used to cloak the thought. It was hard enough to get out the words she had to use, so she didn't intend to add more. "There are a number of matters to be tidied up before I go."

"You don't have to leave now, Ilna," Garric said, crossing his hands before him. He looked awkward and uncomfortable, as though he'd rather face a delegation of hostile nobles or a ravening seawolf.

"I never had to leave," Ilna said, feeling equally uncomfortable but determined that it wouldn't show in her cold expression. "But I don't have any better reason to be in Carcosa now than I did before this happened to my brother. Or Chalcus either."

She shrugged and made a sour face, wishing that she had more talent with words so that she wouldn't confuse people so often when she tried to explain her thinking. Of course, the problem might not have been in the words at all.

"What I mean is . . ." Ilna continued. "Both of us would do anything we could to help Cashel, but I think we have as good a chance of doing that in the Strait as we do here."

"You think they're connected, the Rua and the attacks here in Carcosa?" Liane said, her tone curt and sexless. She was Garric's spy chief, though that wasn't how Ilna usually thought of her. The kingdom's eyes, and very keen ones from what Ilna had witnessed without looking for the evidences.

"Liane, everything's connected," Ilna said, gentle because the reality of the thought was beyond even Ilna's full grasp. To most people, even smart, educated people like Liane bos-Benliman, that truth meant no more than the word *red* did to a blind man. "If I could pull one thread long enough, I'd unravel the whole cosmos."

And on a bad day, I wish I could . . . But recently the days are rarely that bad.

"More direct than that, I don't know," Ilna continued. "But there's something I can do in the north and nothing that we know of here. That's a reason to go."

"Yes," said Garric, "it is."

He cleared his throat. "What do you want from me?"

"Lady Liane," Ilna said, passing over Garric's question. "As you know I've become the guardian of an orphan, Lady Merota bos-Roriman. The journey isn't one I'm willing to subject the child to."

Ilna let the humor of a thought reach her lips in a smile. She went on, "Merota has seen worse, and sometimes through my mistakes, but I'm not happy about it."

She cleared her throat. The other three in the room were as still as statues, their expressions carefully blank.

"Merota has servants and a tutor, of course," Ilna said. "But I would be in your debt, Lady Liane, if you would act as family to the child while Chalcus and I are away. My own life would have been very difficult without my brother's presence, and—"

"I'm honored," said Liane. "I'm honored beyond words. I can't be you, Ilna—"

"I dare say you'll be better," Ilna snapped, waspish despite herself. "For her, probably for anybody. Merota's a lady, after all, and what can I teach her about that?"

"I can't be you," Liane repeated softly. "But I hope I can show Merota as much strength and character as anyone *but* you could, Ilna."

"Thank you," Ilna said. "I'm in your debt."

She turned, and from behind her Liane said, "Which

means you would do anything you could to help me, Ilna, just as you would have done no matter what I'd said a moment ago. As I have never doubted."

Ilna looked back to Liane and Garric. The humor struck her and she laughed—as many times before—because laughing was the choice she found acceptable.

"I'm not good at a lot of things," Ilna said. "I probably haven't told the two of you how lucky you are to have one another, and how lucky Chalcus and I are to know you both. You and Tenoctris will do what can be done for my brother, and Chalcus and I will see to things in the north."

"Yes," said Garric, "I'm quite sure that you will."

And before Ilna was quite sure how to react, Liane stepped forward and embraced her. She wasn't any taller or bigger boned than Ilna herself, and the muscles under her silk garments were just as firm.

Whatever happened with Cashel or the Rua, Ilna was sure of one thing: Liane would look after Merota as well as anyone alive could do.

Chapter Eight

Across the valley dawn had begun to touch the peaks, but the hillside above Cashel was still in darkness. A breeze rustled the leaves of the stunted birches, sounding like distant water.

"Mistress," Cashel said. "It's going to be light enough to see our footing soon, and I think we ought to be on our way."

He'd gone hungry for longer than this, but an empty stomach isn't a good companion on a cold night. He thought of asking how far was it to Lord Bossian, but he didn't suppose it mattered; they'd get there when they got there. . . .

The shimmering cocoon twitched, then split open as Kotia sat up with a worried look on her face. "How late is it?" she demanded, then stared up at the sky. "Oh, Demons of

Hell! I never thought I'd sleep so long! He'll be on us soon, I'm sure of it!"

Kotia hopped out of her shelter and gathered it into a bundle with a few quick movements. She popped the tiny bundle into her satchel again.

Cashel wished Ilna could see the fabric; she'd be fascinated, he knew. That was the worst thing about travel. Cashel was seeing wonderful things, but his friends weren't around to tell about them.

"I can take that," Cashel said, reaching for the satchel. It didn't look heavy, but he was so used to carrying Tenoctris's paraphernalia that the words were a reflex when he was around a female wizard.

"No, you fool!" Kotia said. "Didn't you hear what I said? He'll be on us in a moment! You'll have to fight!"

"Well," said Cashel as he surveyed the landscape, "we may as well start walking until he comes. Which direction is Lord Bossian, mistress?"

He didn't see any sign of a trail. The forest of birch and larch—whose needles were beginning to turn bright yellow—was sparse enough that it wouldn't be an obstacle, but the slopes were steep and there was a lot of loose rock. The girl might dance over it with no problem, but Cashel knew that unless he was careful his weight would start a landslide that could take him with it. Maybe the other side of the valley . . .

He looked to the west, and as he did so there was a glint of vivid red light from the peak opposite. *The sun reflecting from mica in the granite,* Cashel thought.

The glare lit the whole opposite slope, then shrank again to a vivid dazzle. It capered on the peak for a moment, then flashed like lightning to an outcrop halfway to the valley floor. A clump of waist-high larches, stunted by the poor soil, exploded into flame.

"He's coming," Kotia said. Her voice had lost its edge of anger. "Now he'll kill me."

"Get into the cave," Cashel said, starting his quarterstaff into a slow spin in front of him. The broad ledge in front of the cave was the closest thing to flat ground anywhere in sight. "I won't be able to look out for you when things get moving."

Kotia said something, protested probably, but Cashel wasn't listening anymore. He didn't want to clip her with a backswing of the staff, but there wasn't time to argue.

Kakoral flashed to the base of the valley, momentarily out of Cashel's sight among the slender willows. Steam gushed with a sound like rocks cracking.

Cashel placed hand over hand, spinning the staff gradually faster. The ferrules began to blur. He wondered if the demon would leap over him to the slope above and attack from behind. If the fool girl hadn't gotten into the cave, she'd be in serious danger. . . .

The demon flared into view on the slope just below Cashel. He didn't move. There was nothing and then he was there, hunching forward, red and orange like light glinting from jewels, not the warmer color of fire. He stood in a tangle of wild roses; they shriveled away from his clawed feet.

"I am Kakoral!" he said. "I've come for my daughter!"

"If you mean the girl Kotia," Cashel said, speaking in the rhythm of his spinning quarterstaff, "then she's with me now."

The demon was the size of a man when he first appeared—rangy, tall despite his stoop, and with arms so long that his knuckles struck sparks from the ground. His form was of light, not flesh. In the blazing shimmer as Kakoral moved, Cashel glimpsed buildings and forests and spider-limbed monsters.

"With you?" Kakoral thundered. "Did my daughter tell you what she has done?"

"I don't care what she's done," said Cashel. He wasn't shouting, but his voice came out as a husky growl. "Go away and we won't trouble you!"

Without moving, Kakoral was suddenly the height of the peaks that hedged about the valley. His legs were the trunks of great trees, and his clawed fingers reached down from the heavens to pluck Cashel out of the way.

Cashel brought the staff up and around, still spinning. A buttcap smashed into the demon's index finger with a blast of azure wizardlight. To Cashel the shock was like hitting the side of a cliff, but he was used to that. He let the impact reverse his sweep from sunwise to widdershins, punching the other end of the staff into Kakoral's thumb.

The demon gave a great crackling roar. He was man-sized again, glaring at Cashel with a face like a burning skull. Diamonds of blue wizardlight dripped from the ferrules of the spinning quarterstaff and bounced across the landscape before slowly dissipating.

"She is mine," Kakoral said. "She ate the flesh of her mother, and for that I will have her!"

"Go away!" Cashel snarled. He was panting, but he could keep this up for a while longer. Maybe long enough; he'd know when it was over. "She's with—"

Kakoral leaped for Cashel's face and met a ferrule in blue fire and a thunderclap. The demon zigzagged downslope: a flash that disintegrated the trunk of a larch; a flash that cracked a boulder, leaving half standing and the rest a slump of jagged pebbles; a flash that split willows leaning over the streambank, their bark sloughing and the slender whips of their branches drawn up in coils like singed hair.

Kakoral screamed like trees breaking under the weight of winter ice. He flashed toward Cashel and the quarterstaff met him again. The blast shook loose rock from the slope for as far as a good archer could shoot an arrow.

Cashel stood unmoved, rotating the staff before him, sure of himself and now sure of his opponent. The demon caromed downhill again, then in an eyeblink stood where first he'd spoken. Dew wrung from the night air sizzled beneath his feet.

"Tell me your name, champion," Kakoral said, "and I'll give you a gift. Tell me your name, unless you're afraid to."

"I'm not afraid," Cashel growled. He could barely understand his own words; his voice rasped like the sound of nothing living. "I'm Cashel or-Kenset, and I don't want anything of you but your absence!"

The demon laughed like flames chuckling beneath a cauldron. "Perhaps not, Cashel or-Kenset," he said, "but I offer my gift anyway."

He reached into his pulsing chest and came out with what looked like a handful of fire. Cashel braced himself to dodge or bat away the missile, but instead the demon laughed again and opened his hand to let rubies spill onto the ground at Cashel's feet.

"My gift, champion," Kakoral said. "When you're in doubt about your course, break one and let it guide you. They will do no harm to you or my daughter, unless you're afraid of the truth."

"I'm not afraid of you, and I don't need you for a guide," Cashel said. He shuffled a step toward the demon, spinning the quarterstaff faster. "Go now, or I'll speed your way!"

Kakoral laughed; and, laughing, vanished as if he never was. Where moments before the demon had stood hunching, dust motes spun in the first rays of the sun slanting down from the peaks behind.

Cashel let the quarterstaff slow to a halt, then butted it firmly on the ground and leaned onto it. He was shivering so badly that for a moment he was afraid that the staff wouldn't be enough support. Well, he'd sit if he had to.

Kotia walked in front of Cashel and faced him. "I chose well," she said. Her face was set, but a vein in her throat throbbed and her nostrils were flared. "At least if it was me who chose you, I chose well."

"I didn't have anything to do with it," Cashel said. His voice was coming back, but his throat was as dry as flaked granite. "I was fighting a snake and then I was here."

Kotia bent and began picking up the rubies, dropping each into the palm of her left hand. Cashel frowned, then said in more of a snarl than he'd intended, "Leave them! We don't need anything that comes from him."

The girl stood, facing him again with the same still expression. "Are you afraid of the truth?" she said, once again the imperious wizard who had dragged Cashel from the cave of choking fire.

"No!" he said. "Of course not!"

"Neither am I," said Kotia. She eyed an outcrop to the right of where she stood.

"Direct us to Lord Bossian's manor!" she cried, and hurled one of the rubies into the rock.

The jewel shattered in a sizzle of light. Cashel instinctively brought his staff across his body and stepped between Kotia and the flare of red. A tiny simulacrum of Kakoral capered on the outcrop, then spread its arms as though holding up something far bigger than its body. In the air, but as real as the rock and trees and sunlight, appeared a woman and the demon Kakoral. They stood in a workroom lit only by the coals of a great hearth.

"My mother Laterna," Kotia whispered, gripping Cashel's forearm. "That was her laboratory beneath our manor. She was a wizard."

The demon stood arms akimbo, his shimmering form brighter than the coals behind him. He lifted his head back in laughter that Cashel's memory supplied to the silent image. Laterna touched the broach on her left shoulder; a shimmering shift like Kotia's slipped from her body. She stepped toward the demon. He remained motionless except for the way his throat worked as he laughed.

Gripping Kakoral's shoulders with her hands, Laterna lifted herself onto him, then lowered her sex onto his. The demon's fiery arms encircled her while he continued to laugh.

The image faded slowly. The simulacrum on the rock grinned and pointed with one arm. A line of rosy wizardlight streamed along the slope to the north, then vanished behind the high ground.

Kotia stepped a pace back and met Cashel's eyes. "Here," she said, holding out the remainder of the jewels. "Put them in your wallet. We may want them again."

"Right," said Cashel. His skin pickled with the desire to say something to the girl, but he wasn't sure what the words should be. Instead he said, "We'd best be going, then."

The track of wizardlight remained though the imp had disappeared. They started to follow it. Neither of them spoke.

"You've missed the meeting with Vicar Uzinga that was scheduled for the fourth hour," Liane said, holding the four-leafed wax tablet on which she kept Garric's appointments. "And the meeting following it with Lord Waldron about integrating the Count's Household Troops into the Royal Army. We can take the vicar in place of dinner, but I suggest you tell Waldron to consider his recommendations to have been approved. He'll be more flattered by the tacit approval than offended that you've canceled a meeting with him."

Garric frowned. "Frankly, I'd rather see Waldron than the vicar," he said. "I don't have anything to tell Uzinga except to take Reise's advice on every matter where Reise makes a recommendation—and that if he doesn't, he'll be lucky if he *only* loses his office as vicar."

The doors of the reception room were open, waiting for the start of Prince Garric's afternoon levee. The presence of the usher standing in the doorway might not have been enough to keep back the would-be petitioners who packed the hall beyond, but those waiting knew that the detachment of Blood Eagles on guard would take up where the usher's authority left off—with naked swords if necessary.

"I think it's necessary that you—that Prince Garric—say just that to Vicar Uzinga," Liane said. She grinned. "Well, with a little more tact, perhaps."

She sobered and continued, "Remember that Lord Uzinga is a noble. No matter what other people have told him, he won't in his heart believe he's supposed to do what a commoner like Reise suggests. If you tell him that he's to obey your *father* Reise, then there's a much better chance that you *won't* have to remove him from office."

Garric grimaced. "Right, Vicar Uzinga during dinner," he said.

With a sudden smile he added, "Liane, I've suddenly realized something. In any kind of governmental business, the correct choice is always to do the thing you least want to do. Now that I've found the formula, perhaps I can hand my duties over to somebody else and do something I'd like to do instead?"

The crowd in the hallway was noisy. Individually the petitioners spoke in hushed voices, each to his neighbor and supporters. In sum, the noise was like that of gannet rookeries on the spikes of rock off the east coast of Haft. Garric looked at the first hopeful faces in the open doors, sighed, and said, "I suppose we'd better start running them through. The sooner we start, the sooner we'll finish."

Though in his heart he knew he'd never finish, that even

if he listened to complaints, prayers, and suggestions till midnight, there'd still be people waiting with more of the same. But he was more afraid of being cut off from the reality of ordinary citizens' lives the way King Valence had been than he was of being ground down by the minutiae of government.

"I miss you being able to read Celondre to me in the evenings," Liane said with a soft smile.

"I miss being able to get a good night's sleep," Garric muttered, rubbing his temples. He'd said what he meant without thinking, and he cringed even as he heard his response to his lover's gentle romance.

Acting quickly, he turned to Liane and took her small, shapely hands in his. "Liane," he said, ignoring the guards and petitioners and officials and *everybody* else watching. "Tonight I'll read you Celondre. Maybe getting back into old habits will help me sleep without dreams that tell me to make a fool of myself, besides."

Liane looked at him with a shocked expression. *What did I say now?* Garric thought, frustrated and a little angry that he didn't seem to be able to do the right thing even when he tried his hardest.

"Garric?" she said. "You mentioned your dreams. Did you suggest using the Shrine of the Prophesying Sister because of a dream?"

"Well, not that shrine, I didn't even know about it," Garric said, trying to call back the memories. "But yeah, it was a dream that made me think of the Sister at all!"

He could see where Liane was going—where she'd gotten ahead of him—and excitement had washed away his depressed lethargy of moments before. This was progress, this was a way forward that might lead past the wall between Cashel and his friends!

Garric stood. The usher at the door watched eagerly, ready to let through the first of the petitioners.

"Citizens of the Isles!" Garric said in the voice King Carus would have used to bellow orders through the clamor of the battlefield. "I've been called away by a sudden opportunity—"

He'd started to say *emergency* but he'd changed the word

as it started to roll off his tongue. A prince can start a panic by an unfortunate choice of phrase.

"—greatly to the benefit of the kingdom! This audience is canceled!"

"Close the doors!" Liane called to the guards. They probably couldn't hear her over the sudden uproar in the hall, but they got the idea. The usher squeaked, pressed between the door and the petitioners, but the soldiers put their backs into it. They slammed the valves closed, then slid the bronze bar through the staples to make sure they stayed closed.

Liane had already snapped shut the travel desk in which she carried important papers. She was at Garric's side as they turned to the door at the back that opened onto the courtyard. "To Tenoctris?" she said, less a question than an affirmation.

"Right," said Garric, stepping through the door that one of the guards on the portico had already thrown open. He took the desk out of Liane's hand into his own, his left. She could carry it, but they were moving fast and to him it weighed almost nothing.

Keeping his right hand free for his sword was a reflex from King Carus. It came to the surface when Garric was excited, even at times—like this one—when it wasn't necessary.

Though you never knew for sure when it would be necessary.

All the suites around this small garden were held by Garric and his immediate entourage—his friends, not members of the staff. The guards looked surprised but properly held their posts while Garric and Liane ran up the stairs that led to Tenoctris's suite on the second floor. The six guards from the reception room followed, their equipment belts and studded leather aprons clattering.

The noise—meant to frighten enemies when the royal army charged—brought Sharina out onto the landing with the Pewle knife in her hand. She and Garric both had learned hard lessons since they left Barca's Hamlet.

Garric thought of Ilna and Cashel. They'd changed as well, perhaps even more.

"It's all right," he said, stepping into the study as his sister hopped back from the doorway when she saw who was coming. "Liane had an idea and we need to tell Tenoctris."

"Yes?" said the wizard, looking up from the tile floor. She sat on a cushion, probably Sharina's idea because Garric had never seen Tenoctris pay attention to comfort when she had work to do. She'd drawn a large six-pointed star in cinnabar, then written words of power around its margin. On the floor inside the figure were codices, scrolls, and a few loose manuscripts.

"Tenoctris," said Liane, closing the door in the face of the guards following, "it was a dream that led Garric to suggest going to the Shrine of the Sister. I think it was a sending."

"I thought it was just . . ." Garric said. He was embarrassed because the idea hadn't occurred to him immediately. "I'd been worried about the two priesthoods and looking like I was taking sides. And I had a dream of the past, a fantasy I know—the sort of Golden Age that Celondre or Rigal would describe, a sunny day and happy peasants worshipping the Great Gods. But the priest of the Sister was there too, and I thought . . ."

"There's only one active temple to the Sister in Carcosa," Liane said, taking out a notebook that she didn't need. "Someone who wanted Garric—or Garric's friends—to enter a temple of the Sister wouldn't have to specify any particular temple."

"Wonderful!" said Tenoctris. She started to get up, then changed her mind and sank onto the cushion again. Leaning forward she started to shift the books out of the hexagram but paused again.

"I think it would be better for me to do the directional spell from where you were when you had the dream, Garric," she said. "Could we—"

"Yes," said Garric, hoping he didn't sound curt. "What do you need with you?"

"Well, my satchel," Tenoctris said, "and—"

Garric snatched up the satchel and the pot of cinnabar sitting open beside it.

"—perhaps Cantorf's *Dream of Scio,* which should be—"

"I have it," said Sharina, reaching under an open scroll and coming up with the small codex that had been completely hidden beneath it.

"Then let's go," Tenoctris said, rising with Liane's help.

"I wasn't able to trace the attack, but a wizard of my limited powers should be able to determine the source of the dream."

"Power's the easy part of any job," said King Carus, watching as Garric jerked open the door to the inner hallway and his own suite beyond. *"Directing it to the right point is what wins battles—and saves kingdoms, if our luck's in!"*

"The Bird of the Tide," said Chalcus, beaming at the ship lashed to the quay on which he stood with Ilna and Merota. "She's old, I grant you, but still tight as you please. In her day they built with pegs and tenons instead of just trenails holding the strakes to the frames. I'd trust the *Bird* in storms that'd swamp any of the light-built coasters being tacked together on this coast in the past thirty years!"

Six solid-looking men stood together in the stern. They'd stopped murmuring among themselves when Chalcus and the three females appeared, but none of them had spoken to the visitors. Mistress Kaline stood two paces back in prim disapproval.

"She looks trim," said Ilna, which was closer to a lie than she liked to hear come from her mouth. "And of course I trust your judgment on ships as far as I do mine about fabrics, Master Chalcus."

That last was the simple truth, and why Chalcus made her say something as obvious as sunrise was beyond her. "Men!" she was tempted to say; but it wasn't men, she'd heard women as often being fools in the same way.

As for the ship—*The Bird of the Tide* had a deck, which was something, and a single short mast in the middle of it holding a yard that was longer than the vessel itself. At sea the yard would be raised at a slant to spread the triangular sail to the wind. There was a tiny cabin in the stern, enough to hold a tile hearth but no shelter for the crew. In bad weather Ilna supposed they'd all need to be on deck anyway, doing things with sail and ropes and anchors.

The *Bird* was indeed old, so old that the grain of the deck stood out in ridges above the softer, paler sapwood. Four oak planks ran the length of the vessel's sides, sticking out from the pine hull. They were there to rub against stone docks, as they were doing now. They'd been patched at several places with fresh timbers, but the patches were themselves badly worn by now.

And the ship stank. *The Bird of the Tide* had carried generations of men and cargo. They'd left residues, which had decayed into her timbers and still remained as faint, foul ghosts. But Ilna didn't have a delicate sense of smell—few peasants do, not with firewood too dear to waste heating bathwater four months of the year—and this stench, though unfamiliar, wasn't a matter of concern.

"Oh, Ilna," Merota said. She was clinging to Ilna's hand like a child much younger than she was. "I do wish I could come with you. Really, I wouldn't get in the way."

"Ah, child," said Chalcus, stroking the girl's hair gently with a hand whose calluses were like sharkskin. "When Mistress Ilna and I finish our business in the Strait, I'll sail you clear around Haft in this fine vessel as a treat. But for now, it's us alone and you with our friend Liane till we return."

"I just wish . . . " Merota said sadly, but she wasn't arguing. The child had a right to wish for things, but she was already enough of a lady that she didn't whine and embarrass herself trying to change Ilna's mind.

Ilna rarely argued. If the decision was hers to make, she made it; and if not, she accepted the choice someone else made—or fate made, often enough.

"Come aboard and I'll introduce you to the crew, milady," Chalcus said. Now at low tide the deck was more than Ilna's height below the level of the quay, but instead of going down the ladder Chalcus hopped aboard.

He turned and raised his hands. Before Ilna could protest, Merota gave a squeal of delight and leaped into Chalcus's arms.

Frowning as much at what she was doing as what Merota had done, Ilna pinched the sides of her tunic at mid-thigh and jumped lightly to the deck. She told herself she was proving to the crew that she wasn't a lady whom they had to coddle, but a part of her mind was afraid she was showing off. Nobody else would think less of her if she *did* show off, of course, but she wasn't somebody who needed other people to censure her.

"Mistress Ilna," Chalcus said, "let me introduce the crew to you. Our bosun's Hutena, he was a file commander in the Third Regiment until today."

Hutena bowed. He was short and stocky, nearly bald though probably only in his mid-thirties. His limbs were so hairy that the dragon winding up his right arm from wrist to shoulder seemed to be crawling through thickets.

"Nabarbi, Tellura, and Kulit," Chalcus continued. "They're cousins, Blaise fishermen originally but for this past year they've been deck crew on the trireme *Staff of the Shepherd*."

The cousins bowed. They were tall men whose weather-beaten complexions had originally been pale. Kulit wore a fluffy blond moustache; the others were clean shaven.

"And maybe you remember Shausga and Ninon from the *Flying Fish?*" Chalcus said. Ilna did remember them, their faces anyway, from the voyage north on the patrol vessel. Ninon had been the lead oarsman, she was pretty sure.

"Boys," Chalcus said to the crew, "all the cargo's aboard, so we'll be sailing before dawn with the tide. Up to three of you at a time can go ashore if you need to wrap up your affairs—"

"We don't," said Hutena. "We can sail now if you need us to."

Chalcus nodded approvingly. "I shouldn't wonder if a time came on this voyage when we did need to get under way in a fingersnap," he said, "but not tonight. I'll be back aboard with my gear in an hour, and Mistress Ilna will follow . . . ?"

He cocked his head toward her with an eyebrow raised.

"I'll come aboard with you," Ilna said. "I have nothing more to bring but a heavy cloak, and I could do without that if I needed to."

She was showing the sailors she was one of them, just as quick an adaptable as they were; or perhaps she was bragging again. Like so many things, it was a matter of how you viewed it.

"Then in an hour, lads," Chalcus said. He lifted Merota to

his right shoulder and, holding her there with one hand, climbed the vertical ladder to the dock as the child laughed happily.

Ilna followed with what was for her a warm smile. Chalcus was bragging also, but doing it with a verve that she could never imagine in herself. And it was a good thing to tell a crew of strong, skilled men that their new captain was even stronger and *more* skilled.

Over Merota's protests, Chalcus set the girl down on the pavement and sent her a few steps ahead in the company of Mistress Kaline. "So, dear heart . . ." Chalcus said with a sidelong glance at Ilna. "Do you have any questions before we set off on the tide?"

"I'm surprised at the crew," Ilna said frankly. "I'd expected . . ."

She paused to search for a word. Chalcus laughed merrily beside her and said, "Cutthroats and pirates, bloody-handed killers with one eye and an evil leer?"

Ilna laughed also, but with a touch of embarrassment. "Well, not that, exactly; but something closer to that sort than to the men there."

Sobering, Chalcus said, "Those are hard men, dear one, men who've given strokes and taken them in their time. But they'll take orders when they've agreed to, and they'll do their duty because it's their duty, not when it suits them. I sailed with pirates when I was a pirate, but now that I serve a prince, I want men with me as sure of their duty as that prince himself is."

He laughed again and put his arm around her waist. As a rule Ilna didn't like that sort of display in public, but at the moment it seemed appropriate.

"We're honest folk doing the kingdom's business, dear one," Chalcus said. "That strikes me as a more wonderful thing than perhaps it does you, but if it means I can sleep nights without worrying about my bosun cutting my throat— it may be that I can get used to it!"

The balconied windows of Sharina's large bedroom overlooked a courtyard with a large cedar tree and stone planters that had been allowed to grow up in weeds. In the center of her suite was a reception room, it opened onto the inner hallway and also to stairs from the courtyard. The maid's cubicle was curtained off from the reception room and had its own door to the hall.

When Sharina first awakened, she thought she was home in Barca's Hamlet and a hungry puppy was whimpering. When her head cleared, she realized she was hearing the maid.

"Beara?" Sharina called, feeling for the sandals she kept at the side of the bed. "Are you all right?"

Her bedroom had a real wooden door instead of a curtain. The lamp in the reception room leaked light around the panel, but it took a moment for Sharina's eyes to focus through the veil of sleep. She opened the door.

The cryolite urn sat on a claw-footed bronze stand between the windows of the reception room, replacing the black-figured Old Kingdom vase which had been there previously. Hanging from the room's ceiling was a triangular lamp whose corners were molded into grotesquely sharp-chinned faces. A wick lay on each extended tongue; normally one provided a night-light after Sharina had gone to bed.

Tonight a lamp flickered within the urn instead, suffusing the stone's gray-on-gray pattern. It lit the wall paintings showing scenes from the Shepherd's wooing of the Lady. Under its illumination the murals became journeys through Hell: bleak, cynical, and inexorable.

The Shepherd leaned on his staff, his face twisted in demonic glee as he contemplated the future. The sheep around him were pustulent and as terrified of the certainty of their death as so many pox-ridden harlots.

In the next painted cartouche, the Lady reclined on a divan in Her garden. The fruits hanging above were surely poisonous; the doves on her fingertips whispered envious gossip about the whole world else; and the Lady's face was a mask of lust so fierce that neither man nor beast could hope to slake it.

The final panel should have been the couple's holy marriage. Sharina was neither prudish nor more of an innocent than any other peasant raised in daily contact with nature. Even so she felt her breath suck in when she saw the scene as lighted through the stone.

Beara stood by the urn, hiding her face with her raised left arm and trying to reach down inside with the other hand to snuff the lamp wick. It was too deep for her to reach. The girl sobbed bitterly as her arm flailed.

Sharina closed her eyes. The patterns on the ice stone were soothing when the sun lit them from the outside, but they had a wholly different significance when light streamed through them from within. She felt the mottled patterns eating away her flesh like huge cancers.

"Push it over!" she cried. She grabbed the urn's rim and twisted, trying to roll the urn off its stand. In her present hysteria she should've been able to lift the urn overhead and smash it down on the floor in a thousand harmless fragments, but it didn't move. It was as rigid as an iron post driven down to the center of the earth.

Sharina looked for a tool, a spear or a poker that would reach farther into the urn than a human arm. There was nothing in the reception room. She ran back into her bedroom, thinking that the tongs on the charcoal brazier there might serve her need.

The bedroom was decorated with a frieze of birds and vines on a trellis. The light flickering through the open doorway touched them as it had the decoration of the reception room. Sharina felt her stomach tense as she glimpsed what had been a pleasant design: now it made her feel like a corpse watching as the crows and vultures descend.

She reached for the tongs from the cold grill, but they were too short to reach the flame. She could throw them down at the lamp—

No, much better! On the bedside table was a clear glass water pitcher, etched on the inside with a hunting scene. Sharina grabbed it and ran back into the reception room.

The evil glare from the urn repelled her like the door of an open lime kiln, but she'd faced other hard things in her life. Flinging away the tumbler upended to cover the pitcher, Sharina shouted, "Get out of the way, Beara!"

The maid, frightened beyond hope of reasoning, continued to whimper and vainly grope. Sharina grabbed her left shoulder and half-lifted, half-pulled the girl out of the way.

She smashed the pitcher into the mouth of the urn, shattering the glass and releasing its contents in a single gout.

The flood of water shattered the hot earthenware lamp and lifted the oil up the sides of the urn. For an instant there was darkness and peace in the suite. Then a spark from the glowing wick ignited the thin sheet of oil in a flash thousands of times brighter than the original flame.

The light enveloped Sharina. She hung suspended in a chamber of ice that sucked all warmth and all life from her body. Cold squeezed her to a spark and began drawing that into itself.

Sharina thought she heard the maid screaming through the gray hellfire, but perhaps she was screaming herself. Then she was gone.

Chapter Nine

The cryolite urn had been even more delicate than Garric thought: the pieces shattered on the tile floor were eggshell thin. Liane knelt in the debris, supporting Sharina's weeping maid with one arm and holding up a rushlight in the other hand. The tallow-soaked reed pith burned with a pale yellow flame; Liane carried a bundle of them as reading lights in her document case.

"We broke in quick as we could, I swear we did!" said the officer of the guard. "When we heard the screaming, we put our backs to it. I figured if it was just the lady having a good time, well, I'd rather go back to following a plow than make a mistake the other way."

The hall door had been of sturdy beechwood. The overlay of bronze filigree, though meant for decoration, would've slowed the troops who were trying to break in. They'd splintered the panel, half of which still hung from the hinges. The bronze was a lacy tatter trailing into the room.

"You were correct, ensign," Garric said, his hand clenching and unclenching on his sword hilt. "What did you see?"

The guards had brought their lantern with them; that and the rushlight were the only illumination in the reception room. Soldiers and servants were squeezing in from the hall, and troops from the courtyard hammered on the outer door now that they realized there was something wrong.

The screams hadn't been loud enough to alert them. It'd been the sound of soldiers battering down the door with their spear butts that'd warned Garric something was wrong, though his suite was adjacent.

"Just the girl there crying on the floor and the vase all in pieces," the ensign said. "To tell the truth, I thought the girl'd broke the thing and was afraid she'd be whipped to an inch of her life, but then I saw the bed empty—"

He gestured toward the bedroom with the sword in his right hand. The point almost skewered the under-housekeeper who'd run in to see if her staff was the cause of the commotion.

"—and I said, 'Where's your mistress?' to the silly bint, and she starts crying louder than she'd *been* doing, which is plenty loud."

Liane rose to her feet with a supple motion; the maid immediately sank back into the sobbing puddle as she'd been when Garric followed the guards into the room. She'd come from Valles in Reise's entourage, chosen by him and therefore as trustworthy as human judgment could determine.

"Beara said a servant she didn't recognize put a lamp inside the urn," Liane said, speaking loudly enough for Garric to understand over the increasing volume of noise. Lords Waldron and Attaper arrived together from opposite corners of the palace, both trying to take charge. "In the middle of the night she woke up because there was something wrong with the light coming through her curtain."

Liane nodded to the patterned muslin hanging that shadowed the maid's alcove from the rest of the suite.

"She said it was awful," Liane continued with the dry humor that was so much a part of her, even in a crisis. "She can't explain what she means, but judging from her state I'm willing to accept the assessment. She tried to put out the lamp and couldn't, then Sharina did something—"

"Poured water onto it," said Garric, pointing with his bare toe. Fragments of etched glass were mixed with the urn's ice-stone shards.

"Yes, of course," said Liane approvingly. "Sharina poured in water. The urn broke, and Beara says it sucked Sharina somewhere as it did so."

She frowned with concentration and cocked her head toward the door. Garric heard the familiar voice also, barely a chirp among the raucous, angry men.

"Waldron and Attaper!" he roared, determined to be understood. "Bring Lady Tenoctris to me at once, if you please!"

There was a stir by the door. Soldiers moved aside quickly, cursing their fellows who kept them from getting out of the officers' way. The commanders walked Tenoctris the two steps from the doorway, one to either side of the frail old woman. Without their bulk and angry authority, she might as well have been on the other side of the moon for all her chances of reaching Garric.

"Tenoctris," Garric said, so coldly furious that there was no emotion at all in his voice. "Sharina's been attacked or taken away by this urn. Can you learn anything about it here, or is there someplace you might better be?"

"I can possibly determine something here," the old wizard said. "Though . . ."

She looked around doubtfully. "Not, I think," she went on, "while there's so many people around."

"Right," said Garric calmly. In a bellow that rattled the windows he went on, "Clear the room! I want all the soldiers out and all the servants except the girl on the floor. Now!"

There was an immediate shuffle and whispering, then a shift toward the door. It couldn't be called a stampede, but he was being obeyed. That was good, because he was in no mood to be balked. . . .

He looked at Liane. "Will you stay here with Tenoctris, please?" he said. "Help her as she requires?"

"Yes, of course," Liane said. She lit the overhead lamp

with her rushlight, then said to Tenoctris, "You left your equipment in your room? I'll fetch it and be right back."

Garric watched Liane slip out with the last of the Blood Eagles. Many amazing things had happened to him in the past year; Liane was both the most amazing and the most wonderful.

"Lord Attaper," Garric said. "I'll take two companies of the Blood Eagles. Lord Waldron, I want whichever regiment is on standby to come with me also."

"That's Lord Rosen's regiment, your highness," said Waldron with a frown. "They're a Blaise regiment, though."

"Are you saying they're not to be trusted, Waldron?" Garric snapped. Tendons in his throat stood out with his fury.

"What?" said Waldron. The commander of the royal army had spent most of his long life fighting or in preparation to fight. He was stiff-necked, arrogant, and extremely competent. "Of course I trust them, or they wouldn't be on duty!"

"Then I don't care if they're bloody demons from Hell and the Sister commands them!" said Garric. "They'll come with me to the Temple of the Lady of the Sunset. I'm going to turn the place upside down until I get answers about this urn they sent—and I learn what they've done with Sharina!"

Sharina lay on the floor, trembling from a chill greater than that of any winter wind. Her eyes were closed, though it was a moment before she realized that and opened them. She'd been close to death; she'd thought she *was* dead.

She was wearing the shift in which she'd gotten out of bed. It was night and the air was bitter, but even so she was warm by contrast with the place she'd been. She turned her head slowly, afraid that a quick movement would cause the tangled rubble around her to shift and crush her.

When this building's outer wall collapsed, the roof had tilted down to form a lean-to. The tiles had cracked off. Though the substructure of lathes and trusses remained, enough moonlight streamed through the gaps for Sharina to identify her surroundings.

She was in the reception room of her suite—but the palace was a ruin overwhelmed by time and the elements.

The floor humped like a tilled field, and only memory told Sharina she was lying on a mosaic instead of a scatter of sharp-edged gravel.

There could be no doubt, though. A patch of fresco remained on the inner wall from which rain had flaked most of the plaster. The moon shone on it—fittingly, for it showed the face of the Lady who was the Moon in one of Her guises. In the world Sharina'd just left, the same painted visage smiled from a couch in Her garden of peace and delights.

The passage to the hall was blocked by debris. The other doorway had skewed when the wall shifted but it hadn't fallen in. Sharina could see into what had been her bedroom, where now an open fire burned on the floor. The three creatures squatting around it would've looked like gangling, raw-boned men from a distance, but upright each would stand more than twelve feet high.

The creatures' foreheads sloped; their noses were broad and flat, and coarse reddish hair covered their bodies. They didn't wear clothing, but one had a necklace of some sort. Occasionally they made noises, but Sharina couldn't tell whether they were speaking or simply grunting like dogs rolling on the ground. Meat was cooking on the fire; Sharina smelled pork and heard the regular pop and sizzle of dripping fat.

As her eyes adapted, Sharina realized that the objects around her included loot along with the debris of ruin: the creatures in the next room used this half-fallen alcove as a storehouse for the baubles they'd collected, sorting them by type. Beside Sharina was a jumble of gold and silver plate: platters, goblets, and the gilt frame of a hand mirror set with glass beads.

Piled partly on the floor and partly on fallen roof tiles was a tangle of fabric, chosen for shiny threads rather than art. A border decorated with gold braid had been cut or torn from a woolen tapestry; the corner cartouche of the Three Graces dancing remained. Even by moonlight Sharina thought that Ilna would've been interested in the weaver's skill.

On the slant of rubble blocking the hall doorway were swords and daggers whose hilts were decorated with jewels and gold wire. The blades were masses of rust; many of them had been broken. A glaive of perforated brass, some usher's symbol, had survived exposure, but it had never been a weapon.

At the bottom of the pile, visible because of its soft gleam in the moonlight, was a narrow-bladed war axe with gold inlays whose complexity and beauty probably meant nothing to the creatures that had collected it. A spike in the shape of a long nose balanced the axe's single bitt. The blade was a work of art in uncorroded steel, the stylized head of a sharp-featured man with an angry expression.

The creatures in the other room began to eat, tearing chunks of flesh from the carcass without removing it from the fire. Sharina watched them for a long moment, then with a grim expression turned her attention to finding a way out before the owners decided to gloat over their hoard after dinner.

The reception room's only surviving doorway was the one between Sharina and the creatures. The maid's alcove was packed with more of the gathered loot: unguent bottles, jewel boxes, and a few larger containers with shiny metal or sparkling inlays—brass, tin, and glass as well as what humans would've called precious. Even if the door beyond weren't blocked, the treasure would clatter down like a deliberate alarm.

The only possibility of escape was the slanted roof. The beams were spaced a foot and a half apart, far enough for Sharina to wriggle between them easily. The lattice of laths laid across them was the problem. She could easily tear her way through the thin wood, but that'd make noise—particularly if she dislodged one of the few remaining tiles.

Sharina slowly rolled over on her back to survey the roof without getting a crick in her neck. The creatures weren't paying any attention to this room as they grunted and slobbered their way through the meal, but there was a risk one of them might catch a flash of her white face moving in the moonlight.

The back wall, which had originally separated the room from the interior hallway, remained upright. It was the fulcrum supporting the roof beams when the outer wall collapsed. When the tiles slipped downward, they'd pulled the laths some distance with them.

Sharina was sure she could worm through the gap. To reach it, though, she'd have to climb the slope of rubble that had poured through the hall doorway, debris from the other side of the building. That should be possible; and anyway, she didn't have a choice.

She rolled onto her belly again, slowly and carefully, then crawled to the slope on all fours. Tufts of coarse grass grew from the rubble. She could at least hope that their roots had cemented debris into a solid mass that wouldn't slide noisily when she put her weight on it.

She paused, looking at the assortment of weapons in front of her. The only one that remained useful was the axe. It was on the bottom of the pile, and Sharina had no experience with anything bigger than the hatchet by the kitchen door for chopping kindling. Work that required a real axe had been Garric's job from an early age.

The dagger blades were lumps of rust, though, and she was certainly going to need a tool if not a weapon when she got out of this dreadful lair. Reaching carefully into the stack of rusted iron, she worked the axe out—first the head, then the two-foot-long hardwood helve, which ended in an iron knob. The sculptured face glared at her.

Gripping the axe in her right hand, just below the head, Sharina started up the slope. The rubble was as firm as she'd dared pray. The moonlit opening above her was narrower than she liked, but she

"Masters!" screamed the axe. "Masters, a thief is taking me! Masters, I'm being carried away!"

A triple bellow filled the night. Sharina looked over her shoulder. The creatures had risen from the fire and were picking up clubs the size of her body. One of them still held in his free hand the side of ribs he'd been gnawing with massive yellow teeth. They were from a human being, not a pig.

"Masters!" cried the axe. "Kill the thief and drink her blood!"

———

"Oh," said Cashel as they came around the angle of rock. He'd thought the gleam on the peak above was snow or a concentration of quartz. "Oh!"

"Lord Bossian's manor," said Kotia with a smug smile at having finally managed to impress Cashel. "We've arrived, or very nearly so."

The manor was huge. Maybe the buildings scattered over the acres of the palace compound in Valles put together would've added up to this, but Cashel doubted it—and anyway, *these* towers and blocks and terraces were all in one place, one structure.

And though of many different colors, the whole thing was made out of crystal. No wonder sunlight glinting from and through its angles shone for miles above the surrounding crags.

The beads of wizardlight guiding them continued up the hillside, but now the route was paved with textured blue-gray glass instead of being a waste of boulders and pebbles. Cashel cleared his throat. "Ah . . . ?" he said. "Will Lord Bossian be glad to see us, mistress? If you're having trouble with your father and all?"

"I'm having trouble with Lord Ansache, whom I thought was my father, you mean," Kotia said, starting up the pavement with brisk strides. "He and Bossian aren't friends, I assure you. As a matter of fact, Lord Bossian offered to wed me last year, but my—but Ansache refused him."

Her back was straighter than it'd been for most of the morning's hike. Cashel was barefoot, but his soles were hardened to any kind of use. Kotia's slippers hadn't fallen apart on the journey—whatever they were made of was tougher than the light suede it looked like—but they couldn't have cushioned her steps much either. If there'd been much farther to go, Cashel would've been carrying the girl.

Kotia looked at Cashel with an expression that he still couldn't read, though it was becoming familiar. "I doubt Bossian would've taken me in if Kakoral were still pursuing me," she said. "Bossian is a great wizard but he couldn't have protected me against the demon, so he wouldn't have tried. But I had nowhere else to go."

Cashel shrugged. He knew a lot of people felt that way.

For himself, he figured people could generally do a lot more than they thought they could; and if something was bad enough, you did all you could to stop it even if you *did* figure it'd roll right over you.

He glanced sidelong at Kotia. Despite the way she'd made the statement, he got the notion that her opinion of how people ought to behave was pretty close to his own.

Chimes and trilling flutes sounded from the manor. Faces were lining the battlements to watch him and Kotia trudge up the roadway. Goodness, but this was a huge place! Every twist of the path showed Cashel another marvel.

Though all a single structure, the manor was built in at least a double-handful of styles—each in crystal of a different color. The foundations were a drab stone color, yet as clear as seawater on a calm day. The huge block to the east was pink with square towers, arched windows, and tiny round turrets with pointed cupolas on the corners. West of it was a lower, pale yellow, mass of open-topped round towers with colonnaded porticos cantilevered out at several levels.

The central portion was the same blue-gray as the path and had a fusty, antique appearance. The towers flanking the gateway had three sides visible and probably as many behind; tassels and curlicues of contrasting colors draped the walls between circular windows, and the door panels seemed to represent a frozen waterfall.

They opened as Cashel and his companion approached. A middle-aged man stepped out.

The fellow had a short black beard and an air of self-possession; behind him came any number of men and women, servants by the look of them. The leader's clothing was peacock-colored but hemmed with the same rich blue as the sashes cinching the servants' white tunics.

He extended his arm in a sweeping gesture. "Kotia!" he cried. "What an unexpected pleasure! May I hope that your stay will be a long one?"

"As long as you wish, Bossian," Kotia said. "And as your wife, if you still wish that. You should know that Ansache has driven me out of his manor."

"I had heard something about your difficulties," Lord

Bossian said smoothly. He took Kotia by the hand. "I've had my own troubles with Ansache, as you know."

He looked at Cashel, who'd halted at arm's length behind the girl and stood with his quarterstaff vertical in his right hand. Turning again to Kotia, Bossian continued, "You brought a servant with you, my dear? Or perhaps it's an automaton you created with your art?"

"No," said Cashel, his voice a growl. He'd met Bossian's type before, the ones who felt little beside him and decided to make themselves bigger by insults. They seemed always to figure that Cashel wouldn't drive them into the ground like so many tent pegs; and they were right, not for as little as a few words. But Cashel wondered if any of them realized how easily he *could* do that, and how quickly he *had* the times somebody went beyond words to a blow or a gobbet of spit. . . .

"I summoned Master Cashel to scotch a demon who was becoming importunate," Kotia said with the ladylike hauteur that hadn't been in her voice since Kakoral appeared. "He did so in an able fashion."

She gave Bossian a thin smile. "A remarkably able fashion, milord. I told him that you were skilled in the art yourself, and that you could perhaps send him home now that he's accomplished the purpose for which I brought him here."

"Ah!" said Bossian, looking at Cashel in a very different fashion from before. "Indeed. Ah."

Cashel met Bossian's eyes, thinking about what Ilna might have said—or done—to the fellow. Cashel wasn't that way himself—it wouldn't be right for the biggest, strongest man in the borough to act the same as a small woman did—but he wouldn't have minded seeing it happen. Thinking that, he smiled.

Bossian's mouth dropped open and he took a step backward. Kotia must've wondered what was going to happen next also; she touched the back of Cashel's hand on the quarterstaff and said, "Bossian, my friend and I have had a difficult day and night. If you could provide us with refreshment . . . ?"

"Yes, of course!" Bossian said. He clapped the fingers of his right hand against the palm of his left.

"Food and drink in the Summer Plaza!" he cried to the troupe of aides behind him. At once several of them sprinted back into the manor. Shortly after they'd disappeared, bells began to ring in what was either a code or discordant music.

Bossian bowed to Cashel and said, "Sir, I assure you that I'll do everything in my power to speed you to wherever you choose to go. We'll discuss the matter as soon we've eaten. Kotia, my dear?"

He crooked out his elbow.

"May I have the honor of escorting you to dinner?"

Kotia didn't reply, but she took Bossian's arm with practiced courtesy. Together they walked through the fanciful archway; people watching from above began to cheer and wave ribbons.

Cashel followed, feeling a bit funny about the situation. When he thought about the words he'd use to describe what was going on—a pretty young girl thrown out by her father and forced to marry her rich older neighbor—it sounded pretty terrible. The truth, though, to somebody who'd had a day's experience of Kotia, wasn't nearly so one-sided. Or anyway, wasn't one-sided in Bossian's favor.

They walked down a tunnel whose walls were rippling blue; it was like stepping dryshod through the depths of the sea. Kotia and Bossian chatted to one another; Cashel could hear most of the words, but they were discussing things and people that meant nothing to him.

Cashel thought about the world he'd been taken from, feeling sad in a way that didn't often happen to him. Maybe it was the strange fashion light bent in this place. It was *all* strange, and it wasn't where he belonged. He hoped that Tenoctris was all right; and he wished that Sharina was here to explain the parts of this place that she'd understand. It was wonderful the things that Sharina and Garric knew, and they talked to Cashel about them without talking down. . . .

Beyond the tunnel mouth was a courtyard full of people in gorgeous colors, though none quite so brilliant as Bossian himself. The walls and pavement were golden—were pure gold, Cashel would've said from a distance, but close up he could see it was transparent crystal just like the rest.

Instead of shouting, the folk in the courtyard pressed up to Bossian, clasping hands with him while bowing and simpering to Kotia. Other people looked down and smiled from the balconies terraced back from the foundations of the surrounding buildings.

Bossian waved away the mob of greeters and turned to Cashel. "Does the Visitor prey on the regions you come from, sir?" he asked in a friendly enough tone. "I ask because we see portents of his return, and I thought your presence might be connected."

"What are you saying, Lord Bossian?" said Kotia in a voice that could break rocks. "Do you think that I'd have brought a harbinger of the Visitor into our world?"

"Of course not, my dear!" Bossian said, sounding like he was surprised. Maybe he was—though if he hadn't expected Kotia to go for his throat if he played games with words that *might* be insults, he didn't know her as well as Cashel did already. "I just thought we should explore whether he might be a portent, that's all."

The ground started to rise.

Cashel brought his staff over his head, the only place he could hold it crosswise and not bash a lot of people. Even so his left elbow jabbed a solid-looking fellow who caromed back with a shout of amazement. The crowd stopped chattering and stared at Cashel instead.

"Cashel?" Kotia said, calmly but with an artificially blank expression.

The ground—the plate of golden crystal, it wasn't ground!—continued to rise. One edge remained in contact with the tall, smooth-sided cone across from the gateway. The plate curved around the cone and settled into place on the opposite side, several stories higher than it'd been when Cashel first walked onto it.

"I'm sorry, mistress," Cashel said. He lowered his staff, making a little nod of apology to the fellow he'd elbowed. "I just wasn't expecting that to happen."

Then, as the locals started chattering and Bossian mouthed false regrets for not having explained what was going to happen, Cashel said, "And as for the Visitor, I've never heard of anybody who goes by that as a title. If my coming here has something to do with him, it's without me knowing about it. Who is he?"

He thought for a moment and added, "Or she, I guess."

"We'll take the Linden Walk, I think," Bossian said. He looked disconcerted. "Unless you . . . ?"

Cashel gestured brusquely with his left hand toward the broad path bordered with what he would've called basswood trees. "Walking's fine," he said.

Cashel was tired and hungry, and Bossian seemed set on playing tricks on him. He'd have turned around and left if he had any better place to be, and he was just about ready to do that anyway.

Kotia said something sharply into Lord Bossian's ear, then stepped back and took Cashel's arm instead. "Manor Bossian's trees are famous," she said in a coolly cheerful tone. "At Manor Ansache, our parks have a prairie theme."

Her smile was as hard as Ilna's might have been. She added, "And my mother had an extensive fungus garden in the cellars, though Ansache had it grubbed up after she disappeared."

Cashel cleared his throat as they walked along the boulevard. Lord Bossian was a step ahead, talking with several locals and being very careful not to look over his shoulder. There was a little cocoon of open space separating Cashel and Kotia from the others, which suited Cashel fine. He wasn't used to crowds. He said, "Thank you, mistress."

Kotia patted his arm with her free hand. "Is there anything you'd like to see while you're here, Master Cashel?" she said. "There's no reason that you have to rush off, you know."

Cashel noticed Lord Bossian hunch as though somebody'd just hit him on the back of the head. Grinning—Kotia was a *lot* like Ilna, which was a fine thing if you were on her side—he said, "No, mistress, there's people waiting for me back where I was. But thank you."

He'd wondered where the fields supplying this huge building were, but he saw them as he walked along—on roofs and terraces covering the whole manor. As the tree-bordered road curved around a huge tower, Cashel noticed to the north a many-layered pyramid that seemed to be of plantings at every level.

The slopes Cashel'd hiked over for the past day weren't green enough to pasture sheep, so he wondered whether the rainfall was enough for the melons and squash he'd seen among the rows of maize. People who made courtyards move could pump water from deep wells, he supposed.

The slimly-handsome man and woman now walking to either side of Lord Bossian talked about the Visitor in airy voices. Neither of them believed he was coming—or at any rate, they denied they believed that. Bossian made neutral comments. He could've been too high-minded to trouble himself with the matter, but Cashel got the impression that Bossian was afraid to speak clearly, for fear whichever choice he made would bring the Visitor down on him.

"Ah, Kotia?" Cashel said. "Who's the Visitor? I really don't know anything about him." He paused, then added, "At least under that name."

A magnificent waterfall poured from the cleft between two towers—one rosy and decorated with turrets stuck to the sides, the other green and stark, without so much as window ledges to mark its smooth sides. The stream gurgled under the road, twisted, and vanished into a hulking silvery mass whose colonnades seemed to have been spun from cobweb. There was no sign of where so much water could have come from.

"For as far back as history records," Kotia said quietly, "a being has come down from the sky, stayed for a time, and then vanished in the same way as he appeared. We call him the Visitor. Sometimes there's a generation between his visits, sometimes longer than that. While he's here, he does as he wishes—he has that much power."

She turned to meet Cashel's eyes. Without raising her voice she added, "The Visitor remains for varying lengths of time, generally a month or a few months. About a thousand years ago, the Visitor stayed for five years. Everything that happened before then is lost to us now, because civilization ended at that time."

Cashel frowned. "You fight him when he comes?" he said.

Kotia shrugged. "Some have fought," she said. "Some flee. And there have always been some who tried to serve him. The Visitor does as he wishes."

They'd arrived at an array of tables and chairs on half-round terraces. They were set with food and drink, and servants in white tunics were poised discreetly to add more.

Lord Bossian gestured Cashel and Kotia to the circular table at the lowest level. The couple who'd been walking with him took places there also, but they remained standing till Bossian gave them leave.

The male of the pair looked at Cashel and said, "Really, you mustn't get worked up about the Visitor, you know. There's always somebody talking about omens and portents and doom in the stars. It always turns out to be fancy."

"If you've looked at the night sky in the past month, Farran," Kotia said in a voice that was too disgusted to be angry, "you'd have noticed that the stars themselves are different. The constellations in the southeast have changed their alignments! That's no more fancy than sunrise is."

"Ah," said the fellow, turning to the woman with him. "Are you planning to attend Lady Tilduk's gala, Syl?"

Lord Bossian pulled out his own chair; the whole gathering followed his lead, seating themselves in a rush that filled every place on the terraces. Cashel sat carefully, as he always did when he wasn't sure how sturdy his chair would be.

As Kotia settled beside him, she muttered, "The Visitor does as he wishes."

But as she spoke, she eyed Cashel.

Ilna sat with her back to the little cabin and the sun on her left side. Nabarbi was at the steering oar on the opposite railing, so she was as much out of the way as she could be on a small vessel.

She was working on the hand frame in her lap, weaving a cartouche that could become part of a tapestry or set off a garment as need arose. Its measured curves drew the eye and left the beholder feeling marginally more optimistic. Ilna smiled grimly as she worked: the design had a positive effect even on her.

Because the *Bird of the Tide*'s hold was nearly empty, Ilna could've carried any loom she wanted. She couldn't possibly use anything larger while they were at sea, though, and they'd be returning immediately to Carcosa when they'd dealt with this trouble in the Strait.

If they survived, of course. She smiled again. She *was* feeling optimistic.

Their bow was chopping into the sea, a change from the first day out when slow swells from astern lifted the *Bird* in long, queasy arcs. Ilna didn't like the chop, but she hadn't liked the swells either. In all truth she didn't like ships, which put them in the same category as most people and most things. And because of the way she was feeling, she grinned even wider at *that* thought.

"You're a cheerful one today, lass," said Chalcus in a tone of pleased puzzlement. He'd come around the cabin from where he'd been talking to Nabarbi. "I'd feared that bucking the current would've made you uncomfortable."

As compared to what? Ilna thought, but because she was feeling positive—and because she liked to see the pleasure that brought into Chalcus's eyes—she said, "It's not so very bad. I can work—"

She tilted the hand frame as a gesture.

"—and so long as I can work, nothing disturbs me very much."

Chalcus nodded in understanding, though she caught a flash of regret in his expression also. "Most of the north-bound traffic takes the Haft Channel and hugs the mainland," he explained, gesturing to starboard. "That's how the current flows, so even if the wind's from the northeast you can make headway."

He grinned. "If you know what you're doing," he added, "and you're not sailing a pig, which our *Bird* here assuredly is not."

Chalcus patted the railing. He was dressed in tunic and sash, ordinary garb for the captain of a small vessel who expected to help the crew in a crisis; but the sash was bright red silk matching the fillet that confined his hair, and his curved dagger wasn't an ordinary seaman's working blade. Chalcus wasn't a man to pass unnoticed in any company, so he didn't bother trying.

"Ships bound for Carcosa take the Outer Strait and pass north of the Calves," Chalcus continued, "riding south on a current that comes all the way from the Ice Capes. It's those ships that the Rua take, or anyway somebody takes—"

He gave her another grin; Ilna nodded coldly.

"—so we'll be calling in to see Commander Lusius in Terness on the north coast of Corse, that's the northeast island of the Calves. To get there we're slipping between the other two islands, Betsam and Bewld; and that means fighting the current."

"I'd noticed the air was cooler," Ilna said, tying off the completed design. She rose to her feet, looking at the sea for the first time since she'd placed herself against the cabin. The railing wasn't particularly high, but seated on the deck she could see only the sky over it. The water was a murky green as though it was mixed with powdered chalk.

"We'll dock in Terness before the middle of the afternoon, I'd judge," Chalcus said, eyeing the land ahead of them. Ninon stood in the far bow, his right hand on a stay, watching also. "Barring the untoward happening, which is no more a certainty on shipboard than it is with the rest of life, eh, lass?"

"Chalcus," said Ilna. She pointed to the sky high to the northeast. "Are those birds, or . . . ?"

"Ah, you've good eyes, my dear," said Chalcus, following her gaze. "Indeed, it's the *or* of your question, I would say. They're no birds of my acquaintance, for all that they're surely flying."

There were three of them, dipping and swooping in the clear air. Ilna couldn't estimate the distance closer than "many miles away," but that was enough to prove that the creatures were huge. In a sudden simultaneous rush they vanished again over the horizon.

"Shausga and Ninon," Chalcus called. "Go string your bows, I think. Likely we'll not need them, but . . . have them ready regardless. Kulit, take over the lookout."

Chalcus grinned at Ilna with a wolfish good humor that

had nothing funny in it. "And for me, my dear, I think I'll have my sword about me till we dock. Not that we'll need that either, but . . ."

"We'll need it before this voyage is over," said Ilna, folding a swatch of coarse fabric over the hand frame to protect it when she packed it in the hold. "That's why we're here, after all."

She was smiling also. It struck her that there probably wasn't much difference between her expression and that of Chalcus.

And because Ilna really was in a positive mood, she laughed at the thought.

"We should've come double-time," Attaper muttered to Garric as they reached the plaza in front of the Temple of the Lady of the Sunset. "My boys could've taken the gates and held them till the regulars came up."

Ten Blood Eagles were ahead of them; seventy more—companies in the bodyguard regiment were badly understrength because of recent fighting—were behind. Rosen's regiment followed, filling the street eight abreast and singing a Blaise war chant.

The hut beside the temple steps was empty, though the watchman's lighted lantern hung from the hook over his open door. The gates to the compound behind the temple were closed and barred; that might have been normal for the hours before dawn, but an alarm was ringing within and torchlight shimmered behind the walls.

"If you think we could've run ahead and not have those Blaise armsmen decide it was a race, Lord Attaper . . ." Garric said as King Carus in his mind grinned approval. "Then you've seen surprisingly little of the world. Besides, we're not dealing with foreign enemies. These are citizens of the Isles, although they may be a little vague at the moment regarding their duty to the crown."

"We'll sort 'em out," grunted the file leader close behind Garric. "By the *Lady*, we will!"

It struck Garric momentarily as an odd oath. On consideration he decided it was exactly the right one.

The courtyard walls were ten feet high. A man squirmed over them from the other side, then dropped down into the plaza. There were angry shouts within the compound.

Attaper grabbed Garric by the shoulder and held him fast. "Blood Eagles!" he ordered. "Close ranks twenty feet from the wall!"

The wall-jumper trotted toward them, stopping with his hands raised, palms outward, just short of the guards' lowered spears. "Your highness!" he called. "My name's Birossa. I'm Lady Liane's man!"

"Bring him here," said Garric.

"Your highness," said Attaper, "I don't think—"

Instead of shouting in frustration, Garric laughed and twisted away from Attaper's hand, then slipped through the rank of Blood Eagles. The guards were doing their job as they saw it, but Garric's job was to rule the Isles. He wouldn't let his friends keep him from his duty, any more than he would his enemies.

"Master Birossa," he said, ignoring the curses behind him. "What are you doing here?"

"Commanding a squad of temple heavies until just a moment ago," Birossa said. He wore only the simple undertunic that would be covered by a priestly robe when he was fully dressed. "They call them the Lady's Champions, but they're thugs. Lady Liane sent me to Carcosa three weeks ago, and I didn't have any difficulty getting hired. I know how things're laid out inside, so I can guide you."

"That'll be helpful," Garric said quietly. Liane hadn't told him she'd placed a spy in the Lady's camp—and very likely the Shepherd's also; but gathering intelligence before Garric needed it was part of her job, and she did it very well.

"They were alerted by a messenger a few minutes ago," Birossa said, nodding to the compound. "They've called out all the Champions and issued swords."

"Have they indeed?" Garric said, his voice very light. His muscles trembled, and it was with effort he kept from drawing his sword. Attaper was at his side again, but this time the Blood Eagle didn't touch his prince.

The gate was made of heavy timbers with a hawser crossing each leaf diagonally to keep it from sagging. The left panel had an iron-barred window at eye height. Garric walked up to it; Lord Attaper accompanied him, mumbling curses.

"I'm here to see Lord Anda," Garric said, his voice pleasant. The trill of emotion wasn't something the stranger looking out from the bars would find threatening. "Take me to him at once."

There was a brief conversation behind the gate. A different pair of eyes replaced the first. A woman said, "Lord Anda's at his devotions, your highness. As soon as he completes them, I'm sure he'll be glad to admit you."

Garric stepped back, still smiling. He toyed with the hilt of his sword. "Lord Attaper," he said in the same high, cheerful voice, "Open this gate, if you please."

"We've got it, your highness!" cried Lord Lerdain, Garric's fifteen-year-old aide and—significantly at the moment—the son of the Count of Blaise. Garric turned.

"Hup!" cried an officer of the Blaise regiment. Stone scrunched as a pair of armsmen levered an altar over on its side with their spearbutts; six of their fellows caught the toppling stone and lifted it to waist height.

"Hup!" repeated the officer.

"Hi!" cried the men as they started forward, shouting in unison at each stride. The officer ran ran alongside his troops. "Hi! Hi! Hi!"

The Blood Eagles opened a passage as they saw what was coming. Several of them cheered.

"*Hi!*" bellowed the officer. The altarstone was too stubby to use as a ram, but it made a very good missile for six strong men to throw into the center of the gate. The panels lurched open with a crash loud enough to wake the dead.

The six armsmen staggered through first on the inertia of their rush, but Garric with Attaper and a squad of Blood Eagles was immediately behind them. The bronze crossbar hadn't broken, but the stone's impact had torn loose the staples holding it to the gate leaves. The woman who'd spoken to Garric was stretched out with a startled expression and a bloody forehead; the bar had hit her as it spun back.

A large number—scores if not over a hundred—of armed priests had gathered in the courtyard; more were running to join them from the two-story barracks on the left side.

Torches and the lanterns over doorways flickered, emphasizing the nervous haste of the scene. The Blaise troops drew their hooked swords as the Blood Eagles raised their spears to thrust over their locked shields.

Garric stepped between the forces. "Lord Attaper!" he said. "Count to three aloud. When you've finished, deal with any civilian still holding a weapon as a traitor to the kingdom!"

"One!" bellowed Attaper. The armed priests shuddered closer together. One of them shouted a question toward the ornate dwellings lining the right side of the courtyard.

"Monsayd!" called Birossa, who seemed to have squirmed in with the soldiers. A burly priest in the front rank looked up, surprised. "Throw down your sword, you bloody fool. Do you *want* to die? Vaxus, Catual—save your lives, boys!"

Somebody in the rear dropped his sword. At the clang, half-a-dozen more fell. Monsayd looked at his own weapon as if wondering how it got into his hand, then hurled it across the courtyard.

"Two!" said Attaper, but nobody was likely to hear him over the raucous clamor of the rest of the "Lady's Champions" disarming themselves.

Garric caught the spy's eye and said, "Good work, Birossa!"

And good work, Liane. Without her help and her knowledge, the job of being prince would be beyond Garric's capacity. As well as what she brought to the private part of Garric's life . . .

"Back up, away from the swords!" ordered a young Blaise officer with gilt suns on his silvered helmet and breastplate. "Serjeant Bastin, I want those men tied with their sashes to await his highness's determination."

He wasn't formally under Attaper's command, a fact Garric had overlooked in his haste to reach the temple. To the normal rivalry between the Blood Eagles and the regular army was added hostility between Ornifal and Blaise. *By the Shepherd!* Garric snarled mentally. *Do I have to worry about my friends as much as I do my enemies?*

And the answer, of course, was that he did; that this was

part of being a prince. So, because it was his job, he said, "Lord Attaper, take charge here."

He turned to the Blaise officer and went on, "You're Lord Rosen, I believe?"

"Yes, your highness," the fellow said, holding himself in a tense mixture of concern and belligerence. He'd been pushing and knew it; what he didn't know was how Prince Garric of Haft was going to react to his behavior. Lord Lerdain stiffened, midway between Rosen and Garric.

"Turn your troops over to Attaper and come with me," Garric said. "We're going to discuss with the leaders of this place exactly how their gift caused my sister to vanish. Attaper—"

He rotated his head yet again, feeling like a spectator at a ball game.

"—detach twenty of your men to come with us. That ought to be plenty. The ones we'll be talking to aren't the sort to dirty their hands on a sword hilt."

Attaper paused to fight down his urge to protest any time Garric announced he was going to do anything personally. "Yes, your highness!" he said. "Undercaptain Kolstat, take a section along with the prince. Serjeant Bastin—"

The Blaise officer who'd taken charge of battering down the gate.

"—you heard Lord Rosen. Get those men tied!"

"This way, your highness," said Birossa, leading the way toward the freestanding residence at the far end of the residence block on the right. The spy had picked up a sword in the confusion, and the Blood Eagles weren't arguing his right to carry it.

A group of real priests—the aides who'd accompanied Anda when he greeted Prince Garric on the harborfront—were clustered in the doorway, clucking among themselves like hens as a fox approaches. They scattered to either side as Lord Anda strode out, dressed in his full regalia and accompanied by a servant bearing an ornate lantern on a long pole.

"Greetings in the Lady's name, your highness!" Anda said, looking three steps down on Garric from the porch of his residence. "I apologize for my subordinates. They mean well, but they don't appreciate that sometimes temporal affairs take precedence over spiritual matters."

"Bring him to me," Garric said quietly. "Don't hurt him, but—"

Two Blood Eagles tossed their spears to their nearest comrades to free their right hands. Lord Rosen's hands were already free; he took the two lower steps in a single long stride and had Anda by the left arm before a Blood Eagle grabbed the priest's right. Together they jerked Anda down.

The servant with the lantern gave a startled cry and started forward. The Blood Eagle who hadn't gotten a piece of Anda knocked the fellow down with the boss of his shield. Aides twittered and fled as burning oil spread from the smashed lamp.

"Anda," Garric said, his voice trembling, "a lie now will cost you your life. You sent me an ice-stone urn yesterday but I gave it to my sister. She vanished into it a short time ago. Tell me how to get her back unharmed."

Anda straightened; he didn't try to struggle with the men holding him. His jeweled tiara had slipped so that it now hung from his right ear, but he managed not to look ridiculous.

"Your highness," he said, his voice quavering despite an obvious attempt at control, "we didn't send you an urn. Our gift—"

Garric grabbed Anda by the throat with his left hand. He didn't squeeze, but his big hand was tensed to crush the old man's windpipe. "Liar!" he shouted. "Lord Moisin and four temple servants arrived yesterday with the urn as a gift from the Lady!"

"Your highness, we gave you a globe!" Anda cried. "Moisin was sent with a crystal globe from the Old Kingdom, etched with a map of the Isles and the world beyond!"

Garric stepped back, shocked as few other statements could have done. The chief priest was wrong, but he clearly wasn't lying. "Let him go!" he said to Rosen and the guard.

Anda turned to his aides. "Where's Moisin?" he said, his voice rising. "He should be here!"

"This way, your highness," Birossa said, gesturing toward the accommodations block beside Anda's detached dwelling. "Moisin's suite's the one on this side of the second floor."

"Bring Anda," Garric snapped as he started for the outside staircase.

The door at the head of the stairs was painted with an image of the Lady crowned by the setting sun. The soldier preceding Garric lifted his boot to smash though the thin wood; Birossa reached past and flipped the latch instead; it was unlocked.

The interior was dark until a Blood Eagle who'd grabbed a lantern entered and used its candle to light the wicks of a hanging lamp. Garric looked around him. Though there were variations in luxury, the priests of the Lady in Carcosa obviously lived well. Moisin, as one of the highest ranking, lived very well indeed.

The walls were frescoed with hunting scenes, the ornate couches had cushions of lustrous fur, and a section of marble relief from the Old Kingdom was set over the door at the back. Garric thought of the tithes from peasants in Barca's Hamlet who ate bread made of hulls and moldy barley for a month before the first spring crops came in.

King Carus watched in grim silence through Garric's eyes. He hadn't been a peasant himself, but he understood very well what his descendent was feeling.

Garric took his hand away from his sword hilt. He deliberately avoided looking at Lord Anda as his guards—Lord Rosen had turned the duty over to a Blaise regular—hustled him through the doorway.

"Moisin!" Anda cried. He was winded, but his tone now showed anger instead of desperation. To the men around him he added, "Aren't the servants here either? There should be two servants."

Soldiers carrying lights pushed through the inner doorway. A torch flame licked the marble relief; Garric winced, then laughed at his reaction. When so much else was going wrong . . .

Indeed, a beautiful sculpture that had survived a thousand years *did* deserve to be treated better than that; but Garric's first duty was to make the kingdom safe. That way more artists could create more beauty, and ordinary people could sleep soundly in their beds.

The rooms to either side of the inner doorway were for servants, though the beds hadn't been slept in. Beyond was

Moisin's own bedroom, even more richly appointed than the reception room. The ebony bed frame was inset with gold and ivory reliefs, while the coverlet and canopy were of rainbow-patterned silk embroidered in gold thread. Along the walls were storage chests, some of inlaid wood and others of metal or metal banded.

"Open them," Garric said, but the soldiers were already throwing back the lids. If the chest was locked, a spearbutt or a stout sword blade levered into the catch or hinges opened it promptly, even the ones that were meant for strongboxes.

A Blaise soldier set his sword in the latch of an iron casket, smaller than the clothes stores. His partner slammed a boot heel into the unsharpened back of the blade, shearing the locking pins. The chest clanged open.

"There!" cried Anda. "There—don't break it, you fool!"

The last comment was to the armsman reaching one-handed for a crystal globe padded with silken tunics. It wasn't the smartest thing to say to somebody with a hooked sword bare in the other hand, but Garric understood.

"I'll take it," he said, pausing a moment between Anda and the soldier before bending over to lift the globe from its swathing. He raised it carefully. Though larger than a man's head, the crystal was as thin as a soap bubble. In the light of swinging lamps and handheld lanterns Garric couldn't really view the pattern etched *inside* the crystal, but the detail was obvious.

"That was what Moisin was to bring you, your highness!" Anda said. "I swear it was!"

What does a false priest swear by that would make anybody trust him? Garric wondered; but for all that, he didn't doubt that Anda was telling the truth. This globe was worth the throne of Haft to anyone who could appreciate its wonder . . . as Garric certainly could.

"Moisin should be here," Anda said, desperation returning to his voice. "I don't know where he's gone or what he's been playing at. I swear it!"

"Your highness?" said Lord Rosen, tapping the flat of his sword on his thigh. "What would you like us to do now?"

Garric wanted to rub his eyes, but he was afraid to put the globe down in a room crowded with restive soldiers. "Everybody out!" he said after a moment's thought. "Clear the room!"

As the troops filed out, pushing later arrivals ahead of them, Garric set the globe back in its nest and closed the lid. To the trailing pair of Blood Eagles he said, "Carry this, and don't on your lives drop it! Carry it as if it held my soul!"

Then, to Lord Rosen who remained stiffly behind—wondering if he'd been insulted and wondering further how to react if he had been—Garric continued, "Milord, you and I will return to the palace with the Blood Eagles. I'll leave Attaper here to secure the compound and question everybody about where Moisin might have gone."

Now he rubbed his eyes. Smiling grimly he said, "I'm going to see what Tenoctris may have learned about Sharina. And I pray to the Shepherd that she's learned something!"

Chapter Ten

Sharina poised on the pile of rubble, analyzing the situation for a heartbeat. If she tried to crawl through the roof, the creature already hunching in the skewed doorway would grab her ankle with a hand the size of a bear ham and drag her back for a club stroke. Instead she twisted like a cat and leaped down, swinging the axe overhand.

"Blood!" screamed the steel mouth. "Blo—" and the edge sheared through the heavy-browed skull as easily as sunlight penetrates crystal. The rest of the word choked off in a gurgle.

Sharina landed with her feet under her. The axe moved easily; it was balanced like a dream. The creature whose skull she'd split convulsed violently, flinging its arms out to its sides; the club smashed into a sidewall hard enough to shatter into a fibrous broom.

A second creature stuck its arm down through the laths of the roof. Sharina pivoted, almost without thinking, and slashed through the creature's humerus. The bone was thicker than her own whole forearm, but the axe sliced it like gossamer.

"Yes, that's the way to feed Beard!" the axe cried in a throaty treble. "More blood! More blood for—"

The creature jerked back, tearing a barrel-sized hole in the latticework. The lower portion of its arm flailed on the triceps muscle that the narrow axe-blade hadn't severed. The roof beams shifted with a squeal. Sharina leaped, catching a beam in her left hand and pulling herself up.

The roof trembled like a ship's deck. The whole battered structure was shifting toward collapse.

"—Beard to drink!" cried the axe.

The third creature was trying to crawl over the thrashing body of the one with the split skull. The doorway wasn't big enough to hold both giants. The creature with the dangling arm saw Sharina, screamed, and swung its club at her. Before the awkward blow landed, she leaped down onto the back of the third creature. It lurched, dragging its shoulders out of the doorway and glaring at Sharina with eyes further reddened by the firelight.

"The throat!" screamed the axe. "Let me cut her—"

Sharina brought the axe around in a backhanded arc. She was a strong woman and the axe was scarcely more than a hatchet with an unusually long helve, but even so she marveled at how smoothly it moved. It was like watching light shimmer on smooth water.

"—throat!" the axe said.

Sharina didn't feel the blade touch and slip through the creature's neck, but the gush of blood bathed the wall where the frescoes had weathered off. The gout slowed, then spurted again as the creature rose to its feet, lifting its club overhead. The second creature had retrieved its weapon from the pall of dust and splinters raised when it smashed the roof. The dangling arm seemed to be affecting its balance.

Sharina scrambled sideways around the fire and tripped over a human body trussed with bark cord. She was breathing hard and didn't get her feet under her as easily as she expected. The creature whose throat she'd cut toppled slowly backward into the alcove holding the loot, completing the room's destruction with a crash and a pall of debris.

"Feed me!" the axe cried. "Feed me! Fee—"

Swinging the axe with both hands, Sharina leaped toward the only creature still standing. Its left-handed club blow wobbled past like a tree limb whirled in a windstorm. Even stretching to her full height Sharina couldn't reach the creature's skull, but she buried the axe to the helve at the top of the breastbone where the biggest blood vessels lift from the heart.

She dragged her weapon out with a sucking sound and a geyser of blood. The creature cried out and swiped its club sideways. Sharina jumped but the club caught her anyway, lifting her onto the ruin of the room from which she'd emerged. She lay stunned, choking on the dust but unable to move.

The creature dropped its club and staggered forward, clutching the gurgling hole in its chest. Blood welled from between its massive fingers and foamed through its yellow tusks, choking the cries it would otherwise have uttered.

Sharina got her left sleeve over her nose and tried to breathe through it. That didn't help much, but now that she'd started moving she crawled off of the shifting rubble. She still held the axe, though she didn't think she'd be able to swing it.

The creature fell facedown onto the fire, flinging sparks out to the sides. Burning hair added its stench to that of the woman, which the trio had been roasting. Sharina worked her way on all fours around the smothered fire, trying to get upwind.

"Help me," a voice whimpered. "Please. Help me."

Sharina opened her eyes; she hadn't been aware that they were closed. Her stomach roiled with the horror of what she'd just done. She kept remembering the startled expression on the face of the creature as her axe sheared its throat, and then the curtain of blood spraying in all directions. . . .

"Please. . . ."

The tied-up figure was a hollow-cheeked youth; moonlight turned his hair and his sallow complexion much the same color. His simple garments were filthy; but then, so was Sharina's sleeping shift, and she hadn't lain bound by man-eaters for an unguessibly long time.

"Hold still," she croaked, reaching for the cord binding his wrists and ankles together. "If you squirm, I may cut you."

"He's no use to you, mistress!" said the axe. "Come on, let me finish him for you. Look how his throat is just waiting for Beard to cleave it!"

The captive flinched and began to cry soundlessly. Sharina looked at the axe for the first time since she'd drawn it carefully from the pile of rusty trash. The steel was as bright and clean as plate polished for a palace banquet, though its shaft and Sharina's whole right arm were sticky with congealing blood.

"Be silent," she said in a rasping whisper. She short-gripped the weapon and carefully touched the edge to the rope.

"But Beard is still thirsty, mistress," the axe said. Quivering reflections on the back of the blade looked like a mouth there was speaking; maybe it was. "Please, mistress, let Beard drink his blood!"

The tough bark fibers parted without effort on Sharina's part. Though she knew the axe had just split heavy bones, the edge remained as keen as thought.

"Axe," she said in a deadly whisper. "If you don't shut up now, I'll give you all the water in Carcosa harbor to drink. Be silent!"

She paused but heard nothing except possibly a . . . *thirsty* . . . so faint that it might have been the wind through the ruined palace. She cut the youth's ankles free, then his wrists.

"You can move now," she said, leaning back. "What's your name?"

Lady help me, it's so cold . . . But she wasn't sure it was the wind that chilled her as much as her reaction to the few minutes just passed. Only a few minutes.

"I'm Franca," the youth said without meeting Sharina's eyes. He massaged his wrists with the opposite hands; the skin was worn away into a crust of blood. "Franca or-Orrin, but mostly mother called me Franca. And now she's gone."

He started to cry again. His hands stopped rubbing and he clamped his skinny arms tight to his chest.

"Your mother was . . . ?" Sharina said, nodding toward where the fire had been; the woman's feet stuck out from beneath the dead monster's body. Franca's eyes were closed, so she said, "The monsters killed your mother?"

"Of course the Hunters killed the silly woman!" said the axe in a clear, piping voice. "She and her whelp here came right down into Carcosa where the Hunters know every hiding place. But you killed *them,* mistress! Ah, those were fine strokes!"

Sharina looked sourly at the axe, but it was giving her more information than the weeping boy so she didn't snarl again. She needed to learn a lot more if she was to survive, let alone get back to where she belonged.

"Get up, Franca," she said. "We'll roll this Hunter out of the way and then bury your mother."

"Bury Mother?" the boy said. He stared in horror at the creature with the severed arm, then looked squarely at Sharina for the first time. "But why?"

"Because we're human beings," she said, "and that's what people do!"

She set the axe on the base of a fallen column where she could grab it quickly if she had to. It was mumbling to itself, recalling with gusto the slaughter just completed.

All three of the creatures—the Hunters, Sharina now knew to call them—were females. The one she had to move weighed as much as a heifer, but Sharina threw her weight against one of its long arms to roll it off the human corpse. Franca helped without complaint; he was stronger than he looked.

The Hunters had run a broken pike the long way through their victim for a spit. Sharina thought about the situation and decided to leave the shaft where it was.

They carried Franca's mother down into what had been the garden in Sharina's world. Debris choked it, but she'd seen a hollow where they could lay the body and mound a cairn over it. They didn't have the tools to dig even a shallow grave.

"We had to come to the city," Franca muttered, finally responding to the axe's gibe. "Hail flattened our crop and there was nothing to scavenge in Penninvale. Mother thought that maybe in Carcosa there'd be something left, because it was the first place destroyed when She came."

"We'll set her here," Sharina said, wincing as blackberry canes scratched her calves. "Who's the She you say came?"

The night noises were only half-familiar, but the Hunters had probably kept other dangers at a distance. Unless the male of the pack had been off on his own for the night. . . .

"She's God," Franca said. "She came to the world ten years ago. Now She rules everything."

"Everything is better now!" called the axe from the ruined palace above them. "Beard was scarcely alive before She came. Now there's so much more for him to drink!"

"Start covering her," Sharina said, looking around. Most of the roof tiles had poured into the garden when the palace collapsed, and there were manageably larger chunks of rubble as well. She picked up a stone barrel from one of the slim paired columns that had framed the window of her reception room.

"We heard about Her from the people fleeing Carcosa," Franca said. "Horrible monsters tearing down buildings and eating people. We didn't know what to do, so we stayed in Penninvale and for a year everything was all right. Except the winter storms were bad, very bad."

He used a pole, part of a casement, to lever files and a decade of windblown dirt over the body. The rotten wood cracked before he'd made much headway.

"The storms will get worse!" the axe called. "The storms will last longer until there's no longer a thaw and the whole world freezes. But until then there'll be plenty of blood for Beard to drink!"

"There was an early storm that fall," Franca said, lifting handfuls of debris over the corpse. He worked steadily though without enthusiasm. "Out of it came a creature bigger than three houses, all covered with armor, and a pack of Hunters. Mother and I hid in the root cellar and the monster smashed our house down over us. We couldn't see what was happening, but we heard things. And after a week we couldn't hear anything more, so we dug ourselves out.

Everyone was gone, except for the bits that the birds and foxes were eating."

Franca squatted. Sharina thought he was about to lift a larger block, but instead he put his face in his hands and resumed crying. She pivoted a length of stone transom without speaking. It was too heavy for her to lift, but when it shifted, dirt and broken tile cascaded down to cover the woman's face. It wasn't a real burial, but Sharina hoped it was enough for decency in this hellworld.

She stepped back. "May the Lady cover you with Her mantle," she whispered. "May the Shepherd guard you with His staff."

Franca looked up. "They didn't come back," he said. "There was no one left in Penninvale but mother and me, and the monsters stayed away. But we had to leave because there was no food."

"We'll stay here until dawn," Sharina said crisply. "There were some tapestries in the room where I—came here. Maybe we can dig them out for blankets. In the morning we'll go west toward . . ."

She didn't say the words, "Barca's Hamlet," from a sudden fear of what she might call down on the place that had been her home. That was superstition, ignorant foolishness; but the night was cold and she was very much alone despite Franca's helpless presence.

"May the Lady help me," she said.

"There's no point in praying to the Lady in *this* world, mistress!" trilled the axe. "And you needn't pray to Her either, for She's a God who hates Mankind. But with Beard in your hand, ah, there's an ocean of blood to drink before the ice covers us!"

Moonlight streamed through the windows of Garric's suite as the mild breeze cleared the fumes of the recently snuffed lamp. He was briefly aware of the linen sheets and the warmth of Liane beside him; then he slept and, sleeping, dreamed.

He stood in the ruins of a garden. Usually Garric was

alone in his dreams; this time Carus shared his mind as the king did all Garric's waking hours. Phlox and trillium covered the ground, crowding the fallen statue of a winged female that some architect had placed here for interest.

"*No place I've ever seen before,*" Carus muttered, his sword hand flexing. His image in Garric's mind wore a sword; but that too was only an image, an immaterial phantom like the ancient king himself.

"Nor me," said Garric. In the dream he wore the simple woolen tunic he'd gone to bed in. The air was muggy, but the stones underfoot felt cool.

At the back wall stood an altar; around it knelt a dozen or more figures. *Men,* Garric thought, but they slunk off toward the colonnades to either side, still hunched over. *Apes, then, or perhaps bears.*

Garric walked toward the altar. He wasn't sure his own mind guided his motions. Water pooled on worn flagstones and formed a marshy pond in the corner where cattails grew. Frogs trilled from the darkness, their calls punctuated by the coarsely strident shrieks of toads.

The altar was spotted with lichen and miniature forests of blooming moss; no sacrifice had been burned here in a human lifetime or longer, perhaps much longer. On it were heaps of apples, peaches, and a soft, fleshy fruit that looked vaguely like a catalpa pod, unfamiliar to Garric.

"*Bananas,*" Carus said. "*They grow them on the south coast of Shengy, but they don't travel.*"

Garric looked around. An ancient dogwood shaded the altar; its roots had forced apart the sides of the stone planter in which it grew. A stand of elderberries sprouted nearby. Was this Shengy? It seemed much like Haft, though warmer than normal for the season.

The odor of the shambling beasts hung in the air. It was musky; not unpleasant, but strange and therefore disquieting.

"*The moon's closer than it ought to be,*" Carus said. "*Or maybe it's just that the air's so thick. I've been in swamps that didn't seem so muggy.*"

On the altar top was a small ewer, perhaps a scent bottle. Originally it had been clear, but long burial in acid soil gave the glass a frosty rainbow patina. Garric touched it with his fingertip; the surface had the gritty feel he would have expected in the waking world.

Half-concealed behind the ewer was a four-sided prism the size of a man's thumb; Garric picked it up. It was so heavy that he wondered if it were metal rather than crystal, but his fingers were dimly visible through it.

When Garric looked into a flat, it returned a murky reflection of his own face. He rotated the prism slowly. For a moment he stared at an edge as sharp as a sword blade; then his life and his soul scaled off, separating him from Carus and from himself . . . and yet—

He was Garric or-Reise, son of the innkeeper of Barca's Hamlet. His sister, Sharina, was a leggy blond girl who caught the eye of a drover from Ornifal who came to the Sheep Fair; the next year, when Garric and Sharina were eighteen, the drover returned and married her. It was a good match. Sharina wrote once or twice a year, though she never returned to Haft let alone the tiny community in which Garric remained.

When Garric was twenty-three, his father Reise slipped on ice in the inn yard and cracked his head on the pump. He lingered over a month but never recovered his senses. His wife Lora died not long after, apparently pining for her husband. It was a surprise to everybody; Lora was a shrew who'd seemed to dislike Reise even more than she disliked everybody else.

At his parents' death, Garric became master of the inn. It had prospered under his father; it flourished for the stronger, more active, and far more personable Garric. That summer Garric married the daughter of a wealthy farmer on the Carcosa road, and the next spring the first of their twelve children was born.

Garric continued to read the classics. He taught his children to read and write; and if none of them became the scholar he was, they were probably better wives and farmers because they didn't have so many romantic notions confusing them.

When Garric died, full of years and honor, four generations of his descendants attended his funeral. Representatives of the Count of Haft and both priesthoods came from Carcosa, and drovers from distant islands paid their respects at his grave when they arrived for the Sheep Fair in the fall.

He was long remembered as the greatest man ever to live in Barca's Hamlet.

The prism slipped from Garric's fingers. For an instant he was back in the ruined garden; the moon was near the horizon and the eastern sky was pale enough to hide stars. Two figures, immense but unseen, hovered beyond the heavens—

Garric was awake, stifling his shout behind clenched teeth. His muscles were taut and sweat soaked his sheets.

Liane murmured and shifted in the bed. Garric would have gotten up to rinse his face in the washbasin across the room, but he was afraid to waken her. He'd have to explain his nightmare, and no words he used could convey the *horror* of what he'd just lived.

"What did they do to you, lad?" King Carus asked, a wild look in his eyes. His fists knotted and opened, dropping to his hilt and coming away again. *"Did you see them? I did. There were two of them, and they were playing me like a puppet!"*

I was innkeeper in Barca's Hamlet, Garric said in his mind. Immediately he began to relax. He wasn't alone; and even if he had been, the memory of Carus reminded Garric what a man very like him could face and had faced. *But that life couldn't have been. The forces that we've been fighting ever since I left Haft would've overwhelmed Barca's Hamlet and the rest of the Isles long before I died in bed in my old age!*

"Aye," said Carus, smiling at a grim memory. *"I commanded the bodyguard of King Carlake. He put us where it was hottest, and we never failed him. The day an arrow struck me down during the siege of Erdin, my boys went over the wall and took the city. They buried me under a pyramid of ten thousand severed heads!"*

His eyes met Garric's eyes in his mind; both men shuddered. *"Lad,"* Carus whispered. *"A thing like that could have happened. But it never did, I swear that."*

I don't remember King Carlake, Garric thought. *Was he a usurper?*

"*Carlake was the elder brother of Carilan, the King of the Isles who adopted me as his heir,*" Carus explained. "*Carlake might well have made a better king for hard times than his brother did, but the same fever carried him off as did their father and left Carilan king in his place. That world couldn't be, in* our *world.*"

Garric rolled out of bed carefully. He was calm now, able to reassure Liane if she woke, but she continued to sleep soundly.

I saw the figures you're talking about, Garric thought as he poured cool water into the tumbler on the washstand. *Felt them, at any rate. Who do you suppose they were?*

"*They're not Gods, of that I'm sure,*" Carus said. "*I don't believe in Gods, and there's enough trouble without Them meddling too!*"

I believe in the Great Gods, Garric thought as he drank greedily. *But I don't believe They were who I saw. I believe we saw something* very *different. And very evil.*

The banquet had more courses than Cashel had fingers to count them on. All the food was good and most of it was better than that, though he found often enough that he was happier if he avoided looking at stuff before he ate it.

There was wine too. Cashel had drunk ale when he and Ilna could afford it and water when they couldn't, which was often enough. He'd never had so much as a sip of wine till he left home and he hadn't much liked it when he did . . . but what Lord Bossian served was different, sparkly instead of tasting like juice that'd gone bad in the heat.

Syl and Farran pretended that Cashel wasn't at the table. They ate with their right hands only and kept their left raised at funny angles that they adjusted with each new course. Cashel supposed it meant something; to them at least, and the gestures were no more empty than their silly chatter.

Kotia talked to the others with an easy reserve. Cashel guessed she didn't have much use for Syl and Farran—he couldn't see any reason she ought to—but she was polite when she spoke to them and really friendly to Bossian.

The problem was that when Kotia said something to Cashel, Bossian puffed up like a cat when a strange dog comes into the room. She noticed it, all right, and while it didn't seem to make any difference to her, Cashel got uncomfortable. It made him want to pick Bossian up by the seat and scruff, then toss him a few times into the stream till he came to a better understanding of who he was glowering at. . . .

And that wouldn't be right, seeing as Bossian was the host here and he wasn't doing anything wrong, just sort of *oozing* the fact that he'd like to. Cashel started avoiding Kotia's eyes and concentrating on his food. And the wine, of course.

There was music playing, soft pipes and bowed strings; Cashel couldn't tell where the musicians were, but they made a lovely sound. The sky had grown dark but the palace itself glowed with light of the same color as the walls themselves: silver and rose and the pale green of drying hay. The water purling down its channel was steel blue; Cashel could see fish the length of his arm swimming in it.

He was content. Oh, soon he'd start wondering about how to get home, but Lord Bossian had said he'd take care of that. Cashel didn't figure there'd be much delay, what with the choice being to have Cashel for a guest until he did.

It felt good not to be hiking over bare rock and good to have a full belly after a day of hard work and fasting. Cashel swigged his wine and looked up at the stars, wondering if he'd be able to recognize any of the constellations tonight.

The stars began to vanish slowly from one side of the sky to the other, the way an eclipse devours the moon. Cashel blinked and rubbed his eyes with the back of his free hand, wondering if the wine had been even stronger than he thought. He felt a vibration too low to be sound; it trembled up through the chair legs and the soles of his feet, and the walls of the manor shivered with the deep throb.

Syl rose to her feet and screamed. She pointed at the blank heaven, screamed again, and fainted. Cashel lurched up to grab her, knocking over the table as he reached across it. He grabbed the diaphanous sleeve of the woman's tunic, but it tore like spiderweb and left him with wisps as she fell face first on the pavement.

Farran clutched his throat with his left hand, perhaps to choke off a scream of his own. Diners were reacting in various ways, all of them fearful. The raised terraces emptied as they fled babbling, stumbling blindly over one another and the furniture.

Kotia rose and put her hand on Cashel's shoulder, standing close to him. "The Visitor has arrived," she said. "As I'm sure you realized."

Cashel lifted the quarterstaff that he'd laid on the ground behind his chair for want of a better place. He'd been afraid servants would kick it as they attended the tables, but they'd danced around the length of hickory nervously like it was a snake with a bad temper.

"What do you want me to do, mistress?" he asked Kotia quietly.

The blankness overhead flared with azure wizardlight. The stars hadn't disappeared: they'd been hidden behind vastness, a flying mountain passing overhead. But not a mountain either, for the whorls and ridges outlined in light were as surely artificial as the crystal magnificence of Lord Bossian's manor.

The light faded, leaving an afterglow like the smell of decay. The vast darkness passed on and the stars returned. The rumble continued long after the visible cause was gone.

Only Kotia and Bossian remained in the courtyard with Cashel; the three of them and Syl, sprawled unconscious among the tangle of dishes that spilled when Cashel knocked over the table. Kotia trembled, squeezing Cashel's shoulder fiercely. Her eyes were closed, and her lips moved silently.

Bossian looked at Cashel. "Our first business must be to send you home, sir," he said. "If you'll come with me to my workroom, we'll set about the matter immediately."

Kotia's eyes opened. She stepped partly away from Cashel but left her fingertips on his arm.

"Don't you think that perhaps Master Cashel should stay, Bossian?" she said. She gestured toward the now-empty sky with her right hand. "Until we know . . . ?"

"He should not!" Bossian snapped. "Without suggesting your Master Cashel is in any sense responsible for the Visitor's arrival, I *do* insist that he's out of his time and place. That makes him a point of stress at a time when we have very little margin. Besides, if you're really grateful to him for the help he provided you, why would you wish to subject him to the Visitor's attention?"

"Look, I'm not afraid of the Visitor," Cashel said. He felt extremely uncomfortable. Given the chance to fight something instead of standing here in a conversation where so many currents flowed, he'd have fought—anything. "Just tell me what it is I ought to be doing!"

"You're right, of course," Kotia said with a crisp nod to Bossian.

She took her hand from Cashel's arm and met his eyes. She said, "Go with Lord Bossian. He'll be able to help you return if anyone can. I'll leave you here, as there's no point in me becoming involved in a business where my skills would be of no service. Good day, Master Cashel; again, my thanks for your efforts on my behalf, and my good wishes for the success of all your future affairs."

Kotia bowed stiffly, turned, and strode in the direction of the silvery building. Bossian called after her, "I told the servants to ready the suite at the top of the tower. If they haven't, pick any rooms that suit you."

Kotia didn't bother to acknowledge the comment. Cashel guessed that a girl who'd slept out in the mountains with what she could carry wouldn't be too concerned about which room of a palace best suited her.

"Come along then," Bossian said gruffly. "Master Cashel."

He gestured Cashel to stand close to him on the tiled pavement where the table had been set. Cashel obeyed, feeling his guts tighten. He supposed they were going to fly away somewhere. He didn't want to fall off, and he especially didn't want to show Bossian that it bothered him.

Instead of lifting, the circle of pavement around them dropped straight into the ground.

Duzi, was I *wrong!* Cashel thought, and he started to laugh. Streaks of deep red lighted the shaft they slid down, plenty to see Bossian's disgruntled expression by. That made Cashel laugh the harder.

He glanced up. The circle of sky became oval, then closed, so they weren't going quite straight down after all. He thought of asking Bossian how far they had to go, but it didn't matter enough to give his host the satisfaction of thinking Cashel was worried. He wasn't, after all; just curious.

The platform stopped. They didn't enter a room, they *were* in it: where the stripes of red light down the sides of the shaft had been, now there was a dimly-yellow hall of great extent. The ceiling was low enough that Cashel could almost stretch up and touch it with a fingertip, but thick trefoil columns supported it at frequent intervals.

"Come this way if you will," Bossian said, the words polite but nothing in his brusque tone suggesting he cared whether Cashel wanted to obey. The echoes were funny. They made sounds muzzy, and they went on for a very long time.

Bossian led the way around a series of columns. There were benches and tables of various sorts built into the floor. When Bossian passed close, tables lit with one or another of the pastel colors of the crystal towers. The light held until Cashel too had stepped past, then faded. On each were instruments and other items, few of them anything Cashel recognized as a part of his world.

"Here," Bossian said, gesturing to where three curved tables were spaced to form a circle with openings. They glowed the same deep red as the shaft that led down to this place. Each section was crowded with objects: books, tools, and things that might either have been sculptures or trash dug from a midden. "Stand in the center here while I speak the incantation."

He reached into the seeming litter on the nearest table and withdrew a scroll of some shining material. It opened as he lifted it.

"You can send me back?" Cashel said as he walked between two of the raised islands. From what Kotia and Bossian himself had said earlier, he hadn't thought it'd be so simple.

"No, no, not that," Bossian said in irritation as he peered at the scroll. His index finger marked his place, but the winding rods on either end curled through the roll by themselves. "If I could do that, I could send the Visitor away! I *will* provide you with the tools to go by yourself, however."

He glared, at the scroll but not because of what he saw there. "Assuming that there are such tools. As I very much hope there are."

Cashel stood where Bossian told him to. The floor was glossy black, but a many-pointed star had lighted on it. Words in the curving Old Script appeared around the margin, changing as the wizard's finger moved across his scroll.

Cashel didn't like Bossian, but he trusted the fellow to do what he said. To do the best he could, at any rate, and that was as much as you could ask. There were plenty of guys out there who'd be willing to dump a rival in a bad place because of anger and envy. Bossian wasn't like that, and it wasn't just because he was afraid of what Cashel would do to him if he failed—or what Kotia would do if he succeeded.

Not that Cashel was any kind of rival, whatever the wizard might think.

Holding the scroll in his left hand, Bossian extended his right. A wand appeared in it, its color the now-familiar red verging on black. Cashel wasn't sure whether the wand was solid or simply a brief shaft of light.

Bossian pointed at the figure surrounding Cashel and said, *"Bittalos isti bakion . . ."*

Words on the floor flared and vanished. The scroll shifted, one rod taking up its portion of the roll while the other spooled more out. Cashel heard echoes from a place vaster and less cluttered than the room in which he stood.

"Zogenes rake bakion," the wizard said as the light and sound expanded to fill Cashel's awareness. He couldn't see Bossian anymore, but there were other figures beyond the wall of light as deep as a dying coal. He wasn't sure they were human, or at least wholly human.

. . . chuch bain bakaxi . . . the throbbing redness echoed. The sound no longer seemed to have anything to do with a human throat. Cashel's skin prickled as it always did in the presence of wizardry. There was a freezing flash.

Cashel was back in the cellar, dark now save for wisps of rosy foxfire that outlined Bossian. *"Iosalile!"* he shouted.

A thread of pulsing scarlet linked the fourth finger of Cashel's left hand with the table behind which the wizard stood. "There!" Bossian cried, dropping the scroll. He thrust his wand down where the thread touched the array of objects.

The room shone with a soft yellow light that had no source Cashel could locate. The thread of light, the symbols on the floor, and all other signs of wizardry had vanished when the room brightened. He blinked and rubbed his eyes with his left hand.

Bossian reached out, but reaction to the spell he'd just worked caught him. He sagged, his outthrust arms barely able to keep him from sprawling across the table.

Cashel picked up the object the thread had indicated. It was a lump of coal the size of his fist. As the wizard's dizziness passed, his eyes focused on the coal. He glared with what looked like the same puzzlement that Cashel felt.

"What does it do?" Cashel said, handing the lump to Bossian. People in Valles heated with coal, so he knew what it was. Everybody on Haft burned wood or charcoal.

"It has a virtue," Bossian said, turning the piece as he peered at it. "Every item in this hall has been gathered by me or an ancestor of mine because of the power that our art has shown to lie in it. This particular piece was found in the tomb of a great wizard from the time before the Visitor's first arrival."

The coal was smoothly shiny top and bottom, with jags and facets on the sides. The image of a leaf that flared like a trumpet was pressed into the top. The all-directional light cast no shadow, making it hard to get a real feeling for the shape. Cashel frowned, wondering if there was anything somebody like him *could* see; maybe you had to be a wizard.

"But what does it *do*?" Cashel repeated. It was good-quality coal; gleaming black on all surfaces. There were none of the gray speckles of shale he'd seen in cheap stuff.

"To be honest . . ." Bossian said in a muted voice. He set the lump back on the tabletop. "To be honest, I haven't been able to determine that."

He gave Cashel a defensive glare. "But it *is* an object of power, and there's no question that the spell marked it out for you. Why, you saw that yourself!"

"Yes," said Cashel, "but I don't know what it means."

He took the coal again between his thumb and forefinger and looked at it without learning anything more than he had the first time. It was coal; it had a slick feel, and it was lighter than a flint of the same size.

"Well, you're the best one to determine that, sir," Bossian said. He made a gesture with his bare right hand; his wand had vanished. A pastel yellow tunnel suddenly twisted away through the vast hall, while the rest of the room went dark. "I was unable to divine the object's powers when I had leisure to try, which assuredly I do not at this time."

He gestured down the corridor of light. "The path will take you to an exit from the manor," he said.

Cashel looked at Lord Bossian, the coal in his left hand, his quarterstaff in his right. He weighed the lump in his palm, silent as he decided what to do. He didn't like Bossian's attitude, but—

Bossian grimaced. "Master Cashel," he said in a raspy voice, "if I were in a position to help you further I would do so. I am not. I suggest you leave here and work out your own destiny, while we determine ours. And I tell you with all sincerity that I wish the task facing me were as simple as the one facing you—*however* difficult it may seem to you!"

Cashel nodded. "All right, I see that," he said.

The lump was too big to fit in his wallet. He pulled out the neck of his outer tunic and dropped the coal inside; it slipped down to where the sash cinched his garments to his waist, leaving both hands free for the quarterstaff.

Nodding to Bossian, Cashel turned and started down the lighted pathway. His bare feet shuffled on the pavement; that sound was his only companion for a long time, longer than he was sure of. He was glad he'd eaten, but he wished he'd taken a round of bread with him when they left the outdoors banquet.

While Cashel was wondering, not for the first time, how long this was going to last, a stride put him abruptly out on a moonlit slope. He looked across a broad valley. Judging by the vegetation around him, it was better watered than the one where he'd met Kotia.

He turned. In the far distance was a shimmer of light. That

might be the gleaming towers of Lord Bossian's manor, or it might not.

Cashel thought for a time, leaning on his quarterstaff. Then, smiling faintly at his recollection of Kotia insisting they save the gems Kakoral had thrown down, he rummaged one out of his wallet.

Quite a lady, Kotia was . . .

He hurled the ruby into a ledge of rock.

Ilna stood stiffly upright, one hand on the tiny deckhouse as the *Bird of the Tide* eased to an empty quay. As usual on shipboard, her major concern was to keep out of the way of the sailors while they were busy. Four of the men worked the long sweeps; Kulit stood in the bow, looking straight down, and Hutena held a boat pike to push off with if necessary.

"Port side up oars!" Chalcus shouted from the tiller. "Ninon, a dab now—just a dab, laddie, and pat us in."

The harbor at Terness was tight, and the passage between lava cliffs to enter had been tighter yet. The largest vessel Ilna saw was a two-deck warship like the *Flying Fish;* the other ships were part-decked fishing boats.

"Now it may be you're wondering why I didn't sail in, dear heart, rather than stretch the lads' backs by sculling," Chalcus said in a conversational tone as they slid slowly as cold honey toward the quay on the gentle push of Ninon at the starboard bow oar. "It's the way the winds eddy and the entrance, you see, and me being a stranger to these waters. Our *Bird* is a fine, sturdy ship, but I wouldn't care to knock her against those rock walls—"

He crooked a finger back over his left shoulder, toward the harbor narrows.

"—and think of the embarrassment I'd feel with all those folk watching us, eh?"

"Yes," said Ilna, "I see those folk."

The quay was crowded with as many people as it would hold, most of them either servants with scarlet sashes as livery or soldiers in bronze caps but padded jerkins instead of metal body armor. There was a party of their betters as well, folk who thought themselves better, at any rate—a double handful of men in silk and furs and gilded metalwork. In the center of these last, wearing a silvered cuirass set with red stones that might possibly be rubies rather than lesser gems, stood a tall man with black hair and a full pepper-and-salt beard.

"Commander Lusius, as I recall," Chalcus murmured. "And there's no greater rogue unhung, unless it be myself."

Ilna stepped closer to him, reaching instinctively into her left sleeve for the hank of cords she carried there. "Will he recognize you, do you think?" she asked, her voice calm but her mind dancing over possible ways out of the situation if it turned bad.

"I think not," Chalcus said. "I was only one of Captain Mall's crew, many years ago; and when Mall's ship and crew became mine, we did no more business in the Haft trade. But if he does—"

One of Lusius's attendants blew his trumpet and the crowd cheered—halfheartedly, it seemed to Ilna. Hutena'd racked his pike by the mast; he dropped a leather fender stuffed with straw between stone and the hull while Kulit positioned a second fender at the bow. The *Bird of the Tide* thumped the quay without needing the men on shore to draw them in by the mooring ropes.

"—it'll only mean that we each know the other man."

"Captain Chalcus!" Lusius cried, standing arms-akimbo as he looked down into the *Bird*. "Welcome to Terness. I'm Lusius, and I hope you and your lovely companion will accept my hospitality while you're here."

The Commander gave Ilna a broad grin. She tented her fingers very carefully; if she hadn't, they'd have knotted a pattern that— some time in the future—she'd regret having used even on this man. Her mind recalled with satisfaction the greasy *snap* of a chicken's neck as she twisted.

Ilna smiled back at Lusius. The Commander's grin melted away.

"Well now, Commander Lusius . . ." said Chalcus nonchalantly as he fitted a rope loop over the tiller to keep the steering oar from flapping in a current. Shausga and Kulit handed hawsers to attendants on the quay who'd bend them around bollards. "The crew and I will spend our nights aboard the few days we're here fitting a new mast, but I thank you for your offer."

"But you'll dine with me tonight, surely?" Lusius said. "We flatter ourselves that we eat well on Terness, though the food may not be up to the royal banquets you're used to."

He looked around the men close about him, the sneering grin back on his face. Though Terness was a small place by any standards beyond those of Barca's Hamlet, this handful of courtiers was dressed with as much expense—if not taste—as those crowding Garric's receptions in Valles.

"Indeed," said Chalcus easily, standing in a relaxed posture. "I'm a student of the world, Commander; always pleased to meet new folk and sample new fare. What time would it be that you'd wish us to arrive?"

Lusius threw back his head and laughed, resting his left hand on the pommel of his short curved sword. Ilna had learned much about weapons since she left the borough; the Commander's was a real sword with a sturdy blade, capable of lopping off limbs with a strong man swinging it. The sword and the scar trailing down Lusius's neck proved that he hadn't been—and probably wasn't—a man who let others handle all his violence.

He fingered his beard and measured Chalcus with his eyes. "Well, then, shall we say at the eleventh hour, Captain?" he said. "The castle's at the head of Cross Street, that's the one that stretches south from Water Street here. We're simple folk in Terness, so two named streets are all we need."

Lusius turned on his heel and stalked off. His underlings must have been used to his abrupt habits for they instantly leaped aside to form a passage, then fell in behind him.

The *Bird*'s crew relaxed as the local delegation strode away. Ninon set down the short axe he'd been holding behind the mainspar. Hutena had been leaning against the mast; now he wiped on his tunic the hand that'd rested against the boarding pike he'd just racked.

Ilna began plaiting a complex pattern of cords, with no other purpose than to occupy her fingers while she thought. Lusius had a bull neck, but a noose thrown *just* so and twisted would snap it as surely as that of a chicken in the dooryard.

"They know who we are then, cap'n?" Hutena said. He looked uncomfortable speaking, but the eyes of the other men were on him; the bosun's rank meant it was up to him to ask the question that worried all of them.

"Aye, but I never expected to fool Lusius," Chalcus said, watching the last of the Commander's entourage disappear around the corner. Ilna couldn't see up Cross Street from where the *Bird* was docked, but the battlements of a structure on the hill to the south loomed over the roofs of the buildings fronting Water Street. "The only question I had was how he'd react to our arrival; and open acknowledgment of who we are isn't a bad way to react. Not a fool, our Lusius."

"But you'll take him down anyway, cap'n," Hutena said; his words neither quite a statement nor really a question.

"Oh, aye, we'll do that thing," Chalcus said cheerfully, dusting his palms together briskly. "I will; and you will, my fine lads . . ."

He turned and laid a fingertip on Ilna's cheek. "And Mistress Ilna will with her art, which I much expect will be the greatest help of all in the business!"

Chapter Eleven

Tenoctris," Garric said, facing the old wizard beneath a wicker lattice covered with grape vines, "I had a dream. Another dream."

He reached out and touched Liane's hand without meeting her eyes. This was the first she'd heard about the business also.

The roof garden was the closest thing to a private park available to Garric in Carcosa. Trees and brambles covered the mounded ruins of much of the Old Kingdom city, but those tracts were pathless and far more dangerous than a rural woodland like the one which the householders of Barca's Hamlet owned. Rats, feral dogs, and humans as degraded as those beasts lurked in holes they'd dug into ancient tombs and palaces. At night they came out to scour the streets.

Garric had always been more comfortable outside than in, whether he was doing manual labor or reading one of the Old Kingdom texts his father had taught him to love. Rather than discuss the matter in a palace room, he'd asked Tenoctris and Liane to join him in the garden. The dream had made him uncomfortable, so he was easing the process of talking about it by choosing the setting he found most congenial.

Tenoctris nodded, pursing her lips. "Did this one tell you to do something?" she asked. She opened the satchel beside her on the bench and began to finger through the books within it.

A tree frog screamed from somewhere within the grape leaves; rain had fallen just before the dawn, making the frogs active. Garric marveled once again that a gray-green lump no bigger than the first joint of his thumb could make so much noise.

"No, nothing like that," he said. "I was standing in a garden. There was an altar and some offerings on it. I picked up a crystal and . . . saw, I *lived;* I don't know how to explain it. I lived a life that somebody like me might have lived if things had been different. Had been normal."

"A nightmare?" Liane asked, folding her hands in her lap. What he'd said had worried her, so in response she was acting more than usually calm.

"No," Garric said, shaking his head. "Normal life. Taking over the inn, marrying a perfectly nice local girl—"

He grinned wryly; Liane loosened up enough to grin back.

"—and raising a lot of children. If the dream was right, I'd have made a better innkeeper than I do a prince."

"Then the dream was wrong," Tenoctris said calmly, "though I'm sure you'd have been a fine innkeeper as well. Did you recognize the garden, Garric? From other dreams or in the waking world, either one?"

"It could've been here, it could've been in Valles," he said. "Or somewhere that I've never seen at all. It was old and overgrown; there were bananas on an altar, and I thought that the things I saw worshiping were animals instead of men."

He rubbed his eyes, working to recall images that his mind had tried to shut out while he was dreaming. "I'm not sure what they were. I'm not even sure there were real figures instead of just shadows."

Tenoctris closed her satchel again. "I see," she said, getting cautiously to her feet. "I'll admit that this puzzles me, Garric. I'm certain that nobody is working an incantation against you now."

Liane frowned in disbelief; Garric frowned also, but he realized he hadn't felt threatened as he stood in the garden. It was wrong, and it'd disturbed him because he knew how wrong it was, but—

A world where he didn't have the responsibilities of a prince was attractive, even though that world didn't have Liane in it either. *That* thought was the real reason the dream made Garric so angry.

"Oh, yes," Tenoctris repeated. "Quite certain."

She shrugged. "I might well not be able to do anything about an attack," she explained, "but I'd know it was happening. Nothing of the sort is, not through wizardry, that is."

Garric stood, clearing his throat in embarrassment. "I thought I ought to tell somebody about it," he said, "because I didn't the other time. And that one meant something."

"Oh, this dream means something too," Tenoctris said with crisp assurance. "I certainly don't think it's a coincidence, Garric; I just don't believe it was an attack on you or even directed at you . . . which is particularly puzzling."

She smiled again, then went on, "Lord Attaper's been kind enough to provide me with an escort to the Temple of the Lady of the Sunset. I'm told there's an extensive library there. If it doesn't hold the information that I'm searching for either, perhaps there'll be something in the Temple of the Shepherd of the Rock."

"Yes, there may be," Garric said. Liane had risen from the bench beside him; he put his arm around her and hugged her close while still grinning at Tenoctris. "I have some business with the priests of the Shepherd today too. I do, and the army does!"

When Sharina was twelve, she'd seen the Northern Lights in the depths of the coldest winter in the living memory of Barca's Hamlet. At first she'd thought that was what she was seeing now, but the sheets of azure and crimson flared too constantly across the heavens for that.

"Is it always like this at night?" she asked Franca as she added wood to the fire he'd lit with the bow drill he'd made. "The sky, I mean. There's no moon, but it's bright enough to read by."

"The sky?" the youth repeated. "Yeah, it's always like this."

He frowned. "Maybe it wasn't when I was younger, though. Mother used to talk about the stars. I remember seeing them, but not for a long time."

Franca wasn't any better clothed than she was, but he'd apparently become acclimated to the cold. Though he said it was late spring, the wind skirling through the walls of the dry-stone sheep byre seemed as bitter as anything Sharina had felt at the turn of the year at home.

"She makes it this way," said the axe. "Her power lights the whole world, but She drains away all warmth to do it."

He giggled; the sound was like hearing slates rub. The hairs on the back of Sharina's neck stood up.

"One day the ice will have everything," the axe said, "and even the sky will be cold. But until then Beard will drink, won't he, mistress? You'll feed Beard, and Beard will make sure that you eat too, just like today. Until the very end."

Sharina laid another dead limb on the fire. She was afraid to go to sleep, even though she was bone tired. They were burning pieces of trees, which the cold had shattered. Though the wood blazed up easily, the fuel had sunk to a pile of ash after what seemed only moments instead of forming a bed of glowing coals; freezing seemed to have robbed it of all its virtue.

They'd found food on the way: a store of hickory nuts dug

from the trunk of a hollow tree, and the small animals that Beard had sensed cowering in holes. The axe could see through hard soil; with its help Sharina and Franca had blocked exits, then used rusty spearbutts from the Hunters' hoard to dig out victims.

The war axe was a clumsy tool for dispatching a rabbit, let alone a vole, but blood was the price Beard charged for his aid. Sharina couldn't object: without the fresh rabbit skins covering her feet, they'd have frozen before now.

"How much farther do we have to go, Sharina?" Franca asked diffidently. He was older than she was, but he gave her the feeling of being the same child he was when She arrived.

Sometimes Sharina thought her companion was stupid—a half-wit, even—but then he'd surprise her with his observations. Franca had identified the nut store and shinned up to the high entrance like a squirrel himself. Like the world he lived in, Franca had been blighted by Her coming; but there was good left in both of them.

"I've only made this trip once," Sharina said. She smiled; she was very weary, but memory of those spring days with friends warmed her in this cold, friendless place. "That was in the other direction, and anyway, what was true in my world may not be in yours."

Though it certainly seemed to be. Except for Her.

"But I think we should be very close by now, if things *are* the same," she said. "I thought of going on tonight, but I decided it was better to arrive by daylight to see . . ."

To see what? Sharina was afraid of what she might find, but there was no better, no *other,* place from which to start her search for friends in this world. She expected to get bad news when she reached what had been her home, but she preferred to know the worst rather than have an unformed fear looming over her as a bleak, black weight for the rest of her life.

"We never left Penninvale," Franca said. "Till we had to. We shouldn't have left then."

He seemed to have spoken without emotion, but tears began to dribble down his cheeks again. Sharina cleared her throat; she wasn't sure whether to respond or not. At last she said, "I'm hoping that we'll find people in Barca's Hamlet. People I knew in my world."

And what if one of them were Sharina os-Reise? What would that be like? Or Cashel; would he *be* Cashel in this world?

"There's nobody left," Franca said, blubbering openly now. "Nobody in all the world except us and the monsters. Mother, we should have stayed!"

"There's a sound . . ." Sharina said. *It's just the wind,* she thought; but if she'd really thought that she wouldn't have spoken.

"Oh, Mother, Mother—"

"Be silent!" Sharina said, rising to her feet with Beard balanced in front of her body. The walls of the byre were better shelter than she'd realized until she took the buffeting unprotected. The sound could be wind after all, or—

"It's a man and he's trapped!" said the axe. "Oh, he needs help, mistress! He'll surely die if we don't help him!"

"Which way?" said Sharina, squinting against the east wind. She couldn't judge the direction of the cries, let alone the distance. It they'd been blown down on the wind, the fellow might be a mile or more distant.

"The way we've been going!" Beard said. "Not far, mistress, and he needs us badly!"

"Come along, Franca!" Sharina called. She might need an extra pair of hands, especially if the fellow they were going to rescue had been injured in a fall. She thought of herself in the ruined palace; if the walls had collapsed while she was still inside, she might have died in a worse way even than the Hunters had intended for her.

"Don't leave me!" Franca wailed as he staggered to his feet.

Sharina didn't wait for him. Wizardlight pulsing across the heavens gave better illumination than a full moon, so she had no trouble following the path through the woods. It hadn't been used recently, but the encroaching undergrowth didn't keep Sharina from running.

She came out of the trees onto a slope that was still clear. She saw the mill, roofless now, and the inn where she'd grown up; the walls had fallen in and brambles grew from piles of fire-blackened bricks.

Sharina'd found Barca's Hamlet. It was what she'd expected, but she'd prayed in her heart to the Lady that this time she'd be wrong.

The cries were coming from the ruined mill. A male voice cursed and begged the Shepherd's aid, the sort of foolish mixture that desperation dragged from the throats of ordinary people. He didn't sound as though he really expected help to come.

"He's in that stone building!" Beard said. "But be ready, mistress, for you'll need me to—"

The mill pond stored water from high tides and released it to drive the wheel at a measured pace. It was the oldest building in Barca's Hamlet, built in the Old Kingdom of stones so hard and well-fitted that they'd withstood well over a thousand years of weather. During all that time it had continued to serve the surrounding borough at a handsome profit for generations of millers.

The side door, a hundred feet from Sharina, was double height and wide enough for a wagonload of grain to be driven into the milling chamber. The bear that came through that doorway wouldn't have fit anything sized merely for humans. Franca's scream diminished as he turned and ran.

"Blood for Beard to drink!" the axe cried. "Blood for Beard!"

At the Sheep Fairs there was often a peddler from Shengy with a cinnamon-colored bear. When it stood upright to shuffle in a slow dance, it was as tall as a man.

The rangy animal now padding out of the mill was that tall at the shoulder; it must have weighed more than a large ox. It saw Sharina, *whuff*ed, and launched itself at her with no more hesitation than a stooping hawk.

"Blood for—" the axe called.

There wasn't time to think. Five feet short of its victim, the bear lifted its right forepaw for a crushing blow. Sharina stepped within the bear's reach and brought the axe down in an overhand blow. The blade crunched through bone, burying itself to the helve in the bear's broad, flat forehead.

The bear reared onto its hind legs, lifting Sharina until her hands slipped from the shaft and she cartwheeled sideways. *Will it dance now?* she thought hysterically. She was screaming with laughter when she slammed onto the hard ground. Her shoulder went numb, and the world around her had a fuzzy haze as though gray mold grew on everything.

The bear voided its bowels in a gush of liquescent feces. The stench was choking. It toppled slowly forward, then hit like a building collapsing. The ground shook. Except for the initial grunt when the bear saw what it thought was prey, it hadn't made a sound.

The man was still calling from the mill; he didn't realize he was free now.

Sharina could also hear Beard's gurgling joy, muffled by the skull it had split.

The castle was both older and more substantial than Ilna had expected to find in a village on the fringes of the kingdom. Though the two- and three-story buildings that housed Lusius's troops and their families were new, the core of the complex was lichen-covered gray stone that must have been as old as the mill where Ilna lived in Barca's Hamlet.

"An Old Kingdom watchtower," Chalcus said, noticing Ilna's surprise. "Used as a fisherman's hut most of the time since then, I shouldn't wonder, but it seems our Lusius has put it back in shape. A dozen men could hold off an army, as long as they had food."

He grinned at her. "The right dozen men, mind," he added. "But that's true of any fight, isn't it?"

"It's true of more than fights," Ilna said. "Unless to you all life is a fight, and I don't know that I'd argue with that notion."

Chalcus laughed merrily, but the touch of his hand on hers was more than mere whim. "Not everything's a fight, dear heart," he said. "I must learn to save my strength for the times it's needed."

He meant *she* must learn. Well, both of them should; Ilna didn't doubt the truth of that. It seemed very unlikely that she'd ever succeed, however.

The pair of trumpeters stood on the tower battlements, high enough that four levels of arrow slits pierced the stone below them. Their fanfare was slightly out of tune and time with one another. Ilna didn't take a great deal of pleasure in music, but she had no difficulty in telling good from bad. Most was bad, of course, just as with every other form of human activity. These trumpeters fit in quite well with her expectations.

The soldiers who'd met the *Bird of the Tide* on the quay were now drawn up in a double line framing the walk to one of the new buildings rather than the stone tower. When their officer snarled a command, they thumped the butts of their spears into the ground and shouted, "Hail, Captain Chalcus! Hail, Ilna os-Kenset!"

Ilna's face set. She disliked pomp at any time. Here it was obvious besides that their host was toying with them, pretending deference to the high rank he knew they held.

The humor struck her. She chuckled, drawing a glance and a raised eyebrow from Chalcus.

"You said Lusius wasn't a fool," she explained under her breath. "You were wrong: only a fool would mock us if he knew who we were, you and I."

Chalcus laughed again. "True enough, dear heart," he said. "But there's knowing and *knowing*, you see."

They walked side by side through the double rank of soldiers—the Sea Guards, Hutena said they were called. Wealthy drovers and merchants attending the Sheep Fair generally had bodyguards, so even before Ilna left Barca's Hamlet she'd seen a variety of men who made their living by arms. These Guards were a sorry lot despite being turned out with plumes on their helmets for the occasion. Most of them were out of condition; they were dirty, and some of them were already drunk.

The tall doors were open. The building was a single large hall, set now for a banquet. The walls were hung with tapestries which'd been chosen for gaudiness rather than quality. They were of very high quality nonetheless, but Ilna found them an odd mixture. There were hangings from Sandrakkan, Ornifal, red silk from Seres, and a large panel from Pare where they wove goat hair into geometric designs.

Lusius and his aides, a few more than a handful, stood on both sides of a table at the short end opposite the entrance; the two places opposite Lusius remained open. The benches down either long side were for the soldiers; they tramped in after the guests. Servants waited with drink pitchers and handbarrows loaded with food.

"Come in, my honored guests!" Lusius cried. "I greet you not only in my own name but in that of Prince Garric of Haft, whose loyal servant I am!"

Ilna thought of how easily she could kill this smirking man; kill him or better yet knot a pattern that would show him his own soul—thereby causing him to kill himself in horror and despair. She smiled, cheerful and assured.

Chalcus gave his sash a little hitch that settled the sword and dagger held in its folds. For the occasion he wore a short woolen outer tunic of Ilna's own workmanship. From a distance it looked plain, but there was a subtle pattern to the threads that distracted an eye trying to focus on it. It wouldn't protect Chalcus from a chance arrow or a thrust in darkness, but it was the best gift Ilna knew to give to a man like her man.

His inner tunic was orange silk, cut a little longer and higher than the wool one; it matched his sash and the twist of silk about his temples perfectly. His sandals were gilded leather cutwork, a trifle larger than a perfect fit. Ilna knew that if there was trouble Chalcus would kick off his footgear and fight in his bare feet just as he worked on shipboard, but they looked festive.

Ilna's only concession to the occasion was to wear an outer tunic over the woolen undergarment, which would suffice alone on shipboard or in a rural village. The unadorned garments were clean and of the finest craftsmanship—her own. In place of a belt or sash she wore a loosely gathered silken rope that doubled as a noose when she needed one. Because of the cobblestone streets she wore shoes, though she'd have preferred to be barefoot in this warm weather.

Chalcus offered Ilna his elbow for her hand; together they walked to the seats prepared for them—her primly, Chalcus with a swagger. "I'm honored indeed to be the guest of great men like yourself and Prince Garric," he said. "But do you deal in so openhanded a fashion with all your visitors, Commander?"

Lusius snorted. He gave a little wave of his hand; his

courtiers and troops seated themselves with a scuffling of chairs and—for the common soldiers—benches, as Lusius sat down himself. The only people still standing were his guests and the red-robed figure to his right where Ilna had expected to see the Commander's consort.

Her eyes narrowed as she and Chalcus sat as well. She was the only female in the hall, though there'd been women and children in the usual numbers in the dirt plaza in front of the soldiers' quarters. The women were slatterns and their offspring screaming brats; fit companions for men of the quality of the Sea Guards, she supposed.

The figure in red threw back the cowl of his robes. "I am Gaur, the Red Wizard!" he said, making the words sound like a prayer. He wore silk brocade woven in a flame pattern by someone with a great deal of skill. The garments had been embroidered much less ably with gold and silver thread; Ilna supposed the symbols had meaning—very likely were words of power—but they seemed an afterthought.

Gaur was taller than Garric who'd been the tallest man in Barca's Hamlet once he got his growth. He had wiry black hair and black eyebrows that nearly met on his beetling forehead. He looked rangy and powerful, but the whole ensemble was so clearly intended to impress the ignorant that looking at him made Ilna's lips curl in a sneer.

"And I'm Chalcus, the captain of the *Bird of the Tide,* sir," Chalcus said cheerfully. Leaning back in his chair he went on to Lusius, "So, Commander—you provide entertainment with your banquets, eh?"

Ilna took cords from her left sleeve and had started plaiting them before anyone else understood just how calculated had been the insult Chalcus delivered in his pleasant voice. Lusius had been drinking from his embossed gold cup, watching Chalcus over the rim. His eyes opened. He snorted, spraying wine from his nostrils, and doubled over in a coughing fit.

Gaur's hands moved as though he was holding a globe in front of him. "One day, Captain," he said to Chalcus in a grating voice, not loud, "you and I will entertain each other. We will see who laughs the louder then. *Eh?*"

Ilna saw Gaur's tongue move, but she wasn't sure he was speaking further. Images formed in the air between his hands. *Chalcus ran naked across a barren plain. Things came out of the darkness at him, never quite to be glimpsed even when they struck. Each tore away a strip of flesh. Chalcus continued to run, but he was stumbling . . .*

Chalcus laughed. "A good one!" he said. "A touch on me indeed, Master Wizard. Now, Commander—may I hope that your hospitality to your guests extends to the wine I see on your side of the table?"

Gaur sat heavily. Ilna eyed him for a further moment, then put her cords away. The exchange was over—for now. Servants were filling her goblet and Chalcus's with an expensive perfumed wine from Cordin. Ilna didn't like the vintage, but it showed that Lusius wasn't stinting his guests with second-rate drinks.

Gaur was a braggart, a type of person that Ilna found offensive even when she had no better reason to dislike someone; in Gaur's case she was fairly certain that she'd have no trouble in finding better reason. What he had done, however—without preparation or tools—was a remarkable piece of wizardry. Whatever else the Red Wizard might be, he *was* a wizard.

"You ask about visitors here, Captain," Lusius said as servants set fish soup in front of the diners. "We have very few, as the ships in the Carcosa trade are too large to enter Terness harbor. It's a good shelter for those of us who struggle against the flying demons, though. Have you heard of the Rua?"

The man to Ilna's left seized his bowl and drank the contents down. Under other circumstances Ilna might have done the same, but out of pride she ate her soup with the spoon of silver and alabaster that she'd been offered. It was scarcely a point of pride to show that she was more refined than this lot, she thought with a grim smile.

"Indeed we have, Commander," Chalcus said. He'd sopped a torn chunk of rye bread in his bowl and was eating it that way. "Saw them as well, on the horizon as we came up on Terness. Odd creatures, to be sure, but I wonder . . . ?"

He paused, chewing his mouthful as his laughing eyes held Lusius.

"Though they're big for anything flying, these Rua," Chalcus continued, "I wonder that they'd prey on ships so large and well-manned as those that've been their victims. The pirates of the Southern Seas are terrible indeed, they tell me; but they'd never attempt ships the size of those the Rua take. Eh?"

"They're wizards," said Gaur in his grating voice. He'd recovered enough to sit upright, though he wasn't eating. Before him on the table was an agate tureen, silver mounted and covered with a lid polished from the same block of stone. "I struggle, but I am one and the Rua are many hundreds."

The Rua might very well be wizards; they'd arrived here by some means and wizardry was as likely a cause as any other. Ilna doubted the story about them looting the ships, or at any rate doubted that was the whole truth, simply because Gaur had said it. Liars sometimes tell the truth, just as occasionally a stage magician tricked out in red robes could show himself to be a powerful wizard, but she had a bias against believing it.

The food kept coming: a fruit compote; mutton roast; a dish of rice with raisins and ginger. Ilna began to peck at dishes instead of cleaning them, then began to wave courses off untouched. The offerings generally tasted good though unfamiliar—even the fish soup had been remarkably spicy—but there was far too much for a sensible person to eat.

And drink. There were various vintages, some of them doubtless stronger than others, but the total would fill a cauldron big enough to wash the garments of everyone in the hall. Ilna sniffed: if the castle *had* a washing cauldron, it was cobwebbed from disuse.

Ilna asked a servant for beer; he went off—even the servants were male—and returned not long after with a quite passable lager. She nursed her goblet, but even so they were long at the table. The last thing *she* needed to do was to drink enough that she lost control of her behavior.

Chalcus was drinking his share. In the middle of a story about a storm blowing him south so far that he saw icebergs like those that split from the glaciers of the far north, he began to sing, *"The cuckoo, she's a happy bird, she sings as she flies . . ."*

He was probably putting on a show for their hosts, but again—quite a lot of wine had gone down his gullet. Well, Chalcus knew how to take care of himself, drunk or sober, and he had the scars to prove it.

"So, Captain Chalcus . . ." Lusius said. He drank, belched heavily, and banged down his empty goblet. "Have you space in your holds for additional cargo, do you think? We here in the Calves do a fine business in the shell fisheries these last few years."

"She brings us glad tidings, and she tells us no lies," Chalcus sang, completing the stanza and raising his cup to drink. He blinked in apparent surprise to find it empty.

Setting it down he said, "Oh, we've no cargo to speak of, but no need for more than we've got. One chest is all, folderol for one of the lords who's the prince's bosom companion, Tadai his name is. He didn't tell me what was in it, just said it was to go to Chancellor Royhas in Valles. I'm being well-paid for the voyage, so I asked no questions."

A servant filled his cup with wine. As the fellow took the pitcher away, Chalcus drank deeply again.

"Now, I shouldn't've have said that, I know," he went on through a giggle. "I shouldn't be here at all, but our mast is sprung. I need to step a new one before I try the Inner Sea all the way to Ornifal, for all that the worst of the weather should be past by this season. You can't trust the weather, you know."

He tapped the side of his nose with an index finger. "No farther than you can trust men!"

"You're not afraid of the Rua, then?" Lusius said, leaning forward with his elbows on the table.

"Poof!" said Chalcus. "What do I care about some funny-shaped bats? We've bows on the *Bird of the Tide* and men who know how to use them. If these Rua of yours come too close, they'll find they're sprouting goose feathers!"

"Indeed," Lusius said, "indeed. I'm sure that's just what will happen, Captain—but if you have a day or two, would you care to come out with me to the reefs where we fish for shell? I'll be there in my vessel, the *Defender,* because the fishermen daren't to go without my protection. And even so it can be a tricky business, as you'll see."

"I'll be honored to join you, Commander!" Chalcus said. "I and Mistress Ilna, if you don't mind. Sometimes her eyes catch things that mine have not."

"She's welcome, of course," Lusius said. "The *Defender*'s no royal barge, but then, I don't suppose your *Bird* is that either."

Ilna had listened to the exchange with a frown she didn't attempt to conceal. If Chalcus was blabbering for a purpose, her concern was in character; and if he wasn't, if it was the wine talking—then all the better reason to frown.

Gaur had remained silent for most of the meal, glowering at a corner of the vaulted ceiling as though in deep meditation. Now, seeming to awake, he gestured imperiously to a servant and snapped his fingers. The servant brought a canister of gold filigree from a sideboard and set it before the wizard, next to the covered bowl that had been there throughout the dinner.

All eyes were on the Red Wizard, as he no doubt had intended. Ilna heard the man seated next to her curse under his breath and gulp down the rest of his wine.

"Our visitors will have noticed that I myself did not eat," Gaur said, his voice again that of a priest declaiming to an audience of laymen. He lifted the cover from the agate tureen; it was filled to midway with an amber fluid. "I never eat in the presence of others, but in the name of fellowship I like to *feed,* shall we say? Would you care to watch?"

"I'm always ready to be entertained, Master Wizard," Chalcus said in a light tone. He touched his fingertips to the table before him, then lowered his hands to his sash.

Gaur glared at him. His eyes were a black that looked deep red in the lamplight. He twisted off the lid of the filigree container and reached in with thumb and forefinger. "These are flies," he said. "I've pulled off one wing already."

"Ah, every man should have a hobby," Chalcus said brightly. "I knew a fellow once who collected butterflies, so he did."

Gaur's rage couldn't have been fiercer if his eyes had filled with molten lava. He held a fly above the agate bowl. Other flies were beginning to crawl out of the open container, though of course they couldn't go far.

"Watch!" Gaur thundered, dropping the mutilated insect. It twisted on one buzzing wing as it fell into the bowl. The fluid rose to catch it, snatching down the victim while it was still a finger's breadth above the original surface. The fly disintegrated as it sank, leaving a blood-red blotch in the amber. After a few moments the color dissipated.

"Amusing, isn't it?" said Gaur, pinching another fly out of the canister. "They must be alive, you see. My little pet may look like a bowl of water, but it's only interested in living prey."

He dropped the second fly.

Even Ilna who was sober or nearly so saw Chalcus's movement only as a blur. His right hand came up from his sash with the curved dagger and swept across the table. Lamplight turned the steel edge into a shimmer of gold. The stroke was past before anyone else moved.

He slid the blade back into its scabbard.

Gaur snarled like a beast and leaped backward, knocking over his chair. "*Ha!*" Lusius shouted. He flung down the cup in his right hand and covered his eyes with his left forearm, as if he couldn't be hurt if he didn't see the threat.

There were two tiny splashes in the liquid: Chalcus had cut the fly in half as it fell. The portions sank to the bottom of the bowl: as the wizard had claimed, the living fluid ate only live food.

Chalcus stood with an easy motion; Ilna rose with him, her fingers knotting a pattern swiftly.

"My pardon, Commander," Chalcus said. "I fear I've drunk so much that I might become discourteous were I to stay. We'll join you in the morning for a visit to the reefs to see the Rua."

He offered Ilna his arm; they turned and walked out. The soldiers were babbling at increasing volume, but through that Ilna continued to hear the sound of Gaur's bestial snarls.

Cashel threw the jewel against the slab of bare rock behind him; it should've been the mouth of the tunnel by which he'd left Lord Bossian's manor, but by starlight at least it looked as much a part of the mountainside as any other. A stunted cedar tree had draped surface roots across one side of it.

This ruby shattered with the same silent flare as the first one. A tiny image of Kakoral scurried up, then down the rock face like it was a horizontal tabletop. Finally the homunculus paused and glared at Cashel.

"I want to go back to my—" Cashel began. He almost said *home,* but he didn't really know where that was anymore. "I want to go back to my friends. Point me the way."

Still without speaking, the sparkling homunculus made the sweeping introductory gesture of a showman. The shadowed rock became transparent, a window onto the cellar in which Cashel had seen Kotia's mother with her demon lover. Laterna sat on a stool, reading from a thin beechwood plate that she held so that the light of the hearth fell on it. She was alone until the door behind her opened.

Laterna turned to glance over her shoulder. Her face had the look of an ivory carving; it became even harder, even colder.

The man who'd entered was small and trim, fit-looking rather than muscular. His flowing robes had vertical stripes of white alternating with many colors. In the dark cellar the white gave off light, illuminating both the man and his immediate surroundings.

As before, Cashel watched a silent pantomime. The man gestured curtly toward the door with his left hand. He was as angry as the woman, and far more busily so. Laterna flicked out the fingers of her free hand as if she were shooing a fly. She returned to her reading.

The man's robes darkened. If her face had been ivory, his was a waxen death mask. He stepped forward, raising his right arm. He'd been holding a narrow-bladed ice axe along his thigh. He brought it down, spike forward.

Laterna leaped from her stool, flinging the beechwood plaque in the air. It bounced off the ceiling and spun back to lie facedown on the black tile floor. A corner had chipped, but the sheet was mostly whole. Its back was decorated with a gilt sun in the center and a symbolic figure in each corner.

The woman tripped and fell forward. Her arms and legs

jerked, the left side at a quicker tempo than the right. The axe handle waggled for a moment like a pigtail. The body arched, then lay flaccid.

The man hadn't moved since he struck Laterna. Now he raised both hands to his face and stroked his eyebrows with his fingertips. As he started forward, Cashel's window onto the past began to fade.

The last thing Cashel saw before rock replaced the images was the hearth that Laterna had been reading in front of. In its glowing embers, he saw the outlines of Kakoral's face.

The homunculus bowed mockingly to Cashel. It held up both hands, then brought them together overhead in a soundless clap. Streams of red wizardlight curled from each fingertip, spreading into a net that converged on Cashel's chest.

With a cackle of laughter, the little creature vanished. Wizardlight continued to play across Cashel's—

Oh. Not his chest. The lump of coal blazed with cold scarlet light to which the close-woven wool was transparent. Cautiously Cashel reached down the throat of his tunic and brought the coal out. He sat on his haunches, examining it with a care he hadn't taken in Lord Bossian's workroom. The wizardlight slowly faded.

Like any other piece of coal, this one had fracture lines. Even if it'd been whole while it lay in the ground, the process of smashing chunks out of the seam would've twisted it, spreading tiny cracks from where a leaf stem or a grain of sand had been trapped in the mass.

Cashel saw the patterns with great clarity despite having no light but that of the unfamiliar stars. Maybe there was a map? Or . . .

He squeezed with his thumb and forefinger at opposite corners of the irregular lump. Another man would have used a hammer, but steady pressure was enough if you saw the fracture lines as he did, clear as furrows in a fresh-plowed field; and if you were strong enough.

Cashel had always been strong enough.

The lump popped faintly, shearing along a seam too fine for human eyes. Cashel lifted the upper half, holding the lower portion in the palm of his left hand. Inside was a cavity not much bigger than a walnut. Something stirred in it;

then, very carefully it extended a long hind leg and splayed its webbed toes.

There was a toad within the block of coal. It was still alive.

The toad turned its head, looking up at Cashel with one eye, then the other. It drew its outstretched leg back under it.

"It must have been a very long time," the toad said in a rusty voice. "Tell me—who is the King of Kish in this day?"

Chapter Twelve

Commander Lusius's *Defender* was similar enough to the *Flying Fish* that they might have been built in adjacent slips. Ilna hadn't liked traveling on the *Flying Fish,* but it was as clean as you could expect of a wooden box that carried so many men.

The *Defender* was stinkingly filthy. Even Freya, the wife of Ilna's uncle and as lazy a slattern as ever was born, would have said the ship was disgusting.

Ilna smiled faintly. It would've been embarrassing if a man she disliked as much as she did Lusius turned out to share her passion for cleanliness. Not that she'd foreseen much danger of that.

A seawolf was following close astern. It was a big brute, twice the length of a tall man. It swam with lazy sweeps of its tail, back and forth.

Chalcus chatted in the stern with Lusius as one man to another. As one pirate to another, very possibly, so Ilna had made her way to the far bow where her presence wouldn't constrain the discussions. Like her, Chalcus was gathering information that would fit into a pattern—eventually.

Besides, standing in the bow meant she breathed the sea air instead of the *Defender*'s stench.

The fishing fleet was in sight, many handfuls of boats whose crews were a few men apiece. Though they were no more than half the size of the *Bird of the Tide,* they had small central cabins; a skiff was tied to the stern of each one. The crews groped over the sides with long poles.

The Sea Guards rowed the *Defender,* cursing, sweating, and fouling one another, but moving the vessel forward nonetheless. Most people weren't very good at their jobs; Ilna wasn't surprised to find that was true of oarsmen as surely as it was plowmen or weavers. It was neither accident nor charity that caused other women to bring the yarn they'd spun to Ilna, who did the weaving for all Barca's Hamlet. For the most part people arranged things so that a lot of them did the same thing. That way it got done well enough that everybody survived; more or less, and for a time.

A crack crew of men chosen and trained by Chalcus could do much better than these Sea Guards managed, but they were good *enough.* There was only one Chalcus; and one Ilna, for that matter.

And one Prince Garric, Ilna was quite sure. They each had their place in the pattern Someone was weaving.

"The shallows are just ahead!" cried the lookout clinging to the masthead. Neither the spar nor the sail were aboard, but the *Defender*'s mast was stepped to provide a vantage point. Lusius hadn't bothered to fit a platform, though. The sailor shinnied up unaided and clung to the stay rope with his legs wrapped around the pole. "We're entering the shallows!"

Chalcus and the Commander walked forward, Lusius in the lead because there wasn't room enough for two to walk abreast on the catwalk between the oar benches. He carried a light buckler in his left hand.

"The Commander says that the bottom rose into these shallows when the Rua appeared for the first time," Chalcus called cheerfully, indicating the water with a wave of his hand. "I've seen such a shade only once, in a lagoon far to the south."

The railing didn't extend to the far bow; Ilna touched a forestay and leaned over. Though clear, the sea had a violet cast and seemed to be no deeper than the height of a tall man. Pinkish sea lilies waved their jointed tentacles; holes for the breathing tubes of clams pocked the sand covering most of the bottom. She saw no fish.

"It doesn't look like the water I saw on the way north

from Donelle," Ilna said, speaking for the sake of politeness rather than because she thought she had any useful knowledge to add. "I've never seen plants like these either."

"Plants?" repeated Lusius. "Not a one of them, mistress! All these are animals, whatever they look like."

Rincip, the one-eyed man who commanded the Sea Guards and acted as Lusius's chief lieutenant, snarled an order from the stern. Ilna couldn't understand the words, but the crew seemed to. The rowers of the upper bank brought their oars aboard and began arming themselves with weapons stored under the walkway. Most of them strung bows, short but stiff-looking.

"I've got Guards aboard the fishing boats too," Lusius said, "but they're not much use—as you'll see, I shouldn't wonder. Sometimes they'll keep the Rua away till the *Defender* can come up, but mostly they're just there to make sure the men are really bringing up the shell. The bloody cowards are afraid that if they make a good haul, they'll be attacked!"

The *Defender* continued toward the fishing boats, driven by the lower bank of oarsmen. Though they were obviously trying to keep together, the boats had drifted some ways apart. A man couldn't shout from one side of the straggle and be understood on the other.

"What happens if the Rua attack before the *Defender* joins the fishing fleet?" Chalcus asked, his voice a little flatter than usual. He and Ilna had expected to go out at first light when the fishing fleet did, but the warship wasn't ready till mid-morning. If Chalcus hadn't been careful, his tone would've held a sneer for the indiscipline of the Commander's force.

"Oh, they never do that," Lusius said, scanning the heavens. "They've no reason to attack till the boats have a good load of shell, so we sleep in ourselves."

The sea had become even shallower than when Chalcus called Ilna's attention to it, and the bottom now was coral. She still didn't see fish, but there were any number of odd-looking creatures both crawling and attached to the rock. Among them were the little belemnites, walking on clumps of tentacles and dragging their brilliant shells behind.

The reason that patrol vessels wobbled so unpleasantly was that they drew very little water, but even so Ilna wondered if the *Defender* would grind a hole in her hull on the coral. As shallow as this was she could probably stand on the bottom and breathe even though she couldn't swim, but it would be a very long walk to dry land.

"I'd thought your Red Wizard might be with us today," Chalcus said, blocking the sun with his left hand as he surveyed the upper sky. "Struggling with the wizard-demons as he assures us he does."

The Commander looked at him sharply, though there'd been nothing of open mockery in Chalcus's tone. "Gaur has his sanctum in the castle," he said, still frowning slightly. "He works there. Never fear, he's doing whatever he can."

"When do the—" Ilna said, but she swallowed the remainder of the sentence "—Rua arrive." She suddenly understood what the dots Chalcus was watching really were. "I see," she corrected herself. "The Rua have been here all along."

"Aye, the devils!" Lusius said with real venom in his voice. "They pick their time too. They must have eyes like hawks!"

The *Defender* passed within a stone's throw of a fishing boat, close enough that Ilna got a good look at what they were doing. Two men used small nets on the end of poles to scoop belemnites out of the coral. The little shellfish didn't move fast enough to evade the nets, but they were still hard to winkle out from between the coral and hard-shelled anemones. When a fisherman succeeded, he whisked the belemnite aboard and dropped it into a large wickerwork basket in front of the deckhouse.

The third man in the boat was a Sea Guard with a strung bow and three arrows stuck through his sash. He watched with a morose expression as the *Defender* sloshed past.

Now that Ilna had recognized the dots in the high heaven as winged men circling, it was she who noticed when their motion shifted. "Something's changed!" she said. "The Rua are diving, or . . ."

The Rua dipped, then rose instead of plunging down on the fishing fleet. They'd modified their ceaseless circling, but that didn't mean they were attacking.

"They're dropping something!" Chalcus cried. "They've each one let something go as they dived!"

Rincip shouted angry orders; the flutist blowing time for the rowers in the stern swung into a faster tempo. Both helmsmen leaned into their tillers; with only one bank of oars manned, the *Defender* didn't accelerate quickly enough to heel the outside—starboard—steering oar out of the water even in a sharp turn.

"They drop chunks of volcanic glass," Lusius explained grimly. "Big chunks, some as long as your forearm, and the edges sharper'n knife blades. From that height, they can stave in the decking when they hit."

"But can they hit?" Ilna said, frowning. "Surely the Rua can't really aim from that far up?"

"Can't they?" said Lusius. "They'll split your eyeball if you're fool enough to stand watching it come at you!"

With a curl of his lip he said to Chalcus, "Tell me, Captain—will you fill our demons up there with arrow fletching?"

"That I cannot," Chalcus admitted easily. "And do your Rua reach down long nets and snare the shell from your boats, now?"

The crew—the two fisherman and the archer as well—jumped off the stern of a boat that'd drifted to the northern fringe of the fleet. The Sea Guard swam in a noisy crawl, keeping his head above water till he reached the skiff. The fishermen couldn't swim, so they pulled themselves hand over hand along the painter.

Four Rua dived like stooping hawks. The *Defender* continued to wallow forward, but Ilna could see that the Rua would reach the boat long before the patrol vessel came within bowshot.

The chunks of glass smashed into the vessel with the sharp crack of lightning bolts. Shards flew in all directions, catching the sun. A broken plank lifted and spun over the side. Ilna nodded, now understanding why the crew had abandoned the vessel before the missiles struck. Flying pieces would've badly gashed anybody on deck, and she was quite sure that each missile hit within a handsbreadth of where a man had been standing.

There was a stir behind her. The Sea Guards were lifting

wicker shields like siege mantlets out of the hull. Ilna eyed them critically. The woven willow-splits would stop missiles like the ones the Rua were dropping and cushion the impacts besides, but she didn't see how the men on the narrow deck expected to fight with all this defensive truck in the way.

Well, that was probably the answer: the Sea Guards *didn't* expect to fight, any more than the archer aboard the boat that'd been attacked did. Lusius and his men were putting on a show—for the fishermen as well as for her and Chalcus, the spies who Prince Garric had sent. The last thing Lusius really wanted was to defeat the winged men; they alone justified his continued power as Commander of the Strait.

The Rua came out of their dive by arching their chests as if they'd plunged into water, not air; their wings spread only after their bodies had started to curl upward. Quicksilver sunlight danced over the vanes which stiffened the wings' thin membranes.

"Beware to starboard!" Chalcus shouted toward the stern. Because the vessel being attacked was a little off the port bow, Ilna hadn't been paying attention to what was happening on the right side of the ship. Neither had the *Defender*'s officers, apparently, because the fishing boat a stone's throw ahead of them couldn't possibly get clear despite the desperate efforts of the two fishermen on their oars and the Sea Guard who screamed and waved his arms toward the patrol vessel.

Rincip was gabbling something Ilna couldn't understand—she doubted anybody else could, either—and Lusius bellowed, "Sister eat your livers, you fools!" to the fishermen. The men clogging the *Defender*'s deck raised their own racket, trying to see what was happening or just trying to learn from somebody else. None of that was going to help.

"Back port oars!" Chalcus called in a voice that could've doubled for a rock drill.

Only about half the rowers obeyed, and even those didn't all react at the same time. Nonetheless dragging blades and fouled oars pulled the *Defender* enough to the left that she didn't smash straight into the fishing boat. A bow oar struck the boat's stern; the shaft broke just above the blade, and from the scream under Ilna's feet the loom must've slammed into the oarsman's chest hard enough to break ribs. That was a cheap alternative to a crash that could've sunk both vessels.

A splinter of ash from the oar shaft spun into the air. Chalcus reached up without seeming to look and caught the piece. It was the length of a pick handle and sharp as a spear on either end. Lusius grunted in surprise. Chalcus grinned at him and tossed the splinter overboard.

"Well, Captain," Lusius said. "Maybe I should hire you in Rincip's place, do you think? You saved us a bad knock when those fools got in the way."

"Ah, I'm a terrible man when the drink's in me, Commander," Chalcus said with a light laugh. "I'd not wish a scapegrace like me on so nice a fellow as yourself."

Ilna wasn't sure which way the conversation might have gone then—she began knotting a pattern in case it went the wrong way—but the unexpected happened on the far side of the fishing fleet. The *Defender* was only just getting under way again and couldn't possibly reach the attacked vessel in time to take a hand, but several of the other boats were quite close to it. As the Rua flared to land like giant pigeons, the Sea Guard on a nearby boat drew his bow.

The crew of the attacked vessel had gotten aboard the skiff and cast off the painter. One of them—Ilna thought it was the soldier—screamed a horrified warning. The archer loosed nevertheless. Accuracy with a bow takes more training than the Sea Guards probably got, but it was a decent shot aided by the fact that the Rua's wings spread like blankets. The arrow snipped through one of them and thudded into the boat's far gunnel, leaving a neat hole in the wing membrane.

The fishermen on the second vessel immediately jumped over the side. The one who could swim thrashed toward the trailing skiff. The other couldn't and bobbed under the clear water. He got his foot on a coral head and jumped from it in the direction of the skiff as well.

The four Rua launched themselves from the boat on which they'd just landed. The one the arrow struck showed no sign of distress, flapping in a shallow curve that skimmed the calm water. The archer nocked a second arrow, then turned in panic without loosing it; the winged men swooped on him from four directions, arriving simultaneously.

Their wings folded as they hacked at the Sea Guard, flinging bits of flesh into the sea. He continued to scream for a surprisingly long time.

"They've got glass knives," Lusius muttered as he watched the business with a look of disgust. "Sister take them!"

The sea spouted around the fishermen in the water: missiles dropped from the cloudless sky had struck the men squarely. Their mangled bodies sank in spreading clouds of blood. One man's arm had separated.

The *Defender*'s flutist leaned over the railing, staring in amazement at the slaughter. Rincip didn't order him back to his post even though the oarsmen were losing the stroke. Wood clattered as the shafts fouled one another and the patrol vessel began to wallow. The rest of the fishing fleet pulled eastward at the best rate the crews could manage on their oars.

The seawolf drove in purposefully, snapping up body parts and raising its triangular head from the water to swallow. "Our Brother," one of the Sea Guards muttered.

"Eh?" said Chalcus.

Lusius glowered and said, "Just a name."

The skiff tied to the stern of the second boat was sinking: a block of glass had struck it squarely and smashed the bottom out. Ilna was no longer sure the wicker mantlets would stop the missiles—and the Sea Guards were obviously doubtful as well.

"Well, you see," Lusius said in a subdued voice to Chalcus. "It's not so straight and simple as maybe you thought it was."

"Aye," Chalcus said, "there's much thinking to be done on the matter. Much thinking indeed."

The Sea Guards were nervously uncomfortable, and the faces of surviving fishermen showed blank-eyed terror as they rowed past the *Defender* on their way back to port and safety. Ilna supposed the scene she'd just watched was uncommon. Usually the human players would know to flee without the resistance that would lead, as surely as sunrise, to this sort of massacre.

Rua transferred belemnites from the cages on the boats they'd attacked into mesh bags like the one Ilna had examined back in Carcosa. They took off with difficulty, beating their wings hard and staying low above the water until they'd gotten their speed up to that of a running man. Finally they rose and curved away toward the northwest, clutching their loot.

Two boatloads of shell were scarcely a tithe of the fishermen's haul, though. It was a cheap price for Lusius to pay, particularly since the attacks confirmed him as Commander of the Strait. But what had this to do with the merchantmen that were being plundered?

"Put about!" Lusius called to Rincip in the stern. "We may as well go back to Terness. This lot—"

He gestured dismissively toward the fishermen.

"—are done for the day." In a quieter, sneering tone he added to Chalcus, "We'll have trouble enough getting them to go out in the morning. Mark my words!"

Chalcus didn't reply; he was watching the crew of the first boat paddling back to it. The second bobbed empty, apparently abandoned for good. The archer's blood was a red splotch on the near side.

There was colorful movement on the reef. The belemnites clustered around the two corpses and the bits of the third, scavenging a bounteous meal. The sun flared in gorgeous beauty from their shells.

Cashel blinked at the toad. It'd spoken to him, no doubt about that. "I, ah . . ." he said. "Sir, I don't know who the King of Kish is. I've never heard of Kish. Before."

A shooting star streaked across the sky. Its trail was gold, not silvery, and partway into its course it split into two tracks that spat down together. Cashel wondered if that had something to do with the Visitor, then decided that it didn't matter to him either way.

" 'Sir?' " the toad repeated in shrill mockery. "*Sir!* How would you like it if I called you *Mistress,* boy?"

Cashel pondered the question. "I don't know that I'd care much, ah, ma'am," he said. "How would you like me to call you?"

"Well, you might try Evne, since that's my name!" the toad said. "Though as my master, you're free to insult me any way you choose. I have no right to take offense; no, no, not me!"

Cashel set the two pieces of coal on the ground in front of him, the top beside the bottom in which Evne still sat. His staff leaned against the rock behind him. He took it in his hands, letting his fingers caress the polished wood. He'd felt a tingling as the block separated; the touch of the hickory erased it.

"Evne . . ." he said.

The toad turned her head so that she looked straight back at him, disturbing to see. Of course he was talking to a toad, which was pretty disturbing too when he stopped to think about it.

"I never meant to insult you," Cashel said. "And I'm no-body's master, ma'am. Not that I'd insult you if I was."

"You mean you're not the wizard who freed me from my confinement?" the toad said, her head twisting one way, then the other. Her bulging eyes probably saw most everything around her whichever way her face was pointed. "Who did, then?"

"Well, I broke the block open, ah, Evne," Cashel said. "I'm not a wizard, though. The fellow who gave me the coal, Lord Bossian, *he's* a wizard. Maybe it's him you're looking for?"

He was starting to smile at her antics. The toad chirped about like a banty rooster, all prickles and fear of insult. With little men who acted that way, you had to watch that they didn't get too much ale in them and start swinging at the biggest man around—which was always Cashel. Evne wasn't going to do that, so her fuss was just funny.

The toad turned in the hollow so she faced Cashel squarely. She moved with the deliberation of a brood sow rising from the muck, positioning each leg carefully before shifting her body above it.

"You say you're not a wizard," she said, "but you opened my prison?"

"Yes, ma'am," Cashel agreed. "I squeezed till the halves broke."

"And you really don't know who the King of Kish is?" the toad said.

"No, ma'am."

The toad scratched the back of her head with her webbed right foot, continuing to stare at Cashel. "I suppose you expect me to think you're too dumb to lie, is that it?" she said.

"Ma'am," Cashel said, "I don't lie."

He wondered what he ought to do next. Find a place to sleep, he supposed. He'd been looking forward to proper bedding instead of a second night in the open, but he'd survive.

"Well," he said, rising to his feet. "Unless there's something more you need from me, I'll be on my way."

The sky over the peaks behind him brightened with sheets of azure wizardlight. Lord Bossian was at work on something, likely enough. For lack of a better direction to go, Cashel decided he'd head the other way—west, judging from the course of the stars.

"Wait!" Evne said. "Do you *really* not need me? Didn't you free me because there was a question no one else could solve, so you had to come to me?"

Cashel looked down in surprise, then squatted again with his staff balanced across his thighs. "Well, ma'am," he said. "I'm trying to get back to my friends, that's true. But I don't have any notion where they are. Any more—"

He grinned. She was such a funny little thing!

"—than I know about the King of Kish."

"Ah!" said the toad. "Now we come to it! You shouldn't be ashamed to state your problems openly, young man. Who knows what would've happened if you hadn't finally admitted the truth?"

Cashel frowned. "You mean you can help me get back, Evne?" he said. It didn't seem likely, but it wasn't likely he'd be sitting here in a rocky valley talking to a toad either.

"Of course, of course!" the toad said. "There had to be something!"

Cashel didn't know Evne well enough to be sure, but it seemed to him that she was relieved. There were plenty of people who talked about how put upon they were with everybody wanting their help, but who got really huffy if you *didn't* need something. Apparently toads were built the same as people in that way.

"We'll need a mirror," the toad said, looking around

again. If she thought she was going to find a mirror in this landscape, she was more at sea than Cashel was. "Quite a large mirror, big enough to reflect your whole body, my man. And it should be as nearly perfect as possible."

"I don't know where there'd be a mirror, Evne," Cashel said. He thought for a moment. "I guess Lord Bossian has one, but he wouldn't be pleased to see me come back."

He looked over his shoulder, up the slope of shadowed crags and cedars. The blue glare had sunk to occasional flickers, but as Cashel watched, a great bolt shot up into the sky. Clouds absorbed it, shimmering as bright as a huge blue sun for a moment.

"Besides," Cashel said. "His palace wouldn't be a good place to be tonight."

"Well, what could I expect from you?" the toad said. She didn't sound put out, not really. "I shouldn't have expected any better. We'll use water, then. A good-sized pool, perfectly still."

Scratching her head with the other leg, the toad added, "There's often insects around a pond." She looked up sharply and went on, as fiercely as a funny little thing like her could be, "Not that I'm putting my convenience before the duty I owe you for freeing me! I would never do that."

"I'm sure you wouldn't, Evne," Cashel said, having difficulty in keeping the smile from his lips. He found it hard to believe that the toad could really help him return to his own world, but she must know something. She'd lived for ever so long in a block of coal, after all.

He cleared his throat. "Ah . . ." he said, reaching into his wallet and feeling for the remaining jewels. "I'm a stranger here so I'm not sure about where water is, but I've got a jewel, sort of, that'll tell us."

Cashel knew it was going to sound like he'd been lying when he said he wasn't a wizard. It shouldn't matter to him what a toad thought, but it did.

"A fellow gave them to me. A demon did."

Evne made a shrill sound, the sort of call ordinary toads give on summer nights. She didn't speak further.

Grimacing, Cashel rose to his feet. He didn't need to be standing when he did this, but he felt better if he was. The sparks were parts of Kakoral, and Cashel wouldn't have wanted to be squatting down when *that* one came for him.

He threw the ruby against the rock, pretty much the same place that the previous one had hit. He couldn't be sure of that, because when the jewels burst, all the bits vanished like dew in the sunlight.

"Ah!" cried the manikin this time. "You didn't need me, that was what you thought, wasn't it? That's what you said, at least!"

Cashel wondered if there was one sparkling little creature or if each ruby freed a different one. They sure didn't act the same; but neither do people, depending on when you catch them and what their day's been like so far.

"I still don't need you," Cashel said quietly, "but I'd appreciate your help if you'll give it. We're looking for a pool of water we can use for a mirror. Can you direct us, sir?"

"Can I?" said the little man. "*Can* I? Of course I can! But can you face the truth about the woman you protected, *master?*"

"Yes," said Cashel, holding his staff upright at his side. There was no point in saying more when a simple word would do.

The manikin snapped its fingers. A lightning-bright spark flashed into images in place of the solid rock.

When he watched the demon's earlier pictures, Cashel thought he was looking at a scene from the past. This time Cashel watched events that must've taken hours, but he felt no passage of time himself.

The murderer was butchering Laterna's body in the cellar. He'd brought down heavy knives and a stiff-bladed saw since the previous vision, but he was working in a stone tub that had been there beforehand. He'd dumped the dirt and lace-bodied fungus that'd been growing there into a pile on the floor.

The murderer worked with practiced skill, jointing the body and throwing the portions into the hearth that remained the cellar's only light. Fat blazed brightly at each new addition; after it burned away, the flesh continued to blacken and shrivel. The bones remained longer, but they too slowly crumbled.

The murderer never added fuel, nor did the coals change from the sullen red presences they'd been at the beginning. The occasional sparks and flares were always bits of the corpse: a bone cracking, or a globule of fat slipping onto the hearth.

Higher in the cavity a mechanism of pulleys and chains turned a spit. The rib roast there was cooking, not burning. With only the look of the meat to go by, Cashel might have thought it venison.

The silent heat of the hearth had devoured the body almost completely. The murderer took the roast from the spit and arrayed it on the serving platter he had waiting to take it.

The last thing he did before leaving with the covered platter was to change his clothes, throwing the blood-soaked garments onto the coals where they blazed like tinder. Their flickering yellow light showed Cashel parts of the cellars hidden till then by the shadows. Laterna had collected statues and implements, which he'd just as soon not have seen.

As the murderer left, the garments finished burning themselves out. Laterna's bare skull remained in the hearth, shrunken but not quite disintegrated, and the hinted face of Kakoral lowered from the coals.

The scene shifted. Cashel couldn't look away, couldn't even blink, though he wasn't sure that time had passed in the waking world. He couldn't feel his own heart beat, and the sky at the edge of his vision was a frozen painting.

The murderer stood before a round table; seated at the table were Kotia and a youth of Kotia's age but sharing the murderer's own features. Everything in the large room was of the same black, glassy substance, as smooth as the crystal walls of Manor Bossian but as opaque as granite.

There were no servants present. Rolls and vegetables waited on individual serving tables beside each place, but the murderer himself carved thin slices from the roast and set them on the others' plates. They ate, their expressions sullen and distrustful.

Evil glee transfigured the murderer's face. He threw his head back and began to laugh.

Kotia looked at the murderer in wild surmise. She spat out

her second bite of meat; the youth looked from her to the murderer, still chewing as he frowned with puzzlement.

The scene faded to rock. Cashel stood in a nighted valley as thin clouds trailed across the sky above him.

"You see?" cried the capering manikin. "You see! You *see!*"

"I saw," said Cashel. "Where can we find a pool of water, sir?"

The little figure spluttered like a cauldron overflowing. "Don't you care, boy?" it cried. "Even a beast would care!"

"I care," said Cashel. "It was a terrible thing to do to Kotia. Was that Ansache? The man she thought was her father?"

Thinking about Kotia after what he'd seen gave Cashel a queasy feeling, but that wasn't anything he was going to admit to the little demon. He couldn't help how he felt, even if it was wrong, but he could make sure he didn't let that affect what he said or did.

"He was Lord Ansache," said the manikin. "With all the sins that blacken his hands, yet he isn't a cannibal—as the woman you defended is!"

"You have a duty to my master, poppet," Evne said, surprising Cashel and the little demon as well. "Fulfill that duty, or I will send you to the heart of a dead star for all eternity!"

Cashel turned to look at the toad. She'd climbed from the block of coal and had walked up beside him. He lifted her onto his shoulder so there wouldn't be any problem of him stepping in the wrong place. Somehow that latest threat didn't strike him as funny the way Evne's earlier fussing had.

The manikin must have thought the same thing, because in a flat voice it said, "In the hollow of the next valley is Portmayne, a manor vacant since the Visitor arrived a thousand years ago."

A streak of light raced from its tiny arm, off up the slope to the northwest. The line broke into separate glowing dots, then faded completely like the flash of a lightning bug.

"Portmayne had a pool, and it remains," said the manikin. "I tell you this because of my duty—but you will sweat, *master,* if you go there. Out of friendship I suggest that you follow this valley down to the river for your water."

Cashel looked in the direction the demon had pointed. None of the hills in this range seemed exceptionally higher than the others. It meant a climb no worse than that to Lord Bossian's manor and then downhill—which could be tricky, sure, but still easier than the climb.

"How far is the river?" Cashel asked, because he wasn't in a hurry to decide and he knew the right answer might not be as obvious as it seemed to him right now.

"Three days hike," said the manikin. "I say that because you'll be pushing the pace; but if hunger slows you, then four or even five."

Cashel shrugged. "I guess I don't mind sweating some to save my feet that long a scramble over rock," he said. "We'll go to Portmayne."

Cackling with hysterical laughter, the manikin extended his arm again. This time the line of light remained, though the demon vanished.

The night was still. The flashes and sizzle of wizardlight in the east had ceased, and no more shooting stars fell across the heavens.

Cashel let his eyes trace the streak that would guide him in the morning. He thought he could still hear the little demon's laughter.

"Good of you to join me, Lady Estanel," Garric said, bowing to the chief priestess of the Temple of the Shepherd of the Rock. He gestured her to a cushion-spread chair at the corner of the roof garden. An ancient sand myrtle spread above her.

Estanel swished back her white robes and sat gracefully. Bees buzzing among the myrtle's small flowers seemed attracted by the lady's perfume; she ignored them with impressive aplomb.

"My fellow servants of the Shepherd and I are glad to save your time, your highness," she said. She had plump cheeks and her mouth smiled easily, but her eyes were as hard as those of Lord Attaper, who watched from Garric's side. "I'd have said the same even without the example of what happened to my colleagues who serve the Lady of the Sunset."

Lady Estanel had arrived at the palace with the retinue

that both her position and her rank as a wealthy noble required. A dozen ordinary servants had walked beside and behind her sedan chair, and four senior priests followed her in chairs of their own.

There were also thirty burly men, the Little Shepherds; thugs for all their priestly robes. No noble would've been seen in public without their equivalent—but for this visit, the Little Shepherds didn't carry their iron crooks. Garric was quite sure that if he'd had the guards stripped and searched, they'd have been found to be completely unarmed.

He hadn't bothered to do that, because Estanel had entered the palace with only her four aides; the rest of the entourage waited in the street under the eyes of the regiment on guard duty. Estanel was an impressively intelligent woman.

"I suspect that's true, milady," said Garric with a faint smile. "And that should make this interview go more easily than might otherwise be the case."

The aides, three men and a tall, thin woman with a furious expression, were ill at ease. They carried document cases that would ordinarily have been in the hands of servants; there wasn't a table where they could set them down, nor had they been offered seats.

Lady Estanel nodded cautiously. In her hands was a miniature devotional text written on plaques of ivory. Her left thumb turned the leaves one by one, but her whole attention was on Garric.

"You will order . . ." Garric went on calmly. He didn't say, "I want you to order," or "Please will you order," or any other phrasing that might suggest he was giving the priestess an alternative. "Your enforcers, the Little Shepherds, to assemble at noon tomorrow in the Cattle Market. There they will be disarmed and inducted into the royal army as individuals, no more than one man to an existing squad. If things work out, they'll become useful citizens of the kingdom at an honest wage for the work."

"I'm afraid that some of those in the minor orders of the Shepherd wouldn't make good soldiers, your highness," Estanel said. She continued to smile, and her tone showed only mild concern. Her male aides frowned like thunder, and the woman looked as though she were ready to chew rocks.

"Well, milady . . ." Garric said, smiling off into the blue heaven. It was a gorgeous afternoon; daily rain showers for most of the past week had cleared the air and given the sky a gemlike quality. "My understanding is that it works like this: the other men in the squad, the fellows whose lives depend on all the folks around them doing their jobs when Hell's out for breakfast, they hammer on the new guy until he fits into a hole shaped like a soldier. Or else he breaks; they break *him*."

He met her eyes. His smile changed. "It'll be a pity if your thugs mostly wind up in the broken category, but war's a hard business."

King Carus looked on from Garric's mind with an expression that a berserker would've found frightening. *"If training doesn't teach your soldiers hard lessons,"* he said, *"battle will teach them harder lessons yet."*

"Your highness is a stranger," said the youngest of the aides. "You may not appreciate how dangerous a city Carcosa is!"

"You haven't disarmed the Lady's gang!" the female aide shouted in the same heartbeat.

"I have a very good idea of how dangerous Carcosa is," Garric said. The priest to the side of the man who'd spoken had seized his arms as if to restrain him, though the fellow himself seemed shocked by his own outburst. "I came here a few months ago as a simple peasant. That's why I'm taking steps, of which this is one, to change the situation."

He looked at the female aide. "As for the so-called Lady's Champions," he continued, "they'll be mustered the day after tomorrow. Because I have a regiment billeted in the Temple of the Lady of the Sunset, Lord Anda's thugs would assume I was planning a massacre if I called them together first. Since that's *not* my intention, I'm starting with you."

"A massacre would be less trouble than trying to make men of this lot," Attaper growled. It wasn't true and Attaper—unlike Lord Waldron had he made a similar comment—probably didn't mean it, but it was a useful way of reminding the priests of just who held power now and how great that power was.

"Perhaps," said Garric, "but we're going to avoid that if possible. Lady Estanel, do you have any further questions?"

"I will of course give the orders," the priestess said, enunciating every syllable precisely. A bee was crawling along her eyebrows; she didn't twitch or even blink. "Of course, since it's your wish, your highness. But I think it very probable that some of the Little Shepherds will choose to leave the temple's service and go their own way rather than obey me."

Purple and yellow pansies fluttered. Garric let the rising breeze cool the sweat on the side of his neck before he responded.

He was tense, from this interview and from his need to hold in his fury and frustration. He wanted to smash things, to draw his sword and hack an enemy apart . . . but that wouldn't get Cashel back, or Sharina; and it wouldn't help weld the kingdom into a peaceful whole. He had to keep focused on his duty, not his anger.

In Garric's mind, Carus nodded with a wry smile. Few men knew better than the ancient king what it was like to let anger rule you; and how much trouble that could cause for even a strong man.

"My aide, Lady Liane, is going over the roster of the Little Shepherds now," Garric explained quietly. A spy in the temple administration had copied out the names and was now providing descriptions of each of the 212 thugs on the payroll. "While I hope your servants will obey you—and me—without question, those who do not will be treated as traitors to the kingdom."

He cleared his throat into his hand. "I'd thought of offering rewards for information on where they're hiding," he went on, "but Liane tells me that this won't be necessary. The citizens of Carcosa so widely detest your gang that all we need do is put out the word that we're looking for the fugitives to hang. We'll have plenty of help in locating them."

Garric blinked. He was gripping his sword so fiercely that his knuckles were mottled. He took his hand away, shaking his head in mild amazement at how angry he really was.

"I see," said Lady Estanel as she rose to her feet. "Then

with your permission, your highness, my fellows and I will return to our temple immediately. We have a good deal to prepare."

"I have nothing more to discuss," Garric said, giving the priestess a half-bow. "The kingdom appreciates your cooperation."

Lady Estanel's smile was humorless. "The temple's senior priests will lead the Little Shepherds to the Cattle Market tomorrow," she said.

"What?" gasped one of her aides.

Estanel turned and looked at him. "That's correct, Lord Dittic," she said. "I know of no better way to show that my colleagues and I have full confidence in Prince Garric's good faith."

She met Garric's eyes. "As of course we do."

She started for the stairs leading down to where her attendants waited behind the line of guards.

"Lady Estanel?" Garric called to her back. She looked back over her shoulder.

"If you ever decide a secular career is more to your taste than your current religious vocation," Garric said, "please inform me. I assure you that in all I've seen and read of history, I've never heard of a commander conducting a more skillful retreat from an untenable position!"

Even Attaper smiled, and in Garric's mind King Carus laughed in full-throated delight.

Sharina didn't try to stand; she was sure she couldn't manage anything that coordinated. The bear had thrown her onto her left arm, and she'd scraped her elbow badly. Blood from that gouge dripped down her forearm and spread across her palm; she left a line of smudged handprints as she crawled toward the bear on all fours.

"Mistress?" Franca called. He sounded some distance away, but her head had thumped the ground hard. Her vision alternated between being ordinarily sharp and blurring to the point that she had to close her eyes to avoid vertigo.

"Mistress!" Franca repeated. "Where are you?"

The youth's nagging made her furious for an instant, but

the surge of anger steadied her. She suddenly started laughing. *The best bet on where I am is halfway down a bear's gullet,* she thought. And since she wasn't, the whole business seemed funny.

"I'm out here, Franca," she said. She didn't have either the strength or the inclination to shout, so she doubted he could hear her. "It's all right to come back, now."

Sharina rose to a kneeling position and gripped Beard's helve. "Lady help me!" She muttered and lurched to her feet, dragging on the axe with both hands. The bear's hind legs kicked violently. The blade came loose from the skull. Sharina staggered backward, holding the axe out in front of her.

"Oh, good work, mistress!" Beard said. "Oh, you're the one I've been waiting for all these years since I wakened. Straight to the brain, that's you, sucking his life out quicker than spit!"

A man looked out of a second-story window of the mill. He was shaggy and rough-looking, but Sharina didn't suppose she was in shape for a palace reception just now herself. "Hello?" the fellow called.

"The bear's dead," said Sharina. She didn't know if the stranger could hear her either, but the ton of bear sprawled at her feet pretty well spoke for itself. "You can come down, now."

She hoped he would. She didn't think she could climb a flight of stairs to reach him. At the moment she wasn't sure she could walk as far as the mill's doorway, though her strength seemed to be coming back.

The breeze shifted just as Sharina drew in a deep breath, filling her lungs with the stench of the bear's wastes. She doubled up, then vomited her most recent meal of half-cooked rabbit. Immediately she felt better, though she went down on one knee until she was sure she'd regained her balance.

"Shall we kill the fellow when he comes close, mistress?" the axe said. "He's probably dangerous, you know. You can't trust anybody you meet in these hard times."

"Beard," said Sharina. "Why didn't you tell me about the bear?"

"You killed the bear, mistress," the axe said with a desperate brightness. "Oh, nobody could've been quicker than you. Zip! and I was sucking out his brains!"

"Beard," Sharina said. She stood upright again, swaying only slightly. The weight of the axe in her hands helped her to balance. "You wanted a chance to kill the bear, but you were afraid I wouldn't risk my own life to save a stranger if I'd known what the danger was."

"Mistress," said the axe in a subdued voice, "you—"

"Shut up!" said Sharina. She took a deep breath. "I'd have gone. Even for a stranger. He's a human being and I'm human. That's enough."

The man now peered from the doorway, ready to run back to his upstairs shelter if there were any hint of danger. Anger touched Sharina again. Did the fool think the bear was shamming, lying here with its skull cleft to the neck bones?

"Yes, mistress," the axe said. "I'll—"

"Shut *up!*" Sharina said. "The other thing to remember is this: if you ever hide the truth from me again, for *any* reason, I will destroy you if I can. Anyway, I'll bury you where you'll never be found till the ice comes. Do you understand?"

"Yes, mistress," said the axe.

The man who'd been trapped in the mill approached to within ten feet of Sharina, then stopped. From a distance Sharina'd guessed he was in his forties, but close up he was much younger. He had the worn, grayish look of a plow that's spent decades out in the weather, and his breeches were freshly torn. A swipe of the bear's claw had raised a welt on his thigh without quite drawing blood.

"Mistress," he said, nodding acknowledgment. "My name's Scoggin and I guess I'm in your debt for my life."

Scoggin had an ordinary peasant's knife in his belt and a spear made by binding a similar knife blade onto a short shaft. His eyes kept flicking to the axe; he carefully stayed beyond its reach.

He grimaced. "Mistress?" he blurted. "Are you human?"

"Of course I'm human!" Sharina said. Franca had returned from the woods and was sidling toward them, keeping Sharina between him and the stranger. "What did you think I was?"

Scoggin gestured toward the dead bear. "Mistress," he said, "I didn't know."

Sharina smiled despite herself. "Well, I am," she said. "I'm Sharina os-Reise. I was lucky and I've got a very sharp axe."

Franca crept close to Sharina's side, silent and shivering. *How many people had the youth spoken to in the past nine years? Perhaps only his mother and Sharina herself.*

She waggled Beard. The inlaid steel head was as bright as though she'd just polished it, though blood and brains smeared the helve—as they did her own forearms.

"I wouldn't say," she added coldly, remembering how Beard had tricked her into fighting the bear, "that owning this axe was necessarily part of my good luck."

"Mistress, it'll never happen again," the axe chirped. "Beard knows you'll feed him. He trusts you, mistress."

Scoggin stared at the axe in open amazement. He rubbed his eyes with the back of his hand. "It talks?" he said.

"Among other things," Sharina replied crisply. "Now, who else is living in Barca's Hamlet? If you're not sure, I want to search the town before we make further plans."

At the back of her mind she realized she was taking charge. Would she have done that six months ago, before she became "Princess Sharina of Haft?"

She smiled. There was no way of telling, of course, but if she'd changed it was for the better. Given the shape this world was in, the people who'd been making decisions up till now could use some help.

Instead of answering, Scoggin stared in dawning horror and even backed a step. "Pardon, mistress," he said in a trembling voice, "but you're Sharina os-*Reise?* That would be the innkeeper's daughter?"

"Yes," Sharina said. Unexpected hope dawned. "You know my father? Is he—"

"Mistress, he's *dead,*" Scoggin said. "*You're* dead, everybody's dead who was in Barca's Hamlet the day She came! Mistress, who are you? Do you come from Her?"

Sharina sagged. Franca started to whimper and stroked her arm like a frightened kitten cuddling closer to its mother.

A fragment of memory returned to her. She looked at Scoggin and said, "You have a farm in the north of the borough, don't you? On Eiler's Creek?"

Scoggin frowned, but the homely question seemed to relax him. "Aye, I did," he said. "There's no farms now, just scrape for a meal and hope something bigger doesn't find you first; but that was my farm."

"Well," said Sharina, "I'm not the woman you're thinking of; but in another—place, I suppose, or maybe time. Anyway, I was somebody very like the person you mean. I'm not a ghost or a demon, either one."

She took a deep breath and managed a tremulous smile. "What I particularly *am* now," she said, "is hungry. I suppose we could cut chunks off this bear, but if you've got something else, Master Scoggin, I'd prefer to leave the bear until I'm a little more distant from awareness of just what *he* ate."

Scoggin smiled also. "I've a line of snares," he said. "I make a circuit of the borough from here to my old farm in the course of a year, so I don't hunt anyplace out. I just shifted here last night, so there should be plenty for three."

He turned and started toward the ruined inn. "I never saw anything like that bear before," he muttered. "If there's more of them, I don't know what I'll do. Unless you . . . ?"

He looked at Sharina in sudden speculation.

"I don't know what my plans will be until I learn more about this world," Sharina said in a mixture of amusement and irritation. "I don't think it will involve creeping about eating rabbits and watching the ice grow thicker, though."

Scoggin looked away in embarrassment and cleared his throat. *A man who'd stayed alive for the past decade by dealing with short-term problems couldn't be blamed for continuing to think that way,* Sharina realized. Aloud she said, "Were you in Barca's Hamlet when She came, Scoggin? If you don't mind telling me."

"I don't mind," he said. "You saved my life." But he didn't answer for several long moments.

The brick wall and gateposts on the south side of the inn yard had fallen inward, but the culvert under the entrance lane remained. Scoggin knelt beside it and fished out a line of willow bark. The rabbit he'd noosed there had already strangled; he popped it into his game pouch and reset the snare.

"I was coming into town that day," Scoggin said at last. "From midnight on there'd been lightning, I thought it was, and my sheep wouldn't settle down."

He looked at her. "It wasn't lightning," he said. "I know that now. It's in the sky all the time now."

"Yes," said Sharina. "But of course you wouldn't have known that. Go on."

"I set off before dawn," Scoggin said, squatting at a snare across the mouth of a run through brambles along the fallen wall. This one was empty. "I left the sheep with my cousin and his wife; he owned the farm with me and his wife kept house for both of us. I was going to pick up some ale, that was all; for the house and for me."

Scoggin moved to the next snare, at the mouth of what had been a window of the inn's foundation course. Though the building had collapsed into a mound of rubble, the opening was still a trackway for small animals.

The set—a noose of twine with willow springs to snatch it tight when tripped—was obviously empty, but Scoggin knelt by it anyway. He was operating by rote while his conscious mind tried to deal with things he'd kept buried during the past long years.

Still kneeling, he turned his face to Sharina and went on in a stronger voice, "I heard the noise when I got to the big sheepfold. You know where that is?"

"Yes," Sharina said, nodding. The broad stone enclosure on high ground north of the hamlet's first buildings was used to count flocks for drovers taking them out of the borough. It was normally empty.

"I waited there," Scoggin said. "I didn't know what was happening. It sounded like screams and crashing . . . which I guess it was, but I couldn't believe it then. I waited at the sheepfold, just not *comfortable,* you know?"

"Yes," said Sharina. She knew very well.

"I couldn't see the houses because the track curves," Scoggin went on, "but something lifted high enough I could see it. It looked like a beetle grub, only it had a man in its jaws. It was huge, just huge."

He grimaced and stared at the ground. "I don't know who he was, that man," he said. "It didn't matter, it was all of them before it was over. It was near over then, I guess, because a pack of things came up the track heading north. I heard them coming and hid in the brush, so they went past. Some were giants and some looked more like men; but they weren't."

Franca was crying openly now, his head in his hands. Scoggin's description must have been much like what happened in Penninvale a year later. Given the sort of destruction Sharina had seen in Carcosa, events there had followed the same pattern if on a larger scale.

"I started back," Scoggin said. He licked his lips. "Keeping in the woods. I'd seen the, *them,* going north. I didn't know what to do. They'd been to the farm and gone on by the time I got there. It was—"

He turned his hands up helplessly. "Everything was dead. Everybody was dead."

Scoggin rose and walked to where the curb in the center of the inn yard had been knocked into the well it was meant to protect. The snare he'd set there had caught another rabbit; it was still struggling.

"Mine!" Beard called, but Scoggin snapped the animal's neck obliviously and bagged it. He was still operating by reflex, though he seemed calmer now than he had when he began speaking.

"I've been hiding in the woods ever since," Scoggin said. He was limping slightly; perhaps from the bear's swipe, perhaps from older injuries; now that Sharina had been with him for a time, she saw that Scoggin's left arm was crooked where a broken bone had been ill set. "The big packs have gone away—"

His face stiffened. "I thought they had, anyway, because there was nobody left to hunt. The bear, though—that was new. I don't know what it means."

"How did the Hunters arrive here, do you know?" Sharina asked. Her eyes instinctively searched the rubble for bones. There wouldn't be any, of course; the voles would've gnawed them all away in a single winter, let alone a decade.

What her mind knew was one thing; what her heart feared was another.

"Oh, yes," Scoggin said. "It was on the shore, a tunnel of light. It was purple but solid. It was there for years after, but it finally faded away."

"Show me," said Sharina, walking toward the Old Kingdom seawall that protected the east side of Barca's Hamlet from the winter storms that wracked the Inner Sea. She looked out, expecting the view she'd seen every morning when she awakened in her garret bedroom.

The sea had vanished.

She must have gasped. Scoggin looked at her, misunderstanding the surprise, and said, "Yeah, that was Cranmer; he must've touched the side of the tunnel. He froze so solid that he didn't even start to thaw for years, and there's still his hand and some of his arm left."

Scoggin meant the piece of debris on the foreshore. Sharina had taken it for the driftwood and dismissed it from consideration.

"But the *sea*," she said; and then she found it, a glittering line on the horizon. It had drawn back miles from the familiar shore, leaving a waste of shingle, which brush and coarse grasses were beginning to colonize.

"Oh, that," Scoggin said. "Yeah, it's been drying up ever since She came."

He shivered. "That's all right with me," he added. "There were things out in the water the first year or two, huge snakes. The farther away they keep from the land, the better I like it."

"It's the ice," said Beard. "It has to come from somewhere, you know. The sea becomes ice and the ice covers the land . . . but first there'll be more blood for Beard to drink, much more blood."

"What's that?" said Sharina, pointing south toward the glitter just visible beyond the curve of the seawall. She started in that direction, clambering over the rubble of what had been the stables at the back of the inn yard.

"What?" said Scoggin. He leaned outward, learning as Sharina had already realized that he couldn't see much from where they stood. "It was never here before. It might be danger . . ."

He let his voice trail off and followed. To Sharina it didn't look any more or less hostile than the rest of this horrible place, and it was at least a change from stark ruins.

The seawall sloped back a foot for each of the twelve feet it rose from what had been sea level at a spring tide. At its base, drawn up on the rocky beach, was a framework of crystal rods that gleamed with more light than that of the hazy sun.

"It's a ship!" Sharina said. Though it couldn't be an ordinary ship: the rods outlined a vessel but didn't form solid ribs and bulwarks. The lines were too clear for her to doubt her instinct, though.

"But it's up on land," said Scoggin. "And I would've seen it if it's been here even last night!"

Sharina sidestepped down the seawall, touching the stone with her left hand in case she slipped. Beard, chuckling merrily to himself, was in her right. Franca crawled down the slope behind her, but Scoggin stayed at the top wearing a worried frown.

Sharina touched a crystal with the butt of the axe. It made a faint *tick,* more like stone than metal. A shimmer of light, too faint to have color, connected the rods like the skin of a soap bubble.

Scoggin cried out. He jumped down the slope, then turned to face upward with his spear raised.

"Mistress!" Beard shouted. "Mistress! We're—"

A line of men appeared on the seawall, looking down at Sharina and her companions. There were some twenty of them. Most carried bows with nocked arrows; several were already half-drawn.

"—attacked!"

"Good day, sirs!" Sharina called, holding the axe crosswise at waist level. Beard was no threat to the archers above them. "I'm Sharina os-Reise and these are my friends. May I ask who you are?"

Another man hobbled into sight, leaning on a staff of carved whalebone. He wore a short black cape and a peaked cap, both made of what looked like lustrous velvet. He gave

Sharina a look of satisfaction; his staff sizzled against the ground with scarlet wizardlight.

"Ask or not," said the fellow, "I will tell you: I'm Alfdan the Great. Now, set the axe down and move away from it. Otherwise I'll have my men shoot you down and take it from your body."

Alfdan gave a cackle of triumph. "I've been waiting under my Cape of Shadows for almost a day but it's worth the effort—now that I have the axe!"

"Shall we attack, mistress?" Beard whispered. "Mistress, what shall we do?"

The archers began drawing their bows.

"Sail!" called the lookout at the *Defender*'s masthead. "She's a big one, she is!"

"Hey Lusius!" Rincip shouted from the stern. "The timing's right for the Valles ship that turned us down on Pandah. What d'ye want to do?"

"Bring us alongside so I can speak to her captain," Lusius said. His glance fell on Chalcus. With a nod and a half smile, he went on, "No, by the Sister, I'll go aboard and see if I can talk sense into him. And perhaps—"

His smile broadened.

"—our guests would care to board with me?"

"Yes," said Ilna before Chalcus could speak. Lusius was playing with them, pretending to conceal nothing about what was going on in the Strait. All Ilna was sure of was that the Commander was lying. She wasn't about to make the mistake of thinking he had nothing to hide in what he offered freely to show.

Petty officers relayed Rincip's shouted orders to the crew. The Sea Guards were manning both benches again, though their wicker shields cluttered the central aisle. You couldn't get between bow and stern except by walking on the rail itself—easy for Chalcus but probably beyond what most of this crew could manage. After watching the winged men attack, the ability to move around the vessel was less important to them—and their officers—than having protection immediately available.

" 'Turned you down at Pandah,' Master Rincip said?" Chalcus said with an eyebrow raised in question.

"That's right," Lusius said with the falsely open expression Ilna had come to recognize. "I keep a detachment on Pandah so that the ships stopping there to buy supplies can take on Sea Guards as well if they're heading for the Strait. I have a boat meet them to take my men off when they're past the Calves and out of danger."

The *Defender* was closing rapidly with the sailing vessel coming from the northeast. It wasn't as big as the hulks Sidras used as warehouses, but it was an impressively large ship nonetheless; it moved with the wallowing heaviness of a horse swimming. The men who lined the forward railing wore helmets and held spears.

"Lay to!" Lusius bellowed through his cupped hands. "The Commander of the Strait is coming aboard!"

"Will they obey?" Ilna asked.

"They'd best!" Lusius snarled. He must have thought his tone had been too open; he flashed his false smile again and added, "Not that any honest captain would refuse, you see?"

As he spoke, the freighter's huge square sail flapped loose, then began to flutter up to the spar. Horizontal wooden rods—battens—stiffened the fabric. The ship continued to slosh through the swell; it was far too heavy to do anything quickly.

"Why wouldn't a captain choose to have Sea Guards on board when he runs the Strait, Commander?" Chalcus said mildly. "If you don't mind my asking, of course."

Lusius made a sound that was half grunt, half throat-clearing. "There's some that claim the charges are high," he said while keeping his face toward the freighter so he didn't have to look at his guests. "They don't appreciate how much it costs to maintain the patrols."

Suddenly belligerent, he glared at Chalcus. "I have to fund it all myself, you know!" he said. "Not a stiver comes from the Count's treasury. That is, from the Prince, as I now serve him directly."

"Everything has a cost," said Chalcus, nodding as though in agreement. "That's the way of the world, Commander."

"You're bloody well right it is!" Lusius said. "And I'll tell you something else—not one ship with my men aboard has been taken by the Rua! If they want to risk the run themselves, well, it's no fault of mine if they all get their throats slit by demons, is it?"

"None whatever," Chalcus said. He laughed, a cheerful sound to someone who didn't know him as well as Ilna did; and cheerful to her as well, because it didn't bother her to learn that Chalcus viewed the Commander as prey.

The *Defender* turned to starboard, doubling back to match speed with the larger ship as they came alongside. One of the freighter's crewmen tossed down a ladder of rope with wooden rungs; Chalcus caught it and used his foot to lock the lowest rung to the *Defender*'s railing. The freighter's deck was at least twice a man's height above the patrol vessel's, so boarding her without the crew's help—let alone against their resistance—would be extremely difficult.

"After you, Commander," Chalcus said politely. Lusius grunted and scrambled up. He'd eaten and drunk too much for too long to be fit, but he remained a strong man despite his dissipation.

Ilna followed, knowing that Chalcus wouldn't release the bottom of the ladder until she was safely on deck. The side ropes were made of some coarse fiber, unfamiliar to her. As she climbed, gripping the ropes, she felt images of sun-blasted badlands where the dust blew about plants whose leaves were clumps of daggers.

She clambered over the railing to find herself midway along the big vessel's deck. A forest of heavy ropes slanted upward to brace the single mast, and the boat in the chocks forward was larger than the vessels in the Terness fishing fleet.

Chalcus sprang to the deck beside her. He landed on the balls of his feet, then touched Ilna's elbow to warn of his presence.

Lusius was facing a middle-aged man in a serviceable tunic of blue wool and a younger, softer fellow wearing silk and a thick gold seal ring. The spearmen stood to either side of them, Blaise armsmen with hooked swords in belt scabbards and tattoos on their right forearms.

"I'm Ohert, captain of the *Queen of Heaven*," said the

middle-aged man, "and this is Master Pointin. I've taken you aboard so I can tell you to your face that we neither want nor need your louse-ridden drunks aboard."

"We wouldn't want them if they were free," the silk-clad Pointin chimed in. "That we'd pay the fee you demand—well, the notion's absurd."

The guards glared at Lusius, acting as hostile as they could without offering open threats. Much of the attitude was put on for the purpose, but Ilna didn't doubt that those fellows were willing to chop the Commander to fish bait if the captain told them to.

Lusius must also have recognized that. "Captain Ohert," he said without the bluster and mocking superiority that had been general with him previously, "You're making a mistake, and I only pray to the Lady that your mistake not be fatal. You've not sailed these waters since the demon Rua came up from the Underworld to loot ships and slaughter sailors. You may think our charges high—"

"I think they're absurd!" said Pointin. "I told you that, my man!"

"—but it would be more expensive yet to let the Rua take the ship and your lives as well, would it not? What is it that you're carrying, Captain?"

"It's none of your business what our cargo is!" Pointin said. "Now, you've got your answer, so take yourself back to your own ship and let honest men be on with their business."

"You're carrying tapestries," Ilna said, scarcely aware that she was speaking until after the words had come out. The aura of the woven goods in the vessel's several holds had flooded her ever since she'd boarded the freighter. She didn't think she'd ever been around such a *mass* of fabric before.

"They had a spy in Valles!" the captain cried in distress. Lusius turned toward Ilna with a frown of amazement; Chalcus stepped between them with a vague, friendly smile.

Images cascaded through Ilna's mind: *armored heroes, women dressed in gold and silver threads, and animals from myth. Forests and gardens and cities with high walls and fanciful turrets. . . .*

She shook her head, trying to return to her present sur-roundings. The tapestries' workmanship was generally mediocre and not infrequently poor, distorted figures on gapped, ill-woven grounds; but occasionally, burning through the trash like the sun on a hazy day, there was a piece—often a single panel or a cartoon in a hanging of slight merit otherwise—whose craftsmanship took Ilna's breath away.

And it was all in her mind, hidden from her eyes in burlap-covered bales beneath the freighter's thick deck timbers. All in her mind . . .

"All right, you know we're carrying tapestry!" the super-cargo said. "With the Prince of Haft ruling the Isles, there's going to be a market for the best sort of furnishings in Car-cosa. *Palace* furnishings very likely, and the Pollin family will be there with the goods to sell long before anybody else sees the opportunity. We'll not pay a third the cargo's value to put your thugs on board, either. We've got real soldiers to deal with anybody who thinks he can rob us!"

"The Strait isn't like the valleys of Blaise," Lusius said, bobbing his bearded chin in acknowledgment of the leader of the freighter's guards. "My men understand the demons and know how to deal with them."

From what Ilna had seen, the Sea Guards understood well enough to avoid fighting the Rua whenever it was possible to run away instead. But ships *were* being stripped, and she didn't see how Lusius could be responsible for that. This freighter's crew was probably equal in number to the Sea Guards; between the vessel's high decks and the Blaise armsmen—*real* soldiers, as the supercargo had said—they could beat off the *Defender* with ease.

"We've listened to you," Ohert said. "Now get off my ship. And you needn't think half our crew'll be coming ashore in Terness when we anchor off the harbor tonight—everybody's staying aboard, and there'll be a proper watch kept, I promise you!"

"I've warned you and that's all I can do," Lusius said with a sad shake of his head. "My guests and I will return to Terness."

He started for the ladder, then looked back over his shoulder. "I hope you and your crew have a good night, Captain Ohert," Lusius added. "But I greatly doubt that you will."

Ilna smiled minusculely. The first half of the Commander's statement was a lie, but she was inclined to believe the second part.

Chapter Thirteen

D o you think we can trust Kakoral?" Cashel said as he climbed the slope, stepping sideways because it was so steep. Every so often he switched so the other foot led; otherwise he'd likely get a cramp in the leg that'd been higher. Cashel figured this was a place he'd best be in good shape.

"Trust him?" said Evne, riding on Cashel's left shoulder. She could've been in his wallet or in a fold of his tunic, but he'd thought this way was most companionable; she'd seemed satisfied with the suggestion. "Trust him to use us and deceive us and cast us away when it suits him, the way males generally do? Is that what you mean?"

"Well, no," said Cashel. *Companionable* wasn't the word everybody'd have used about Evne, but because he'd grown up with Ilna, the toad's manner made him feel right at home. "I meant, would this red line—"

The dots of wizardlight climbed the slope ahead of them, faint but as visible now against the bright sun as they'd been when they first appeared at night. Cashel'd found that the track the light plotted either sloped less or had firmer footing than any of the alternatives nearby.

"—take us to the nearest water, like he said?"

The toad snorted. Her hoarse voice was louder than Cashel would've expected from a little toad, but she seemed to talk normally from her lipless mouth. Her throat sack fluttered as she spoke.

"Oh, that he has no choice about," she said. "You bested

him, didn't you? You're his master, just as you're mine. But he's not your friend, Cashel. The demon serves you because he must and because it suits him; don't ever imagine that he helps because it suits *you*."

Cashel thought about it. After a moment he said, "I guess that's true for most people, Evne. It's true for me, anyway. If I help somebody, it's because I feel better for doing it than I would if I didn't help."

"Faugh!" said Evne. "It's nothing like that. You're a fool. Most men are fools; but they aren't most of them fools the way *you* are, master."

Cashel chuckled. It really was like being home with his sister.

The track had actually been more down than up, but there'd been a lot of both. They'd hiked—well, Cashel had—from morning to mid-afternoon in getting from where Bossian put him out to where they were now. This was the steepest rise of the trek so far.

Evne didn't know how much farther they had to go either; Cashel figured they'd just keep on till they got there. It was pretty much the way he did most things in life, by putting one foot in front of the other till the job was done.

He gripped one of the dwarf birches rooted in the rock to help him up the last step to what he thought was a broad ledge. It was a flat-topped ridge instead. Filling the broad valley beyond was a jumble of shattered marble. From it grew pines, cottonwoods, and clumps of spiky silkgrass waving stalks of yellow-white flowers.

"Oh!" he said. "I guess we're here."

"Brilliant," said the toad. "Do you guess the sun will rise in the east tomorrow morning too?"

Cashel smiled broadly as he surveyed the vast ruins. Portmayne must have been as large as Manor Bossian, but its walls had been built of vari-colored marbles instead of crystal. There'd been a central tower whose stone was brilliantly white with a blue undertone. It must've been higher than any tree gets, because when it toppled it reached almost to where Cashel stood.

He eyed the fragments carefully. The tower had shattered when it hit the stony ground, but it seemed to have been all one piece till then—like an eggshell rather than a building constructed from carved blocks. Lightning had burned a ragged line down the side of the tower, turning the stone a powdery white like a leper's skin. The bolt had torn its way from the battlements to the ground; maybe that was what threw the tower down.

"The tank is there to the north," Evne said. "Just beyond where the travertine wing collapsed."

It wasn't just the tower, of course: the whole manor was flattened as thoroughly as a stomped-on anthill. He'd done that when he was younger; stepped on anthills. . . .

"Yes, ma'am," Cashel said. "Where the sedges are growing, you mean. I just wanted to get a look at things before I went wandering down into them, you know; in case."

He gave his quarterstaff a spin, then reversed its direction. It felt good to swing the iron-shod hickory, Duzi *knew* it did. Cashel wasn't a lazy man, but he walked from necessity rather than pleasure. It seemed like walking was most of what he'd been doing since Kotia brought him to this place, so using his arms and shoulders for a bit was a special treat.

"Far be it from me to tell my master what to do," the toad said tartly. "Though I did consider that there might be insects around the tank, and that it's been some while since I last ate."

"Right, we'll head on now," said Cashel, suiting his action to his words by starting down the slope with long strides. The soil was different on this side of the ridge; instead of being red clay, it was more of a yellowish brown with shiny, silvery chunks of galena ore in it.

"Don't let me put you out," said the toad, but she didn't say it very loudly. "After all, I've waited at least seven thousand years; what difference would another few weeks make?"

Cashel wondered about the utter ruin, how it'd happened. Lightning might've struck a high tower easy enough, but that didn't explain all the rest of the buildings. Well, that'd been a long time ago. He didn't guess it mattered anymore.

Birds chirped and fluttered in short hops among the trees. Cashel saw a wren with fluff in its beak and a number of other little gray fellows he might not have identified for sure even if they'd been flitting in a hedgerow back in Barca's Hamlet where the animals were familiar.

Sheep wouldn't have been happy in this country. There was too much stone, and the silkgrass would cut their lips as they grazed. Goats would've done well enough, but Cashel didn't like goats. They had minds of their own, more than sheep did; but they weren't really any smarter than sheep. Being contrary, they managed to get into more trouble as well as not being as nice to be around.

Cashel grinned and spun his quarterstaff overhead for the fun of it. There were plenty of people who reminded him of goats too.

He wished Garric was here to play his pipes as they walked through the rubble of the fallen manor. Or Sharina; either of his friends could've told Cashel things about the broken stones, what the buildings'd looked like originally and what the reliefs cut into them meant.

"Or you could ask me," said the toad unexpectedly. Had he spoken aloud? "I'd tell you that the frieze we just passed shows the first Lady Portmayne receiving eternal wisdom from figures representing Sky, Earth, and Sea. Those folks shown ankle height around her are her adoring subjects."

"Oh!" said Cashel. "I hadn't been thinking about you, Evne."

"Given how rarely you seem to think of anything, I won't feel insulted," the toad said. "And as for those adoring subjects, I daresay they or their equally adoring descendents wished Lady Portmayne had received some other form of eternal wisdom—perhaps that of cabbage worms. Because what she did receive didn't help the folk of Portmayne in the least when the Visitor arrived and threw down their walls."

Cashel walked past a fallen colonnade; the shafts were of deep red stone with white seashells embedded, but the bases and capitals had been black and had green veins. It must have been lovely, once upon a time.

"Would cabbage worms have been able to stop the Visitor, Evne?" he asked.

"Faugh, you're a fool!" she said. Then in a different tone—a tone very like the one that Ilna used when she was being careful to say no more than she was sure of, "The Visitor would claim, I believe, that no one and no thing could stop him. Thus far he's had no reason to change his opinion."

The tank was of white marble, carved all around with columns that were part of the same block as the rest of the structure. A gently sloped mound raised the bottom some distance above the surrounding plain. The slope must originally have been sodded—a few tufts of real grass still grew there—but now dark green sedge covered it. Sedges need a lot of water, and if they were getting it around here the tank must leak.

Cashel stood at the base of the mound and eyed the structure. It was as broad as he could've thrown a stone and more than twice as long. The marble sides were sheer and double Cashel's height, which could be a problem. He figured he'd climb onto the base and see if he could lift himself from there to get a grip on top of the cornice. If that didn't work, well, he'd try something different.

"You think the hardest part of this business will be to get to the top of the tank?" the toad said quietly.

"Well, yes, but it shouldn't be too hard," Cashel said. "I think I can—"

"You're wrong about that being the hard part," the toad said. "There was a dragon sleeping in the tank. It's awakened now, and it plans to eat you."

"Oh," said Cashel, looking up again. A broad snout rose over the cornice; above it were a pair of wide-set eyes, staring at Cashel through slit pupils.

The dragon's head was not only bronze colored, it had the sheen of metal in the afternoon sun. It lifted out of the marble tank and began to flow down toward Cashel like a river of dark honey. The head looked a little like a crocodile's, but the snakelike body walked on more pairs of short, bowed legs than Cashel had fingers to count them on. It was as thick as he was through the chest, and he couldn't be sure how long it was because it was still coiling out of the tank. Water gleamed on its bronze scales.

"Evne," Cashel said. He scooped the toad into his cupped left hand and put her down in a patch of grass. "I'm going to move to the right, I think. You go the other way so you don't get trampled, all right?"

"You could run, Master Cashel!" the toad said.

"I don't think I could," said Cashel. "Anyway, I'm not going to try."

He knew what the little image of Kakoral had meant about being sorry if they didn't hike down to the river instead of searching for the water here at Portmayne; though Cashel wasn't sure that was true. In a place like this, there'd likely have been trouble waiting at the river too; and anyway, how would he have gotten a decent reflection from flowing water?

Anyway, he'd made his choice and he'd live with it. Or not, he supposed.

Cashel started moving to his right the way he said he'd do. He eased back a little from the base of the mound also. No point in letting the dragon use the higher ground to spring on him. Not that it looked like springing was part of its usual act, but you could never tell.

As Cashel sidled backward, he began spinning his quarterstaff. It made a low thrum, a familiar sound and a soothing one.

He wondered what the creature ate when people didn't come along. He hadn't seen any animals bigger than the few doves, and there weren't buzzards circling in the pale blue sky either. If there wasn't food here for a buzzard, he didn't see how you could feed a dragon that seemed to be the size of a trireme.

The slope had been backfilled with clean dirt, but when the dragon's forequarters reached the natural soil its claws began to click on stones. Once Cashel saw a spark when a claw ticked a half-buried chunk of quartz.

Cashel swept his surroundings with quick jerks of his head, never losing the dragon from at least his peripheral vision. A sprawled jumble of pink marble—the remains of a tower once nearly as tall as the manor's central spire—would shortly keep him from retreating any farther. That meant he'd either have to wait or attack himself, and he figured attacking—

The dragon, three double paces distant, lifted its head on a sinuous curve of its forebody. Cashel, spinning the quarter-staff sunwise before him, strode forward. The dragon struck down. Cashel met it with his staff end-on; the dragon recoiled in a flash of blue wizardlight.

Cashel's body tingled; he couldn't hear anything but the whirring in his ears. He reversed the staff and struck with the other ferrule—half a swing, half a battering ram punch with his shoulders behind it. There was another flash. The dragon rolled away from the blow, its scales black and dinted where the iron had smashed them. The air stank of brimstone.

The dragon opened its mouth and roared like a mill grinding without grain between the stones, a rasping, terrible sound. Each canine tooth was as long as Cashel's whole hand, and the interlocking side teeth weren't much smaller.

Cashel stepped forward again and struck with his left hand leading. A blast of azure light blinded him; he couldn't feel anything. He struck again, right hand foremost. He was moving on instinct and the skill of long practice, swinging a staff he couldn't feel into an enemy he couldn't see.

Light flared, piercing him bone-deep. This shock threw his surroundings into focus in stark black and white. The dragon's left eyetooth spun into the bright heavens. Hot fog surrounded the beast: the water slicking its scales boiled off like drops from the sides of a heated cauldron.

The dragon roared again, a sound Cashel felt though he still couldn't hear. Its jaws were big enough to swallow a man in one gulp, even a man as big as Cashel. The creature's breath stank like a smithy, not a slaughterhouse.

He stepped forward and rammed the quarterstaff like a spear into the dragon's palette, crushing through the light bones. The creature jerked back, lifting its forebody while Cashel still clung to the staff deep in its skull. He could see the ground as clearly as he could the ridged grain of his quarterstaff: every pebble, every sprig of sage, every bird track. It seemed to be far below him.

The dragon writhed into a tight knot. Blue-white flames jetted from its maw and outlined the individual scales of its squirming body; sedge sizzled and blackened at the creature's touch.

Cashel was flying free. He held his quarterstaff.
Nothing else in the world mattered.

Sharina faced the archers above her, hesitating when the answer was obvious to anybody. Scoggin tossed his spear onto the shingle at his feet and looked at her with a desperate expression.

"Throw down the axe, woman!" he cried. "Throw it down or they'll kill us all!" Sharina didn't *like* Beard, and she'd lived all her previous life without owning a talking axe ... but that didn't mean anybody had a right to take it away from her. She wondered what Cashel would do, or her brother Garric?

The truth was that they'd drop the axe without question. They didn't need to prove their courage to anybody—

And neither did she. She bent over and set Beard down gently. As a fine tool alone she owed the axe better than to be tossed onto hard stone.

"Wait, mistress!" the axe cried. "We're being attacked! I promised I'd warn you!"

"I know we're being attacked!" Sharina said in fury. "They're standing all around us with bows aimed. I'm giving you up."

"Not them, mistress," said Beard. His metal voice was as pure and piercing as the note of a bell. "The men are no danger, now that the fauns have come back!"

"What?" said Alfdan, looking over his shoulder. He gave a cry of angry wonder and pointed his staff in the direction of the hamlet. He began to chant in a high singsong voice, then choked to a halt. He swayed, on the verge of collapse. He must be exhausted from the wizardry involved in keeping his ambush concealed until Sharina walked into it.

"I can fight them, mistress!" Beard said. "I can drink their blood too, just like men's."

Sharina couldn't see anything from where she stood at the base of the seawall. One of Alfdan's men shot toward the new danger. He gave a shout of horror, tried to nock another arrow, and dropped it in nervousness.

"Come on!" Sharina cried, running up the steep slope

more easily than she'd descended it. Emotions fired her now; emotions and the delighted, shrieking bloodlust of the axe in her hands.

Four or five archers were shooting; the others either scuttled down the seawall or stood in terror with their bows half-drawn. Sharina reached the top; Franca was with her but Scoggin hadn't followed.

Five creatures covered in lustrous blue fur were coming from the ruins of Barca's Hamlet. They were in a line spread from north to south, converging on Alfdan's band. They were somewhat taller than men, but much more of their height was in their legs; their thighs were as hugely muscled as a grasshopper's. Tiny curling horns grew at the top of their foreheads, and their faces had the calm majesty of ivory statues.

The creatures were male. Their genitals were pony-sized and erect, in obscene contrast to their saintly expressions.

The archers were shooting at the nearest of the five, the one in the middle of the line. Several arrows stuck out of his chest; one was through his calf; and one protruded from the socket of his left eye. He walked with high, mincing steps.

"I'll drink the blood of fauns!" chuckled Beard. His helve quivered in Sharina's hands; for the moment the weapon weighed almost nothing. "Oh, mistress, you're so good to Beard!"

"To the ship," Alfdan wheezed. "We can't—"

The nearest faun raised his edged club of dense bone over his head. He trilled like a frog in springtime, hideously magnified, and leaped thirty feet onto the wizard.

Sharina stepped forward, swinging Beard in a downward slant. The axe sheared off the faun's raised left arm and sank into his neck, severing the spine. The creature spurted steaming, sulfur-colored blood and made a spastic leap. It landed well out on the dry seabed.

Alfdan sprawled where the faun had thrown him. Another of the creatures sprang onto the man to the left. He tried to fend off the attack with his bowstaff. The faun swung his club overhand, striking straight down and pulping the man's head. A man nearby thrust with his short sword. The blade left a steaming gash in the faun's hide but skidded off the ribs.

Sharina brought Beard around backhand and sank the spike in the faun's temple. This one sprang straight in the air, its limbs flailing wildly like bits of twine caught in a high wind. Sharina kept her grip on the axe handle, knowing it would be certain death if she lost her weapon.

"Behind you, Sharina!" Franca cried.

She spun, swinging the axe in a horizontal arc that ripped the full depth of its blade through a faun's ribs and breastbone. The creature's gushing blood burned where it spattered her forearms. The creature toppled down the seawall, holding the club it hadn't had time to use.

Sharina paused, gasping through her open mouth. The axe slobbered joyfully. Its edge was keen enough to split a ray of light, but the effort of jumping and whirling still took all Sharina's strength.

The two remaining fauns approached her from opposite sides, more circumspect now than their fellows had been. They walked on their toes; though their feet weren't really hoofs, the four lesser toes were on the way to growing together.

Scoggin had crawled up to the edge of the seawall, clutching his spear. He thrust into the ankle of the faun to Sharina's right, tripping it over on top of him.

Sharina met the other faun's descending blow, lopping its long bony fingers off against a club made from a seabeast's shoulderblade. That was what she'd been trying to do, but she'd felt Beard twitch in her hand at mid-stroke; the axe was adding its own increment to her strength and athleticism.

The bone club smashed into the top of the seawall and leaped out of the creature's maimed hands. The faun screamed musically and reached for Sharina with its thumbs and stubs of fingers. She drove Beard into the creature's forehead and heard the steel gurgle, "So much blood! Rich blood!"

The faun did a backflip to thrash like a dying beetle. Sharina jerked the blade free. Her arms felt swollen and her vision was blurred. The faun Scoggin had disabled lay on the ground with a dozen men on him, holding down his rangy body and stabbing. One of Alfdan's archers used a broken arrow as a poniard, punching it again and again into the faun's throat. Each thrust brought a spurt of searing blood, but the faun continued to struggle.

Sharina staggered over to the melee. She was afraid she'd hit one of the men if she swung normally.

"Give me room," she gasped, only half able to hear her own voice. Nobody in the surging mass reacted. Short-gripping Beard, she turned the axe over and pushed the spike through the faun's upper chest as though it were a dagger blade.

The creature arched its back violently, flinging away the men holding it. It continued to convulse until it rolled over the seawall to lie on the shingle not far from the glowing crystal ship.

Sharina rested on all fours. She didn't know whether her eyes were open or closed; she couldn't see anything through the roaring white fire that consumed her lungs and throat.

Voices coalesced out of the sea of noise. Men were talking, apparently to themselves rather than each other; nobody seemed to be listening to anybody else. Sharina heard prayers and curses and long half-coherent babbling about how close death had come—and passed by.

"There it is," Alfdan said. He spoke in a heavy, breathy voice, forcing out each syllable between his wheezing. "Take the axe from her and bring it to me."

Sharina heard the words, but they hung as if in a vacuum that was wholly separate from her and the world in her mind.

"Take it!" Alfdan said. "Faugh, I'll get it myself."

She felt a tug and suddenly was alert again. She held Beard in both hands; the steel was crooning in an undertone punctuated by sucking sounds and giggles. Alfdan had just tried to pull the axe away from her.

Sharina jerked back and rose to a kneeling position. Dizziness washed over her, but it was gone as quickly as it came. She braced the butt of the axe on the ground and used the helve as a cane as she rose to her feet.

"Oh, he's an enemy, mistress," Beard said. "Let's finish him too, a little dessert for Beard after the luscious fauns you fed him!"

"Kill her!" Alfdan shouted, jumping back. He stumbled,

tangling his feet with his carved staff. "Quickly, shoot her down!"

Scoggin raised his spear; Franca fitted an arrow to the string of the bow he must have taken from a man the fauns slew. The youth's eyes were open and staring, but there was no more intellect behind them than there was in those of a rat cornered by a weasel.

"Stop!" said Sharina. She put a hand on Franca's shoulder and shifted her body so that she stood between Scoggin and the wizard. "There'll be no more killing of men by other men, not here. There's few enough of us left as it is."

A faun sprawled on the ground beside her, its complexion turning from blue to purplish as the blood drained out of it. Its hands were shockingly long, its palm and fingers both twice the length of a human being's.

"She's right," a man said. "Lady help me, it would've broke my neck in the next heartbeat if she hadn't killed it when she did. Alfdan, let 'er be."

The wizard had lost his cap though he still wore the black cape. Sharina couldn't tell what the material was; it seemed to absorb light without having a color of its own.

He looked about the circle of his men. "All right," he said, trying to sound as if he were still in control. "But she must hand over the axe. Then she can do as she likes."

"Beard is—" Sharina said. She almost said, "mine," but her thought was quicker than her tongue. "—my companion. You will not take him from me, Master Alfdan."

"I will have it!" Alfdan shouted, his face transfused with fury.

"Drink his blood!" shrilled the axe.

"No!" said Sharina. "Both of you, be silent! There will be no more killing!"

"Alfdan," said the man who'd spoken a moment before, a big fellow with auburn hair and a beard that was nearly brunette. "She saved our lives, yours too. If we need the axe, ask her nice to come along with us. And if she doesn't want to, well, that's all right too. We don't, and *you* don't, force her to do nothing."

"That's right, Alfdan," said another man. "Neal's speaking for me."

Alfdan suddenly relaxed. "Yes, I see the sense of that," he said. He managed a weak-kneed bow; he was as wrung out as Sharina herself. "Pardon me, mistress, this has been . . ."

He gestured around him with a trembling left hand. "I'm not myself. None of us are ourselves. Will you come sit with me in the Queen Ship so that we can discuss the future?"

Sharina looked at the shimmering crystalline vessel that had drawn her into Alfdan's trap in the first place. "Yes," she said. "Let's do that."

With Beard muttering in her hand, she walked down the seawall again. This time she didn't brace herself with a hand.

Garric was dreaming. . . .

He and Carus walked into the garden they'd entered the previous night. It was the same location but a different age; the stonework was sharper and beds of carefully tended flowers lined the paths.

"The moon isn't right," Carus said, locking his palms together to keep from fidgeting with his sword hilt. In this dream the king was dressed as he often did in Garric's mind, wearing a short blue tunic over breeches and knee-high cavalry boots. His sword hung from the left side of his broad leather belt, its weight balanced by the dagger and traveler's wallet on the right.

Garric looked at the full moon through the branches of a fruit tree. The orb seemed bigger than he was used to, but it also had a deep golden cast as though there were more than distance between it and him.

"Nothing right's here," he said. "We're dreaming."

Did ghosts dream? Was the Carus beside him only a dream himself?

The trees were in bloom. Garric thought they were pears, though there'd been only apple orchards in the borough so he wasn't sure. The perfume of their white blossoms was faint but noticeable in the moonlight.

Garric walked toward the altar in shadow at the back wall, but as he moved he felt his consciousness swirl away. He was being lifted by a pair of figures so faint that the stars twinkled through them, so huge that their presence filled the cosmos.

There was no Garric, no seeing or hearing; time wasn't the same. There was warmth and water and eventually surging excitement as he/it *grew*.

Sunlight flooded and faded; moon and stars had no meaning anymore. Rain fell and the soil dried again; and fell and dried, and fell. . . . Always there were the Presences, tending and protecting him/it.

The days became shorter, the sunlight weaker. Garric felt his leaves slough away. He'd been only vaguely aware of them, the way a man might be aware of his skin. The cold came, as painless as a cloud covering the sun for a moment. He felt his young limbs being trimmed; the Presences flowed about him, as omnipresent as the breeze.

Spring followed and *growth;* richer and fuller than before, and wholly engaging. His/its limbs were being trained. His/its leaves unfolded, soaking in sun and converting nutrients, processes too complex for a human mind to fathom but utterly a part of the mindless being he/it now was. His/its buds bloomed in lustful profusion and the bees brought fulfillment that flowed through every vein and rootlet. He/it *was*.

Sun and rain, warmth and cold; and always the Presences were there to guard and guide him/it. Every year brought growth, every spring meant blossoms. Life was good, joy was eternal, and always the Presences. . . .

He/it felt a tugging. He/it resisted, but he had no strength to change what was happening. His existence flowed out and upward, bodiless for an uncertain time.

For an instant, Garric or-Reise stood in the moonlit garden again. King Carus was at his side, his face twisted in a look of fury.

The ancient pear tree beside them no longer curved its gnarled branches into a ragged oval. The trunk had been stunted to knee height, and its two remaining limbs were trained in a cordon that ran parallel to the path. Great white blossoms bloomed on stubs like miniature trees which grew upward from the horizontal limbs.

Garric's consciousness roared on. He sat up with a shout.

His sword hung from a rack at the head of the bed. He'd half-drawn its watered steel blade when he realized where he was—and that it was really *him* again, not a dream phantasm.

"Garric?" said Liane, her voice so sweetly modulated that it all but concealed her fear.

A footed lamp in the form of a three-headed dragon stood in a niche across the room; one wick burned as a night-light. Garric shot his sword back home in its sheath and padded over to the lamp. His hands were shaking. He tried to light the other wicks from the first, but he couldn't even get the scrap of tow he intended for a spill to catch from the existing flame.

Liane took the tow from his trembling fingers and lit the wicks. She glanced at a second lamp, but instead of lighting it also she crushed the spill out on the bottom of the niche. She faced Garric and put her hands on his shoulders without speaking further. He hugged her hard against him.

"I was a tree," he said. He closed his eyes tightly. "They made me grow exactly where they wanted me to grow."

He drew in a deep breath. "I don't know who they are, Liane," he said. "But I know what they intend."

"They won't succeed," Liane said, her voice calm but her heart hammering like a bird's. "You won't let them, Garric. None of us will let them do that."

"Read to me," Garric whispered into her hair. "I don't care what—just civilized words, my love. Because what they are isn't civilized. It isn't even human."

Obediently Liane lifted the lamp out of the niche with one hand. With the other she guided Garric back to the bed and sat him beside her on the edge. She set the lamp on the nightstand and opened the book she'd been reading earlier in the evening.

" '*I know my own language only from letters,*' " she read aloud, her voice a glow of amber in the darkness. " '*If I could not write, I would be mute. . . .*' "

She paused with a look of horror. Garric started to laugh. His choked giggles built quickly to bellowing guffaws just this side of hysteria. She'd been reading Pendill's *Letters from Exile,* and because of her nervousness she hadn't remembered the subject matter when she picked it up in haste at Garric's direction.

After a moment, Liane began to laugh also. She set the book back on the table and embraced him. "Oh, Garric, we *will* win this, you know," she gasped between gusts of laughter.

"*Aye*," growled the king in Garric's mind. "*And when it's time to split skulls, we'll do that too, lad; you and me!*"

Ilna awakened in her bedroll on the stern an instant before the lookout's cry roused everybody aboard the *Bird of the Tide*. The sky to the north rippled and flared crimson.

"Get the oars out," Chalcus ordered calmly from the door to the tiny deckhouse. "Nabarbi and Tellura to port, Shausga and Ninon starboard. Kulit—"

Kulit was on watch; he'd sounded the alarm.

"—stay there in the bow to conn us through the passage."

In a break from his usual blithe cheerfulness, Chalcus added in a snarl, "Sister take those bloody rocks, and may they not take *us* before we're even out of this harbor!"

Ilna glanced at the stars; it was past midnight. The moon was waxing and not yet visible in Terness Harbor, though on the open sea it would probably be above the horizon.

The weapons were stored in the deckhouse, sheltered from the weather. Chalcus took out a bow, set one end on the deck, and leaned his weight on the other until the staff curved; then he slipped the bow cord into its notch. Bow-staves cracked if left with the cord taut, so an archer only strung his weapon when he was about to use it.

Night lay on the drystone huts built up the hillside; the town was dark as only a peasant village or the deep forest can be. No lights gleamed from the fishing boats. A muted clang came from the *Defender*, moored across the harbor. The narrow-hulled patrol vessel rocked even in the still wa-ter of the harbor; the hammer hanging beside the alarm gong in the stern occasionally brushed it as they both swung.

"What's it that's happening out there, Captain?" Hutena

asked as he took the first bow as Chalcus began to string the next. The four crewmen told off to row were fitting their long oars onto the thole pins. They worked with their usual skill, never wasting a motion, but there was a silent tension to the task tonight.

"Ah, that's what we're going out to learn, lads," Chalcus said. He passed the second bow to the bosun who gathered it with the first in his right hand. He held them by their tips. "Wizards' work, that we know from the sky."

He nodded as he strung the third bow, a particularly stiff one. Its core of black wood from Shengy was laminated between a layer of whalebone on the face and a backing of ox sinew. "Which wizards those would be, and what their intent is—those things we need to be closer to learn."

Chalcus grinned broadly at Ilna. "Not so, dear heart?" he asked.

"I can't tell anything from here," Ilna said. Smiling faintly because the situation really did amuse her, she added, "Of course I may not be able to tell anything when we're in the middle of whatever unpleasant business is going on, either."

"Indeed, we may not," Chalcus agreed equably. "And we may all have our heads taken for trophies in the airy halls of the birdmen. If any of you lads would stay ashore tonight, the dock's a short step now but a very long one if you wait."

"We're with you," Hutena grunted. He reached for the third bow.

"This bow is for me, I think, Master Bosun," Chalcus said mildly. He straightened, surveying the crew. "Does Hutena speak for you all, then?"

Nobody replied. Hutena said, "Cast off the bow line, Kulit. I've already gotten the stern."

Kulit loosed the line, then took a boat-pike from the mast rack and joined the bosun in shoving the *Bird of the Tide* away from the quay. The rowers took up the stroke, falling into a rhythm without external command.

The bosun set a bow between each pair of oarsmen while Chalcus brought out bundles of arrows. Ilna thought about the attack on the fishermen; if the Rua chose, they could drive the *Bird*'s crew into the hold as easily as they'd cleared the decks of the open boats. But she was increasingly less convinced that the winged men had anything to do with the attacks on merchantmen in the Strait.

The *Bird of the Tide* made for the harbor entrance. Kulit called low-voiced bearings from the bow, but the oarsmen needed little correction. Their faces had the set, unhappy expressions of men about to go out in a drenching rainstorm. They didn't look frightened; and perhaps they weren't.

That there were no lights in the village of Terness was only to be expected; Ilna would've been surprised if any fisherman had been wasting lamp oil at this time of night. The castle was equally dark, though, and that was another matter. She'd seen enough palaces and noblemen's mansions to know that there should be the gleam of a lantern in the guardroom, the glow of fires beneath the ovens where bread for the company was baking.

She smiled tightly again. In this particular place, she didn't suppose the lord would be reading far into the night; but it was likely enough that the wink of a rushlight through a shutter would indicate that a clerk had been late finishing his accounts.

The stars shone as bright points undimmed by a haze of wizardlight. Whatever had awakened her was over now. That part of it, at any rate.

Chalcus distributed short cutlasses to the crew, all but Hutena who had his own broad-bladed hatchet thrust through his belt. The short, curving cutlasses looked clumsy to Ilna, but they were as keen as Chalcus thought they should be—working edges rather than being sharpened chisel-thin and sure to break at the first hard stroke. They must have suited the men using them or else they'd have had something different. Blades were no business of hers, anyway.

Another gush of wizardlight stained the sky as the *Bird of the Tide* negotiated the last of the narrows. The cliffs on either side of the vessel stood out starkly against the scarlet glare above them. Ilna felt the hairs on the backs of her arms rise; her nose wrinkled in irritation at her body's inability not to react.

"Dead ahead on the horizon," Kulit called, his voice strong but just a half tone higher than Ilna had heard it on other occasions. "I saw a mast when the . . . when the sky was bright, you know?"

Chalcus hopped to the top of the deckhouse, the highest vantage on the *Bird* since they'd unstepped the mast and left it back on the quay. "Row on, lads," he said in a tone of quiet excitement. "That's the *Queen of Heaven* or another so like her it makes no never mind. There's lights aboard her, and it's more lights than any captain would burn while anchored in calm weather. We'll learn something soon or I'll know the reason why."

He dropped beside Ilna again and crossed his hands before him. "Had I left the mast up," he said, "we'd have a better view as you doubtless are thinking. But we'd have been visible from farther out as well, and that concerned me more than what *we* could see."

"I wasn't thinking anything of the sort," said Ilna tartly. "I assumed you knew your business; and I certainly *don't* know your business."

She was knotting and loosing patterns as she spoke. She'd taken the cords out of her sleeve almost as soon as she awakened, and she'd been working—and unworking—them ever since. She saw Chalcus glance at the latest version and quickly cupped it between her palms. He couldn't have gotten a clear enough look anyway, but—

"That wouldn't be a good thing to see," Ilna said without letting her voice display her terror at what had almost happened. "I'm nervous, you see, and when I'm nervous my mind calms itself by thinking of dark places to send my enemies."

"Ah!" said Chalcus. "I can understand how that might be." He laughed merrily and hugged her with his left arm, though his eyes continued to scan the sea ahead of them.

The *Bird of the Tide* drove over the slow swells. The steering oar was raised and lashed to the rail where it didn't drag against the vessel's progress. Ilna knew there was a current because of what the sailors had told her and from the way bubbles of foam slowly drifted right to left, but Nabarbi and Tellura on the port side oars were compensating for it by taking longer strokes than their shipmates to starboard.

"There's the *Queen* or her twin . . ." said Chalcus, pitching his voice just loud enough to be heard over the faint squeal of the rowlocks. The crew had tallowed them just after nightfall, before they opened their bedrolls to sleep. "And there's boats in the water beside her, low ones. Hutena, were any of the fishing boats missing from the harbor tonight?"

"They were not," said the bosun, standing with a hand on the tiller and a hand on his axe head, ready at instant need to drop the steering oar into the water. "Every boat that went out this morning came back to harbor, saving the one you say the demons took. And every boat that came back was there in her berth as we put out."

"My thought as well," said Chalcus with a smile. "And there's more and bigger vessels by the *Queen* than one poor fishing boat that was left for the Rua."

Wizardlight pulsed in the deep sea, spreading outward like a ripple on a pond. It silhouetted the merchantman, now little more than a bowshot away, and two long, low barges moored to it. An instant later the *Bird of the Tide* was suspended in crimson purity. Fish, caught in the same clarity, hung lower in the light-shot void, and arrowing through the sea toward the merchantman was the great seawolf Ilna had glimpsed from the deck of the *Defender.*

The flash spread on and vanished. It hadn't affected Ilna's night vision.

"Dear one, do you know what it was that just happened?" Chalcus asked in a voice all the crew could hear. He held his bow in his left hand with an arrow between his fingers, but his right hand wasn't on the cord. The light had shown everything nearby; the air was empty of Rua and of every other thing beneath the clouds.

"Beyond the obvious, that there's a wizard working," Ilna said, "I know nothing at all."

She tried to keep the irritation out of her voice. She realized that the crew, brave men though they were, needed or at least deserved reassurance, so she had to be willing to offer it.

A question formed in Ilna's mind and resolved itself; she chuckled, but she didn't explain the reason when Chalcus raised a quizzical eyebrow. She'd thought, *How can telling the men that we're completely ignorant be reassuring?* And the answer came as swiftly: *We've told them they're as well off as the people putting them to this risk; and that's not what they'd assume if we failed to tell them.*

"A hard pull and we'll come up alongside the barge at the stern," Chalcus said. "Hutena, have you seen ships like that before?"

"Grain scows on the River Erd," Kulit answered in the place of the silent bosun. "A hundred feet long and forty broad, but they'll swim in water that won't come to your waist."

"There's marshes on the west side of the castle where you could land a barge," said Shausga. "I sailed the Carcosa run when I was a lad. Though why you'd want to berth there with Terness Harbor so good, I don't see."

"Indeed, a marsh?" said Chalcus. "It'd conceal your barges from an agent of Prince Garric with his eye on the *Defender,* would it not?"

"They're not hidden now," said Ilna. "Wherever they land and sail from, we can see the barges as soon as they're used."

"Aye, my love," said Chalcus. "And so could anyone else who put out when he saw wizardry in the sky at night. But would, do you think, every agent choose to do that? And if he did, or she did—would their crew obey the orders to put out?"

Chalcus laughed, but quietly. They were coming up on the *Queen of Heaven* and her attendant barges. In a conversational tone he went on, "Conn us around, Kulit, starboard to starboard with the barge. Not that I think they'll try to chase us down, this lot, but for the craftsmanship of the thing."

He grinned at Ilna. She smiled back, touched by the humor but aware also of the patterns that formed and scattered under the play of her fingers.

There were many lights on the merchantman's deck, more than Ilna could count with both hands. She heard men's voices, often that of Commander Lusius himself, shouting angry orders.

"Won't they see us coming?" she asked in a quiet voice, almost a whisper. *"Don't* they see us?"

Things splashed into the sea, followed moments later by a swirl of water and the *clop* of great jaws. Ilna'd seen the sea-wolf; now she knew why it followed whenever Lusius put out to sea.

"Not this lot," Chalcus murmured. "Not till we tread on their toes, and maybe not even then."

"We're going aboard, Captain?" asked Hutena as the *Bird of the Tide* slipped toward the barge with a soapy ease. Shausga and Ninon shipped their long oars; crewmen on the port side backed water to kill the vessel's remaining momentum. "We know who the pirates are already, don't we?"

"I think we know who," said Chalcus. "But not how, and just possibly not who either—since our Lusius wouldn't be one to leave a derelict with a full hold. You and I will board her, Hutena, while the others will wait ready to cast off."

"And I'm coming, of course," said Ilna. She'd made a choice of the pattern to have in her hands; she'd chosen or her fingers had, either one. She sometimes thought that her hands had not only more skill than her conscious mind but more wisdom as well. If she'd been wise, she'd be rich and powerful beyond all other folk—but she wouldn't be Ilna os-Kenset anymore, and that was a greater price than she was willing to pay for anything in the world or beyond it.

"Of course you are, my heart," said Chalcus, striding forward to hand his bow and the bundle of arrows to Kulit. "Of course you'll come with us, or there'd be no reason for us to be here at all."

Thick hawsers at bow and stern lashed the barge to the merchantman. A coarse swatch of rope netting draped over the bigger ship's side provided a ladder, which several at a time could climb. A few worked on the barge by the light of several lanterns, stowing bales that the larger number who'd gone aboard threw over the merchantman's railing.

The men were Lusius's Sea Guards, though for the most part they were in tunics rather than linen cuirasses and only a few wore their swords. That was a factor Chalcus would have noticed from the moment the *Bird of the Tide* drew within bowshot; it explained why he was blithely taking the

Bird's handful into the midst of the much greater number of Lusius's men.

The Sea Guards used many lamps, more than the work itself required, on the *Queen of Heaven* and the pair of barges. Lamplight illuminated only a small circle around each flame, and by doing so hid whatever was beyond those circles more thoroughly than the darkness itself. Lusius' men so feared what might be lurking aboard the merchantman that they ignored the possibility another ship might slip up on them.

The *Bird* thumped alongside the barge. Shausga and Ninon looped ropes around two of the oarlocks that lined the other ship's gunwales. Though the barge was by far the larger vessel, its deck was actually lower than the *Bird*'s. Ilna and Chalcus hopped aboard together.

"Hey!" cried a Sea Guard as he and his fellows turned to see what had struck them. "Com—"

Ilna saved his life by spreading the pattern she'd knotted. She held it out so that lantern light fell squarely on its seemingly effortless artistry.

The man who'd spoken doubled up, spewing vomit that appeared to be mostly wine. Those nearby retched and covered their eyes. A man who'd been at a distance so that he'd gotten only a slanted view of the pattern called, "What? What?" in the voice of one waking from a nightmare.

Hutena cracked him hard over the head with the peen of his axe. "Tie these scuts up while we're gone!" the bosun ordered over his shoulder. He grabbed the boarding net a moment after Chalcus and Ilna had started up.

Ilna's eyes watered. She sneezed fiercely, smothering the sound in the shoulder of her tunic. The *Queen of Heaven* reeked of brimstone. Had it been a grain ship, it might have been fumigated before setting out on this voyage, but there was no call to worry about rats seriously damaging a cargo of tapestries. Besides, the smell hadn't clung to the timbers when they'd boarded the ship with Commander Lusius.

The netting was made from the same sword-leafed desert plant as the rope Ilna had handled earlier. It had a clean, dry feel, and the strands had been twisted by a careful workman who knew her business. There was nothing so simple that there wasn't a right way to do it—or for most people in Ilna's experience, a wrong way.

"Hey, what's going on down there?" a man called from the *Queen*'s railing. "Stop playing the fool or we'll tip this bloody tapestry on your bloody heads!"

Chalcus vaulted the railing, using his left arm as a pivot. He hadn't drawn his inward-curving sword, but Ilna knew how quickly the weapon could appear in his hand when he wished.

The Sea Guard screamed and stumbled back, crossing his hands before his face as if to keep from seeing his own on-coming doom. There'd been four of them lugging a rolled hanging, a full weight for them all together. *Silk with gold and silver wires on a wool backing; valuable no doubt but journeyman's work, exceptional only in the value of the raw materials . . .* The others jumped away also, and one started to draw his sword.

"Gently, lad, there's no need for that," Chalcus said, taking the man's sword wrist with fingers that Ilna had seen bend iron nails. The Sea Guard gasped in pain; then Hutena mounted the railing behind him and quieted him with another rap from the axe.

"Who are you?" demanded the Sea Guard who'd first spoken. He wasn't armed, which may have been the reason his tone changed from hectoring to merely inquisitive in the course of a short sentence. "Sister take you, I didn't see you when I looked over the side, and I thought . . ."

He didn't bother to explain what he'd thought. Ilna could've guessed closely enough, even without a pair of Sea Guards coming out of the deckhouse hauling a corpse between them.

Part of a corpse: a man's head and shoulders, with the torso below that ending in a ragged slant at mid-chest. Ilna believed that the victim was the chief of the Blaise armsmen.

The men dragging the torso had sour expressions, and their minds didn't take in the things their eyes glanced over. They walked past the group around Chalcus and tossed the fragment into the sea between the two barges.

"We're guests of the Commander, don't you recall?"

Chalcus said. "Now, where is it he would be, friend? For we've business for his ears only."

"You're . . . ?" the Sea Guard said. He shook his head in puzzlement. "Well, I don't know, in one of the holds, I suppose, but—"

"Hoy, Commander!" Rincip bellowed, striding out of one of several open doors on the side of the deckhouse. He held a lantern high in his left hand. "There's a strongbox but there's money bags all over—hey!"

His eyes fell on Chalcus, then Ilna. "Where'd *you* come from!"

"In a crisis like this, all men must stand together," said Chalcus, stepping toward Lusius's second in command. "Not so, Master Rincip?"

Rincip touched his sword pommel but didn't let his fingers close around its shagreen grip. After only a moment's thought he pointedly lifted his hand away.

"Civilians have no business here!" he snarled, but he didn't try to keep Chalcus and Ilna from entering the cabin he'd just left.

A lighted candle burned in a free-swinging holder hung from the ceiling. It threw a pale tallow illumination over the interior of the cabin, sufficient to see by even before Rincip followed them back in with the lantern.

A bed frame was folded out from the wall. The mattress was a common one of waxed linen filled with straw, but the bedclothes—now mostly tumbled on the floor—were silk. Instead of an ordinary sea chest roped to floor bitts so that it didn't skid around the cabin in bad weather, the wealthy occupant's large chest was cross-strapped with iron and padlocked to the bitts. The lid had a hasp and staple also, but the padlock that should have secured it was missing.

Three heavy leather money bags closed with lead seals lay on the floor. Beside them was a document case and several thick codices. Ilna recognized those last as ledgers, though she couldn't have read them even if they weren't in cipher—as they almost certainly were.

On the floor, half-covered by the bedding, was a man's hand and wrist. The hook-bladed sword it'd been holding lay beside it. One of the long bones of the forearm was still attached, broken off at the elbow end. The muscles had been stripped away, but some tendons still dangled.

Smiling in friendly innocence, Chalcus gripped the hasp of the strongbox in his left hand and tugged. The lid didn't rise; it was fastened even though the external lock was missing.

"What's this about money?" said Lusius, stepping into the cabin with a Sea Guard holding a lantern. "There should be a specie chest—you!"

Four men and Ilna crowded the cabin. Hutena remained on deck, very possibly overlooked in darkness and the confusion. Chalcus had a way of drawing eyes to him, which— given the bosun's demonstrated ability to think and act quickly—could be the key to escaping a situation that was literally—Ilna smiled—getting tighter by the moment.

"Aye, Commander," Chalcus said. "We saw the trouble in the sky and came to it, like good citizens of the Isles. And what should we find but you and your men?"

"It's my job to be here!" Lusius said. He didn't reach for his sword; the cabin was too cramped for sword work, and he'd seen what Chalcus's dagger could do in less time than a victim could blink. "You don't claim that I did this, do you?"

The commander thrust his boot under the bunk and hooked out the severed hand. "We saw the light, same as you did, and came to it as quick as possible. We were too late to save the crew, just as I warned the fools would happen if they didn't take my guards on board."

He didn't mention that his troops were looting the merchantman's holds. In all fairness, Ilna didn't suppose she'd met ten men in her lifetime who'd have passed up a valuable cargo whose owners had been reduced to a scatter of body parts.

"And your wizard Gaur?" Chalcus asked. "Where would he be, Commander?"

Lusius shrugged. "Back in his bed, I suppose," he said. "Gaur doesn't leave the castle often, and he never goes aboard a ship."

Ilna stood silent with her hands cupped over the fabric of cords that she would display if she needed to. Getting out of the cabin would be possible if not easy; getting down the

side of the *Queen of Heaven* with a troop of hostile soldiers
above them . . . that would be another matter, a problem to
solve when they must.

The Commander's look hardened and he drew himself up.
"Now, Captain," he said, "there's the matter of how *you*
came to be here. For the time being I'm willing to accept
your story, though many folk would find it unlikely that any
man went unbidden into wizardry unless his duty required
him. What I say is this: get back to your ship, and get back to
Terness—now. By my order as Commander of the Strait."

Ilna sneezed again from the brimstone in the air. Bits of a
pattern connected in her mind. While Lusius spoke in an increasingly louder voice and Chalcus faced him with his
hands on his hips, Ilna bent forward and grasped the sword
on the floor of the cabin.

"Watch her!" Rincip shouted, grasping Ilna's shoulder;
she wriggled free. Chalcus caught Rincip's neck in one hand
and jerked him away.

Ilna used the sturdy sword as a pry bar, her left hand reversed on the grip and her right on the pommel. She rammed
the point into the seam of the strongbox's latch, then levered
upward. After a moment's resistance the lid flew open.

The supercargo, Pointin, crouched like a hare in her form
within. He leaped up screaming, blind with fear. The iron
straps protecting the chest were held on with large rivets.
Pointin had used a silk sleeve from his sleeping tunic to tie
together mushroomed rivet-heads on the side and lid of the
chest.

"By the Sister!" Lusius swore.

"Don't!" cried Chalcus, holding Rincip back with his
right hand, his left poised.

The Sea Guard who'd come in with Lusius grasped his
sword hilt. Ilna brought the Blaise sword around in a short
arc. The back of the blade wasn't sharpened, but it broke the
soldier's wrist bones with a crunch. He screamed and
dropped the lantern in his other hand. Oil spilled but didn't
catch fire for the moment.

"You're human!" Pointin cried. He'd been shoving away
the air; now he lowered his hands. "Wha . . . where are the
demons? Have they gone?"

Chalcus punched Rincip in the stomach, then kneed him in the jaw as he doubled up. Lusius's deputy thumped to the floor and lay still, groaning and bleeding from the mouth.

"Now, Commander Lusius . . ." Chalcus said. His eyes hadn't moved from the Commander's during the moments it'd taken him to put Rincip out of the way. "We'll leave the *Queen of Heaven* to you and your fellows to deal with, as you demand. But for safety's sake, you'll come as far as the deck of the *Bird of the Tide* with us. We'll climb down the netting with you on the side of my dagger hand."

Chalcus spoke pleasantly enough, but Ilna noticed he hadn't worded the statement as a question even for the sake of conventional politeness. Lusius glared, gathering his thoughts for a response.

Before he could make one, Ilna said, "No, the Commander will climb down after you so that if anything's thrown over the side it'll land on *his* head."

Chalcus opened his mouth for a protest. "And as he climbs," Ilna said, loosing the silken rope that served her for a sash, "he'll have my noose around his neck—"

She tossed the running loop. Lusius bellowed in surprise and jerked his head back. The noose slipped over his head anyway and settled to his shoulders. Ilna tugged the soft rope tight—but not stranglingly tight—before Lusius got his hand up to throw it off. His lips twisted in a snarl, but he was smart enough to take his hand away before Ilna choked him to the floor, gasping and helpless.

"—to remind him that his duty is to escort us clear."

"Right," said Chalcus with the quick decisiveness that was the difference between life and death when time was short and the risks uncertain. "Pointin, going out of the cabin you'll follow Mistress Ilna and the Commander, and I'll bring up the rear."

Ilna put a finger's weight of pressure on the noose. Lusius grimaced and started for the cabin door.

"But where are you taking me?" the supercargo demanded in a tone that started high and ended as a falsetto.

"Some place other than the belly of a seawolf with what's left of your friends," Ilna snapped. "If that's not reason enough, I've got enough cord here to put a loop in the other end too and drag you along with the Commander!"

Pointin's face registered shock; he didn't respond for a moment. Chalcus took him by the shoulder and headed him toward the door. Pointin raised his feet high enough to clear the side of the box in which he stood, but he moved in a slack-mouthed daze.

Ilna curled her lips under in irritation with herself. She had years of experience in telling people unpalatable truths, and never once had it seemed a good idea afterward. If she kept doing it nonetheless, she must be as great a fool as most of the rest of humanity.

The air outside was cool enough to be a surprise. She'd expected to see the Sea Guards waiting with their weapons drawn, but the interplay inside the cabin had gone unnoticed by most of those aboard. They had their own concerns, hauling heavy fabrics from the ship's several holds and disposing of the remnants of the vessel's crew.

Splashes and the swirling attacks of Our Brother sounded unabated. Whatever had killed the crew was a messy eater. The scattered fragments reminded Ilna of what was left of a chicken devoured by rats—feathers and feet and perhaps the head after the back of the skull was gnawed open to lick out the brain.

"Hutena, you lead," Chalcus said. "Quickly, man."

The bosun was over the railing like a great, squat spider. He continued to hold the hatchet instead of slipping the helve through his belt to free the other hand.

"Say, Commander, how many of these rolls are we supposed to bring up?" asked a soldier who'd seen Lusius and hadn't noticed anything wrong. "We'll never empty her in one night—nor three if I'm a judge."

Ilna smiled tightly and pulled with the care she'd have taken to place a thread in her weaving. "Later!" Lusius growled.

"But look—"

"Later, Dover!" Lusius shouted. "Do you want to feed Our Brother, is that it?"

The Sea Guard snarled a curse and backed away. Chalcus prodded Pointin to the railing; when the supercargo simply stood there, Chalcus lifted him one-handed and dangled him over the side. Only then did Pointin grasp the ropes and begin descending, clumsily but with increasing speed.

Ilna climbed the rail, paying out a little more line as she did so. The boarding net was an old friend by now, a brief transport to a dry place without the slurp/*clop!* of a seawolf gobbling human tidbits. Lusius followed with the speed of long practice.

When the Commander was well over the side and unable to change his mind, Chalcus dropped like an ape leaping from a tree. He caught the net halfway down, swung himself beneath Ilna, and dropped the rest of the way to the barge to join Hutena and Pointin.

The crew of the barge had recovered from the shock Ilna'd given them, but they weren't ready for more. One of them cried out when he saw her; all of them backed into the relative darkness of the bow.

"What did you do to them, mistress?" Hutena murmured wonderingly as he gripped the Commander's shoulder.

Ilna whipped off her noose as easily as she'd caught Lusius in it. "I made their heads spin," she said, doubling and redoubling the rope before she looped it back around her waist. "That's all."

And if she'd wanted, she could've knotted another pattern that would make those who viewed it leap into the sea to quench the flames they felt blazing from their eye sockets . . . but there'd been no need, and Ilna was trying to learn a sense of proportion in the punishments she paid out to those who opposed the right as she saw it.

But it was very hard. They all deserved to die; and Ilna os-Kenset deserved to die also, as she well knew. . . .

She hitched up the drape of her modestly-long tunic and jumped aboard the *Bird of the Tide.* Some day she'd receive the justice she deserved; but until then she'd live and continue to make amends in the best way she could.

"Cast off!" Chalcus ordered, but the crew was already shoving them clear of the barge. Lusius stood glaring after them. "You're free to return to your investigations, Commander. And no doubt we'll meet again in good time, after you've returned to Terness, not so?"

Chalcus laughed as the oarsmen pulled hard for the harbor. Ilna did not. The sound of the seawolf slapping the water again and again as it leaped for morsels could be heard for miles against the quiet sea.

'There's some wine in the cup here," said a voice in Cashel's ear. "You'll feel better if you can drink it."

Cashel opened . . . well, no, his eyes were already open. They suddenly focused, though. He blinked twice, clearing them, and thought about getting up. He tried to raise his head first, then thought better of moving at all for at least a little while.

It was late evening. He could tell that because he faced west as he lay on the mound at the base of the marble tank, and so he saw the sun setting. If he hadn't been looking that direction, he'd have just had to guess about the time of day.

Evne waddled around Cashel's head to face him. "Of course if you prefer to lie here feeling sorry for yourself . . ." she said.

Cashel started to laugh. It was just what he needed to do, though the first wracking gulps of air almost killed him. His bruised chest bounced again and again on the ground, and there was nothing he could do to stop it.

He finally got his laughter enough under control to sit up. It was a good thing he'd landed on the mound rather than digging a trench with his nose across the stony plain. He felt dizzy for a moment and closed his eyes, then realized that was a bad idea and opened them again. When he didn't have the horizon to look at, he got vertigo.

"You knew I'd get mad if you said I was feeling sorry for myself," Cashel said. "And then I'd see how you'd fooled me, so I'd laugh and that'd bring me around. You're really smart, Evne."

"Yes, I am," the toad said. "Now the wine."

Cashel looked down at her affectionately. "I don't like—" he said.

"I didn't ask if you liked it," the toad said. "I said you'd feel better for drinking it. Though of course—"

Cashel took the cup waiting beside where his right hand had been holding the quarterstaff. Duzi, he'd really bruised the knuckles; though he didn't suppose that was such a terrible thing, given what might've happened when he came down.

The cup was crystal and as clear as the air around it. He drank the pale green liquid in three gulps. There weren't any bubbles in it, but it prickled like there were.

"Oh!" he said wonderingly. "That's wine, Evne? It doesn't taste like any wine I've had before."

"No," said the toad. "I don't suppose it does."

Cashel looked around him, which saved him asking where the wine—and the cup—came from. There were any number of folk, both in bright clothing and in servants' garb, standing among the ruins below the tank and staring up at Cashel. Near each handful of people was a curvy, boatlike thing with a long stem and stempiece—sort of milkweed pods grown to giant size.

"Where did *they* come from?" he asked amazed. And as rough as the slopes had been even for him, how did this lot of soft-living folk from the manors manage to get here near as quick as he had and carry those boats with them besides?

"Some are from Manor Bossian, I believe," said the toad, "but mostly they fled from Manor Ansache when the Visitor destroyed it. And there may be a few—"

She moved her head in a series of short twitches rather than a smooth arc as she eyed the crowd below them.

"—from other places as well, running before they're forced to run."

The toad paused, rubbing the back of her own neck with her long right leg. She added, "They flew here in their airboats when they learned you'd killed the dragon. They're afraid, you see, and they're looking for somebody strong to protect them."

"I'm not . . ." Cashel said. He didn't know how to continue the sentence, so he let his voice trail off. "Should I do something, Evne? I mean, about them?"

The toad sniffed. "You're not required to do anything,"

she said. "And at the moment, master, I don't see that you're *able* to do very much. Including stand up."

Cashel cleared his throat. "Yeah, that had better wait for a time," he agreed. Because he didn't want to think about *all* those people watching him and expecting him to do—something, whatever—he turned his head to the side and saw the dragon for the first time since he'd awakened after the fight.

"Duzi!" he said. The little herdsman's God of Barca's Hamlet didn't seem a grand enough deity to name as he looked on the thing he'd been fighting, so he added, "May the Shepherd help me, Evne. I couldn't have beaten *that!*"

"Really?" said the toad. "Then my eyes must have gone bad while I was imprisoned in that block of coal. It's not surprising after seven thousand years, I suppose, but I very distinctly saw you hammering the creature to death."

The dragon was a long sagging bronze tube. Some of the scales had dropped off, leaving gaps through which Cashel saw what seemed to be a web of wires. The body stretched from the top of the mound to well out into the plain, plus however how much of its length was still in the tank. Black smudges on pedestals of rocky soil showed where tufts of silkgrass had burned when the creature rolled over them during its flaming death throes, and it'd seared a broad wedge of the slope's juicier vegetation as well.

"Evne," Cashel said, "I couldn't have stopped it any better than I could've stopped a herd of oxen if they'd stampeded at me. It's just too big, it *weighs* too much. I'm strong, sure, but nobody's that strong."

"That might have been so if it'd been a real snake," the toad said, "but it wasn't—it was wizard's work. So you fought it as one wizard to another, and you were the stronger. It certainly gives the lie to those who claim intelligence and erudition are prerequisites for wizardry, doesn't it?"

Cashel sighed. He didn't know what either *erudition* or *prerequisites* were, but *intelligence* was a word he understood. He could figure out what the toad meant easily enough.

He ran the quarterstaff through his hands, letting his fingertips check the hickory for damage that his eyes couldn't see. The iron buttcaps were now rainbow colored from the energy they'd channeled during the battle, but the staff itself was unmarked. It remained the same straight, smooth friend as it'd been since he turned it out of a branch.

The closest spectators to Cashel were well-dressed folk in a group at the bottom of the mound. One of them was Syl, the woman who'd sat at Bossian's table during dinner, though the men didn't include the Farran who'd been with her. Cashel didn't recognize the others, which wasn't surprising; but seeing Syl made him wonder uneasily about Kotia.

"I told the refugees that I'd summon them in the event you deigned to grant them an audience," Evne said in a cool tone. "Otherwise they should keep their distance or it'd be the worse for them."

Cashel grinned. "They took orders from a little toad?" he said.

Evne rotated her head to put him in the middle of her two bulging eyes. "They may have thought," she said, "that so great a wizard as yourself would have a familiar who could herself blast them to ashes. And they may have been right."

Two of the men were arguing with Syl; one put a hand on her shoulder, turning her so that she faced the mound "Lord Cashel?" she called.

"Shall I order them away?" the toad said with no emotion at all.

"No, no," Cashel muttered. "That's all right."

Loudly to Syl he said, "Mistress, you can come up if you like. But I don't think I can help you."

He hadn't meant for the whole group of them—six, a handful and the thumb of his other hand—to come, but they all did. That was maybe a good thing: two of the men carried a crystal hamper between them. More of that wine and some food—Cashel's stomach rumbled in excitement—would go down a treat.

Manor Ansache destroyed, the toad had said, and Syl here from Manor Bossian. Well, it wasn't his world and these folk *sure* weren't his friends.

Their clothing was just as fine as it'd been at the banquet the night before, but it'd now seen harder use than it was meant for. The tall, blond man who'd been most insistent about Syl calling to Cashel had lost the sleeve of his tunic; there was even a scratch on his bare shoulder. The rest were tousled looking, and the long aquamarine gown of the other woman—older than Syl by quite a lot—was seared across the train.

"My master will accept your gift of further viands," Evne said. Listening to her voice you'd think she was looking down her nose as spoke, but she didn't have a nose. "And scraps of chopped meat for his loyal servant wouldn't come amiss . . . though the pair of damselflies that fell my lot as he rested will suffice if they must."

The men with the hamper immediately set it down; it started to slide. Cursing, the blond man blocked it with his foot and jerked the lid open.

"Lord Cashel . . ." Syl said. She hadn't been injured, but she looked like she'd been dragged through a drainpipe. Her eyes flicked nervously, and there was nothing in her expression to remind Cashel of the haughty, elfin girl she'd been when he met her. "We didn't realize that Lord Bossian had summoned you to destroy the Visitor. If we seemed less than attentive previously—"

"If you seemed like a nitwit who was more worried about the shade of her hair ribbon than the fact her world was ending, you mean," said Evne. "As of course you were."

Syl instinctively reached up to touch her hair. The ribbon was a green so faint it might have passed for white. She realized what she'd done and grimaced.

"Whatever," she muttered. "Anyway, we've come to say that we'll put everything we've managed to escape with at your service."

Which was different from, "ourselves at your service," thought Cashel as he took a flat loaf from the hamper while one of the men refilled the crystal cup. He couldn't imagine any service this lot could be, of course; to him or to anybody, themselves included.

"Ma'am . . ." he said as he bit down and found to his surprise that the loaf was meat or anyway tasted like meat instead of being bread. *Duzi!* but he was hungry. "Ah, what I meant to say is that Bossian didn't summon me anywhere. He helped me some but that was because he wanted to be shut of me."

Cashel paused, both to swallow what he'd been chewing and to collect his words. He knew what he meant, now and most times, but often he had a hard time finding the right words.

"It was Kotia who brought me here," he said carefully. "To your world, I mean. And now I'm going back."

"But milord . . ." said the blond man. His face twisted up in a funny way; Cashel thought for a moment that he was going to spit at him. That had happened to Cashel before, though it'd never turned out to be a good idea for the fellow spitting . . .

Instead the blond man sank down on his knees and started to cry, and it was absolutely the first time in Cashel's life that *that* had happened. If he'd had to pick between the experiences he guessed he'd have taken the spitting, because then he knew exactly what to do.

"Milord, milord, *please*," the fellow blubbered. "You slew the dragon, surely you can slay the Visitor also. Milord, if you abandon us we have nothing, *no* one."

The others weren't crying but they looked like they were ready to, all but Syl who patted her hair ribbon with a distant expression. Shuving or-Gansel had that kind of look on his face when the oak he'd been felling split partway up the trunk and leaped back on him. It didn't change even when he died, an hour or so after Cashel and Shuving's son had gotten ten the tree off him.

Cashel gulped the wine; it tingled all the way to his toes. Pretty soon he'd be ready to stand up; Duzi, he was probably ready now. He said, "Sir—"

Before he could come up with a way to continue, the fellow grabbed Cashel's knees with soft, clammy hands. Cashel jumped to his feet, spilling the refill of wine that another of the locals was pouring from a bottle with a serpent neck.

"*Don't* do that," Cashel said. He slammed his staff into the dirt, holding it vertically in front of him like a narrow wall.

The blond man jerked back. Now the older woman started to cry, a little soft, *"Whoop, whoop, whoop,"* through the hands covering her face.

"Kotia brought me here," Cashel went on. He had a flash of dizziness, but nothing worse than what generally happened if he stood up quickly after squatting. "She saved my life, I guess—"

The place he'd been before Kotia took him out wasn't somewhere he'd have wanted to live much longer, even if he'd been able to.

"—and I paid her back by bringing her safe to Lord Bossian to marry. She and I are quits, now, and for the rest of you . . ."

He shook his head, wishing he could find a better way of saying what he felt. "Look, I'm sorry about your troubles, but I can't fix everything. Even if I could fight your Visitor, which I don't see that I could."

Cashel bent down. He set his cup on the ground—the slope wasn't quite too steep for it to stand on its base—and turned his palm up before the toad.

"Come on, Evne," he said. "We'll be leaving now. I think you'd best ride inside my tunic while I climb onto the tank."

The toad didn't hop into his palm as he expected. Syl looked at Cashel, her face as calm as a corpse's, and said, "Lady Kotia won't be marrying Lord Bossian. The Visitor came to Manor Bossian after he'd destroyed Manor Ansache. He destroyed the Crimson Tower and demanded Kotia or else he'd destroy the whole manor."

"He . . ." Cashel said, trying to get his mind around what he'd just heard. "What . . . what did Lord Bossian do?"

The blond man had gotten to his feet again. "What did he do?" he repeated in a shrill, half-mocking tone. "What could he do? He sent the girl to the Visitor, of course!"

Cashel didn't speak. He'd been stroking his quarterstaff with his left hand, but he stopped that too. He felt a vein in his throat throbbing.

"She didn't object," Syl said. She was no longer detached; she watched Cashel closely. "She was walking toward the Visitor's ship even before Bossian sent to bring her."

"Yeah," said Cashel at last. He couldn't have recognized his own voice. "She'd have done that."

He licked his lips; they were very dry. "Lord Bossian's a wizard. Why didn't he stop the, the Visitor?"

"He couldn't!" crowed the blond man, coming closer to being hammered into the ground like a tent peg than he probably realized. "Nobody can stop the Visitor!"

"Then why didn't he try!" Cashel shouted and they all but one stumbled back; all of them except Syl, and she was smiling now.

"The Visitor stays in the middle of the Great Swamp when he's on this world," said Evne, sounding like a teacher. "All the streams on this side of the hills drain into it, and there's no outlet."

"I can't fix everything," Cashel said, starting to get his normal voice back. He reached down again and this time Evne hopped into his palm. He straightened.

"I can't fix everything," Cashel repeated, "but there's things I *will* fix regardless. Now—"

He eyed the group of locals without affection.

"—how do I get to the Great Swamp?"

Chapter Fourteen

The *Bird of the Tide* moved with the same heavy ease as the rolling sea. Ilna didn't like boats, but the *Bird* was a part of the sea in the same fashion that her shuttle became part of the fabric it wove. The oarsmen kept up a deliberate pace that nonetheless drove them toward Terness with surprising speed. The *Queen of Heaven* and the barges looting it were already out of sight.

"Captain Ohert had doubled the watch," said Pointin, sitting with his back to the deckhouse. He'd sipped from the sack of wine Chalcus offered him as soon as they got aboard, but now he was cradling the sewn goatskin like it was all that kept him from sinking into the deeps.

"The regular sailors, I mean," he went on; mumbling, exhausted from fatigue and fear. "Half the guards were awake too, and the other half were sleeping armed and with their boots on."

"Land in sight, sir," called Kulit from the bow. Hutena stood near enough to Ilna, Chalcus, and the supercargo that he could have helped if called to, but not so close that he had to overhear.

Ilna smiled faintly. The crewmen had conducted themselves all this night with skill and quiet courage, but they were deathly afraid of wizardry. Hutena didn't want to hear the details of what had struck the *Queen of Heaven,* and the oarsmen let their eyes rest anywhere but on Pointin's face.

Chalcus had chosen his men well. Of course.

"I was asleep," Pointin said. "Why shouldn't I be? I didn't think that thieving rogue Lusius would dare anything since he knew we were on our guard, and anyway I wouldn't have known what to look for."

He lifted the wineskin, then stared at it as if he wasn't sure what it was or what its purpose might me. He lowered it again, frowning and silent. His eyes had gone unfocused.

"What awakened you, Master Pointin?" Chalcus asked in a mild voice. He hadn't spoken much, letting the supercargo tell his story in bits and pieces as they came to the surface of his mind. Imposing a form on the telling might have thrown the man into shock and locked his tongue.

Ilna could see that Pointin was on the verge of collapse, even with delicate handling. She'd said nothing at all, but the patterns that her fingers knotted in the light of the now-risen moon were as soothing as the glow of embers to an awakened sleeper.

"It was the light," Pointin said, frowning now with concentration. "It came through the walls of my cabin. It was blue; I guess I'd call it blue, but I've never seen anything like it."

He looked up with a desperate expression. "I don't know how to describe it!" he said.

"We know the sort of light you mean," said Ilna quietly. She spread a pattern, then folded it between her palms and began to unpick the fabric as quickly as her touch had formed it. "We know why it would awaken you."

"I heard people shouting on deck," Pointin went on. "I ran out immediately; I thought the ship had caught fire and I'd burn."

He shook his head, then deliberately raised the wineskin to his lips and sucked at its contents. He looked calmer as he lowered the skin, but a muscle in his left cheek was twitching.

"It was worse," he said. "Fire I could've understood."

The rocks framing the entrance of Terness Harbor loomed ahead of the *Bird of the Tide;* the oarsmen had stroked their way back with no more than an occasional glance over the shoulder. Kulit began calling low-voiced directions; Hutena lifted the boarding pike that lay on the deck beside him and held it ready for fending off.

"We *fell,*" Pointin said. His plump face grew taut again and his arms began to tremble. Hutena had given the supercargo his bad weather cloak to cover the silk sleeping tunic, but the fellow still trembled uncontrollably.

"It wasn't really falling, not at first anyway," he said, "but it felt like . . ."

He looked from Chalcus to Ilna and back. "Did you ever take a step in the dark and the ground wasn't there?" he said. "That's what it was like, the feeling in your gut that the ground wasn't there."

Pointin drank again, this time slobbering wine over his face and throat. "The sky was dark and yellow," he said, his voice rising. "The sea was gone. There were rocks around us and the air was hot, blazing hot. It stank of brimstone. I can still smell it on my clothes. I can still smell it!"

"Yes," said Ilna, spreading a new pattern before the supercargo. "We can smell it too, but you're safe now."

She wondered if that was really true. Pointin was as safe as the rest of them were, she supposed. That was enough for *her* sense of honesty.

Pointin nodded three times with seeming determination. "The deck tipped and threw me against the cabin again," he said. "If it had tipped the other way it might've put me over the railing, but it didn't. We were on dry land and the ship had rolled to one side of the keel."

He giggled. "One side or the other, and it didn't throw me out."

"Did you know where you were?" Chalcus said, loudly enough to drag Pointin back from the brink to which his rising laughter was rushing. "Was it a land you'd seen before, my fellow?"

"Land?" said the supercargo. "It was no land, it was the Underworld! There was almost no light and what there was came from the whole yellow sky. Clouds swirled all around us—thicker or thinner but never *thin*. There wasn't any sun, that I know. I saw spires of rock, and the wind was blowing. I saw red fire on the horizon. I think it was a volcano, but I don't know for sure."

He slurped wine, then choked and sneezed some out of his nostrils. Chalcus whipped off the bandanna he used as a headband and offered it to Pointin. The fellow mopped himself, then handed the bandanna back with a grateful smile. Chalcus folded the cloth one-handed at his side.

"I saw something coming toward us," Pointin said. "Out of the fog, out of the shadows. It was on two legs but . . ."

The silence lingered. "Was it a man?" Chalcus asked softly.

"It wasn't human," said Pointin. "I don't think it was human. It glittered, even in that light, and it was huge. I . . . I went into my cabin and hid in the specie chest."

He looked up fiercely again. "We couldn't fight demons!" he shouted. Lowering his eyes he went on in a less angrily defensive tone, "Anyway, I'm not a soldier. I couldn't have done any good that way. But the chest was iron and iron has strength against demons, so I've heard."

"So I believe," murmured Chalcus, but the way his fingers stroked the eared pommel of his sword showed Ilna that he wasn't simply agreeing with the supercargo. "Could you hear what was happening before you got into the chest?"

Pointin shrugged. His shoulders were hunched and his knees drawn up as though he was still trying to hide in the iron box. "I heard shouts," he said. "Captain Ohert called something about getting the cover off the stern hold. The covers were cleated to stay firm in a storm; I doubt they'd have been able to get one open in time to hide below."

"Nor would it have done them much good if they'd managed," Chalcus said, his lips smiling faintly but his eyes focused on another time, another life. "There's always some who try, though, thinking it better to hide than to fight."

The *Bird of the Tide* had reached the harbor narrows. Ilna heard an oar blade scrape rock and a muffled curse from Nabarbi, but neither Hutena nor Kulit needed to push off with their pikes.

"I'd just closed the lid over me when I heard my cabin door open," said Pointin.

"There'd been screams from on deck. I thought . . . whatever it was, whatever it was had come for me. I hadn't had time to tie the lid yet."

He licked his lips feverishly. His hands clenched the flaccid wineskin, squeezing an occasional drip onto his tunic. He didn't notice it.

"It wasn't that," Pointin continued, "it was men—two of the guards, I think. I couldn't hear the words but they were talking with Blaise accents. And then the door broke in and . . ."

He shrugged again. "There was shouting," he said. "The words didn't mean anything, just, you know, shouting?"

"I know," whispered Chalcus.

"There was a fight," Pointin said. "I could hear things breaking. And there were more screams and, and . . ."

Ilna spread her latest pattern before the supercargo. When his eyes finally took it in, he lost some of his pallid tension and began to breathe normally again. "I heard crunching," he said. "It must have been very loud for me to hear it. And after a while the screaming stopped. Then there was nothing. I don't know for how long."

"How were you able to breathe?" Ilna said. What room there'd been in the treasure chest was scarcely enough for Pointin's doubled-up body.

"I'd tied the lid closed," he said, casual about the question because his mind was reliving horrors instead. "The silk had enough stretch for the lid to raise a crack when I needed to breathe. The air stank of brimstone, but I had to breathe."

Ilna wouldn't pretend she liked Pointin, but he was smart *and* quick-witted, which was a different thing. The fact that he'd used his wits solely to preserve his own life shouldn't matter to her, since she couldn't imagine there was anything he could've done to affect what happened to the rest of those aboard the *Queen of Heaven.*

It did matter, though. Ilna knew other smart, quick-witted people who wouldn't've made the decision Pointin did. No more than she'd have done that herself.

He looked up, his expression puzzled again. "There was another *change,*" he said. "A fall like before, only a splash and I could feel the ship was floating again. And then I heard voices, but I was afraid t-t-to . . ."

"Did you see the wizardlight?" Chalcus said, his voice calm and calming. "Like what awakened you?"

"No," said Pointin. "I was in the chest, though. Perhaps the iron . . . ?

"Perhaps the iron," Chalcus agreed softly.

"Ship the starboard oars!" Hutena ordered. The *Bird of the Tide* was easing back to the slip she'd left hours before. The eastern sky was almost bright enough to read by.

Ilna smiled. If you could read, of course; which the supercargo alone of those aboard the vessel was able to do.

"Well, Master Pointin," Chalcus said, "we're here in Terness. While I won't tell you what to do, I think you'd be wise to stay aboard the *Bird,* cramped though you'll find her, until we've stepped our mast and are able to sail for Valles. We'll do that tomorrow morning, nothing else appearing."

"But what about Commander Lusius?" Pointin said. "When he comes back, won't he try to take me away?"

"That one?" said Chalcus as the *Bird of the Tide* thudded gently into her berth. Kulit and Nabarbi hopped up to the dock, holding lines. "Not openly, not even in Terness. He thinks we have Prince Garric's ear, and he knows word would get out if he slaughtered us. Something will come, I think; but not openly, and not till late night."

Chalcus laughed. He drew his dagger and threw it up, juggling it from hand to hand while he continued to watch the supercargo.

"He knows that his business is with us, now, not just you, my good fellow," Chalcus said.

"Yes," said Ilna as she looped her hank of cords away in her sleeve for use at another time. "And our business is with him!"

The crystal vessel—the Queen Ship, Alfdan had called it—was only a little more comfortable to sit on than it'd looked to Sharina from outside. The planes of blurry light were solid, but they were also slick as ice. The deck's slight angle—the beach sloped, and the ship hadn't nosed straight into it—meant that Sharina had to cling to the mast or she'd have slid back onto the shingle as surely as sunset.

Holding on wasn't easy either. The mast was of the same immaterial solidity as the deck, so it tried to slip through her fingers.

"I'm a wizard," Alfdan said, sounding more defensive than he had any reason to be. "A real wizard!"

He'd placed himself on the high side of the deck and braced himself against the mast with an outstretched foot. Sharina was sure that if she tried the same technique she'd slide just as she was doing now; it was a matter of practice and perfect balance.

"I never doubted it," she said. "You—you and your men, you were completely concealed. Even from Beard here."

"It wouldn't have stopped me from killing every one of them!" the axe muttered—also in a defensive tone, and with as little cause. "Arrows indeed! Beard would've drunk all their blood before *they* could bring my mistress down!"

Sharina smiled. The axe showed more enthusiasm about the prospect of her bleeding to death atop a mound of mangled corpses than she could muster, but that was true of many of Beard's enthusiasms.

"Yes, well . . ." said Alfdan, lowering his eyes. "I didn't want you to think that because I use devices like the Cape of Shadows—"

He plucked the hem of his sleeve. When he moved, the cape fluttered like an ordinary garment, but though the shape changed Sharina couldn't see folds or wrinkles. It was a swatch of blackness, not fabric.

"—and the Queen Ship, that I'm not a wizard. But it's true

that my power would be . . . not great . . . without them to aid me. Except in one thing."

Up close, Alfdan was an ordinary looking man. He was thin and nervous, but so was Franca; so were most people in this world, Sharina supposed. Most of the few who survived.

"I can find objects of power," the wizard explained. "See them, feel them, know where they'll be. I knew the axe Beard would be coming here, so we waited for it."

He nodded. The axe lay across her lap with her left hand on the grip.

"Do you know what Beard is?" Alfdan said, his deep-set eyes focusing on hers.

"She knows that Beard could split you scalp to crutch, little man," the axe said with unexpected venom. "She knows that he'll be *glad* to drink your blood, thin and sour though he knows it'll be!"

"I know that Beard's the reason that we're still alive, most of us," Sharina said, "after the fauns attacked. That makes him my friend. I don't need to hear anything about him that he doesn't choose to tell me."

"Whatever you please," Alfdan said, licking his lips and turning his head to the side. "I hadn't expected the fauns. Did you . . ."

He met her eyes again.

"Had you seen the fauns before?" he said. "Had they been pursuing you?"

Beard cackled with glee. "Do you think you're the only one who can see things before they happen, wizardling?" he said before Sharina could reply. "They weren't following us, but they may have been waiting just as you were. Or they may have been waiting for you!"

Alfdan played with his hem again, staring intently as if he saw something important in its lack of being. "I found the Cape of Shadows," he said, "in a casket among the roots of an ancient tree that had fallen that morning. The roots pulled the casket up from the ground with them, and I was there to find it!"

"And this ship too, I suppose?" Sharina said. She'd have tapped the deck, but she needed both her hands. She felt

Beard quiver with words too faint to hear; it was like having a purring cat on her lap, a cat of sharp-edged steel.

"Yes, the Queen Ship," the wizard agreed absently. "It was in a cave on Ornifal. The entrance had been under water for millennia, but I found it when the sea receded. In another day—"

He looked up fiercely again. Sharina wondered how much of Alfdan's jumpy behavior was from fatigue and how much was simply madness.

"—a glacier would have covered it and locked it away for all time. Except that I found it!"

"I see that," Sharina said quietly, stroking the axe in her lap as she thought of glaciers on Ornifal. "What has that to do with me?"

She wasn't afraid of Alfdan. She wouldn't have been afraid of him even without Beard, but she knew that Alfdan, like an injured dog, might snap at her out of pain and blind fury. She didn't want that to happen, but there's no way to control what a madman may do. She'd deal with whatever happened.

"The Queen Ship sails over the sea, not in it," Alfdan said, calm and seemingly reasonable again. "Over the sea or the land either one—it doesn't matter to the ship."

"All right," said Sharina. Her fingers were slipping. She shifted her grip, snatching at the mast before she could begin to slide off the deck.

What does this ship of light weigh? Could a man or a hundred men lift it from the beach using ordinary muscles instead of wizardry?

"We're searching for the Key of Reyazel," Alfdan said, lifting his head and speaking in a consciously portentous voice. "Will you come with us, Sharina os-Reise?"

Sharina frowned. "Why should I?" she said bluntly. Did Alfdan think he could compel her by his art, now that his men had refused to use force on her?

Could the wizard compel her by his art, whatever he thought?

"You're alone," Alfdan said. "We are many, and—"

"Franca is with me," Sharina said.

Alfdan sniffed. "Yes, I saw him," he said. "A sturdy help, I'm sure!"

"And Beard is with her, wizard," said the axe with ringing clarity. "Mistress, let me kill him now. The others will follow you, see if they don't!"

"We are many," Alfdan repeated, wetting his lips with his tongue again. "And I have the treasures that allow us to flourish even in this world. The Cape of Shadows, the Queen Ship; other objects now, and perhaps in the future *many* more objects. If you slew me . . . if you were *able* to slay me, as this one wishes . . . they'd be quite useless to you."

Sharina looked at the wizard. She neither liked nor trusted him, but he was certainly right that she couldn't use tools that required wizardry; nor, she suspected, was she likely to meet another wizard—in this place or anywhere—whom she'd like or trust any better than she did Alfdan.

She smiled. If she hadn't met Tenoctris, she'd have believed all wizards were arrogantly self-willed, and that most were actively evil besides.

Alfdan misunderstood her expression. "Do you doubt me?" he demanded. "Do you think—"

"I know you're a wizard," Sharina said, raising her voice enough to ride over his. "I know I'm not and that I could no more use your cape than I could fly. But I'm still not convinced that we should join you, Master Alfdan."

The wizard leaned back and chuckled, suddenly at ease again. "Well, mistress," he said. "The fauns were looking for something, were they not? Or do you believe it was chance that brought a pack of them here, now?"

Sharina kept a strait face. "I don't suppose it was chance," she said. "I don't think it was, no."

"So they might have been looking for me, but nothing of the sort has happened to me in the past," Alfdan said. "Never in the ten years since She came. But you, mistress . . . you just came to our world, you say. If their friends or many more of their friends come looking for you again, would you rather run from them on your two legs? Or would you sail away with us on the Queen Ship?"

"I see," said Sharina, her hand motionless on Beard's helve. "Yes, that's a reason to join you. Now, Master Alfdan, tell me why you *want* us with you?"

"Because the axe in your hands is almost better than having it in mine, mistress," the wizard said. He laughed again, but this time the humor trailed off in a giggle that was close to something else. "There's finding the Key of Reyazel, which I can do easily; and there's bringing it up from where it lies. If you and your axe will agree to fetch me the Key of Reyazel, then you're welcome to all the protection to be had from my band and my art, I assure you."

"There'll be things to kill," Beard said in a steely whisper. "Blood to drink, mistress, much blood for Beard to drink!"

"I'll get this key for you . . ." said Sharina. "If you take me where I want to go in exchange."

"Where is that?" said Alfdan with a frown.

"I don't know," she said. She smiled without humor. "I just arrived. Does it matter?"

Alfdan shrugged. "I don't suppose so," he said. "All right, mistress. But first you must fetch the key."

He and the axe both began to laugh in high-pitched voices.

"Sit in the middle, Lord Cashel," Syl said as she got into the bow of the craft and knelt facing backward. "Getchin will guide the boat. He's good at that."

"He weighs too much," said Getchin, the blond man. He stood in the stern, holding a slender crystal rod about as long as his arms would spread. "You shouldn't come with us, Syl."

"He doesn't weigh more than Elpel and Gromis both," Syl said composedly. "Not quite."

Cashel looked doubtfully at the vessel he was supposed to get into. Not only was it shaped like a pastel pink milkweed pod, it seemed to be equally flimsy. He wasn't much happier about the prospect than Getchin was.

"Are you sure I won't just step through the bottom?" Cashel said.

"It makes no difference to me, since I'll be carried whether you enter the airboat or hike on your own legs, master," said Evne from his shoulder. "But it's three days journey if you walk it, so we'd best be getting on . . . unless it's your plan to bury Kotia instead of rescuing her?"

"I don't have a plan," Cashel muttered, stepping over the boat's curved side. It had a warm, firm roughness to his bare feet, the feel of a thick, newly-sawn plank. "I just thought somebody ought to . . ."

Cashel thought somebody ought to give the Visitor some of what he was dishing out to other folks. Saying that— and saying that he meant to be the fellow who did it— sounded like bragging. If things worked out, Cashel wouldn't need talk; and if they didn't, well, at the end he wouldn't have to worry that he'd made a fool of himself in addition to losing a fight.

"Well sit down, then," said Getchin peevishly. "And keep your weight balanced, if you would!"

Cashel looked at the blond man. Getchin was as tall as he was, but he was only of middling build and soft besides. He glared at Cashel, then flushed. No one spoke until Cashel turned and seated himself with his usual care. The boat's interior was hollow with neither thwarts nor furnishings of any kind. Cashel held his quarterstaff across the gunwales before him.

"Getchin hopes to replace the late Farran in Syl's affections, master," the toad said in a voice that folks deep in the circle of spectators could hear clearly. "He regards you as a rival, so he regrets that Syl insists on coming along at the start of your heroic endeavor."

"Look, let's get moving, can we?" Cashel said. He didn't look over his shoulder at Getchin, and he wished that Syl wasn't seated staring right into his face.

"Getchin is a fool," Syl said distinctly. "To believe *he* has any chance, I mean."

The toad laughed. The boat lifted, jerking forward with a wobbly violence like a skiff rowed by an angry man. Someone on the ground cheered, and then the whole crowd was shouting, "Lord Cashel!" and "Long live the wizard Cashel!"

Syl smiled faintly. Her eyes looked through Cashel, not at him.

The boat slanted upward till it was about a furlong above the ground. It steadied too; they trembled a little when Cashel turned his head to look around, but nothing serious.

He half-expected Getchin to say something anyway, but the fellow just stood there in the stern with his crystal rod held out crossways like a rope walker using a balance pole. He didn't seem to notice Cashel—or Syl, either one.

"At the beginning of the First Cycle . . ." Evne said. She sounded like one of the priests reading the Hymn of the Lady to the assembled borough at the end of the Tithe Procession. "A moon fell to earth. Its impact formed a great bowl surrounded by ranges of mountains."

"What do you mean, *the First Cycle?*" Syl asked, looking at the toad on Cashel's left shoulder.

"This is the Seventeenth Cycle," Evne said. "I can't imagine why you would ask, except to satisfy intellectual curiosity . . . which rather surprises me, given the source."

Syl smiled at her. "Thank you, Mistress Toad," she said. "Pray continue."

"The manors are built on the peaks," Evne said. "The streams that flow inward drain into the bowl and form a swamp because there's no outlet. More than water sinks toward the center and collects, so human arts aren't sufficient to allow the airboats to fly into the swamp. You will go on foot from the edge, master."

"There's power in the air above the Great Swamp, Lord Cashel," Syl said. "Our boats rise or fall or simply come apart if they venture there. . . . But of course there's no reason to go there at all."

"There's no reason to leave the manor!" Getchin snarled. Lapsing into a desperate whine he added, "Oh, *why* did this happen to me?"

"One answer might be that it spared some useful person from discomfort," said Evne. "Though I don't expect that that's true."

Cashel smiled. When he noticed that Syl was smiling also, at him, he blushed.

Clearing his throat he said, "But the Visitor flies there?"

"The Visitor does as he wills," Evne agreed. "Or so he has always done."

They'd risen considerably higher. Cashel could see the ridges curving beneath him the way ripples spread on a pond. There wasn't enough forest to color the general gray rock background, but creeks glittered jaggedly. On more peaks than Cashel could count with his fingers stood manors built of a variety of gleaming materials.

Several of them were in ruins. The manors had no enemy except the Visitor, but he seemed sufficient.

A sea of fog rose over the ridge ahead. "The Great Swamp," Evne said. "You'll find the air there warmer, master. A great deal of power has settled in the basin."

"There's monsters in the swamp," Syl said. "Sometimes the mist clears and they've been seen. But you slew the dragon of Portmayne, Lord Cashel. You don't fear monsters, do you?"

Cashel smiled. "I don't guess I do," he said. Maybe it was bragging to say that, but he wasn't going to lie; and anyway, Syl was a pretty thing in her way.

"I'm setting us down," Getchin said in a hoarse voice. "I don't dare go any closer. It isn't possible!"

"Not for him, at any rate," Evne said with an audible sniff. "But this is good enough, master. The ground here on the south edge of the basin is firmer than that to the east and north, though there's little enough to choose."

The boat slid downward and past the tops of trees clinging to cracks in the rock. There were hardwoods here, oaks and beeches, and down on the valley floor grew a few tall, straight-trunked trees with shiny, oval leaves and big flowers.

Ahead was a patch of warm mist. They drove into it, slowed, and set down on a plain of pulpy grasses. There were low banks a stone's throw to either side. The trickle meandering down the center of the plain must be a roaring freshet in the spring.

"All right, get out," Getchin said, standing with his wand upright before him. "*Please,* Mas . . . that is, Lord Cashel. It's not safe here!"

Cashel rose and stepped out of the boat. Though it rested on a narrow keel, it didn't topple over the way an ordinary ship would do if the tide left it on dry ground. He wondered how they made it do that.

"Wait," said Syl, getting out behind him. She untied her

hair ribbon, a pale green color like the middle band of the rainbow. Cashel had never seen cloth of that shade before.

"Syl, we mustn't—" Getchin whined.

"Shut up, you fool!" said Syl, stretching the ribbon between her hands. Evne laughed from Cashel's shoulder.

"Lord Cashel," the girl said. "Stretch out your left arm, if you would be so good."

"Ma'am . . . ?" said Cashel, but he obeyed. Syl looped the ribbon over his sleeve above the biceps and tied it into a quick square knot. It wasn't tight around his arm, but the friction of cloth to cloth would hold it against his tunic unless things got too active . . . as of course they might.

"I'd like you to wear this token as you go forward," Syl said. "In memory of Manor Bossian, let us say. It shouldn't get in your way."

Cashel frowned. "It's likely to get lost, mistress," he said. "I'll have other things on my mind, and—"

"Then it gets lost!" Syl said. "It's only a ribbon, after all. But you'll wear it till then?"

"I guess I will, yes," Cashel said. "Evne, I think we'd best—"

"Am I holding you up, master?" the toad snapped. "Are you waiting for me to pick you up and walk off with you?"

"Right," muttered Cashel as he turned, giving his quarterstaff a slow spin. Glancing back over his shoulder, being careful not to meet Syl's eyes, he said, "Thanks for carrying me this far. I hope things go well for you."

He started off, walking faster than he'd usually have done. He didn't want any more conversation. He heard Getchin ask Syl to get back into the boat—and her snarl at him in a voice like an angry cat.

But she didn't call to Cashel, and he was just as happy about that. He wouldn't have answered, but he wouldn't have been happy not to.

"Atten-*shun!*" bellowed a voice with the twanging accent of Northern Ornifal as Garric walked into courtyard of the barracks of the 4th Company of the Carcosa City Watch. A squad of Blood Eagles was in front of him, another squad behind, and the remainder of the demi-company had taken key positions in the barracks before Lord Attaper would permit Garric's visit to go ahead.

"Permit!" snorted Carus in Garric's mind. *"Every bodyguard is born an old lady, it seems to me."*

Perhaps, thought Garric. *But it's generally easier to go along with them, and in this case Attaper may have a point.*

Liane walked primly to his left. A Blood Eagle—one of *her* guards—was a pace behind her, carrying the traveling desk with her documents. The guards had explained that they'd rather carry the gear themselves than worry about a servant being that close, and everybody from Liane on down had insisted that Prince Garric couldn't do servants' work in public.

"Generally easier to go along with them," Carus parroted back with a gust of laughter.

"Your highness!" shouted the commander, a former cavalry decarch named Pascus or-Pascus. "The Fourth Company is all present to receive you!"

Garric smiled faintly. Normally the report would've been, "All present or accounted for," because there were always men on sick leave or detached service. Not today: every man on the muster rolls of the newly-constituted company was here to greet their prince.

"Some of them look like they'll be on their backs in bed as soon as you've left the compound, though," Carus noted with amusement. That was true enough, and their commander himself had a febrile brightness that suggested he was still suffering from his injuries.

Pascus had been among the first troopers to batter their way through the back wall of the Temple of the Mistress in Donelle; he'd lost half his left foot in the fighting there. His family had been retainers of Lord Waldron's family for as far back as parish records went, but even without the army commander's enthusiastic recommendation Pascus would've been an obvious choice for promotion to a job in the City Watch.

"Captain Pascus," Garric said, "tell your men to stand easy."

His voice rang across the courtyard loudly enough that Liane winced. Garric hadn't learned to call orders through the clangor of a battlefield the way Carus had, but a shepherd shouts most of the time if he expects to be heard by another human being.

"Stand easy!" Pascus ordered, just as loudly. "Your prince will address you!"

Until the morning before, these barracks had been the stables and servants quarters of one of the private houses owned by the priesthoods—the priests of the Lady, as it happened, but it made Garric's blood boil to attach Her name or the Shepherd's either one to gangs of thugs. Lord Anda had donated the buildings to the kingdom on behalf of his priesthood; without protest, which was just as well.

A part of Garric and the whole of King Carus wanted to hang the man whose gift had snatched Sharina away to the-Shepherd-knew-where. It wasn't entirely fair to blame Anda for that, because the urn wasn't really his gift—but that same part of Garric wasn't in a mood to be fair, either.

The buildings were easy to come by. Filling them with men who'd act to defend the law and the citizenry rather than this or that individual who believed wealth and strength made them the law—that was more difficult. The process had brought Garric here to the northern corner of the city.

Garric stepped through the line of Blood Eagles and surveyed the new members of the City Watch. The members of the new City Watch, in fact; Carcosa hadn't had a public force to maintain order since the fall of the Old Kingdom.

"You men haven't worked together before," Garric said. He wore his silvered breastplate and the helmet with the gilt wings flaring to either side. This was a public occasion, one on which his job was to be *seen*. "You're starting out with fresh companions and officers to protect the safety of all the residents of this city. Not just the rich ones, not just the ones who can afford to hire muscle . . . though them too, so long as they're behaving as good citizens."

The company was lined up in four ranks of twenty-five men each. They wore linen cuirasses and protective headgear, though there hadn't been time to standardize that as yet. For the most part they were in iron caps confiscated from the temple thugs, but some men wore leather hats and those who came from the army—Pascus among them—had generally kept their bronze helmets.

"You don't work for me," Garric said, his voice echoing. "You don't work for the Vicar of Haft, either, though your salaries will be paid through his office. And you particularly don't work for an individual nobleman anymore, those of you who used to be in private households."

The City Watch—the whole body, not just this company, though Liane had seen to it that the individual companies were widely mixed also—came from assorted backgrounds. Some—including all those who started out with rank in the new organization—were former soldiers from the royal army who'd been pensioned for age or wounds or who simply wanted to retire. Many of those would be abandoning families on Ornifal or elsewhere, but right now Garric and the kingdom had more pressing problems.

Others had been members of Count Lascarg's household troops, but most were former retainers of the city's noble families. King Carus smiled broadly. *"If I'd had a fellow as clever as your Lord Tadai,"* he remarked, *"I might not've gotten myself in so much trouble by solving all my troubles with a sword. Though I'd probably have thrown a table at him for disagreeing with me and he'd have left. The Shepherd knows I did that often enough;* that *or worse."*

Liane had drawn up the rosters with the help of her spies and a group of noncoms seconded from the royal army and the Blood Eagles both; Lords Waldron and Attaper had checked the results. She'd suggested that households be limited to four bodyguards apiece to create an immediate pool of personnel for the Watch.

Lord Tadai had suggested a refinement: anyone appearing in public with more than four male attendants between the ages of eighteen and forty-five was taxed at the rate of a hundred gold Riders per man, per year, payable immediately. After that had been enforced—reasonably politely, but with the royal army stationed in Carcosa there wasn't going to be resistance—a few times, the nobles had released most of their guards. If you couldn't display them in public, there wasn't any point in having them.

"You serve the citizens," Garric said. "Everyone who wants to live in peace with his neighbors. Your job is to make it possible for them to do that—and my job is the same as yours!"

Each watchman had a sturdy three-foot club of oak or hickory. They weren't quarterstaffs, but they weren't mere batons of office either. A quarterstaff was a wonderful weapon—a wonderful *tool*—in trained hands, but training took time, and even so it was awkward to use in a building or a narrow alley.

Besides clubs, the watchmen carried short, slender swords like those of the troops of the royal phalanx. The phalanx used long pikes as its primary weapon, but at close quarters or in an ambush the men had their blades. Carcosa was too dangerous a city at present for Garric to expect men to patrol it with a club and a rattle to summon good citizens to their aid.

"You've been chosen because my advisors and I believe you're responsible men," Garric said. "You have a responsible job. And be very clear, fellow soldiers, that I will *hold* you responsible for the way you perform this job!"

He put his hands on his hips. The company cheered—the cheers led, he noticed, by the veterans of the royal army, but joined quickly enough and with equal enthusiasm by the rest of the watchmen.

Garric saluted, thumping his right fist against his left forearm—the gesture made more sense if you knew that it had originated among soldiers with a spear in their right hand and a shield on their left arm—and turned on his heel. The company continued to cheer as the prince and his considerable entourage left the compound.

"We'll go to the barracks of the First Company now," Liane said, her fingers flipping the boards of a notebook whose contents she had memorized, "then back to the palace for meetings until the tenth hour. We'll visit the Sixth Company before we eat, then get the rest tomorrow."

Garric grimaced as he handed Liane into her sedan chair; she couldn't possibly walk any distance wearing thick-soled court buskins. Everyone—everyone concerned with protocol—would've been happier if Garric had ridden in another chair or at least on a horse, but he wasn't a good enough horseman to risk that on the cobblestone streets. As for being carried in a sedan chair—he'd have died first.

"I'd rather be doing something real," he muttered to her.

Liane touched the side of his chin to get his attention. "Your highness," she said, her tone formal despite the intimacy of her gesture. "If you sail from island to island crushing opponents and public order collapses behind you as soon as you leave, the kingdom will fall just as surely as if you never left your palace in Valles. This *is* real. This is telling the men that you depend on that you *do* depend on them. Nobody else could tell them that and have them really believe it. And they need to believe it, or there'll be no more peace in Carcosa when you leave than there's been for the past thousand years."

Garric patted her hand, then set it in her lap. "To the headquarters of the First Company of the City Watch, Under-Captain Houil," he said to the commander of the escort.

The bearers lifted Liane's chair. The whole procession set off at a stiff pace through streets bordered both by modern buildings and the ruins of far more impressive ones.

"It's easier to go along with them, lad," said King Carus when he got control of his laughter. *"Especially when they're dead right. As I know to my cost from having done it wrong a thousand years ago when I was king!"*

Chapter Fifteen

Does the Visitor have guards out here in the swamp, Evne?" Cashel asked as he probed the bottom of the stream. It was only a handsbreadth deep, but the water was so black with dissolved leaves that he could no more see through it than he could've seen into a stone wall.

"Jump over this," the toad said. "Don't put your foot in it."

Cashel butted his staff in the water and pivoted over it to the other side instead of crossing in two steps as he'd other-

wise have done. He landed on a sprawling mat of cypress
roots and picked his way over them carefully; his mud-slick
feet were likely to slide on the smooth bark.

"There's a flatworm in the water," Evne said. Cashel
hadn't been going to ask for an explanation, though he was
interested to hear it. "Even if I had a chance to talk with it,
which I wouldn't because it never comes above the surface,
it probably wouldn't listen. Flatworms are very stupid, even
by human standards."

The trees, mostly cypress though there were others Cashel
didn't recognize, crossed branches. They didn't exactly hide
the sky, because the warm mist did that. In the few open
patches above, the sun was just a brighter blur than the vapors around it.

"The Visitor neither knows nor cares what humans are doing until he has a use for them," the toad said, getting around
to answering Cashel's question. "He doesn't have guards because he doesn't see a threat . . . which is not to say that
you'll be able to walk straight into his ship. That is protected
against enemies he fears as he fears nothing on *this* world."

"Evne?" Cashel said. He was frowning. "Why does the
Visitor come here, anyway? And if he comes, why does he
leave, then?"

The toad snorted. "Why does Lord Bossian have dinner
now in the West Tower, now in the Plaza?" she said.
"Whim, that's all. Merely the whim of one who thinks he's
all-powerful."

They'd reached another body of water, this one too broad
to jump. Bubbles rose to the surface and hung there as a
dirty froth before finally bursting; there was no current at all.

Cashel checked; he didn't find bottom at what would've
been mid-chest if he'd jumped in. The jet-black water
drained cleanly off his quarterstaff, leaving the hickory wet
but not gummy.

"There's a fallen log to the right," the toad said. "There,
where the yellow iris grows on the bank. It's underwater, but
only ankle deep."

"All right," said Cashel, making his careful way toward
the nodding yellow flags. "Ah, that's a snake on the branch
overhead."

He didn't add, isn't it? to make a question out of the observation, because he had no doubt at all once his mind had registered the fact that one gnarled, blotchy tree limb was twice as thick as the others. Even so he wasn't sure which way the snake lay until the flicker of an inner lid wiping its gleaming black eye caught his attention.

"I wondered when you'd notice him," the toad said, but Cashel thought he heard approval in her tone. The truth was he'd noticed the snake as soon as there was any reason to; if he'd been able to cross where he first struck the water, the long body wouldn't have been of any more importance to him than the branch on which it sprawled.

"Ho, serpent!" Evne called. "Do you know me?"

The snake turned its head, lowering it slightly to hang on an *S*-curve of its neck. "What if I do?" it said. Its forked tongue took several quick, nervous sips of the air. "You have no power over me here!"

Cashel didn't like the snake's tone—Duzi! he didn't like the fact he was listening to a snake talk!—but he kept walking forward along the overgrown bank, picking his footing carefully among the roots and knotted bog plants. It wasn't a time he'd choose to hurry, regardless.

"You're lucky I don't have any reason to show you that you're wrong!" said Evne with the archly superior tone she used when she was being formal instead of insulting people in a common fashion. "Am I correct that there are no creatures of a sort to be threatening in the waters near your ford?"

"You know there's not," the snake said, letting more of his body loop down. It moved as smoothly as oil spreading. "You know I'd have killed them if there were."

"So I hoped," the toad said. "And I also hope you'll let us pass on our way without a problem."

Cashel paused and wiped his quarterstaff with his wad of raw wool. It might be that he needed a clean grip on the hickory soon.

The snake hissed its laughter. "You may hope that all you like, but you've no reason to expect it," it said. "This is my ford and my hunting ground."

Cashel started forward again. They were getting pretty close. He wasn't sure how far the snake could launch itself, but it was a *very* big snake.

"I've two reasons," said Evne. "First, because I've asked you politely—"

The snake hissed even louder. Its head began to sway back and forth, swinging a trifle lower with each movement.

"—and second," Evne continued, "because my master will smash your head in if you don't!"

"Does he think that?" rasped the snake. When its jaws were closed, it seemed to smile, but the two fangs that unfolded whenever it spoke were as long as Cashel's hand.

"*I* think that, serpent!" said the toad. "Do you doubt me?"

Cashel raised his staff to mid-chest with his hands spread a comfortable distance for thrusting with one ferrule or the other. Nobody moved for a moment.

"Faugh!" said the snake. Its body slid back up on the branch as easily as it'd lowered. "I ate just the other day. Somebody else can have the pleasure of swallowing you."

"We can go on now, master," Evne said. Cashel was already picking his way forward, not fast but fast enough. His toes found the log and started forward, balancing with his staff.

He kept his face turned up, watching the snake. It stayed as still as the branch it lay on. Walking like this it was better not to look down anyway.

The ground on the far side was higher and a lot firmer than what Cashel had just come through. When he'd put a moss-draped pin oak between him and the snake, he said, "Do all the animals in this swamp talk, Evne?"

"None of them talk," the toad said. "Not so that you could understand, anyway."

"But—"

"Except that you're with me, of course," she added. "That was too obvious to bother mentioning."

"Ah," said Cashel. There was a spiderweb in his path. He started to brush it away with his staff, then decided to go around the other side of the tree instead. A web that big would be a lot of work, even for a spider the size of both Cashel's hands spread.

"Evne?" he said. "Who are you?"

The toad laughed without humor. "Me?" she said. "I'm your servant, great master. Your guide and humble companion."

Cashel sighed. He didn't suppose it mattered. He didn't doubt that Evne was on his side . . . in her own way.

A damselfly glittered past, an iridescent blue body and shimmering crystal wings. Cashel snatched with his right hand, then brought the trapped morsel close to his left shoulder.

"I thought you might be hungry," he said as he opened his fingers. The toad's long tongue patted his palm before the insect could flutter free.

They continued on for a time in silence broken only by the occasional slosh of Cashel's bare feet. After a while Evne began to sing about a frog who went a-courting.

She had a pleasant voice, for a toad.

Alfdan's band climbed aboard the Queen Ship. Their air of quiet resignation reminded Sharina of peasants heading for the fields on the third day of the harvest—tired from what has gone before and well aware that this day too will be long and hard, but that it must be faced.

Ordinary folk didn't like wizards or wizardry. These men were here because Alfdan was the closest thing they had to a hope of safety.

Scoggin was among the first to board. Sharina reached out to pull him up, but Scoggin had braced his spearbutt in the ground. To her surprise he stretched back his free hand to help Franca. They seated themselves to either side of Sharina, linking their hands around the mast to keep from sliding off.

Beard chuckled, muttering things that Sharina couldn't hear clearly and probably wouldn't have wanted to. Like Alfdan, the axe was a valuable associate but not a completely comfortable one.

"What do we do now, Mistress Sharina?" Franca asked.

"I've promised to help the wizard find a key," she said. "I don't have any more information than that. He'll take me where I request after I've found the key. I don't know where that is yet."

Scoggin snorted. "Suits me," he said. "Away from here is a good start."

He looked at the men now crowding the ship's deck. There were seventeen in the band and Alfdan himself; plus now Sharina and her two companions. "They aren't a bad lot," Scoggin went on in a low voice. "The rest of 'em, I mean. I haven't had anybody around since, well, for a long time."

It struck Sharina that Scoggin and Franca had attached themselves to her for the same reason the wizard had been able to gather his entourage. She and Alfdan were willing to lead in a world where most of the survivors had lost purpose.

Alfdan stood in the stern of the vessel. Though the deck was crowded, there was a clear space in front of him for as far as he could have swung his bone staff. He tapped the deck and said, *"Aieth."* There was a quick flicker of crimson.

Keeping a hand on the mast, Sharina stood to see over the heads of the men seated between her and the wizard. Scoggin cursed under his breath, but he braced her foot with his own.

A many-pointed symbol had appeared on—in the shimmering deck before Alfdan. The figure and the words of power crawling around its perimeter were spaces in the plane of light, chill air through which Sharina saw the rocky beach without the intervening glow.

"Thotho squaleth ouer," Alfdan called. His staff was upright and motionless on the deck. The words of power spun around the symbol faster as he spoke them. *"Melchou melcha ael."*

He lifted his staff and pointed it out toward the distant sea. Though he continued to chant, a rushing sound like the winds of an approaching storm blurred the words. Sharina could no longer hear them clearly.

The deck came level. The prow rotated seaward in line with the staff as though the vessel were pivoting on its mast. The deck now had a tacky grip on the rabbit-skin boots when Sharina shifted her feet.

"Pissadara!" Alfdan shouted. The unfelt wind roared

around them, making Sharina's marrow tremble; the Queen Ship slid forward.

She'd expected to hear the crunch and scrape of shingle against their keel as she would've done if an ordinary vessel were being dragged into the water, but the only vibration was the high tremble of the wind. She and the others on the ship's deck were in an existence of their own, cut off from the world around them as if by thick diamond walls.

The ship accelerated, moving faster than any real vessel could have done. They reached the new shoreline, at least a mile beyond where the coast had been when Sharina was growing up in Barca's Hamlet. The water had a sluggish, gelid appearance, and the surf seemed to cling a long time to the beach before rolling back. The Queen Ship sped outward, leaving the swells as unmarked by its passage as the land had been.

Alfdan pointed his staff southward; the vessel obediently followed the wizard's direction. Sharina braced herself, expecting to be flung toward the outside of the curve as she would have been in a carriage, but she had no feel of them turning—beyond what her eyes told her about the way the world moved around her.

Alfdan's band was beginning to relax. Men talked among themselves in the manner of old associates in familiar surroundings. Several took food out of their packs or swigged from skins of liquid—wine, beer or water, Sharina couldn't tell. Franca watched them longingly.

Neal, the big auburn man, was seated on the other side of the mast from Sharina. She leaned sideways and called, "Neal? As we're a part of your band now, you need to feed us. We left our rations back at Barca's Hamlet when you waylaid us."

"Oh, good eating for Beard in Barca's Hamlet," said the axe, jolted out of his low-voiced litany by the key word *feed*. "Blood and brains, blood and brains and rich marrow for Beard!"

Neal looked disconcerted, then switched his gaze from Beard to Sharina herself. "Food?" he said. "Oh, food."

"We had a whole bear," said Franca. "Mistress Sharina

killed it. We could have dried the meat and lived on it for months!"

"Here, mistress," said Neal, rummaging in his wallet. "It's smoked fish, that's mostly what we have. We build weirs and Alfdan calls fish into them. He has a lure. Lugin, give the mistress some of that wine."

"And for my companions," said Sharina sharply. "We're all together now."

She squatted to take the packet, a slab of dark, oily fish wrapped in an unfamiliar large leaf. After she broke off a chunk—it flaked when she twisted—she handed the rest to Scoggin. He started to bolt it, then caught the sudden hardening of Sharina's eye. He quickly divided the piece with Franca.

Neither of her companions was used to being part of society. They'd been surviving in a harsh world where being quick was the difference between life and death. They had to readjust to caring about other human beings.

"How long have you been with Master Alfdan?" she asked Neal through a mouthful of fish. It tasted wonderful, but the oily richness hitting her empty stomach made her gorge rise. She paused, hoping she wouldn't vomit.

"Me?" said Neal, chewing on a similar fillet. "Three years, near enough. He found me on Tisamur, when he was searching for the Stone Mirror."

He nodded toward Alfdan, standing statue straight. He held out the staff as he mouthed inaudible words of power. The script at the wizard's feet continued to turn in silent regularity like thin clouds scudding across a summer sky.

"He uses the mirror to find things," Neal explained. "Just a little pebble, you'd think, no different from any other that you'd turn up with your plow. But Alfdan sees things in it."

"Burness's been with Alfdan from the start," Neal said, nodding to a balding, older man talking volubly and with hand gestures to two others in the bow. "They were both rooming in a tenement on Erdin when She first came. Alfdan told fortunes and made charms, you know the sort of thing."

Sharina nodded. "I know," she agreed.

She looked over her shoulder at Alfdan. She wondered how long he could keep the staff out straight.

Alfdan would've been a conjurer, a hedge wizard; but not altogether a charlatan. There was somebody like him in every neighborhood of the larger cities; similar folk traveled through the borough, setting up their booths during the Sheep Fair and occasionally in other seasons as well.

"Alfdan took Burness with him," Neal said. "There were two other guys too, Burness says. One I never met, but Tadli was the man the faun killed just now on the shore. He'd lasted a long time, though."

Neal grimaced and chewed in silence for a time, his eyes on the horizon. Sharina thought she saw something moving there, on the surface of the gray sea or in the sky just above it. Neal's attention was on his memories.

When She came, when the weather chilled and the night sky began to ripple with wizardlight, Alfdan learned he could find objects of power. Perhaps the talent had always been in him but too weak to be noticed; perhaps Her power and the changes She wrought in the world squeezed Alfdan's mind into a pattern completely new to it.

"He's Alfdan the Great, now," Neal said in a wondering voice, still looking beyond his present company. "He does amazing things. I've seen him do things that I couldn't imagine being done. Wonderful things!"

"And Alfdan will freeze," said Beard, "and *you* will freeze, and all the wonderful toys your great wizard is collecting, they'll freeze also. Because they're just toys—he gathers them to have them, not to use them. But my mistress—"

The axe laughed as musically as an infant watching a hanging bauble turn in the wind.

"—she'll use Beard. Beard will drink his fill many times more before the ice comes!"

Neal shivered. "Does it have to talk?" he muttered.

"Beard tells me things that I need to know," Sharina said, though she understood Neal's discomfort. "But perhaps, friend axe, you can keep your opinions more to yourself while we're in such close quarters?"

"Hmpff!" said Beard. "It won't change anything, whether I say things or I don't, you know."

Though the axe did subside with that remark. He began to

sing in a low voice, *"They struck with swords and hard they struck till blood ran down like rain. . . ."*

Neal sank into gloomy introspection, his eyes on his hands folded in his lap. He obviously didn't want to think about a doom he couldn't avoid. Sharina didn't have any better answers than Neal did—neither to his problems nor to the more complicated business of getting herself back to the world *she* knew; but she hadn't given up trying.

She smiled. She wasn't going to give up, but she didn't see even a path to an answer to anything. It was funny if you thought about it in the right way.

Men in the bow murmured, nudging one another and looking toward the southwest. Nobody spoke. Sharina turned, squinting to sharpen her vision.

Something was coming toward them, either on the sea or flying just above it. At first she thought it was a bird with long, sparkling wings, but when it changed course slightly she saw that it was a fish whose pectoral fins were each as long as its body. A figure rode on its back and waved a wand or spear. It wasn't human, though at first she'd thought it was.

Alfdan moved for the first time since they'd started south: he pointed his staff a few degrees to the right of its previous bearing. The great fish squirmed through the air in a desperate attempt to follow, but it fell inexorably behind. Finally it vanished in a haze of crimson wizardlight.

"What was that?" Sharina said to Neal. "Have you seen it before?"

Neal remained silent, lost in his bleak considerations.

"We've seen that sort of thing, sure," said another man. "They're not real, we figure. They're mirages, because lots of times they just scatter away after a while."

Beard laughed. "Oh, they're real," he said. "As real as you are when you're here on the Queen Ship. The ship doesn't sail in the world you're from, you know; and the place your great Alfdan has taken you has its own residents."

The man who'd told Sharina that what they'd seen was a mirage gaped. He must not have heard the axe speak before.

"Are those things dangerous, Beard?" Sharina asked. She turned back in the direction she'd last seen the fish and its rider. The sky was empty and the sea was its usual turgid gray. "The residents?"

"Not unless they catch you, mistress," the axe said with its usual enthusiasm. "If they catch you, they'll kill you all! Beard will be alone in this place with nothing, no blood to drink ever again."

Did the axe think he'd frighten her, or did he just have a wry sense of humor? Well, Sharina'd been places before where if you couldn't laugh at horrors you had nothing whatever to laugh at.

"We'll hope that they don't catch us, then," she said with a faint smile. "I'd hate to leave so good a friend as you, Beard, in such a terrible place."

The axe laughed merrily. His voice was a pleasant tenor when he was at ease, but when he saw the hope of slaughter his tones rose till they were indistinguishable from a small brass bell ringing a tocsin.

"Oh, yes, mistress," he said. "You'll treat Beard well, he's sure you will. Ah, Beard hasn't had a master like you in thousands of years, *thousands.*"

Sharina continued to smile. It was always good to have friends; and in this world, Beard wasn't a bad friend to have.

"Look, mistress," Franca said. Instead of touching her shoulder, he extended his pointing finger past her face, then lowered it.

Sharina turned and saw trees on the horizon. "Are there islands here?" she said. There hadn't been—she hadn't *seen*—islands in this portion of the Inner Sea when she'd crossed it in her own world, but if the sea level was dropping perhaps . . .

"They walk on water, mistress," Beard said. "They came down from where the Ice Capes were. Now it's all ice there for hundreds of miles south, so the trees have had to move."

"How do trees walk?" Scoggin demanded. "They can't! They never did before!"

"Did you think it was only wizards who gained power when She came?" the axe chuckled. "It wasn't. Some wizards, and some—other things. Perhaps they now call themselves Larch the Great, do you think?"

"Look, Layson," said Scoggin, leaning sideways so that he could see the man who'd been speaking. They must have exchanged names while Sharina was talking with the wizard. "What is it that that fellow—"

He waggled a finger toward the stern. Like many other people Sharina'd met, Scoggin didn't choose to name wizards—any more than they would demons—for fear of what they might be calling to them.

"—plans to do? Is it like the axe says, he's just sailing around till we all freeze?"

Neal turned, awakening from his state of detachment. "Do you have a better idea, Scoggin?" he said. His tone was questioning, not a sarcastic snarl. "Because he's keeping us alive, it seems to me."

"He didn't keep Tadli alive just now," Franca said unexpectedly. Because he was so quiet, it was easy to forget his presence—and the fact that he heard and understood things.

"He didn't keep any of you alive just now!" Beard said. "My mistress and I kept you alive!"

"What do you say, mistress?" Layson said. "What would you do?"

Alfdan had adjusted his wand again, returning them to their previous course. Did he have some tool of art to tell him where to steer? Sharina saw another grove of trees to the west, but they were too far away for her to make out any details before the Queen Ship left them behind.

Alfdan stood fixed by the strain of his art; everyone else was waiting for her reply. It didn't make sense except in human terms, but Sharina'd learned since she left home that the answer to the question, "Why me?" was always, "Because you will." These men wanted her to lead them, because they knew she was willing to lead.

"You talk about Her," Sharina said. "When *She* came, when *She* made things change. Where is She?"

Men looked at one another or at their hands. She wasn't sure they'd have given her an answer even if they had one. "Maybe Alfdan knows," muttered someone seated behind her.

"She is in the north," said Beard, speaking in a precise, pedantic voice. "She is in the farthest north, from where everything is south. She is in a palace beneath the ice, and there She weaves the fate of the world. Ice and death and silence!"

"Then . . ." said Sharina. There was no other answer, after all, though her mouth had gone dry. "Then I think that's where we should be going, or at least I should."

"And Beard should go, mistress!" the axe caroled. "Oh, so very much blood to drink before they slay you, mistress, so many monsters and halfmen and so much blood!"

Alfdan's wand thumped against the shining deck before him. The Queen Ship slid to a silent halt at the base of a craggy headland. The narrow cliff beyond and that of the similar headland opposite were nearly vertical; they framed a narrow fjord. Here and there grasses sprouted from cracks in the rock.

They'd reached their destination without anyone except the wizard being aware they were approaching land.

Alfdan wavered with the effort of the task he'd just accomplished. He tried to sit but he was already collapsing when two of his men caught him with the skill of experience.

The deck was again as slick as the film over melting ice; men slid off, then scrambled out of the way of their fellows. Sharina let herself follow, holding Beard up in both hands to avoid an accident. The axe chuckled.

She landed on her heels, flexing her legs to take the shock. Even so she winced: her makeshift boots were thin protection against bare rock.

Sharina walked down to the narrow shoreline, looking into the fjord. The water was dark blue but clear; she could see the rock wall continue to slope jaggedly into an abyss.

"There's where you're going, mistress," Beard said happily. "There's where you and Beard are going soon!"

"Oh bye-bye good woman, I'm gone," Chalcus chanted, leading his six crewmen down the dock. As they walked, hauling on a hawser reeved over the top of a pair of shearlegs, the *Bird of the Tide*'s new mast rose in tiny jerks toward vertical. Without the shearlegs to give them leverage, they wouldn't have been able to start the pole from the horizontal.

"You gonna miss me, you'll see," Chalcus sang, taking another short step with each weighted syllable.

Ilna, waiting at the base of the mast with a wedge and

maul, thought again how much his voice reminded her of liquid gold, smooth and pure and perfectly beautiful. No sign of the effort—and she knew how much effort it was for seven men without pulleys to replace a mast—could be heard in the chantey. She called, "Once more!"

"A rider, she's a rider I know," Chalcus caroled, and the mast quivered straight according to the plumb line tacked into the side of the mast partner that would shortly hold it.

"Enough!" called Ilna and dropped her wedge into the slot. She stepped back and brought the maul around in a three-quarters circle to slam the tapered oak home.

Hutena had insisted—*insisted*—that Ilna should stand back and let one of the crewmen or Captain Chalcus himself set the wedge. Ilna didn't flatter herself that she could be of any real help on the line; she was strong for a woman, but she simply didn't weigh enough to matter with what was more a job of lifting than pulling. But the notion that she couldn't use a mallet—or a hatchet either one—as well as any man in Barca's Hamlet or this crew, *that* she would not have.

She wasn't sure she'd convinced the bosun, but she certainly convinced him that he should keep his opinions to himself when they clashed with hers. All the while Chalcus had stood with his back to the pair of them, whistling a merry tune called "I am a Noted Pirate," and juggling the knives of all five crewmen while they pretended to watch him instead of the argument.

Ilna smiled wryly. She supposed she'd been better entertainment than the juggling, but the men hadn't wanted her to catch their eyes when she was in a temper like that.

Four men continued to brace the hawser while the others ran back to catch the stay ropes already hanging from the collars. Ilna moved to the rail, giving the sailors as much room to do their work as the *Bird* allowed. Chalcus ran the forestay to the bow, then set his foot against a bitt and tensioned the rope before he took a quick lashing through the deadeyes. Ilna heard the mast groan as it strained. Chalcus wasn't a big man, but she'd met few who were stronger.

With the stays temporarily fastened, the men on the dock returned, coiling the hawser as they came. Chalcus swaggered toward Ilna, adjusting his sash. He was proud of the show he'd just put on and well aware that Ilna'd seen and understood how impressive it was.

She smiled wryly. She'd always felt it was wrong to boast, and maybe it was; but Chalcus wasn't any more proud than she was, of what she did and of what he did also. Maybe the willingness to flaunt what was fully worthy of pride was a more honest attitude than her own.

Anyway, she certainly wasn't going to change Chalcus. Nor would he change her, she suspected.

"I was beginning to worry about the good Commander," he said. "If he simply let us go on about our business we'd be lost, wouldn't we? But he's not so subtle a man as that, I'm pleased to see."

Chalcus nodded toward Cross Street, leading down from the castle, but the rattle of ironshod wheels on cobblestones would've drawn Ilna's attention anyway. A two-wheeled cart came around the corner, guided by four servants on the paired poles front and back. They must've struggled to keep the weight from running away from them on the slope, but now they got their footing properly and continued toward the *Bird of the Tide*.

At a muttered command from Hutena, he and the men with him dropped the hawser on the dock and boarded the ship quickly. Hutena gestured to the deckhouse; Chalcus grinned and shook his head minusculely.

He sees no need for weapons, Ilna thought. And—being Chalcus—he was certainly right when he answered that sort of question. Nevertheless Ilna leaned the maul against the railing and unobtrusively readied the silken noose around her waist.

The servants rolled their rumbling burden up the dock to the *Bird*'s stern lines. "Captain Chalcus?" called one of the men on the forepoles doubtfully, looking from the bosun to Chalcus.

Hutena gestured to Chalcus, who said, "We've not purchased stores in this port, my man. Your goods are for another vessel."

Ilna thought he was overacting the mincing innocent, but perhaps you couldn't do that so long as you played into the hopes of your audience. Certainly the servant looked relieved and said, "This isn't a purchase, sir, but a gift from the Commander for your aid last night. It's not everybody who'd have taken the risks you did to come out and help."

Ilna smiled grimly. The servant's last statement was as true as Chalcus's sword, of that she was certain. If Lusius had dreamed anybody'd dare row to the scene of a wizard's attack, he'd at least have posted sentries while he looted the *Queen of Heaven*.

"A gift?" said Chalcus, still acting the babe in the woods. "Why, that looks like a jar of wine?"

"Yessir," said the servant eagerly. "One of the best vintages from the Commander's cellars. Besides beef roast and boiled chicken, all for thanks."

Chalcus laughed merrily. "Why, Commander Lusius is a gentleman beyond compare," he said. "Speaking for myself, I've always found good wine to be as much of a meal as a sailor needs, but perhaps some of my men will find use for the meat as well."

He looked around the crew. They watched, grim-faced and worried.

"Now there's only one thing . . ." Chalcus went on, facing the servants again. "I hope Commander Lusius won't take it amiss that I intend to move the *Bird* and settle near the harbor mouth tonight. I've a new anchor line and I want to see that she doesn't chafe when she's fully paid out. Eh?"

The servants looked at one another. Finally the leader said, "Well, sir, there's no traffic in the harbor during darkness. If you don't want to be tied up to the dock, I guess that's your business."

"Aye, it is," Chalcus said. "But assure the Commander that it isn't that I fear pilfering thieves might slip aboard in his harbor while my men and I are at our ease tonight, will you?"

He turned to his crewmen. "Bring our dinner, boys," he said. "And then we'll unship the oars and shift the ship, as I said . . . before we eat, eh?"

Chalcus grinned. Ilna was the only one who smiled back at him, though the crew jumped to the dock without further direction. They began to unload the handcart.

Ilna trusted Chalcus, of course, but the men did as well. From her viewpoint, this was the opportunity she and Chalcus had been waiting for, the reason they'd kept Pointin aboard and held him cowering out of sight in the hold: he was the bait to force Lusius and his henchmen to act.

If Lusius struck and they weren't able to parry—well, then he was the better man and deserved to kill them. The crew, brave men though they were, might feel otherwise, but Ilna had too keen an appreciation of justice to believe that the weaker and less skillful *should* survive.

She was also sure, though, that even if Lusius won, he'd know he'd been in a fight.

The trunk of the pond cypress looked as dead as white bone, but tiny, dark green leaves sprouted from its branches. The trunk just beyond it surely *was* dead, but an air plant growing from a crotch threw down sprays of much brighter foliage. Beyond were grasses, green mixed with the russet stems of last year's growth, spreading into the blurred gray blanket of air.

A shrill cry sounded. Cashel looked up. It sounded like a bird—a big bird—and might've come from overhead, but he couldn't see anything beyond the usual swirls of mist.

He stepped onto the meadow. It undulated away from his foot the way a slow swell trembles over the surface of the sea. By reflex Cashel held his staff out crosswise before him to spread his weight if he broke through. He'd had a great plenty of experience with bogs; sheep *would* go after juicy green morsels on soil where their pointy little feet couldn't possibly support them.

"I'm not sure this will hold me, Mistress Evne," Cashel said. He didn't take another step for now, just made sure that he had his balance as the grasses continued to move.

"Oh, it would hold you, master," the toad said. "But unless you turn back now, there's a creature who'll dine on your flesh for anything I can do to stop her."

"I didn't come this far to turn back," said Cashel, hearing his voice turn huskier with each syllable. "And I don't guess I ever asked you or any soul else to do my fighting for me."

He stepped back into the scrub of turkey oaks, spaced well apart and none of them much taller than he was. He didn't doubt Evne when she said the meadow'd support him, but that didn't mean it was good footing in a fight.

The bird screamed again. It *was* a bird; he could see it now, fluttering toward him on wings that should've been too small to keep it in the air. It got bigger with every jerk of its wings. It wasn't *in* the air; it wasn't even in the same world as Cashel yet, but it was coming toward him quickly.

Very quickly.

He braced himself to strike, but he wasn't sure of the timing because he didn't know where the bird—

It stood before him and kicked a three-clawed foot. The bird was half again Cashel's height and probably outweighed him, though he knew how deceptively light birds were with their feathers and hollow bones. Maybe not this bird, though.

Cashel shifted left and brought his staff around sunwise, leading with his left hand. The kick slashed past him, snatching away a length of the whorled border Ilna had woven into the hem of his outer tunic.

The bird—leaped/flew/*shrank* upward; Cashel wasn't sure of the movement, only that his quarterstaff sliced the air and the bird was now dropping on him claws first. He jumped to his right, using the staff as a brace and a pivot to bring him back around.

The bird kicked a scrub oak to splinters and strings of bark. It turned its head and long beak over its stubby wing as Cashel drove the butt of his staff like a spear toward its midsection. The bird hopped/flew/shrank away, but not quite quickly enough. The ferrule touched solid flesh in a flash and sizzle of blue wizardlight.

The bird jumped clear, leaving a stench of burned feathers in the air. It watched Cashel, turning its narrow head slightly so that first one eye, then the other, was on him. Cashel, gasping through his open mouth, stared back.

He'd thought the bird was golden as it came toward him, but now that it stood at rest its feathers seemed bronze or even black. Over them lay a rainbow sheen like that of oil on a sunlit pond. Its beak was long and hooked, but its nostrils were the simple ovals of a buzzard instead of complex shapes like eagles and falcons.

The bird's wings were shorter than Cashel's own arms. It couldn't have flown through the air with them.

"You've met your match, bird!" called Evne from a tuffet

of grass some distance out in the open meadow. Cashel
guessed he must've thrown her off as he swung and dodged,
because she was farther away than he thought a little toad
could jump. "Let us pass or it'll be the worse for you!"

The bird cocked its head toward Cashel. It raised a crest
of feathers so nearly colorless that they shimmered like a
fish's fins, then lowered them again.

"Does the toad let or hinder the phoenix?" the bird said.
"Creep through the muck and eat bugs, slimy one!"

Cashel stepped forward. The bird drew its head back and
leaped, striking with both splayed feet. Cashel stabbed,
holding one end of his staff with both hands. The bird
flew/jumped/shrank over him. For an instant it seemed no
more than sparrow sized, a spot in the heavens; then it was
on the ground behind him and he recovered his staff, thrusting backward instead of trying to turn.

The buttcap slammed into the bird's keeled breastbone
with a crash and azure flare that numbed Cashel's arms to
the elbows. The bird screamed wordlessly and staggered
back. The feathers of its breast were blackened like a
chicken singed for plucking.

"Have you learned manners, bird?" Evne crowed. She
clung awkwardly to the grass stems, her legs stretched in
four separate directions. "Does the phoenix now know who
is master in this—"

The bird spun and struck at the toad, its wings lifting.
Cashel's staff caught it in the upper ribs; he felt bones crack
under his iron.

The bird's feet left the ground, lifted by the impact rather
than conscious evasion. It gave a strangled squawk as it tumbled sideways over the crouching toad. She'd tricked the bird,
drawn its attention to her so that Cashel could strike. . . .

He staggered forward, wheezing and only half aware of
his surroundings. The bird was at the far end of a tunnel, and
even that view was through a red haze of fatigue. Cashel
moved with the punctuated violence of a jagged rock rolling
downhill, lurching from one side to the other but never
changing its ultimate direction.

The bird eyed him. Its tongue quivered as it gave another

shrill scream. Its legs bunched, then straightened. Cashel thrust with his staff.

The bird shrank away into the heavens. For a moment it was a glitter in the mist; then it was gone, vanished like a rainbow when the air clears. Cashel sprawled forward as the meadow sloshed and rolled beneath him.

He didn't know how long he lay there. His first conscious thought was that breathing no longer felt like he was jabbing knives down into his lungs. He opened his eyes very carefully. Evne squatted within handsbreadth of his nose, rubbing her pale belly with a webbed forefoot.

"You've decided to rejoin me, I see," the toad said.

"The bird's gone?" said Cashel. He didn't try to move. He wasn't sure he could move just now, and he sure didn't see a good reason to.

"I'll say she's gone!" Evne said complacently. "Gone and wishing she'd never come, if I'm any judge."

"What do I do next?" Cashel said. It seemed a little funny to be carrying on a conversation with his cheek pressed down into boggy soil, but he'd been laughed at before.

"Next?" said the toad. "Next you try your luck against the Visitor himself, master. Unless you decide to turn and run instead."

She laughed. "Which you won't do," she added, "because you're very stupid, and very determined. Though it's just possible that you're even stronger than you're stupid!"

Chapter Sixteen

The *Bird of the Tide* was anchored near the harbor mouth, as far from the docks as was possible in the enclosed waters. The vessel undulated slowly as the current out of Terness Harbor tugged at the anchor line.

Commander Lusius, dressed in fur-trimmed velvet, stood

in the shadows of the quay. With him hunched three men; their clothing would've been nondescript were it not for the swords they wore.

The *Bird* was as silent as death; there was no sound from aboard her save the creak of the line working against the scuttle as she moved. A lantern hung from the mast, arm's length below the furled sail. It guttered on the last of its oil, but the faint glow showed what the men on the dock wanted to see.

One of the vessel's crewmen sprawled in the bow with an arm over the railing. Three more lay amidships; two on their backs, the other facedown. The man who'd begun the night on watch leaned against the sternpost, utterly motionless. The woman's legs stuck out of the small deckhouse; she hadn't moved either.

"There's two I don't see," muttered one of the nondescript men. "And the fellow from the merchantman, he must be aboard too."

"They're in the hold, Rincip," Lusius growled. "The supercargo is, at any rate. And they're just as dead as the others. The poison doesn't care whether you can see the bodies or not."

"Let's get it over with," muttered another of the men as he climbed into the skiff tied to the stern of the nearest fishing vessel. "The moon'll be up in an hour. I don't want an audience of rube fishermen while I send corpses to the bottom of the harbor with their bellies filled with ballast."

"Yeah, all right," said Rincip. He and the third Sea Guard boarded the skiff and unshipped the oars. Lusius watched with his arms folded across his chest as his men rowed toward the *Bird of the Tide*.

The harbor was quiet. The fishermen couldn't rake belemnites from the shoals during darkness, and nothing about Terness—neither the Commander and his men, nor the Rua who now ruled the region's skies—encouraged simple folk to be out at night. The water carried the slight thump of the skiff touching the larger vessel's side to where Lusius stood.

Two of the Sea Guards gripped the *Bird*'s gunwale while the other scrambled aboard carrying the painter. He looped it to the rail. Rincip had just followed his man over the railing when the woman in the deckhouse sat up. There was a shimmer in the dim light; Rincip squawked and jerked forward, clawing at his neck.

The vessel's crewmen were all moving—fast. The Sea Guard on deck got his hand to his sword hilt before the captain made a quick swipe with his own slim blade. Lusius swore as the Guard toppled backward over the rail in a spray of blood. His head hit the water some distance from the rest of the body.

"Don't or I'll—" the *Bird*'s bosun shouted as the Sea Guard in the skiff tried to cut the painter with his sword. The rest of the sentence probably would've been "—kill you!" but he didn't bother finishing it after he thrust down with a boarding pike.

The Sea Guard went over the side and sank as soon as the bosun managed to jerk his pike free. The two-handed stroke had driven the spearhead the length of a tall man's forearm through the Guard's chest cavity.

Lusius swore in a monotone as he ran back toward the castle, trying to stay in the shadows. Oars scraped and squealed as the *Bird of the Tide* got underway.

He'd almost shouted to rouse the tower watch, but he caught himself in time. He'd seen what Captain Chalcus could do with a dagger and now a sword. Lusius didn't intend to prove with his own body that the fellow was just as skilled with a bow.

And besides, there was a better way to deal with Prince Garric's spies. . . .

The faces of men, each announcing his own name, jostled one another through Garric's mind as he lay in bed. He was tired, desperately tired, but he couldn't sleep because the literal army of men he'd met and inspected today wouldn't let him.

"It's part of the job, lad," Carus said in his mind. *"Just like going over tax assessments is part of the job; though that one I never could do, not even to keep my officials honest."*

Iron clanged against stone in the garden below. Garric tensed, ready to leap for the sword hanging from the rack by the bed; glad at a chance for action but so tired that he was afraid he'd stumble over his own feet.

A soldier cursed; his officer snarled him to silence. Garric relaxed with a smile. A guard had dropped his spear; Prince Garric wasn't the only tired person awake tonight in the palace.

Smiling, Garric dropped off into the sleep that frustration had denied him. When he realized that the dream had him again, it was too late to rouse himself . . . and he was so tired, he might not have wanted to return to that restless consciousness anyway.

He was in the garden as before. The moon must have been full; branches stood out against the sky even though it was drizzling. The air was cooler than on the previous times he'd been dragged into this place, though the blossoming pear trees meant it must be late spring.

Carus wasn't with him. Garric was alone on a dank, chill night, and something waited for him beside the altar at the back of the garden. He walked forward because he *had* to: the great figures beyond the sky were again forcing him to.

The compulsion wasn't necessary. There was no place to flee in this dream and besides—Garric was the descendent and successor of King Carus, the greatest warrior the Isles had ever known. He wasn't going to run from the thing that rose onto its hind legs and snarled at his approach.

He couldn't get a good look at the creature. The diffused light hid as much as it displayed, but Garric also had the awareness that things didn't always stay the same even while he looked at them.

The creature had a bestial head with great tusks jutting from the upper and lower jaws, but except for a bristly mane down the middle of the back its body was as hairless as a man's. It had short legs and a long, broad torso; on its hind legs it stood as tall as Garric. Its arms were half again the length of his own.

Garric had been looking for a weapon from the moment he realized the situation. He saw fallen branches, but they were probably rotten and wouldn't be effective clubs against so large a creature anyway.

The ape growled. He was going to call it an ape, though

part of Garric's mind feared that it was nothing of the sort.

The ape gave a rasping bellow and hunched onto the knuckles of its hands. Other beasts watched and waited in shadowed corners of the garden. They chittered quietly among themselves.

Garric grabbed the edge of a stone planter that roots had fractured. The ape grunted explosively and lunged forward. The slab resisted; the weight of dirt held it where it was. Garric screamed in frustration and tore the piece free, bringing it around in both hands. As the ape dug its clawed fingers into his shoulders, he smashed the stone into three fragments against its forehead.

The beast flung Garric away with a started cry. His right thigh slammed the trunk of pear tree, a numbing blow.

He got up, using his hands and left leg to raise his body. His right leg was barely able to hold him upright, but he didn't think the bone was broken. The ape staggered backward, apparently dazed. It patted doubtfully at its forehead with its left hand. The pressure cut was bleeding freely; blood dripped from the deep brow ridges.

The fractured planter lay between Garric and the ape. He might have been able to lift the stone shell, three-quarters of the original object, if he had time to empty the dirt from it. He doubted the ape would give him the time, and anyway he wasn't sure his leg was up to walking just yet. Much as he'd have liked to charge while the ape seemed dizzy, he guessed he was going to wait for it to come to him.

The ape rose onto its hind legs. It stared at its great left hand, black with blood in the moonlight, and gave another snarling roar.

Garric seized the branch above him, then jerked down with all his strength. The brittle pear wood broke where the limb met the trunk. As the ape charged, Garric brought the long branch around as a spear tipped with jagged splinters.

He meant to thrust it into the ape's throat, but the long crooked brush of twigs and blossoms tangled in the branch above and fouled his stroke. The ragged tip gouged the beast's shoulder as its clawed hands closed on Garric's neck. He drove both bare heels into the ape's belly, but it was like kicking an oak.

The beast raised him overhead. Garric's vision blurred and turned red. He tried to pull the ape's hands apart, but he wasn't sure his fingers were gripping. The ape swung him like a flail into the pear tree. He felt his ribs crack.

Red shifted toward blackness and the world went dark. Garric felt himself moving again. He was vaguely aware of another shock; then it was over, except for pain beyond anything he'd ever imagined.

He woke up in his bed.

Liane breathed softly beside him; sleeping dreamlessly or dreaming ordinary human dreams. Garric grinned despite himself; his heart was hammering and all his muscles were tense, but this time he hadn't leaped out of bed with a shout. His mind hadn't expected him to be able to move after all the bones of his torso had shattered against a tree trunk.

"Now that was a hard one, lad," Carus murmured. The image of the ancient king was the same as always, dressed in trousers and tunic with a long sword at his side; the way he'd generally been when he went about the business of government. *"They're trying to break us to their will, I'd guess. Make us say we'll serve them."*

I won't, thought Garric. His hands gently explored his rib cage and right thigh as he convinced himself that he wasn't really a cripple dying in agony. *No matter how often they kill me.*

But a part at the back of his mind wondered how much longer this could go on without affecting him, no matter how brave he was consciously.

I fought an ape, he thought. *It beat me to death against a tree. Was it the same with you?*

Carus smiled. *"It was an ape, I guess,"* he said. *"But I killed it instead of the other way round."*

How? thought Garric, touching the medal he wore on a neck thong. It had been struck for the coronation of King Carus; he wore it at all times. *I mean—were we in the same body? Or did you have a weapon?*

The ancient king's smile became rueful. *"A weapon?"* he said. *"Not exactly, lad. You see . . ."*

He paused, smiling again in real embarrassment. *"You see,"* Carus went on, *"I've been places that you haven't been.*

I tore the thing's throat out with my teeth. I don't have much recollection of it while it was happening, but . . . it wasn't the first time it'd happened to me, lad. And the other time it wasn't a beast's throat when my sword had broken."

I see, thought Garric. *Well, your highness, I'm glad the Good has folk like you to defend it.*

He breathed deeply, then added, *Maybe between us we can arrange that other people don't have to learn how to fight monsters without weapons.*

Liane awoke to Garric's laughter. She turned to him with a warm smile.

Sharina sat wrapped in the fur of some large animal she didn't recognize, drinking mulled wine and looking down into the waters of the fjord. She didn't want much in her stomach before she dived, but the warmer she started out, the longer she'd be able to continue.

Neal had supplied both the fur and the hot drink. He appeared to be the generally accepted leader while Alfdan recovered from the strain of his art.

The band's driftwood fire crackled with flashing enthusiasm. Rainbow-colored flames spurted whenever heat opened a pocket of sea salt. Franca and especially Scoggin, sitting on opposite sides of her, glanced nervously at the blaze. They'd survived the decade of Her rule by creeping through the shadows. They saw an open fire as a frightening beacon drawing in terrors, known and unknown.

"I suppose they know what they're doing," Sharina said to the men; *her* men, beside but not part of the wizard's band, the way oil lies on water. "Alfdan's protected them so far."

"Alfdan isn't protecting them now," Scoggin muttered, glancing sourly toward where the wizard lay on a bed of furs. He was beginning to stir: Layson helped him sit upright while another man waited with a mug of soup. It'd be some time before he was ready to use his art again, though.

Some of the men had tied driftwood into a raft using ropes from their stores. It was a clumsy-looking thing and didn't have a real deck, but it'd do as a fishing float . . . or a diving platform.

"There's nothing on land here to fear," Beard said. "Anyway, they have me and my mistress, don't they?"

"What about the water, axe?" Franca said. "That's where Mistress Sharina has to go, isn't it?"

"There are things in the fjord," the axe said. "But the mistress will have Beard, so the danger will be greater for the other things. If they come to the mistress and Beard, there will be *so* much blood!"

Sharina wasn't clear on how useful an axe would be under water, but Beard's enthusiasm seemed genuine and he was the expert in killing things. She grinned. Everybody ought to have a talent. . . .

A slab of stone wrapped in fishing net sat in the middle of the raft. It was heavy enough that the man who brought it aboard had waddled with it cradled against his chest. Sharina would ride it down, saving time that would be too short anyway. The raft's crew could draw the stone up by the rope attached to the net's lines in case she had to dive again.

This was going to be very unpleasant, but she'd said that she'd do it. Besides, the bargain would get her the opportunity that she wanted.

Which would be even more unpleasant.

Alfdan rose with Layson's help and stepped carefully to Sharina. Scoggin started to get up but settled back when he realized Sharina didn't intend to do so.

"So, mistress!" the wizard said. "Are you ready to carry out your promise?"

"Yes," said Sharina. She smiled. Beard had been across her knees. She turned the axe upright, its butt on the ground and the pointed steel face glaring at Alfdan. "Of course. What is your plan?"

Until she knew in detail what was expected of her, she had no intention of shrugging off the fur and standing. She'd move when it was time to; until then she'd wait.

"We'll go out to the center of the inlet," Alfdan said, taking what looked like a stream-washed pebble from an ermine purse. Sharina remembered what Neal had said about the Stone Mirror. "I'll guide you. Then you'll swim down to the key where Lady Sodann cast it and bring it back to me."

Except for Neal and another man finishing the raft, the

band had gathered quietly around Alfdan and Sharina. They listened openly but in silence; they weren't part of the business nor did they want to be, but they knew their future might depend on what was said.

"If the key's so valuable," Scoggin demanded with deliberate hostility, "then why did this lady throw it away?"

" 'This lady' as you call her," Alfdan said with a look of irritation, "tried to dispose of the Key of Reyazel because Baron Hortsmain, her beloved, used it to enter a place from which he could not return. This is scarcely your concern, my man, as I'm the one who'll be using the key. And both Sodann and Hortsmain have been dead these five thousand years!"

Sharina looked at the fjord, then toward the raft. She set down her empty mug. "Is that ready?" she called to Neal.

"Yes, mistress," Neal said, eyeing the slope above them, his bow ready. It seemed to Sharina that only a bird could come down on them from the heights.

"Then so am I," said Sharina as she stood, pinching the fur closed at the throat with her left hand. "We've got the light, and I don't suppose things will change for the better if we wait."

Beard gave a ringing laugh. "In ten more years the water'll be barely half this depth," he said. "Of course the ice will have come down from the hills to cover it by then, too."

Rather than reply, Sharina started for the raft. Scoggin and Franca fell in beside her. The youth clutched the section of spear he used for a dagger. "We're coming too!" he said to Alfdan with more vehemence than Sharina'd thought he was capable of.

"All right," said the wizard nonchalantly. "You two can paddle. Neal, I'll want you along also."

The big man nodded glumly. "Colran, lend me your spear," he said, holding out his bow and five arrows to a blond spearman in exchange. "This won't be much use if something comes up from the water."

"Nothing will threaten us," Alfdan said in irritation.

Neal ignored him. With the spear in his hand he said to the circle of his fellows, "Come on, carry this into the water."

The band leaped to the task, grunting and muttering as

they gripped the lengths of wood lashed together in a thick mat. Beard tittered disconcertingly. "They're all afraid if there's a delay, Master Wizard will decide some of them should come along as well."

"There's no danger!" Alfdan said.

The axe sniffed. "Is that what you think, wizard?" he said.

"We're allies now," Sharina said quietly, holding the axe so close to her lips that her breath fogged the steel. "Don't bait Alfdan. It's not polite."

"Polite!" Beard said. "Polite to what?"

But he spoke in a tiny voice and subsided after that slight protest.

Sharina took off her rabbit-skin sandals and left them on the shore before she stepped into the water. The fjord had an eerie chill, as though she were walking in a basin of frozen knife blades. The raft swayed and rippled as she and the others boarded; water slapped and squirted through the openings between the interlaid logs.

Sharina squatted at the side, her hip braced against the stone that she'd use for her descent. Franca and Scoggin moved them out in a wobbly, half-circular course; their paddles were almost as crude as the beams from which the raft was woven.

Alfdan's men watched at the shoreline with expressions of morose anticipation. Some of them were rubbing their legs dry. The walls of the fjord were as sheer as the sides of an axe cut. . . .

"So much blood!" Beard chortled.

Sharina laughed. Scoggin looked at her in amazement. "It's nice that somebody's looking forward to this," she explained.

Alfdan remained standing, staring into the pebble. His lips moved, but Sharina couldn't hear words if he was even speaking. Neal sat on the stone with his spear between his legs; he held the wizard steady.

"Downstream!" Alfdan said. "Another twenty feet or so. We're far enough out already."

The raft began to rotate; even the most experienced boatmen would've had trouble controlling so clumsy a craft, and neither Scoggin nor Franca were that. There was very little current in the fjord, but that little complicated the business.

"Here!" Alfdan called. He continued looking at his pebble, facing off at an angle to the far shore. "This is far enough. Stop here!"

As if it were that simple, Sharina thought as she stood; but to some people, the wizard apparently among them, it *was* that simple: they gave orders and other people carried them out at whatever cost to themselves. She dropped the fur and stripped off her tunic before squatting again to grip the stone against her belly.

"How far down is the key?" she asked.

"It doesn't matter!" cried Alfdan. "We're drifting past! Get down there!"

Sharina lifted the stone slightly, using her left hand and three fingers of her right. The raft billowed; water sloshed over her feet. She turned and straddle-walked two steps to the edge, then rolled over the side. The water was a quick, unpleasant shock; then she was aware only of the weight crushing in on her as she plunged downward.

She let go of the stone with her right hand as soon as she was over the side. The fingers of her left held the netting firmly, while her right hand now gripped only Beard's helve.

The water was blue and clear and at first empty; bubbles dribbled from the net fibers as the depth squeezed them. Sharina began to see crystalline planes jutting up past her, as steep as the cliffs of the fjord. It was as though the water had compressed itself solid. Perhaps the pressure was affecting her sight. . . .

The rock she clung to was covered with bubbles that'd been trapped in cracks when she went over the side. Water swirled about it as they dropped, distorting her sight, but beyond that the planes of a separate world were growing more real. She couldn't see the bottom, but things of pulp and blubber crawled up slabs of crystal from an unguessibly deep abyss.

The rock crunched onto the bottom of the fjord, kicking out a spray of stream-washed quartz nuggets the size of walnuts or smaller. Sharina couldn't see the key; she couldn't see anything but a blurred, dim waste of stone. She let go of the weight and breaststroked over the plain. Beard's narrow blade winked; she thought she heard him singing.

No more! Sharina drove upward for the surface. Her lungs

were burning and her sight had blurred from lack of air. The crystal walls had vanished but she felt the creatures continuing to crawl toward her like huge gelatinous ticks; out of sight but still present. She couldn't see the raft and the light was dimming—

Sharina broke surface, gasping and blind. She blew a roar of froth with her lips. She couldn't see anything until she realized that her eyes were tight shut.

She was arm's length upstream from the raft; it thrashed and rocked. Neal was hauling the rock up hand over hand as Franca coiled the line behind him. Scoggin slashed the water furiously with his paddle to keep the clumsy craft from drifting farther.

Sharina kicked herself to the raft and caught the end of a branch in her left hand. She didn't feel cold, but her lungs were a mass of fire that subsided only slowly as she dragged in great breaths.

Alfdan looked up from his pebble. He glanced around till his eyes lit on Sharina. "It's still there!" he cried angrily. "You haven't brought it up!"

"Shut up, you fool!" Scoggin snarled. Neal looked over his shoulder; he nodded. He'd raised the netted stone to the surface and belayed the line around the end of a log near where Sharina clung. The raft tilted toward it; neither Franca nor the wizard had sense enough to move to the opposite side for balance.

"I'm getting my breath," Sharina said. The words didn't want to come; her throat was stiff. "I'll go back in a moment."

"Mistress, do you want to try another day?" said Neal.

"No, I'll—" Sharina said.

"She must get it immediately!" said Alfdan. "If I wait—"

Beard actually twisted in Sharina's hand, lifting his razor-keen edge above the water like a shark breaking surface. "I'll kill him!" the axe squealed, raging instead of speaking with his usual sanguine anticipation.

Sharina gripped the netting with her left hand. "I'm ready," she said. Neal loosed the rope; she plunged again into the depths of the fjord.

Sharina had thought the crystal planes were a hallucination and perhaps they were, but they were back again as she drove deeper. When she'd looked down from the surface Sharina had been able to see the quartz bottom, wavering and faint beneath the filter of blue water. Now she no longer could: as when she dived the first time, the depths slid all the way to the center of the world. The things that lived there were climbing toward her again, and this time they were closer.

The stone hit and scattered pebbles. The other world shifted out of sight the way a reflection disappears when a mirror tilts; but it was still there and its creatures were still there, sliding closer, ready to grip and suck and drain her not only of blood but of her very soul.

Sharina couldn't see the key, but Beard was pulling to her right. She frog-kicked in that direction. The plain of shimmering pebbles jerked by beneath her, fading as her breath failed. There was no key—

She saw it, golden and the only warmth in a waste of white and blue. She didn't know how far away it was—a foot, a yard, a furlong; it didn't matter.

Too far. Sharina broke for the surface, thinking she'd left it too long till the instant her control failed and she sucked in not seawater but air after all. She collapsed and lay still, scarcely aware that somebody was cradling her head to allow her to breathe.

"Mistress?" a voice begged. "Mistress, are you all right?"

Sharina opened her eyes. Franca was beside her, kicking to stay in place as he supported her head. Neal had taken the other paddle and with Scoggin was thrashing the raft toward her against the slight current. The men's expressions were grim.

Alfdan squatted to keep from falling over. He seemed angry, but he was pointedly not looking at Sharina or his other companions. The tableau made Sharina smile—and that brought her back to sudden full awareness. Alfdan had his own view of the world, but he'd learned this wasn't the time to try to impose it on angry, armed men who hadn't liked him very much to begin with.

"Get her aboard!" Scoggin said. "She's done for the day!"

Alfdan started to rise, then settled back on his haunches looking even angrier than he had shortly before. The raft

was close, now; Sharina could no longer see Neal on the opposite side. Franca grabbed a projection with one hand and
drew her in.

*Funny that she'd never realized that Franca could swim. A
good thing that he could, although she was all right now; or
would be shortly. . . .*

"Neal, help me lift her," Scoggin said as he leaned over
the side to grasp Sharina's right arm. The raft shuddered and
tilted again, though not so much. Neal had raised the stone
and snubbed it off at the back of the craft where it counter-
weighted the crew.

She must have been under water a long time if Neal had
been able to lift the stone. She smiled faintly. *I must have
been under water as long as it felt.*

"Get back," she said. "I'm all right."

Scoggin continued to tug; Neal was reaching down also.

"Stop that!" Sharina said. She hadn't thought she had
enough energy to get angry, but she'd been wrong; Beard
twitched hopefully in her hand, though he didn't speak. "I'm
going down again! I know where the key is, now."

"Mistress, you shouldn't . . ." Neal said, then straightened
back abruptly. The axe had lifted without Sharina's conscious volition.

"You've seen it?" Alfdan said eagerly, turning toward her.
"You can get it up, then?"

Sharina lay on her side, fully in control of her body again.
Franca held her shoulder, but he was shivering violently and
seemed barely able to keep himself above the surface now.
He was the one they ought to be pulling onto the raft. . . .

"It's on the bottom, just lying there," Sharina said. "I just
need to be in the right place. Beard, will you guide me?"

"I will guide you, mistress," said the axe. "I think they're
afraid of Beard. They haven't come quite close enough; but
perhaps when you take the key they will."

"Well, friend axe," Sharina said, "we both have something
to look forward to. Though it's not the same thing."

She looked up at Neal. "Bring the rock around to me," she
said. "I'm ready to go down. And then get Franca up before
he freezes to death!"

Sharina didn't feel cold. In truth, she didn't feel much of

anything. She viewed her body as she might have viewed a horse, considering the work it had done this day and deciding how much longer it'd be able to go on before it dropped in the traces.

Long enough, she thought. Long enough.

Neal straddle-walked across the raft with the stone in his arms; the wooden fabric wobbled and groaned at each step. He squatted at the edge. Alfdan, startled into awareness of his immediate surroundings, gave a sharp cry and hopped to the other side as the raft tilted.

Sharina reached up and caught the netting in her left hand. "Ready!" she said, drawing in a deep breath.

Neal shoved the weight outward into the water. It streamed downward, trailing bubbles and Sharina's lithe body.

She was no longer conscious of the water. In her mind she flew down canyons of planes joined at right angles. Creatures squeezed out of the cracks where they'd been hiding while Sharina was on the surface. Other creatures, mountainously huge, continued up from the depths of time toward her.

Beard trilled a war song that sliced through the water like the point of an arrow. Sharina could see the things poise—things of no shape or a thousand shapes, filled with the mindless malevolence of spiders. But they did not, would not, *dared* not launch themselves onto her while the axe sang.

The stone weight crunched onto the bed of the fjord. Beard tugged her to the right again.

Sharina breaststroked over the quartz. The key congealed into focus from a distant blur; it was gold and ornate but not large, no longer than her little finger. She snatched it in her left hand and kicked upward.

The metal tingled against her palm. She wondered if the key was burning into her, and clutched it more firmly so that she wouldn't drop it if it was.

A thing came at her, dropping like a jumping spider at the end of a train of its own substance. Sharina twisted and slashed out with Beard. There was no water to resist the blow; the place they fought in was not the fjord whose icy depths enfolded her body.

The axe slid through the creature and beyond, dragging a gelatinous trail behind the steel. The creature folded in on itself. Sharina brought the axe back around in a figure eight. Her head broke the surface and she was sucking in cold, clean air again.

The water about her was clear. There was no sign of the crystal canyons nor the monsters that infested them, but Beard was caroling in delighted triumph.

Cashel got up slowly and carefully. He ached all over, but the bird actually hadn't touched him. The way he felt was entirely what he'd done to himself.

"That would cover most people's problems," the toad said. "*I* think."

Cashel frowned as he considered. "I just meant I'd pushed pretty hard while I was fighting the bird," he explained. "I'm feeling the strain."

He paused. "You must have been hearing me think," he said.

The toad sniffed. "If you want to call it thinking," she said. "And yes, you made a great effort, physically as well. What do you do when your greatest effort isn't enough, master?"

Cashel frowned again, thinking back as carefully as he could. "I don't know," he said at last. "I don't remember that ever happening. I just don't know."

"Well, pick me up," said Evne, "and I'll take you to another chance to find out. Life with you is certainly more colorful than it had been for the previous seven thousand years."

Obediently Cashel put his right palm flat on the ground in front of the toad. She hopped onto his fingers and he lifted her to his shoulder again.

"Thanks for drawing the bird's eyes off me, Mistress Evne," he said. "It helped a lot. And it was a brave thing to do."

"It would only have been brave," said the toad with her usual tartness, "if I'd thought you might be too slow to deal with the phoenix before she snapped me up. I'm not that unobservant."

Evne pointed with her left hind foot, a gesture that made Cashel grin with surprise. He had to squint to see her, so close to his eyes as she was. "Cross this bog and go through the belt of fir trees. I'll show you what to do then."

Cashel resumed his way over the meadow with his staff out before him. The ripples were disconcerting at first, but they spread in a rhythm. By the third step he'd suited his pace to how the bog was going to react. It gave him no trouble from then on, though he was still glad to reach firm ground.

That meant forcing his way through the prickly, steep-sloping branches of firs growing too close together for their own good, though. He edged through with his right side leading so he wouldn't risk brushing Evne off. The toad shifted closer to his neck, but she didn't seem terribly concerned.

It struck Cashel that he didn't hear birds among these trees. There was a funny buzzing sound, something like swarms of cicadas at a great distance. It was the wrong season for cicadas, though, and besides—

He pushed through the last of the firs. It wasn't a wide belt, probably no more than he could've spanned with his staff laid out twice, but it'd been so dense that he was beyond the trees before he realized they were ending. Before him shimmered a purple dome covering everything for as far as he could see to right or left. A belt of bare ground, no wider than he could reach across with his arm, bordered the dome and separated it from the firs.

"If you touch the barrier," the toad said, "it will kill you. It'll probably kill me too, as I deserve for serving a fool."

"I won't touch it, then," Cashel said politely. "That'd be a poor way to repay a friend who's been so much help, Mistress Evne."

The toad snorted. "Walk to your left along the barrier," she said. "We'll come to a slough shortly."

Cashel walked carefully; his shoulders were broad enough that he'd bump the dome on his right if the fir branches didn't scrape their dark green needles along his left arm. Evne walked to the front of his collar and clung there, a clammy bump against his throat. He didn't say anything.

The buzzing sound came from the dome. Cashel thought he could see things inside it, but that might just have been the play of the sun falling on a solid surface through patches of mist.

The shiny violet color gave him a nasty feeling, and the hair on his right arm prickled. He probably wouldn't have touched it even without the toad's warning.

A furlong from where he'd started, Cashel saw open water in front of him. The water was brown-black under a gray film of dust and pollen; it sizzled where the base of the dome cut across it. Just as the fir trees grew only so close to the violet curve, the water's surface within a finger's breadth of it was clear of scum.

"Now," said Evne, "set me down and swim under the barrier just as I do. It's no thicker than one of your Sharina's hairs, but it'll fry you to ash if you come up beneath it. Do you understand?"

Cashel squatted at the edge of the still water and lifted the toad from his shoulder. "I understand, mistress," he said. "But I can't swim."

"Well then *crawl,* you fool!" the toad snarled. "The water's barely deep enough to float a rowboat! Or if you prefer, jump straight into the barrier and blast your huge gross body to atoms!"

"Crawling sounds fine, mistress," Cashel said quietly. He probed the slough with his left hand instead of using his quarterstaff. The water was warm—blood warm, it seemed—and he was pushing his fingers into soft mud before half his forearm was wet.

"Then do it," snapped Evne. She leaped, a clumsy, splay-footed motion. For a moment she paused beneath the water's grimy surface; then her long hind legs kicked again and she vanished beneath the edge of the dome.

Cashel settled himself carefully in the water, on his belly after taking time to consider it. He didn't like the thought of squirming under the dome without seeing for sure how close he was, but he guessed he'd have an easier job digging down into the mud if he went face first.

Cashel slid his staff forward, keeping it well down in the muck. The last thing he wanted was to have it burned out of his hands before he even got close to the Visitor. He figured things were going to be tough enough as it was.

The staff was under the barrier. He pushed it with the heels of his hands, then sloshed his head under and hauled himself forward using his hands and elbows both. He didn't like water and he hated not being able to see, but nobody'd forced him to be here. Anyway, he wasn't one to complain about his work.

Cashel crawled till he couldn't hold his breath any longer. At last he jerked his head up, blowing the air out of his lungs and gasping in more. He shook himself violently, then rubbed his eyes with the back of his hand to clear some of the mud away before he opened them and looked around.

The place where he'd crossed under the dome was twice his length behind him, marked by the trail of mud spreading back to it. Evne was behind him also. His quarterstaff floated just above the surface, and she sat in the middle of it.

"Have you decided to come back for me and your staff?" she asked. "Or are you going to swim to the center of the Visitor's lair on your own? I don't recommend that, but you're the master."

"I wouldn't care to be without either one of you, mistress," Cashel said as he sloshed to the toad.

The landscape on this side of the dome was a bit different from what Cashel'd come through to reach it. On the dry land there was grass, mostly blue-stem, instead of trees. Reeds grew in the water. The air was clear instead of warm, gray fog, and the light had just the least bit of something strange. Rather than a color, there was an odd *sharpness* to objects. He didn't see anything like the great glowing hill that'd flown over Manor Bossian while he'd been dining there.

When Cashel looked back the way he'd come, he was scarcely aware of the dome. The air shimmered the way it might do above a hot rock in the summer sun; that was all.

With Evne back on his shoulder, Cashel wiped down his quarterstaff. The wallet's waxed leather kept its contents dry under any conditions short of floating alongside a dead whale, and the lanolin in the wool shed water anyway.

"There!" said the toad with satisfaction. She was peering at a perfectly ordinary patch of air, so far as Cashel could tell. "I was beginning to think that we'd have to get in by our own efforts."

She swiveled her little head toward him. "I don't say we

wouldn't have done so," she said. "But I prefer to avoid the labor if I can. We'll have plenty of use for our strength later on."

Cashel squeezed the wool dry and put it away. He'd need it again, he figured, if things worked out.

The air just beyond his staff's reach started to twist and turn gray. Images were forming in it. Cashel had the feeling that he was looking at a rolled tapestry where both the base and the figures were woven in transparent thread. He could almost see what was there. . . .

He stepped onto firm ground, a better place to use his staff. It also put him closer to where the air was changing: not much closer, but enough.

"Do you want to get down, Evne?" he asked, his voice husky.

"No," she said. "We'll need to move quickly in a moment."

"You're right about that," said Cashel.

The distortion vanished; a man in white robes stood in its place. He was over the water, but his gilded sandals didn't dimple the surface. In his right hand was an athame, a wizard's knife. His was forged from metal of the same violet hue as the dome seen from the outside; words of power in the Old Script wrapped around the blade in bands.

Cashel smiled in pleased surprise. "You're Ansache!" he cried. "Did you come to get your daughter free too?"

"I am Lord Ansache, seneschal to the Visitor," the man said, obviously startled. "I have no daughter, and as for why I came here—"

He raised his athame so that it pointed straight up.

"I came to cleanse the Visitor's park of the monkey that crawled in under the barrier!"

Cashel thrust the butt of his staff at Ansache's face.

"Iaththa," Ansache cried. A bolt of red wizardlight sprang at Cashel from the peak of the dome. It met a bubble of blue fire expanding from the tip of his staff and vanished.

Cashel staggered, then thrust again. Ansache screamed and flung himself backward. He turned and ran, changing angle to Cashel with every step.

"Follow!" Evne shouted. "Don't let him get away!"

"He's not," Cashel grunted as he stumbled after the running man. "He won't!"

He wasn't in the marshy landscape anymore. He ran down a tunnel with mirrored walls, seeing himself on all sides and multiple copies of Ansache in front of him. The reflections crowded him, constantly warning that somebody was coming at him with a quarterstaff from the corners of his eyes.

Cashel's arms tingled all the way back to the shoulder. They felt like he'd slammed his staff into a cliff face instead of having it stop in a flash of wizardlight. His legs didn't work quite the way they should've; he rocked from side to side as he ran, as if he'd been carrying a heavy stone all the past hour.

Ansache wasn't in good shape either, though. He staggered like a drunk, flailing his arms. The purple athame seemed to be dragging him to the right. Wizardry, even failed wizardry like Ansache's, took a lot out of the fellow using it.

Ansache disappeared. Cashel was in a grove of fruit trees. An animal that looked like an armored possum stood on its hind legs to lick branches clean with a long tongue. It was as big as an ox. When it saw Cashel, it turned and raised its forepaws with blunt, black claws as long as Cashel's fingers. It uttered a hissing squeal.

"Through it!" Evne cried. "That's the pathway!"

Cashel sprang toward the beast, his staff slantwise across his body to beat aside the claws when they swung toward him. The scene— the beast and the grove, both—vanished.

Cashel was in the mirrored corridor again. Ansache gave a cry of horror and despair, then lurched another step onward and disappeared.

Cashel followed. He'd follow till he died. It wasn't a conscious decision anymore, it was just the way things were going to be till the business ended one way or the other.

He stepped onto ice and skidded. He chopped his staff down; the ferrule gouged a purchase from the slick black surface. It was blazingly cold, freezing his feet because his calluses had been softened by tramping through the bog. The only light came from the sullen red flare that silhouetted ruined buildings on the horizon.

The ice was clear. Beneath it, staring up at Cashel through

fans of stress marks, was the face of a giant. His mouth, large enough to swallow Cashel whole, opened in a bellow that made the world vibrate.

"Down his throat!" said Evne. "You'll have to break the ice!"

Cashel swung the staff in a half arc. An azure glitter trailed the ferrules the way sparks stream from a quickly-spun torch. The opposite buttcap slammed into the ice in a silent, mind-numbing blue glare. A thousand tiny cracks shivered across the surface, clouding the face beneath it.

The mouth shouted again. The ice blew apart like sea foam shredded by a gale. Cashel jumped or fell—he wasn't sure which, just that he'd managed to get through—down the roaring tunnel beneath him.

He was in the hall of mirrors again. Ansache, sobbing with terror, stabbed his athame into the wall beside him. Instead of shattering as Cashel expected it to do, the world itself curled back from the point like a sheet of isinglass touched by a hot spark. An edge of reality coiled over the wall and the wizard together, leaving a different universe expanding into the place where the corridor had been.

Cashel stood on a hot, windswept plain. In all directions were hills eroded from the yellow, chalky earth. He raised his left arm to breathe through the sleeve of his tunic and filter out the dust.

"Which way is Ansache?" he said to the toad on his shoulder.

"Ansache doesn't matter anymore," Evne said. "To save himself he opened a passage for you onto the ship. Now we'll find the Visitor."

Hutena was on the port tiller; Kulit in the bow as lookout again. The other four crewmen were on the oars, pulling hard. They wore the set expressions of men who knew that they'll be at the task for a long time—but that the faster they worked, the better off they'd be.

Rincip knelt facing sternward, his wrists and ankles bound to the bitts holding the mainstay. Chalcus had stripped him, cutting his tunics off with long strokes of his dagger. It would've been as simple to undress the prisoner normally, but Ilna supposed the dagger—and the nudity itself—was for its effect.

That seemed scarcely necessary; Rincip was terrified, both of what had happened and of what he feared would be next. He looked ready to offer his mother's soul if his captors demanded it. But Chalcus wasn't a man to take unnecessary chances, probably because his life had involved so many risks that he *hadn't* been able to avoid.

Pointin had gotten out of the hold, for the first time since the *Bird of the Tide* came in sight of Terness Harbor after his rescue the night before. He sat against the starboard gunwale and stared at the captive Sea Guard. His face showed no emotion, no expression at all.

"So, Master Rincip . . ." Chalcus said. He sat cross-legged facing the captive. As he spoke, he stropped his curved dagger on the ball of his callused foot. "I've some questions for you. If you answer them promptly and honestly, we'll put you into your skiff and you can wait for your friends to pick you up when they come chasing us . . . as they surely will and as surely will fail, for in the hours it takes the Commander to get a crew together, I'll have the *Bird* across shoals where your *Defender* can't follow without ripping her bottom out."

"You're lying," Rincip whispered through dry lips. "You'll kill me whatever I do."

Despite the words, Ilna thought she heard hope in the Sea Guard's tone. Until Chalcus made the offer, Rincip hadn't even imagined that he might survive this night.

Chalcus laughed merrily. "I've killed too many men to count, my friend," he said. "Men, and it might be women and children too; I was a hard fellow when I was younger. I don't need to add to the number, though it won't bother me greatly if that happens. Regardless, we're towing your little boat behind us, which we would not do except I'm willing to set you free on it."

"Ship your oars and raise sail!" Hutena shouted. The four rowers lifted the sweeps from the oarlocks and pulled them aboard.

Ilna glanced over her shoulder. The castle's watchtower was now below the horizon, but she'd seen it a few minutes earlier when she last looked. She didn't doubt that it'd take at least an hour before Lusius could muster enough of a crew to take the patrol vessel out, but that didn't matter. Everybody aboard the *Bird of the Tide* knew that Lusius would choose wizardry rather than swords to solve this problem. That way it couldn't be traced back to him.

"If you don't talk willingly," Chalcus continued in the same playfully cheerful tone, "Mistress Ilna here will weave you a pattern that brings the words out regardless. Then too you'll go over the side; but bound as you are and without the skiff. You may be floating when your friends arrive; but you won't, I think, be in any different state than if I'd slit your throat to give you a quick end . . . which I will not."

"What do you want to know?" Rincip asked in a guarded, hopeful tone. "I'm not . . . I mean, the Commander plays things pretty close. I don't know much."

"But you know that Lusius is behind the attacks on shipping, do you not?" Chalcus said. "The *Queen of Heaven* and others before her, a dozen ships or so?"

"Yeah, he must be," Rincip said. *Admitted* would've been the wrong word to use since the Commander's deputy was so determinedly separating himself from the business. "He knows to take us out in the barges before anything happens. But it's that demon Gaur who does it and I don't know how. He stays back in the castle, down in his rooms where the dungeons were. I'm not sure even Lusius knows what Gaur does."

Nabarbi loosed a line; the sail slatted down. Ninon and Shausga drew it taut by adjusting the foot ropes. Ilna hadn't noticed enough change in the breeze to justify switching to sail now, but she wasn't a sailor and these men certainly were. Sure enough, the *Bird* continued on its way; as fast or perhaps a trifle faster than the oars had driven it.

Rincip licked his lips and glanced longingly at the skin of wine that the crewmen were passing around now that their hands were free of the oars. Ilna said, her voice harsher than she'd expected, "We said we'd spare your life. We didn't say that we'd treat you as a friend. Tell us about the attacks!"

"All right, all right," Rincip muttered. "It's always the same. Lusius knows where to go. We wait; the sea's empty, there's nothing there, and then there's a flash and the ship is on the sea rocking and stinking of sulphur. Always the same."

He closed his eyes, moving his head side to side as if he was trying to clear something from it. "I try not to look when I know the light is going to come, but it doesn't help," he said. "It comes right through you. You see it in your brain even if your eyes're covered."

"And when the ship appears . . ." said Chalcus mildly, ignoring Rincip's trembling terror. "Do you board and slay the crew?"

The captive laughed harshly. "There's no crew!" he said. "There's nobody, not a soul alive ever till that one there—"

He jerked his chin toward Pointin since his hands were tied behind him.

"—hid in the iron chest just now. There's parts of bodies, torn parts and chewed like shrews that a cat brings back. We throw them in the sea to Our Brother, but it's not us who kills them."

"You've been training the seawolf for the whole time, then?" Chalcus said with a broad, hard smile. "A clever man, our Lusius."

"You don't know the half of it," said Rincip. "Did you think it was chance the beast is named Our Brother?"

"Go on," said Chalcus; still smiling, his right index finger playing with the eared pommel of his inward-curving sword.

"Lusius and his twin Ausius bribed Lascarg to send him here as Commander of the Strait," Rincip explained. "They were as much a pair as your two hands are. The first night Ausius fell into the sea and a seawolf ate him before we could get a line over to draw him up. Ever since then the seawolf's followed whenever Lusius puts out, in the *Defender* or the barges either one. And Lusius never goes aboard one of the fishing boats, because Our Brother is big enough to capsize them . . . and he thinks that's what he'd do."

"Did Lusius throw his brother to the beast?" Ilna said. "Stab him and throw the body in?"

Rincip shrugged. "It was night," he said. "They were in the far bow of the *Defender*. Lusius says his brother leaned over holding a stay to look at the seawolf and his hand slipped. Maybe that's what happened."

He scrunched up; if his hands had been free, he'd have been covering his eyes with them, Ilna was sure. He said, "I wish I'd never got into this. We're all afraid, we'd all like to quit. I think the Commander's as scared as the rest of us, but what can we do?"

"You can get very rich, I'm thinking," said Chalcus pleasantly. "From the shell alone, a tidy sum; and with what comes out of the bellies of the ships you loot—richer yet. I know better than most how quickly that gold flows away, but having it means a fine time while it lasts."

"You don't know," Rincip said, shaking his head miserably. "Sure, I've seen bodies before, but just pieces, always pieces . . . And I kept thinking, what if it gets loose? What if it comes after me?"

"What *it?*" Ilna said. "What's the thing that does the killing?"

"I don't know," Rincip said, his voice rising. "I don't know, I don't want ever to know. But I'm afraid!"

Which surely was the truth, given that where he was *now* didn't frighten him as much as Gaur's monster did. If the thing was Gaur's at all . . .

"What do you think, dear one?" Chalcus asked her.

Ilna pursed her lips but it was a moment before she decided how to speak. At last she said, "He's telling the truth, surely, but I don't see that he's any further use to us. Except as a witness, I suppose, but you said we'd let him go."

Chalcus grinned and pulled his dagger from his sash. "So I did," he said. He reached out; Rincip flinched as far away as the cords twisted from his own silk tunic allowed, but Chalcus slipped the dagger behind him.

The bonds parted; Rincip sprawled on the deck, dragging tags of severed cord. Chalcus had cut him loose without seeing the knots or touching the prisoner's skin.

He sheathed his dagger and grinned at Ilna. She grinned back. His was a personality very different from hers, but he showed an equal attention to craftsmanship.

"Get in your skiff, Master Rincip," Chalcus said, gesturing toward the painter tied to a stern bitt. "Go over the side and I'll cast you off. There's oars in the boat, but you may as well wait for the Commander to come by."

"It wouldn't bother me to knock him in the head first," said Hutena, speaking for the first time as his hands gripped the tiller fiercely. He glared at the man who'd talked so casually about aiding in the slaughter of hundreds of sailors much like Hutena himself.

"Nor would it bother me, bosun," Chalcus said with a merry laugh, "but we'll not do that, not just now."

He gestured to the cowering Rincip with the finger that a moment before had been playing with his sword hilt. "Get over the side, my man," he said. "I won't make the offer a third time."

Scrambling and looking back toward Hutena, Rincip tripped over the low railing. He bellowed with shock and fear in the moment he splashed into the water. He must have caught the painter, though, for it jerked violently.

Chalcus cut the skiff loose with a single swift motion of his sword. He sheathed the weapon and said, to Hutena and perhaps to more than the few souls aboard the *Bird of the Tide,* "If every man were hanged who deserved it, friend bosun, I greatly fear that you'd be serving a different captain now."

"You're not like Rincip, Captain," Hutena growled. "He's not a man, he's a jackal without the balls to kill for himself. But I guess we can leave him for others if you say so."

Chalcus looked back over the stern, his lips in a hard, bright smile. Ilna followed his gaze; the skiff was almost lost in the slow swells in the *Bird*'s wake.

"They'll be following in the *Defender*," Chalcus said musingly. "The barges'll still be loaded with what they took from the *Queen of Heaven.* And they know the *Defender* can't catch us before we make the shoals where she can't follow. . . ."

"I just want to get away," said Pointin, staring at the deck between his knees. "I don't care where. Just away!"

There was a cyan flicker in the night sky. If Ilna hadn't known what it really was, she might have guessed it was heat lightning.

"And so we shall, I do hope," said Chalcus. "But first we'll make a detour to a place Master Gaur wishes us to see."

"Captain?" called Kulit from the bow. The sailor's face was carefully composed to hide the fear inside. All the men held weapons, but they clearly shared Ilna's doubt as to how useful that would be.

"Aye, lads," said Chalcus. "It's now that we earn our pay, I'm thinking."

Azure wizardlight flared again, this time as a continuous solid bowl pulsing across the sky directly above the *Bird of the Tide*. It pulsed, and Ilna felt herself falling though nothing around her changed.

For a moment she heard Pointin's terrified screams. Then the roar of wizardry overwhelmed every other sound.

Chapter Seventeen

The mechanical birds trilled tunes as golden as their own flashing wings. That was the only soothing thing going on in the audience room this morning.

Garric sat grim-faced at the head of the conference table. Lord Tadai, Lord Waldron, and Master Reise ("representing the Vicar") were arguing over the size, makeup, siting, and especially the funding of the garrison that would remain in Haft when the royal army accompanied Prince Garric to Sandrakkan, the next stage of his progress. The army commander was heated, the acting chancellor was suave, the former palace servant was self-effacing—and none of the three of them would move a hairbreadth from his initial mutually-exclusive position.

"*There's no perfect decision!*" Carus said. Garric was dizzy with silent frustration but the ancient king was in a livid rage. "*You should just do it, do anything, and be done!*"

Before Garric could make any response beyond the first

twitch of a smile, Carus realized what he'd said and guffawed loudly. *"Aye, lad,"* he said. *"You should decide by throwing knucklebones and let the kingdom go smash. The way I did, because I wouldn't spend time on anything that didn't involve a sword."*

Each of the principals had several aides carrying document cases. A staff captain and one of Tadai's section heads, both junior members of the Ornifal nobility, snarled at one another beside the silver birdcage; if they'd been allowed to carry swords in the presence of the prince, they'd have been using them. The pair of Blood Eagles on duty watched with superior smiles.

Liane sat demurely beside Garric with a waxed notepad in her hand and a rank of part-opened scrolls laid on the table before her. To look at her she was wholly focused on her documents, oblivious of the discussion going on. Garric was quite sure that if asked, Liane could repeat verbatim any portion of the argument and counterarguments; which was more than *he* could do, and he'd been trying to follow it.

The door opened. A guard outside whispered to one inside, then a nondescript man entered. He walked around the room against the wall to Liane, then stooped and whispered to her lowered head. Garric smiled again. He didn't know the details—yet—but he knew that if the fellow'd been allowed in now, something more important than a council meeting was about to occur.

Liane nodded to the messenger—one of her spies, obviously—and stood expectantly. Nobody but Garric paid any attention.

Garric stood also and slapped the table. Everyone jumped; Lord Waldron reached reflexively for the hilt of the sword, which he wasn't wearing.

"Gentlemen," said Garric. His tone and expression were stiff, just short of angry. "Lady Liane has an announcement."

"An emergency requiring Prince Garric's presence with troops has arisen at the Shrine of the Sister," Liane said. As she spoke, she set her scrolls back each into its place in her traveling desk, then closed the inlaid lid over the cavity.

"Right," said Waldron, no longer angry. To an aide he went on, "Alert Lord Tosli. We'll take the whole palace regiment, so go next to the camp and tell Lord Mayne or who-ever's on duty in his headquarters to bring his regiment at once to replace Tosli's men."

"But about the point we're discussing . . . ?" said Tadai.

"For the time being . . ." Garric said. "That is, until I give different orders, Lord Insto's regiment—" which had the highest number of sickness-related casualties; they'd suf-fered badly on the voyage from Valles and hadn't recovered yet "—will be billeted on the northern arm of the harbor—" which the troops could easily fortify with a short wall across the base of the peninsula before they had time to build a proper fort. "They'll cause less irritation to ordinary citizens there than if they were living in the middle of the city. They'll be concentrated, but they can deploy either by land or sea to wherever they're needed."

Reise nodded; Waldron shrugged, impatient to get mov-ing. Garric knew from Liane's phrasing that this wasn't an emergency in which seconds counted, so he could use the summons as a way to finish a discussion that would go on for many further hours if merely adjourned.

"But the source of the regiment's pay hasn't been de-cided," Tadai said. "I—"

"If I may?" Liane said sharply, looking toward Garric. She reopened her notebook but didn't glance down at it.

"Speak," said Garric, curtly formal.

"Two-thirds of the regiment's pay might come from the Vicar's revenues," Liane said, "with the remainder from the royal treasury in acknowledgment of your right to withdraw the troops without notice should the need arise."

"Done," said Garric. "Lord Tadai, prepare the decree for my signature. Lord Insto will be under the command of the Vicar until and unless I recall the regiment to the royal army."

"I don't like the idea of my legates taking orders from civilians, your highness!" Waldron said, frozen in the middle of his stride toward the door.

"*My* legates, if you please, Lord Waldron," Garric said coldly. "And I prefer that system to having two competing authorities in one jurisdiction."

He broke the chill rebuff with a smile. "Since the Vicar,

Lord Uzinga, is your wife's nephew and the man you recommended for the post, Waldron, I think you ought to be able to work things out. Now, let's get moving."

"Well, but there's the principle . . . ," Waldron was muttering as he and Garric stepped into the hall together. It was a silly enough comment that the old warrior choked off the rest of the thought before he embarrassed himself further.

His aides and Garric's—Lord Lerdain was carrying Liane's traveling desk; from what Garric could tell the youth was besotted with Liane, but he was too much in awe of her to get himself into trouble by saying the wrong thing—were right behind them. The rest of the guard detachment formed around them in the hallway. The captain on duty handed Waldron his sword; during military operations the rules changed, even for the Blood Eagles.

The door slammed, leaving Reise and Tadai behind to wrestle with the problem of converting Garric's decision into the legally appropriate arrangement of words. The whole entourage started down the corridor in an echoing crash of hobnailed boots and jangling armor.

"Your highness!" Liane said, shouting to be heard.

"Eh?" said Garric, gesturing her forward into the space between him and Lord Waldron. "What is it that's going on at the Shrine of the Sister?"

"Nothing, your highness," Liane said, not quite so shrilly as before. "I want to call on the Temple of the Shepherd of the Rock, but I didn't want to say that in the room with the mechanical birds in it."

"The birds?" Garric said, frowning. "The present from the priests of the Shepherd, you mean?"

"Yes, in a way," said Liane. "But it occurred to me that just as Lord Anda didn't know about the urn, so the birds you were given in the name of the Shepherd may not have been what Lady Estanel and her colleagues thought they were sending you. I've just received information that my guess was correct. That doesn't tell me why someone wanted to put that cage of birds close to you, but one of the possibilities is that they were listening to what was said in their presence."

"Can't say I'm sorry," snapped Lord Waldron, who'd

heard as well. "I don't need anything to do with the Sister except send the kingdom's enemies to greet her!"

"Can't say I do either," agreed Garric. And, as they burst out of the side entrance to the courtyard where the duty regiment was already drawn up, he lifted Liane with his left arm alone and kissed her.

Cashel looked about the windblown waste to get his bearings. To tell the truth, that didn't put him much ahead of where he'd been at the start. The sun was a bright blur beyond veils of fine yellow dust. Since he didn't know the time of day, all that told him was which direction wasn't north.

"Walk toward that boulder on the right," Evne said in a muffled voice, crouching on a fold inside his inner tunic. This must be an awful place if you were a toad. It wasn't a good one even for Cashel, who'd gotten used to most kinds of weather.

Cashel obediently turned and started walking, though he couldn't see any boulder. He was headed into the wind now, so he had to close his eyes to slits to see anything.

"This doesn't seem much like a ship, Evne," he said.

"The Visitor doesn't use a ship of the sort humans build when he goes from world to world," the toad said. "His device, if you prefer that word, already exists in all of the places where he makes his home. He merely changes his present reality to appear in one place or another."

She paused, then added, "Well, I see you haven't understood a single word that I've said."

"Ma'am," corrected Cashel, "I understood all the words, I think. I just don't see how they fit together; but that's all right because you understand."

He didn't see the boulder till he was just short of clacking it with the ferrule of his staff, slanted out in front of him. "Where do we go now, Evne?" he asked.

A thing with a hard gray carapace and many legs stood up on the other side of the boulder. It was far the biggest thing in the landscape. For a moment it towered motionless over Cashel; then a jointed proboscis with two savage fangs at the tip unfolded toward him.

"It's an illusion!" warned the toad. "Touch the boulder with your bare hand. If you back away, you'll never be able to leave this place, nor will I!"

Cashel pressed his left palm against the warm, wind-scoured limestone. The creature's fangs sure looked real. They were as white as old bone, and the ends had a slight corkscrew shape.

The rock didn't so much give way as suck him in, turning inside out and engulfing Cashel. He gasped with surprise; the part of his mind that he didn't control had been expecting the fangs, so the shock of sudden change seemed like the fatal stroke. Realizing how he'd tricked himself, he burst out laughing.

"I'm glad you're so pleased," Evne said sourly as she crawled out onto his shoulder again.

Cashel looked around. They were on a rocky slope. Besides tufts of short grass, there were bushes and some good-sized pine trees scattered among the outcrops. The wind was noticeably cool, though not enough to be a problem, and wisps of clouds trailed across the pale blue sky.

Cashel shook his tunics out as much as he could, sending a pall of yellow dust downwind. He blew his nose with his fingers. That helped him breathe, but the back of his throat still tasted like alkaline mud.

"Well, this is a nicer place to be than where we just left," he said reasonably.

"Do you think so?" said Evne. "*That* isn't an illusion."

Ah! She meant the cat that had risen from the shelter of a ledge half a furlong up the slope from her and Cashel. Its coat had a mottled black-on-gray pattern. Cashel's first thought was that Ilna'd really like to see the creature . . . and could you turn the fur into yarn?

The cat flattened. Rather than relaxing out of the wind, it faced Cashel and pressed against the rock like a bolt in a cocked crossbow. Its tail began to twitch; the tip was a tuft of black.

"Where is it we want to go from here, Evne?" Cashel asked. The outcrop behind him looked exactly the same as the one he'd seen in the yellow wasteland, except that this one had gray-green lichen growing on it and blowing dust had scrubbed the other clean.

He rotated the quarterstaff in a slow figure eight before him, working kinks out of his muscles. If the cat charged, he'd want to meet it with one ferrule and then the other.

"You see the ledge the cat is standing on?" the toad said. "You'll need to touch the rock face below her. Or not, of course, if you want to stay here for the rest of your life."

"No, that's not what I want," said Cashel with a sigh. He'd hoped that all he'd need to do was turn around and push against the rock behind him, leaving the cat to its—to her, apparently—own devices. He'd *hoped* that, but he hadn't expected it.

He started toward the outcrop. It was one step uphill for every two steps forward, and the footing wasn't the best either because of loose rock. He didn't guess it'd slow the cat down much, though; she must be used to it.

She watched Cashel coming toward her with tilted green eyes. Her head twisted; then she opened her jaws wide and screamed. The sound was metallic and so loud it waked echoes from the slopes for a mile down the canyon.

The cat's long fur made her look bigger than she was, but Cashel had lifted enough animals out of trouble on his shoulders to know that she *was* big. He judged she'd weigh more than a ram though probably less than a yearling bull; as much as two men of Cashel's own size, which wasn't very many men.

Her eyeteeth were longer than his index fingers. They'd stab to his vitals if once they closed on his torso.

"You're just going to walk straight up to her, master?" said the toad. "That's your whole plan?"

"Yes'm," Cashel agreed. "I'm surely not going to turn my back, and I don't see any gain in waiting for her to decide how she wants to best work things."

The cat jumped to the slope beneath her ledge. Cashel's staff quivered. Part of his mind judged the path she'd trace to his throat: a leap to *there,* and a second leap—spraying back pebbles and an uprooted clump of grass, arrow straight, black claws splayed out before her—

The cat stopped and screamed again. It was an awful

sound, worse than the cry of a rabbit in a leg snare. She turned, as supple as a great gray-furred serpent, and bounded back uphill. She'd vanished over the crest before Cashel had time to let out the breath he'd been holding without knowing it.

"Well, I'm glad to see that," he said as he continued to walk up the slope, breathing more normally now. Mind, he wasn't letting down his guard.

"She could have killed you, you know," Evne said sharply. "You're strong, but she's stronger still, and she has claws and fangs."

"Yes'm," Cashel said. "I was worried about the way things were going to work out."

"Why did you just go walking on, then?" the toad demanded.

"Well, Mistress Evne . . ." Cashel said, frowning as he tried to understand the question. "She was between us and where we were going. I had to keep on."

The toad laughed shrilly. After a moment she said, "My first thought was that so complete a simpleton wouldn't remember to breathe. Then I recalled that you had, after all, taken the correct course and that *simple* isn't necessarily the same as *simpleton*."

Cashel couldn't see anything useful to say, so he said nothing. Evne hadn't asked a question, after all.

As he came to the outcrop, he saw where the cat had been sharpening her claws on the pine tree a little way to the side. She'd torn the bark into fuzzy russet shreds for near as high up the trunk as Cashel could've reached with his quarterstaff. He guessed she'd been bigger even than he'd thought.

"Do I push on this the way I did the other one, mistress?" he asked, standing a little back from the rock and looking around him instead of staring in front. A slab of limestone wasn't ordinarily much of a threat, but other things in the valley besides the cat might be.

"Yes, touch the patch of white lichen," said Evne. "These are all worlds—"

Cashel set his palm on the blotch; it looked like a face. The world folded in and spat him out the other side of it, just as it had before.

"—where the Visitor dwells part of the time."

Cashel was standing in a forest of moderate-sized hard-woods. The trees were nowhere near as thick as the biggest ones in the common forest of Barca's Hamlet—he could've circled the largest of these with his spread arms—but a tap with his staff confirmed what he'd guessed: the wood was very dense, probably as hard as dogwood.

He looked behind him. Instead of a natural outcrop, he was in front of an ancient stone wall built from squared blocks without mortar. A patch of lichen much like the one he'd seen before spread across two layers.

Cashel frowned. "Evne?" he said. "There at the first place, in the dust; did the Visitor put that mirage there to scare off people like me?"

"Are there other people like you?" the toad said in a mocking tone. Then, answering the question, she said, "No, the race that used to live there used the illusions to drive *their* enemies away from nexi of power. It didn't work with the Visitor, of course; but it angered him."

"Ah," said Cashel. That explained what she meant by "the race that *used* to live" here.

Cashel judged it was early spring, though it felt as warm as summer in the borough. The trees hadn't leafed out enough to stunt the lush undergrowth. There were grasses, but lots of soft-leafed plants as well.

Sheep would love this forage, though woods were apt to hide dangers. Hide them from the shepherd, that is; if there was anything so obviously dangerous that a sheep *wouldn't* walk into it, Cashel hadn't found it.

"In a moment!" Evne said peevishly, though Cashel hadn't gotten the question, "Which way do we go now?" beyond the tip of his tongue. "This is a maze, a very complex maze, and neither of us want me to misjudge."

Cashel smiled faintly. It wasn't the first time he'd been snapped at for asking a question somebody else wasn't ready to answer. Though it might have been the first time anybody'd snapped at him for what he hadn't gotten around to saying.

Instinct or maybe the sound made Cashel look to his left.

For a moment there was nothing to see; then a clump of small-leafed stems growing from a common base disappeared. Where the clump had been was a round head near as big as a horse's, attached to a body covered with brown fur. It was a good-sized creature, though it didn't have any legs Cashel could see. It chewed sideways.

"Yes, in that direction, I believe," the toad said. She sounded—not hesitant but *guarded,* extremely careful in what she said. "Past that family of herbivores. Be careful; they can be dangerous."

At the sound of her voice half a handful of other brown heads rose through the undergrowth like sheep when they're alarmed. They didn't look like any animals Cashel had seen before. They reminded him a bit of huge caterpillars, but they had hides like cows.

The first one hissed like a kettle on the boil and lifted a row of spines from the mane down the middle of its back. Those just back of its head were as long as Cashel's forearm. The whole family did the same thing. The others didn't have spikes nearly as long, but they weren't anything Cashel wanted poking into him either.

"The spines are poisonous," Evne said. "They won't kill you outright, but you may get gangrene when the wounds start to fester."

"I'll try not to let that happen," Cashel said calmly. He touched the top of the wall beside him. It wasn't as high as he was; he could vault to the top with the help of his staff if he had to, though he'd rather avoid that.

"Now, I'm going to leave you to your business, sheep," he said, walking slowly to his left. He kept one ferrule out between him and the animals, but he didn't point his staff so close at them that they'd take it for a threat. "I'm headed off where I'll never trouble you again."

They turned together to keep facing him as he moved, hissing louder than before. They were more like a sounder of hogs than a herd of sheep; he might have to get up on that wall—

"*There was a wealthy merchant. . . .*" sang the toad. "*In Valles town did dwell . . .*"

The animals went silent as suddenly as a hen when her neck's wrung.

"*He had an only daughter...*" Evne continued. "*The truth to you I'll tell....*"

Cashel sidled along a little faster, always keeping his face to the animals and his staff out. He put several good-sized trees between them and the herd.

"*Lay the lily oh, oh lay the lily oh,*" sang Evne.

Cashel couldn't see any of the creatures. He'd just reached the end of the wall when he heard a thumping rush—diminishing. They were going in the other direction. From the sound, they were hunching along like so many inchworms.

Cashel grinned. That was something he'd like to see, but not so badly he was going to chase after the herd.

"Thank you, Evne," he said. "I'd just been thinking that if Garric was here, he could've played them a tune on his pipes like he did the sheep sometimes when they were spooky from a storm coming."

The toad sniffed. "Don't mention it," she said. "I certainly didn't want to walk the rest of the way to the nexus myself. Not to mention deal with what happens after that."

She pointed with a hind leg again and added, "A little to the right here. It shouldn't be very—"

Cashel saw the stone and nodded his staff toward it.

"Yes, that's it," said Evne brusquely. "Touch the bust of the god Ruhk there on top."

Cashel hadn't realized it was a worked stone. Now that Evne told him, he could see it was built from several layers rather than a single block, but he still couldn't imagine how she knew the lump was supposed to be anything or anybody.

He took a last look around the forest. It'd been a nice place compared to some, and it reminded him of home. If Ruhk didn't have a fancy statue, well, strangers seeing the scratches on the stone above the pasture south of Barca's Hamlet probably wouldn't guess the shepherds left offerings to Duzi there.

Cashel laid his palm on the stone. He felt himself sucked into a waste of blinding light and his own mirrored image infinitely repeated.

"He's trapped us!" Evne said from Cashel's shoulder. She spoke in a distinct voice, a little louder than usual. "I don't see a way out from our side."

The mirrored walls were flowing closed like cold honey. Cashel tried to swing his quarterstaff, but the ferrules were already fixed in the matrix. He couldn't move his feet, and the glittering pressure moved up his calves.

"The Visitor may keep us alive for a time," said Evne. She was still free on his shoulder, not that there was any place for her to go. "Or of course he may not."

Cashel twisted his staff again. The thick hickory flexed, but even he couldn't make it move any more than that. The mirrored faces crawled toward his hands, engulfing the wood on their way.

Cashel reached into his wallet and removed the last of the rubies Kakoral had given him. It wasn't much of a hope, but it was the best one going.

"Another thirty seconds, I'd judge," said Evne. "A little longer for me if I hop onto your head, but I don't know that I'll bother."

Cashel didn't trust the walls. They were hard enough where they held him, but he guessed that they'd suck in anything he threw at them. He held the red jewel over his head, squeezing it between his thumbs. Nobody was strong enough to break a ruby with his bare hands, but this wasn't exactly a ruby . . .

A thought struck him; he laughed.

"Yes," said Evne, "the Visitor knows he's in a fight this time."

And as she spoke, there was a red flash and the stone powdered between Cashel's thumbs.

The clumsy raft touched while it was still several yards out in the fjord; a length of driftwood had sagged out of its lashings to drag beneath the surface. Sharina roused herself as men from the shore splashed out to pull them onto the beach.

The fur she'd been lying on was soaked, but it'd kept her from being splashed from between the logs every time the paddlers slopped the raft forward. Scoggin glanced at her with concern; Franca was huddled in a ball with Neal's short cape over him. He doubtless would've been concerned, but he hadn't recovered from his own dip into the water.

"I'm all right," she said, and managed to stand up to prove it. *All right* didn't necessarily mean *good,* but she was certainly feeling better. She thought she'd be able to keep food down shortly, and that should help a lot.

Sharina walked across the wobbling raft and hopped to the stone beach without stepping into the water again. Doing that was pointless except as an exercise, but proving that she had her strength and balance back was oddly more satisfying than the fact she'd retrieved the Key of Reyazel. Part of her wondered if the world wouldn't have been better off with the key remaining at the bottom of the fjord.

She grinned as she pulled her shift on, transferring Beard from one hand to the other so that she never had to put him down.

"You've got a right to be happy about what you've done, mistress," Neal said. He was helping—*carrying* would be a more descriptive word—Alfdan to dry land. The wizard's efforts had cost him as much as diving had Sharina, though Alfdan had a blankly beatific expression and was mumbling. Hs hands were clasped together over the key; he looked down at it through the opening between his thumbs.

"Do I?" Sharina said. "Perhaps. But what I was thinking is that *this* world can't be harmed very much by me bringing up the key."

"Get the mistress another fur!" Neal shouted, still supporting the trembling wizard. "By the Lady, don't any of you have sense?"

"I'm all right," Sharina said. "But get something for Franca."

Several men grabbed robes from their packs and trotted over to her. Sharina handed the first to Franca—he took it with a grateful smile—and wrapped a sheepskin around her shoulders wool side inward. It felt good, though she really hadn't been cold without the cover. She wondered if that had something to do with holding Beard; he was certainly more than an axe that talked.

Alfdan began hobbling up the slope toward the ruined tower. Neal followed him, protesting, "Sir, I think you should rest before you do anything more. You're not—"

"No, you fool!" the wizard snarled with more animation than seemed likely in his weakness. "I have the key now and I'm going to use it!"

Neal looked over his shoulder at Sharina, raising an eyebrow in question. Sharina laughed. *Why not?*

"Yes, all right," she said, starting after Neal and the wizard. "I may as well see what the thing does. Beard and I worked hard enough to get it."

She wasn't surprised that the whole band trailed along as soon as she said she was going with Alfdan. Nor was she surprised to hear the axe protest, "Oh, mistress, it wasn't work, it was the greatest pleasure Beard has had in all the ages of his life! You're a wonderful mistress to bring Beard an Elemental's life to drink! And there'll be more, Beard knows there'll be more before the ice takes all!"

Sharina smiled wryly. Beard was probably right about her having to kill additional things that she'd rather never have known existed. And he might be right about the ice too; but if he was, well, she'd have died long before it happened.

Alfdan had straightened and was taking quick, short steps like an old man who'd gotten into his stride. He held the Key of Reyazel out in his left hand as though it were a talisman. It flashed warmly as it jerked back and forth in time with his steps.

"What's the tower for, mistress?" Scoggin asked politely. He and Franca walked on either side of her, staking their claim to her authority as well as being protective. "It doesn't make any sense to build a fort halfway up a hill, does it?"

"I don't know either," Sharina said. It was flattering that everyone here thought she was an authority, but it also seemed silly; she wasn't even from this world! Though—

"Beard," she said. "Do you know about the tower?"

"That?" the axe said dismissively. "A customs post, that's all. It was on the shore before the sea fell."

Beard sighed and went on, "Nothing there to kill. Nothing anywhere around here to kill . . . unless we go back into the fjord?"

"No," said Sharina firmly. "We're not going to do that."

The slope became abruptly steeper. Alfdan dropped onto

one hand and the knuckles of the other, still clutching the key. Neal bent to help, but the wizard gained strength as he neared his goal. He stood upright again on the flat apron before the tower's door. It was on the landward side so storm surges wouldn't batter it.

"But it's open," a man said doubtfully. "By the Sister, it's only hanging by the one hinge!"

Sharina stepped to side of the wizard as he contemplated the door. It was thick oak, cross-braced with more oak, but the last occupant to leave the tower hadn't latched it. Years of wind battering the heavy panel back and forth had broken the upper hinge, leaving the door half-open and askew.

"I'd like to see the key," she said quietly.

"No!" Alfdan cried, hiding the golden sheen in both hands and clutching them tight to his breast. "It's mine!"

"It's yours," Sharina agreed, calm-voiced but frowning. "I'd like to look at it, though. I had other things on my mind when I saw it before."

"My mistress killed an Elemental to fetch the key to the surface," said Beard in an eager singsong. "A wizard's blood isn't much for taste, but Beard would drink it down regardless."

"Let her see the thing," said Layson. "Let us all see it! She fetched it up, and the rest of us have a right too."

With the desperate eyes of a rabbit searching for escape, Alfdan looked at Neal on his other side. Neal gave a dismissive jerk of his head. "Let Mistress Sharina see it," he said.

Terrified, his mouth working, Alfdan held the key out between his left thumb and forefinger. He turned his head away so that he wouldn't have to look at it or Sharina. She took it, feeling him resist for a moment.

Save that it was gold instead of brass, the Key of Reyazel was much like what Sharina's mother used for the lock of the inn's pantry in Barca's Hamlet. The shaft was flat on one end and flared into four pins of varied length at the other. The user stuck the pins into the curving slots of the lockplate and rotated the key to open the latch.

The door of the abandoned tower had a lock, but its key would've been a huge iron thing with a pair of hooks to engage holes in the heavy bar on the inside. It was no more like the Key of Reyazel than it was like an oil lamp; and as the man had said ago, the door was open.

Turning, Sharina offered the key to Neal. He shook his head, flaring his auburn hair. "Layson?" she asked. "Anyone?"

"That's all right," Layson muttered, scowling at his boots. "But we got a right to see it, that's all I meant."

"Yeah, let's get on with it," said a man at the back of the crowd. There wasn't room for everybody on the apron, so some of the band had climbed up the slope for a better view of what was going on.

Sharina returned the key to Alfdan. He took it, smirking at her. The pause had settled him back into his normal personality. That wasn't entirely a good thing, but Sharina supposed it was better than wondering what a dazed, half-mad wizard was going to do next.

Alfdan thrust the Key of Reyazel into the latch opening. Holding it there, he raised his whalebone staff overhead and said in a low voice, *"Herewet."* He twisted the key in his left hand.

A door opened; not the door of the tower but a half-glimpsed thing of light and surfaces reminding Sharina of what she'd seen when she dived into the fjord. Beyond was a beach flooded with warm sunlight. The wizard cried in triumph and stumbled through, leaving the key in the lock.

Sharina hesitated, but not long enough for anyone outside her mind to notice. She'd rather not have entered the world through the door at least until she'd had a good look at it from this side, but she and Beard needed to be close by Alfdan to protect him.

If anything happened to the wizard, the rest of them were probably marooned here for the rest of their lives. Given how barren the region was, that might not be a very long sentence.

Within the portal, the ground was sandy clay: dry, cream colored and as solid as rock beneath Sharina's bare feet. Alfdan was walking toward the sea with the same short, quick steps that had brought him to the tower. She dropped the sheepskin and caught up with him in a few long strides, holding the axe in both hands.

The sun was hot. A strong breeze blew from the sea,

pulling the wizard's robe and Sharina's shift back in the direction they'd come. Her feet scuffed into the surface, pure sand now.

"Wait, mistress!" Franca called; she looked over her shoulder. He and Scoggin were trotting toward her. The rest of the band was now on the beach also, looking around with cautious pleasure. The doorway was a slot of emptiness in the bright air.

They were at the end of a semicircular bay. The sea beyond stretched north and south to the horizon, swelling and subsiding with slow majesty. The water was a chalky green near the shore but pale ultramarine where it met the sky.

"It's here," Alfdan said. "Somewhere close, it must be. . . ."

He wasn't looking at her; Sharina wasn't sure that the wizard knew he was speaking aloud. "What's here?" she asked. "What are we looking for?"

"Mistress . . . ?" said the axe. Beard's tone was diffident, unlike anything she'd heard from his steel lips in the past. "I don't think you should stay here. If I could see the thing, I would try to eat its soul, but I'm not sure . . ."

"Whose soul?" Sharina said sharply. She was suddenly angry, though she knew she was overreacting. Exhaustion and hunger had stripped away her normal patience. "What is it that's here?"

"Mistress, I don't know," said Beard. "And I'm not sure we can kill it, you and Beard."

What had been merely a swell in the open sea rose into a great curling surge as it swept into the bay. It licked the shoreline with a roar and a trail of foam, washing thirty yards up the beach in a thin sheet, then spun its way back out to sea. The water was shockingly cold, but it splashed no higher than Sharina's ankles.

Alfdan gave a gasp of wonder. He poked the firm sand with his wand, then squatted to dig with both hands. Sharina watched him, holding Beard ready.

"Ah!" the wizard cried. He rose holding a ring set with a tiny amethyst, barely a wink of purple against the narrow gold bezel. "The Pantropic! The specific against all poisons, here!"

He slipped the ring onto his left little finger and turned gleefully to the company. "No venom can touch me now!" he cried. "I'm safe! I'm safe!"

"Who wanted to poison you before?" Franca asked, frowning.

"You're not such a fool as some wizards I know, boy," said Beard loudly. "It's a toy that does nothing except add to Master Great One's collection. None of them mean anything to him, nor to the ice that will have him and them all in no great time."

"Look!" cried a man standing at the sea edge. He'd suddenly dug in the sand with his spearbutt. "Look at this diamond!"

"I don't much like this place," Layson said, holding a nocked arrow to his bow. He'd walked slowly toward Sharina and her companions, looking around watchfully.

"You're right not to like it," said Beard. "But it likes you all very much."

"We've found what we came for," Sharina said, aware that she sounded harsh. "Now let's get back."

She touched Alfdan's sleeve. She didn't have to pull hard as she'd thought she might: he came with no more than guidance.

"Oh!" cried Franca, rising from the sand where he'd knelt, holding up an object. "Oh! My father's charm! I thought it'd been . . ."

Sharina looked at it, a disk of porcelain with a relief of the Shepherd leaning on his staff between a pair of fruit trees. It was pierced to be hung from a thong. Priests sold them when they came through Barca's Hamlet with the Tithe Procession; several people in the borough had similar ones, more as talismans than for deeper religious reasons.

It hadn't brought much luck for Franca's father; but then this was one of thousands of identical disks and might have nothing to do with the man . . .

Franca turned it over and showed Sharina the name clumsily scratched on the back. "Orrin!" he said. "My father!"

She felt cold. "Let's get out of here!" she said, loud enough that they could all hear. Most of the band was now digging at the sea's edge and chirruping in delight.

"The currents sweep things into this bay and leave them," Alfdan said, looking around with a critical eye. "There's probably more things here. Things of unimaginable value!"

"You think the sea brought you that ring, wizard?" Beard said. "Do you really think that?"

"I didn't say the sea!" Alfdan said. "There's more currents than those in the water, axe!"

"So there are," said Beard. "And who controls them, do you know? *I* don't; but I don't want my mistress to learn!"

"Leave him if he wants to stay!" Layson muttered. "I'm going back."

"Come!" said Sharina, pulling the wizard's arm. She stepped and her toe stubbed something. *A bit of driftwood,* she thought as she glanced down reflexively; but she'd flipped up the weathered back to expose a surface of fresh yellow pine with a crude carving.

Sharina picked it up. She was trembling. "Mistress?" said Scoggin in concern.

Somebody'd carved a figure of the Lady on the scrap of wood; the sort of thing that a traveler might make when he wanted to pray of an evening in a distant place. You had to know what the scratches *must* be to identify the image, and you couldn't possibly tell who'd made them.

But Sharina knew. "Nonnus . . ." she whispered.

With sudden certainty, she turned and flung the scrap toward the sea. "Come!" she said. "Now!"

She strode toward the doorway, no longer concerned whether Alfdan and the rest followed her or not. Scoggin and Layson were quickly at her side. Franca trotted along after when he saw them leaving. The wizard was coming, and the others as well.

"What was that, mistress?" Scoggin asked, now more concerned about her than he was for their surroundings. "That you found?"

"The man who carved that died for me," Sharina said. She wiped her eyes with the back of her hand, but everything was still a blur. "Died for me and the world, I suppose; but for me. I don't know why it was here, but I know that whatever rules this place isn't a friend of mine. So I gave it back."

She stepped through the doorway, into chill air and a sky

in which the sun was already hidden beneath the high cliffs. She'd forgotten the sheepskin but she didn't care; the relief was as great as what she'd felt when she breathed again after her third plunge into the fjord.

Neal walked back to the doorway with a stunned expression. He held something cupped in his left hand, but he wasn't looking at it or even toward his hand. Alfdan followed, reaching for the key as he passed through. He stopped when he realized that a handful of men were still on the beach side of the portal.

"Come along!" the wizard shouted peevishly. "You won't be able to return after I take the key out!"

That brought them at a shambling run. Two were chattering toward one another with animation; toward, not to, because neither could've been listening to what the other said. The rest were in a state of numb concern, their expressions much like Neal's.

Alfdan twisted the key. "Wait!" said Neal, putting his right hand over the wizard's. He flung the object in his left hand back through the opening, then turned away. Sharina caught a glimpse of something spinning in the sunlight; a miniature painted on ivory.

Alfdan withdrew the key; they were all standing before a gutted tower, its door sagging inward. Neal caught Sharina's eye and muttered, "What did I want with that? She's been dead all these years!"

"Yes," said Sharina. "I understand."

She turned to the wizard and said, "I've carried out my part of the bargain; now it's your turn. Take me to the farthest north. Take me to where She is."

"Are you mad?" Alfdan said. "You'd find nothing there but your death!"

"I'll die anyway," Sharina said. "Sooner or later. If we kill Her, perhaps it'll be later."

"Go, then," Alfdan snarled. "But you'll go alone. When I said I'd carry you where you wanted to go, I didn't mean I'd commit suicide. I'll not take you to Her!"

"If he'll not keep his bargain with us, mistress," said Beard in a coyly musing tone, "then there's no reason for him to live, is there?"

The wizard backed away and stumbled. "There's no need for that," Sharina said sharply to her axe.

"There's no need for threats," Neal said in near echo. "Master Alfdan, you and Mistress Sharina made a bargain. She kept her part; and you'll keep yours."

"Are you *all* mad, then?" Alfdan said, looking around the circle of his followers. "Do you want to die? That's all you can possibly do if you go to Her!"

"I don't . . ." Burness began in a small voice.

"Shut up, old man!" Layson snarled. "We didn't make a bargain with the wizard, but *she* did; and he's going to keep it or she won't have to kill him. I will!"

Alfdan rubbed his forehead; the amethyst on his finger winked like a fairy's eye. "It'll take days," he said. "Even in the Queen Ship."

"Oh, days are fine," said Beard. "We have days and weeks and months before the ice covers all."

He tittered like a steel skeleton. "Days and weeks and months, yes," he said. "But not years, no, not if you don't kill Her very quickly. For She'll have drained all warmth and all power from this world and there'll be no blood left for Beard to drink!"

Blue wizardlight flared in a roaring sphere around the *Bird of the Tide*. When it vanished, Ilna had the momentary impression that she was blind and seeing stark black-and-white images of the Hell inside her mind.

The *Bird* tipped to its left, crunching on cracked rock. The vessel's hull was shallow so she didn't go all the way over on her side, but the mast now tilted at an angle halfway between the horizon and the roiling yellow sky. The air stank fiercely of brimstone, making Ilna's eyes water and her bare skin sting.

Pointin had fallen against the port railing hard enough to knock the breath out of him. That kept him silent, the one good thing Ilna could find in this situation.

No! She was unharmed, Chalcus and the crew were unharmed—and they were all in the place they'd chosen to go in order to do their duty. She had no reason whatever for complaint.

Ilna braced her left foot on the railing and squinted to save her eyeballs as much as she could while she looked at the landscape. It was an awful place.

Spikes of rock, cut deeper where layers rested on one another, rose from flat, cracked terrain. The wind that had ravaged them whipped around the *Bird* now, rocking her violently. Chalcus and the men leaped to the lines, bringing the spar clattering down; there was no time to furl the sail properly.

Ilna hadn't noticed any orders passing. The sailors all knew what had to be done and did it. She could learn to like sailors; competent ones, at any rate . . . though the only problem she had with competent people in *any* walk of life was that she found so few of them.

There was little in the landscape but rock and heat and the sulfurous wind. On the horizon something pulsed orange-red, possibly a volcano. Except for that, Ilna couldn't see anything farther away than she could fling a stone. The sun was a huge dull blur through clouds ranging from sepia to a yellow so dark it could scarcely be called a color.

Something shrieked in the distance; or maybe it was just wind through the rocks.

"What happens now?" Tellura asked, his voice muffled. He was holding the bosom of his tunic over his mouth and nose to breathe. "Are they going to smother us? Is that it?"

Ilna doubted that a layer of coarse wool would help much with the brimstone; besides, she needed her hands for other things. Her fingers formed knots in yarn with the flawless certainty of raindrops falling on a pond.

"Not that," Chalcus said. He held his incurved sword in one hand, the dagger in the other. "There'll be company, have no doubt, my friends."

Hutena was the only crewman who'd seen the fragments of human bodies on the *Queen of Heaven*. Bad though this air was to breathe, no one could imagine it had caused *that* slaughter.

Chalcus gestured toward the higher railing. "Kulit and

Nabarbi," he said, "keep watch to starboard side. We don't know which direction it'll come fr—"

Pointin screamed piercingly. Ilna turned.

A huge thing shambled out of the swirling darkness. It walked on two legs and had two long arms as well, dangling near the ground as it hunched forward. Nothing else about it was manlike. Hard, smooth plates like insect armor covered its limbs and body.

Shausga drew his bowstring to his right ear and loosed. The arrow cracked against the creature's narrow chest and glanced off.

The creature raised its arms, opening the pincers in place of hands. It came on, gurgling like the last wine from a bottle.

Chapter Eighteen

Ilna stepped over the railing, lowering herself carefully to the ground. She could've jumped, but she wasn't sure of the footing—and she was *quite* sure that she couldn't afford to fall on her face at this juncture.

"It's twenty feet tall!" Ninon cried. "By the *Gods,* it's a demon from Hell!"

Ilna smiled faintly. The creature might or might not be a demon, but it wasn't *from* anywhere: it had stayed home. The *Bird of the Tide* and her crew were the ones who weren't where they belonged. She walked forward, holding the knotted pattern between her hands.

Another arrow, then two in quick succession, struck the creature. Two skidded away like rays of light from polished steel; the third *whack*ed the ridge between the creature's bulging, faceted eyes. The shaft shattered and spun off in the wind like a handful of rye straw.

Ilna kept walking. She hoped there was enough light for the creature to see her pattern. Animals didn't see things the same way humans did.

She smiled more broadly. It would be—briefly—a pity if this thing's eyesight wasn't good enough to slip into the trap she'd so skillfully woven for it.

The air had been hot, but the ground was oven-hot. Ilna almost stepped on one of the cracks zigzagging across the rough stone; heat radiating up from it struck her callused foot a punishing blow. When she glanced down, she saw a tremble of orange light at the bottom of the narrow crevice: molten rock flowed between the solid plates.

The creature rubbed its elbows against the sides of its torso, making a shrieking sound like that of a cicada hugely magnified. It stretched a jointed arm toward Ilna's face, the pincers opening fully. Each curved blade was as long as a sickle's.

Ilna spread her knotted pattern above her head. If it didn't work, she didn't want Chalcus to think that her last act had been to hide her eyes from the sight of death reaching toward her.

The creature staggered. Its arm froze in midair and its mouth opened slightly; the jaw plates spread sideways, not up and down. Its breath reeked like a tanner's yard, rotted foulness and the savage bite of lye.

Ilna didn't move; her eyes were blind with tears from the brimstone. Behind her Chalcus shouted words that the wind whipped in the other direction. Men ran past Ilna on either side; they were blurs of movement, not individuals.

An axe rang; Hutena gave a high-pitched cry of triumph. Ilna blinked, bringing the scene into sudden focus. She realized she'd been afraid to take her eyes off the creature for fear that it too would look away and break the binding spell.

The creature began to topple sideways. The bosun wrenched his axe out of its right knee in a wave of syrupy blood. The other sailors hacked with their blunt-tipped swords, aiming at the knees and ankles. Their blades generally clanged and bounced back, leaving lines scored across the creature's hard casing.

The creature hit the ground with the point of its shoulder, cracking the rock. It continued to stare at Ilna, its eyes like those of a landed fish. Chalcus stepped close, judged his victim, and stabbed through the creature's open mouth with the quick skill of a wasp paralyzing a spider.

The creature leaped like a beheaded chicken, both legs spasming; the right one flailed sideways at the broken knee. Chalcus wouldn't let go of his sword, so it pulled his feet off the ground. He kicked at the creature's chest with a great cry and jerked his blade free.

The creature toppled again. It half turned, its eyes sightless when the brain behind them died. It crashed into a needle of wind-carved rock, wavered there for a moment, then flopped onto its back. Its limbs waggled like a dying beetle's.

"Back to the ship, my lads!" Chalcus called, hoarse from the searing atmosphere. "We don't want to be left here when Lusius and his fellows call the *Bird* home, as they surely will."

Ilna lowered her hands, bunching the pattern together between them again. Hot as this place was, she'd felt a chill as the creature died. She hadn't killed the thing with her art—she doubted that she'd have been able to kill it or she would have tried—but there'd been a link between her and her giant victim there at the end.

Everyone was all right. Chalcus and the six sailors were, at least; she didn't see Pointin, but the supercargo would be in the hold out of sight unless he'd become a different man from the one who'd survived the attack on the *Queen of Heaven*.

"You took no harm in the business, my dear one?" Chalcus said, suddenly at her side. He'd sheathed his dagger so he could wipe the sword blade with the tail of his silk sash. The creature's blood had congealed to a tarry smear.

"No," Ilna said, "though I'll be glad to leave this place. I wonder if Lusius and his wizard know where they're sending ships or if it's just that they're ready to be looted when they come back?"

"Sir!" cried Shausga, pointing with his sword toward an arch that the wind had carved from the surrounding rock. He was left-handed. "Mistress Ilna, *there!*"

A monster like the first came through the arch. In the whirling shadows Ilna thought it was smaller, but once clear of the rock it rose onto its hind legs. Tall as the first creature had been, this stood half again as high.

"Right, well, we know the job now, lads, so it won't be so hard," said Chalcus. He hacked to clear his throat, then whipped his sword in a shimmering figure eight. The steel was as clean as it'd been when he boarded the *Bird* in Carcosa. "But I think we'll wait here close by our good vessel, as we know now how the business will go."

Another shrilling cry sounded, very close though Ilna couldn't tell the direction in this waste of rock and fire and darkness. The creature walking toward them hadn't made the terrible sound. Its arms were lifted, the elbows splayed out to the sides.

"What's that?" Kulit said, his voice rising. "Where is it? What are we going to do?"

"Master Chalcus!" Ilna said. "Take this, if you will. You've seen how to use it."

She held the pattern to him, bunched; Chalcus sheathed his weapons with quick understanding, then reached for the fabric. Ilna placed it in his hands deliberately, making sure the correct side would be outward when he spread it to the monster.

"All right, lads," Chalcus said, turning with a grin that might well be genuine. "We know the drill, so Mistress Ilna is letting us handle it ourselves. Let's get on with it, hey?"

The ground shuddered; Ilna turned. She'd thought the sheer rock to the left was a butte. Now she saw that it was two walls standing close together; between them lurched a third monster.

Ilna walked toward the creature, smiling faintly. She'd taken more lengths of yarn out of her sleeve and was knotting them. At worst, devouring her might delay the creature long enough that Chalcus and the crew could dispatch their opponent and turn their attention to the new threat.

"All right, boys!" Hutena snarled behind her. "You heard the captain!"

Ilna'd thought of giving the fabric to the bosun or another of the crewmen, freeing Chalcus to do whatever was most important—

But holding the pattern steady before the oncoming monster *was* the most important thing, beyond question. The sailors' courage went beyond the standard even of brave men, but Ilna knew from her own experience just how heavy the weight of the creature's eyes felt. Chalcus wouldn't fail.

Whether Ilna would succeed in knotting a second pattern in the time she had—that was another matter. If she didn't— her smile was broad—she wouldn't have to worry about listening to reproaches on her performance.

The creature walking toward her wasn't as tall as the other two, but it looked as broad as both of them together. Its chestplate was flat instead of having a keel down the center. A different breed or simply the other sex? She didn't suppose it mattered.

The thing's arms unfolded toward her with the smooth certainty of a pair of bluefish driving their prey together for the kill. The pincers clacked open; the inner edges were black and undulating.

Ilna raised the new pattern high. For an instant she didn't know whether the figure her fingers had knotted was complete, only that she'd run out of time to do more.

The creature froze. If Ilna'd believed in the Gods, she'd have thanked Them. Smiling wryly, she whispered a prayer of thanks anyway. She'd much rather seem a fool for thanking nonexistent beings than she wanted to seem ungrateful.

There were shouts and cries behind her, then the clang of steel on armor that was very nearly as hard. Ilna's eyesight blurred from the rasping sulphurous wind. She blinked repeatedly but didn't notice much improvement. Well, there was very little in this place that she wanted to see anyway.

She felt the ground shake through the soles of her feet. There was a tremendous crash, then a lesser shock and crash. The sailors had brought down the creature Chalcus held for them. It had hit the rock like a felled tree and bounced.

"Come on, boys!" Chalcus croaked in a voice scarcely his and scarcely human. "If anything happens to the mistress, then Sister take my soul if I'll bother to go back!"

Ilna felt herself swaying. She continued to stare at the

monster, but it'd become a pulsing haze whose color shifted from orange to purple and back.

Polished sword blades flashed brighter than the yellow light they reflected. The creature lowed like a bull, the first sound Ilna had heard come from the mouth of one of them.

"Get her clear!" Chalcus shouted. "Don't let the green devil—"

Hutena caught Ilna around the waist and dragged her back. "You numskull!" she shouted, her voice trembling an octave higher with fury. "You've killed us—"

The monster fell forward, smashing the rock. Had Ilna not moved—had Hutena not moved her—she'd have been pulped as surely as a fool of a woodsman who trips in front of the tree he's toppled.

The bosun set Ilna on her feet again. "Aboard the *Bird!*" a voice called from a great distance. "Quick! You can feel it coming!"

Ilna took a step, wobbled, and felt Hutena lift her again in his left arm. He had the axe in the other hand, its head black and gummy with the blood of the monsters it had brought down.

Now that Ilna no longer focused on her own art, she felt the ripples of power which'd warned Chalcus that Lusius's wizard was at work again. Once she even thought she saw an azure flicker, but that could've been a trick of her eyes or mind rather than Gaur's doing.

Hutena lifted Ilna over the *Bird*'s railing, passing her to Kulit. She felt a flash of anger at being treated like an invalid when she could've boarded by herself—

And so she could've done, but the men hadn't been sure and therefore hadn't taken any chances. There wasn't time for a mistake, and there wasn't time for the pride of Ilna os-Kenset either. There was never time for that!

Chalcus brought up the rear, his sword and dagger out. He'd wrapped Ilna's loose fabric of knots around his waist. The sash fouled with monster's blood lay crinkled on the ground behind him.

Chalcus caught Ilna's eyes and grinned; but he stumbled as he jumped to the railing and had to catch himself. "I've a better appreciation for your work now, dear heart," he said, not whispering but in a voice few others could hear. "And I'll take all day as stroke oar on a trireme before I'll play at being you again."

She smiled in acknowledgment, but the comment made her imagine being at a warship's oar all day. It was an absurd notion . . . and yet she'd do it if she had to, poorly beyond question but do it regardless.

Another wash of power made Ilna's skin prickle. The blue quiver on the masthead and the tips of the spar couldn't have been her imagination this time.

"Into the hold, lads," Chalcus ordered, his voice gaining strength as he returned to his familiar occupations. "No sound, now, till I give the word."

Nabarbi slid the hatch cover away; it'd lain part open when the crew returned to the vessel. "Captain!" he shouted.

Pointin lay on his back beside the ironbound chest that was the *Bird*'s only cargo. The smell of camphor filled the hold, strong enough to be noticed despite this hellworld's brimstone stench.

Ilna had seen many dead men, and no few corpses of men who'd died horribly. She had never seen a look of more consummate agony than that on the supercargo's distorted face.

"May the shepherd save us if he's let them out!" Hutena cried.

Chalcus hopped into the shallow hold. "He didn't," he said. "He reached in to empty the chest for his own use, but he got no farther. And if he had, we'd still have no choice but to take the risk. Briskly, lads! There's not much time."

Ilna helped herself into the hold by her arms. She could still see the ravaged landscape over the portside railing. A pair of creatures, similar to the others but half the size, had come out. They were tearing chunks of flesh from the last one slain. She wondered if they were the dead monster's cubs.

"Shall we throw him out?" Hutena said, prodding Pointin's corpse with his foot.

"He's not in our way," said Chalcus. "Given what he paid to avoid being eaten by our demon friends here, I think we can carry him back for a burial in the sea he knew."

Two sailors lifted the hatch cover overhead and set it back

askew on the coaming. Ilna could see wedges of the burning sky on all four sides.

There was a roaring azure flash. Ilna was falling again, gripped by wizardry.

"Ah, the great wizard is landing," said Beard, jarring Sharina out of her reverie. Her eyes passed over the seascape and occasional islands that the Queen Ship sailed by, but the view meant nothing to her. Images struck her mind and glanced off like reflections from the surface of a pond.

"What?" Sharina murmured. Directly ahead was a gravel island which before the sea level dropped would have been only a few yards in diameter. It was several times as large now, but vegetation hadn't had time to spread far from the small birches on the original rocky peak. Brush straggled downward in a ragged ring, and sea oats nodded in the easterly wind.

"Why?" Sharina said, correcting herself now that she'd really looked at the islet toward which the ship was dropping. "There isn't anything here."

"That's safer, mistress," said Neal. "For us just stopping, I mean. We'll sleep here and go on in the morning, when Alfdan's had a chance to recover."

"Oh," said Sharina, looking over her shoulder. "Of course."

The wizard stood upright by the help of two of his men. His features were as tight as a skull's. Sharina knew how much effort went into wizardry, but because she wasn't a wizard herself her unconscious mind discounted it unless she really thought about the matter.

She grinned. Maybe she could trick herself into thinking of wizards as people swimming long distances through a sea of power. She understood swimming.

The Queen Ship grounded with a soft crunch. Alfdan's men were already on their feet. Franca remained asleep, rolled as tightly as a pillbug and muttering under his breath. Scoggin shook him.

"Wakey, wakey, lad," Scoggin said. "It's dry land for a while, which I don't regret."

Franca jerked alert as the ship tilted onto its side, but Scoggin still had to keep a hand on the youth to keep him from slipping onto the gravel. Sharina noticed the interplay with a slight smile. The disaster that was destroying this world seemed to be making men—these men, at any rate— behave better than she'd have expected of villagers during an ordinary winter in Barca's Hamlet.

"Tasleen, get a fire going," Neal ordered with nonchalant authority. Tasleen, a small, dark fellow from Dalopo, had an almost magical skill with a fire bow. "Some of the rest of you gather driftwood."

Franca grabbed the gray, salt-dried trunk of a tree whose bark had weathered off in the distant past. Scoggin gripped the piece by another stub branch and said, "There's a righteous plenty of *that* here, even if there's bloody little else."

"Mistress lend me axe to split kindling?" Tasleen asked, reaching out to take the axe in anticipation of her agreement.

"Mistress split stupid savage's skull so Beard eat brains!" the axe said indignantly. "*Chew* yourself some kindling, buckteeth!"

Tasleen's face darkened with fury. Then he looked from Sharina to the axe and remembered who it was who'd spoken. He backed away, muttering a protective charm under his breath.

"The idea!" Beard huffed. "Using me to chop driftwood!"

"Hey!" said Layson, who'd walked toward a lump farther down the beach. "Here's a sea chest. What do you s'pose it has in it?"

Nothing of the least possible interest to any of us, would've been Sharina's guess; but there was no need to guess. The chest had a keyhole covered by a sliding panel, but either it wasn't locked or the lock had corroded away over the years. Layson jerked the lid open: the chest was empty.

"Tranek and Coffley, get your lines out," Neal ordered. "With luck we can catch some fish before we lose the sun."

He looked at Sharina and added, "We're all right for provisions, but I don't know how things are going to be if we keep going north."

He and Sharina both eyed the sun. It was higher above the horizon than she'd have expected for as many hours as it'd been since sunrise. It was summertime, and they were already at high latitudes.

"Do you think we can really defeat Her, mistress?" Neal asked in a near whisper, his eyes on the horizon.

"I don't know," said Sharina. "I hope so."

A seagull screamed in the western sky. It sounded like a lost soul.

"I really don't know. . . ."

The Arcade of the Shepherd was a large rectangular precinct with colonnaded shops on the lower level. The priests' offices and living quarters were on the upper two floors. If the gates at the north end were closed it would become a blank-walled fortress.

As Garric and his troops clashed up the cobblestone street toward the Arcade, a pair of priests and a trumpeter trotted out of the watchtower into the gateway. The trumpeter blew a brassy summons. One of the priests prostrated himself in greeting while the other—a priestess, Garric thought—ran into the precinct to deliver a detailed message to the High Priestess.

"Huh!" said Lord Waldron. He'd rather have been on horseback, but when Prince Garric insisted on walking, the old nobleman had refused to ride as a matter of military ctiquette. "I thought maybe they'd try to keep us out."

"Lady Estanel's far too intelligent to do that," Garric said. "And I'll be very surprised if there's a weapon more dangerous than a fly whisk in the hands of a priest. The lady knows better than to fight battles she can't win."

"Though she's not one I'd push into a corner, lad," noted King Carus. *"If it's go down fighting or simply give up, the lady's one who'd fight like a demon."*

The troops with Garric at their head entered the gateway eight abreast. Liane in a sedan chair followed Garric, Waldron and their military aides. Four tough-looking men, one of them the fellow who'd brought Liane the message in the council meeting, walked beside the chair.

The Arcade was a fashionable shopping district and fairly busy at this time in the afternoon. Civilians gaped as the soldiers appeared. Some of them were entertained but most looked frightened and ducked within shops in hope of hiding.

Garric grimaced. There was no benefit to him or the kingdom in scaring citizens needlessly, but he *was* going to need the troops. There wouldn't be any trouble from the priests, but he might have to react instantly to the information they gave him.

At the south end of the plaza stood the Temple of the Shepherd of the Rock itself, a shapely structure built narrower than the available space so that it would seem higher. The capitals of the six tall, slim columns across the front were more ornate than anything Garric had seen before, except perhaps for the tangle of multiflora roses, which seemed to have been the sculptor's inspiration.

"Your highness," said Liane, jumping out of her sedan chair. "While you greet Lady Estanel, my associates and I will sequester Lady Panya, the priestess who brought the gift."

She and her four men trotted into the arcade on the right and up the open staircase leading to the priestly quarters. Garric glanced at Lady Estanel and a gaggle of aides coming out of the low building beside the temple, detached from the arcade itself. They could wait.

"Waldron!" he said. "Tell the high priestess to join me in Lady Panya's quarters!"

Garric and the platoon of Blood Eagles guarding him followed Liane. He heard Waldron pass the order along to a junior officer and fall in behind.

Garric grimaced, stopped, and gestured the army commander to his side. "Lord Waldron," he said. "I was in haste and may have seemed impolite. That was not my intention."

Waldron's narrow face had been a mass of hard planes. It broke into an expression of pleasure. "I accept your apology, your highness," he said.

One part of Garric's mind was astounded at the arrogance that allowed the old man to believe he'd had a right to be angry at his prince's brusqueness. But Garric also knew that the same stiff-necked pride meant Waldron would sacrifice his life and whole household to guard Prince Garric, his sworn liege. People weren't simple, and it was Garric's business to treat every one of them as an individual—for the sake of the kingdom.

They went up the stairs together. Liane and her spies had gone into the first suite off the stairhead. The Blood Eagles ahead of Garric were binding three temple servants who lay on their bellies on the floor of the third-level portico.

The higher-ranking priests of the Shepherd lived just as well as those of the Lady. Garric strode into the suite, through the reception room and the bedroom to the small water garden at the rear where Liane and two of her men stood with Lady Panya bos-Parriman.

Garric had only a vague recollection of the priestess who'd brought the cage of mechanical birds; she'd been a face among hundreds, another person whose opinions were more important to her than they were to the kingdom. She'd been good-looking in a slim, severe fashion; the sort of woman who strove to be imposing rather than enticing.

Now Panya looked like a browsing ewe with her neck caught in the crotch of a sapling. She twisted furiously in the grip of the men bending her arms back and lashing her wrists with a rawhide strap.

"She was climbing over the wall," Liane said, gesturing toward the parapet. It was only five feet above the terrace floor, but the drop to the ground beyond was a good thirty feet. "I don't know if she was trying to escape or if it was a suicide attempt."

"Let me go!" Panya shouted. Her eyes twitched in all directions; they didn't seem to focus. "I'm a priestess of the Shepherd! He'll strike you down for blasphemy!"

"I'm sure Prince Garric is acting in accordance with the will of the Shepherd in seeing to the needs of the kingdom, Lady Panya," said Lady Estanel, startling Garric with the unexpectedness of her voice at his elbow. In between phrases she breathed in half-suppressed gasps. "Obey the prince and know that you're obeying the Great Gods who work through him."

The high priestess was red-faced with exertion. She must have run half the length of the plaza and then up two flights of stairs to arrive so quickly, but her expression was as calm as that of the statue of the Shepherd in the temple below.

"Who told you to bring the cage of birds to Prince Garric in place of the gift the temple sent you with?" Liane asked. She didn't raise her voice, but she spoke with cold hostility. No one who knew her socially would've imagined the words came from sweet-natured Liane bos-Benliman.

"The temple gave me the cage!" Panya said. "I did what I was told!"

"We sent you an Old Kingdom manuscript of Celondre's *Odes,* your highness," the high priestess murmured. She frowned at Panya. "With an inscription in Celondre's own hand."

"Mistress?" the spy who'd entered the council chamber said to Liane. She nodded but turned her head, biting her lip.

The spy gripped Panya by the hair and kicked her feet out from under her. His fellow stepped out of the way.

Panya cried out as she fell forward. The spy thrust her face into the basin of the fountain and held her there in a flurry of froth, then lifted her again. He didn't release her. The priestess gasped and spluttered, crying uncontrollably.

Liane turned. "Mistress," she said, "your head will go under water each time you refuse to answer me. Each time will be longer. Eventually you will answer or you will die with your lungs on fire. Who sent you with the cage of birds?"

"I can't—" the priestess said. The spy thrust her forward.

"I'll tell!" she screamed. "I'll tell you!"

"Talk," said Liane. There was more mercy in a flash of lightning than in her voice. "Quickly."

"Count Lascarg's twins came to me," Panya said. She closed her eyes; her neck muscles were taut so that her head didn't hang painfully from the spy's grip on her hair. "Monine and Tanus. They said I had to help them or they'd, they'd say things about me."

Garric nodded in grim understanding. His enemies had corrupted Moisin, the priest of the Lady, with money, but they'd used blackmail to control the Shepherd's emissary.

"Go on," said Liane. Garric was glad she had enough stomach to conduct the interview. He wasn't sure he could do it himself.

"There wasn't any harm," Panya said desperately. "The

birds would sing, that's all, and nobody would tell, would say that I . . ."

She closed her eyes again, her lips working silently.

"Do the birds report what they hear to Monine and Tanus?" Liane asked. "Is that why you were to give them to Prince Garric?"

"I don't know," Panya said. She or her conscience must have felt the spy's hand twitch. Her eyes opened again and she screamed, "I really don't know!"

"It doesn't matter," said Garric. "We'll learn from the other end. Lord Waldron, I'd like you to take charge here with Lord Tosli's regiment while I return to the palace. It's crucial that no one leave the precinct to get word back to Lascarg's spawn."

"Tosli can take care of that," Waldron said. "He's a good officer, for all that his family's bloody Valles merchants. And if you're worried that this is a lot of running back and forth for an old man like me—"

That was *exactly* what Garric was worried about.

"—then don't be. I can march the legs off you and half the Blood Eagles, even if I do prefer riding a horse!"

"Let's go," Garric said, starting for the stairway. Lord Waldron was exaggerating—*probably* exaggerating—but if he said he was ready to jog back to the palace, Garric wasn't fool enough to call him a liar.

"Your highness?" Liane called to his back. "What would you like done with Lady Panya?"

"She doesn't matter now!" Garric said. "Let her go, for all I care."

He was out of the suite when he heard Lady Estanel say, "The temple will deal with the traitor, milady. Because I assure you, we care very much about her actions!"

Garric didn't laugh the way the king in his mind did; but neither did he go back to insist on mercy for a woman who'd been a traitor to her God and the kingdom both. Monine and Tanus, the dimly glimpsed puppeteers who'd toyed with him and Carus in dreams, were his present concern.

"Aye, lad, it'll be a pleasure to see them dance on a rope instead of us for a change," growled the king through a sav-

age smile. *"Assuming we take them alive, which wouldn't be my choice!"*

A crimson flash from the jewel shattering between Cashel's thumbs turned the walls gripping him transparent. He still couldn't move, but he could see where he was. That didn't make him comfortable, exactly, but at least it was a change.

The demon Kakoral stood in front of him, laughing with a sound like a thatch roof ablaze. His body was a thousand shades of red, but now that Cashel saw the demon close-up he got the impression that the skin had no color at all—that instead it reflected the light of a different world.

The room was vast beyond anything Cashel had seen—except the sky from the deck of a ship at sea. Girders of light slanted from unguessible heights to the walls and floor. Cashel instinctively grasped their pattern, though his conscious mind couldn't *understand* it at all.

"Well, Master Cashel," Kakoral said. "I thought I'd come myself this time, since you've proved to me that Kotia is not only Laterna's offspring but mine as well."

Besides the structural members, a spiderweb of fine lines trailed through the interior space. Where they intersected, objects hung. Some were tiny, no bigger than a pear, but others seemed the size of large buildings. Kotia hung nude in a transparent enclosure like Cashel's own, slightly higher and a half bowshot away.

"I didn't prove anything," Cashel said, frowning as he tried to puzzle out the question. "I just came to get her out."

He paused, frowning harder. "If I could."

"He means that Kotia found you for her champion," said Evne on Cashel's shoulder. "Did you think that was a little thing, master?"

A gray globe was forming in the middle of the room. Cashel was good at judging sizes, but this thing tricked his eyes in a fashion he didn't understand. If he had to guess he'd have said it was large; *very* large, too large even for this huge space. But he also felt he could've spanned it with his arms if he'd been free to climb the cobwebs of light to where it hung.

"I don't think finding me counts for much, seeings as I'm trussed here like a chicken at market," Cashel said.

Kakoral roared with laughter. His body seemed to swell to the scale of the room. "You brought me through the Visitor's defenses, Master Cashel," he said. "That was enough to suit me. It will suit him too, like a hemp collar!"

The demon reached out a foreclaw toward Kotia. The crystal cage exploded in a crimson flash, leaving the girl sprawled in the air. She rubbed her biceps; she'd been spread-eagled in her prison like a hide pegged out for drying.

The globe was now a perfect solid with the glint of steel. It stabbed a needle of blue wizardlight toward Kakoral.

Toward where Kakoral *had* been. The bolt ripped a deep furrow across the floor, mounding material like smelter slag up on either side. The demon was a furlong high in the air, his hands spread.

Axeblades of red fire chopped at the globe and glanced off with ripping sounds. One sheared a girder and the other sparkled through a swath of the fine cords crisscrossing the interior. A second blue needle stabbed and missed.

The demon and the Visitor's globe rose in alternating pulses, leapfrogging one another and blasting wizardlight as they went. Neither of the opponents seemed to exist in the spaces between their successive stages.

Cashel followed the battle until even the searing flares of azure and crimson twinkled like the stars seen through horsetail clouds. He lowered his head, sighed, and gave a tentative pull at the quarterstaff. He'd hoped he'd find that the invisible substance binding him had softened since last he tried moving. It hadn't.

"I wish Kakoral had cut me loose before he left," Cashel said, as much to himself as to Evne. He smiled. "I guess he had other things on his mind, though."

"So do you, master," the toad said, pointing with her right leg. "I rather thought we'd be seeing that one again."

Cashel turned his head. Ansache was walking toward him, down a line of light that seemed to have no more substance than the sun's reflection in a pond. The wizard held his violet athame vertically in front of him like a ceremonial mace.

Cashel strained again. It didn't help any more than he'd thought it would. "Ah, Evne?" he said. "Can you stop the fellow? Because I can't, not tied up like this, and I don't think he has anything good in mind."

"While the Great Lord of All Worlds deals with your pet, vermin . . ." Ansache said, pointing the tip of his athame at Cashel. "I will rid his domain of you!"

"Oh, I don't think either of us need to exert ourselves, master," the toad said, rubbing her pale belly with a forepaw. "Let Lady Kotia do it, why don't we? She's had time to rest."

"Brido ithi lothion!" Ansache called, looking along his athame like a soldier sighting a catapult.

"Phrene noumothili!" said Kotia from behind Cashel. A web of red wizardlight wrapped Ansache. It looked like the dazzle of a faceted jewel in full sunlight, but there was a roaring crackle as well. Ansache screamed.

Cashel turned his head. Kotia was walking toward them from the place where she'd been confined. In front of her, spinning in midair, was a golden disk—one of the objects Cashel had seen suspended from threads of light.

"Oba lari krithi!" Kotia said. The golden disk slowed perceptibly; from it shot scarlet sparks that danced down over Ansache and tightened the bonds already in place. Ansache screamed again, but on a diminishing note. His shroud of red light collapsed to a point.

Ansache's athame clattered to the floor, blackened and smoking. Kotia frowned at it. *"Rali thonou bo!"* she said. The shimmering metal vanished in a thunderous crash, leaving motes of soot dancing in the air where it had been.

The disk settled with a hum that grew deeper as the spinning slowed. When it finally stopped with a liquid chime against the floor, the hum stopped also.

Kotia rubbed her forehead with both hands. Cashel waited till she'd lowered them and her eyes had cleared of the fatigue of the wizardry she'd completed.

"I'm glad to see you again, mistress," he said. "Would you get me loose from how I'm held here? If you can, I mean."

"What?" said Kotia, frowning. She looked at him closely, then gave a warm smile. "Yes, of course."

She bent to raise the golden disk, then waved a dismissive

hand at it. "Faugh, there's no need," she said. She touched the quarterstaff, apparently hanging in the air, with her index finger.

"*Boea boa nerpha,*" she said in a firm, quiet voice.

The staff dropped into Cashel's waiting hand. His legs and lower body were free, and he felt like he'd just set down a heavy weight. It'd bothered him to be trapped that way; bothered him more than he'd realized till it was over.

"I see being a guest of the Visitor has brought you more in touch with your father, girl," Evne said as she walked down Cashel's left arm and perched on the back of his hand where it held his staff. Her tiny claws prickled but her feet had a clammy stickiness that he found oddly pleasant.

"And who are you?" Kotia said, her eyes hardening as they focused on the little toad.

"She's my friend Evne," Cashel said, surprised at the hostility in Kotia's tone. "I wouldn't have gotten here without her, mistress. I wouldn't have come close."

"And I suppose you think she's a toad?" Kotia said to Cashel, raising an eyebrow.

"I *am* a toad, girl," Evne said in a tone every bit as cold as Kotia's. "Unless you insist on having things a different way."

Kotia laughed with a mocking undertone. "No, of course not," she said. "I don't suppose it matters."

"Not for me, it doesn't," the toad agreed. "Nor for you either, I would judge."

Cashel had heard every word of the exchange. The girl and the toad might've been chanting gibberish for all the sense he made out of it. He'd been around people—and especially around women—enough to know not to ask them to explain what was going on, though.

Kotia looked in the direction of the ceiling. The flickers of wizardlight were too distant for Cashel's excellent eyes to make out, though he still felt the tremble of the accompanying roar through his soles.

"There's no way to get out before it's over, I suppose?" Kotia said to Evne.

"No," the toad said. "But it shouldn't be long now."

Cashel saw the light again as she spoke: glittering, then glaring; blue and red intertwined in a savage purple rhythm, spinning around the edges of the vast room. The battle was descending as swiftly as the opponents had risen out of sight.

Not long.

"Mistress Evne," he said. "Get back on my shoulder, if you please. Or get down so that I won't hurt you if I move."

"You're going to fight the Visitor if he defeats a demon, master?" the toad asked in a mocking tone.

"Yes, ma'am," said Cashel. "I am."

"Of course," said Kotia in a quiet voice. Evne hopped to Cashel's neckline in a single motion, the most graceful thing Cashel had known her to do.

The thunder of the downrushing combat filled the air. Not long at all . . .

Chapter Nineteen

Sharina awakened. The stars were dim points in a sky pulsing crimson and azure with light as cruelly cold as icebergs. She didn't know what had aroused her. The night was silent, save for the sighing wind.

"The great wizard has gone off again, mistress," said the axe her cheek rested on. "I wouldn't care what happened to him, of course; but if we're abandoned here, there'll be only your companions for Beard to dine on."

"Gone?" said Sharina, jerking upright and throwing off the bearskin wrapping her. "He took the ship?"

She leaped to her feet, then felt a surge of relief. She could see the Queen Ship's mast through the branches of a birch tree, on the other side of the little island. She and the rest of the band had moved to the western edge to sleep out of the constant wind.

"Not the ship," Beard said disdainfully. "He's using the Key of Reyazel again."

"But there's no—" Sharina said.

"Is there not the sea chest, mistress?" the axe snapped. "Do you think it matters what the keyhole opens in this world? It does not! Only that there be a keyhole."

All those in the camp were asleep in their furs. At Sharina's side Scoggin and Franca shared the mantle of a huge bison; they hadn't awakened during her conversation with Beard. She thought of shaking Scoggin alert, but there was no point in that: the only threat was that Alfdan would get himself killed, and with Beard she was as well able to prevent that as all the rest of the band combined.

Sharina strode to the crest of the island, directly into the wind's cold buffeting. The birches rustled like malicious whisperers as she passed. She wondered if she'd have thought that in another place, or on a night that wasn't lighted by ripples of wizardlight. Perhaps one day she'd be at another place again and thereby able to answer the question. . . .

The lid of the sea chest had been flung back. The key winked in the gutted lock, gleaming red or blue as the light washed across the heavens. The chest's interior was a shimmer of alien moonlight, a leprous white contrast to the present sky roiling with wizardry. The chest had become a passage.

Sharina hesitated. The world she stood in was an evil twin to the one where she'd been born, but her memory of the treasure-strewn beach was so powerfully unpleasant that even these surroundings were preferable.

"You're right about the danger," Beard said morosely. Then in a more cheerful tone he added, "Of course, if something happened to you there, somebody might come to the beach later and take me out with them. I'm a greater prize than any foolish poison antidote!"

"I'm glad you're comfortable on that score," Sharina said with a wry smile. "It's good to have a companion who looks on the bright side."

The chest was sunk almost to its lid in the gravel; she stepped over the slight lip and stood at the edge of the curving bay, under the light of a moon like none she had ever seen. It was huge, and instead of the familiar craters and seas the looming face was banded like the wall of a sandstone canyon. This wasn't the world she knew, even in the distant past or future.

Alfdan walked slowly along the edge of the water, poking his wand into the sand in front of him like a woodcock probing for worms. A swell moved toward the shore, breaking into froth and fury as it reached the shallows.

"Alfdan!" Sharina called. The wizard turned and looked, then resumed his course.

"May the Lady help me!" Sharina muttered, furious and frightened both. She jogged toward Alfdan as the wave combed up the sand, spurting high as it struck the wizard's legs.

Sharina splashed through the shallows, listening to the sea growl. Alfdan jerked his head toward her, raising his wand. "Get away from me!" he snarled. "It's here and I'm going to find it!"

"Oh mistress, if Beard only could . . ." the axe whimpered miserably. "When we leave the island, then can Beard kill him? Please, mistress, please let Beard kill him?"

"Silence!" Sharina said, speaking to the wizard or the axe or perhaps to her own angry desire to split Alfdan from pate to navel. She caught the whalebone wand with her left hand, then jabbed the butt of the axe into the wizard's belly. He gave a despairing cry and fell to his knees. The last of the surf foamed seaward past him.

"Get up!" Sharina said. Alfdan dropped his wand when she punched him, but she held it. Her first thought was to throw the dense bone into the sea, but the wizard needed the tool for his art . . . and all the rest of them needed the wizard if they were to get off this barren islet, let alone reach Her dwelling.

Alfdan ignored her, bending over. Sharina thought he was going to vomit; instead he began to scrabble in the hard sand. She stuck the wand upright in the ground and grabbed the back of his collar.

"Here!" the wizard cried, rising to his feet without her having to pull him. "I knew it was here!"

He held a strip of vellum, curling but apparently undamaged despite the sand that clung to it. There was a drawing on one side, a map as best Sharina could tell by moonlight.

"It's part of Master Amoes's record of his travels through the world he found under the surface of the moon!" Alfdan said triumphantly.

Sharina blinked. "But you're not going there, are you?" she said.

"Of course not!" Alfdan snapped, rolling the parchment without bothering to brush off the last of the sand. "The moon's been dead for all the ages since Amoes's day."

Beard tittered mockingly. "It'd be an act of mercy for Beard to drink his blood, mistress," he said. "But he'll take us to better pastures, so we will let him live."

Sharina shivered. "Come!" she said, tugging Alfdan's sleeve. He came without protest, pulling up his wand when he passed by.

Sharina stepped on something hard and square. She didn't look down; her face was as rigid as an executioner's. Whatever the thing was, it belonged to this place; and humans *didn't* belong here.

The door to the world they'd left was a rectangle of gravel and flotsam, the beach where the sea chest lay. She motioned Alfdan through ahead of her: she'd come to bring him back and there wasn't room for both of them to leave together. When she stepped onto the opening, the bay vanished and she was standing on the rocky island. The wizard reached for the key.

Sharina batted his hand away and took the key herself. Alfdan yelped in surprise.

Sharina was trembling with relief beyond anything she could put in words. "I'll hold this till we're done with you," she said, putting the small golden key into a fold of her sash. She didn't have a proper purse in this place, in this world.

Alfdan grabbed for it. She held Beard in front of her, the edge outward in a glittering warning more effective than a spoken threat. "It's mine!" Alfdan said, recoiling.

"Yes," said Sharina. "And when you've delivered me to Her palace, I'll give it back to you. I won't care what happens to you then."

She started back to the sheltered side of the island. "But I warn you, wizard," she added over her shoulder. "As bad as the place you're taking me may be, you'll be going to a worse one if you use the Key of Reyazel again!"

"Master?" said Evne, back on Cashel's shoulder where she seemed to prefer to ride. "There's a cauldron near the wall to the right, a hundred feet up. Do you think you could turn it upside down if it were on the floor?"

Cashel looked upward. Kotia extended her index finger and muttered words Cashel didn't catch. A red spark from her finger snapped to a great bronze curve.

"Oh," said Cashel. He'd been looking in the right place, but he hadn't realized anything so big could be a cauldron. He'd been thinking of something like the inn's washing tub, the largest vessel in Barca's Hamlet. That wouldn't have been a shadow of the huge thing hanging from cobweb strands of light.

"Yeah, I guess so," Cashel said. It depended on how thick the metal was, but even if it turned out to be a lot thicker than he expected . . . "I guess I can, sure."

Evne extended her left hind leg; a delicate pink membrane webbed the base of the three toes. Azure lightning crackled at the tip of the middle claw, just that; no more than the sound a man makes popping his fingers. The cauldron was on the floor instead of high in the air. It hadn't moved, it just *was*.

"I don't think we should wait," said Evne, looking up at the descending thunder.

"Right," said Cashel. He didn't like to run or often do it, but now he broke into a lumbering trot. The cauldron was deceptively far away. The size of the room was really amazing.

The demon and the globe were in sight again, swirling in tight circles around a common center as they ripped at one another with weapons of light. Blasts that missed their targets tore across the room, as little affected by objects hanging in the way as arrows are of dust motes.

Red wizardlight slashed a knot of crystal curves. Half the structure vanished in glare and molten gobbets; the rest—itself the size of any building in Barca's Hamlet—crashed to the floor not far from Cashel and his companions.

He ducked instinctively. The jagged chunk that would otherwise have brained him sailed overhead.

Kotia stayed at his side without running; she'd picked up the golden disk on her way by. Her long legs scissored as quickly as Ilna's fingers moved when she was weaving, but her face retained a look of faint amusement.

Especially, Kotia never looked at Evne. The toad for her own part was singing what sounded like, *"Send a flea to heave a tree."*

Cashel thought they were both being silly, but it sure beat screaming and carrying on about what was happening the way a lot of people would've done. He hadn't been around toads enough—socially, that is—to know how they usually behaved.

Not all the blows the pair battling downward struck at each other missed. A spear of blue light stabbed Kakoral square in the chest. For an instant the demon gleamed translucent purple; then he was crimson again, carving at the Visitor with blades of hellfire from both clawed hands. The vast room pulsed with the echoing combat.

Cashel reached the cauldron. He could just touch the rim if he stood on his toes, but his weight wouldn't be enough to make it move. It sat on its broad bottom, not on legs.

"I guess then . . ." Cashel said as he considered the problem. He thrust the quarterstaff out to Kotia without bothering to face her. "Hold this for me."

He squatted, placing his hands under the base where the curved sides met the flat bottom. He was counting on the cauldron to be heavy enough that he wouldn't have to chock the opposite side to keep it from skidding along the floor, but that seemed a safe enough bet. . . .

Something exploded not far overhead. A rain of greenish pebbles cascaded down, rattling on the bronze and making Cashel's skin prickle wherever they touched.

"Now!" he shouted, straightening with the strength of his legs and shoulders both. The cauldron lifted smoothly. Cashel walked forward, placing his hands farther down the bottom as the inertia of the bronze helped to rotate it.

"Yes!" cried Kotia. The cauldron teetered past its far edge and began to fall onto its rim.

The globe rapped out blue spears as quick as a woodpecker taps, striking Kakoral in repeated thunderclaps. Cashel looked up. The demon swelled and thinned into a figure of fiery cloud; the girders of light and dangling objects were clearly visible through his body. The Visitor's globe shrank and shimmered into a ball no bigger than a melon.

The cauldron hit with a bell note so clear and loud that Cashel could hear it through the cataclysm tearing the air apart just overhead. Kotia's lips were moving, but no sound a human throat could make would be audible now.

"Under the cauldron!" Evne said. She didn't shout; instead her words clicked out in pauses of the blasting chaos.

The cauldron's near edge rocked waist high on the inertia that'd carried it over. Kotia ducked under; Cashel followed a half step behind. The bronze lip hung for what seemed a long time, then rang down again. It clanged back and forth repeatedly till finally coming to rest with only a tingling hum to remind Cashel of its presence.

With the cauldron's rim flat on the smooth floor, there was no light at all inside. The roaring battle was a vibrating presence but no longer noise in the usual sense. There was plenty of room inside, so Cashel didn't expect the air to get stuffy till long after something good or bad had happened to change things.

"Shall I provide a view?" Evne said in an arch tone.

"Don't strain yourself!" said Kotia. Her golden disk suddenly appeared in midair. Its light didn't touch anything else, though: the hollow bronze was just as dark as it'd been before.

"*Mecha melchou ael,*" Kotia said. The disk began to spin, accelerating rapidly. "*Balamin aoubes—*"

The disk was a shiver of light, a golden reflection instead of a solid object. It made a high-pitched sound—or at least something did, raising the hairs on the back of Cashel's neck.

"*Aobar!*" said Kotia. Beyond where the disk spun, the bronze became transparent. The crackling flames of the battle lit the interior. Kotia had a pinched look, though she seemed not so much weak as worn to Cashel.

The Visitor stabbed a jagged trident of blue fire, missing Kakoral because the demon was suddenly above the globe.

The blast splashed the cauldron, igniting the bronze with quivering brilliance. The flash made Cashel blink, but he didn't feel anything unusual.

"The uses this vessel's been put to over the ages," Evne said, "have . . . hardened it, let's say. I won't say that it's indestructible, but I don't think anything we'll see today could harm it."

"Did the Visitor make it?" Cashel asked, frowning. He'd gotten out his wad of wool to polish his staff. Touching the hickory always steadied him.

"The Visitor makes nothing!" Evne said. She was angry; Cashel had never heard her angry before. "The Visitor takes and destroys, only that."

"Until now, I think," said Kotia, looking upward with a faint smile. "Until he met my father."

The toad laughed appreciatively.

It didn't look that way to Cashel. No longer did the Visitor jump nervously about the room: his globe was a diamond-bright glitter, hovering and unmoved. By contrast Kakoral had spread into a crimson fog, too thin to have shape. The Visitor's bolts lanced through the demon's substance unhindered, ripping whatever other objects they touched. Many girders had been severed, and the whole structure was beginning to shift around its axis.

"Yes," said Evne. "He has him now."

The red mist sucked down. *Being swallowed,* Cashel thought, but instead Kakoral coalesced again out of the vapor. For an instant he stood as a giant in whose belly the globe sparkled with evil fury; then the demon shrank again to the size of a man and the solidity of a blazing crimson anvil.

Cashel heard a muffled pop. Kakoral shook with titanic laughter. He raised his head and opened his mouth wide. Flames shot out, momentarily purple but shifting quickly to the same rose red that Cashel saw winking across the valley when the demon first appeared to him.

The jet of fire spread into a channel of Hell-light as broad as a mill flume. The objects suspended throughout the enormous space tumbled downward, untouched themselves but released when the threads supporting them flared away. The walls of the ship began to burn.

Kakoral closed his mouth. He turned and bowed to the overturned cauldron, his arms spread back like a courtier's. Above the demon—unthinkably far above him and racing higher—scarlet flames continued to blaze in the portion of the Visitor's ship that they hadn't yet devoured.

Kakoral straightened; and, straightening, vanished.

"Oh!" said Cashel. He cleared his throat, then ran a hand along the rim of the cauldron. It wouldn't be hard to get enough purchase to lift it again.

"Ah?" he said. Evne and Kotia were still looking upward. "Would you like me to lift—"

"Not unless you want us all to die," said the toad.

"You'd better cover your eyes," said Kotia. She closed hers and folded the crook of her elbow over them. Cashel did the same.

The world beyond the walls of the cauldron went crimson. The light was as cold as the depths of the sea, streaming through Cashel's flesh and soul together.

Thought stopped, everything stopped. Cashel didn't know how long the light lasted; the flooding glare had the feel of eternity. He was squeezing the quarterstaff; if nothing else existed, that did, and Cashel or-Kenset did while he held it.

Kotia touched his wrist. "It's over," she said. Her voice came from far away. "The power that drained into this basin over the ages has been voided back to where the Visitor came from."

Cashel opened his eyes. He, Kotia, and the toad on his shoulder were in the middle of what'd been a bog like what he'd seen on his way to the Visitor. The rushes were sere now, and tussocks stood up from cracked mud rather than marsh.

"The process involved heat," said Evne. She gave a grim chuckle. "Not nearly as much heat as on the other end of the channel, though. I don't think there will be more Visitors to trouble us."

Kotia turned to Cashel. He couldn't read her expression. "Now, if you would please lift the cauldron again, milord?" she said. "We'll have callers shortly."

She saw his expression and quirked a smile. "No, not that kind," she said. "The display will summon folk from all the manors to see what has happened. Airboats can safely fly into the basin now."

Cashel handed the girl his quarterstaff again, politely this time because he wasn't in a hurry to get them all under cover. He squatted and positioned his hands under the curve of the rim.

"I wonder if Lord Bossian will be among those arriving?" the toad said.

"Yes," said Kotia. "I've been wondering that too."

They both laughed. It was the sort of sound that made Cashel glad the two of them weren't his enemies.

"Nobody's entered the Count's wing since Lady Liane sent the warning, your highness," Attaper said as he and a company of Blood Eagles met Garric at the west entrance to the palace. "A few servants came out on normal business, but we're holding them as ordered."

"As ordered?" said Garric, frowning in surprise. "Lady Liane?"

"Yes, her messenger arrived with your orders that nobody should enter or leave Count Lascarg's quarters," Attaper said, frowning in turn. "By the Shepherd, your highness! Were the seal and signature forgeries?"

"No, milord!" Liane herself said as she hopped from her sedan chair. Her bearers must've run all the way from the temple: they were covered in sweat but grinning. The coins Liane spun them winked gold. "Say rather that Prince Garric was too busy to be aware of all the details he was taking care of in the crisis."

Garric grinned. That was a charitable way of putting it. In truth it hadn't crossed his mind to send someone ahead to put a discreet guard on Monine and Tanus. Well, he didn't have to think about that sort of thing. He had Liane, praise be the Shepherd!

Garric took the steps two treads at a time. Guards trotted ahead of him. Lord Mayne, the legate commanding the regiment that'd just arrived from the camp on the harbor, had linked arms with Lord Waldron to exchange information as they both pounded along immediately behind. A pair of palace ushers holding silver-banded wands high led the procession down the branching corridors. The household staff was no longer the proper concern of Master Reise, the Vicar's advisor . . . but as he ran past, Garric saw his father watching alertly from an alcove, pressed between the wall and a statue where he wouldn't interfere with the Prince's haste.

The double doors to the wing of the palace that Count Lascarg still occupied were closed. In the vaulted hall outside waited a squad of Blood Eagles instead of a doorkeeper from the count's household.

"Get us in!" Garric ordered as the guards straightened to attention. He hoped the raid would take Monine and Tanus by surprise, but there was no time to waste.

The noncom of the guard detail pushed at the panels where they joined, seeing whether they were barred from the inside. They didn't give.

Four men of Garric's escort were already carrying an ancient statue from a niche down the hall. It'd been a caryatid, a woman's torso with a fish-scaled base, which might once have supported the roof of a loggia in an Old Kingdom water garden. As the noncom stepped clear, the men carrying the statue jogged forward and with a collective grunt smashed its flat head into the door.

The panels sprang open; the heavy oaken bar ripped out of its staples and crashed to the floor. The right-hand panel banged into the servant dozing on a stool at the side. He fell off with a cry of pain.

"This way!" cried one of Liane's spies, charging through the anteroom and down the corridor to the right. He wasn't the man who'd led the way into the Temple of the Shepherd. Soldiers, Garric, and Lord Waldron—who'd kept up just as he'd said he would—clashed after the spy in their cleated boots. A group of female servants—three or four of them—gossiping in a side hall squealed and ran the other way.

Lascarg's rooms looked dingy and had a smell of neglect. Garric wondered if that was a change or if the rest of the building had also been dirty and rundown before his own staff took over. He'd been too busy to care, but thinking back he remembered squads of servants working in the hallways with stiff brushes and buckets that breathed the biting tang of lye.

It wasn't just dirt creating the oppressive atmosphere, though. One side of this corridor gave onto a courtyard, but shuttered blinds closed the portico despite the pleasant weather. Only through cracks between warped panels did Garric see sunlight or foliage.

A servant in tawdry finery—his tunics stained but hemmed with cloth of gold—heard the crashing footsteps and peered from a doorway. He stared for an instant at what was coming toward him, bleated, and ran down the hall in the other direction. He carried a writing case until it brushed the wainscoting and flew free, scattering documents, quills, and rushlights unnoticed on the floor.

Garric didn't blame the fellow. He supposed Lord Mayne's entire regiment was following down the hallway. Maybe the whole army was; Duzi knew how Lord Waldron's orders might have been garbled!

The spy reached the door the servant had run from and jumped inside. Garric followed, slamming a hand against the doorjamb so that he didn't skid on the worn stone flooring. He wasn't wearing hobnails like the regular soldiers, but his boots had hard soles.

Count Lascarg sat at a table with a top of colored marble on massive wooden legs. Before him was a mixing bowl, a water pitcher, and an ornate gold cup whose stem was in the form of a couple making love. The pitcher was full: Lascarg had been drinking his wine undiluted, and drinking it in considerable quantity from the look of him.

A servant—a girl of no more than twelve years—stood beside him with a wine dipper. She stared at the doorway, her eyes so open they seemed to fill her white face. The dipper shook violently in her hand.

"You've come to kill me!" Lascarg said, lurching to his feet. His tunic hadn't been changed in days, perhaps longer. He fumbled at his side where the hilt of a sword would've been if he were wearing one. He wasn't.

"Where's your children?" Garric said. "Where's Monine and Tanus?"

"Go on then, just do it!" Lascarg said. He swayed and fell

forward, knocking over the bowl and pitcher. Clinging to the table, he began to cry.

The girl pointed her dipper toward the small arched door in an alcove. Garric thought it was to a service staircase. The nearest soldier took two strides and kicked it down, staggering backward at the impact. Garric lunged through the opening.

He hadn't been conscious of drawing his sword, but it was out in his hand. The image of Carus watched through Garric's eyes, grinning and poised.

Garric grinned back. With a friend like that sharing his mind, he never need worry about being unprepared for battle.

He'd burst into an overgrown garden: the garden of his dreams, his nightmares. To the right was a pavilion that ivy was taking over; that was the building the ape men had shambled from. Seen by daylight, the altar was an ancient stone bench supported by stone barrels from a fallen pillar.

Moisin, the priest who'd brought the urn to Garric, lay naked across the altar. His back was to the stone. His wrists and ankles were tied to the barrels so that his chest arched.

Behind the altar, two chanting teenagers poised silvery knives over the priest. Their dark hair was cut to shoulder length, and their faces were identically androgynous.

The tabard of the twin on the left showed a hint of breasts, so that was probably Monine. Tanus wore a similar garment, embroidered in colored swirls. Garric could see the twins' faces clearly, but something about the tabards blurred his vision when he tried to place the figures in context with their surroundings.

"Samanax asma samou!" Monine and Tanus shouted together. They drove their knives down, Monine slashing Moisin's throat while her brother ripped his blade through the cartilage joining the victim's ribs to his breastbone. Blood gushed in fountains that seemed too huge to come from a single human being.

"Keep back, your highness!" somebody behind shouted as Garric ducked under a tree branch on his way toward the altar. The pears were done blooming, but the fruit hadn't set yet.

Moisin jerked against his bonds and fell back, his eyes staring and his mouth slackly open. A lens with an icy purple rim formed where previously there'd been only the brick wall at the back of the garden. The opening was big enough to drive a wagon through. Within it, muted walls of the same color as the rim shimmered.

The twins turned toward the lens. Garric slashed at their backs: honor had no more place in this business than it did in dealing with ticks and leeches. The tip of his patterned steel blade zinged against the bricks well to the side of where he'd been sure Monine was standing. *Those tabards . . .*

The twins stepped through the lens. They remained faintly visible as they ran down the tunnel of light beyond.

"Get them, lad!" shouted King Carus, but Garric didn't need anybody prodding him to follow. He leaped to the top of the altar, the ball of his foot on the stone but his boot touching the priest's flaccid corpse.

"Your highness!" a soldier behind him cried. "Don't—"

Garric leaped into the lens. He felt a shock as though he'd dived through a hole in a frozen river. Monine and Tanus were ahead of him, their figures shrinking more than a few seconds of distance should have caused.

From behind in the waking world Garric heard, "Follow your prince!" He didn't know how much use a regiment—or the whole army—would be in whatever business there was on this side of the gateway, but Prince Garric had lost the right to object to other people's decisions when he jumped into the portal alone.

He raised his sword high and shouted, "Carus and the Isles!" He wasn't sure if his men could hear his words, but they made him feel better and that was worth something.

"Garric and the Isles!" cried other distance-muted voices. *"Forward!"*

For an instant Ilna felt herself suspended in the crackling blue limbo. Then the *Bird of the Tide* slapped water thunderously, sloshing from side to side. The hatch cover that they'd deliberately left askew jounced half off its frame.

Nabarbi snarled, "Sister take it!" and reached up to grab the cover.

"Leave it!" Chalcus said. He continued more mildly, "The

Defender's not so tall a ship that we need worry that they'll be peering down on us as they approach. Hutena, you and Ninon ready the jug if you will. Or perhaps I—"

"No, we'll do it!" the bosun said, though he didn't look happy. Well, there was little enough to be happy about in the present situation; save that it was the one that Ilna and her companions had worked very hard to bring about.

Hutena and the seaman together swung back the lid of the ironbound chest. The odor of camphor flooded the hold. Ilna turned to Chalcus and said in a conversational voice, "You brought reef snakes from Sidras's store."

"We brought *all* the reef snakes from Sidras's store, dear heart," Chalcus said with a grin fit for a crocodile. "Seventeen of them; and I have great hopes for the result when they go to join the Commander's crew."

When the *Bird* wallowed to starboard, Ilna could see the patrol vessel thrashing toward them with both layers of oarsmen rowing. She supposed the *Defender*'d reached this stretch of sea not long after Gaur's wizardry had sent the *Bird* into his fire-shot Hell. Lusius would've lain to until his prey returned to the waking world so he and his gang could loot it.

Ilna smiled as she ran her noose between her fingers. The night was too dark for her to be confident that her patterns would be effective, but a silken cord tight around an enemy's neck was *always* effective.

Muttering instructions to one another, Hutena and Ninon gripped the rim of the stoppered ceramic jug nestled in a bed of sand and camphor within the strongbox. The jug had a line of holes at the neck—so that the serpents within could breathe, Ilna realized, but a man with small hands like the late Master Pointin might have stuck his fingers through them when he tried to empty the chest so he could hide. The camphor fumes had kept the snakes relatively sluggish during the voyage, but the jouncing and heat of their translation to the Hellworld must've aroused them enough to respond when the supercargo offered them his fingers.

The sailors lifted the jug out of the box. They kept as clear of the openings as they would've done so many live coals.

The *Bird of the Tide* had steadied after it splashed back into the waking world. Now the vessel began to roll again on the bow wave of the approaching *Defender.* "Back water!" shouted a hoarse voice with an Ornifal accent.

The *Bird* rocked more violently; a pair of grappling irons thumped onto her deck. "Snub them up!" ordered Lusius's voice. "Casadein, get that pitch ready. After we've seen what they were carrying in their hold, we'll burn her to her waterline!"

Chalcus rotated his head to meet the eyes of everyone in the hold with him. He grinned and said, "Now!" emphatically but without shouting.

Tellura and Kulit threw the hatch cover back the rest of the way. Chalcus, Shausga, and Nabarbi leaped up onto the deck; Chalcus had his sword and dagger both ready, while the ordinary seamen leaned back into the hold and grasped the rim of the jug Hutena and Ninon were raising to them.

A Sea Guard with a sword in one hand and a lantern in the other had just jumped from the *Defender*'s deck to the *Bird*'s. He screamed with angry frustration at the men coming out of the hold. Chalcus thrust through his eye socket and into his brain.

The Sea Guard sprang backward convulsively, toppling over the gunwale as the ships recoiled from their first contact. As he fell, Shausga and Nabarbi hurled the jug onto the patrol vessel with all their strength. It shattered among the oarsmen rising from their benches.

Ilna followed the men, holding her noose slack in both hands. Many of the *Defender*'s crew held lanterns as they prepared to board. In the bow stood a pair of Guards with a large wooden bucket and a flaring torch: the pitch Lusius had mentioned, ready to destroy the *Bird of the Tide* as soon as his men had looted her.

A pair of Sea Guards wobbled on the patrol vessel's railing, swords in their hands. Nabarbi snatched the boat pike from its socket on the mast. As the nearer of the Guards jumped, Nabarbi thrust him through the chest, shoving him back into his comrade.

Both Guards fell into the sea. Our Brother rose in a fountain of spray to meet them. The big seawolf's jaws clopped shut, tossing an arm that still clutched a sword back aboard the *Defender*.

At least a dozen Sea Guards screamed simultaneously, sounding like they were being disemboweled. The lower rank of oarsmen wouldn't normally have risen until their fellows in the upper rank had cleared the walkway. Now the deck lifted like the ground during an earthquake as men lunged upward to escape the death slithering down through the ventilators onto them.

Chalcus jumped aboard the *Defender,* his sword and dagger gleaming in the lanternlight. The men with the bucket and torch went down, as suddenly dead as if they'd been lightning struck. The torch fell to the deck; Chalcus kicked the bucket of pitch over beside it, then sprang backward onto the *Bird.* He moved with the formal grace of a peasant dancing with ram's horns bound to his feet at a borough fete. The pitch roared into flame, spreading as it burned.

Hutena hacked at a grappling iron with his axe. The leader was chain, but a clean blow using the *Bird*'s gunwale as a chopping block parted it in a shower of sparks. The vessels began to swing apart, though the grapnel farther astern still bound them.

"We're afire!" a Sea Guard screamed. "We're afire! Oh Lady help us!"

Ilna noted that she hadn't heard Rincip's voice. Perhaps Lusius hadn't bothered to pick up his former second-in-command in his haste to run down the *Bird of the Tide.* That might have been the best luck yet in Rincip's whole miserable life. . . .

A group of Sea Guards—more than a handful; in the confusion and scattered light, numbers were even more doubtful than usual—leaped from the patrol vessel to the *Bird.* Chalcus and his crew met them. Ilna stayed back, letting the fight weave into her consciousness. When the pattern required her action, she would act.

Shausga and Ninon were cutting at the remaining grappling iron. Their cutlasses didn't have the authority of the axe and they were getting in each other's way besides. At least one of the would-be boarders missed his footing and went straight into the sea boiling with the blood-maddened violence of Our Brother.

Nabarbi had dropped the pike and was wrestling with a Sea Guard. Ilna twitched her noose back to throw, but as she did so Nabarbi slammed his dirk to the hilt in the Guard's chest. He flung the dead man from him with one arm, clearing his weapon by tugging on it with the other. The great seawolf leaped so high to meet the victim that Ilna glimpsed his wedge-shaped head over the gunwale.

Chalcus was killing with single thrusts, using his dagger to block his opponents' strokes. His slim, curved blade didn't seem sturdy enough to stop the Sea Guards' stout swords, but Ilna saw Chalcus lock one of them in a shower of sparks. When the Guard fell back, his neck cut through to the spine, the sword flew out of his hand. The dagger had cut a deep notch in the heavier blade.

The *Bird* was free of boarders again, all but the man who sprawled half into the open hatch. Convulsions had thrown him there when Hutena crushed his skull with the axe. Ninon's two-handed blow had finally severed the grapnel's line, and the ships were drifting apart.

The *Defender*'s bow was fully ablaze. The roar of the flames was louder even than the screams of men still trapped on the lower deck with the reef snakes.

Lusius climbed out on the bitts holding the steering oar; he'd thrown away his helmet but his silver breastplate gleamed in the light of his burning vessel. He looked down at the sea, then up again at the *Bird* already ten feet distant. He was clinging to the end of the steering oar, leaning forward but unwilling to risk the leap.

"Jump, man!" Chalcus shouted. "I'll spare your life!"

He reached out with his free hand, but not even the outstretched boarding pike would've touched his fingers. "Sister take the fool," Chalcus said in a voice of calm disgust. He sheathed his sword and dagger with a skill that was far more remarkable than the way he drew them. "We've questions for him, though, so—"

As Chalcus stepped to the *Bird*'s gunwale, Ilna cast her noose with a side-arm motion. It dropped neatly over the Commander's head and outstretched arm.

"Jump, you fool!" she shouted in a voice that would've pierced bronze. When Lusius still hesitated, Ilna braced her right foot on the gunwale and jerked back with all her considerable strength. Lusius gave a despairing cry as he flew toward her.

More hands grasped the silken rope—Chalcus took it in front of her and at least two of the sailors grabbed the end trailing behind. The Commander splashed into the sea.

"Pull!" Chalcus bellowed, tugging upward with the whole strength of his back. His tunic ripped as the muscles bunched under it. Ilna sat down on the deck—the deck and Hutena's legs as the bosun fell down behind her.

Lusius grabbed the gunwale with both hands and started to lift himself over. His polished breastplate was flopping loose: he must have tried to take off the heavy armor when he realized he had to abandon the *Defender.*

Chalcus dropped the lasso and grabbed the Commander's right wrist. As he did so, Lusius gave a terrible scream and slid backward. Nabarbi stepped to the gunwale, holding the pike overhead in both hands. He stabbed straight down.

Lusius screamed again but Chalcus lifted him over the side and flopped him belly first on the *Bird*'s deck. The Commander's right leg had been severed raggedly above the knee; blood spurted from the big artery that had been pulled several inches free of the torn muscles.

The men were shouting. The dead Sea Guard from the first attack had worn a waist sash as well as carrying his sword and dagger on a leather belt. Ilna freed the sash with a quick pull, then looped it over Lusius's right thigh and tightened it for a tourniquet.

"I'll take it, mistress," Hutena said. He laid his axe helve across the simple hitch, then knotted the free ends of the sash over the wood to give him leverage. He twisted, squeezing off the blood that still dribbled from the open artery.

Ilna rose, swaying slightly. Lusius was a heavy man and for a moment she'd supported his weight by herself. She had the strength to do it, but that didn't mean her body didn't have to pay for her exertions.

She glanced over the side. The two vessels continued to drift apart. The *Defender* was burning from bow to stern.

She saw a man, his hair and clothing ablaze, try to climb over the railing. He fell backward instead.

The flames hammered reflections from the sea. Debris floated between the vessels, mostly bodies and body parts. Our Brother swam in tight circles, his tail lashing from side to side. The pike shaft slanted up from his neck, waving in counterpoint to the movements of the tail.

"And now, Commander Lusius," Chalcus said in a bantering tone, "we've some questions about your tame wizard and his lair. I hope you'll choose to answer them, because—"

Chalcus laughed. The sound was as ominous as the clop of the reptile's jaws when they took Lusius's leg off.

"—I believe your seawolf friend has already eaten as much as is good for him. I wouldn't want to give him indigestion by sending the rest of you to join your leg!"

Sharina'd been lying with her head over the bow of the Queen Ship, peering into the depths. The water was gray but clear, like the sky before the first color of dawn.

She could see to the bottom, miles below. On it crawled monsters, and through the water swam greater monsters. The teeth of the creature peering out of a deep trench must themselves have been as long as the ship; its ribbon-shaped body pulsed with azure and crimson wizardlight.

"Oh, they're real," Beard said, answering a question that hadn't gotten beyond the surface of Sharina's mind. "You're not seeing them with your ordinary eyes, of course. Although those eyes *would* show you the ice sheet ahead."

"Mistress?" said Scoggin. She jerked her head around. Scoggin and Franca wore worried looks, their eyes flicking from her to the horizon.

"What's . . . ?" Scoggin went on, gesturing with the hand he'd stretched out to touch Sharina's shoulder if she hadn't responded. "That we're coming to?"

The men of Alfdan's band, all those who weren't sleeping, stared toward the dark line ahead also. The wizard himself stood in a capsule of his art, speaking words of power through his tight lips.

"Beard says we're coming to the ice sheet," Sharina said,

turning again and sitting up so that she could look at what she'd just identified to the others. A jagged boundary separated the pale gray sea from the sky washed with wizardlight. It was the charcoal shadow of a vertical edge where the ice met open water.

To the north were humps and hillocks and glitter, white except where ice threw back the sky's reflections in a form harsher than the original. The sullen sea was almost as still as the frozen waste beyond, but bits of debris moved in slow circles at its margin.

"What'll we do now, Mistress Sharina?" Layson asked, speaking with the touch of belligerence that meant he was nervous.

"Do?" repeated Beard with a metallic sneer. "Why don't you do exactly what you're doing now, my man? Nothing! Squatting on your haunches, waiting for the Great Wizard to call a halt. This ship makes no more matter of sailing over ice than it does over water—or over the heads of fools like you, I suppose!"

Layson grimaced but he didn't look too put out by Beard's insult. The men seemed to regard the axe and Sharina herself as their best hope of survival. They might be right . . . which was either frightening or amusing, depending on the mood Sharina was in when the thought recurred to her.

She glanced at Alfdan in the stern. Neal stood nearby, but the wizard didn't need anyone to support him at the moment. He'd been gaining strength as the Queen Ship coursed northward.

Despite the power of Alfdan's art, he provided only temporary respite, not long-term hope, for the men gathered around him. To the wizard they were only tools to help him achieve his ends; and those ends were as ultimately trivial as those of a child picking up shells on the seashore.

The ship had seemed to sail just above the swells of the sluggish sea. Without appearing to rise the bow slid over the sheer edge of the icepack, though it was a yard or more higher than the water at the point the keel crossed. Men murmured to one another, looking out nervously.

"It's awful," Franca said quietly. "It's empty, it's just a desert."

"It's the same sea," Sharina said. "Freezing didn't make it real land."

"Or make it a desert," said Beard. The axe had been cheerful in his waspish fashion ever since they set out for Her residence. "There's life here too, you know. In the ice and beneath it."

"What?" said Sharina. She lay flat again, looking down as she had previously. For a moment all she saw was white and the evil shimmer of the sky, picked out occasionally by a tree trunk or some other flotsam that the ice had engulfed. Then, slowly, she began to see deeper.

"Franca!" Sharina said. "Scoggin? What do you see . . . ?"

She pointed with her left hand. She was holding Beard tight against her chest with the other; as if he were a kitten instead of an axe.

The two men leaned close, peering at the ice. Sharina looked from one to the other; both wore puzzled expressions.

"Mistress?" said Franca. "I see ice. Is that what you mean?"

Sharina swallowed. "No," she said, gazing into the depths again. "But it doesn't matter. I thought I saw animals below the ice, that's all."

She *knew* she saw animals below the ice. The ship passed over an ammonite, one of the Great Old Ones who'd been Gods before there were men to worship them. The coiled shell of this one was the size of Count Lascarg's palace. Rather than eight arms like an octopus or the ten of a squid, the ammonite waved more tentacles than Sharina could count in her brief glimpse. They interwove like a tangle of brambles, forming a pattern that was obviously evil even though it had no meaning for her.

"Beard?" Sharina whispered. She didn't want the others to hear her; she was afraid she was going mad. "What is it? Why am I seeing things when the others don't?"

"Did the others dive for the Key of Reyazel?" the axe asked ironically. "Why no, I don't suppose they did! And you weren't diving through water, mistress. You know that, don't you?"

"I guess," Sharina said, clutching the axe more tightly. "I guess I do."

"It changed you," Beard said. He giggled. "You should be thankful: you see the truth where others see only the surface."

Sharina stared at a school of fish, their bodies bright with bands of wizardlight. No one of them was as long as her arm, but there were hundreds in the school. They moved together like the scales of a snake, and their teeth were like daggers.

The Queen Ship was a world of its own, neither hot nor cold; the air was motionless though always breathable. Outside in the world through which the ship voyaged, however, winds swirled snow so hard it carved the ice into shapes from nightmare.

Alfdan muttered words of command. The vessel changed course slightly, taking it up a valley where the ice had lifted in long ridges to either side. The wizard seemed to be keeping his part of the bargain. It would've been nice if he'd been a person Sharina could like or even respect, but—she grinned—she'd learned long before leaving Barca's Hamlet that you couldn't expect that in life.

Her smile faded. She'd been looking at the gleaming surface but found her vision entering the crumpled ridges. Great worms gnawed tunnels through the ice; their jaws were like the toothed bronze rams of warships. Black armor covered their segmented bodies, but Sharina saw their long coils of intestine pulsing as the worms digested something. . . .

"Algae grows in the ice," Beard said in his mockingly superior tone. "Algae of a sort, that is. And the worms eat it."

"There's enough light here for algae?" Sharina said, frowning.

"Light?" said the axe. "Of course there's light! Look at the sky."

"Oh . . ." said Sharina, glancing up reflexively. The washes of evil color were so constant and vivid now that they hid the stars completely. For an instant she began to see shapes in the wizardlight, but she looked away quickly. What she saw in the water and ice was bad enough.

"I wouldn't have thought that sort of light would make things grow," she whispered.

"Make *those* things grow?" Beard said with a laugh. "Oh,

yes, mistress. There are many things that flourish in this light and this place. They just aren't things that have any use for men."

Sharina sat up. Franca and Scoggin were on either side, watching her with concern. They hadn't broken in on her dialogue with Beard, but they must have heard at least part of it.

"I'm seeing things beneath the surface," she said to them in a deliberate voice. "I hope this won't go on forever."

Beard laughed again. "Never fear, mistress," he said. "Not even I will go on forever."

Scoggin forced a smile. Neither man spoke.

The wizard muttered another command in a harsh, clipped tone like that of a squirrel complaining. The ship slanted to the right and mounted the ice ridge without slowing. In the distance ahead gleamed orange-red light, a harsh color but a natural one in contrast to the sheets of crimson covering the sky.

Layson pointed. "A volcano!" he said. "We saw volcanoes on the coast of Laut when Alfdan was getting that medallion."

"We're nearing the Ice Capes," said a man. His left cheek and forearm were tattooed in a complex spiral pattern, but Sharina didn't know his name. "Where they used to be, I guess. That must be Mount Yanek."

The Queen Ship raced over the ice field, now banded with stretches of black ice where leads had opened and refrozen. Once Sharina thought she saw eyes staring at her from the solid mass; the head of a monstrous thing, motionless but not dead. Perhaps it had been an illusion, shadows distorted by the rippling ice.

Beard laughed. She didn't ask him why.

The volcano grew from a lump and glow on the horizon into a mountain streaked with orange flame. Tentacles of lava touched the ice encircling its base. Great bubbles of steam rose and whirled southward on the wind.

The ship began to slow; the tone of its progress changed to a deep thrumming instead of a scream like that of chorus frogs in springtime. Sharina and the men glanced back at Alfdan. The wizard began to sway, so Neal quickly gripped him by the shoulders.

The Queen Ship touched the ice with a skirling vibration. Azure wizardlight crackled about them in an egg-shaped pattern, the broader end toward the bow. Mount Yanek covered the northern horizon, though its slopes were still a half-mile distant. The volcano's rough stone absorbed the rippling glare of the sky instead of reflecting it the way the ice did; Yanek stood as a black wedge detailed only by its own savage orange veins.

"Mistress?" Layson said, his voice rising between the syllables. "Why is it we're stopping here? There's no shelter!"

Nor was there. The ship coasted to a halt and overbalanced onto its right side. When the vessel lost way, the wind ripped across them. The flecks of snow that'd merely given the gusts visual presence to those inside the cocoon of Alfdan's wizardry now cut like a sandstorm.

Sharina tugged the bearskin close, but the wind lashed her legs and the rabbit-skin sandals were little protection against the ice underfoot. She and the others dropped to the ground and hunched in the lee of the Queen Ship. It was slight protection but there was nothing else in this landscape.

Neal lifted Alfdan from the ship. The wizard was mumbling. Neal, bending his ear close to Alfdan's lips, frowned in incomprehension. Alfdan waved or pointed to the east.

"What he's trying to say . . . ," Beard said in a loud, piercing tone, "is that if you dig into the dip there in front of you, you'll find that it's a hole filled with windblown snow that you can go through in time not to freeze. It leads to a tunnel in the ice that'll shelter you for the night."

The axe laughed. "Assuming that the beetle who dug the hole doesn't come back, of course," he added. "The grubs eat the algae, as you saw—but the adults need more nourishing fare to breed."

Sharina stamped across the frozen terrain. Even with her feet numbing, she could feel the change from solid ice to the crunch of grains barely cemented by contact and the pressure of the driving wind.

"Here, start digging!" she shouted. "Neal, get them digging!"

Scoggin and Franca had come with her. They bent and chopped at the ground with their spearpoints, sending ice up to sail away on the wind in flurries. The rest of the band joined immediately, except for Neal who—holding the wizard in one arm like a half-empty grain sack—took charge.

"Moster, Dalha, and Toldus!" he said, raising his voice against the wind. "Lay your capes on the ground. The rest of you, dump the spoil on the cloth. Dalha, you idiot, lay your cape on the downwind side!"

Sharina nodded approval. The band didn't have proper digging equipment, so without an expedient like the one Neal'd chosen they'd just shove the ice around in the hole rather than removing it. The men he'd told to take off their warm coverings had done so without argument. They trusted Neal to act in all their benefit.

And they trusted Sharina as well, because they were men with a desperate need to trust *some*body. They hadn't lost their faith in God, exactly, but it was all too clear that She was against them.

"Wah!" Burness shouted as he and another man slid out of sight. The rest of those in the pit either scrambled out or thrust whatever they were digging with into the side to hold them steady.

"Hey, we're in a tunnel!" Burness cried, his voice a deep echo of its normal self. Those outside the pit bent over the edge to listen, while the men clinging to the sloping walls cocked their heads. "Hey, there's a *house* down here!"

"If you all plan to stand here and end your miserable lives by freezing," said Beard loudly enough for the whole band to hear him distinctly, "then I won't try to change your minds. But otherwise, don't you think it'd be a good idea to get under cover now that you're able to?"

Sharina pointed to the hole with the butt of the axe. "Franca!" she said. "Go."

The youth's jaw dropped slackly, but he jumped into the hole without hesitating. She expected him to go feet-first, but instead he dived with his arms out before him as if he were entering the water.

As soon as Franca had disappeared, the rest of the band slid or scrambled to follow him. Shouts and complaints reverberated. Sharina, Scoggin, and Neal, holding the comatose wizard, were the only ones who remained in the wind.

"Go!" Neal said to her. "Scoggin, you follow and I'll hand Alfdan to you through the hole, all right?"

Sharina set her bearskin on the ice and slid to the bottom of the slope. She spread her feet to either side of the opening to catch herself, then dropped through holding Beard overhead. She didn't want to open somebody up when she hit the ground.

Actually, she landed on Layson, on all fours and trying to get up. He snarled a curse, then realized who it was. "Here, mistress!" he said and whisked her out of the way before Scoggin dropped where she'd been.

The roof of the tunnel was about six feet high. The floor was stone, an ancient lava flow; it was warm beneath the skin of water trickling over it. The frozen walls shone azure and crimson in concert with the sky; instead of filtering the wizardlight, the ice seemed to amplify the glow into evil brilliance.

At the inland end of the tunnel was a house, just as Burness had said. It was a low, dome built from the rib bones of whales; feathers of baleen chinked the interstices. It must have dated from well before She came: a shelter for whalers trying out their catch on shore and perhaps wintering over if they were caught when the seas skirting the Ice Capes froze early.

"The ground's warm!" one of the men said. He must only now have noticed it. "Why's that?"

"The volcano, Bayber," Layson snapped as he helped Scoggin bring Alfdan up the tunnel. They transported the wizard with his arms over their shoulders. His toes dragged. "There's a vein of lava under the rock here, I shouldn't wonder. What we saw up on top of the mountain had to come from somewhere, right?"

"You mean we're sitting *on* lava?" a short, shaggy man demanded. "Hey! What if it breaks out?"

"If you had nothing worse to worry about than the volcano," said Beard in a clear, cutting tone, "then you'd live longer than I expect to be the case."

The axe chortled metallically and added, "But oh, it will be a splendid time! The *lives* Beard and his mistress will drink, oh! Splendid!"

"Can't you shut him up?" Burness muttered, but it wasn't a serious complaint. Sharina recalled that he'd been with Alfdan the longest, which meant he'd seen more of the wizard's companions die than anybody else in the band. The others might pretend to themselves that Alfdan would save them, but Burness couldn't do that.

"Hush, Master Beard!" Sharina said in the crisp voice she'd have used to an affectionate drunk when she was serving drinks in her father's taproom. "You're discourteous."

The axe sniffed, but he subsided.

Several of the men had already entered the building. It was fairly large, twenty feet by ten the long and short ways. "Hey, there were people here," Offlan said. "The ashes in the hearth still have the shape of the wood!"

"That's not wood," said Beard. "There's no wood here. They were burning bones, and of those there's no lack."

Looking at the edges of the tunnel, Sharina saw that the bottom of the ice had been chiseled out for some distance along the former shoreline. The strand would've been covered by the debris the whalers had left. The bones' fatty marrow would make them excellent fuel once they'd been chopped from the ice.

"Where'd they go, then?" Neal said. He'd followed Scoggin and Layson, nervous about leaving Alfdan in their care but unwilling to insist that they let him carry the wizard instead. "There's nowhere but the other way in the tunnel, is there?"

"There's down a beetle's belly," said Beard. "Which is where they went, all three of them, and only last night. They'd lived here ten years, ever since she came and the ice locked in their boat; and now they're gone. Mostly."

"Oh," said Sharina, glancing at something glistening in the water, half-hidden where the ice had been dug out. It was a right foot, shoeless and filthy looking, severed raggedly at the ankle. "I see what you mean."

"The tunnel goes down to the water," called one of the pair of men who'd gone in the other direction without anybody telling them to. "There's a trotline out to sea on driftwood floats."

"All right," said Neal, forceful again once the wizard had

been laid on the stone floor wrapped in a sheepskin robe. "We'll stay here tonight. There's room in the hut for all of us, I think. In the morning . . . when Alfdan gets his strength back, anyway, we'll go on. I guess we're pretty close by now to where we're going."

Sharina looked at the building. Its sturdy door had been fashioned of ships' timbers, but it'd been smashed off its jamb; the splintered wood was still fresh. The sealskin latch cord still dangled from a hole near the top of the panel.

"The beetle dug down through the ice," Beard said, "but its body was too large for the tunnel. It extended its jaw—it's hinged, you see—and plucked them out of the house one and one and the third. And then it went away . . . for a time."

"I think . . ." said Sharina, looking around her. The stone was wet everywhere, but that was true within the hut as well as outside it; and the water wasn't cold, not really. "I think I'll sleep out here. The rest of you can have the hut, if you like."

"Don't you like the decor, mistress?" Beard asked mockingly. "I think it's quite attractive, in its way."

"I don't," said Sharina, squatting to pat the rock where a natural hollow looked like it might cradle her hip.

Sharina didn't fear death, but she'd never regarded it as her friend, either. The dismembered foot proved that the house of bones was no protection . . . and the structure was too clear a symbol of this world that She ruled for Sharina to want to sleep in its false shelter.

Chapter Twenty

Cashel sat on a dried tussock, polishing his quarterstaff and watching airboats from many different manors arrive. He wasn't sure he'd ever seen so many people in one place before, even when Garric was addressing the biggest crowds that could hear him in Valles. They just kept coming in, boat after boat from all directions.

Kotia'd taken charge of things. Every time a new group arrived, the lord of the manor came over and talked to her before doing anything else. Nobody at all came near where Cashel sat, but every time he looked around he saw eyes staring at him.

"That's Lady Raki," said Evne, perched as usual on Cashel's shoulder. She was rubbing herself down with one hind leg, then the other; grooming, Cashel guessed, though it wasn't a subject he wanted to get into with a toad. "She's mistress of Manor Rakon on the north side of the basin. It's suspended on threads over the Frozen Sea."

Initially Cashel'd been worried about whether Kotia was going to have trouble being surrounded by her world's most powerful people. He relaxed almost at once. Kotia didn't need his support to take care of those folk or anybody else.

"And my goodness, there's Lord Bossian," said Evne, pointing her long foot at a particularly ornate airboat approaching from the west. It looked like three hulls joined together and the whole thing covered by a canopy of rainbow-colored fabric. "I was wondering when he'd decide to show his face."

Cashel watched the big airboat slanting down at a majestic pace. "I wouldn't have guessed Bossian wanted to come around," he said. "I'd have thought he'd be embarrassed, to tell the truth."

Evne sniffed. "Embarrassed? *Him?*" she said. "Anyway, he's just as much afraid of you as he was of the Visitor. He's coming to see what he can do to keep you from destroying him."

Her long tongue licked out. She chuckled and added, "From squashing him like a bug!"

The airboat settled to the ground close enough that Cashel could've thrown a rock to it if he'd had any need to. It held more people than Cashel could count on his fingers. He recognized a few of them from dinner at Manor Bossian all that time ago, though he didn't recall their names if he'd even heard them. Except for Lord Bossian, of course.

"He doesn't need to be afraid of me," Cashel said.

"Doesn't he?" said Evne. "No, I don't suppose he does. But he needs to be very much afraid of your friend Kotia, master."

Lord Bossian got out of his airboat. He looked a good ten years older than he had when Cashel last saw him, worn and gray. He was wearing clean clothes, but he had a line of angry blisters on his left cheek: something hot had splashed him in the recent past.

Bossian looked at Kotia, then deliberately turned and started walking toward Cashel. A man and a woman followed, but the rest of those from the airboat hung back.

"Lord Bossian!" Kotia said. The nearly spherical Lady Raki and two lords of manor were standing near Kotia. They quickly shifted so they weren't between Kotia and Bossian.

Bossian glanced over his shoulder. The man and woman with him stopped where they were.

"Lady Kotia," Bossian said in a loud voice. "I'm going to offer my congratulations to Lord Cashel, the great wizard who has conquered the Visitor!"

He took another half step. Kotia stretched out her right hand and spoke under her breath. A ring of crackling fire, bright as Kakoral's heart, roared up around him.

Bossian screamed and stopped where he was. The vividly dressed crowd gave a collective gasp and fled outward. Some people threw themselves into airboats or behind them.

Cashel got up and walked toward Bossian, leaning his staff over his right shoulder so it wouldn't look like he was planning to do anything with it. He'd been really tired after all the business in the Visitor's ship, but he figured he was back in shape now. That was a good thing, seeing as Kotia was her full prickly self.

The ring of fire vanished in an eyeblink, just as it'd appeared. The ground it'd sprung from wasn't scorched.

"The girl formed an illusion rather than real flame," Evne said in a tone of appraisal. "As she could easily have done, of course. Her father and the Visitor between them have awakened what was already in her."

Maybe the fire hadn't been real, but even after it disappeared Bossian couldn't have been more afraid if he'd had a knife point pricking his eye. He stood trembling, unwilling even to turn his head to look squarely at Cashel.

Kotia was walking over from the other direction. "Indeed, Lord Cashel *is* master here, Bossian," she said, plenty loud enough for others to hear even after they'd scrambled back. "Therefore politeness dictates he not be disturbed unless he requests to be; and if politeness fails, his friends have other means!"

"It's all right, Kotia," Cashel said. "Bossian, you can relax. Nobody's going to hurt you."

He gave Kotia a friendly smile. He didn't care for people talking about him like he wasn't there, but Kotia had a right to be angry. Bossian hadn't owed anything to a stranger like Cashel, but he'd taken Kotia under his protection—until there was something to protect her against.

"He isn't worth anybody's concern, is he, milord?" Kotia said. She stepped to Cashel's right side, looking at Bossian with the kind of expression you'd give a scrawny ewe who wasn't worth pasturage even until fall. Cashel noticed that Kotia was being a lot more deferential to him than she'd been when it was just the two of them and Evne.

The toad padded softly around Cashel's neck and squatted on his right shoulder; he shifted the quarterstaff. Evne's feet tickled, but this probably wouldn't be a good time to laugh.

Bossian cleared his throat. The two people who'd started toward Cashel with him were now with the rest of the group behind the big airboat. "I came to congratulate you, milord," he said. "Ah, to thank you for driving away the Visitor."

"Drive the Visitor away?" Evne said in rising incredulity. "Is that what you think? You worm! Master Cashel *destroyed* the Visitor. As though he never was!"

"Well, it wasn't really me. . . ." Cashel muttered, but he didn't try to make himself heard. It was all pretty complicated, and he didn't guess he needed to explain things to Bossian. *Worm* was a good enough description for the man, though it occurred to him that when a toad used the word it might mean something a little different.

"I beg your pardon, Lord Cashel," Bossian said, licking

his lips and looking about as nervous as he had when Kotia looped the fire around him. He was staring at the air between Cashel's right shoulder and Kotia without meeting the eyes of either of them. "I didn't mean . . . that is . . ."

He cleared his throat and tried again, this time looking straight at Cashel. "The collection of objects of power here in the Basin is quite remarkable," he said. "I suppose they were gathered by the Visitor?"

"Of course they were gathered by the Visitor," Evne said in a mocking falsetto. "On some twenty worlds besides this one, I might add. Perhaps more—I haven't had a chance to do a proper inventory yet."

Bossian stared at her. For the first time he seemed to have taken in the fact that a toad was talking to him.

"Her name's Evne," Cashel said. "You gave her to me in the lump of coal."

He paused, then added, "Thank you. I wouldn't have gotten very far without her."

"With the objects I see here . . ." Bossian went on, looking to one side and then the other reflexively. "You'll be able to raise an impressive manor—"

"A unique manor," Kotia corrected. "A manor beyond any other in the world!"

Bossian grimaced. "Yes, I'm sure that's so," he said. "A unique manor. With these objects, your power is greater than that of all of us combined."

"I should've thought that became obvious when my master destroyed the Visitor," Evne said, rubbing the back of her head with her forefeet. "Even a worm should've realized that."

"I'm not going to build a manor," Cashel said. "Even if I knew how, I mean. I just want to go home."

He shook his head, trying to clear the nonsense out of it. He didn't see why he had to explain stuff like this. It was bad enough any time when people jumped to conclusions about him, and *these* conclusions didn't make a bit of sense. Why would he want to stay here?

"Look, when I first got here," Cashel continued before any of the others jumped in with another comment, "Kotia thought you could send me back home, Lord Bossian. Is that right? Can you?"

"*I* can, Lord Cashel," Kotia said. Her face was unreadable. "If that's what you really want."

With a sudden, fierce expression, she put her hand over the back of Cashel's right hand. She said, "There's nothing in this world that the man who conquered the Visitor can't have, you know. Nothing!"

Cashel shook his head. He didn't pull his hand away, though Kotia's touch made him feel uncomfortable. "There's nothing here that I want, mistress," he said. "Except to go home."

Kotia met his eyes for a long moment. She stepped back, perfectly the lady. "Yes," she said, "I see that. I'll take care of the matter as soon as you wish, milord."

"Since you won't be able to take away all the objects that you, ah, fell heir to," said Lord Bossian, "I suppose those of us holding existing manors should divide them among—"

Evne laughed incredulously. Her voice was really a lot louder than ought to come from a little toad.

"No, I am not going to divide Lord Cashel's property with you, *Lord* Bossian," Kotia said with sneering emphasis. She looked around the huge gathering. It seemed to Cashel that there were more airboats than he'd seen of anything except wavetops in a storm. "Nor with the others. Some of you are cowards and *all* of you are weaklings compared to Cashel. And compared to me!"

"Where will you build your manor, girl?" the toad asked. "Right here in the middle of the Basin, I suppose?"

"It won't be my manor!" Kotia said. "I'll build it for Lord Cashel. If ever he chooses to return, it'll be waiting for him. Everything will be waiting for him!"

"He won't come back, girl," said Evne. There was more in her voice than a simple statement, but Cashel couldn't be sure quite what it was. "You know that, don't you?"

"Do I?" said Kotia bitterly. Then, glaring at Bossian, she snapped, "Go away, milord. Go back to your manor. If I have need of you here, I'll summon you." She sniffed. "As well I may."

Bossian blinked at her, then backed away. When he was half the distance to his airboat he turned and trotted the rest of the way, calling to his companions.

"You could do better," the toad said, looking at Kotia.

Kotia shrugged. "No doubt," she said. "But the thought amuses me."

Her face went grimly blank again. "What about you, Mistress Toad?" she said. "I can return you to your own shape now, of course. Is that what you want?"

Evne stretched one hind leg, then the other. "I've been a toad so long . . ." she said. She turned her head toward Cashel. She was so close that he could only see her out of one eye.

She looked back at Kotia. "The emotions aren't as fierce in this shape," she said. "All I ever got from human emotions was to be locked into a block of coal." She laughed, only partly in amusement, then added, "Thank you, girl, but I think I'll leave things as they are. I'd miss the taste of flies, and my neighbors would speak harshly of me if I didn't give up the sport of catching them."

"I can see the advantage," Kotia said, smiling wryly as she looked from Evne to Cashel himself. "Well, if you change your mind . . ."

People were gathering the various bits and pieces that'd fallen to the ground when the ship burned. Now that Kotia wasn't flinging around flames and angry shouts, folks came up in groups with what they'd found. Kotia must've given orders when people talked to her as they arrived.

Even parts of things that'd broken seemed worth gathering up. The big glass *something* that hadn't missed Cashel by much when it fell was arriving in any number of fragments, carried reverently in the lifted skirts of servants' tunics.

There was a lord or lady at the head of each group, but they weren't doing the work of carrying things. Well, Cashel hadn't expected they would be.

"I guess I'm ready to go, mistress," Cashel said. He raised an eyebrow. "Unless there's more I need to do here?"

"No, we may as well get on with it," Kotia said. "The lingering ambiance of the ship will aid the process—not that it should be very difficult."

She looked at the assembly. The gold disk she'd taken before the Visitor's defeat was in her right hand. Cashel hadn't seen it there a moment ago, but he wasn't sure whether it'd appeared, enlarged from a seed of itself, or if he just hadn't noticed it.

"Return to your manors for the time being," Kotia said. The disk spun, lifting out of her hand. She didn't raise her voice, but Cashel heard her words echoing back faintly from the circle of distant hills. "I'll invite you back when it's safe to come, but right now I have work to do. What's about to happen will seriously endanger anyone who's too close to it and who lacks the power to protect himself."

"Which means all of you," said Evne. As with Kotia—but without any help from the disk—she was speaking to the whole huge crowd. "That's especially true for you who fancy yourself as wizards. Don't stay around or you may not even have time for regrets."

No question about everybody being able to hear the two, well, females. Even at the back of the crowd, ordinary people ran for the airboats. The lords and ladies with their courtiers started out being more dignified about their leaving, but the panic spread like fire in dry grass. Lady Raki running with her skirts hiked up was as comical as a fat lamb gamboling in springtime, and some of the other nobles were even funnier.

"I know you would've avoided them when you raised your manor, girl," Evne said, looking at Kotia. "But I wanted to see them scamper."

Kotia ran her left index finger over the rim of the disk, now at rest in her hand again. "Do you *know* that?" she said nonchalantly. "Perhaps you're right, then."

She looked up, nodding to Cashel but then focusing her hard gaze on Evne. "You're welcome to stay with me, you know, Mistress Toad," she said.

"I'm *welcome* to stay wherever I choose, girl," Evne said. "Don't mistake me for one of those."

She lifted her body on three legs to sweep the right hind leg in an arc across a portion of the spectators rushing off more quickly than they'd arrived.

"There was once one who could gainsay me," the toad continued. She spoke with certainty and an absolute lack of emotion. Again she reminded Cashel of his sister when she was very, very angry. "But not, I think, for seven thousand years."

Kotia stared at her, balancing the disk in her palm. "Yes, I believe you're correct," she said, as calmly as the toad. "But I don't intend that we should ever become certain."

She smiled. "Lord Cashel?" she continued in a wholly different tone. "If you're ready, we can proceed."

"Sure," said Cashel. He cleared his throat. "Ah, do we have to find a mirror?"

"Yes," said Evne. She extended her hind leg again. There was a *spat!* of blue fire. A circle of grass and dried mud nearby became as smooth and clear as the surface of a dewdrop.

"Stand in the center, if you would, Lord Cashel," Kotia said quietly. "Mistress Toad, what is your will?"

Evne walked down Cashel's forearm to the back of his hand. "I'll accept your offer of hospitality, girl," she said. "I expect it to be interesting. If not—"

She turned her head to look up at Cashel.

"—quite as interesting as the past two days."

Kotia stretched out her left hand. Evne hopped to it. The toad looked graceless in the air with her four legs splayed in different directions, but she landed precisely in Kotia's palm and tucked herself back together.

Cashel cleared his throat again. "I guess I'll be going, then," he said. He nodded—twice, once to each of them, though with them both together it didn't make much difference. He stepped carefully onto the circle. He expected it to be slick because it was perfectly smooth, but his feet didn't slide at all. He felt like he was standing in empty air, but the surface was faintly warm as well as being solid.

Cashel turned, holding his staff crosswise. You never knew what you were going to run into when you were dealing with wizards.

"I'm ready!" he said, meeting the two sets of eyes. Kotia and Evne looked as cold and hard as crags in the winter sea. It was a really good thing they weren't his enemies.

"Ene psa enesgaph," they said, speaking together. *"Selbi-outh sarba . . ."*

Cashel's surroundings began to spin, though he himself

didn't move. Evne and Kotia faded from sight, all but their eyes; their eyes remained fixed like the constellation of the Seven Oxen in the northern sky.

"Thaoos sieche thur . . ." the voices said. Blue fire danced soundlessly about Cashel, concealing everything else but the eyes. *"Spanton kwilm!"*

Cashel was falling into himself. Everything vanished, light and sound and feeling.

In his mind someone whispered, "Farewell, Lord Cashel." He wasn't sure, but he thought it might be both women speaking together.

Garric's steps had been soundless from the moment he entered the lens of light in the garden; now his boots clacked on ice so cold and hard that it was dry. He saw the twins running ahead of him—or perhaps it was only one of them, his/her figure multiplied by reflection in the ice walls.

The ceilings were as high as those of the audience chamber in the royal palace in Valles, ribbed and coffered with ice. Ropes of blue and red wizardlight twined in helixes at the core of each beam and plate; at any distance the ice looked purple.

The walls were sometimes clear, sometimes mirrors that might throw back either a perfect image or a distorted mockery of the original. When the man-shaped monster shambled out of a side-aisle Garric hadn't seen till that moment, his first thought was that he was seeing the reflection of a man, perhaps even himself.

The creature gave a high-pitched laugh and raised its club, the trunk of a fir tree split and slain by a frost beyond what even its cold-adapted fibers could bear. High as the ceiling was, the tree struck it: the monster was real and just as huge as it seemed.

"Haft and the Isles!" Garric shouted, rushing before the creature could come to terms with what for it were narrow confines. Its forehead sloped sharply from thick brow ridges. It was naked except for a coat of coarse reddish hair, incrementally thicker on its scalp and in a mane along its spine; and it was almost twenty feet high.

The creature swung a slanting blow at Garric. He flattened against the wall. The club struck the ice behind him and rebounded, scattering a haze of splinters. Garric cut upward, catching the monster's wrist with the sweet spot of his sword just a handsbreadth from the tip. His steel crunched through cartilage and small bones.

The monster jerked its arm back. When the fingers lost strength, the club slipped and flew against the opposite wall of the corridor. Garric hacked at the inside of the creature's right ankle, cutting deep again.

The creature screamed, grabbed at Garric with its left hand, and toppled forward when its leg gave way. It twisted in the air, still trying to seize him, but Garric jumped past, beyond the creature's reach.

He looked down the range of gleaming, branching corridors. It would've been a maze even without the reflection, but as it was . . .

He couldn't see the twins. Another of the gangling monsters came down the corridor toward him, doubled by the mirroring walls. It raised its weapon, a crudely forged iron trident. The reflection was carrying a simple spear, point down as if preparing to gig frogs.

There were two of the creatures, each as tall as the first. There'd be more following them, and still worse things besides. Garric looked over his shoulder for the soldiers who'd come through the portal with him.

The creature he'd crippled was squirming after him on its belly. Beyond it a tunnel of light twisted toward the world Garric came from. He remembered how the distance between him and the twins had seemed greater than it should have been. The portal wasn't a simple hole in space, and there wasn't a regiment of infantry rushing to their prince's support.

But Tenoctris was there, and also Liane supporting the old wizard with her left arm while holding the satchel of paraphernalia in her right. Tenoctris seated herself cross-legged on the ice. Liane dropped the bag beside her and ran on, reaching into her sleeve.

"Watch!—" cried Garric, starting back to deal with the monster he'd thought he could leave for the soldiers behind him. It reached out with its uninjured left arm; its fingernails were blunt and black, like a dog's claws.

Liane grabbed the shock of hair at the peak of the creature's scalp and drew her right hand and little dagger around its throat. The arc of the blade was as quick as a ripple shimmering on a pond. The ghost in Garric's mind gave a shout of delight.

Blood, brighter than a man's, gushed out. It steamed as it pooled on the ice. Liane's dagger had an ivory hilt and a gold-chased blade no longer than Garric's index finger, but the steel was so good that it held a wire edge even when slicing corded muscles. The great veins and arteries near the surface of the creature's neck let its life out even faster than a thrust through the heart could have done.

Tenoctris dribbled a triangle of black dust—powdered charcoal or maybe iron filings—on the ice before her. She began chanting even before she'd completed the figure.

"She'll guide the troops through!" Liane said, gasping for breath. Her right forearm and her tunic from the waist down were covered in orange-red blood. "We have to hold back the Hunters a few minutes more!"

"Right," said Garric, turning to face the things that Liane called Hunters. He supposed that Tenoctris had named the creatures; they were nothing Liane would've found in the classical literature that was one of the joys the two of them shared. "We'll hold."

The Hunters came toward him at a loose-limbed gait, giggling and apparently unaware of each other's presence. They didn't seem to be hurrying, but their long legs covered a considerable distance with each stride.

Garric drew his dagger with his left hand. For the most part the shorter blade was only there on his belt to balance the weight of his sword, but this time it might be useful. "Keep back," he muttered to Liane. "I may have to move—"

The creature with the trident cocked his arm back. Liane gripped her cuffs and spread her outer tunic wide, shouting, "Here! Here!"

Garric sprang forward as both Hunters thrust at Liane. The one holding the spear was on the left, nearer him, so he cut through the back of the creature's wrist. The spear came loose from the Hunter's nerveless fingers and clattered down the corridor. It ripped Liane's tunics, nicking her right thigh as she sprang back to safety from the expected spear thrust.

The Hunters collided with one another and recoiled, grunting in surprise. Garric sank his dagger into the knee of the creature he'd already wounded. As it bent to grab him, he leaped upward, using the imbedded dagger like a climbing iron to give his outstretched sword a few extra inches of reach. He stabbed the Hunter in the belly and jerked the blade back as he fell. When the point withdrew, coils of intestine and dark, stinking fluid spilled onto the ice.

The creature gave a despairing wail and batted Garric into the wall with its good hand. His head hit the ice; his ears rang and he could see things only in black and white. The Hunter reached for him again but vomited a great flag of blood and slowly collapsed on the ice.

The uninjured Hunter had chopped the ground where Liane stood taunting it. It raised its trident again and stamped toward her. Garric tried to get between the creature and Liane but his foot didn't rise as much as he intended it to; he stumbled on the faintly-twitching arm of the Hunter he'd killed. Liane poised between the slavering monster and Tenoctris. She was unable to move without exposing the old wizard—and therefore unwilling to move.

"Hah!" grunted the Hunter. There was a meat-axe *thwock!* The creature arched backward. A spear-shaft stuck up from the middle of its face; the steel head had penetrated the thin bones at the bridge of the nose and grunched into the back of the skull.

"Garric and the Isles!" Lord Waldron said, holding his long cavalry sword high as he ran past Liane and Tenoctris. He hadn't thrown the spear; that had come from the Blood Eagle skirting the women on the other side. The soldier was tugging his own shorter blade from its scabbard.

A line of crimson fire led from Tenoctris's drawing and down the twisting tunnel. Scores of soldiers, a mixture of the bodyguard regiment and regular infantry, packed the opening between worlds, following the light the old wizard had sent to guide them.

"Your highness!" Waldron said. "I sent Lord Valser back

to the camp with orders. The whole army will report to the palace and follow Mayne's regiment through that wall of light. Was that right?"

Garric looked down corridors shimmering in a pattern as complex as that of the veins of a hazel leaf. The Hunters were dead; soldiers had just finished hacking the one he'd crippled early into a mass as bloody and shapeless as a cow's afterbirth. But in the distance, from a score of mirrored branchings, came an army of half-men and not-men; some with swords, some with fangs and claws as long as daggers.

"Yes, milord," said Garric. He wiped his blade clean with the skirt of his tunic because the monsters he'd slain with it didn't have clothing he could use for the purpose. "That was a very good idea indeed. And I only hope that they don't waste time in getting here!"

"*Now* will you wake, mistress?" Sharina dreamed Beard was saying to her in a cave of glowing ice.

Sharina came alert, throwing off the bearskin and raising the axe to strike in whichever direction danger appeared. She was breathing hard, shocked to have slept so soundly and frightened by the threat that lowered over her unseen.

The night was as peaceful as night ever was in this world. The ice walls glowed with wizardry and from far down the tunnel the sea moaned, but at least there was no wind in the cave.

Several of the band besides Scoggin and Franca were sleeping outside. The others were in the bone cabin, but the rasp of snoring through the open doorway indicated that all was well there too. Nothing moved but the wizardlight, and its pulses were as slight and sluggish as the steps of an old man.

"What . . . ?" Sharina began in puzzlement.

"The reason you should be concerned," said the axe waspishly, "is that Alfdan removed the Key of Reyazel from your sash and has reentered the world it unlocks. Unless you find this an attractive place to spend the rest of your life, you might consider fetching him back."

Sharina stood, weighing the axe in her hand. She was

coldly furious. The cabin door had been lying on the stones where the beetle's violence had flung it. Now it leaned against the bone wall, and the ground which it'd covered was a hole into the sandy beach.

Sharina started for it. "I don't see how I could've missed him taking the key away," she said.

"He *is* a wizard, mistress," said Beard, "and one of his toys is the eyestone of a sloth. It let him cast a sleep spell deeper than even I could wake you from until he'd taken himself away. Did you suppose all these folk were sleeping naturally—that none of them would be wakeful in *this* place?"

Sharina hadn't thought the cabin door had a keyhole; nor did it in the ordinary sense, but the flange of the gold key stuck up from the notch through which the latch cord had been led. She glared as she paused at the doorway in the ground; but there'd be time enough to decide how to deal with the key for once and for all *after* she retrieved Alfdan.

The sun was setting on the beach beyond. Beard said, "If you're afraid to enter, then you may as well go back to sleep, mistress. You'll need your strength for when the beetle comes or something worse does."

Sharina stepped into the sunset. She didn't bother responding to the axe's gibe. He was right, after all.

Alfdan stood at the tide line; the oval sun threw his shadow far up the sand. The sea had drawn back, but a great swell was lifting beyond the jaws of land.

"Alfdan!" Sharina called. She started toward him. The air felt warm and the dry sand was very warm in contrast to the ice cave. "Wizard!"

The sea rolled into the narrow bay, curling and foaming. Sharina didn't suppose Alfdan could've heard her calling over the sound of the surf, much less that he'd have returned if he had. She began to run, her feet sinking deeper as she reached sand that hadn't been compacted with clay.

Beard pumped back and forth in her hand. She'd have to be careful when she reached Alfdan lest she slice the wizard open in an accident that her anger wouldn't completely regret.

The surf carved another curving slice across the strand,

washing Alfdan's legs and springing up in droplets of spray. As it withdrew, the wizard bent and lifted something large from the sand.

"Alfdan!" Sharina shouted. "Leave it!"

The wizard heard her and turned. The object in his hands was a helmet whose rim spread into fanciful flares. The metal shone in the sunset like fresh blood.

"Leave it!" Sharina repeated, still twenty feet away. She felt Beard rise in her hand, but whether that was by her will or by the axe's she couldn't be sure.

Alfdan set the helmet over his head, just as she'd known he'd do. The flaring rim framed his narrow face. He took his hands from the metal and his eyes brightened in beatific delight. "This is . . ." he said. "I can see everything from the beginning of—"

Sharina halted. She was within arm's length of the wizard. His eyes suddenly lost their focus though he didn't look away. "That's odd," he said. "It's almost as if . . ."

"Mistress," said Beard. "You should get out of this place. Now."

"I don't—" said Alfdan. His face went pale; then he screamed like a hog when the butcher clamps its nose for slaughter. He grabbed the helmet with both hands and tried unsuccessfully to lift it.

"Alfdan!" Sharina said, seizing the broad rim with her free hand. It burned her; she jerked her fingers away, leaving bits of skin sticking to the metal.

"Mistress, get *out*," the axe said with an urgency that she'd never heard in his steely voice before. At the moment she was too concerned with the wizard to appreciate Beard's tone. "Get out now. He's already dead!"

Alfdan lowered his hands. His expression was blank. Though his eyes were open, the corneas had become featureless and silvery.

"Help me!" the wizard screamed. He stuck out his tongue but it wasn't a tongue, wasn't flesh: a tendril of shimmering metal waggled toward Sharina.

"Get out, mistress!" Beard shrieked as Sharina swung at the extending tentacle, gripping the helve with both hands. Beard's edge had sheared bone like butter, but it glanced off

the tongue without marking it. The shock threw Sharina backward onto the sand, her arms numb to the elbows.

Alfdan—the thing that had been Alfdan—took a tottering step toward her. The metal tongue continued to lengthen, moving with the circular, questing motion of an ivy shoot but immeasurably faster.

Sharina scuttled backward on her feet and left hand. When she'd lengthened the distance between her and the creature enough to risk it, she got up and ran. She didn't look over her shoulder; that would've slowed her down—and besides, she was afraid of what she might see.

Only when Sharina jumped through the portal with a cry of triumph did she look back. The creature was staggering after her. As best as Sharina could tell in silhouette against the red sun, the helmet had closed over Alfdan's face. The tendril continued to elongate; by now it stretched half the remaining distance to the opening.

Sharina slammed the door flat on the wet stone. The echoing crash roused sleeping men with shouts of fear and surprise. She reached for the key winking in the wizardlight, but as her fingers closed on the flange she paused.

"Mistress!" cried Neal, his bow strung and an arrow nocked. "Where's Master Alfdan? I can't find him!"

Instead of withdrawing the Key of Reyazel from the door notch, Sharina pushed it inward. It shouldn't have moved; there was nothing on the other side of the thick panel but a slab of smooth rock. Nevertheless the key slipped downward and vanished.

"Where's Alfdan?" Neal shouted. "Where?"

He was a big man, holding a weapon and utterly distraught. At another time he would have frightened Sharina.

Not now. Neal was merely human.

"I suppose Alfdan's in Hell," she said calmly. "He was so determined to go there that I couldn't stop him."

"But . . ." said Neal, staggering back as though she'd stabbed him through the body. "But how . . . ?"

"Then we're marooned here," said Burness, hugging his broad-bladed spear to his chest. "We'll never leave. We'll freeze or we'll starve, but we'll never leave!"

Franca began to whimper. He extended the hand that

didn't hold his dagger, pointing toward the wall of the cave. A lens of violet light was forming in the ice.

Sharina watched the opening, waggling the axe to make sure that her hands had their strength back. They seemed to be all right, though her left fingertips burned like the fire itself.

"I don't think we'll freeze or starve either one," she said with cold detachment. "We can't go to Her without Alfdan's art, but it seems that She is coming to us."

"Many lives to drink," whispered Beard, shivering in her hands with anticipation.

Ilna settled her tunics neatly as the *Bird of the Tide* brushed to a halt against the stone quay. The watchman in the tower had vanished as soon as he was sure that the *Bird* had entered Terness Harbor alone, not in company with the *Defender*.

Hutena and Shausga jumped to the quay with ropes while the oarsmen stowed their long sweeps. "I guess they'll be waiting for us, eh, Captain?" said Ninon, careful not to look at Chalcus because he was afraid his concern would show.

"You mean because I waved to the watchman, lad?" Chalcus said with a grin. He set a tip of his bow on the deck and bent it with his knee, then slid the thick cord into the upper notch. "Ah, no, we couldn't help him seeing us, could we? What I was doing was giving what few folk are left in the castle, servants most like, time to vacate before our arrival. I don't think they'll want to greet us, especially when they hear their Commander's bound to our mast."

He gave Lusius an appraising glance. "Most of their Commander, that is."

The sailors laughed. "Hey, Kulit would've jumped in and got the Commander's leg back from that seawolf, wouldn't you, Kulit?" Nabarbi said, ruffling his friend's curly hair. "You should've asked him."

Ilna smiled coldly as she stepped onto the quay and looked back at Lusius. He was unconscious; in shock, she supposed, and very likely to die . . . but he'd die shortly in any case. They'd never promised Lusius his life, only that they wouldn't feed him to the seawolf; and that was more of a concession than he'd granted to his brother, after all.

"Master Bosun?" Chalcus said to Hutena as he hooked a

quiver of arrows onto his sash. "I'm leaving the rest of the lads here while Mistress Ilna and I visit the castle, but I'd be grateful if you'd come along with us with the maul. I don't expect to meet anybody there till we get into the cellars, but it may be there's locked doors in the way."

He hefted the powerful bow with a grin. "I may have my hands full, you see."

"I can carry the maul," Ilna said with a frown.

"Your hands, dear heart," Chalcus said with an edge in his voice, "may be a great deal fuller than mine. Not so?"

Ilna nodded, her lips tight with irritation at herself. When she'd left Barca's Hamlet for the wider world, she'd often found men who treated her as though she couldn't do real work because she was a slim girl. That wasn't a mistake anybody'd made in the borough; nor made twice nowadays either, but Ilna was always on edge expecting what to her was an insult.

This was Chalcus. And even if it hadn't been—if some foppish courtier had made the comment—there wasn't time now to feel insulted!

"Sure, I'll go," the bosun said, his voice calm if not precisely eager. He patted the head of his axe to make sure the helve was thrust firmly under his belt, then leaned down into the hold and came up with the maul Ilna'd used to set the mast wedges. The massive head was from the root of a white oak, banded around both faces with iron.

"Captain?" said Ninon. "We'll all go. You know that!"

"I know you would, indeed," Chalcus said with his easy smile, "but this time you'll serve me and our prince better for waiting here by the ship. Who knows how quickly we'll need to put off again, eh, lads?"

"Aye, that's not half the truth," said Kulit. He'd taken another bow from the deckhouse and was stringing it. As he spoke, he looked up the hill toward the castle.

"Dear heart and bosun?" said Chalcus. His left index finger tapped his quiver, the hilt of his dagger, and last his sword. "Shall we be off?"

"Yes," said Ilna, striding up the street and wishing it was dirt rather than cobblestone, even though she'd worn boots. She hated stone . . .

She smiled. Reminding herself how much she hated stone was a better thing to do than worrying about what they'd find in the dungeons of Lusius's castle; and what might find them there.

"Stone's hard for feet used to a deck," Hutena said, putting words to Ilna's thought. He slanted the maul's shaft over his shoulder, then changed his mind and carried the big tool in both hands. He was on the right side as they walked up the twisting street abreast; Chalcus was on the left and Ilna, smiling broader and letting her fingers knot the pattern they found appropriate, was in the middle.

Nobody was out on the street. Occasionally Ilna caught a glimpse of eyes through the crack in a shutter. A baby cried desperately behind the counter of a used clothing shop as they passed, but neither it nor the mother hushing it were visible.

"What're they afraid of?" Hutena said, frowning with anger and frustration.

The same thing you are, Ilna thought, but instead of that she said, "They don't know what's going to happen any better than we do. The difference is that they've decided to hide and let it happen to them, whereas we're choosing to deal with it on our own terms."

"Yeah, I guess so," the bosun muttered. He gave her an appreciative smile and hefted the maul. "I'd rather be us."

"Yes, me too," said Ilna with a wintry smile of her own. Perhaps she was learning to tell the truth in a way that other people didn't find offensive. That'd be a useful skill, though she'd use it to supplement her instinctive responses rather than replace them.

The street grew steeper and switched back; the only buildings this high up the hill were three-story structures whose upper floors were laid back along the slope. The castle loomed like part of the crag. The outer gate was open.

"Do you know "The Single Girl," Master Bosun?" said Chalcus cheerily, his right middle and index fingers touching the nock of the arrow on his bow string. *"When I was single, I went dressed so fine . . ."*

"Aye, I know it," said Hutena. "But we'll sing another time if you please, sir."

Chalcus laughed. They'd reached the gate. Nothing moved but the wind.

Chalcus slipped through the gateway, drawing the bow to his cheek in the same sweeping motion. A cat yowled and sprang from a trash pile. The bow string went back to Chalcus's ear; then he relaxed with a gust of embarrassed laughter.

"I'm not the man I once was if a little cat makes me jump," he said as Ilna and the bosun joined him. He was smiling, but the comment wasn't altogether a joke.

"We're none of us the people we wish we were," Ilna said, sharply because she understood perfectly the thing Chalcus hadn't been willing to put in words. "We never were. As for what matters—you'll do for this."

She smiled, coldly because in a crisis she was always cold; but with enormous affection. "And you'll do for me."

Chalcus set the bow against the inner side of the curtain wall, dropped the arrow back into his quiver, and set the quiver beside the bow. He drew his sword, keeping his left hand free. "I think from here on I'll not worry about what there might be beyond the reach of my blade," he said with a grin.

The buildings around the ancient watchtower were empty—abandoned, not just closed around their cowering inhabitants. "I figured there'd be servants still," Hutena said. "Are they that scared of us?"

"It's not us they're worried about," Chalcus said. "It's what they think we'll let loose that scares them, eh?"

Ilna sniffed. "Then we'll have to be careful not to let it loose," she said.

The tower's outer door was closed. Hutena raised his maul in anticipation, but when Chalcus pulled on the great iron ring, only its weight resisted. The interior was dank and spartan, a military post whose thick walls filled most of what seemed from the outside to be interior space.

A stone staircase ran around the walls. Every fifth step—the thumb of Ilna's hand—was broader and had an arrow slit. The only light came from the slits and from the open trap door that gave onto the roof platform.

Set into the base of the staircase was a small, heavy door with a peaked arch. Chalcus tried it with his left hand; the panel had no more give than the stone jambs that held it. Chalcus moved back and nodded to the bosun.

Hutena stepped to the side of the doorway and eyed it for a moment as he waggled the maul to work his shoulder muscles loose. The panel was hung to open inward. There were staples for a bar on this side from the days the cellars were a dungeon, but they'd rusted to nubs.

"Huh!" the bosun said as he swung, stepping into the blow so that his whole body drove the massive oak head. It crashed into the lock, smashing the plate loose and splintering the internal bolt out of the panel.

Hutena backed away, breathing hard. Chalcus shoved the door open with the toes of his left foot. Air puffed out, chill and stinking of ancient slaughter. The stairs leading down were lighted faintly from below.

"I'll lead," Chalcus said, speaking quietly. He drew his dagger.

Ilna looked at Hutena. The bosun had leaned the maul against the jamb and was trying to slide the short axe from his belt. His hands trembled and his eyes were fixed on a damp patch of wall across the circular room.

"Master Hutena," she said crisply. "I'd like you to wait here and keep people from coming at us from behind. I don't like stone walls, and I certainly don't want to be blocked into this place while I'm busy with—"

She smiled with about as little humor as she felt; she wasn't joking about her dislike of stone.

"—other matters."

"Sir?" the bosun said. He tried to keep a straight face, but his relief was obvious to anyone.

"Aye, and I should've thought of it myself," Chalcus said, shaking his head in feigned irritation. "Indeed, that's all we'd need—locked in a dungeon with no company but a dead wizard."

To Ilna, in a faintly thinner voice, he went on, "Ready, dear heart?"

"Yes," she said; and she followed her man down the narrow steps.

The staircase was steep, but its flights were straight and reversed at landings instead of spiraling like those of the tower above. The treads had been cut from the rock of the hillside, and they were so old that the feet of those passing up and down them had worn them concave.

Ilna couldn't imagine what would have justified such an amount of traffic. Perhaps these steps were much older than the tower built over them, though it dated to the Old Kingdom of a thousand years ago.

There were two handfuls of steps in each flight. Looking over Chalcus's shoulder as she turned onto the third flight, Ilna saw a doorway at the bottom. The iron door hung askew; the upper hinge had rusted away, and the lower one was a red mass that would've crumbled if anybody tugged hard enough to swing the door closed.

Chalcus paused three steps up from the bottom. Ilna could hear the wind whispering, and a slight breeze traced her ankles.

"Eh?" murmured Chalcus. He didn't turn his head.

"Go on," said Ilna, also in a quiet voice. Smashing down the door'd made enough noise to wake the dead, but it still didn't seem right to talk loudly.

The pattern Ilna'd woven was in her left hand, the silk lasso in her right. She didn't know which she'd need—or if either would help—but she was as ready as she could be.

Chalcus jumped a double pace into the room below, as smooth as water flowing down the steps but much, much faster. He poised, motionless except for quick movements of his head.

"I'm behind you!" Ilna said sharply, halting an arm's length back of Chalcus. Her eyes swept the circular room beyond.

Its width was four or five times her height. Its illumination came from slots in the upper walls that must've been cut through the crag on which the tower stood. Ilna wouldn't have guessed that any useful amount of light could trickle through such long narrow passages, but in what otherwise would've been total darkness her eyes quickly adapted to see shapes if not colors. Nothing was moving.

The ceiling had been hollowed into a natural dome. The

builders had trusted the strength of the living rock without adding supporting pillars. Ilna smiled faintly. Given how old this room must be, they'd been right.

There was no furniture except chests of wood and metal around the walls. Some were covered with animal skins to make adequate benches, and other furs and skins were heaped in several places on the floor.

The room stank like a tanyard. The light slits ventilated it, but even so the stench of death and rotting blood squeezed Ilna's lungs like a pillow over her face. More than just the smell went into the oppressive atmosphere; foul things had happened here. Utterly foul.

Chalcus started edging sunwise around the periphery, the sword in his right hand waggling like a snake's questing tongue. Ilna remained where she was, waiting for the pattern to change.

A slab of basalt lay in the middle of the room. Crude tools had shaped it more or less into a rectangle. There was a groove down the center and a hole in the stone floor beneath it for a drain. Blood coated the slab and the floor both. The latest outpouring gleamed in the faint light; it looked fresh enough to be tacky to the touch, which Ilna had no intention of testing.

She saw no sign of the bodies of the sacrificial animals. Human sacrifices, she supposed.

Two thin, mirror-polished sheets of stone—one of banded agate, the other something bluish and translucent, perhaps topaz—stood upright on either side of the basalt. Ilna frowned, trying to determine what was *wrong* with the stone mirrors. She felt there was movement in them, but her eyes saw them only as stone.

Chalcus neared one of the piles of furs. He was grinning faintly. His right foot slid forward in another slow step. Without warning he lunged instead, his curved sword stabbing down like the sting of a spider-killing wasp. The point clicked against the stone floor and withdrew as smoothly as it had gone in.

Chalcus shook his head, still smiling. He resumed his slow shuffle.

Ilna had turned her head minusculely when Chalcus thrust; she saw the change in the agate mirror at the corner of her eye. From this slightly different angle she was looking at the hellworld the *Bird of the Tide* had dropped into. A pool of molten sulfur, yellow as bile, bubbled beneath the window of stone; she thought she could see one of the pincer-armed monsters hunch between spikes of rock in the near distance.

"Chalcus," she said in a quiet voice. "These plates are doors of some kind. Gaur may not be—"

Gaur stood up from the heap of furs and bullhides to her right, across the room from Chalcus. The wizard was taller than she'd remembered, raw-boned and powerful. For an instant she thought he was wearing animal skins hair-side out, but that was a trick of the dim light: Gaur was nude and covered with fur like a beast. He growled softly.

Chalcus shifted his stance to face the wizard. Gaur was unarmed, but so big a man could be dangerous regardless. He'd sent a ship and crew from this world to another, though. That would be exhausting for even a very powerful wizard, and from the look of him Gaur hadn't had time to fully recover.

Ilna dropped her knotted pattern back into her sleeve. There wasn't enough light down here for her to trust its effect.

Chalcus sidled toward the wizard, his sword advanced and his left hand not far from the hilt of the slender dagger. Gaur hunched, his eyes fixed on the swordsman. He growled louder, then—

Gaur's body slumped inward, not shrinking as Ilna first thought but changing: the face flattened into long jaws, the chest grew deeper, and the arms formed into forelegs. For a heartbeat Gaur crouched on his bed of skins as a huge black-furred wolf; then he sprang at Chalcus's throat.

Ilna arched her noose over the thick beast neck, tightening as she pulled with all her strength. The wolf outweighed her by twice or more, but even so she jerked its head around even as the beast snatched her off her feet.

Chalcus's sword slipped in behind the wolf's shoulder blade, grating on ribs as it sliced through and out the other side. Gaur crunched sideways onto the stone floor. Chalcus tugged his blade free; there was a gush of blood.

Ilna'd fallen onto her knees and left hand. She started to rise, still holding the noose tight. The beast was twitching.

The wolf rolled, getting its legs under it again. This time it glared at Ilna. The wound through its chest had closed, though a flag of blood still matted the dark fur.

Gaur snarled and leaped. Ilna threw herself backward, knowing there was no escape. Chalcus caught the wolf's hind leg with his left hand and hacked at the beast's neck, using his edge rather than the point this time.

Gaur twisted in the air and slammed onto the floor again. The inward-curving sword had cut deep into his spine. Still holding the wolf's ankle, Chalcus lifted his sword to repeat the blow; a line of blood drops curled off the blade.

The gaping wound started to close as soon as the steel withdrew. Gaur turned his head toward Chalcus and snarled loud enough to make the stone mirrors vibrate.

Ilna lunged backward, pulling on the noose with both hands. She tripped over the basalt slab and sprawled, doubling her knees up to her chest.

Gaur leaped at her, his beast strength pulling his hind leg through Chalcus's grasp. Chalcus gave a cry of fury and stabbed, driving his point up through the wolf's diaphragm into its chest, but the beast completed its pounce. Its forepaws, each the size of Ilna's hands with the fingers spread, jolted her shoulders down on the basalt.

The pattern was complete.

Ilna kicked upward as she rolled in a backward somersault. She couldn't have lifted Gaur's weight but she didn't have to: the wolf's own inertia carried him over and past her, through the sheet of agate sullen with the light of another world. The growl turned midway into a scream.

Ilna looked into the agate window. Gaur, his head and torso again a man's, plunged into the pool of boiling sulfur. The thick fluid plopped as it closed over the body and then blasted outward. The wizard's flesh had cooked to vapor in an instant.

Ilna ducked as a blob of molten sulfur spat from the pool

to splash over the basalt. It hardened into a thin sheet whose dry reek cut through the stench of old blood.

Ilna straightened, breathing hard. The agate was a smooth mirror again; only from one narrow angle was it a gateway to Hell.

"I lost my noose," she said in a shaky voice. "I've had it for a long time."

"Dear heart, dear love," Chalcus said. He was ignoring Gaur's blood drying on his sword, though he usually kept the steel as scrupulously clean as the bright curve of the waxing moon. "There'll be a thousand cords, there'll be all the silk on the island of Seres now that you're safe. I almost lost *you*."

Ilna walked around the upper end of the slab, wiping her hands on her tunic. "I didn't think . . ." she said. "All the strands had to be placed just so . . ."

She smiled weakly at Chalcus. "That's true of any pattern, of course. But when it's yarn, the strands don't fight your placement."

As Ilna stepped past the sheet of blue topaz, she caught the hint of movement again. She glanced to the side. What she'd thought was clear stone had shadows in it: man-sized, growing—

Chalcus shouted. She tried to draw back but she was too late. The clawed fingers of a pair of Rua, fine-boned but strong as steel, closed on her upper arms, pulling her toward them into the topaz mirror.

As Ilna fell, she heard Chalcus shout again.

Chapter Twenty-one

I'll take over here, your highness!" said Lord Waldron, glancing back over his shoulder to judge how many troops had arrived. It looked to Garric like several score, a mix of Blood Eagles and regular infantry from Lord Mayne's regiment; the passage from the palace garden was packed with more men. "One quick charge'll sweep these scum away!"

"By the Shepherd, lad!" Carus snarled in Garric's mind. *"Don't let that bloody cavalryman throw them away!"*

Nor shall I, Garric thought. Aloud he said, "No, milord. I haven't time to explain my strategy here—"

Carus guffawed, Garric's only strategy was to keep from spreading his force into a maze of corridors where the unknown numbers of enemies would have all the advantages. Simple though the plan was, it was a considerable improvement on Lord Waldron's notion of hurling his troops at the enemy in heroic disregard of what might be in ambush behind these gleaming walls.

He stepped in front of the soldiers and turned his back to the army of monsters. "Soldiers of the Isles!" he shouted. "Form ranks five abreast. We'll advance at a walk. The front two ranks will throw spears on my command, the rest of you keep yours till we know more about the situation."

Things would've been disorganized even if all the men had been from the same unit. As it was, besides the Blood Eagles and Mayne's regiment, there were members of half-a-dozen other commands who'd been in the palace for one reason or another. They'd rushed to follow their prince when it looked like action.

This was exactly what good soldiers *should* do, of course, but it turned confusion into chaos. Every man in earshot of Garric, some thirty or forty of them, pushed forward to get into the front rank.

"Fellow soldiers!" Garric bellowed. "Save your shoving for the enemy or you'll be cleaning latrines for the rest of your army careers! If any of us live long enough to have careers, which we won't if you don't stop acting like schoolboys. There'll be plenty of fighting for all of us this day, as sure as I love the Isles."

The commotion settled into a reasonable array, though Garric noticed that there were six men, not five, in each rank. That'd be a hindrance for good sword work, but with the enemy channeled straight ahead by the ice walls it might be as well as not to have more weight up front.

Waldron laid his hand on a Blood Eagle's shoulder to

move the man back and take his place. "Milord!" Garric said, stepping between Waldron and the soldier. "I need you to stay here where the passage enters this ice world. Make sure everyone coming through knows to follow the men in front of them and not go down other corridors. They can fight if they're attacked from the flanks, but they're *not* to leave the path that I've chosen."

The path that Tenoctris had chosen, of course, but there was no need for technicalities. The old wizard's thin crimson line continued to stretch back to Carcosa and the sunshine of late spring. A similar trace of blue wizardlight now curled from the triangle also and gleamed down the corridor filled with oncoming beastmen.

"No, your highness," Waldron said with an angry wave of his left hand to brush the notion away. "Mayne can handle that, or—"

"No, Lord Waldron!" Garric said, with King Carus's iron in his voice. "My army commander will take charge of the matter. For the moment that means you. Are you resigning rather than take an order framed for the kingdom's good?"

"Faugh, you're a boy!" Waldron shouted. He slammed his long sword back in its scabbard. "But you'll never say a bor-Warriman didn't do his duty!"

He stalked back to where the passage through nothingness opened into the ice world, every inch a man. *"And a soldier besides, rather than just a warrior,"* said Carus thoughtfully. *"Which is a harder task than many realize, and a task I failed at more often than I care to remember."*

Officers were bellowing the troops into order as they stepped onto the ice. Invariably the men's set expressions warmed into relief as they left the passage. These corridors weren't like home—Garric smiled with black humor; at least not home to anybody in the royal army—but ice was a natural thing compared to the glowing nothingness they'd crossed to get here.

Garric and the king in his mind both blinked in a surge of pride. In training and discipline, these were the best troops the Isles had seen in a thousand years; and in courage they were the equal of any men who'd ever lived!

Garric pushed his way toward the front of his force as it

tramped up the corridor, filling the corridor as a piston does the cylinder of a pump. Men cursed when he bumped them, but they let him by when they realized who he was. Lord Mayne was in the front rank; Garric halted behind him, squeezing between two veterans—both of them noncoms from Mayne's regiment.

One man muttered, "You hadn't ought to be here, sir."

The other nodded but said, "Aye, though it's an honor to see your highness this way. Wait till I tell my grandnephews that I stood beside Prince Garric hisself when we sent all them demons back to Hell!"

"They're a bit beforehand on that," said the image of Carus with a gust of laughter. *"But a soldier who thinks that way's generally worth two of the other kind!"*

"By your leave, your highness?" called Lord Mayne, cocking his head but keeping an eye on the squadrons of monsters ahead. "We'll shortly be in javelin range."

Mayne was a pudgy fellow, the younger son of a family of wealthy Valles merchants. He hadn't been raised to hunting and other rural sports like the nobles from Northern Ornifal who provided most of the officers in the royal army. Bringing his regiment double-time from the camp had winded him, whereas Lord Waldron twice Mayne's age and more—had run back and forth between the palace and the Temple of the Shepherd without signs of effort.

But Mayne was in the front rank, thinking about the practical questions of war instead of his fears or hope of honor. He held his rank by Lord Tadai's recommendation; for which Tadai deserved the thanks of his prince and the kingdom.

The hostile army wasn't of demons, but it looked a formidable enough crew regardless. Garric wasn't sure any two of the enemy were the same, nor were any of them human. He saw something that looked like a stork, but it stood ten feet tall and had two heads with long bills. Beside it tramped a squat figure wearing half-armor and a closed helmet; it had four arms, each holding a double-bitted axe, and it walked on a pair of legs like a sow's. Beside that was a goat with the head of a great cat. Beside that—but it didn't matter: they'd all die, or Garric would die and the Isles with him.

"You may give the order, milord!" Garric said.

The leading ranks canted back the eight-foot spears in their right arms. Some of the soldiers were probably left-handed. In this as in all other things, the needs of the army overrode personal preference: the shield *must* be on the left arm to keep an even front in closed ranks, so the spear and sword were always in the right.

"Leading ranks, ready spears!" Mayne said, his voice suddenly a cricket chirp. The troops had prepared when they heard Garric, but discipline required that their own officer give the command. "Loose!"

The army of monsters was a hundred and fifty feet away, much closer than usual for the volley of javelins that opened a battle. The corridor's ribbed ceiling—though high for a building—prevented the soldiers from arching their spears high for maximum range. Even so, the missiles crashed into the beasts and halfmen with devastating effect.

The goat-lion spun, biting and kicking in mad fury at the spear wobbling in its haunches. Other creatures fell under the beast's sudden onslaught or slashed in response when their instinctive rage overwhelmed the control of the wizard directing them.

While the troll in half-armor was in mid-stride, a spear clanged on his helmet. He toppled and the chaotic rush of his fellows swept over him. The troll's axes chopped mindlessly, lopping pieces off the creatures stumbling past him.

The legs of the two-headed stork kicked in the air, occasionally visible over the throng of its fellows. A spear had punched through the base of its double neck and thrown the creature over on its back.

The creatures that met the swordsmen of Garric's first line were already bleeding from wounds their fellows had inflicted. The Blood Eagle on the right edge of the line thundered, "Gut'em, boys!" an instant before contact.

"Haft and the Isles!" Garric cried. Everybody in the royal army was shouting, but the sum of their voices was a wordless snarl more terrible than the screams and whistling that came from the mob of monsters.

Claws tore at heavy shields, while short swords cut and thrust through flesh in a score of inhuman forms. A manlike figure with a two-handed sword and the head of a blue-feathered hawk shrieked as he went down under quick chops by a pair of soldiers; their hobnails trampled the body as they passed on. The creature's big sword had notched a shield but done no other damage.

Lord Mayne, who didn't have a shield, was battling what looked like a lizard on its hind legs wielding butcher knives in both hands. Mayne held the thing's right wrist in his free hand, but the other knife was blocking his sword and the long jaws were reaching for his throat. Garric judged his moment and thrust over Mayne's right shoulder, piercing the lizard's brain through an eye socket. His blade sparkled; the creature's scales were iron or something equally hard.

A scorpion the size of an ox scrabbled down the corridor. In place of eyes it had a curved crystalline bowl from which two wizened manlike figures peered. The beast's pink body was gashed and dripping ichor from the ruck of injured, maddened monsters it'd had to fight through to reach its intended enemy.

A pincer with jaws the length of a forearm reached for Garric over the wall of shields. He brought his long sword in an overhead arc, his left hand on the pommel to add strength to his right arm. His blade crunched through chitin, severing the pincer's hooked upper jaw. The muscle within was bright yellow.

The scorpion's weight hit the human line. Garric, off-balance from the sword stroke, lost his footing when the soldiers ahead staggered backward. He fell onto the ice, holding his dripping sword straight up. All he could see was bulging calf muscles and the metal-studded leather kilts of men slashing at a horrific enemy.

A spear flew overhead. Garric wasn't in a position—literally—to say it was a bad idea, though by the Shepherd! it *seemed* like a bad one.

The struggle with the scorpion ended. Garric regained his feet as fresh troops from the rear ranks pushed forward to take the place of the men who'd killed the creature. Swords had chopped off the scorpion's pincers and four pairs of legs, then repeatedly driven through the body's hard pink casing.

The crystal head was shattered. There was no sign of the two miniature figures Garric had glimpsed.

The mob of beasts had become a pile of corpses, more untidy even than the wrack of battle usually was. Blood and ichor of a score of shades stained both the twitching bodies and the equipment of the troops who'd cut them to bits.

There'd been human casualties too, some of them fatal even though the troops wore heavy armor. Lord Mayne was dead, his throat torn out by the barbels of a creature that looked like a catfish on six legs. A Blood Eagle captain had taken the legate's place, reforming the front ranks with men whose swords hadn't been dulled by battle.

"Here sir, we'll get you up there!" growled one of the noncoms who'd flanked Garric a moment before. He grabbed Garric firmly by the left biceps and pulled him forward.

"Make way for his highness, you bloody fools!" shouted his fellow, using his spearbutt as a baton to separate the men in the rank ahead. The veterans had not only survived, they'd retrieved spears from the slaughtered monsters. The irons were straight though smeared with purple ichor. The two seemed to have adopted Garric.

"Not the worst thing that could happen to a commander, lad," said Carus. Because the ghost lacked a physical presence he hadn't felt the dizzy wave of exhaustion that'd swept over Garric, but a lifetime of remembered battles left his image as tense as Garric had ever seen him. *"Nothing against your Blood Eagles, but soldiers who've gotten as old as those fellows have in the front ranks know something more than about being brave."*

The royal army was advancing again; the corridor ahead was empty. Soldiers grunted as they speared monstrous bodies that already looked dead. These men were veterans, and they knew a quick thrust was the cheapest insurance there was.

Garric squirmed through the second rank. "Captain—" he said.

"Degtel," said Carus, filling in the name that Garric must've heard but hadn't remembered.

"—Degtel," Garric continued, as smoothly as if the name had been on the tip of his tongue. Carus chuckled in his mind. "We'll proceed, following the line of light. Keep the pace down to that of a route march as you've been doing. Hurrying's likely to get us somewhere we want to avoid."

They'd reached a rotunda from which seven corridors branched. The walls quivered: some with crimson light, others with azure. Tenoctris's gleaming guide bent to follow a red one. Garric knew he should be glad of any illumination, but his heart would've preferred blackness to this wizardlight.

"May I ask your highness where we *do* want to go?" Degtel asked over his shoulder. He was a young man, quite handsome, and—judging by the quality of the gold inlays on his black armor—from a very wealthy family.

There were—there seemed to be—shapes frozen into the walls, and the floor was so clear that Garric could see things moving beneath the ice. Once the movement was accompanied by a flash of teeth, any of which was as long as a man.

"We're going to the place Lady Tenoctris's art tells us will bring an end to the business," Garric said. He grinned at a sort of humor he wouldn't've have known if he didn't share his mind with a warrior like Carus. "Or to Hell, of course, if we get there first."

Degtel, as surely a warrior as the ancient king, barked laughter.

"If it's Hell," said the veteran on Garric's right, "then we'll bring an escort with us like the Sister never saw before!"

"*That's* the bloody truth!" agreed his partner on the left.

Garric laughed with the others. There were no longer any questions or vexed decisions. The task was quite simple, and the only doubt was whether their swordarms were strong enough to accomplish it.

Something far down the corridor was coming toward them. *Quite simple . . .*

The direction of *down* changed more times than Cashel could count. Light flickered the way lightning stutters between cloud tops instead of crossing in a single bolt. Cashel didn't move, so he kept his balance when the shifting stopped.

The whirlpool of wizardlight vanished and with it the sensation of movement. Cashel's feet were planted on firm ground—a little damp, mossy rather than grass-covered. He was standing under a pear tree in a garden; part of the Count's palace, he guessed, though not a part he'd seen before. There were any number of soldiers coming through the door in the building, but a pair of cavalry officers from Lord Waldron's staff were there to keep the newcomers from crowding in too fast.

Cashel must've just popped out of the air so far as the soldiers tramping past were concerned, but nobody said anything or even looked surprised. As a matter of fact, they didn't really look *at* him, even the men whose eyes were turned in his direction.

The line coming out of the palace led to a narrow stone table at the back wall of the garden. Behind it, mostly where the brick wall ought to be, was a shimmering purple oval. Soldiers climbed steps made from lengths of pillars set on end, then jumped through the disk of light. An officer in high boots stood at the base of the steps, using his sword like a baton to keep men from rushing up before the fellow ahead was through the disk.

There were three steps: a section of column not much thicker than Cashel's thigh; a taller section that was also about twice as big around; and another of the little columns set on top of another big one. They didn't have a proper foundation, so a Blood Eagle noncom squatted beside the double step to brace it.

Beside the table lay a dead man, opened up like a fish for frying. There was blood all over the stone and the ground around it, which explained why the corpse's skin had the pale yellow look of beeswax. Cashel hoped he'd deserved it; but he didn't know what you'd have to do to deserve what happened to *that* fellow.

"What's happening?" Cashel said to a man in line. The fellow kept shuffling forward, so Cashel walked along with him. "Where're you going?"

"We're going to Hell to fight demons," the soldier muttered. He didn't look up as he spoke. "Some demon grabbed

Prince Garric and the whole army's supposed to go get him back. That's what *I* heard, anyhow."

"We're going to Hell, *that's* no rumor!" said the man ahead over his shoulder. "Look at that thing we're supposed to jump through! It's wizard work!"

"Just sitting down to dinner and the trumpet sounds," said the first man. "We don't even get to die on a full stomach. May the Sister take all wizards!"

"Well, there's some good ones," Cashel said mildly. He frowned. "One good one, anyhow."

He'd met his share of wizards since Tenoctris washed ashore in Barca's Hamlet, but even if pushed he couldn't think of another that he'd really call "good." There's been no few *powerful* wizards, which was a different thing; and the Sister was welcome to every one of them so far as Cashel was concerned.

He and the two soldiers were nearing the base of the steps up to the purple disk. Neither man seemed frightened, for all they said they expected to die. They weren't happy, but they kept shuffling forward as fast as the line allowed. The man Cashel'd started talking to snugged up a buckle on his breastplate that he'd missed in his hasty departure from camp.

Cashel nodded in understanding. He guessed that was what he looked like when he went out to the byre in a rainstorm to calm the sheep. He knew he'd be cold and miserable, and the folks who owned the flock wouldn't bother to thank him. It was his job, though, and somebody had to do it.

"I think the sheep appreciate it," Cashel said aloud. The soldiers were lost again in their thoughts. They probably didn't hear what he said, and if they had they wouldn't have understood it.

"Hold it!" snapped the officer at the base of the steps as the first of the two soldiers who'd been talking with Cashel started up. He stuck his long sword out. The man ahead was still climbing.

"I'll go up ahead of them, sir," Cashel said politely to the officer. He wished he'd had room to give his staff a trial spin, but this garden with the trees and all the soldiers in it was just too tight for that. "I'm a friend of Garric's."

Cashel put his foot on the bottom step. The officer's face went red. He grabbed the throat of Cashel's tunic with his left hand and raised his sword. "You peasant scum!" he shouted. "You'll get out of here now or I'll feed you to the dogs in pieces!"

"Lord Artis!" said the Blood Eagle who'd been chocking the steps. He straightened, holding his hands up toward the staff officer. His blackened-bronze helmet had its crest crosswise instead of front and back; that meant he had some rank also, though Cashel had never tried to keep that sort of thing straight. "He really is a friend of his highness! That's Lord Cashel!"

"I don't care if he's King Valence the Third!" the officer shouted. "Civilians haven't any business in this affair!"

"Garric's friends do, though," said Cashel in a growl that he could barely understand himself. He hadn't realized how angry he was that something'd happened to Garric while he was off in a place where he rightly didn't have any business.

The officer was nervous too and probably angry that orders kept him back here and not up with the fighting. At another time Cashel might've sympathized with him.

But not now.

Cashel rapped the officer's right hand with his quarterstaff; the man shouted and dropped his sword. Cashel grabbed him by the throat and took a step toward the back wall. The fellow'd lost his grip on Cashel's tunic when the staff numbed his other hand; his face, red to start with, bulged and turned purple.

Cashel cocked his right arm, then straightened it in something between pushing and throwing. The officer flew over the brick wall. It wasn't a clean toss—his heels caught on the coping and flipped him into what would probably be a complete somersault when he landed on the other side—but it was enough to get the fellow out of Cashel's way.

"I'm going to find Garric now," Cashel said to the Blood Eagle in a husky voice. He was breathing hard.

"So are the rest of us, milord," said the Blood Eagle, gesturing toward the lens of purple light. "Just don't hold the line up, if you please."

"Right," said Cashel. He climbed the steps deliberately,

planting his feet with care because he knew that somebody with his weight'd push the steps over if he came down skew. With the staff angled in front of him, he stepped into the disk.

"Bloody wizard's work!" muttered the soldier following on his heels.

"Master Alfdan's gone!" cried Werbeg, a big man who'd been a wine merchant before She came. "What'll we do! We can't run!"

"We'll fight, of course," said Sharina, raising her voice to be heard though she didn't shout. "Line up to either side of me. I've got the axe and I'll, I'll try . . ."

Werbeg's panic disgusted Sharina. She was very frightened. Her legs shook. She watched the portal open to spew hellspawn in the certainty that she was about to die; but she was human and this was evil, so *of course* she'd fight.

"Oh, many more lives!" Beard chortled. "Rivers of blood for Beard to drink, blood and lives and hot, steaming brains!"

The men had wadded a buffalo robe into a plug for the hole by which they'd entered the cavern; wind-swirled ice crystals had set it in place. There was probably ice inches thick over it now. They could break it clear, but not instantly, and what kind of escape would the glacial desert of the surface provide?

Neal looked around the company, holding an arrow between two fingers to his bow's handgrip. He seemed to have recovered from his shock at losing Alfdan. "You other archers," he said in a commanding voice. "Nock an arrow and get ready. Dalin, your bow's not strung! String it, man! Do you want to die?"

The rim of violet light rotated slowly like a bit boring through wood. The center of the circle remained gray, but it was becoming paler and increasingly translucent even as the edge solidified into what looked like shimmering purple metal.

Old Burness knelt and started whimpering. He had a hunting spear with a broad engraved head and a crossbar below it to keep a maddened boar from running his body up the shaft and gutting the man who'd speared him. Even rusty it was an effective weapon—but not in Burness's hands.

Neal must've thought the same thing. He caught Sharina's eye, then snapped, "Franca, trade that spear you've got with Burness. Quick now!"

Franca's spear was actually the head and two feet of shaft from a weapon broken in the fight with the fauns. The youth looked startled. He started toward Burness, then paused in doubt.

"Burness!" Neal said. "Now! Give your spear to somebody who'll use it!"

"Franca, take it," Sharina said. "I need you by me."

In her heart she didn't feel she needed anything: she was about to die, and there wasn't room for any other awareness. Franca hesitated no longer; he snatched away the boar spear and pressed the stub shaft of his own into Burness's hand. The older man stood up, hugging the exiguous weapon. He continued to sniffle, but at least he looked willing to defend himself.

The center of the disk of light had become soap-bubble thin. Figures waited beyond it, some of them beasts and the others bestial at least from the distortion.

The membrane vanished as though it never was. "Kill!" screamed Sharina as she lunged forward. She hadn't had the least intention of giving that battle cry until she and the moment merged.

A thing with the forequarters of a lion and lizard haunches leaped to meet her. It wore iron gauntlets whose tips were knives.

"Kill!" cried Beard and Sharina together, and their mutual stroke split the creature's flat skull like an eggshell. It arched its back as violently as a catapult releasing, lifting Sharina into the air. An arrow from behind her grazed her left calf, then vanished down the gullet of the froglike creature waiting with its huge jaws open. That was probably chance, but it was a lucky chance for her. . . .

Sharina came down in the midst of monsters. She wouldn't have been able to stand upright were it not for the crowd of enemies. She swung—*Beard* swung; the steel killer's own volition guided it—right and left. The edge ripped apart an octopus on human legs, and the axe in recovering spiked the temple of a faun like the ones who'd attacked Alfdan's band on the shore of Barca's Hamlet.

In the space cleared by the falling monsters, Sharina spun widdershins on the balls of her feet, using Beard's narrow blade like a scythe. There was a shower of sparks as the axe sheared through scales, fangs, and the iron carapace of a creature that looked like a giant helmet walking on crabs' legs. She felt no resistance to the blow. Blood and ichor gouted as monsters collapsed or fell apart.

Beard laughed like a demon. The axe *was* a demon, as horrible and far more deadly than the thing with a hedgehog's face and hands like balls of needles that he beheaded at the end of his circular sweep. Beard was *her* demon for now, and at this juncture she'd willingly take him against all the saints who ever lived.

"Save the mistress!" cried Franca in a voice as squeaky as a six-year-old's. He rammed his boar spear into the throat of a snake crawling on hundreds of tiny legs as it struck at Sharina. The creature writhed onto its back, fanged jaws working convulsively and spraying a mist of saffron poison.

Men and monsters battled behind Sharina. Toward her came a spider the size of a haywain. It walked on long glass legs; its body was either clear or dazzling with prismatic reflections, depending on the angle of the light. Its mandibles clicked against one another, dripping green venom from their tips.

"Blood and brains!" Beard shrieked. "Blood and—"

Sharina swung the axe high, using the full length of her arms and both hands on the helve. The reasoning part of her mind wondered if Beard wouldn't shatter on the glittering thing the way an ordinary axe would break if driven into a granite cliff.

Reason didn't control Sharina's actions at this instant. She was filled with the same bloodlust that Beard caroled as his bright steel face shed ropes of blood. As the spider reached for her with its forelegs, she smashed the axe into the middle of the creature's flat face.

A flash of crimson wizardlight pierced the ice in all directions. It illuminated both the sea bottom and cloud-huge bladders with dangling tentacles that swam through the sky above the ceiling of coruscance. The spider disintegrated into shimmering dust finer than jeweler's rouge.

The corridor ahead was empty save for a small man or woman sauntering toward them from a furlong away. Sharina looked behind her, at carnage. Half the band was down, dead or crippled, and all the survivors except her were bleeding.

Burness was dead; his blackened, bloated body was almost unrecognizable. He'd lost his grip on the half-spear in his final convulsions. The man-sized creature that killed him, a black-and-red-striped wasp walking on its hind legs, lay nearby. The short shaft stuck out of its faceted right eye.

Scoggin and Franca were both alive, though the older man had been stabbed or bitten through the left shoulder. Franca'd packed the wound with a portion of Burness's silk sash and was wrapping it with the rest of the sash to hold the wad in. The youth showed a deft hand for basic wound dressing.

Sharina reached down to rub the inside of her right calf, then looked at what she was doing and giggled. She was bleeding after all, though not badly. The arrow'd broken the skin and the cut itched like fury.

Her giggle became a loud chuckle. If the wound were worse—if the arrow'd smashed a bone, say—she'd have been in shock and wouldn't feel any discomfort.

"What do we do now, mistress?" Neal asked. Blood matted the left side of his scalp, but his eyes focused and his voice was firm. Instead of his bow he held a sledge hammer, its shaft forged from the same piece of iron as the head. Sharina hadn't seen the weapon before; one of the slaughtered monsters must have carried it.

"We'll continue up this corridor," Sharina said, speaking firmly to give the impression she knew what she was doing. Though in a manner of speaking, she *did* know: either they went on or they went back, and *back* meant an ice desert where the only life was hostile to men. "I think we'd better get going at once, before She sends something else against us."

"She's already sent something, mistress," said Beard in a dreamy, sated voice. "See him coming? His name's Tanus."

Sharina turned again to the figure she'd discounted in the

immediate aftermath of the battle. Tanus was now within fifty feet, a pale youth with short blond hair and a supercilious grin.

Sharina's eyes narrowed. She couldn't be sure of *how* close Tanus was because the tabard he wore over his tunics was woven in a pattern that didn't allow her eyes to focus. In his right hand was a curved knife with a silvery blade. It looked like a ceremonial tool, but the blood smearing it was so fresh that it still dripped.

"You're one of Count Lascarg's children, aren't you?" Sharina said. She recalled the face, but without Beard's identification she'd have had to guess whether the androgynous features were male or female. "What are you doing here?"

"I'm here to kill you," Tanus said in a thin, childish voice. "I'm going to kill you all."

"Tell the Sister that!" said Werbeg on a rising intonation. He took two steps forward and flung his javelin at Tanus's chest with all his strength. When the missile left his hand the point was almost in contact with the youth. It missed, clattering down the ice corridor.

Tanus laughed. He slashed at Werbeg, cutting his throat in the middle of a scream of terror.

Neal snarled and brought the hammer around in a horizontal stroke that should have torn Tanus in half. The force of the blow saved Neal's life by jerking him to the side when the sledge didn't connect. The youth's knife opened the skin over his back ribs instead of gutting him.

Sharina moved without thinking, swinging Beard high. Tanus faced her with an expression of ecstasy. She saw his moon-bladed knife sliding toward her belly. The axe twisted in her hands, keen edge slanting away from the grinning face of the youth who was about to kill her.

The thunk! of contact surprised her. Beard had split the youth's skull down to the bridge of his nose.

Sharina waggled the helve in a reflex she'd learned since she came to this world. The axe came free, slobbering joyfully. Tanus crumpled to his knees and fell backward. When his tabard rucked up, she could see him clearly; but not until then.

"Oh, it's been a long time since Beard fed on wizard

brains!" the axe said. "Oh, mistress, you're so good to Beard!"

Sharina felt a wash of dizziness as if her mind were a flag in the breeze. The things that'd just happened didn't touch her—now. But they would. She'd done things before that came back to her in the third watch of the night, when dawn was a distant hope and past horrors ruled the darkness.

A slim, blond youth was dead and she'd killed him. She didn't regret what she'd done, but she regretted very much what she'd had to do.

"Lady, may the soul of Tanus find peace in You," she whispered. "And may the souls of those who kill in Your name find peace as well."

"Mistress?" said Neal, his face contorted with pain as Franca bandaged his shallow wound. "Down there, the way the, this one—"

His boot spurned Tanus's body; it was already rigid because of the way Beard had split the youth's brain.

"—came at us. There's more people."

Sharina looked up. She squinted, but even so she couldn't tell more than that there were figures. They didn't seem far away, but the rippling azure light within the walls of this corridor distorted vision.

"All right," Sharina said, slanting Beard's helve over her shoulder for the time being. Her arms were tired, her soul was tired, but she knew the axe would be ready to strike no matter how she carried him. "We'll deal with them next."

Some of Beard's personality was entering hers. For the present, that was desirable—and she no longer believed in a personal future.

Sharina started forward, resigned to death but unconcerned about it. She and her demon companion had more strokes to give the forces of Evil before that happened.

Roaring blue wizardlight left Ilna blind and deaf, but she could still feel. The winged men's fingers were short but as strong as whalebone; they held her arms like crabs' pincers, hard enough to cut the skin. Then the creatures released her and she fell.

She threw out her hands to catch herself, wondering as she did whether the Rua had dropped her into the pool of boiling sulfur or if there was a worse place than that. At this instant Ilna couldn't imagine a more unpleasant death than the sulfur, but she'd seen enough of the world to know that it could always get worse.

The globe of blue light surrounding her sucked in and vanished. Her feet landed inches below, on bare rock at the edge of a dead volcano. The slope stretched down before her, its red-brown surface pitted and gullied by the rain. The shallow sea ran up on the shore and spewed foam. The water was the ultramarine hue of yarn dyed with eggplant peel.

Chalcus dropped beside her, his sword lifted and his left arm thrown back for balance. He crouched, sweeping his head right and left, taking in all his surroundings.

The Rua who'd dragged Ilna through the topaz lens hovered just beyond the rim of the cliff, their translucent vans bowed to catch the updraft. Chalcus thrust at the nearer of the pair; she canted her wings a trifle and ballooned up beyond reach of the curved sword.

"We are allies, Ilna os-Kenset!" cried her mate. His voice was squeaky and piercing, but perfectly understandable even over the moan of the wind.

Hundreds of the winged men soared and wheeled in the sky overhead, some of them so high that the wispy clouds blurred their shrunken outlines. Ilna looked behind her. The cone's outer slope was a harsh cliff only spotted with vegetation, but grass and gnarled shrubs with gray leaves covered the far side of the crater's sheltered interior.

"Take us back to where we belong, then!" Ilna said. She grimaced to hear the words, then quickly corrected herself with, "Take us back to where we were."

She knew by now that she didn't belong anywhere. This windswept cliff hadn't much to recommend it, but considered by itself it was an improvement on Gaur's stinking dungeon.

"We will return you to your world, sister," said the female Rua, sliding sideways through the air so that she hung closer to Ilna but remained well beyond reach of Chalcus's blade. "But first we must talk."

"The only right you have to ask that is that we're completely in your power, not so?" said Chalcus in a ringing voice.

He laughed and sheathed his sword in a curving gesture as graceful as a fish leaping, then went on, "Which is a right I've asserted too often myself to deny to another. If Mistress Ilna will bear with me, I'm interested to hear what you winged folk have to say."

"All right," said Ilna. "I don't mind having the smell of Gaur's den washed out of my nose. But we have business in the place we came from."

She pointed to the ground beside her. "Come," she said. "Land. You may be comfortable fluttering out there, but I'm not comfortable watching you. And besides, I want to get out of this wind!"

The noose that served Ilna also as a sash had burned in a pool of sulfur with Gaur. The updraft would lift her tunics completely over her head if she didn't fight them down. In addition to distracting her, the loss of dignity made Ilna furious—the more so because she realized how absurd the concern was under the circumstances.

The Rua landed in perfect concert, the male on the other side of Chalcus and the female beside Ilna. With their wings folded to their sides they looked like walking skeletons, though they were nearly the height of the human pair.

"You brought us here to talk," Ilna said, backing from the cliff edge and smoothing her tunics. Three steps toward the interior of the crater there was still wind, but it was no longer an uprushing torrent. "Talk then."

She supposed she sounded curt and unfriendly, but she'd never been good at pretense. The Rua had brought her here for their own reasons. Those might be perfectly good reasons, but the fact didn't require that Ilna pretend an affection for the winged men that she didn't feel.

"You killed the wizard Gaur, mistress," the female said. "He was your enemy and our enemy as well. Will you now kill Her? She is a greater enemy to your world and our world and all worlds of the cosmos!"

"Who do you mean by Her?" Ilna said. She was on edge both from fatigue and the emotions seething through her during the struggle with the wolfman. "If you can't make sense, then send us back!"

She deliberately turned and walked toward the opposite slope to look into the crater. When she looked down at a slant the inner wall looked as green as a meadow, though Ilna knew that the vegetation was actually quite sparse. It grew only where dirt collected in pockets of the rock. There were beehive-shaped dwellings with windows of some translucent material in walls of shaped stone, but there were no fields or grazing animals. This would be good country for goats. . . .

"She is a great wizard, mistress," said the male Rua. "Her world is freezing because of the power She drains from it with her wizardry."

"She is reaching into our world and yours, mistress," said the female. "She will destroy both worlds and destroy all worlds, unless you stop Her."

Ilna turned to them again, scowling in frustration. "But why are you telling me this?" she snapped. "You're the wizards. I suppose we'll help—I'll help, that is—"

"We both will help as we can, indeed," said Chalcus with a little bow to the female. The Rua were almost hairless; the female's breasts were flat, distinguishable only because they softened the ridges of the flight muscles so prominent on the male. "But I think that Mistress Ilna will be far the greater help; and the pair of you think so as well."

"We are wizards, yes," the male chirped in perfectly formed syllables. "But we could not overcome Gaur. How could we hope to overcome Her?"

"She moved the shoals where the belemnites grow from our world to yours, mistress," continued the female, "to bring wealth to her disciple Gaur. Without the shell, the wings of our kits—"

Both Rua spread their wings. They unfolded like fans, narrow strips of skin as fine as sea foam alternating with struts of denser material that shimmered like nacre in the sunlight. Ilna remembered the belemnites' similar rainbow hues.

"—do not harden."

"We could not wrest our shoals back from Her grip," said the male. As he spoke, his struts clicked together in se-

quence, folding and stretching the skin between each pair.
Ilna nodded in appreciation of the muscular control required to do that. "We could only open a gateway to your
world so we could continue to hunt the shell our kits must
have. And for our strength, even holding the gateway open
was a struggle."

"Dear heart . . . ?" said Chalcus. Instead of pointing, he
nodded outward. The Rua looked toward the sea also, turning their heads without moving their torsos. Ilna could understand the importance of so flexible a neck to a flying
creature, but it was disconcerting to watch.

She sniffed in irritation at herself and let her eyes follow
the line of Chalcus's gaze to a monster undulating through
the sea. Only the top of its great head showed above the surface, but because the pale water was so clear she could see
the whole line of the creature's snakelike body. It was as
long as a warship. When it turned its flat head toward the
land and opened its jaws, Ilna could see individual teeth.

"The thing that attacked Garric's ship," she said. "The
whale."

"She sent that creature's mate to your world to aid minions of Hers," the male Rua said.

"Not Gaur but others," added the female. "Your enemies
but not ours, save that all who serve Her are the enemies of
all who do not."

"It seems, dear heart," said Chalcus with a lifted eyebrow, "that whoever She may be, She's brought us into this
fight."

Ilna sniffed. "And you were going to walk away from it
otherwise?" she said coldly.

"Aye, you have me there, my love," Chalcus said, smiling
in wicked merriment. "It's not my habit to walk away from
fights, that is so."

"No," said Ilna crisply. "Nor is it mine."

She looked from one Rua to the other. "What needs to be
done to . . . ?"

She turned her palms up. "To overcome her, you say. To
kill Her, I suppose."

"We do not know," said the male. "But we have watched
you, mistress."

"We could not overcome Gaur," said the female, "but we saw you slay him."

Ilna grimaced. "From what you say, Gaur's mistress will be a worse knot to untangle," she said. "And Gaur wasn't an easy one."

She shrugged. "Still, we said we'll do what we can. How do we reach Her?"

"We will open a gateway for you, mistress," said the Rua together. They turned and plunged off the cliff edge, rising on the updraft like dandelion seeds.

Ilna watched, frowning in puzzlement as the Rua spiraled to join their kin in the high skies. The air before her took on a faint opalescence in the same shape as the mirror of blue topaz in Gaur's den.

"Ah!" she said. "Chalcus, the pattern of their flight—all of them together? Do you see what they're weaving?"

"No, my heart," the sailor said in a tone as silvery as the *sring!* of his sword against the scabbard as he drew it. "But I think shortly there may be use for the things I *do* understand."

Chapter Twenty-two

The corridor ahead forked; for the seventh time, Garric thought, though he doubted he could recall the particular pattern of the branchings that'd get them out of this place by the portal they'd entered through. He supposed there was still a solid line of men behind him, marking the route better than the white pebbles of the folktale.

Carus grinned in his mind. Right, worrying about getting back could wait till they'd survived getting to where they were going.

Tenoctris's trail of light bent to the right, down the branch whose walls glowed red like those of the corridor Garric was in at present. In the middle distance the sullen crimson became a dot of purple.

"Prester?" he said to the noncom on his right; he'd learned the men's names as they marched together into frozen Hell. "How far do you guess we've come? It must be miles."

"That's Pont you want, your highness," Prester said. He leaned forward and called to his partner on Garric's left, "Pont! The Prince here wants t' know how far we come."

"Three thousan seven hunnert fiffee three," Pont said. "Paces. Four, five . . ."

"Got it, Pont," said Garric, breaking in on what was likely to be a very long sequence as Pont called out a number every time his right heel came down.

"Pont was in the engineering section back when he was a nugget," Prester explained with a proprietorial nod. "His job was route measurer. The habit's stuck with him all these years."

A thousand double paces equaled a mile, so they'd come three and three-quarters miles. Garric had no way of guessing how much farther they had to go. Maybe he should've made commissary arrangements before he went charging through that hole in the world. . . .

"Your highness, there's something in the tunnel ahead of us!" called the Blood Eagle who'd taken charge of the front rank. He pointed his spear forward.

"Right," said Garric, peering past the shields and helmets of the men ahead of him. He was taller than the pair directly in front, but they'd both slipped their horsehair crests into the slots on top of their helmets during the past half hour of uneventful march. Their care was commendable, but at the moment Garric wished he'd had a less-obstructed view. Not that what he saw was anything he looked forward to meeting.

There hadn't been any fighting since they'd killed the giant scorpion. Garric hadn't consciously expected that to be the last, but when he saw the creature ahead he realized that emotionally he'd hoped that everything would be peaceful. Now reality clattered toward him on more legs than he could count. He felt as though he'd been dropped into ice water.

"Your highness," said Lord Escot, turning to look back at Garric past the cheek piece of his silvered helmet. Escot was commander of the second regiment to enter this ice world.

He'd trotted up through the column to the front to take the place of Lord Mayne. "It's time for you to retire."

He was a landholder from Northern Ornifal, cut from the same cloth as Lord Waldron though thirty years younger. He wasn't an officer Garric had ever warmed to; so far as he could recall, Escot had never said a word about anything but horses save in response to a direct question.

"Aye, lad," agreed Carus in his mind. *"He's thick as two short planks. But he's here where he belongs, and how smart do you have to be to stand in the front rank in a business like this?"*

Point taken, agreed Garric. Aloud he said, "Carry on with your duties, milord. I will do the same—from here, where I can see what's going on."

"Oh, aye, lad," said Carus with a savage grin. *"And I suppose you'll take off your sword now and give it to one of the fellows who're fighting while we stand by and watch?"*

I've too much of your blood for that, thought Garric as he grinned in response to his ancient ancestor. Escot took the expression as meant for him and blinked in surprise. "Of course, as you say, your highness," he blurted and faced front again.

"Silly twit," said Prester in an undertone.

"He'll do to stop a spear, though," replied Pont. Apparently counting paces was so ingrained that it didn't interfere with him carrying on a conversation—or fighting, for that matter. "Bloody officer."

From the way the two noncoms talked, Garric decided they'd promoted *him* to line soldier . . . and that *was* a promotion, so far as Pont and Prester were concerned.

What had been a purple blur when Garric's column entered this corridor became a circular volume beneath a dome whose surface was ribbed for strength. Eight corridors merged in it, including the one the troops were in.

The rotunda was about thirty double paces across, and as best as Garric could tell in a quick glance the room's ceiling was the same height as the diameter. Threads of red and blue light twisted about one another at the core of the walls and of the piers framing the arched corridor mouths, turning the ice violet. The ice floor beneath must have been feet or even scores of feet thick, but again Garric saw monsters twisting in the phosphorescent water.

The creature coming down the corridor directly across the rotunda was more like a centipede than anything else Garric had seen, and more like a nightmare than anything alive. It had side-hinged mandibles and a chitinous maw whose interior was a mass of jagged plates rotating against one another like millstones.

The thin azure guideline passed through the monster. The only way to where Garric needed to go was by the same route: through the monster.

"Double time!" he shouted. He and his troops might be able to block the centipede before it got to the rotunda where each of its pincer-tipped legs was a deadly weapon.

"Charge!" cried Lord Escot, slanting his sword forward and breaking into a run. As Carus said, Escot was bright enough for his present position.

The troops were happy to run also. The ranks spread to either side as the column entered the rotunda where there was room. The clear floor was so hard that hobnails skidded instead of digging in. It was much like running on stone, because the extreme cold also meant the footing was dry and not nearly as slippery as ice normally would be.

The blended wizardlight had an oppressive weight. The huge room seemed dimmer than the corridors feeding it, though that was an illusion: Garric could see the men around him more clearly than he had before.

He could also see deep into the ice walls. The vast pillars supporting the dome were hollow. Within them were plants whose roots grew through the ice floor in broad nets to reach the sea beneath. Their twisted stems and the leaves spreading against the inner walls of their enclosures struck Garric with a pathos that he couldn't understand until he caught a glimpse of a flower that wasn't hidden by the foliage. It was shaped like the red mouth of a woman screaming, and the petals moved as he looked at them.

The center of the rotunda allowed Garric to look down all eight corridors. He had his sword out, but as much as he wanted to kill something to wipe the image of the plants from his mind he knew he needed to act as commander rather than swordsman for the time being. His men depended on him, and so did the kingdom.

"Hold up!" he shouted to his informal bodyguards. Prester and Pont obediently halted, facing back with their shields outthrust to fend away the troops pouring into the rotunda at a dead run. If the noncoms had an opinion about what Garric was doing, they kept it to themselves.

Glittering figures marched toward the rotunda down the second corridor to the left of Garric's column. They were too distant for him to see details beyond the fact that the walls' blue glow sparkled on scores of sharp points.

"Well, you didn't think they were going to send dancing girls to greet us, did you?" laughed Carus. *"Mind, I remember places where I lost more troops to what they caught from the women than I did to the spears of the men."*

A junior officer was running past. He was armed in Blaise fashion and affected flaring mustachios that he had to fill out with a fall because he was too young to grow proper ones himself.

"Ensign!" Garric said. He pointed to the startled youth, then the approaching enemy. "Yes, you! Take a hundred men and block that blue corridor. Don't go any distance down it, just far enough that you've got a little room to retreat without letting them into this rotunda."

"Sir?" said the ensign, gaping like a cod at a fishmonger's.

Swearing silently, Garric looked around for another officer in the rush of troops. Prester shouted, "Suter! Get your ass over here to his highness!"

A husky warrant officer trotting past—he must have been fifty if not older—turned in mid-stride. "Who do you think *you* are giving me orders, Prester?" he said.

"Prince Garric here wants you to help the young gentleman—" Prester nodded to the blinking ensign "—organize a company to block that tunnel there."

"Sister take me!" Suter said. He slapped his spear against his shield boss in salute to Garric. "Yes *sir,* your highness!"

Turning to the stream of troops, Suter stretched out his spear as a baffle and bellowed, "All right, soldiers! We got a job to do! Vedres, start'em down that corridor. I'll be up with you quick as I can. Sir—" to the ensign "—you just follow Vedres there and he'll put you right."

The ensign turned and jogged off with the file closer who was presumably named Vedres. The youth looked immeasurably relieved to be getting out of Prince Garric's presence.

"Silly twit," muttered Pont, eyeing the ensign's back. Suter was shunting the incoming stream of soldiers toward the corridor where Vedres formed them in ranks about a hundred feet down from the rotunda. The ensign—whatever his name was—struck a pose in the front rank, which was actually quite a useful thing to do. A young officer like that had no real purpose except to be brave and thereby to provide a spiritual anchor to the line soldiers who'd be doing the fighting.

"Yeah, but he'll serve to stop a spear," said Prester with a complacent smile. "And if that bunion Suter stops another one, well, that's cream with my strawberries."

Garric tried to swallow his smile. Then deciding that this was as good a place for humor as any in the world, he let his grin spread. When the noncoms grinned back at him, he laughed out loud while in his mind Carus laughed just as merrily.

Lord Escot and his troops met the centipede a short spearcast before the creature reached the rotunda. "Loose!" called the Blood Eagle in the front rank, his voice echoing over the crash of boots and the centipede's pincered feet.

The spears flew in a ragged volley, wobbling because they were thrown by running men. Even so most struck their target because the centipede's armored body nearly filled the tunnel. Some glanced off, but half-a-dozen missiles cracked the monster's headplate and penetrated deeply enough to dangle.

The centipede continued forward with the relentless certainty of water gushing through a pipe. The creature towered over the men as they charged home with drawn swords.

"We'll need to—" Garric said, his stomach suddenly knotting.

They'd have to meet the centipede in the rotunda and attack it from all sides, because it was obvious that no number of men could stop the creature in a head-on encounter. The casualties from that—the men torn to pieces by the pincers and flung across the rotunda—would be in the hundreds.

"Garric!" Liane called from behind him.

Garric spun, his face going coldly blank to hide the horror in his heart. He'd known that one of those bodies the centipede mangled might be his, but that was part of his job. Liane would be back where she and Tenoctris could return through the portal if things went disastrously wrong. She'd be *safe*.

But instead here she was, running toward him at the head of a forest of pikes. "I brought a company of the phalanx!" she explained, gasping for breath as she clasped arms with him. "The s-soldiers made an aisle for me so that I could get them through. I thought you might need them!"

"By the Shepherd! we do," Garric said. He glanced over exactly what Liane had brought him.

Master Ortron, commander of half the phalanx, stood facing the other way as he formed his men into ranks in the rotunda. Ortron was a commoner who knew that the officers and men of the older regiments looked down on his men. The pikemen doubled as oarsmen in the fleet, and they'd been recruited from farm laborers and the urban poor instead of the yeoman farmers who made up the heavy infantry.

Ortron and the men under him were convinced that their phalanx could cut the heart out of any army in the Isles; and on the proper terrain, they were right. This might be an even better opportunity to test the effectiveness of their twenty-foot pikes than against human enemies.

"Ortron," Garric shouted, "form them by sections—" blocks of nominally a hundred men, eight ranks deep "—and take over from the infantry that's fighting the centipede, the bug over there!"

The passages of this ice maze were higher than those of any palace Garric had seen in his own world, but even so the pikes must've been a close fit when troops jogged down the corridors carrying them upright. Just moving with the long weapons took a great deal of training and coordination; using them effectively in battle was even more difficult. But a fully trained phalanx was as deadly a weapon as anything under the sun—and perhaps as deadly as anything in this icy hellworld as well.

Garric gestured toward the target he'd set Ortron. As he did so he saw his aide Lord Lerdain burst from the crowd of soldiers. The boy was flushed and his cuirass wasn't properly buckled; he must have been in his quarters asleep when all this broke open.

"Your highness!" Lerdain cried. "I got here as—"

"Yes," interrupted Garric. He pointed to the corridor where swords flashed in the wizardlight as men hacked at the centipede. "Tell Lord Escot or whoever's in charge now—"

Whoever's still alive now.

"—to clear out of the way and give the phalanx their chance."

Lerdain turned without replying and shoved into the crowd battling the centipede. "Prince Garric's orders!" he bawled. "Make way for the pikes! Make way or die like fools with pike points in your backs!"

Lerdain's father was the autocrat of one of the two—with Sandrakkan—most powerful islands in the kingdom. Another fifteen-year-old might've lacked the self-confidence to deliver Garric's message in a fashion that battling soldiers might listen to, but not Lord Lerdain.

Ortron shouted an order; his men lowered their pikes. The weapons of the first three ranks were horizontal, a hedge of points. The shafts of the remaining five ranks slanted up at the increasing angles necessitated by the tight formation. If the men in front fell or their pikes were broken, those in the rear would step forward to replace them.

"Advance!" Ortron ordered, stepping to the side to watch the dress of the ranks as his men stepped off on their left feet. He walked along, frowning critically as they advanced.

To look at him, Ortron was completely oblivious of the huge monster rippling in his direction . . . and the impression was probably true: the centipede was the business of Ortron's men; *his* business was with the men themselves.

"What about Tenoctris?" Garric asked Liane, trying to hide his frown. The line of light they were following shone thin but strong as it vanished into the centipede's armored head, but if the old wizard was left to her own devices as hundreds of armored men rushed past in tight quarters, an accident was almost inevitable.

"A squad leader from the Blood Eagles wrenched his knee fighting the Hunters when we arrived," Liane said, having gotten her breath back in the past moments. "He's helping Tenoctris. He's not afraid of what she does because his grandmother worked spells. And I had to lead the pikemen—the troops in the corridor would have made way for another soldier."

Garric grinned and gave her shoulder a squeeze. Liane was right. Of course.

For the most part, the regular infantry battling the centipede ignored Lerdain's orders; they were focused on the monster whose advance was slowed more by the time it took to devour the men it killed than anything the survivors were able to do with their swords. They'd have ignored Garric himself if he'd thrown himself among them. He couldn't have done that unless he'd been willing to let the rest of the chaos take care of itself . . . which it would surely have done, and taken care of all hope for the Kingdom besides.

Ortron barked an order. "Ho!" bellowed the men of the phalanx as they struck home, their points rising slightly to clear the struggling infantry. The shout wasn't as effective from only a hundred or so men as it would've been with the whole eight thousand, but the rotunda's echoing dome gave it a respectable presence.

The centipede might've been deaf for all Garric knew, but it wasn't immune to the crunching impact of a dozen pike points. The giant creature lurched upward, raising its head and several body segments in the air. "Ho!" shouted the phalanx as the section's right feet stamped forward in perfect unison, driving the pikes deeper.

The breastplates of the men in each rank slammed against the backplates of the men directly ahead. Instead of fighting as a hundred soldiers, the phalanx was a single unit with sharp steel fangs. Their combined weight and the thrust of all their powerful legs together stabbed the pike points into the centipede.

The pikes were of close-grained ash or hickory. Even so the strain bowed, then snapped, several of them. The men whose shafts had broken continued to jab the splintered ends at the monster. The ragged wood couldn't penetrate undamaged armor, but when it lodged in the thinner, flexible fabric covering the joints it sometimes gouged its way into the flesh beneath.

The infantry who'd been trapped between the centipede and the multiple bulk of the phalanx had to duck or be thrown to the floor when the two collided. Now that the centipede's forequarters had lifted, they either stood or scuttled forward under the long body to hack at its leg joints.

Lord Escot had lost his helmet. His long red hair swirled with the violence of the strokes as his long sword hacked forehand and backhand. "Escomann and Ornifal!" he cried in a high tenor voice. "Escomann over all!"

Something between a smile and a grimace quirked Garric's lips. It wasn't the most satisfactory battle cry from the kingdom's viewpoint, but under the circumstances he guessed he'd allow the Ornifal noble his whims.

Pont and Prester must've thought much the same thing. "Huh!" said Prester, his eyes narrowing as he watched Lord Escot. "He's still a silly twit, but . . ."

"Yeah," agreed his mate. "If I had him for two weeks in my section, I might be able to make something out of him regardless."

Despite the size of the rotunda, it'd begun filling with troops when the men in the lead couldn't advance any farther because the centipede blocked the way. Garric no longer had unobstructed vision down the other corridors. If the route wasn't cleared quickly—and he didn't see how it could be, since even dead the centipede's corpse would fill half the corridor—the crush of men would become dangerous.

If only there were something he could stand on to—

"Prester!" he said aloud. "Can you lift me onto your shoulders? I'll yell to the men at the entrance corridor to halt in place. Maybe they'll obey if they can see me."

"I'll lift you, Garric," said a familiar voice. There, pushing through the soldiers as though they were blades of oats in a field, was the massive form of Cashel or-Kenset.

And never more welcome!

Cashel didn't mind the press of men the way he had when he'd first entered a big city, though that hadn't been so very long ago. He'd found if he just pretended all the people were sheep, it was the same as shearing time in the spring. He'd always liked shearing time. Of course sheep didn't wave swords and spears as they milled about.

"Cashel!" Garric cried. From a distance you'd never take this nobleman in gilt and silvered armor for the boy Cashel'd grown up with in Barca's Hamlet, but when he smiled— Cashel smiled in response—*that* was Garric. "Right, I'll stand on your shoulders. Just like old times!"

Cashel laid his staff crosswise in front of him, his arms slanting down. There wasn't room for him to do that without bumping people out of the way, so he bumped them out of the way.

A glittering officer pitched forward when the staff whacked him in the small of the back; he bleated angrily and turned. One of the pair of old soldiers standing with Garric poked a spearbutt at the fellow's face and said, "Mind what you say to the Prince here, cap'n!"

The officer looked like he still might've argued the matter, but Liane stepped in front of him. "Do you dare jostle his highness, my man?" she said in a voice as cold as the floor underfoot. *That* seemed to take care of the problem.

Garric set his right boot on the staff like it was a fence rail. As he pushed off with his left leg Cashel lifted his arms, bringing his friend's weight up so that Garric just stepped over, one foot on either of Cashel's shoulders.

Holding firm as a statue, Cashel turned his staff vertical and clashed the ferrule down on the ice. With three points to brace him, he figured he could stand here even if he had to support the ceiling instead of just Garric. The thought made him smile.

One of the old soldiers rubbed his chin with the knuckles of the hand gripping his spear. "They grow many more your size back where you come from, lad?" he asked.

"They grow better than that," Cashel said, letting his smile spread in pride. "They grew Garric in Barca's Hamlet too!"

"Lord Menzis!" Garric shouted. Through a megaphone of his hands, Cashel supposed, though standing underneath his friend and facing the other way there wasn't any way he could tell for sure. "Halt the flow for the moment! Send word back to hold in place!"

Herding sheep gave you good lungs, not that sheep were much more likely to heed you than trees were. Shouting at least made you feel like you were doing something as you pounded across the meadow hoping to reach the ewe that'd mire herself sure if she took one more step into the marsh. . . .

Cashel had a pretty good view of what was happening down the tunnel where a huge centipede was trying to bull through a solid mass of pikemen. *Had been trying,* rather than *was,* because by now the monster writhed like a worm on a hook. Any number of hooks, in fact, because there were more pikes punched through its yellow armor than Cashel could count on both hands.

The men kept shoving forward. By now the folks in the front rank, those whose pikes hadn't broken anyhow, must've had their points halfway into the creature's vitals. It was either trying to escape or else it was just curling up to die the way centipedes of the usual size did.

"Cashel, turn left!" Garric said, sharply but not in a bellow meant to be heard across the huge domed room. "I'm going to shift some men down the other corridors to give us some room in here."

Cashel obediently shuffled partway around, careful to keep his shoulders level. He was pretty sure that Garric could balance even if the fellow under him broke into a dead run, but that wasn't a reason for Cashel to do his own job badly.

The adjustment put Cashel looking down one of the blue tunnels while Garric shouted to an officer on the other side of the room. There was fighting going on in that tunnel too, and—Cashel frowned—it didn't look like it was going very well. Plenty of soldiers were trying to crowd in, but the sounds coming out of the tunnel were screams, not battle cries. Cashel couldn't see what they were fighting because it didn't tower over the soldiers the way the centipede did, but besides the screams he could hear an off-key clinking/clattering. It wasn't quite right for either metal or stone but seemed a bit of both.

"Garric?" he said, making sure his friend was going to hear him. He'd herded far more sheep than Garric had. "You'd better look at this on my—"

He felt Garric's weight shift as he twisted to look over his shoulder.

"—side," Cashel went on. "I'm turning some more."

A fellow squeezed out of the crowd at the tunnel mouth and staggered toward Garric. He was an officer—a nobleman, anyway, and that meant an officer—because his breastplate was molded with a design of people and gods. The metal, bronze under the gilding, had been slashed in strips, deep enough that blood dribbled out of the cuts. The officer, just a boy really, had lost his sword and his helmet besides.

"Steady!" called Garric. He jumped down, landing squarely. Cashel put out the hand that wasn't on his quarterstaff to brace his friend, but Garric didn't need the help.

"Your highness!" the boy bleated. "We can't stop them! They're not alive, they're just ice, and our swords only chip them without doing any harm! They'll kill us all if we don't get away!"

"Do we have hammers?" Garric said. "Maybe the men can use their shields for clubs. We can't cut ice, but if we break it up—"

"I'll see what I can do, Garric," Cashel said. He lifted his staff overhead and gave it a trial spin, the only way he could do that without knocking down any number of people in these cramped quarters. The hall was a lot like a sheep byre on a winter night.

He strode toward the tunnel mouth, shouldering men out of the way when he needed to. He didn't bother to wait for Garric to agree; he and his quarterstaff were the best choice for the job. Cashel didn't need anybody, even a close friend, to tell him so.

Close up to the tunnel, the soldiers were packed too tight for even Cashel to shove them aside without breaking bones or worse. "Make way!" he said. "Garric sent me! Ah, *Prince* Garric sent me!"

From where he was now, Cashel could hear the screams even better. Blood sprayed high enough for him to see over the heads of the men ahead, and once a man's arm flew up.

For a moment not much happened. He was about to use his staff as a lever when somebody shouted, "It's the big wizard! Let him through! He can sort'em out!"

Cashel frowned. He wasn't any kind of wizard, but he'd always told himself he didn't care what people called him and this didn't seem the time to get huffy about it.

Sure enough, men peeled away from the back of the crowd. When the ones behind stopped pushing, the soldiers actually facing the enemy broke like the plug squirting from a squeezed waterskin.

Cashel stepped forward, spinning his staff. He saw the enemy for the first time.

They were man-sized and more or less man-shaped, but he wasn't sure he'd have seen they were individual figures if it hadn't been for the wizardlight quivering at their core—some red and some blue. Their arms ended in blades of the same cold, clear ice as their bodies. There was no doubt about the edges being sharp: all those in the front row were gory, and the ground was smeared with the blood, bits of equipment, and severed limbs left behind by soldiers who'd withdrawn into the rotunda.

The icemen stumped along more like hoarfrost spreading across bare dirt than the way men walk, but they had the same purposeful direction as plow oxen. They weren't going to stop; they had to *be* stopped.

Well, that's what Cashel had come to do.

He strode into them, swinging his staff sunwise as a feint. An iceman on his right lurched ahead of its fellows, an arm extended toward Cashel. The limb looked more like a spear than a sword held in a human's arm.

Cashel reversed the staff's spin, bringing a buttcap against the iceman's featureless head in a stroke that would've knocked in a thick door. The creature flew apart like an icicle dropped onto stone. The wizardlight filling it flashed out in a crimson thunderbolt.

The blast seemed to stun the rest of the icemen for an instant. Cashel felt only a mild tingling in his hands, nothing that prevented him from slamming the opposite ferrule into the midriff of another creature. It blew itself apart just like the first, rocking the nearest of its fellows the way a flung stone throws ripples across a pond.

Cashel'd intended to strike quickly and back away to judge how effective he'd been; he'd never fought anything like these icemen before, and the first thing you do in a fight is take the measure of the other fellow. There wasn't much doubt that hard, quick blows were the right medicine, and if each time he struck he numbed the survivors too—

Plenty of people had said that Cashel wasn't very bright, but nobody'd ever doubted he understood how to win fights. He continued forward, striking right and left with the thunderous speed of raindrops in a thunderstorm.

Shards of ice stung and even bruised the bare skin of his face and arms. He ignored that as he ignored the shouts of the men behind him. The quarterstaff wasn't long enough that he could clear the passage as he walked down the middle, so he punched a hole through the glittering creatures. The ones on the sides came at him from behind—but not without him noticing, because he kept his head moving in quick jerks to either side. He saw motion, not figures, at the edges of his vision but that was enough to warn him.

There might be too many of them, before and behind, for him to strike them all before they cut him to collops like the poor dead soldiers whose bodies he shuffled through as he advanced. If that happened, it happened. He'd do what he could till he died.

There were three figures in front of him. Cashel struck right, left, and right. The silent, searing gusts of light left him blinking away afterimages. There was movement behind him. He turned and stumbled to his knees; his legs bent like ivy runners. He slammed down the butt of his quarterstaff and clung to the shaft to keep from sprawling face-first on the ice.

Two surviving icemen approached him, splotches of red and blue as Cashel's blurry eyes tried to focus. He tried to heave himself to his feet. He couldn't move.

There was additional movement; Cashel's vision cleared. The young officer who'd gasped to Garric a tale of unstoppable monsters stood behind this remaining pair of them. He held the butt portion of a pikestaff, which had broken at the handgrip; it was thicker and filled with lead to balance the weight of the front two-thirds of the long shaft.

The youth swung the club over his head. He smashed first one, then the other iceman into light and shards as cold as death.

More men ran past the young officer, grasping Cashel's arms and helping him up. One of them tried to take the quarterstaff. "No!" Cashel said in a snarl that was scarcely human.

The youth dropped his broken pike and held out his right arm to Cashel. "Milord," he said. His voice was a croak. "Milord!"

Cashel shrugged off the hands of well-meaning soldiers trying to support him. He took a step forward on his own, feeling strength start to return as he moved.

He took his right hand from the quarterstaff and clasped arms with the youth who'd saved his life. The boy was slender as a reed and trembling with fear and reaction; it was like holding a sparrow.

There was a great shout from the rotunda. "C'mon, milord," Cashel said in a rusty, hesitant voice. "They need us there. Our job's not done yet."

Ilna saw the hole growing, not in the sky but in the world itself. Layers peeled back so that a pulsing absence of light replaced the open air with its view of clouds scudding over a background of chalky blue. When she judged the passage was open—a matter of only a few heartbeats from when the rupture appeared; the Rua were as skillful in their arts as Ilna was in her own—she nodded approvingly and said to Chalcus, "All right. Let's go."

"Dear heart?" he said, meeting her eyes with a worried expression. "Go where? I don't see . . ."

He waggled his sword. To him the point danced in air as empty as it was before the winged men wove their patterns in the sky.

Ilna smiled crisply and extended her right hand to his left. "Come," she said. "I'll lead."

She stepped forward, into a textured emptiness that she understood; and Chalcus came with her, into something he couldn't even see. He'd have done the same thing, she knew, if she'd jumped off the cliff instead. All the more reason not to fail him . . . but then, Ilna had never been able to understand people who considered failure an acceptable choice.

Ilna moved through the passage much as she'd have walked across a familiar room in the darkness. The Rua had cut an opening between their world and another, not so much by art as with the same dogged skill that a beetle uses to bore through wood. It followed paths of lesser difficulty rather than taking the shortest route through the cosmos.

Ilna wasn't sure that she could have created the pattern herself—her different skills didn't lend themselves to a task of this sort—but she could understand it as easily as she understood how to breathe. She moved forward, feeling nothing under her feet but moving anyway. Chalcus's fingers tightened minutely, an extra pressure she wouldn't have noticed except that she knew how perfectly controlled his movements usually were.

She saw and heard nothing. She could feel Chalcus's hand, but she touched nothing of this world or place or not-place they moved through. When she turned slightly to the left—as she did—or pausing for a moment—as she did also, not out of indecision but because the way wasn't yet clear—she made easy, natural choices.

After an uncertain length of time, she stepped into light and cold; a real world, solid to a fault and less welcoming than the featureless dark through which the Rua had gnawed their passage. She stood at the juncture of three high tunnels in the ice. Two of them had walls of red light; the third was blue. The ice where they joined was a sullen mauve, pulsing with the slow rhythm of a snake's throat contracting to drag down its latest victim.

Chalcus was beside her, looking in all directions. He detached his hand from Ilna's and *flick-flicked* his sword through the air. He was just proving that his muscles worked the way they should, she supposed; though being Chalcus, he might have decided to slash some dust mote in half as well.

"So, dear one . . ." he said. "Did our winged friends tell you which way we go from here?"

He continued to scan their surroundings, but with less urgency. When Chalcus first reappeared beside her, he'd thrashed about like a dog being swarmed by hornets. The three long, straight passages were empty for as far as Ilna could see. That didn't mean danger couldn't threaten them at any instant, but it made it less likely that it *would*.

"No," said Ilna, her lips pursing as she looked at the ice about her. "You heard everything they said to me. But . . ."

Things were frozen in the walls—tiny fish, no more than a finger's-length long, with bits of weed and other flotsam like what the sea threw up on the beach of Barca's Hamlet; but fragments of corpses as well. Some of the pieces came from men or maybe men, but others couldn't possibly have been human.

"Chalcus," she said, "we need to go down this blue tunnel. I'm sure we do."

"Aye," he said, smiling like a brilliant sunrise; his cheerful humor was never more welcome than in a grim setting like this. "I knew you'd find the route, dear heart. Whatever the pattern is, *you* can see it."

"Perhaps, but that's not what I mean," said Ilna, irritated despite herself at flattery when there wasn't time for it. There was never time for flattery . . . though of course what Chalcus had said was true, or at least she'd be surprised to learn it wasn't true.

"Chalcus, I recognize this place." She gestured with her right hand. "I've never seen it before, but I *remember* it, I remember watching it being built."

"In a vision you mean, dearest?" he said. His eyes never rested on her longer than they did on any other thing about him, but his voice was warm with real concern. "A dream, perhaps?"

"Nothing," snapped Ilna. "I don't recall ever seeing this, any of this, before. But I remember *it*, do you see? And I don't know how!"

"Then let's go on," said Chalcus with a faint, hard smile. "The sooner we've come to the end of this business, the sooner we'll never have to think about the place again. For though I won't say I've never been in a place that less appealed to me, dearest—"

Chuckling, he waggled his sword as a curved pointer.

"—I will say I've never been in a place that less appealed to me an' I was sober enough to remember."

Ilna nodded coldly. "Yes," she said. "Let's go."

But before she stepped forward, she touched Chalcus's left hand again with her fingertips. He twisted his palm upward to squeeze her in turn.

They both wore shoes that they'd put on aboard the *Bird of the Tide* to walk the cobblestone streets of Terness and the passages of Lusius's castle. Ilna didn't like shoes, but now the thick leather soles kept her feet from freezing as might've happened otherwise. The cold wasn't the worst of the discomfort, but it was a discomfort.

Her footsteps and those of Chalcus beside her were lost in the creaks and groaning that she supposed were the ice working. She'd heard similar sounds on the very coldest winters while she was growing up, when the shore of the Inner Sea froze out toward the eastern horizon.

She wasn't sure that was what she was hearing, though, because sometimes she thought she saw movement in the clear, glowing ice. That might have been a trick of the light or distortion from unseen fractures as she glanced while walking past, but in this place there were other possibilities. She remembered sheets of wizardlight acting as warp and woof, weaving tunnels out of open water. Things had begun to grow in it at once, the way weevils appear in meal left uncovered. . . .

They neared an intersection; not a simple *Y* this time but a joining of five tunnels. The plaza in the middle had high, flat walls, one for each tunnel. Chalcus held up his left hand.

"We take the second one to the right," Ilna said.

"And so we shall, dearest," Chalcus replied, his dagger now out as well as the sword. "But first I—"

Chalcus swung into the intersection, his sword and the dagger slashing in opposite directions. He landed flat-footed in the center of the space, his head twitching to either side while his body poised to react to a threat from any direction.

He relaxed, not that anybody but Ilna would've recognized the difference. "Only us, dearest," Chalcus said, his eyes continuing to search the four tunnels besides the one she was in. "We can go on, I'm thinking . . . and I'm thinking that the less time we spend in one place, the better off we are."

"Yes," said Ilna. She grimaced. "Chalcus, let me go ahead."

"I—" he said, protest in his voice but without turning to face her.

"There's as much risk from behind as there is ahead," she said sharply. "I . . . I'm remembering things that I've never seen, Master Chalcus. I'm afraid that if I'm in the rear, I'll get lost in what never happened. And I'll miss what's creeping up on us."

She paused. *I can tell him the truth,* she thought; and, with a fierce anger blurted, "Chalcus, I hate this! I'm going mad, and I can't trust my own mind!"

He gestured her ahead of him with his empty left hand. "I much misdoubt that you're going mad, dear one," he said with a grin that only a fool would think amusing. "I think instead that there's someone very clever in this place who is not our friend; and the quicker we've slit that someone's throat, the better. Not so?"

"So," agreed Ilna striding across the intersection and proceeding up a corridor glowing the same deep red as a demon's eyes. In her memory the roots of a Tree grew through the ice, sucking nourishment out of the world itself. The root that formed this tunnel still filled it, though not in a fashion that the eyes of her body could see.

She strode on. The Tree's bark was as smooth as human skin, and its branches waved like serpents, writhed like the tentacles of the great ammonites, the Old Ones of the Deep. There was no evil in the cosmos that a tendril of the Tree's roots did not touch. . . .

Ilna came to another intersection and stepped through it without pausing. She no longer feared things that might wait in ambush. Nothing could surprise her in her present state.

She smiled; the curve of her lips was as hard and cold as the ice itself.

She'd known the Tree in Hell—a year ago or a lifetime, depending on how you counted time. In exchange for Ilna's soul, the Tree had taught her to weave as only Gods and demons could, and she'd used her new skill to the Tree's ends.

There'd been no more effective minion of evil than Ilna os-Kenset—till Garric had freed her. Neither Garric nor anything else could free Ilna from the memory of what she had done in those months when she fed the Tree's tendrils.

Ilna reached another intersection. She was barely conscious of it. The floor here bore footprints crossing left to right. They looked human, but whatever had made them was so heavy that its feet had sunk into the ice, stressing it white in blotches around each print.

Ilna walked on. A figure ahead sauntered toward them.

"Chalcus," she said, "there's an enemy coming, a girl."

"I see her," Chalcus said appraisingly. "I couldn't have told her for a girl, though, at this distance."

"Her name is Monine," said Ilna. It no longer bothered her that she remembered what she hadn't seen. "She's a wizard and very dangerous."

"Danger?" said Chalcus. He laughed. "In this place, what else would we find?"

His sword cut a tight figure eight, making the cold air whistle.

"I'll lead, shall I, dear one?" he said, stepping past Ilna with the sword slanted out to his side. Its point quivered like the nose of a hound straining as it waits for its leash to be slipped.

"Chalcus, be careful," Ilna said. "She's not what she seems."

"Ah," Chalcus said, his low voice as eager as his blade. "But I *am* what I seem, dear heart."

They neared the sexless figure walking down the center of the tunnel. Monine's lips curved in a bloodless smile. Her knife echoed the curve, and there was blood enough for any number of smiles on its blade.

"So, Mistress Monine," Chalcus called. "Have you business with us? If not, then my friend and I are willing to pass by and forget we've met."

"I have the business of killing you," said Monine. She laughed, a high, glittering sound like jade wind chimes. "But I've always found killing more pleasure than business, and it will be a particular pleasure this time."

"Chalcus, the cloth of her tabard!" Ilna said. No eye but hers could've traced the pattern woven in brilliant colors, but even Ilna was helpless against it. The fabric was a net, catching eyes—even Ilna's—and snatching them away from their intent as surely as a fisherman draws his catch from the sea. "You won't be able to see her! She won't—"

Chalcus slashed, a blow as quick and smooth as the play of light on a dewdrop. His sword touched nothing. Monine's knife came up arrow-swift; swifter yet, Chalcus's dagger blocked the stroke with the ring of steel on steel.

He hopped back, his mouth open and his breath a cloud before him in the still, cold air. He lunged, his sword a curved extension of his right arm. His steel punctured emptiness, and again Monine stabbed for his heart. Her blade sang on the slim dagger, locking it guard to guard. Sparks showered and Chalcus jumped back again.

Ilna held her cords ready but she didn't knot a pattern because it'd be useless—the tabard would trap her art as surely as it trapped her eyes and the eyes of as good a swordsman as had ever been born. Instead she backed, giving Chalcus space to retreat—as he did again when his sword flicked and missed, and the bloody knife sought him.

Chalcus had shown himself able to anticipate the knife even if his eyes couldn't find the wielder; perhaps he and Ilna could back all the way to where they entered this maze. But if they were going to retreat to where they entered, then they might as well have stayed with the Rua or better still in their own world. In this place, there was more than a likelihood of something coming from the other direction to find them if they didn't move ahead quickly.

Chalcus struck—low this time, aiming at the sexless wizard's feet but glancing along the stone-hard ice. Stab/*clash* as sacrificial knife met dagger, but this time the edge stopped close enough to mark Chalcus's tunic with a line of blood from some other victim's lungs. He jumped back flat-footed, so Monine's second stroke cut the air instead of severing his ribs at mid-chest.

The slender wizard seemed tireless. Her smile never faltered, her steps and slashes were as steady as the beat of a millstone driven by the stream's relentless force. If—

Chalcus laughed and closed his eyes. He stepped forward, his curved sword singing in a short arc.

Monine screamed and collapsed. Ilna thought the sound continued to echo long after the wizard's severed head had spun and danced to a halt far down the tunnel of ice. Blood spouted, then dribbled from the neck stump. As it soaked into Monine's rumpled tabard, her corpse took on clearer lines against the floor.

Chalcus toed the knife out of the wizard's hand. "I've seen sickles that'd be less clumsy in a knife fight," he mused aloud, "and the blade's heavy enough for a trireme's ram. But for all that it nearly did for me, did it not?"

"There's nearly," said Ilna in a terse voice, "and there's what she is. Dead. Nearly will do."

Chalcus jerked a sleeve off Monine's tunic and wiped his blade clean of her blood. "She could fool my eyes," he said in the soft lilt that he'd have used to describe Ilna's hair or the curve of her neck. "But not my hand, I thought; and I was right."

"What if she'd struck at you when you closed your eyes?" Ilna asked mildly.

Chalcus snorted; he lifted an edge of the tabard with his sword point, then let it flop down again. "Strike?" he said. "When she saw her death coming on my sword edge? No love, not that one."

He grinned at her. "She's not you, you see."

"Apparently not," Ilna said, looking down the tunnel. Monine's head had come to rest on the stump of her neck. The shock of decapitation had lifted the corners of her mouth; from a distance the rictus looked like a mocking grin.

"Not yet, at least," Ilna added. "Come, then. We have a little farther yet to go."

Sharina led the way down the corridor. Franca was on her right, Scoggin on the left. Either man was a little behind her and far enough to the side to be safe when she began to swing the axe. The remainder of the band, eight men and some of them limping along with wounds, spread to either side.

The glowing walls made Sharina feel as though she were walking in a tunnel of light. She'd thought at first she might get used to it, but she'd been wrong. Faint though the glow was, it jabbed into her consciousness like the brush of nettles on her skin; every step, every heartbeat.

The figures at the other end of the tunnel shimmered as if seen across an expanse of sunlit desert, but she could see that there were many of them, far more than her band had killed on entering this realm. The points of their weapons winked like the stars on a winter night.

Beard had been singing softly. Now in a regretful voice he said, "I don't mind if we kill the ones waiting for us ahead. Not me, not Beard; blood is blood. But *you* might want to know that those are your friends, mistress."

Ah. Now that she'd been told, Sharina saw that the shields of the figures ahead were the familiar long ovals of the royal army, and that the ranks showed a degree of order that she'd never seen among the minions of chaos.

"These are friends!" she shouted, turning her head to the right, then left to make eye contact with her men. "I'll talk to them when we get closer. There'll be an officer who recognizes me, I'm sure."

Actually, she *wasn't* sure. Nobody in the royal army had seen Princess Sharina dressed in a bearskin over the remnants of her sleeping shift, carrying an axe at the head of a band as ragged as she herself was. And what her hair must look like!

In an undertone she went on, "Thank you, Beard. For telling me they were friends."

"Oh, you'd have figured it out before we killed anybody, mistress," the axe said. He sounded as if he were trying to convince himself. "And anyway, there'll be more blood for Beard to drink. Much more, don't you think?"

"I'm sure there will be," said Sharina. But less sure that she wouldn't have gone tearing into Garric's army, oblivious of everything except for the fact that they were in front of her.

"Mistress?" said Beard. "All I think about is what I'm going to get a chance to kill next; that's the way Beard is, how Beard was made to be. But you humans aren't supposed to be like that."

She'd forgotten that the axe heard her thoughts....
"You're right, Beard," Sharina said. "And we humans especially shouldn't become focused on how we're going to die. It's good to have friends who warn us when we get off the right road."

"Humph!" said the axe, a kind of metallic snort. "*I drink blood.*"

They'd come within a hundred feet of the royal line. One of the men in the front row was a Blood Eagle, but judging from shield facings the other troops were a mixture of two or three regular regiments. Had there been a disaster?

"Ready!" called an officer, slanting his sword forward. The spears of the men in the front ranks came back, ready to throw.

"Wait!" cried Sharina. She gripped Beard just below the head and waved the butt in the air, hoping that looked pacific. The axe was giggling. "Wait, we're friends!"

A big, barrel-chested man in gold-chased black armor forced his way to the front of the formation. Lord Attaper, and a welcome sight.

"That's Princess Sharina, you fools!" Attaper cried. "Platt, are you blind or have you gone mad? Lower your spears!"

Sharina trotted forward, wobbling for the first couple steps. She was suddenly aware that she'd almost been killed by her friends. Garric would've been very angry when he heard about it.

The axe giggled again; so did she.

"Lord Attaper," Sharina gasped as she reached the line. Scoggin and Franca were with her, and despite what she'd said the rest of the band was close behind. "These are my friends. We've come to kill the wizard who's destroying this world. Ah, *Her.*"

The royal troops looked either puzzled or embarrassed. The officer who'd been about to order Sharina killed stood rigid, facing straight ahead so that he wouldn't have to meet her eyes.

"I'll get you to the prince," Attaper said. "He'll be glad you're safe."

"Safe," echoed Beard. "Safe? Oh, what marvelous jesters these soldiers are! But there'll be enough blood for everyone, for Beard and these soldiers and more besides than all of us can drink!"

Attaper looked first at Sharina, then down at the axe. His eyes widened; then he looked away, toward the men following her. He gestured with his chin and said, "Is this lot with you, your highness?"

"Yes," she said, her voice sharper than she'd really intended because of what she heard as an implied insult. These men had followed her here—to Hell!—because she'd asked them to. "These are my companions. They'll come with me to see my brother."

"Right," said Attaper, gesturing with both arms to clear a passage through the close-packed troops. "We need to get them inside so that Captain—"

He looked with hard eyes at the stiff, flushing officer.

"—Platt doesn't have another brainstorm!"

Sharina turned to her men. "Follow me and keep close!" she ordered.

She clutched Beard to her chest so she wouldn't slash somebody as she squeezed between the soldiers. "As if they were going to do anything else," said the axe. "You're the only thing in this place that they trust. Why, you're the only thing in this place they're not terrified of!"

Attaper led them into a huge domed chamber, larger than any of the similar junctions Sharina and her band had seen on their way through the ice maze. It was full of milling soldiers.

Here and there officers were trying to organize their units, causing greater confusion than there would have been without their efforts. Except for the commander of the Blood Eagles leading them, Sharina didn't suppose she and her band could possibly have gotten through—even with Garric himself, standing on a pedestal, shouting to them at the top of his lungs.

"It's not a pedestal," Beard said. "Your brother's standing on the shoulders of a man named Cashel or-Kenset. Is this possibly of interest to you, mistress?"

"Cashel!" Sharina cried. "Cashel!"

She started to slip past Attaper—she could have, slim and strong and because she was female likely to be treated with deference that these nervous armed men would never have given another of their own. But she'd have had to leave behind the band who'd followed her, *her* men.

Sharina smiled. Cashel could wait a few minutes. He'd understand if anyone alive would understand.

Garric jumped to the ground as Attaper wove Sharina and her companions closer. He vanished for a moment behind the wall of troops, then reappeared in front of Attaper with Cashel at his side. They moved like whales bellying through a sea of armed men. Liane followed closely, and a pair of noncoms trailed her, looking bemused. They were apparently attached to Garric though they weren't Blood Eagles and Sharina didn't recall seeing them before.

Sharina hugged Cashel awkwardly because both of them had something in their right hands. He was used to doing things while holding the quarterstaff, but she had to remind herself that Beard had sheared everything he'd touched save the metallic monster Alfdan had fed himself to.

Cashel was a mountain, a tower against everything hostile. Holding him and being held brought order to the cosmos. It was the first peace Sharina had known since the urn in her bedroom had sucked her into the world She ravaged.

She patted Cashel once more between the shoulder blades, then leaned back and broke the embrace. She took a deep breath.

"Garric?" she said, turning to indicate the band who'd come with her. Franca was glaring at Cashel; Scoggin rested his left hand on the youth's shoulder. The others stood close behind. Some looked ill at ease to be crowded by men in armor, but Neal and Layson in particular stood straight and looked the curious soldiers around them in the eye. "These are my companions. They helped me and fought for me. I'm responsible for them."

"For that they'll be honored as they deserve when we have the leisure to do so," said Garric, glancing about the confusion with a smile that reminded her of the brother she'd grown up with. "Which at present we certainly do not. But—"

"Your highness!" said Lord Lerdain, pushing back through the crowd. "The centipede's dead or dead enough that we can get by! Lord Escot and Master Ortron are advancing!"

Lerdain had gotten a bang on the side of his face; the present puffiness would become a bad bruise in a few hours. He no longer seemed the pudgy fifteen-year-old he'd been a few months before when he became Prince Garric's aide.

"Right!" said Garric, turning toward one of the corridors branching off this great junction. "Tell them I'm coming."

Looking past him Sharina saw the chitinous, pincered leg of an insect large enough that its legs could scrape the high ceiling when it lay on its back. The sight gave her stomach a sudden jolt. *But we killed that already!* her mind told her; but they hadn't, not this particular creature nor even one exactly like it. And what else was waiting before they reached Her?

"Sharina," Cashel said, "I've to go with Garric. I'll be back when, well, you know."

Garric and his pair of soldiers were already pushing forward; Attaper followed with a set expression and his hand on the ivory hilt of his sword. The bodyguard commander obviously had his own opinion of what was reasonable behavior for his prince, and as obviously he knew to hold his tongue at this juncture.

Sharina hesitated, caught between concern for her ragged followers and her desire to stay with Garric and Cashel now that she'd finally been reunited with them. Though she didn't suppose she had any business fighting now, since there were soldiers with the training and equipment to—

"Mistress, you must take me to the front!" Beard cried. "Has Beard not been a good servant to you? Will you starve Beard of the blood he deserves?"

"But—" Sharina said. Cashel and Garric were already out of sight beyond the currents of milling soldiers. She couldn't let her whim and an axe's blood lust take her where a girl without armor would only be in the way of men in a hard battle!

"Do you think they can fight what waits for them, mistress?" Beard said, his voice rising in peevish anger. "They can't, you know. They'll only die when they face an Elemental! But Beard and his mistress, they can drink even that life. Please, mistress!"

"An Elemental . . . ?" Sharina repeated softly.

"Oh, She's a great wizard, the greatest of wizards," the axe, crooned. "No one could bind an Elemental! But She bound one and drew it here, and it will swallow all the souls it finds unless Beard drinks its soul instead."

Sharina shuddered as she remembered diving into the fjord to bring up the Key of Reyazel. Her mind had been numb then, so focused on the brutal strain of the dive that the horror of the things guarding the key had slid off her like filth from a wall of ice. Thinking back on the event forced her to understand exactly how foul the things had been—and how unutterably awful it would have been to be engulfed by one of them.

"Neal," Sharina said sharply. "Take charge till I return. Hold the men here. Stay together and don't get in the way of the, the soldiers with better equipment."

"But mistress!" Layson begged.

"Stay here!" she snarled. "Franca, you and Scoggin too!"

"You didn't dive into the fjord with her," said Beard in a piercing, sneering tone. "If you come now you'll die the same way, the very same way, and your souls will die forever!"

Sharina's eyes met Liane's; Liane nodded. Sharina turned sharply. "Neal," she said, "obey Lady Liane here as though she were me. She'll take care of you!"

She turned again and slipped off through the crowd, holding the axe over her head. Behind her, her former companions stood like scarecrows with gaping mouths. They eyed Liane and clutched their weapons like shipwrecked sailors holding spars.

"Make way for Princess Sharina!" Beard cried; his ringing voice cut through the clamor, jerking startled men about and opening gaps that a slim, determined woman could stride through. "Make way for Beard's mistress!"

I'm not abandoning Franca and the rest. I'm giving them a chance to live, which they wouldn't have had if they came with me now. The fact that Sharina knew her litany was objectively true didn't keep her from feeling sick to her stomach at having left behind frightened men who depended on her.

Beard gave a metallic titter. "My mistress doesn't fear anything, of course," the axe said. "She knows that Beard'll drink himself fat on blood before she dies. Oh, fortunate mistress to have such a servant as Beard!"

Which was also objectively true, and Sharina's laughter at *that* thought washed away her empty queasiness at the way she'd treated her companions. Anyway, she didn't have any choice but to go. She knew her brother and Cashel would fight the Elemental if she wasn't there, and she didn't doubt Beard's claim that it would devour them.

"We will kill it as we killed its sibling in the deeps," Beard caroled in response. "As we drank the soul of something that'd swallowed a thousand souls. Oh, mistress, Beard will chant your praise till the sun dies!"

The Old Kingdom poet Celondre had claimed his work was more lasting than bronze. Beard was going to outlast Celondre, at least in this place, so Sharina supposed she'd achieved immortality of a sort. . . .

She laughed, wondering if she was becoming hysterical. The axe laughed with her.

She reached the archway where the corridor joined the great rotunda. Here the troops were packed so tightly that even she couldn't squeeze through. "Make way for Princess Sharina!" Beard cried shrilly.

That didn't change anything directly, but a Blood Eagle in the crowd ahead of her looked over his shoulder. Sharina found his face vaguely familiar; he'd probably been in her guard detachment at some point.

"Say, that *is* the princess!" he said. "Say! Don't crowd her highness, you dogs! Have you lost all honor?"

Between shouting and prying with the butt of his spear, the Blood Eagle opened a space for her to join him. "Let the princess through!" he bellowed as he started pushing forward through the ruck. "Pass the word up there that Princess Sharina's coming through!"

The Blood Eagle cocked his head toward her again. He was an older man whose nose had been broken at least twice.

"File Closer Gondor, your highness," he said in a respectful voice. "I don't suppose you remember, but—"

"I do indeed, Gondor," Sharina said. That was half a lie, but this wasn't a time for pleasantries. "Carry on."

Which Gondor did, using the side of his shield like a plowshare to carve a furrow through the crowd. Sharina's name alone hadn't been enough to make a path, but her name *and* brute force succeeded.

"Brute force, oh yes," said Beard. "Brute force, but especially Beard's fine edge to drink their blood!"

The corridor was half-blocked—more than half—by the twisted body of the segmented, many-legged monster. The gigantic corpse still twitched. Its movements and the sulfurous, stomach-roiling stench of the blood leaking from the creature's wounds made even veteran soldiers pause as they reached it, delaying the advance more than the constriction itself did.

"Oh, go on past, File Closer!" Beard said. "The worst that can happen if one of those legs kicks is it'll kill you. Much worse will happen if the Elemental sucks you down, as it surely will if Beard and his mistress don't stop it!"

Gondor lurched forward, clambering over a limb the size of a fallen hickory. The bristles sprouting from its joints were as long as Sharina's arm and as stiff as blackberry canes.

Sharina hadn't seen Gondor hesitate, but she supposed thoughts along those lines must have been going through the soldier's mind. They'd certainly been going through hers; but the axe was right. She *had* to get ahead of Cashel and Garric.

The waving legs cast shadows against the lighted ceiling, a foul echo of the way breeze-blown limbs dapple the sunlight falling on the floor of a forest. Soldiers picked their way through with dogged courage, trying not to look in any direction as they squeezed past obstacles of quivering saffron chitin. They shifted aside to let Gondor and Sharina go by: the Blood Eagle driven by the presence of the girl behind him, while she pressed on out of blind determination.

Sharina'd decided she had to reach the front of the column. Now she was driving onward without allowing herself to think further. She knew there wasn't anything new to consider, nor any thoughts that she wanted to dwell on.

The great centipede's final segments were curled against the ceiling. One of the legs stroked like a metronome, the jaws of its pincers scraping parallel channels. Shavings drifted over Sharina, chilling her more than ice alone should have done. She shook herself, concentrating on what was ahead.

Troops who'd gotten past the centipede moved quickly along the corridor, widening the gap between them and the bulk of the army. The men who'd crossed the obstacle immediately preceding Gondor and Sharina were doubletiming to catch up with their fellows.

"Can you keep up if we run, mistress?" Gondor asked.

"Let's see, shall we?" Sharina said distantly. He was being solicitous; he really *didn't* know she'd regularly outrun any of the men in Barca's Hamlet, so it wasn't fair for her to react as if somebody'd just branded her for stealing.

She shrugged off her bearskin—she doubted that she'd be in this place long enough to freeze to death, one way or the other—and broke into a long-legged stride. Her hair streamed back, though smoke-stained and greasy it was more of a clump than the gossamer blond fabric that'd been her pride when she was a girl.

Sharina hadn't been a girl in longer than days or years could express.

The hundred or so troops ahead marched down the corridor in a tight mass, though they weren't so much in formation as a mixture of two formations. Part of the force was regular heavy infantry from several regiments, but half or more were members of the phalanx. Many of the latter'd lost their long pikes. Sharina had already seen the broken shafts, the butt ends littering the ice beneath the dead centipede and the slender points black with ichor dripping from the wounds they'd punched in the creature's armor.

Cashel's quarterstaff showed above the ranks of soldiers, moving to the front like a standard. Garric and the rest of his entourage must be close to him, though Sharina suspected Cashel was leading.

She smiled faintly. Cashel was a very gentle man, but when he pushed, others made way. *Her* Cashel.

"Princess Sharina to join her brother!" Beard cried as she reached the formation. A man swore, but because Garric and his followers had already disarrayed the ranks Sharina had less difficulty getting through than she'd expected. Gondor was somewhere behind her. Had he *really* thought he in his armor could outrun Sharina os-Reise? And yes, he probably had; but he wouldn't think that again.

She worked her way up to Cashel; Garric and the others were to the side, forming a partial rank just behind the front of the formation. "Garric, Cashel!" Sharina said. "You've got to let me through. The thing that's coming won't be harmed by your weapons!"

Garric looked back awkwardly past the cheek flare of his helmet; Cashel turned also, his smile of greeting turning quickly to a troubled frown. "Sharina," Garric said, "this isn't a business for you. I—"

"It's a business for Beard and for no others!" said the axe, causing Garric's eyes to widen. "Any of you can face the Elemental—but you'll die and spend eternity in torment! Beard and his mistress will drink its life instead."

"Look, if the axe is necessary," Lord Attaper said, "I'll take it and—"

"No," said Sharina.

"Out of her cold dead hands!" said Beard. "If you think you can, which you will not—for Beard will eat your brains if you try."

Sharina didn't know why she was so furiously determined that she alone would handle Beard. She and the axe had survived horrors together; perhaps it was that. But beyond that, she'd faced Elementals before. Attaper hadn't, none of the others had.

"Your highness?" called Master Ortron, now marching on the left side of the front rank. A helmetless nobleman was on the right; Sharina could imagine the confusion that would cause if Garric hadn't been present. "There's something funny about the passage ahead. I don't see the light we're following."

Sharina cocked her head toward Garric to see between the shoulders of two men in the front rank. Fifty feet away the deep blue undertone of the present corridor became a murky yellow-gray like nothing she'd seen in these caves. She could still make out the walls and ceiling—or thought she could—but the thread of wizardlight blurred and vanished like a fishline plunging into the sea. The line of troops continued forward at a measured pace.

"The Elemental's waiting," said the axe. "It's waiting to swallow every soul that comes to it, but it isn't waiting for Beard."

"Sir, we're not afraid!" the nobleman cried. "Come on, men!"

"Stop him!" Sharina shouted. The fool could draw the whole force with him unless—

"Charge!" the noble cried, waving his sword as he broke into a run.

"Knock him down, Herther!" Master Ortron roared. There were three pikemen in the front rank. Two of them— one was presumably named Herther—swung their long shafts sideways, one cracking the nobleman across the temple and the other sweeping his ankles out from under him. He crashed into the wall and flopped to the floor on his back.

"Let me by," Sharina said in a desperate murmur. She didn't raise her voice for fear she'd scream with fear and frustration.

"Sharina . . ." Garric said with a troubled frown. The troops continued to march toward certain death; the front ranks divided enough to keep from trampling the fallen officer, but the men behind probably couldn't see the poor fellow until they were on top of him. They were nearing the change in light.

"Garric, let her go," said Cashel. "I don't like it, but I trust her. Whatever she says, I trust her."

Garric nodded, his face still furrowed with worry. *"Regi-*

ment . . ." he said in a voice that thundered over the clash of boots and jingling equipment. *"Halt!"*

The boots crashed down one more time. The echoes continued to roll; from farther back in the corridor came the sound of men running to join the main body.

"Sister, I wish it were me," Garric said with a lopsided grin. He turned. "Make room for Princess Sharina!"

"Oh, mistress, Beard will eat again!" the axe trilled as Sharina slipped between soldiers, her shoulder brushing the man on her right. "Oh, mistress, you've brought Beard to such feasting. No one else in this world will hold Beard until you're gone!"

Nice that somebody's happy, Sharina thought. And not for the first time; but she was here not only by her choice but by her insistence. Of course if Beard wasn't just exaggerating as a compliment, there was no other choice that gave anybody a chance at survival.

The change in light was just ahead. Some of the pikes reached into it; their shafts seemed to kink slightly as though they'd been thrust into water. *As though they were reaching into the water covering the Key of Reyazel.* . . .

She hadn't come here *not* to act. Sharina stepped through the insubstantial barrier.

She didn't look over her shoulder, but she knew the world behind her had vanished. She was in the fjord again, and the enfolding chill penetrated her soul. Planes of light jutted up, intersecting and interpenetrating one another. They had no color, but their textures differed as surely as walls of sandstone and granite and shale.

Sharina drifted onward, downward, instinctively holding her breath. If she took this place into her body, she would never return.

She couldn't see the thing that was waiting for her. It was like walking through a nighted forest, watched from the darkness but unable to see anything herself. Beard tugged like a leashed hound. She couldn't hear him in this wilderness of planes and soul-numbing cold, but the helve trembled in her hand as the steel mouth laughed.

Someday Sharina would die. Perhaps this was the day she

would die forever, her soul devoured by a force that was alien to all life. She felt the chill and she felt the presence of hidden doom; and she continued onward because that was what she'd come to do.

She'd lost track of direction. There were no more walls and floor than there'd been when she sank through the waters of the fjord.

Her lungs began to ache. She knew that they'd shortly be ablaze with white fire but she *couldn't* breathe, didn't dare to breathe.

The axe twisted in her hand. Sharina looked upward and it was there, rippling down onto her like a mass of silk in the summer when the young spiders balloon off on the breeze. She struck or Beard struck in her hand. The Elemental divided to either side of the blow, untouched by the steel. It came on undeterred, spreading around her to right and left the way the tide rises on a narrow isthmus.

Sharina backhanded her weapon. The spike parted the Elemental's tenuous form like smoke, its substance leaking like honey oozing from a comb dropped on hot stone.

Beard screamed in triumph. The planes of non-light, noncolor fell into shards that crumbled in turn to specks too small for sight, then evaporated.

Sharina slumped forward. She heard Cashel cry, *"Shar—"* but the remainder of her name was lost as a sea of darkness surged over her mind. She knew she'd hit the floor, but she didn't feel the impact.

Chapter Twenty-three

Ilna walked through the tunnels at a deliberate pace. She didn't run because she wasn't good at running; and besides, there was no need: she'd get where she was going soon enough, and possibly sooner than that.

Behind her Chalcus sang in an undertone, *"I've seen the*

fruits of rambling, I know its hardships well . . ." Ilna was aware of his presence, but he was part of a world that had ended when she entered these frozen halls.

"I've crossed the Southern Ocean, rode down the streets of Hell . . ."

Ilna's personal memories were fading. In their place she remembered how She had built this palace beneath the ice to channel the powers on which the cosmos turned. As Ilna walked, she saw the necessity of each angle, of every knob or divot in the walls.

It was a work of the greatest craftsmanship; but craftsmanship alone wouldn't have made the place the focus that it was. That had required materials and the willingness to use them.

". . . been up above the Ice Capes, where the shaggy giants roam . . ."

Through Her eyes Ilna looked down on the sea of faces staring up at Her on the ice throne. They were cutthroats, pirates, killers; bad men before She enlisted them in Her army, and since then become worse. There was no act too vile for them to commit for Her, and few that they had not committed already. Now they would do one further thing: She raised Her hands.

"I tell you from experience, you'd better stay at home."

Ilna turned right, into a tunnel lower and narrower than the others had been. At its end was a slab of blank ice, which alone of the walls in this place wasn't filled from within by wizardlight. Ilna saw herself reflected from a surface as blackly perfect as polished obsidian.

"Dear one . . . ?" said the voice from behind her. She made a silent, brushing motion with her left hand, the sort of gesture she'd have used to flick away a fly.

In a memory not Ilna's, Her hands began to weave in the air. The brutal faces below watched in frightened fascination. Most bore scars—brands and cropped ears as frequently as knife slashes; teeth smashed out or rotted out during lives as savage as those of wild beasts. They were bound to Her by fear of Her power and fear of the revenge those they had wronged would take if ever they left Her protection; but Her art, even if used to help them, frightened them also.

Ilna's lips gave a smile as cold as the black reflection. She'd killed in the past and would kill again soon if she was able to. She'd have had no more mercy for the men who stared at Her than she would for a chicken she needed for dinner; no more mercy than they were about to receive . . .

Wizardlight streamed from Her hands in gossamer splendor, crossing and interweaving in a pattern that none of those watching beneath the great ice dome could appreciate. The men fidgeted, fingering weapons and glancing covertly at their fellows. The light rippled like gauze as it spread above them. Its color was too subtle for words to describe or eyes to grasp.

Her pattern finally reached the curving walls of the chamber. For a moment nothing happened save that the light pulsed the way breath throbs in the throat membrane of a waiting lizard.

The fabric settled.

The gang of killers tried to flee, screaming curses in a score of languages. They had no more chance than minnows within a closing purse net. Palpable light drifted over them, coating those it touched the way oil spreads over still water.

At first contact, men froze where they stood. The net shimmered, as beautiful as the rainbow hues of a snake's eye, and it continued to sink.

A few of the band, shorter than the others or quicker thinking, dropped to their hands and knees to crawl toward the corridors feeding the great hall. Some slithered on their bellies at the end—crying, praying, or shouting curses depending on their temperaments—but the wizardlight settled onto them also.

Ilna reached the end of the narrow passage. She looked into the black reflection of her own eyes, remembering a past that those eyes had never seen.

The glowing net began to congeal the way pudding sets. Its color deepened and became more saturated without changing hue. The forms trapped beneath it blurred and lost definition. Their flesh and souls together dissolved. Light began to spread *through* the walls of ice that had been dark with the gloom of polar winter.

Still clutching their weapons, the corpses settled into the ice, shrinking to skeletons. The floor engulfed them. Above, looking out into the world Her art ruled, She wove the cosmos into patterns of devastation and inexorable doom.

Ilna smiled.

"So, dear heart, shall we try another tunnel?" said Chalcus with false, lilting brightness.

Ilna took the bone-cased knife from her sleeve. The blade of worn steel was only finger-long, but it sufficed for all her tasks: trimming selvage, gutting rabbits, and slicing swatches of cowhide into laces for Cashel's winter boots.

Instead of chipping at the ice, Ilna turned the knife over in her hand, still cased. She paused, letting her mind locate the nexus in what the eyes of her body saw as a blank, smooth wall.

She tapped with the bone hilt. The slab of ice disintegrated into crystals smaller than snowflakes, smaller even than the dust motes that float in beams of sunlight.

Chalcus gave a cry of wonder. He stepped through the sudden opening, his sword and dagger poised. Ilna, smiling like a coiled spring, followed.

Cashel watched Sharina's slender body shrink as she strode into the yellowish light. She seemed to be flying away with each step, not just walking.

Cashel held his quarterstaff in both hands. He didn't squeeze it out of frustration, just held the smooth hickory with the grip he'd use to put a ferrule through the skull of anyone or anything that tried to hurt Sharina—if he could. She was so tiny, now; a little poppet he could've held in his hand.

Her axe glittered brightly. Cashel hoped and prayed that Sharina knew what she was doing, the way he'd told Garric she did; but he didn't doubt at all that the axe knew *its* business.

The distant doll of Sharina turned and slashed over her head. There wasn't anything near her. She reversed the stroke without hesitation, bringing the spiked end of the axe around.

Cashel'd used an axe in his time, felling trees for his neighbors and shaping the logs; he nodded in pleased approval as he watched. Sure, that narrow-bladed war axe was a different thing from the heavy tools he'd worked with, but motions like Sharina'd just made took wrists and shoulders that few men could boast of. Oh, she was a *fine* girl!

The air above her went red as a smear of blood. Cashel shouted and strode forward, his staff crossways in front of him. He didn't know or care what dangers Sharina might be facing, just that right now he'd rather die than let her face them alone.

The wall of light collapsed inward before Cashel stepped through it. Sharina was just ahead, full-sized and toppling onto the ice.

There wasn't blood in the air or on the floor below, but there was a stink as bad as anything Cashel'd ever smelled. It reminded him of the time a great shark washed up on the beach of Barca's Hamlet. The fish had been so rotten that its gill rakers hung as tatters of cartilage, but even so this was worse.

It didn't matter. It wouldn't have mattered if there'd been a wall of pike points between him and Sharina: Cashel was going through. He scooped her in the crook of his left arm. Her lips moved, though if she was saying anything Cashel couldn't hear the words.

She held the axe in both hands. It was talking enough for both of them, chortling, "Two Elementals, two of them, oh Beard never dreamed he would serve a master who would feed him Elementals!"

The axe didn't stop there but it didn't say anything new either, so Cashel ignored the rest like he would a breeze whispering through the trees. Garric, Lord Attaper, and the two soldiers with Garric had come running up only a heartbeat behind Cashel.

Garric put two fingertips on his sister's throat and nodded with relief. "Her heart's beating fine!" he said. "She's just—"

His voice didn't so much trail off as simply stop, because he didn't have any better notion of what'd happened to Sharina than Cashel did. He guessed she was exhausted. Two swipes with the axe weren't much for a healthy girl, but Cashel knew from his own experience that when you got in with wizards and their art it took more out of you than it seemed like it ought to've done.

"She's strong and well," the axe said. "She'll soon bring Beard to more blood and souls! Oh, what a fine mistress!"

It wasn't the sort of talk that generally appealed to Cashel, but hearing that the axe thought Sharina would be all right made it a pleasure this time. He felt her stir, twisting her head against his chest. He could probably set her down on her feet shortly, though he wasn't sure he would.

"Your highness?" said Master Ortron, about the only officer Cashel'd met that he liked as a person. Ortron was an ordinary fellow, not a noble, and he'd been happy to show Cashel how to handle a pike in return for lessons with a quarterstaff. "Are we to hold here, or . . . ?"

"Duzi, no!" Garric said. "We'll resume—"

He paused, looking sharply at his sister, then Cashel. "Cashel?" he continued. "Can you—"

"Sure," said Cashel, rocking Sharina gently in his arm the way he'd have soothed a baby. Of *course* he could carry Sharina.

He noticed that a couple of the soldiers had picked up the officer who'd been knocked silly for his own good. Cashel was glad of that. The fellow didn't have any more sense than a sheep did, but Cashel'd spent so much of his life looking after sheep that he couldn't help feeling sorry for the man.

"All right, Master Ortron, resume your advance," Garric said. He quirked a smile and added, "We'll go on till we get where we're going."

"Your highness!" called somebody from the back of the formation. Cashel wasn't tall enough to see past the mass of soldiers; he didn't think even Garric was, not with them wearing helmets like they were. "The passage has closed behind us! Let me through, you fools! I have to report to Prince Garric!"

"There's something up ahead of us too," said one of the soldiers with Garric. "Looks to me like it's a solid wall up there."

Cashel had a clear field of view ahead. There was no doubt about it: the tunnel had closed off since after Sharina made the light come back the way it was down here: not normal, maybe, but normal for this place. As for being solid, though . . .

"The wall at the end's coming toward us," Cashel said, loud enough for the others to hear him if they'd wanted to. Everybody was looking instead at the officer who'd just come through the formation. He was an older fellow with curled, hennaed moustaches; a regimental commander, though not somebody Cashel knew by name.

Garric did, though. "What happened to the passage, Lord Portus?" he said.

"Behind me!" Portus said, gesturing with a flourish back the way he'd come. "I heard a shout and saw that sheets of ice were growing from either side of the wall. There were several men following closely, but they were cut off from me when the ice joined. They began to attack it with their weapons, but it continued to thicken until I couldn't even see them through it."

Portus took off his gilded helmet and wiped his forehead with the wad of cambric he kept between the leather straps that suspended the bronze above his scalp. "I came on at once. I, ah . . .

"I thought the ice was following me," he said into the hollow of his helmet. He looked up to meet Garric's eyes. "Your highness, I think it *is* following me. The wall is growing toward us!"

"Garric, so's the one in front of us," Cashel said, this time loud enough that they *had* to listen. He pointed with his quarterstaff. "There!"

He wasn't exactly angry—he was used to people not paying attention to what he said since he generally let the words stand for themselves. You had to put a lot of fuss and flailing about into the way you said the words to get sheep and most people to listen, and Cashel only did that when he had to.

"Oh, well," said one of the soldiers who'd been looking after Garric. "Maybe her ladyship'll chop a hole in it with her axe, do you think?"

"She's not a ladyship, Prester," the other man said. "She's a princess!"

"And Beard," said the axe sharply, "is not a navvy's pick! Try to cut ice with me, Squad Leader Prester, and you'll find just how quickly I bounce back and empty your skull of what passes for brains!"

"If we advance behind the pikes, as many of them as we've still got . . . ?" Master Ortron said. He didn't sound real confident, showing that he was the sensible man Cashel had always taken him for.

"Garric," said Cashel, "hold Sharina for me. She's coming around fine, but . . ."

He passed Sharina to her brother without waiting to see if Garric had an opinion. Cashel needed both hands and somebody needed to watch over Sharina for a little while yet; there wasn't anything to discuss.

Cashel stepped forward, balancing his staff before him in both hands. "Anything I can do to help, Cashel?" Garric said.

"I think this one's for me," Cashel said as he began to spin the staff. "I haven't been doing much since I got here."

Cashel wasn't too proud to let somebody help, especially not a friend like Garric, but he didn't see much anybody else could do. It wasn't certain he could do much either, but he figured he and his quarterstaff had the best chance going.

The thin blue thread that Tenoctris had sent out for a guide disappeared into the plug that'd grown across the tunnel since Sharina cleared the other thing out of the way. The new wall of ice didn't move fast, not even as fast as Cashel ambled toward it at a sheep's pace. The ice didn't *have* to be quick to do what it was planning—or anyway what the wizard behind it planned. Cashel appreciated the value of steady over fast as well as any man living.

He spun the staff in a slant before him, first high on his right side and then doing a tricky crossover that brought the left side high instead. He kept on walking, reversing the spin from sunwise to widdershins by changing hands again behind his back.

None of this had anything to do with how he planned to use the quarterstaff when he got to the wall, but Cashel knew in his heart that there was more going on than just him loosening up his muscles before he needed them for real. He wasn't exactly showing off for the watching soldiers, but—

Well, if this was the last time he was able to put his staff through its paces, he wanted it to be a display he and the familiar hickory could be proud of. And it might very well be the last time.

The quarterstaff's ferrules sparkled with wizardlight, then streamed a dazzling blue disk encircling Cashel as he walked on. His skin prickled; he didn't recall starting to smile, but he was smiling now and he guessed he would till this was over one way or the other.

The ice wall was close. The roof of these tunnels was twice as high as Cashel could reach with the staff held up in one hand, but the barrier right in front of him looked higher even than that. It was like facing a mountain that reached all the way to the stars, though there wouldn't be any stars where it was, just black ice on forever.

When Cashel had entered the Visitor's ship, he'd been trapped like a bug in hot sap. This business might end the same way, with the ice before him squeezing hard against the ice and Cashel part of a red mush that included Sharina and all the soldiers. So far, though, he had plenty of room to swing his staff.

He kept the iron-capped hickory spinning as rapidly as he could control it—which was a good deal faster than anybody else he knew could, even Garric. Cashel didn't move forward but the ice did, in a more delicate step than a human could manage.

The staff's whirling ferrule brushed the sheer black face. Instead of the tiny *click* that Cashel expected to feel but not hear, the world exploded in a crash of blinding blue wizardlight. His arms went numb to the shoulders. He felt as he had the day when, too young to know better, he'd been clinging to a tree during a thunderstorm and lightning struck the next tree but one.

He was Cashel or-Kenset: he didn't drop his staff, and though he lost the rhythm of the spin for a moment he still brought the other ferrule around in a straight-on slam. The blow would've put his staff a handsbreadth deep into a sea wolf's thick skull.

Touching the ice had brought a thunderbolt. This time the shock threw Cashel to the ground, deaf and blinded to everything but orange and purple afterimages that alternated faster than his heart was beating.

He didn't feel the floor as he hit it, but when instinct drove him to reverse his stroke he found he was sitting on the ice and twice his own length back from the wall. He got up without thinking—there was no time to think, this was a *fight*—by crunching one end of the staff down beside him and poling himself up as much by the strength of his shoulders as with his legs.

Cashel stepped forward. He supposed the men behind him were shouting, but he wouldn't have paid attention even if he could hear anything beyond the roar of that last impact.

He could see now, but his vision was focused down to a circle of the wall right in front of him. At the edges even that started to gray out; beyond the space he could've spanned with his arms spread, Cashel's world just didn't exist. All he saw—all he cared about for as long as this fight lasted, whether he lived or died—was the target for his next blow.

He spun the quarterstaff overhead, keeping its momentum up. He took another step and a third. The wall wasn't where it'd been when he got up and started for it again, but Cashel was used to opponents retreating when he came at them. He was moving faster than it was. As he took a fourth long stride he turned the staff's rotation into forward motion. He punched a butt cap into the ice with all his weight and strength thrusting it.

Wizardlight held Cashel in a sphere of lightning-cored needles, each of them stabbing into the marrow of his bones. It would've been agony if he could really feel, but the pain was so intense that his mind floated above it. He marveled that his flesh didn't blacken and slough away.

He was sitting on the ice again. Men were running past him, their mouths open with shouts that Cashel couldn't hear. Sharina knelt at his side. He couldn't hear her either, but her left hand stroked his cheek. Warmth and feeling returned to his body, the pain draining away as though Sharina's gentle fingers had lanced a boil.

Cashel lurched to his feet. In the wall of ice was a gap he could've driven a yoke of oxen through. The edges still sizzled as azure light ate them away. Garric and his soldiers were clambering through the opening to the chamber beyond.

"Cashel?" Sharina said. "Can you walk?"

"I can run," growled Cashel, and he started forward again.

Sharina's heart leaped as she watched a sphere of nothingness engulf Cashel as he drove his staff into the center of the ice. It looked black because it had neither hue nor reflection, an absence of anything.

The emptiness vanished; maybe it'd been an illusion. Cashel flew back as though something huge had kicked him, but he still held his quarterstaff.

Sharina ran to him. She had a funny, detached feeling. She didn't hurt nor even feel tired, but she wasn't sure that it was her own strength that moved her limbs. Beard was more than an axe—she'd known that from the moment she picked him up and he started shouting—but she was beginning to wonder how *much* more than an axe he was.

"Beard *serves* his mistress," the axe sang, his voice ringing through the echoing cacophony. "Beard would never treat his mistress the way the Augenhelm did Alfdan, the Great Fool of a Wizard!"

Sharina felt cold terror stab through her mind as she recalled Alfdan's last moments; then she laughed. "Beard," she said, "without you, all my friends would be dead and the kingdom dying too. If that means you destroy me—well, I won't be happy about it, but I'd have done the same if I'd known ahead of time."

She knelt beside Cashel, stroking his cheek with the hand that didn't hold the axe. He'd smashed a huge hole in the ice. Instead of the corridor they'd been following, there was a vast domed hall on the other side of the gap. Cashel had opened more than a mere physical barrier.

Garric and his immediate companions climbed through the opening, but the ordinary soldiers were hesitating when they realized that a blue quiver of wizardlight continued to eat the gap still wider. Cashel made a rumbling sound in his throat; he blinked and his face flushed away the frozen pallor of a moment before. He rose to his feet, an awkward, inexorable movement like that of an ox rousing from sleep, and bunched his great shoulder muscles.

"Mistress, there's great danger for your friends beyond!" said Beard urgently. He tittered and went on, "Much danger for them, and much blood for Beard to drink!"

"Cashel?" Sharina said. Master Ortron had lashed the men of his phalanx into motion with a tongue rough as chipped lava, and the regular infantrymen were moving also out of embarrassment to lag behind troops they felt were their social inferiors. "Can you walk?"

"I can run," growled Cashel. He started forward, holding his quarterstaff up at a slant before him.

"Let us by!" Sharina cried, because she wasn't sure whether Cashel was aware of anything beyond the fact that he *was* going through, whoever or whatever happened to be in the way. Maybe he wasn't ready to face the dangers on the other side of the opening, but Sharina didn't want to leave him behind. Even without Beard's prodding she wouldn't have stayed back herself.

Besides, she'd never seen a time that Cashel *wasn't* ready to face what was before him.

The soldiers made way. As Sharina danced through the opening, moving like a breeze beside Cashel's avalanche, she heard Master Ortron snarl, "There, you pansies! Will you let a wisp of a girl go where you're afraid to?"

"Wisp of a girl!" Beard chortled. "My mistress, a wisp of a girl?"

The hall within seemed empty at first glance only because it was huge beyond the standards of enclosed space. The entire royal palace in Valles, scores of separate buildings spreading across many acres, would've been lost beneath the huge dome. Here as elsewhere in these caverns the ice shone with a core of wizardlight, but the ceiling and walls were so distant that the figures within were dim shadows.

The floor was clear as diamond. Plankton in the water beneath shone faintly red or blue instead of the yellow-green of the sea off Barca's Hamlet in springtime. Through the glowing water swam monsters that were large even by the standards of this place. Their teeth gleamed as their platter-sized eyes stared longingly at the creatures above them.

Garric, Attaper and the two soldiers with them were in a tight circle surrounded by a pack of Hunters like the ones Sharina had killed when she'd been sucked into this world. There must've been seven of the gangling giants to begin with, but one was down with a javelin sticking up from an eye socket and another staggered in tight circles trying to pull out the similar missile imbedded to the wood in her breastbone. It was amazing that she was still alive since the iron must be through her heart, but she was no longer a danger to the men.

The remaining five were. One raised a club made from a whale's shoulder blade to swing at Garric. Cashel stepped close with quick right and left blows from his quarterstaff. The Hunter gave a guttural cry and toppled backward, his knee joints smashed.

"Blood!" shrilled Beard as Sharina rushed the Hunter whose great iron sword threatened the soldier to Garric's right. "Blood! Blood! Blo—"

Sharina swung, cutting the Hunter's left hamstring. The creature fell, twisting toward the injury.

The soldier lunged forward, thrusting into the Hunter's thigh as Sharina ducked under the falling body to reach the next enemy. When he withdrew his short blade, a column of blood spouted high from the wound: he'd sliced the Hunter's femoral artery. From the way the soldier moved, that stroke had been no more of an accident than the way he'd thrown his javelin through a previous Hunter's eye.

A Hunter crashed his club, a section of tree trunk, down at Lord Attaper. The Blood Eagle didn't carry a shield. His long sword slashed, not in a vain attempt to block the stroke but trying rather to skew it to the side enough to miss.

He was almost succesful, but the wood brushing his left shoulder flung him sprawling; the thigh-thick club splintered without marking the ice. A fish scraped teeth the length of a man across the bottom of the crystalline barrier, trying to get at either combatant.

Sharina leaped over Attaper and swung high, shearing the throat of the stooping Hunter. Its blood sprayed in a steaming torrent over the ice.

"Blood and brains!" said the axe.

The other soldier of Garric's entourage jabbed the edge of his shield into a Hunter's groin, doubling his opponent up, while the point of its great spear skidded on the ice where the soldier had been a moment before. That put the creature's skull within Sharina's reach. She buried Beard's edge in the Hunter's temple, then twisted it free. Her victim bounded away like a headless chicken.

The remaining Hunter was staggering backward, making wordless cries and waving its arms above its head like a pair of bloody fountains. Garric crouched, gasping as he used a swatch of his tunic to wipe the blade that had just lopped off the creature's hands.

Additional monsters lumbered toward them, Hunters and things still more terrible. Sharina saw a pair of beetles with iridescent wing cases; they picked their way across the ice on legs the size of trees. But more troops were pouring through the opening as well, their weapons and armor catching highlights from the cold purple glow.

Garric straightened, throwing down the rag. He looked back at the soldiers entering the hall, then slanted his sword forward.

"Follow me!" he called. He jogged toward the center of a room so large that his shout didn't echo.

The difference between what Garric was doing and the nobleman's identical order to charge the Elemental was that this was the right time for it. A headlong assault might not succeed, but no other means could possibly succeed.

Garric was measuring his stride, leading his troops but not running away from them. Cashel followed, though for him it was probably his best speed. Sharina paused instead of going off with them immediately; she sucked in deep breaths and took a good look at the situation.

"Nothing left *here* to kill," Beard fumed, but he knew as

well as she did that she could catch up with the others before there was more fighting. And there certainly would be more fighting.

Skeins of crimson and azure wizardlight wove upward from the middle of the hall. Their patterns were as breathtakingly complex as the iridescence of a soap bubble. The tapestry of light had the searing perfection of the surface of the sun.

"Much blood!" the axe said. "Much more blood though not Her blood, not even with this fine mistress . . . but oh! if we *could* drink Her blood . . ."

The lines and ribbons and cables of light spread from a nub raised from the floor. *Just a bump of ice,* Sharina thought, denying what her eyes suggested.

"You know better!" Beard cackled. "You know it's a throne, mistress; and you know who sits on the throne!"

It *was* a throne, of ice so clear that only surface reflections limned its form. On it a great white blob quivered in concert with the pulsing wizardlight.

"To drink Her blood!" said the axe. "Oh, if only Beard could drink Her blood!"

Lord Attaper had gotten to his feet, but when he took a step his face went white and he stumbled. Despite the pain, a broken collarbone if not worse, he continued to shuffle forward.

One of the common soldiers who'd accompanied Garric set his right heel on the head of the javelin he'd pulled from the Hunter's eye and lifted the shaft judiciously to straighten the iron. The head back of the point wasn't hardened, so it would bend in an enemy's shield and prevent him from pulling it out to throw back. This veteran obviously had experience with field expedients.

The chest-speared Hunter had finally collapsed face upward. The other soldier was trying to free his javelin from the corpse. The missile had penetrated so deeply that the point was probably in the creature's spine.

"Leave it, Pont!" the first soldier cried. "Time's a-wasting!"

The pair broke into a lumbering jog. "That's all right for you to say, Prester," Pont muttered, "but I notice that you waited till you had yours loose!"

Sharina loped along with them. A segmented worm that looked like a glacier squirmed toward the invaders, but despite its size at least the leading company of soldiers would be past before it could block the route to the throne. No point in fighting needlessly; there'd be more than enough that couldn't be avoided.

"We got the princess with us, Pont," Prester said.

"And a bloody good thing it is too," his partner agreed. "Thanks, your highness. You saved my ass back there, I shouldn't wonder."

"Your highness!" somebody shouted in a breathy voice. "I'm coming!"

Sharina glanced over her shoulder and saw Gondor, the Blood Eagle who'd gotten her into the corridor to begin with, running across the ice to catch up. He'd lost his spear somewhere.

She felt a momentary pang at having abandoned a man who'd been of significant help. But—the men who'd attached themselves to her after Alfdan's death hoped she'd be their salvation. Gondor in contrast regarded her as a child he had to protect. While the Blood Eagle's concern was no less real than that of the civilians, it wasn't something Sharina needed to worry about while matters were in their present state.

"You needn't worry about civilians either, mistress," the axe said in an excited chant. "Only worry about feeding Beard; the rest will come!"

That was close enough to the truth that Sharina smiled. Beard couldn't save the kingdom by himself, but by putting the axe in the places that best suited it Sharina would be performing the best service to the kingdom that was within *her* power.

She and the soldiers joined Garric, who nodded, and Cashel, who smiled. Cashel ran with his quarterstaff crosswise in front of him. So far as Sharina could tell he'd fully recovered from the effort of smashing open Her sanctum, but in a fight Cashel focused on his opponent alone.

Half-a-dozen others, members of the phalanx who'd lost their pikes, were already with Garric. To allow them to handle their heavy primary weapon, pikemen wore linen corselets instead of metal body armor. Their light shields were supported by a neck strap and they carried long daggers rather than proper swords. Without their pikes they were much more agile than regular infantrymen burdened by full armor.

More troops followed, alone and in small groups as they emerged through the wall of the chamber. Sharina felt a stab of despair. They seemed so very few against the size of this enormous hall.

"Better hold up, your princeship!" Prester called. "We want to take this lot in close order!"

"Take his right, Prester," Pont said. "You keep between us, your highness. We got shields, you see."

This lot was a pack of wolves the size of heifers, loping across the ice. Their coats would've been white under normal light; here they had an evil violet shimmer. Their eyes glowed yellow-orange and had no pupils.

"Halt, we'll fight them here!" Garric ordered. He took three strides, each shorter than the one before, so he didn't fall. This ice gave good footing, but slowing on a hard surface was always risky. "You men watch my back. I don't have a shield so I'll be out in front where I can do some good."

"Stay behind me, your highness!" Gondor said to Sharina. "I'll try to keep them off you!"

"Keep out of my way," Cashel said, stepping forward as Garric did. He moved to the left so that even if he extended his staff full-length in one hand, the outer ferrule wouldn't touch his friend.

"Mistress, we must be in front!" Beard said. "Mistress, you mustn't keep Beard back from his food!"

"Of course not," Sharina agreed. She glanced at the Blood Eagle and said sharply, "File Closer Gondor, keep anything from getting behind me but stay far enough back that you don't foul my axe. If I kill you by accident I'll regret it; but Beard will not, I assure you."

Gondor looked shocked, but he closed his mouth with his protest unspoken. Sharina stepped past the line of soldiers and placed herself as far to her brother's right as Cashel was to his left. Beard took up a lot of room in a hot fight. . . .

The wolves were on them, a loose *V* led by a brute nearer

the size of an ox than a heifer. Its mouth was open; slaver dripped through teeth as long as a man's fingers. It bunched its huge body to leap on Garric.

A javelin struck the point of its right shoulder at an angle that took the head through the beast's heart and the blood vessels leading from it. Instead of leaping, the wolf twisted in the air and somersaulted, its jaws splintering the spear shaft in dying fury.

Sharina stepped forward, swinging Beard in a slanting overhead stroke. She used the strength of both arms with her right hand leading on the helve. The axe screamed, "Kill!" but she screamed also. *"The Isles!"* she thought it was, but she was barely a spectator of her own actions at this moment.

Beard's narrow edge crunched just behind the left orbit of the wolf coming at her. The beast's thunderous snarl turned into a yelp. The eyes' inner light winked out as the animal skidded past in a flaccid heap, dragging Sharina around as she tugged her axe loose.

She felt rather than saw a second wolf as large as the one she'd killed leap toward her. Gondor was between it and her, his shield raised. The beast knocked him backward and slammed him onto the ice with forepaws each the size of a soup plate.

As the wolf's jaws opened to snap off the pinioned Blood Eagle's head, Sharina brought Beard around to bury his spike where the spine entered the back of the wolf's great head.

The wolf convulsed, arching backward. Sharina jerked her axe free; the beast gave a spastic leap that flung it thirty yards sideways.

There were no more wolves in front of her. Sharina turned. All of them were down. A pikeman sat astride the neck of a beast that still thrashed though its legs had collapsed under it. He clung to its left ear and stabbed its throat repeatedly, apparently unaware that its eyes were empty and its tongue lolled onto the ice.

Cashel got to his feet, pulling out the wool from his wallet. He wiped blood and brains from one buttcap of his quarterstaff. His face had an expression of perfect calm, as though he were currying an ox after they'd spent the day plowing. He felt Sharina glance at him and gave her a smile.

Garric tried to rub his eyes with the back of his left hand. He'd been drenched with blood; it dripped from him and his sword to the ice. Either Prester or Pont—they were as bloody as Garric, and Sharina couldn't tell them apart—handed him a rag he'd carried in the hollow boss of his shield. A wolf's teeth had reduced the shield itself to splinters, though it was made of thick cross-laminated birch.

Garric stepped around a wolf quivering in its death throes. He'd cut through its throat with what must have been a single stroke. More men had run up during the fight, replacing the casualties—but there'd been many casualties.

Garric wiped the patterned steel of his sword, then slanted the blade again toward the throne. They were within bowshot now.

"Haft and the Isles!" he shouted as he started forward again, stumbling for the first step but getting his feet properly under him by the second.

"Haft and the Isles!" Sharina croaked as she shambled after him.

"Kill them all and drink their blood!" cried Beard; and that was a good war cry too.

Within bowshot, Garric thought as he jogged toward the throne. He was a good archer—he'd been a good one, anyway, in the days when he minded sheep. Archery required constant practice to keep the muscles toned as well as the skill to know what to do in the first place.

It wasn't really very long since he'd been a boy in Barca's Hamlet though it felt like a lifetime. He could probably put two arrows out of three through the center of the blob seated on the ice throne . . . if he had a bow.

And if pigs had wings, they could fly. Which wasn't a result anybody wished who knew more about pigs than that they liked the taste of pork.

King Carus laughed with Garric, then said, *"Don't worry, lad. It'll be more satisfying to do the job with your sword."*

The battle with the wolves was hazy in Garric's mind. His

eyes had only seen what his ancient ancestor's instincts told
them to focus on: shapes blurred except where Carus saw a
chance to strike or a need to dodge. At one point in the fight
he'd buried his dagger in a wolf's eye, so deeply that he had
to release the hilt as the beast bounded away snapping at the
air. Though the steel had destroyed the wolf's brain, its muscles still burned with blood lust.

At another point—before? after?—he'd slashed through
the foreleg of a white-furred monster, then jumped to the
right as it rolled over the missing limb. He didn't know
what'd happened to the wounded animal afterward. He'd
been past it, using both arms to swing his sword. His blade
had met the neck of the wolf bounding toward him, shearing
it in a broad diagonal.

There'd been blood before. When Garric opened the
throat of the great wolf looming over him, the whole world
became a sticky red torrent. He'd struck the ice on his shoulder and rolled to his feet in the same motion. After that he
could see the things about him normally again, because he'd
had nothing more to kill.

For the moment.

The figure on the throne raised hands like suet puddings.
In concert with Her gesture, wisps of wizardlight spun like
dust devils before Garric and his companions.

"Wizardry!" snarled the ghost of King Carus. *"May the
Lady smite all wizards down for their sins!"*

That's our job, not the Lady's, thought Garric. The
whirling funnels of light drained into the ice; only a glow remained. Then the hard surface shattered, erupting like mud
when frogs crawl to the surface of a dried pond during the
first rains. Skeletons clothed in wizardlight rose from their
icy graves, holding swords and spears with rust-pitted
blades.

The wizard on the throne continued to weave. The whole
surface between Garric and the throne was breaking open.
Some of the skeletons were of bone so old it was splitting,
while others still had not only ligaments but flesh clinging
to them.

"Haft and the Isles!" Garric shouted, shocked despite

himself at the sight. He wasn't sure that anyone but Cashel would follow him into the dreadful array.

"Hey, the dumb barbarians haven't got armor!" bellowed Pont.

"Let's get stuck in, boys!" cried his partner Prester. "It's party time!"

I'll make them nobles for that bit of bravado! thought Garric joyfully. Then peasant caution made him add, *If any of us survive.*

"It's not bravado," Carus explained. "They mean it. And they're right!"

A skeleton ran at Garric holding a spear over its right shoulder in both fleshless hands. *Whatever was animating the corpse must be powerful, but it hadn't had even rudimentary weapons training. . . .*

Instead of waiting to sidestep the awkward thrust, Garric backhanded his sword through the skeleton's right elbow. The spear twitched sideways and Garric's edge crunched deep in the naked spine. The creature folded backward.

Garric snatched the spear from the twice-dead thing's nerveless grip, then used the shaft to parry the cleaver-like blade that another skeleton swung at him from the left. He thrust his own sword through the creature's chest cavity, both edges grating on bone.

The haze of crimson light that clothed the creature dissipated as suddenly as a reflection vanishing when the angle changes. The skeleton collapsed onto the ice, already starting to disarticulate.

Garric saw movement to his right and was whirling to deal with it when Pont stepped past. The veteran crushed skeletal ribs with the upper edge of his shield, struck the skull of a second creature with the edge of his short, heavy sword—ancient bone powdered at the impact—and broke a third's knee and the thighbone above it with the hobnailed sole of his boot. When it fell, he smashed the thing's chest with the other boot.

To Garric's other side Prester proceeded in much the same fashion, though he was using a pikeman's lighter shield: there was never a moment that one limb or another wasn't moving and never a motion that wasn't lethal. It was like watching pistons working in pump shafts, inexorably shoving everything before them.

"Haft and the Isles!" somebody cried over the tumult.

Garric strode forward between the two veterans. He didn't have a shield to strike with, but his longer arm and longer blade helped him keep even with the older men.

His left hand stabbed the spear he'd appropriated through the thin nasal bones of a skull. The creature behind that one hacked at Garric's extended arm with a sword so dull it bruised worse than it cut. Garric didn't quite drop the spear, but he was clumsy when he lunged and with a half cut, half thrust, lopped off the head of the creature that'd wounded him.

Another of the things drove its spear upward into Garric's breastplate, banging deeply enough through the bronze to draw blood as well as knocking his breath out. The stroke would've gone deeper yet if the spearpoint hadn't broken.

The creature pulled the weapon back for a finishing thrust. Garric stood, paralyzed from the blow to his diaphragm. Pont, almost absently, shattered the skeleton's pelvis with the lower edge of his shield. When it fell, he drove the heel of his boot like a battering ram into its neck.

Garric got his breath back. He stepped forward, his sword raised.

"Yeah, and I'll bugger your sisters too!" Prester shouted as he thrust and chopped and continued to advance. He didn't move quickly, but neither did he halt or even pause. It was like watching sap drip on a warm spring day.

Cashel's quarterstaff struck right and left with the regularity of a water clock, smashing a skull or a fleshless rib cage with every blow. Whenever an animate skeleton thrust at him, a ferrule batted the weapon back and crushed the thing wielding it. What'd been an army of hideous monsters as numerous as stalks in a barley field, was going down as surely as that barley at harvest time.

The footing became as much of a danger as the creatures themselves. In rising from their frozen tombs, the skeletons had left craters of shattered ice. Garric set his boot on a hole filled with treacherous fragments. Only instincts he'd honed

while following sheep into bogs warned him not to rest his
weight on that foot.

A skeleton swung a double-bitted axe down at him. Garric
caught the helve with the point of his upraised sword and
skidded the axe to the side, then flicked his blade to the right
to lift the skull from the neck vertebrae. If he'd carried
through with the lunge he'd intended, his leg would've sunk
beneath him. The creature's blow would've split him up the
back like a sheep butterflied for roasting.

Sharina's axe wove figure eights before her, clearing a
space as broad even as Cashel's quarterstaff. The axe was
shouting or singing in the sort of joy displayed at coronations and for sudden windfalls; its edge clipped through
whatever it met—wood or bone or rusty iron. Garric didn't
know how long his sister could keep up the effort, but by
now there was little more need for it. A single rank of skeletons separated him and his immediate companions from the
figure on the ice throne.

Garric chose his final opponent, the skeleton of a man
who when alive ages previously must've been seven feet tall.
It raised its sword for a vertical chop; instead of the deliberate swordsmanship he'd demonstrated till this moment, Garric did the same.

They swung down at one another, their blades crossing in
a clanging tocsin. Sparks flew. Wizardry gave the skeleton's
limbs enormous strength, but the salt-pitted sword snapped
on the watered steel of Garric's blade.

Garric thrust through the creature's mouth, scattering
teeth like hail stones and lifting the top of the bare skull. The
skeleton flew backward, the broken sword dropping from its
right hand as its left arm came loose at the shoulder.

Garric had reached the foot of the great throne; he looked
up for the first time since the skeletons began to rise from
the ice. The wizard seated above him must have weighed as
much as a full-grown ox. Her body was a mushroom of fat
on legs whose drooping calves swaddled tiny feet the way
rich cloth drapes an altar. Her arms were so monstrous they
appeared to have no elbows. Her fingers, though thick as
sausages, seemed delicate by contrast with the bloated
palms.

She was looking at Garric. Her cheeks were so puffy that Her eyes seemed to be set at the bottom of deep tunnels, but Garric recognized Her nonetheless.

He was looking at his childhood friend, Ilna os-Kenset.

And as he realized that, the net of wizardlight that She had woven in the air dropped onto Garric, freezing him in his tracks.

As Ilna entered the huge domed hall that she'd seen so recently through Her eyes, the net of wizardlight drifted down over her. Ilna's expression was colder than the winter stars.

The Tree growing from the enthroned figure dominated the vast chamber. Its trunk was deceptive, as thin and supple as a willow's at first glance. At the back of Ilna's mind she had the impression that the Tree was too thick for even this huge room to hold. Its leafless limbs squirmed on currents of wizardlight, brushing over every peak and valley of the world; branching and spreading to branch again.

Chalcus saw Her net falling. He threw up his left hand to keep it from tangling him, but that touch froze him. The net continued to settle, draping his head and shoulders. Ilna stepped around him and continued toward the center of the hall.

The Tree in its full splendor looked as it had when Ilna first saw it in Hell. What she'd brought back with her to the waking world had been a relatively slight thing, but it would have grown.

Grown to look like this towering monster, visible only to her of all those in this chamber.

Soldiers were gathered in the center of the room; more men had been running toward them from an entrance close to where Ilna had shattered her own door in the wall. In a scene much like the one she'd just viewed through Her memory, a net of wizardlight had locked most of the men stiffly. A few were trying to crawl away; none of them would succeed.

The chamber held inhuman creatures of more sorts than Ilna had fingers to count them. Her net had trapped those as well; it would convert them to Her purposes in the same fashion, if nothing prevented that from happening.

Ilna smiled like light dancing from a sword blade. Something would prevent it.

She walked forward, feeling a faint tingle from the wizardlight eddying about her. The net was at shoulder level now and dropping lower.

Nearby crouched a thing whose body was a great cat's but whose eagle's head was crowned with great green feathers. A group of soldiers braced themselves to receive it, their shields raised; two of the men had javelins cocked to throw. The encounter had become a tableau when Her net had fallen across it. In their concern with each other, neither monster nor men had been aware of what was settling on them.

Ilna detoured around the corpse of a giant with a brow that jutted like a warship's ram to protect its single central eye. It lay on its back with three pikes, two broken and one whole, sticking up from its chest. Judging from how deep the pikes were driven in, the creature must have run itself onto the points and continued struggling forward on pillar-like legs until death finally caught up with it.

Ilna sniffed. That massive skull must hold a brain no bigger than a squirrel's. Of course there were plenty of ordinary men she'd say the same about.

Garric and Cashel were where she expected to find them, in the middle of the front line. Sharina was there too, her blond hair draped about her shoulders like a shroud. She'd been swinging an axe when the net halted her in mid-stroke.

As white as a slug and fatter than Ilna had believed a human could become, She sat on the throne looking out over the frozen soldiers. Of course She wasn't human anymore; Her soul was merely the soil in which the Tree had sprouted to spread its tendrils across the world.

The net of light reached the floor, locking Garric and his whole army beneath its spell. From the throne Her hands wove power in subtle patterns; those hands and Ilna herself were the only things moving in the huge room.

She turned Her head toward Ilna. Her fat white fingers .wisted; crimson wizardlight looped out to knot around Ilna like a snake throttling a vole.

The coil slipped through Ilna as if her body were water; she felt only the quivering chill she'd get from a draft when a winter storm rattles the shutters. She walked on, looking up and smiling more broadly. She met the deep-set eyes of the thing she hadn't allowed herself to become.

"Who are you?" shouted the thing on the throne.

"I'm Ilna os-Kenset," said Ilna. "I'm who you used to be, when you were human."

This close to the throne, Ilna had to choose her footing with care. The ice was broken into chunks, and everywhere lay the skeletons of the men who'd followed Her until she tore out their blood and souls to feed her wizardry.

"I have power over you!" She cried from the throne. Her fingers writhed again, molding forces into a tool and sending them curling toward Ilna as an azure noose. "I have power over all things!"

Ilna shrugged through this coil as she had the first one, as she had the net that held the others in the chamber. "You don't have any power except what the Tree allows you," she said calmly. "And the Tree has no power over me *now*— since I broke away from it."

Ilna looked up at the round face and bloated white body. "As you did not in your world," she said. "And as you can't ever do now."

"Ilna?" said a voice Ilna knew well. "I'm so glad you've come back!"

It was not Her voice. It was the voice of the friend Ilna never had, the one who understood her and cared about her, as nobody had ever cared about Ilna os-Kenset.

It was the voice of the Tree.

"You have no business with me," Ilna said. "Not any longer."

She wasn't sure her lips were moving. The huge ice hall faded to flickers at the edge of her awareness. She stood in a gray limbo with neither light nor texture. Before her was the Tree, its sinuous branches weaving a slow dance of mastery and evil.

Ilna smiled; and if it was a grim expression, there was pride in it nonetheless. *Not mastery over me. Not any longer.*

"None of them understand you, Ilna," said the Tree; its voice was soothing, loving. "I'll make sure that you get what you deserve."

"You have no—" Ilna shouted, but the remainder of the words froze on her lips. Time stopped, then flowed down a channel different from the one that she had lived.

The vagabond Kenset brought Ilna to Barca's Hamlet as an infant, but divine parentage already shone from her face. As a child she never lacked for anything. Barca's Hamlet became known as a paradise on earth where winters were moderate and crops bountiful. This blissful series of events was rightly credited to the presence of the Divine Ilna.

Some of those in the borough found the pain of their own inadequacy too much to bear in the light of the Divine Ilna. Her uncle Katchin and his slattern wife swam out to sea one night; their bodies were never recovered. The next day Garric's shrewish, self-important mother Lora hanged herself in the panty of the inn. Neighbors regarded the deaths as part of the blessings Ilna brought on the community.

Ilna allowed Garric to attend her. It pleased her to see the light of adoration in his eyes. He never presumed to touch her, of course, realizing that no human was worthy of the Divine Ilna. She was whole in herself, a fit subject for worship but unmoved by it as by all else around her.

Around Her; She was divine.

Realizing the inadequacy of their resources, the folk of the borough carried Her in state to Carcosa. The ancient capital received Her with fitting enthusiasm, rebuilding the Old Kingdom palace for Her. Delegations arrived from Sandrakkan and Ornifal, from Blaise and from rocky islets too small to have a name recognized by any but the handful of fishermen inhabiting them.

The rich and powerful brought gold and jewels and sometimes tapestries; She looked with amused contempt on the finest fabric that humans could weave. The poor could offer only their worship, but that they gave Her unstintingly.

On every isle, in every home, voices rose in praise for the Divine Ilna. What had been a kingdom became a temple, as a new and eternal Golden Age came to the Isles.

"What you deserve . . ." the voice whispered affectionately.

Ilna laughed, a harsh, bitter sound that shattered the illusion. She stood among the frozen figures beneath the great dome again. "What I deserve," she said as the Tree swayed in a vain, desperate attempt to touch her, "is to die—because of the harm I did when I listened to you before. Never again."

She stepped forward. She'd reached the line of soldiers and squeezed between them, sometimes ducking under an outstretched blade or a thrusting shield. The men were in tight ranks, but Ilna was a slender woman.

Garric stood with his sword raised and his right foot lifting from the ice to lunge toward the creature above him. Ilna touched her friend's shoulder in a protective gesture. She smiled at Her, thinking with a rare surge of pride, *Despite the evil which I did and can never repay, I didn't become* that; *and I might have.*

"You have no power over me either!" She said. "However great your art, you can't touch me!"

"Is that what you think?" said Ilna. She chuckled and slipped her little knife from its bone sheath. The keen steel edge winked like a demon's tongue. "What I think is that I'll reach a vein with this eventually, even if I have to dig for a while."

She mounted the lowest step, grinning like a cat.

The creature on the throne screamed in warbling terror. *I didn't become a coward, either,* Ilna thought, and climbed the next step.

The throne trembled. She was straining to stand, channeling forces to lift a body too massive for human muscles to move.

"You can't run from me!" Ilna said. "You can't run from yourself, Ilna os-Kenset!"

The Tree shuddered as its bed shifted, rocking like the surf in a storm. Ilna struggled onto the third step despite the rippling violence.

The vast white form screamed again; then She toppled sideways, unable to balance the mass on Her tiny feet. She struck the floor with the weight not only of Her body but also the load of trembling evil that grew from it.

There was a soggy crash, then a roar. The ice, already weakened when the dead climbed out of it, broke open.

Water just warmer than the ice fountained from the hole,

then dropped back. A second geyser, this time tinged with blood, followed an instant later. The things swimming beneath the chamber were feeding.

Wizardlight began to fade from the walls the way sparks do after they've been flung onto a stone hearth. Ilna swayed; then the throne pitched with greater violence and she fell backward.

Chapter Twenty-four

The net that'd held them the way winter ice coats a gargoyle dissolved. Garric, free to move again, saw Ilna fall backward. He sheathed his sword with a skill that'd become unconscious when he awakened the spirit of King Carus in his mind and caught Ilna with both hands. She was a solid weight to arms fatigued by the brutal fighting, but Garric figured he could carry her as far as he needed to go.

The glow in the cavern walls suddenly dimmed. Garric could see men in silhouette, but the floor strewn with corpses and debris was in darkness.

Garric turned his head. *The door we entered by is—*

As the thought leaped through his mind, the trail of light Tenoctris had sent to guide them brightened to a fierce blue glare. Now it lit the route instead of just indicating it.

"Cashel, hold your sister!" Garric said, swinging Ilna toward his friend.

The steps up the throne were twice the normal height; he jumped rather than stepping. Behind he heard Ilna say, "I'm perfectly all right! I just slipped!"

That was doubtless true—Garric doubted Ilna even understood why anybody would *want* to lie—but he hadn't had time to check. Tenoctris's blazing guide ended above the seat, quivering like a plucked lute string. Garric turned and set one leg to either side of the light. Through a megaphone of his hands he bellowed, "Go back! Get out of here fast!"

A cornicene somewhere in the chamber blew "Retreat" on his coiled horn. Garric was happier to hear that sound than he'd have been if a priest assured him that the Lady would fold his soul to her bosom when he died. He didn't trust priests—

And he *sure* didn't trust this warren of chambers and tunnels. He could hear the ice groaning, louder with each passing moment. More than the strength of the material had kept Her palace from collapsing; and though Garric was very glad that Her power had drained away when she died, he'd prefer not to be buried in the heart of a glacier.

The cornicene repeated his call. Many of the soldiers were already turning. There was nothing about this frozen darkness that made men want to remain if they were offered an excuse to leave. For a moment Garric thought he heard an echo; then he realized that a signaler back down the tunnel was relaying the call on a trumpet. All the humans in the chamber, Her throne room, were following the guide back to their own world.

Thought of his men made Garric look around the hall in sudden concern. The things that were *not* men, Her minions—where were they? Retreating in near darkness could be more dangerous than—

"*They're running, lad,*" said Carus, whose experience had let him see more through Garric's eyes than Garric himself had. "*As soon as She went into the drink, they took off for the exits. Running or crawling, if they were the sorts that crawl. I'd say a lot of those creatures had a good notion of what was going to come to them next if something hadn't happened to Her instead.*"

Garric glanced down beside him reflexively. The water was generally as black as the ice that had covered it, but it roiled. Occasionally fangs glinted above the surface as a latecomer or perhaps just an optimist snapped at the diluting blood.

"*It wasn't your friend,*" Carus said softly.

Someone was jogging toward the center of the hall, against the flow of soldiers heading for the exit. Garric touched his hilt, uncertain in the halflight; then he saw a shimmer as the figure sheathed his curved sword: Chalcus.

Garric relaxed. Ilna stepped forward and embraced the sailor.

No, agreed Garric. *It wasn't my Ilna. It couldn't have been her.*

It could have been me, Ilna thought. She trembled with fear of what hadn't quite happened. *It was me, She was me!*

"Dear heart?" said Chalcus. "I've been cut more times than ever so great a scholar could count, but the truth is I've never learned to like it. If you must prick me, prick away; but otherwise . . . ?"

"Oh!" said Ilna. She stepped back and slipped her blade into its case, then returned the little tool to her sleeve. She didn't ordinarily think of a knife as a weapon; her instinct was for the noose, but that was shriveling in a pool of sulfur on a world she hoped never to revisit. She'd completely forgotten that she held the blade in her hand when she threw her arms around Chalcus's neck.

Garric climbed down from the ice throne, stepping as awkwardly as an ox descending a steep bank instead of the catlike grace with which he'd mounted. Ilna smiled in her mind. Many things were easier to do when you didn't have time to think about them.

The rod of light shone from above, throwing pools of shadow over men's feet and turning their faces into grotesque masks. Garric looked at his friends and said, "We need to get moving too. As a matter of fact, the rest of you go on ahead and I'll—"

"We'll stay with you, Garric," Cashel said. He didn't raise his voice more than required by the sound of the ice in its dying agony, but the fact he interrupted was itself enough to surprise those who knew him.

"Yes," said Ilna. "We've been apart long enough."

"Now that we've decided we're going to stick together . . ." said a grizzled soldier at Garric's side. He had the heavy breastplate and sword of a regular infantryman, but for some reason he was carrying a pikeman's shield. "Can we maybe do it a little closer to the way out of this place?"

He nodded to where the guide disappeared into a tunnel. Nearby stood another soldier who'd have been his near double even if they hadn't both been drenched in blood. He'd lifted his helmet to scratch the bald spot in the middle of his scalp. "Why wouldn't we stick together, Prester?" he asked as he settled the helmet back in place. "There's no loot *here* worth having; and anyway, I never minded sharing with somebody who'd watch my back."

"Right, let's get on," Garric said, nodding to the soldiers shuffling toward the exit. They were already some distance away, though they weren't moving fast. "And Pont? You and Prester aren't going to lack for drinking money for the rest of your lives, if that's what you're thinking about."

"To tell the truth, your princeship . . ." said the man who must be Prester. "There were times today I thought I had enough coin for the rest of my life in my purse already . . . and all of that was a lead groat!"

Chalcus was the first to laugh, but they all joined in as they started forward. The laughter and companionship were better than sunlight in this place; though Ilna'd be glad to reach sunlight also.

Where the centipede's body narrowed the tunnel to one person at a time, Sharina followed Cashel and Gondor was immediately behind her. Garric and his entourage—Attaper and the two veterans—brought up the rear.

The first time Sharina'd passed the centipede, she'd scraped herself on the bristles sprouting from a leg joint. The break in the skin had begun to fester. She moved carefully now instead of scrambling over the chitinous obstacles with the haste her instincts urged. She really wanted to be out of this place!

Though the huge corpse still twitched, men passed it without the bunching and hesitation Sharina had seen when they were going the other way. Maybe that was because the vivid light that guided the troops hid rather than illuminated the legs pressing against the dark ceiling; and maybe it was just that they were leaving. These were brave men or they'd never have come this way at all, but leaving didn't require that they struggle against their hope of survival at every step.

"We didn't drink Her blood," murmured the axe in a faint, musical tone, "but we drank deep, blood and brains and souls. What will happen now to poor Beard, though?"

What would happen to any of them? Sharina thought with a stab of longing for her placid existence as a girl. Now she lived in a world where she might get up in the middle of the night because of a funny light and find herself dragged into a place ruled by a wizard for Her own evil purposes. . . .

"It's the same world, mistress," the axe said. "You just understand what you didn't understand when you were younger. Perhaps you'd rather be ignorant?"

Sharina smiled wryly. "No," she said. "I'd rather know the truth. I just wish the truth was different, sometimes."

"And because you do know the truth, mistress, and act on what you know . . ." said the axe. "The truth becomes a little different, a little better, for other people. And Beard drinks his fill for a time, a brief time."

Sharina was holding the axe in her right hand. With the fingers of her left she stroked the helve, then the steel head. Beard chuckled as if from deep in his throat. The sound trembled through Sharina's fingertips, reminding her of a cat purring; a very large cat.

She laughed and reached forward to touch Cashel's shoulder. Together they entered the rotunda where she'd first rejoined her friends and the army.

There were still many people here, but nothing like the crowd there'd been when Sharina arrived. The exit corridor was broad enough to let the soldiers march in squad ranks, and there wasn't a monster's corpse along the route to narrow it. Even so the rotunda's human contents didn't drain quickly. Sharina hadn't believed how long it took a large body of troops to march off in column until she'd seen the process twice: the second time to convince her that something hadn't gone horribly wrong on the first occasion.

"Garric!" Liane called and came running as soon as she saw him past Cashel's broad shoulders. Sharina smiled as she stepped out of Liane's way.

"Mistress!" Franca and Scoggin cried together. They and the rest of the ragged band rushed forward with an enthusiasm that caused Cashel to set his staff crosswise between them and Sharina.

That was reflex on Cashel's part—he knew as well as Sharina did that they intended no harm. But it was also true that frightened men carrying weapons could trip in their haste. An edge didn't care whether it cut by chance or by design.

Beard laughed. "Some of us care, mistress," he said.

Master Ortron and several other officers had descended on Garric, who talked to them with one arm around Liane. She held her waxed tablet out at an angle to the light so that she could read the notes she'd been making.

Attaper stepped over to the Blood Eagles, by now a full company under a captain. While the regular troops filed out of the rotunda, the highest-ranking Blood Eagle present had held the bodyguards in ordered ranks until Garric and their commander reappeared. That didn't delay the general departure and it salved their honor.

Many men worried about honor, which meant they were often silly. But Sharina'd met men who didn't worry about honor at all, and they were far worse than silly.

"Mistress, what shall we do?" Neal asked. He'd found a spear to take the place of the hammer he'd dropped when Tanus slashed him. The remainder of Alfdan's band—eight of them now—looked at Neal with sidelong glances at Sharina; only Scoggin and Franca were willing to face her directly.

"My brother Garric—" Sharina said. "Prince Garric, that is, he's said he'll make sure you're taken care of."

"Will he?" said Beard unexpectedly. "And what about the men in your world who were the same as these till She came? Will the prince kill them so that your friends can have their families and livelihoods back?"

Sharina frowned with real anger. "Of course not, but they'll have *some* life!" she said.

"And all the rest in their world?" the axe demanded. "The scattered ones and twos and the families still surviving? She's gone, but Her creatures still roam the Isles, you know."

"I'm not going to leave them in the ice!" Sharina snapped. The ragged men glanced from her to the axe, listening with mingled fear and horror. "They wouldn't stand a chance up on the surface, and these tunnels are no place to live even if they weren't going to collapse soon!"

Indeed, the ice seemed to moan louder with each passing moment. Shortly it'd be time for Garric and his companions to fall in at the end of the column exiting the rotunda. Sharina knew her brother wouldn't leave before his troops were clear, any more than he or Cashel would've abandoned their flocks when danger threatened.

"Ah, but the tunnels go to other places in this world, mistress," said the axe. "If these men went now to a valley in this world's Ornifal, they might be able to save what's left of a village barricaded against a pack of Her wolves. There's fourteen men, but some are old; and there's thirty women, and there's children besides."

Cashel stood as silent as a crag. He'd turned his staff vertical and planted one end on the floor beside Sharina now that he was sure the men weren't going to trample her.

"But I don't . . ." Sharina said.

I don't know where any of these tunnels lead, except the one that goes back to the edge of the frozen sea and the one down which light leads me home.

I don't want to stay in this ravaged world myself!

"But I know, mistress," the axe said. "And I want to stay; with these men, if you're leaving."

"Beard, you want to stay here?" Sharina said, shocked by the unexpectedness of it. She wouldn't—Princess Sharina wouldn't—need the axe, but she'd assumed after what they'd gone through . . .

"Mistress, if Beard goes to your world, he becomes a lump of iron," the axe said. "There She won't have awakened him. Would you do that to one whom you've fed so well in the past, when there's so much more for him here to eat?"

The Blood Eagle captain shouted an order over the creak of the ice. His company came to attention. There was already a gap between them and the end of the shuffling column of regulars.

"Sharina?" called Garric. "Time to go."

Without looking up, she waved a hand to indicate that she'd heard. She opened her mouth to object to the axe, then said instead, "Neal and all the rest of you?"

She glanced from Scoggin to Franca, adding, "Both of you as well. You can come to my world where you'll have some sort of jobs. Or you can let Beard lead you to a place in your world where you're needed and you can make a difference. Which? Quickly!"

"Will you come with us to Ornifal, mistress?" Franca asked. They'd of course been listening to what she and the axe said, deciding their future for them.

"No, she won't come with you," said Beard in a rising, sneering tone. "And you'll never see her again if you come to the mistress's world either. She's a fine lady, you fools! You'll have your farms and your shops, and you can bore people who'll think you're lying when you say you helped Princess Sharina save your world—which you then abandoned!"

"But you'll be *safe,*" Sharina said.

Garric waited; Attaper spoke in his ear, but Garric gestured him back curtly. Both men's eyes were on Sharina.

"Mistress," said Neal. "If we go to this place in Ornifal—"

"The place with the women," Layson amplified.

"—who would carry your axe?"

"Here," said Sharina, turning Beard to offer the grip to Neal.

The big man shied as if the helve were a snake. "Mistress!" he said, his hands trembling despite their grip on his spear shaft. "Not me, mistress, *please!*"

The rest of the band had backed away also. They'd seen a great deal of wizardry when they followed Alfdan. That had made them more, not less, afraid of it.

"I'll take Beard," Franca said. He looked down at the axe and added, "If he'll have me?"

"I'll serve you, young master," said the axe. "Oh, wolves' blood first and then who knows what we'll drink?"

In a voice like an alarm bell, Beard went on, "Quickly, though! Quickly!"

Franca grasped the axe. He hesitated a moment, then offered his hunting spear, bloody now, to Sharina.

I don't need this! she thought, but she took it.

"Let's go!" Garric ordered with a peremptory gesture. He started off at a trot to join the end of the column.

Sharina touched Cashel's arm; he nodded and they followed Garric. Behind them a screamed order brought the bodyguard company off to a crashing double-time.

Franca's band jogged toward another of the arched corridors. Sharina could hear Beard calling directions in a voice that pierced like an awl. They'd be in darkness most of the way, she supposed; but she also supposed they'd be all right. Beard had never failed *her,* after all.

She reached out with her left hand and squeezed Cashel's forearm as they ran, just for the companionship. Her eyes stung. She was angry at herself for being so silly, but she couldn't stop the tears.

"Go on ahead," Cashel said to Sharina as the last of the regular soldiers walked through the lens of light. Their forms shrank faster than their strides justified. "I'll stay with Tenoctris."

He squeezed her hand as she stepped into the light, her head high and her spear glinting.

Garric hesitated also. Attaper gripped him by the elbow. "Your highness, nobody doubts your courage. Now let's get back to our world so that you can take charge!"

Garric met Cashel's eyes, grinned in embarrassment, and obeyed. He and Attaper vanished into the lens, still arm in arm. The company of Blood Eagles followed, man by man across each rank, from the front to the rear.

"You can go too," Cashel said to the soldier who knelt with a supporting arm around Tenoctris's shoulders. The old wizard looked pale as a wraith, but she continued to mumble a chant as she tapped the corners of her triangle in sequence. A line of light lifted from the center of the marking and split—one arm blue and brilliant stretching back down the corridor, the other faint and red where it entered the lens.

The soldier glared. His right leg stuck out straight; splints made from broken spear shafts were bound above and below the knee.

"I been with her this long," he snapped. "Guess I'll take her the rest of the way. Beat it, farm boy!"

Cashel nodded. "Are you going to carry her back?" he

asked calmly. "Because I guess you know she won't be able to walk."

The soldier gaped in sudden horror. Cashel gave him a warm smile. "Go on through, friend," he said. "I'll be along with Tenoctris. You've done a great job, but for this I'll do better."

He squatted to Tenoctris's other side and placed his arm below the soldier's. The man sucked in his lips, then nodded. "Right," he said. "I'll wait for you on the other end."

He staggered to his feet. The last of the bodyguards were entering the lens. A pair of them took the injured soldier's arms over their shoulders and walked in, holding him upright.

Cashel looked up. Nobody was left but him, the old wizard, and the fellow who commanded Garric's army—Lord Waldron. "Go on, sir," Cashel said to the old man. "I'll bring Tenoctris."

"Get out of here, boy!" Waldron snarled. "I obeyed orders to stay while the others went on to fight, but the Sister eat my kidneys if I *leave* before everybody else is gone!"

"Right," said Cashel. "I can see that."

He slid his arm under Tenoctris's haunches. "It's time for us to go, Tenoctris," he said calmly and lifted her, still chanting. The guiding line vanished, but they didn't need it now.

Cradling the old woman to his chest, the quarterstaff upright in his other hand, Cashel walked into the disk that became a corkscrew tunnel as soon as he entered. He could see the miniature figures of the soldiers ahead of him, but even without them he wouldn't have gotten lost.

He glanced over his shoulder. Lord Waldron was following, as stiffly upright as Cashel's staff—though he seemed to be walking on his side because of what this place did to eyesight.

Tenoctris mumbled something. "We'll be out of this in a moment, Tenoctris," Cashel said. "You can get a proper rest, then. You did a wonderful job. You saved everybody."

That was pretty much true, but it was true for a lot of people. Cashel included, he guessed.

Shortly Cashel would step out into sunlight again. Sharina'd be there waiting for him, and likely Garric and Ilna besides. They'd done a good job, all of them. They could relax for a time, he hoped.

And if something else happened, as it probably would . . . well, Cashel had been a shepherd. He'd gone out every day with his flock, because they might need him. That was what Garric was doing now, only instead of sheep he had the whole Isles to watch over. That was how it was supposed to be.

And Garric had friends to help him watch. That was how it was supposed to be too.

Cashel stepped into the sunlit palace garden, onto the altar and then down to the ground where he handed Tenoctris to the soldier who'd been helping her in the tunnel. There was a lot of shouting, but it was happy shouting. Sharina threw her arms around Cashel and he kissed her, right there in public with ever so many people looking on.

At least for now, things were the way they were supposed to be.

Look For

MASTER
of the
CAULDRON

(0-8125-6170-8)

by DAVID DRAKE

Available now
from Tom Doherty Associates